ALSO BY MICHAEL ISENBERG

Full Asylum

The Thread of Reason

The Thread of Reason

A Novel by
Michael Isenberg

Monteferro Press
Boston

Cover illustration based on "The Assassination of Nizam al-Mulk" in Rashid ad-Din Tabib, *Jami al-tavarikh*, Topkapi Museum, Istanbul, Hazine Library Manuscript #1653, folio 360b (14th/15th century).

ISBN 978-0-9853297-5-4
Library of Congress Control Number: 2018900053

10 9 8 7 6 5 4 3 2 1

اجرام که ساکنان این ایوانند   اسباب تردد خردمندانن

هان تاسر رشته خرد گم نکنی   کانان که مدبرند سرگردانن

Objects that dwell in the Vault of the Skies
Whisper of Caution to Men who are wise.
       Grasp tightly the end of Reason's Thread. For
The Clever grow reckless—brought down by Lies!

—Omar Khayyam, *The Rubaiyat*

Contents

Historical Note

This is a work of fiction. Omar Khayyam, Abu Hamid Ghazali, the sultan Malik-shah, the caliph al-Muqtadi, and indeed most of the named characters in this book were historical figures, and the assassination of Nizam al-Mulk occurred more or less as I describe it. However, since the chronicles of the time were terse, it was up to me to fill in the gaps surrounding the event. In particular, the idea that Malik-shah tasked Khayyam and Ghazali with solving the mystery of who was behind it is an invention on my part. I don't think it's far-fetched, however. After all, they were probably the two smartest people the sultan had in his employ. Although historians have pondered the same mystery for centuries, as far as I know the solution that Omar came up with, acting as my proxy, is entirely original.

Real life does not, in general, make for good storytelling. Events are seldom arranged neatly into beginning, middle, climax, and end. The characters—and there are far too many of them—rudely insist on coming and going without any consideration as to what they symbolize or their role in the plot. With that in mind, I rearranged slightly the sequence of some events and I combined some historical figures into single characters. In particular, the character Mahmud is based on the historical Mahmud, who was the son of Sultan Malik-shah, combined with Ja'far, who was the son of Caliph al-Muqtadi and *grandson* of Malik-shah. Similarly, the character Taj al-Mulk is based on the historical Taj al-Mulk, a senior official who was the reputed rival of Nizam al-Mulk, combined with Tutush, the brother of Malik-shah. I beg the indulgence of historians for these liberties.

Incidentally, names ending in *al-Mulk*, *ad-Dawla*, and so on are, strictly speaking, not names at all but titles. *Nizam al-Mulk* was the title of Hasan ibn Ali at-Tusi and means "The Order of the Kingdom." Similarly, *Taj al-Mulk* was the title of Abu'l-Ghana'im Marzban ibn Khusrau Firuz ash-Shirazi and means "The Crown of the Kingdom." Despite the similarities in their titles, Taj al-Mulk and Nizam al-Mulk were not related. Titles were (in principle) awarded on merit and were highly sought after by sultans and officials alike.

Many of my characters were authors themselves, and I quote from translations of their works liberally, as well as from the Quran and the Hadith. Throughout the quotations, I made minor changes in spelling, capitalization, place names, and so forth for the purposes of clarity and consistency with the rest of this book.

In his *History of the English-Speaking Peoples*, Winston Churchill told one of the many legends of Rosamunde, mistress to Henry Plantagenet. He followed it up with a disclaimer: tedious researchers had proven the darn thing wasn't true. Churchill saw no reason to let that get in the way of a good story; he included it in his book anyway.[1] I feel the same about the story of the pact between Omar Khayyam, Nizam al-Mulk, and Hasan-i Sabbah, as well as the story of the secret Garden of the Assassins. They're just too famous—and too good—to leave out. I hope historians will approve of, or at least forgive, my solutions to the very real difficulties raised by the tedious researchers.

For more information about the history behind *The Thread of Reason*, please see the notes at the end of the book and visit my website, www.ThreadOfReason.com.

Michael Isenberg
Boston, MA
December 31, 2017

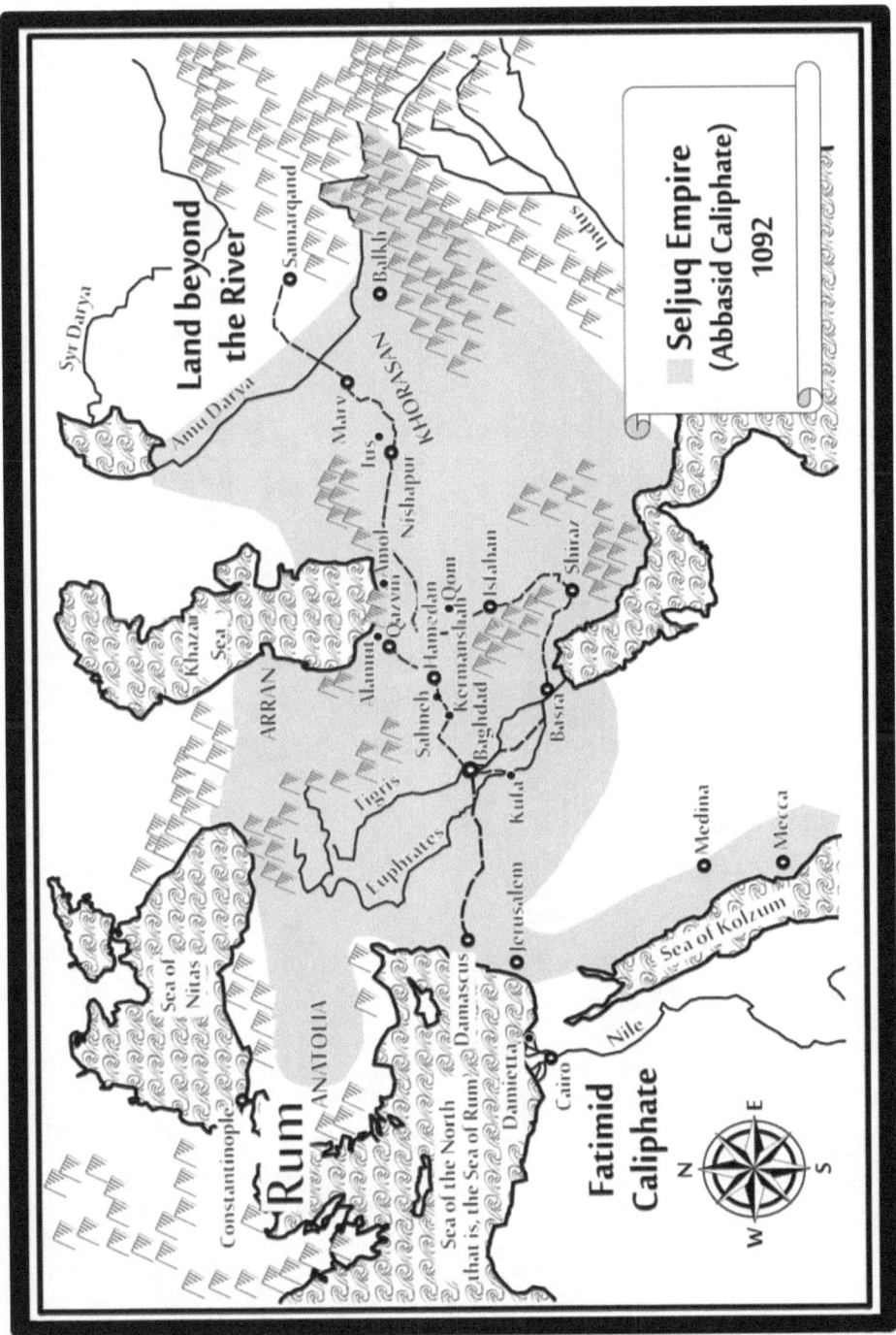

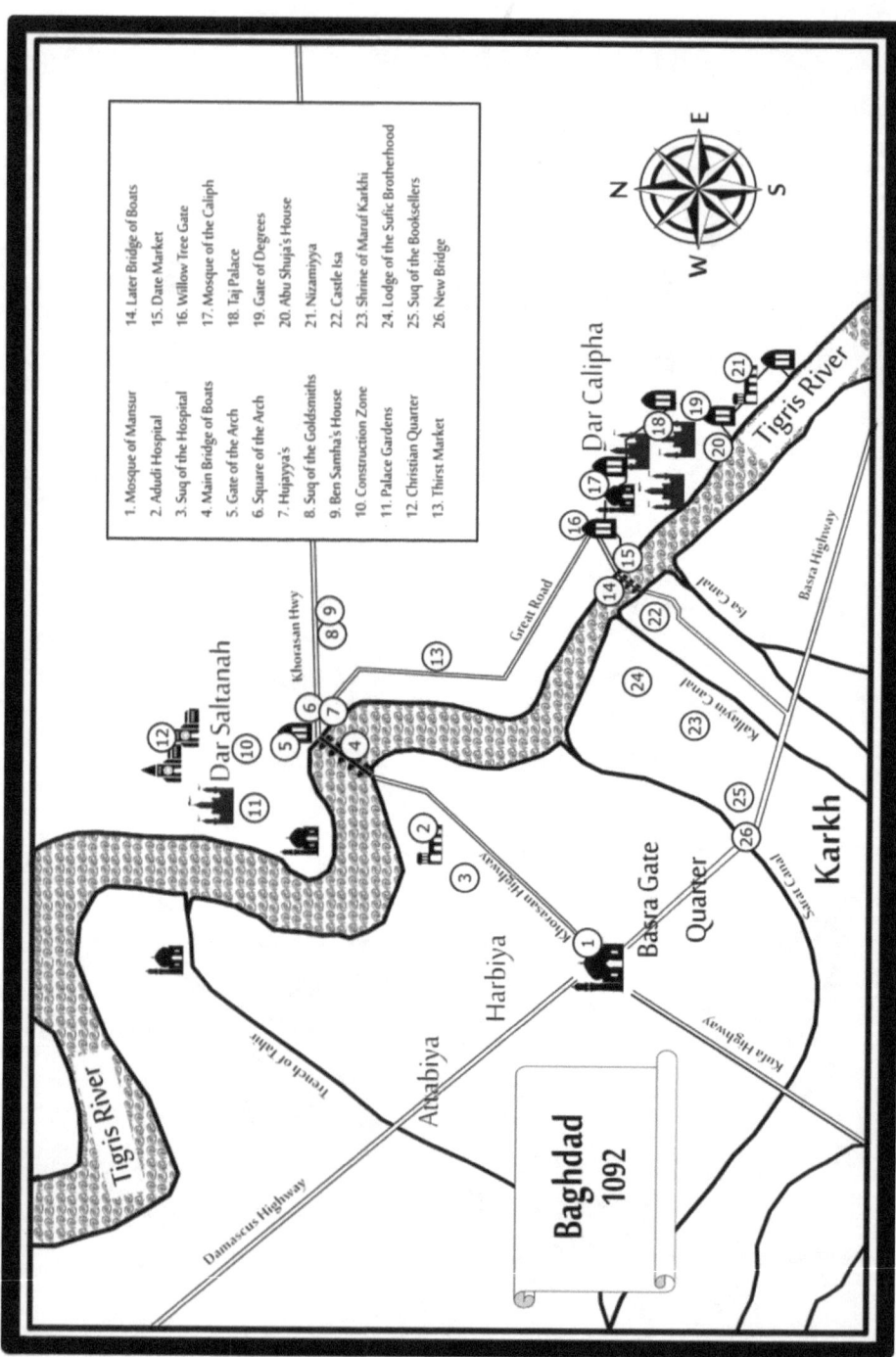

1. Mosque of Mansur
2. Adudi Hospital
3. Suq of the Hospital
4. Main Bridge of Boats
5. Gate of the Arch
6. Square of the Arch
7. Hujayya's
8. Suq of the Goldsmiths
9. Ben Samha's House
10. Construction Zone
11. Palace Gardens
12. Christian Quarter
13. Thirst Market
14. Later Bridge of Boats
15. Date Market
16. Willow Tree Gate
17. Mosque of the Caliph
18. Taj Palace
19. Gate of Degrees
20. Abu Shuja's House
21. Nizamiyya
22. Castle Isa
23. Shrine of Maruf Karkhi
24. Lodge of the Sufic Brotherhood
25. Suq of the Booksellers
26. New Bridge

Baghdad
1092

Dramatis Personae

OMAR KHAYYAM (Abu'l-Fath Omar ibn Ibrahim Khayyam)—astronomer and sometime poet

KHULD—his daughter

THE COURT OF THE SELJUQS

MALIK-SHAH, THE SULTAN (Sahib al-Jalal, the Sultan Malik-shah, Son of Alp Arslan the Seljuq, King of the East and the West, Glory of the Nation, Master of the World, Builder of Bridges, and Slasher of Taxes)—ruler of the Seljuq Empire

ABU NASIR (Abu Nasir ibn Ali, called *Abba* Nasir prior to his conversion from Judaism to Islam)—chief of intelligence

ABU'L-FADL QUMMI—successor to Taj al-Mulk as finance minister

BERK-YARUQ—oldest surviving son of Malik-shah and presumptive heir to the throne

FAKHR AL-MULK—son of Nizam al-Mulk; childhood friend of Omar Khayyam and Hasan-i Sabbah

FULANA—daughter of Malik-shah and Terken Khatun; wife of al-Muqtadi; mother of Mahmud; died 1090

GOHARA'IN—an emir; formerly a rival to Nizam al-Mulk

MAHMUD (Mahmud ibn Abu'l-Qasim; later given the regnal name al-Muslih B'illah)—son of al-Muqtadi and Fulana; grandson of Malik-shah and Terken Khatun

MU'AYYAD AL-MULK—son of Nizam al-Mulk

NIZAM AL-MULK (Nizam al-Mulk Hasan ibn Ali at-Tusi, the Nizam)—the grand vizier

NUSH-TEGIN—cupbearer to Malik-shah

RAQIM—a clerk

SAFARIYYA—third wife of the sultan Malik-shah; mother of Tapar and Sanjar

SANJAR—son of Malik-shah and Safariyya

TAJ AL-MULK (Taj al-Mulk Abu'l-Ghana'im Tutush ibn Alp Arslan)—brother and finance minister to Malik-shah

TAPAR—son of Malik-shah and Safariyya

TERKEN KHATUN—first wife of the sultan Malik-shah; mother of Fulana

YALBARD—an emir and head of security

ZUBAYDA—second wife of the sultan Malik-shah; mother of Berk-yaruq

THE COURT OF THE ABBASIDS

AL-MUQTADI, THE CALIPH (Commander of the Faithful, Scion of the House of Abbas, the Caliph Abu'l-Qasim Abdullah ibn Muhammad al-Muqtadi B'illah)—nominally, the leader of all Muslims

ABU SHUJA (Abu Shuja Muhammad ibn al-Husain Zahir ad-Din ar-Rudhrawari)—former vizier to al-Muqtadi, now under house arrest

ABU'L-ABBAS—son of al-Muqtadi and presumptive heir to the throne

AMID AD-DAWLA (Amid ad-Dawla ibn Fakhr ad-Dawla Jahir)—the caliph's vizier; son-in-law to Nizam al-Mulk

THE NIZAMIYYA

GHAZALI (Abu Hamid Muhammad ibn Muhammad al-Ghazali)—chief professor

BAGHDADI (Muhammad al-Baghdadi)—a student

GHAZI (Abu Ishaq al-Ghazi)—a poet

HUMAYDI (Abu Abdullah al-Humaydi)—deputy to Ghazali

SHIHAB AL-ISLAM—scholar at the Nizamiyya and nephew to Nizam al-Mulk

TAMIMI (Abu Muhammad at-Tamimi)—professor of shari'ah

TOGHRAI (Abu Ismail al-Husain ibn Ali at-Toghrai)—poet and author of several books on alchemy

OTHER CHARACTERS

ABU ALI BASHIR—a pharmacist in the Suq of the Hospital

THE BLIND IMAM (Abu Muhammad Emir)—chief Quran reader at the Mosque of Mansur

ABU TAHIR (Abu Tahir Wahid al-Arrani)—ward of the Ja'far family

AHMAD GHAZALI—a Sufi mystic; brother to Abu Hamid Ghazali

BEN EL—a Basra tax farmer and protégé of Nizam al-Mulk; died 1079 or 80

BEN SAMHA (Abba Saad ben Samha)—a merchant; banker to Malik-shah and jeweler to Terken Khatun

HARIRI (Abu Muhammad Qasim ibn Ali al-Hariri al-Basri)—an aspiring poet

HASAN-I SABBAH—childhood friend of Omar Khayyam and Fakhr al-Mulk

HUJAYYA—a tavern owner

IBN YASIR—a rug seller

IZMA—wife of ibn Yasir

LINA—serving girl at Hujayya's Tavern

MISRI (Commander Abu Dhafir al-Misri)—second in command at Alamut

MORDECAI—grandson of ben Samha

QUTAYYA (Qutayya bint Fakhr al-Ma'ali al-Ja'far)—last descendant of the Ja'fari dynasty of Qazvin merchants

SAAD—son of ben Samha

SHAMI (Abu Bakr Muhammad ibn Muzaffar ash-Shami)—chief qadi (judge) of Baghdad

THE THREAD OF REASON

PROLOGUE

NEAR THE VILLAGE OF SAHNEH, KERMANSHAH PROVINCE
FRIDAY, 10 RAMADAN 485
Jalali Date: 29 Mehr 471
Julian Date: 15 October 1092

O Allah! There is nothing easy but what You make easy, and if it be Your will, You change the difficult into the easy.

Silently, Abu Tahir recited the invocation and surveilled the scene around him. The wavering orange torchlight created the illusion that the tents were breathing. *Allah preserve me from those torches*, he thought. They killed his night vision, and that was going to complicate his escape.

He had chosen the third row of the crowd—close enough to the front to push forward when the time came, not so close as to be conspicuous. The people around him were mostly poor, their coarse woolen garments belted tightly against the October chill. Many gripped small scrolls of paper. If only they could get their petitions into the hands of Nizam al-Mulk, the grand vizier, he could put a sack of flour by their cooking fire, rebuild their ruined mosque, or punish the local emir who took more in taxes than the Shari'ah allowed.

But a row of soldiers barred their way to the great man. Beyond the pointed Turkish helmets, Abu Tahir could see him talking to the so-called Master of the World, the sultan Malik-shah, their two figures framed in the rectangle of light that marked the entrance to the sultan's pavilion. Nizam al-Mulk looked exactly as Abu Tahir expected; it was reassuring that the description he had received from his sheikh had been accurate. The Nizam wore a simple robe of fine silk, the scarlet and ivory chessboard collar its

16

only ornament. A carefully groomed white beard and an immaculate white turban framed his face; Nizam al-Mulk was simultaneously elegant and austere.

But Abu Tahir had expected the sultan, Malik-shah, to be taller. He had never seen a sultan in real life. He and Qutayya used to devour the stories in the *Shah-nama*;[2] the rulers in them were always "tall as a cypress tree, with a face like the full moon." Malik-shah resembled a steppe-dwelling shrub more than a stately cypress: knotted and tough (despite his flowery silk robes), but stunted by the wind-cursed climate of central Asia. As for his face, it was round enough, but after a lifetime of hunting and war, it had tanned far darker than any full moon.

Qutayya. Why did he have to think of her tonight? He wished he had back all the hours that he had spent with her at her parents' low table, their little legs folded under them on the cushions, the *Shah-nama* open between them to one of its colorful illustrations. He remembered the lock of black hair that used to come loose from under her hijab as she leaned forward to turn the pages—he had brushed it back for her with his fingers many times. But Rostam and Khosrau and the other heroes of the *Shah-nama* were infidels, cursed to live in the Time of Ignorance, before the Messenger Muhammad, may the prayer and peace of Allah be upon him. They knew not Allah, so they were not the sort of heroes Muslim children should read about. And Abu Tahir certainly shouldn't have read books with pictures in them. The Hadith was clear about that.[3] *Instead of reading the* Shah-nama, *I should have been studying more Hadith. And Qutayya should have been helping her mother. It was wrong of her father to teach her to read. That was how the trouble started.*

The memory of Qutayya made him tense. He fell back on his training. *Think about Allah at all times and you will find serenity. Give every silver dirham of effort to your task and Allah will be pleased with you.*

He looked back toward the entrance to the pavilion. Malik-shah and Nizam al-Mulk were still talking. At this distance, Abu Tahir couldn't distinguish the sultan's words, but he was clearly furious about something. As for Nizam al-Mulk, he seemed unfazed.

*   *   *

"I serve at your pleasure, O Master of the World," Nizam al-Mulk said. "If the service I offer is no longer satisfactory—"

"It's *not* satisfactory," Malik-shah interjected angrily. "It's not satisfactory at all. It's *sikking un*satisfactory!"

"Then of course I won't stand in the way of whomever the Master of the World names to replace me. I'm an old man. I've served you for twenty years and your father before you for ten. My retirement is long overdue. I've never been on the hajj. Nothing would please me more than to travel to Mecca and spend the rest of the days Allah has allotted to me sweeping out the Kaaba.[4] And it will be a great opportunity for you."

"Opportunity?" Malik-shah asked nervously.

"A *great* opportunity. It will take my replacement some time to learn all the lessons of governing that it took me a lifetime to acquire. In the meantime the Master of the World would necessarily need to be more involved in day-to-day affairs."

"What affairs?"

"Oh, the minutiae that fills my days. How many dinars to mint and how many to borrow. How to cover payrolls until the taxes come in. Determining which reports from our spies to believe. It's all quite fascinating. Although I'm afraid it would cut into your hunting time."

Then Nizam al-Mulk fell silent.

The trouble with men who like to talk is when they finally shut up it throws everyone off. As the silence dragged on, Malik-shah grew increasingly uncomfortable. Desperate for something to say, the best he could come up with was "There's no need to be hasty. My displeasure is with your grandson. I never said anything about being dissatisfied with *your* services."

"Well, I'm glad that's settled," the Nizam replied. He peered off into the western sky, as if looking for some landmark. But no landmarks were visible. Even the stars were in hiding, washed away by the light of the torches and a setting moon about two-thirds full. "I believe we'll reach the Zagros Mountains tomorrow," he said. "That puts us in Baghdad on the twenty-second or the twenty-third, *inshallah*." If it be the will of Allah.

"So another twelve days or so," Malik-shah said, grateful for the change of subject. "Is everything set for our arrival?"

"Ben Samha is taking care of it. The palace will be ready. He also reports that construction of the Mosque of the Sultan is on schedule. The foundation is complete. You'll tour it while you're there."

"I still can't believe you put a Jew in charge of the mosque."

"If there's one thing I've tried to impress on the Master of the World over the years, it's always to hire the best man for the job."

"When do we see that *peech* al-Muqtadi?"

"If by that vulgar expression you mean the Commander of the Faithful, we're expected at the Dar Calipha during the afternoon of Eid al-Fitr. Any time the sultan and the caliph get together is an occasion. But this will be one for the history books. Between the festival and the—"

"Never mind. I only asked because I want to make sure there's time for hunting."

"Affairs of state first, O Master of the World. But as soon as we're finished with the caliph . . ."

"Just make sure the quivers are full and the game is teeming."

Nizam al-Mulk embraced the sultan farewell and, leaning on a cane, walked slowly to his litter, which awaited him in the road in front of the pavilion. The four bearers—all dressed in brown caftans over orange robes and pointed Turkish caps with broad, turned-up brims—snapped to attention as he approached. They raised the litter a little higher, the better for the old man to ease himself into the seat. The Nizam took his time settling into the cushions. Then he ordered, "To my wives' pavilion," and the bearers set off at a trot along the central avenue that ran through the sultan's encampment.

They passed one tent after another. A ring of troops jogged along with them like a protective shell, although their commander was intimidating enough to keep unwanted intruders away all by himself. He was tall with a powerful build; the thick leather cuirass that girded his chest and torso made it seem more powerful still. He marched with precision; his gait told the world that he was a lifelong soldier, born to obey orders. But the fierce way his eyes glared above his long, white mustachios and the even fiercer way that he wielded his long, bronze-headed mace carried a warning: the commander giving the orders better be worthy. He maintained pace at the front, accompanied by Fakhr al-Mulk, son to the Nizam.

The tide of petitioners alternately washed up against the moving formation and retreated from its advance, all the while jostling to get the attention of the man at its center. "Nizam! Nizam!" they yelled, waving their little scrolls of paper over their heads.

Fakhr al-Mulk noticed a white-haired woman in a ragged shawl, struggling to keep up. "That one, Yalbard," he ordered the commander.

Yalbard looked crestfallen. "She's just an old woman," he said.

"Don't let my father hear you say that," said Fakhr al-Mulk. "Unless you want the speech about how the regime exists solely to serve old women—especially poverty-stricken old women. He usually accompanies it with a long story about a starving widow and the caliph Omar, may Allah be satisfied with him. For myself, I'm not satisfied with him at all; I'm tired of that story. I have heard my father tell it a thousand times. He included it in his book, which I had to edit. And it's required in the curriculum in the nine universities he started, which I have to inspect. I prefer to forgo the torture of hearing it again."

"As you wish, sir. But I was hoping for someone more imposing."

"Whatever for?"

"So the Nizam knows what sort of people we guard him from."

"That's the genius of picking the old woman."

"How's that, sir?"

"When my father sees her approach, he'll know you kept all the imposing people away."

Yalbard hadn't thought of that. Happy now, he signaled to his men with a vigorous thrust of his mace. A soldier broke ranks and hustled the woman through the gap in the circle, then sealed it up again before the rest of the petitioners could rush in. Not that they didn't try.

"Stand back," Yalbard shouted. "No one gets through unless I say so!"

The old woman prostrated herself in the dust in front of the litter and held up her petition. Nizam al-Mulk raised his hand for the procession to stop. He took the scroll from her hand and bid her rise.

"What's your name?" he asked.

"My name is Baysan. I come from a village near Nahavand."

Nizam al-Mulk scowled. Nahavand was fifteen farasangs away—a few hours by post horse, but a five-day journey for an old woman on foot. "Bring something for her to sit on," he ordered.

A soldier found a wooden box in a nearby tent. When the woman was settled, Nizam al-Mulk asked, "What brought you all this way, Baysan?"

"Food, my lord. I don't have any."

The Nizam gestured for her to continue.

"My husband and I had two sons, but they both died of smallpox when they were children. So it was only my husband and me. Five years ago, he died too."

"Then you're a widow." The Nizam looked up and addressed the crowd at large. "There's a famous story about the caliph Omar ibn Khattab—may Allah be satisfied with him—and a widow."

Fakhr al-Mulk groaned. "Damn," he whispered to Yalbard. "He's going to tell it anyway."

"One night, the caliph was riding on patrol near Medina with Abu Zaid ibn Aslam. Seeing a fire in an abandoned building, they went to investigate. They found an empty cauldron on the fire, two sleeping children, and their mother cursing the name of Omar. He asked what had brought her to this ruin in the middle of the night. 'O sir,' she said, not recognizing him. 'I'm a poor widow and I can't afford food for my starving children. So I brought them out to this abandoned building so my neighbors wouldn't hear them cry. I put the cauldron on the fire and told them to go to sleep, and when they wake up, a feast will await them.'

"'What will you do when they wake up?' Omar asked.

"'Tell them the same thing all over again.'

"Omar rode off to fetch sacks of flour, rice, and peas, and a jar of cooking oil from his own house. Abu Zaid wanted to help him carry them, but Omar wouldn't hear of it. 'You can bear this burden of victuals today, Abu Zaid,' he said. 'But then who will bear the burden of my sins on Judgment Day?'

"When they got back to the ruin, the caliph made the stew himself while the woman made the bread. The children were fed. 'How can I ever thank you?' the woman asked.

"'I ask only one thing in return,' Omar replied. 'Do not curse the name of Omar.'"

A buzz of appreciation passed through the crowd. Those who had heard the story before buzzed the loudest. Turning back to the widow, Nizam al-Mulk said, "Tell me, Baysan, was your husband your only means of support?"

"I was his, my lord. He never did amount to much. I was a seamstress, embroidering fabrics and selling them to the passing merchants. But my eyesight is not so good. I can't sew anymore. I had a few dinars, but they ran out this summer. And so now I have nothing to eat."

Nizam al-Mulk called out his orders. "Give her one hundred maunds of flour, one hundred maunds of rice, and one hundred maunds of peas," he said. "And enough oil to cook it."

"But I can't carry all that," the widow protested. "Six donkeys couldn't carry all that!"

"And give her seven donkeys."

The woman took his hand and kissed it. "May Allah bless you for your generosity."

*   *   *

Abu Tahir didn't share the murmured admiration of the crowd. Generosity with the public treasury was no generosity at all. He had heard the tales of the massive Shah Diz fortress, on the outskirts of Isfahan. Few could enter, but everyone knew what was inside: the royal treasury. Millions of gold dinars, the rightful property of the Muslim community, hoarded by the sultan and his vizier.

As the procession resumed its forward progress, Abu Tahir hurried along with the rest of the petitioners. He remembered the things he had seen on his travels. His sheikh had instructed him to observe carefully how the Seljuqs had defiled the land. He obeyed scrupulously.

In Qazvin he saw an army settling in for the winter. Having attempted to besiege the fortress of Alamut, and failing miserably by the will of Allah, the soldiers gave themselves over to besieging wine shops and brothels, with somewhat more success. In Saveh the mosque library was defiled by a collection of astrolabes and celestial spheres—instruments of foreign sciences that sought to uncover what Allah had made hidden.

But the city of Hamadan was the worst. For two weeks he waited for the sultan to arrive on his way to Baghdad. Abu Tahir had been too anxious to stay in the safe house; he spent the time walking around the city.

The stalls of over two hundred moneylenders blighted the marketplaces. The Quran was unequivocal about what Allah would do with them: *Those who devour usury . . . are the fellows of the Fire, and they shall dwell therein for aye.*[5]

Some thirty thousand spawn of the Cursed Tribe made their homes in Hamadan's Jew Town. Some of their houses stretched to four and five stories—much nicer than most of the Muslim houses. The Jews traveled on horseback with comfortable saddles. They wore no identifying patches on their clothes. Apparently Nizam al-Mulk's regard for the caliph Omar didn't go so far as enforcing the Ordinance of Omar.

Truly it was an age of heresy, atheism, and decadence. Abu Tahir was blessed that his sheikh, by the grace of Allah, had chosen him to be the instrument that would kill not merely a man but a corrupt, sin-infested, spiritually impoverished civilization.

*   *   *

"Now that we've given my father his obligatory impoverished widow," Fakhr al-Mulk said, "let's have some fun. Those two men over there look more prosperous than the others. The way they're glaring at each other, they should provide us with some amusement."

Yalbard gave the order to let them through. This time Nizam al-Mulk did not stop the procession. The petitioners had to trot alongside the litter. One of the men was middle-aged, the other quite advanced in years.

"I know you," Nizam al-Mulk said to the younger of the two. "You're the qadi of Borujerd. We met when I gave you your diploma of investiture. Why have you come here tonight?"

"To defend myself from this quack, my lord. Not satisfied with spreading lies about me all over Borujerd, he now brings his falsehoods to you."

Nizam al-Mulk regarded the other man sternly. "The qadi is the senior judge in the city," he said. "A false attack on him is an attack on the law itself. Are you sure what you say is justified?"

23

"Justified, validated, and warranted, my lord."

"He called you a quack. Are you a physician?"

"For forty years, my lord. During the summer, this man called me to his house to treat him for a fever. Which I did, with cooling foods and a preparation of willow bark. He recovered completely and then refused to pay me."

The qadi interrupted angrily. "Everyone knows the treatment for fever is bleeding. You have to get the heat out of the blood. If I recovered, it was because it was the will of Allah, and not a potion he made from trees. As far as I'm concerned, he agreed to treat me and then didn't deliver."

"When you preside in your own court," Nizam al-Mulk asked, "what punishment do you give to those who do not keep their agreements?"

"The whole of commerce depends on people delivering on their promises. So I punish breach of contract severely. The offending party must meet his obligations three times over. Then he must ride an ass through the streets of Borujerd for not less than three hours, bareheaded and dressed in sackcloth, and carrying a sign that says, 'This is the fate of those who break their agreements.'"

"A just punishment indeed," said Nizam al-Mulk to the qadi. "And that is the punishment I give you."

The qadi hesitated. He fell a couple steps behind the litter and scrambled to catch up. "Don't you mean that's the punishment you give the doctor?"

"No, I mean you. You drank his prescription and you recovered. The doctor delivered on his end of the agreement. On top of that, when you didn't pay the doctor, you counted on him having no recourse, since his complaint was against none other than the chief officer in charge of enforcing the law. There is no practice that stinks to Allah more than abuse of power by those charged with administering His shari'ah. I have always taken the gravest view of such offenses. You will pay this physician three times what you owe him and be shamed in the streets of Borujerd as you would have shamed him. Further, you are relieved of office immediately."

The former qadi tried to argue. "But I've done nothing wrong. I told you the truth. My recovery was entirely due to the will of Allah."

"I believe you," said Nizam al-Mulk. "Nothing on earth happens except by the will of Allah. Including your punishment."

*   *   *

As if Nizam al-Mulk knows anything about the will of Allah, thought Abu Tahir. *But he's going to find out.*

The procession hurried by a gap between the tents, a side street. Abu Tahir strained to see where it led, but the view was as black as a caliph's shawl. As he feared, the torches were destroying his night vision. Once he crossed the border into the shadows, he would have to stumble in the dark until his eyesight recovered. The sluggish seconds would ooze away like pitch. Plenty of time for a fatal mistake.

He had listened attentively when the sheikh told him to prepare for martyrdom. But he didn't believe it then. Now he considered the possibility in earnest: he might never return to his home. The hero's welcome he had imagined for himself, the congratulations of his sheikh, and the glow of pride on Qutayya's face—none of it may ever occur. And the thought made him happy. In a matter of minutes he would be with the Messenger Muhammad and his Companions, may the prayer and peace of Allah be upon them. For *those who are slain in Allah's cause, their works shall not go wrong; He will guide them and set right their mind; and will make them enter into Paradise which He has told them of . . . a blissful place—gardens and vineyards, and youthful girls with swelling breasts and a brimming cup.*[6]

He noticed the tension in his face and hands and the anxiety in the pit of his stomach. The sheikh had warned him to expect this too. *Be thou patient then; verily, Allah's promise is true!* He reminded himself that his sheikh wouldn't have chosen him for this mission if he doubted the outcome. "If I had two men like you," his sheikh had said, "I could turn the empire upside down." He submitted to the exercises the sheikh had given him to achieve tranquility. Breathe. *La ilaha illa-llah.* Breathe. *La ilaha illa-llah.*

He started to inch his way to the front of the crowd. It was a painstaking process, slipping between the other petitioners, making progress a finger's-breadth at a time. Finally he reached the first row. The only thing between himself and Nizam al-Mulk was the circle of soldiers. *There are so many of them,* he thought. *But, then, the Muslims were outnumbered at Badr and won a glorious victory. When Allah decrees the outcome, what do the numbers matter?*

He felt for the dagger in his sleeve, tried the point, and ran his finger along the edge one more time. It was sharp enough. *To kill with a dull knife is forbidden. An animal must not be made to suffer.*

La ilaha illa-llah. La ilaha illa-llah. La ilaha illa-llah. It was time.

*　　*　　*

They noticed him at the same time, the Sufi mystic who had suddenly materialized in the front row of the crowd. He was a young man, only nineteen or twenty, but his beard, tapering to a point, was well filled in. He wore the pale blue robe of the ascetic; its many patches, along with his ragged white turban, were witnesses to his vow of poverty. His face was smooth with the serenity of one who gives little thought to this world. Maybe his body still lingered here, but his mind was already in the Garden of Paradise. It was a look that men of action like Fakhr al-Mulk and Emir Yalbard could never understand, and so it filled them with respect. They nodded to each other. Of course they would let him through.

He took his time approaching the litter. The hem of his robe dragged in the dust and flattened tufts of grass. His feet were barely visible; he seemed to glide preternaturally across the ground. When he saw the petitioner, Nizam al-Mulk ordered the procession to stop again. All eyes were on Nizam al-Mulk and the Sufi, their faces orange in the torchlight. Sensing the change in their neighbors, even the loudest members of the crowd abruptly stopped their conversations and looked around, confused, to see what was happening. The crowd stood in religious silence, as if gathered around a sacred fire.

The Sufi was now an arm's length away from Nizam al-Mulk, who had traded his usual bearing of authority for one of humility. To receive a Sufic *baraka* during Ramadan was a double blessing. "*As-salamu alaykum,*" he said. Peace upon you, friend. Then he began another story for the benefit of the crowd.

"When I was a young man," he said, "I served an emir who was brutal; he cared for nothing but his wine and his dogs. One day a Sufi said to me, 'Serve a man who will do you good. Do not serve today those who will be eaten by dogs tomorrow.' Of course, I did not know what that meant, but true to the Sufi's prediction, I found out the following night. The dogs killed some trespassers on the palace grounds. The emir, who had been drinking as usual, stumbled outside to see what was going on. Not recognizing him, the dogs attacked and tore their own drunken master to shreds. It became clear to me that the Sufi possessed knowledge that our conventional methods of inquiry cannot fathom. Ever since, I've been a patron of Sufism.

"And so," he said, turning back to the petitioner, "how may I serve you, blessed Sufi?"

Using his right hand, the Sufi reached into the left sleeve of his robe as if to retrieve a petition. Nizam al-Mulk held out his own hand to receive it. But instead of a petition, a dagger gleamed in the Sufi's hand. "Serve with your life!" he yelled.

Then, with a war cry of *Allahu akbar*, he thrust the knife into Nizam al-Mulk's chest with all the strength that months of training had given him. Clothes and skin were no obstacle to the blade's sharp point. It scraped past a rib. He felt the resistance of the heart, the resistance of a chunk of raw meat pierced by a cooking spit. The killer angrily drove the knife deeper. The force of his attack caused one of the bearers to stumble; the litter and its occupant listed at an odd angle.

When the killer yanked the dagger out, a spray of blood came with it, soaking the sleeve of his dagger arm and spattering his face.

Then he ran.

*　　　*　　　*

The viciousness of the murder is what made his escape possible. For one long moment, everyone was too shocked to react. Their hesitation lasted just long enough for him to plow down a guard and muscle his way out of the crowd.

As Abu Tahir fled down a darkened side street, he prayed for Allah to keep him from tripping on an exposed root or a stray item of baggage. His head start was slim; already he heard Yalbard, his wits recovered, ordering the men to give chase. The killer pushed himself to run faster.

Before his conversion, he had been seduced by wine. It had turned him away from Allah, precisely as the Quran had warned; it was the *abomination of Satan's work.*[7] And yet he persisted in trying to capture that one brief phase of drunkenness that made him very, very happy. That was how he felt tonight, with no intoxicant other than his faith. He had done it. The painstaking planning and hard physical training, the journey to Hamadan and the anxious weeks spent there, the farasangs of stalking the sultan's caravan and the wait for just the right moment—they had paid off. Tonight he had succeeded not only at killing a man; he had declared jihad against an empire.

Spurred by giddiness, Abu Tahir tore between the rows of tents. Most were dark; a few had light leaking through the seams. In an open area that served as a kitchen, he glimpsed servants kneading bread for breakfast. Beyond that, music floated from a tent. As he rushed past it, he saw through the open flap a sable-haired beauty plucking the strings of a lyre while four or five couples in various states of semi-dress embraced on brocade-covered couches.

He heard the shouting and tramping of his pursuers, but he was too well trained to turn to see how many there were—or how close. Doing so would slow him down. Instead he tried to evade them by rounding a corner into another street. This one was completely dark. The black outlines of the tents were in sharp focus; his night vision was returning. His torch-wielding pursuers had no such advantage. Allah was with him. All he needed to do was stay beyond the range of their light.

A tree loomed. He grabbed the trunk and pivoted himself around another corner. Instantly he realized his mistake. The alley he had turned into ended with a rectangle of bright light. But it was too late to turn back—his pursuers had already rounded the corner behind him and blocked his escape.

He ran toward the light at the far end of the alley and burst into a square; it turned out to be a food market. Merchants were setting up their stalls; they would be ready when the faithful arrived before sunrise to buy their *suhur*, the predawn breakfast, in advance of the day's fast. Fruit sellers unloaded apples and dates onto plank tables. Porters lugged sacks of barley and rice. Zigzagging to avoid one porter, he crashed into another, knocking a sack of lentils to the ground, where it split open and spilled. He pushed onward. In two seconds he dashed across the open space to the far end of the square, where he leaped over a table, disappeared down another alley, and ran past a large tent.

A guy rope was stretched from the corner of the tent to a wooden stake jammed into the ground. But with the light of the market his night vision was destroyed again and he didn't see the rope. He just knew that his foot had caught on something, and he was sprawled in the dust with brutal pain where his chin hit. Then army boots and sword points surrounded him.

A soldier grabbed Abu Tahir's wrist and twisted it until agony made him drop the blood-covered dagger. Another soldier frisked him roughly from head to foot. When it was certain he had no other weapons, he was ordered onto his knees, with his hands clasped behind his head.

Several more squadrons marched up with torches amid shouting and confusion. Yalbard arrived and barked orders in Turkish to command his men into a semblance of order. Just in time too: the beat of hooves was heard and the soldiers parted to make way for an elegant horse bearing Sultan Malik-shah.

Yalbard handed the dagger to the sultan. Malik-shah turned it over several times and inspected it thoughtfully. The blood was already dry.

He prodded his horse forward, toward the prisoner. The horse stamped uneasily; Malik-shah calmed it with the reins.

The prisoner looked up at the sultan. Malik-shah didn't look so short now, glaring down at him angrily from his horse. In fact, he looked terrifying.

Abu Tahir remembered the story of how the sultan's father, Alp Arslan, had died. When a prisoner with a knife had broken loose and rushed him, Alp Arslan decided to show off. He ordered the guards to stand down and faced his attacker one-on-one. But the attacker got lucky—Alp Arslan slipped, the attacker stabbed him, and the teenaged Malik-shah ascended to the throne.

Allah had been on the killer's side earlier tonight and struck down Nizam al-Mulk. Perhaps Allah was still on his side and his capture was part of a larger plan. If only he could goad Malik-shah's well-known vanity, it might afford him the opportunity for a second assassination.

Abu Tahir locked eyes with the sultan and he knew: Malik-shah was thinking about his father as well.

But Malik-shah had learned from his father's folly and wasn't taking any chances. He quietly uttered two words:

"Kill him."

CHAPTER 1

THE MALIK-SHAH OBSERVATORY, ISFAHAN, IRAN
SUNDAY, 12 RAMADAN 485
1 Abán 471
17 October 1092

*T*he immenseness and complexity of the armillary sphere always astonished first-time visitors. A dozen or so brass rings, each with a diameter equal to the combined height of five tall men, were mounted on a central axis. Some, arranged in regular lines of latitude and longitude, formed the skeleton of a globe; others orbited at bewildering angles. Some were smooth; their polished surfaces gleamed in the moonlight without interruption. Others were broken into regular intervals by numbered tick marks etched into the metal. One of them—it was more of a band than a ring—was inscribed with the constellations of the zodiac; disks of inlaid silver represented the stars. At the center, a smaller sphere, this one solid, impersonated the Earth. The inlay here displayed the landmasses of Asia, Africa, and Europe. A five-pointed star marked the location of Isfahan; a somewhat larger star, Mecca.

But the visitor climbing the tower was no first-timer. He bounded up the stairs with the assurance of someone who knew where he was going. He reached the top step, emerged onto the platform, and paused to feel the cold air. He liked feeling the cold inside of him. To feel cold is to feel. To feel is to be alive. And to feel anything when most of the citizens of Isfahan were undergoing the dull routine of preparing to slide under their warm blankets and become unconscious made him feel special. Given who he was, it was funny that he had to work at feeling special. Seeing the armillary sphere made him feel special too. Few people ever got to see one; even fewer understood what they were seeing.

He wasn't alone on the platform. Inside the sphere the black outline of a man moved about, guided by the pathetic flame of a single oil lamp, shaded against the wind. The man looked through a sighting tube and then slipped between two rings, taking care not to trip on his robe. He pushed on a crank; the rings rotated. Then he returned to the tube and repeated the procedure two or three times. The visitor waited for the man to notice him, but the latter was immersed in his calibrations and the former was thirteen years old: not an age for patience. Unable to refrain from interrupting, the visitor called out, "Khwaja Omar!"

Snapping his head up from the instrument, Khwaja Omar—Abu'l-Fath Omar ibn Ibrahim Khayyam—was startled to see someone else on the platform. But he recovered quickly. He stretched his arms in an exaggerated gesture of welcome and recited theatrically:

"When all the temple is prepared within,
Why lags the drowsy worshipper outside?"[8]

The visitor took that as an invitation. He approached the armillary sphere, climbed over a ring, and joined Khwaja Omar inside.

With the visitor's face now illumined by the lamplight, Omar recognized him. "Berk-yaruq. It's you," he said. Then with too much familiarity, given his guest's lofty status, he added, "I suppose your father still wants you to be a sultan instead of an astronomer."

"To be a son of Malik-shah is to prepare for the throne," Berk-yaruq replied gravely. After a pause he added, with some frustration, "Not that anything's official."

"He wants to make you work for it," Omar said, and then changed the subject. "How did you manage to abscond from the palace?"

Berk-yaruq smiled. Listening to Khwaja Omar always made him smile. The Astronomer Royal's voice was quite deep, which would have made it authoritative were it not for an atrocious working-class accent. That, combined with the occasional and incongruous use of ostentatious words like "abscond," made for a surprisingly comical and friendly effect. He emphasized the word, drawing out the "o", as if he enjoyed the sound of it.

31

Abscond. His critics, and there were many of them, said he was in love with the sound of his own voice. His friends, there were many of them too, said it was the sound of the Persian language that inspired his love.

"I snuck past the guards," Berk-yaruq replied. "They're not really that good." Placing one hand on the armillary sphere, he asked, "What are we observing tonight?"

Omar recited:

"That inverted Bowl we call The Sky,
Whereunder crawling coop'd we live and die."[9]

"I don't know that verse," Berk-yaruq replied. "Is it one of yours?"
"That way I know it's good."
"Do you have a verse that's a little more specific?"
Omar obliged:

"Up from Earth's Centre through the Seventh Gate
I rose, and on the Throne of Saturn sate."[10]

"Saturn," said Berk-yaruq. "What time does it rise?"
Khwaja Omar checked the level of a water clock shaped like a dancing girl clapping a tambourine. "About an hour. Over there." He pointed along the sighting tube to a location on the horizon. "In Leo."

The prospect of Saturn rising caused him to grow nostalgic. "When your father commissioned this place—"

"Eighteen years ago."

"Before you were born. We made our first observations and Saturn was over there." He swept his arm across the sky and kept going until he was pointing at the ground. "You can't see it now, but it was in Sagittarius. Almost two-thirds of the way around. If I keep this up for another twelve years, it will be there again, back where it started—assuming your father doesn't cut off my funding—"

"If I'm sultan, you will receive a lot of funding."

"*When* you're the sultan. And thank you. This place isn't cheap. But if I can keep it going twelve more years, I'll be the first man ever to record an entire orbit of Saturn."

"You'll go down in history."

"It's not so I can go down in history. Well, not *just* so I can go down in history. A complete set of observations is of great scientific interest." He turned the crank again for another adjustment. As the rings orbited the sphere, he recited:

"Perplex'd by the celest'l Midnight Show;
'Tis a sort of Magic-Lantern, We know.
    The Sun is the Flame, and the World the Lamp,
And We the Figures who around it go!"[11]

The verse bothered Berk-yaruq. It took a moment before he realized why. "That's not right," he said.

"What's wrong about it?" Omar asked, smiling that Berk-yaruq had caught on.

"You describe a universe where the sun is at the center and we revolve around it. It should be the other way around. The earth is at the center and the sun revolves around *us*."

"Are you sure about that?"

"It's what all the astronomers believed, ever since Ptolemy, in the time of the ancient Greeks."

"Not all the astronomers. Biruni thought Ptolemy was erroneous."

"And was he?"

"That's what I aim to find out."

"How will you do that?"

"With extremely precise measurements—of Saturn."

"Why Saturn?"

"It has the longest orbit. The poor planet takes thirty years to go all the way around." He swept his arm in a big circle. "If I can get a lot of measurements, a complete set, measured to a few arc minutes, we can compare the measurements with Ptolemy and see who's right—Ptolemy or Biruni."

"If anyone can get better data, you can," Berk-yaruq said. "Your accurate measurement of the length of the year made the Jalali calendar a success." He groaned inwardly. *Can I say that any more stiffly? But at least now he knows I'm familiar with his work.*

"I'm flattered that you are interested in the doings of your mere servant," Omar said. "And I am impressed that you have grasped that traffic on the street of flattery moves both ways. That's how a sultan thinks."

They watched the night sky for a while. The observatory commanded the top of a hill, a short distance outside the city walls. From this vantage, the sky really was an inverted bowl. Underneath, pale brick buildings glowed bluish-white in the moonlight. The twin minarets of the Grand Mosque dominated the skyline. At opposite ends of the mosque the Dome of Nizam al-Mulk and the Dome of Taj al-Mulk, named after the men who had paid for them, faced each other icily. A chilly breeze carried the muffled chants of the congregation up the hillside.

"It's cold," Berk-yaruq said.

"It is a cold, unfeeling world," Khwaja Omar replied. "For astronomers in their observatories and sultans on the field of battle."

"I know a cure for that."

"With all due respect, O Sahib as-Sumu al-Malaki, that isn't a good idea."

"You let me last time."

"Yes, but I shouldn't have. I don't think your father approves of you drinking wine."

"He holds drinking parties twice a week."

"He's a grown-up."

"I'm thirteen!"

Omar chuckled. "Teenagers always cite their age as an argument why they should be treated as adults, but it never occurs to them how young that makes them sound to those of us in our forties."

Failing at reason, Berk-yaruq resorted to poetry:

"Ah, my Belovéd, fill the Cup that clears
TO-DAY of past Regrets and future Fears—
    To-morrow!—Why, To-morrow I may be
Myself with Yesterday's Sev'n Thousand Years."[12]

"That's right," Omar replied. "Quote me against myself. Muhammad's tomb! With such an eminent authority ranged against me, I concede the argument. I won't be the first philosopher accused of corrupting

34

the youth." He reached into a pocket of his robe and produced a clay bottle. After removing the stopper, he handed the bottle to Berk-yaruq, who took a swig. The wine formed a warm ball in his stomach. One more swig, and then he handed the bottle back to Omar.

Omar satisfied his own thirst and was about to pass the bottle back. But instead he abruptly pointed to the east and exclaimed, "Look!" Berk-yaruq's gaze followed the moving finger. Most of the stars twinkled palely tonight; they couldn't compete with the nearly full moon. But the bright dot of light appearing just over the horizon was primed for a fight. "Saturn," Khwaja Omar said.

He looked through the sighting tube and made a small adjustment. "What do you think? Is it centered?"

They changed places. Berk-yaruq peered through the tube and confirmed that the instrument was aligned. Omar was about to read the bearing off the ring when he changed his mind. "You do it," he told Berk-yaruq.

As Khwaja Omar held the oil lamp over his shoulder, the prince read the longitude off the zodiac ring. "Six degrees in the sign of Leo."

"How many minutes?"

"It looks like six degrees exactly."

Omar rewarded Berk-yaruq with the bottle; it doubled as a diversion while Omar surreptitiously checked the measurement. He dipped a reed pen into an inkwell perched on one of the more horizontal rings and made an entry in his notebook: *Six degrees. Zero minutes.* Then he sprinkled dust from a shaker onto the page to blot it.

Upon blowing the dust away and closing the notebook, Omar said, "I'm going to take another measurement in a couple of hours, when it's not so close to the horizon. You're welcome to stay."

Berk-yaruq settled onto a cushion for the wait, keeping the bottle close by. Omar began the process of moving the sighting tube and rotating the rings to adjust the sphere for his next observation. After some time had passed, Berk-yaruq said, "It's nice that you allow me to spend time with you. Most of the other scholars in my father's court seem to feel like they're not doing their jobs if they're not giving me a lecture about something. I was so relieved when Abu Hamid Ghazali was transferred to Baghdad. He kept telling me to repent from my sins."

"He probably thinks all thirteen-year-olds are brimming with sin." Encouraged by Berk-yaruq's laugh, Omar did his Ghazali imitation. "The mortal world is a foul old hag who killed all of her husbands," he said in a tone of smug self-righteousness. "Only dimwits fall into the error of becoming too attached to her. And when you have sexual intercourse with your wife, be sure you lie with your head pointed toward Mecca."

"Which head?" Berk-yaruq snickered.

"And say the correct prayers before and after intercourse. Praise be to Allah, who made us out of fluids."

When the joking was over, an uncomfortable silence lingered. Khwaja Omar clearly had second thoughts—and a little guilt—about setting a bad example for the young by poking fun at a scholar as eminent as Ghazali.

"All kidding aside, O Sahib as-Sumu al-Malaki," he said, "it behooves you to listen to Professor Ghazali. There's no one—not in Isfahan, not in Baghdad, not in Cairo—there's no one who knows the Shari'ah better than Abu Hamid Ghazali."

"Is he a friend of yours?" Berk-yaruq asked.

The prince hadn't intended that to be a difficult question, but Khwaja Omar had to think about it. When he finally answered, he said, "We're friends when the wind is from the west."

"And when it's from the east?"

"Storm clouds roll in."

Khwaja Omar's more serious tone put Berk-yaruq in a meditative mood. The young man was quiet for a good ten minutes or so, looking at the stars and thinking, but eventually he felt the need to talk about what was on his mind.

"Khwaja Omar," he said, "do you think it's odd that my father hasn't officially named me heir to the throne?"

"Don't worry about it. You're the oldest son. Or at least the oldest who has not yet passed behind the Door of Darkness."[13]

Astronomers probably don't know about political matters, Berk-yaruq thought. *Especially Persian astronomers*. So he explained it.

"The House of Seljuq is Turkish. We have our own tribal customs; the rule about the first-born son succeeding his father isn't one of them. The

36

crown goes to a warrior. It could easily be one of my brothers. Or my sister's son. Or an uncle."

"Your sister's son is four," Omar said. "Your brothers are children too."

"They won't always be."

"No, but you'll always have a head start on them."

"I don't have a head start on my uncle. Taj al-Mulk has real battlefield experience."

"You have experience."

"No, I don't."

"You gave the guards the slip tonight. That takes strategy and stealth."

But Berk-yaruq wouldn't let Khwaja Omar dismiss the subject with a joke. "What if something happens to my father and there's no official heir? There will be a civil war."

"*W'allah!* Your father is thirty-eight years old. He isn't going anywhere. He'll reign over us for many years to come—and probably keep you in suspense the whole time."

"You don't know that. My grandfather was cut down in his prime."

"And Nizam al-Mulk was there to make sure the right thing got done, and that there was an orderly transition of power and no civil war. And he'll do it again if it's necessary. Which it won't be."

Berk-yaruq was caught off guard by the vehemence of Khwaja Omar's response. He wondered if the succession was something he should be discussing outside the palace. *But this is what grown-ups talk about, isn't it? Political matters?* He took another swig from the bottle while Khwaja Omar got on with his work.

Unnatural silence precedes the news of unnatural death. That was the kind of silence that settled over the tower. The breeze died; the noises of the city died with it. The sound that broke the silence was barely audible at first, merely a faint drumming in the distance. Berk-yaruq and Khwaja Omar couldn't have said when they first noticed it. But it quickly grew in volume: approaching hoofbeats.

"Someone from the palace must have discovered you're missing," Omar said.

But when they searched the landscape, they discovered the new arrivals were not coming from the palace: three horses, one of them riderless, galloped in from the northwest, along the road from Qom.

When they reached the entrance to the tower, the horses split up. Two of them, including the riderless one, stopped; the third sped on toward the city. Omar and Berk-yaruq heard someone sprint up the steps; whoever it was, he was in a hurry.

A soldier emerged onto the platform. "I'm looking for Omar Khayyam," he announced in the voice he reserved for official soldiering business.

"I am Omar Khayyam."

"By the command of Sahib al-Jalal, the Sultan Malik-shah, Son of Alp Arslan the Seljuq, King of the East and the West, Glory of the Nation, Master of the World, Builder of Bridges, and Slasher of Taxes, you are hereby ordered to accompany me immediately to the village of Sahneh in the province of Kermanshah." He handed Omar an official-looking document.

Omar took it over to the oil lamp and bent over to read it.

"What is it?" Berk-yaruq asked.

"It is not good. Go back to the palace," Omar replied.

"Tell me."

Omar hesitated. But Berk-yaruq was old enough; he didn't need to be sheltered. Omar put his hands on the prince's shoulders and looked him in the eye. "Nizam al-Mulk is dead."

The tears would come later. For now, all Berk-yaruq could say was "It has to be a mistake."

"It is not a mistake," said the soldier. "I saw it myself. A man in a Sufi robe with a dagger attacked the Nizam."

"What happened to this dog?" Berk-yaruq demanded.

"The sultan took care of that."

Omar's tears would come later too. After arrangements had been made. "I've got to pack," he muttered, distracted. "And I've got to get cash for expenses. I've got to talk to my staff about rearranging the observation schedule while I'm gone. Then there's the grocer and the laundrywoman . . . It all shouldn't take more than a couple of days, really. So we can leave promptly after morning prayers on Wednesday . . . Thursday at the latest."

"You misunderstand me," the soldier said. "The Sahib al-Jalal said *immediately*. That means now. There's a horse waiting for you downstairs." He pivoted sharply and headed to the exit, leaving no doubt that he expected Omar to follow.

When Omar was almost to the stairs, he remembered something. He looked over his shoulder and called to the prince, "Berk-yaruq, tell my daughter what happened." Then he disappeared down into the staircase.

And thus Berk-yaruq, Sahib as-Sumu al-Malaki, prince of the House of Seljuq, son of Malik-shah the sultan, presumed throughout the land to be the heir to throne, even if it wasn't official, was demoted to messenger boy. He stood alone on the platform and contemplated the vicissitudes of fate.

CHAPTER 2

NEAR THE VILLAGE OF SAHNEH, KERMANSHAH PROVINCE
TUESDAY, 14 RAMADAN 485
3 Abán 471

19 October 1092

*O*mar was embarrassed to enter the sultan's presence stinking of sweat and horses. But the soldier hadn't given him a choice. "Orders," he explained.

The two men hadn't slept since they left Isfahan. A cry of "Sultan's business!" from the soldier was enough to cause fresh horses and a scrap of bread to appear instantly at each posting station, spaced every three farasangs along their route. The same cry scattered slow-moving caravans to the sides of the road, allowing Omar and his escort to hurtle past. They sped north past the outline of mountain ridges, black against the moonlit sky, the soldier staying just far enough ahead of Omar to discourage conversation.

At midday, near the city of Qom, they veered west to cut through the Farahan district. Late afternoon found them picking their way through a narrow valley. On both sides of the road, craggy peaks glowed gold in the light of the fast-sinking sun. Tiny villages were wedged into the folds at the bases of the cliffs, each village dominated by the turquoise dome of a single minaret poking above the housetops.

Emerging from the valley, the pair entered a desert of salt flats. The earth gleamed white under the nearly full moon. The packed crust was as hard and smooth as pavement, and the horses glided over it at demonic speed. They flew along the shore of a saltwater lake with a noose of wooden shacks around it. In the daytime these structures teemed with laborers preparing and packaging salt for market. Now the buildings were silent and desolate. The lake itself was so dark it appeared as if Allah had declined to create this particular spot of universe, leaving an irregular black patch of nonexistence. The sharply focused beam of the moon's reflection and a whiff of sulphur were all that could escape being swallowed by its surface.

Sometime during the night, the countryside had become mountainous. The curves in the road became more frequent as it weaved among the bases of the mountains. By morning they reached Rudhrawar, rich farm country with mountains all around. The reds and golds of autumn spread to the tree lines like enamel on a brightly painted bowl. Acres of *crocus sativus*—the saffron crocus—painted the valley floor purple, petals blinking open beneath the rising sun. Even at this hour, teams of peasant women in brightly colored hijabs were at work gathering the flowers into baskets. Allah had been generous this year: the saffron harvest was abundant. Once the stigmas and styles were extracted, the spice merchants of Hamadan and Nahavand would pay generously for the aromatic threads. Rudhrawar families would eat well in front of warm fires this winter. Optimism was in the air. Everyone worked cheerfully. One robust woman pointed to something inside a flower she had picked and laughed raucously, leaving Omar to speculate about what she thought was so funny about a plant's genitalia.

Beyond Rudhrawar, Omar and his escort merged onto the Khorasan Highway. The road was wider now; heavy traffic—all on the sultan's business—slowed them down, but they had only another six farasangs to travel until they galloped into Sahneh.

It was noon when the sultan Malik-shah's camp burst into view. Omar noticed two men guarding the entrance. There seemed to be something wrong with them. When Omar realized what it was, he halted abruptly. The men had no bodies. They were merely heads on pikes. The necks were cleanly severed. The expressions were almost peaceful, the eyes closed, the mouths only slightly open, as if the men were sleeping and might open their eyes at any moment. In a way, Omar thought this sight was more gruesome than if the heads had been battered and bruised and the faces frozen in an expression of horror.

But Omar's escort didn't slow at the display. Omar had to spur his horse to catch up. The two riders dashed through crowds of people who tried to go about their business despite the necessity of leaping out of the path of charging horses on the main thoroughfare. Omar and his escort halted only when they arrived at the sultan's pavilion. The soldier bounded off his horse and said a few words to a guard. Not as young as the soldier, nor as hardened to life on the road, Omar dismounted with effort; he was stiff with the aches and pains of forty hours' jostling in the saddle. The soldier took both horses by the reins and disappeared around a corner, leaving Omar at the entrance. Omar wasn't prepared for what he found inside.

Taking leave of the sun, Omar found that his eyes needed a moment to adjust to the gloom. The sultan's tent was vast. Rumor had it that he played polo inside it on rainy days. It looked like a place where a party had been held, but everyone had gone home. Emptiness stretched between the ornately decorated fabric of the walls. It was bare of furniture except for a group of couches that seemed too small for the space. At the center of the group was a brass brazier, but no fire burned inside; there was only a heap of gray ashes. On one of the couches, Malik-shah lay curled in a pitiful state. His head was uncovered, his long black hair disheveled. His beard had not been trimmed since the murder, and he had replaced the silk gown he had worn that night with a garment of sackcloth.

"Sahib al-Jalal," Omar said softly.

Upon seeing Omar, the sultan rose from the couch and embraced him tightly without saying a word. Tears wet his beard; his shoulders convulsed with his sobs.

When Omar saw what the murder had done to his friend and king, the monstrousness of it struck him like a thousand maunds of bricks. He shook with sobs of his own. Nizam al-Mulk had been a generous patron to him. Maybe the fatigue of his journey had made him overly sentimental, but all Omar wanted was to hear the Nizam tell the story about the caliph Omar and the poor widow one more time.

Malik-shah spoke first. "I still can't believe it," he said in Persian. "I always thought that Nizam al-Mulk was indestructible."

"So did I," Omar replied. "I can barely remember a time when he wasn't a huge influence in my life. I assumed he would always be there."

Malik-shah sat down on the couch and gestured for Omar to sit beside him. "When I was a child, I thought my father was indestructible," Malik-shah said.

"The Martyr Sultan," Omar replied.

"He was struck down by a murderer's dagger too," he said. "Then Nizam al-Mulk stepped in and took charge. It's strange how things come full circle."

Omar didn't answer. He thought it would be good for Malik-shah to talk a bit.

"Everything I've accomplished . . . if it hadn't been for Nizam al-Mulk, I literally wouldn't have survived the first week. My uncle Qavurt wanted the throne for himself and rebelled. Nizam al-Mulk captured him. Uncle Qavurt tried to barter for his life with a box of letters he said implicated his coconspirators. I wanted to be harsh to the conspirators and lenient to my uncle. He was of the same blood as me, after all. But Nizam al-Mulk threw the box of letters into the fire and had Qavurt strangled with his own bowstring. He was right, of course. I was eighteen years old; I didn't know a thing back then.

"Then the army started looting. The Nizam asked me for authority to get them under control. I still remember exactly what I said to him: 'I hand over to you all affairs, great and small. You are my father now.'"

Omar knew how Malik-shah felt. When Omar had left home to study in the madrasa and started spending so much time at the home of his friend Fakhr al-Mulk, Fakhr al-Mulk's father, the Nizam, became more of a father to him than the tent maker who was his real father.

"I behaved so badly on Friday," the sultan lamented. "Unleashing my fury upon him over . . . over nothing. An ill-considered remark about my crown resting on his inkwell. Although, between us, it disturbed me even more that he didn't compliment my ring. The last thing I said to him was 'Just make sure the quivers are full and the game is teeming.' If I knew that a few minutes later . . ." He began to sob again.

Omar waited for Malik-shah to cry himself out. Then he asked, "So now what happens?"

"First I have to decide whether to continue our journey to Baghdad or turn around and go back to Isfahan," the sultan replied.

"Why wouldn't you go on?"

"I have important plans for when we get to Baghdad. But I'm not sure if I can carry them out without the Nizam at my side. I feel like my boat sank and I'm struggling to keep my head above water."

"I assume you'll appoint someone to succeed him. No one can ever replace him, of course. But I'm sure whoever you appoint can get the job done. So you'll have a new boat."

"I still have to figure out who I should appoint."

"What are the choices?"

"Nizam al-Mulk's oldest, Fakhr al-Mulk. And my brother, Taj al-Mulk."

"I don't know Taj al-Mulk too well, but I can put in a good word for Fakhr al-Mulk. We went to school together. He's smart, loyal, ambitious."

"Don't you think he's *too* ambitious?"

"Where did that idea come from? Did he push too hard for the job?"

"On the contrary. He's busy preparing to return to Isfahan to bury his father."

"That shows more piety than ambition," Omar said. "He could continue on to Baghdad with you. He knows the risk of leaving your side. Out of sight, out of mind. He's doing the right thing anyway. Consider that."

"I will," the sultan said thoughtfully. "I'll make a decision soon."

"When I'm stuck on a problem at the observatory, I ask myself, what would Avicenna do?[14] You should try the same thing. Not what would Avicenna do, of course. What would Nizam al-Mulk do? How would he advise you?"

"I don't know, but it would probably be couched in a long story." The sultan smiled sadly. "I never thought I would say this," he added, "but I'm going to miss his stories."

"You know why he told them, don't you? All those stories about the great kings of the past. And then he wrote a collection of them, and published the collection, and called the collection *The Book of Politics*?"

"If you asked me that a week ago, I would have said he did it to be a pain in my ass. And possibly to bore me into agreeing with him."

"And suppose I were to ask you now?"

The sultan replied slowly as his thoughts struggled to keep up with his words. "If you asked me now . . . I'd have to say . . . Nizam al-Mulk wanted me to be ready for the day when he was no longer here to guide me."

"Exactly!" Omar said. "Those stories, they were for you. They can all be summed up in three words: be a king."

"You and the Nizam had something in common," he said. "You both always gave me good advice."

"My advice isn't that good. At least not so good that you brought me a hundred farasangs to hear it."

"But still, I'm going to follow it," the sultan replied. "A king would go on to Baghdad and finish what he started. So that's what we're going to do. We'll leave first thing in the morning." He sat up and donned authority as if he were putting on a new robe. The friend-to-friend part of the meeting was over; the sultan-to-subject part was about to begin.

"Good as your advice is," the sultan said, "you're right, I did have something more specific in mind for you. I want you to find out who murdered Nizam al-Mulk."

"I heard you already took care of that."

"I executed the man who wielded the knife. But I don't believe he acted alone. I want you to investigate the murder and find out who hired him."

Omar didn't know what to say. If someone really had ordered the murder, then that man needed to be brought to justice. The nation owed that to the Nizam. *Omar* owed that to the Nizam. It was an important mission that the sultan was giving him. Too important to leave to an amateur.

"I'm not a *shurta*," he stammered. "I'm not a detective."

"So?" the sultan replied.

"I'm hopeless at court intrigue. This business needs someone who actually has experience with this kind of thing."

"You're one of the two smartest people I know. That counts for something."

"That's the same reason you gave me an observatory. In two weeks Saturn goes into retrograde. I have to be at my instruments—so that all that money you spent on them goes to good use."

"Saturn can wait to go into retrograde until you find the murderer."

Omar was tempted to explain that he didn't actually control when Saturn went into retrograde. But sensing the sultan's growing frustration with him, he had the good sense to take a different tack.

"I'm not trying to be difficult," he said. "But I'm the wrong man for the job."

"I trust you. That makes you the right man."

"There must be other people you trust."

Malik-shah signaled for Omar to wait a moment. He walked over to a chest, raised the lid, and removed an object wrapped in cloth. Returning to Omar, he unwrapped the cloth to reveal a dagger.

Omar examined it carefully. It was an expensive piece of cutlery. Damascus steel blade. Leather-covered handle with gold filigree. A large blue gemstone was embedded in the handle. Omar wasn't a jeweler, but he believed it was some sort of sapphire.

"Is this the murder weapon?" Omar asked.

"No," the sultan replied. "It's the murder weapon's twin brother."

"Twin brother? Where did it come from?"

"My bed."

Omar looked at the sultan blankly.

Malik-shah explained. "After the murder of the Nizam and the chase after the killer, I returned to my pavilion. I was worn out from the long day and the tragic events. All I wanted to do was go to sleep. When I got to my bed, the dagger was lying on my pillow, as if on display."

"'Display' is the right word."

"Oh, yes. Whoever left it there wanted me to see it."

"It's a message of some sort. A warning. 'You're next' or 'We can get you too.'"

"Now you understand my concern."

"You must have had guards on your bedchamber," Omar said. "Did they see anything?"

"Someone lured them away with a jug of wine. We found them sleeping it off nearby."

"Could they identify who it was?"

"Not anymore."

Omar remembered the two heads he had seen on pikes when he rode into the camp.

"It could have been anyone," Malik-shah said. "Do you understand why I can't trust anyone around me?"

"But why me?"

"Remember when Nizam al-Mulk first introduced you to me?" Malik-shah asked. Omar nodded. Malik-shah continued, "He told me he had offered to make you governor of Nishapur. You were twenty-six years old, and he was giving you a huge opportunity and you turned him down. You told him you wanted a stipend to study the stars instead. And that's why I trust you: your ambitions draw you in a direction other than power, which will ensure the integrity of your investigation. On top of that, everyone around me is mired in bureaucracy. I need someone who will move quickly. This dagger is a threat on my life. I need whoever is responsible for it apprehended before he can make good on that threat."

Omar couldn't keep arguing. Not when the stakes were Malik-shah's life and Malik-shah—his friend—was asking him for help. "Okay," he said. "You win. I'll do it."

"Dark forces are at work. But promise me that no matter what happens, you'll see it through to the end."

"I promise." He contemplated the dagger again. "They killed Nizam al-Mulk and sent you this dagger as a warning. There's something they want you to do. Or not do. Do you have any idea what that might be?"

"It could be anything."

Omar tried to think. "What did you and the Nizam do this year? You were with the army in the Land beyond the River, right?"

"That's right. The *sikking* Qarakhanids rebelled. We were bringing them back under our control."

"Did you win?"

"There were still pockets of resistance when we had to break off for the winter. We'll go back in the spring to destroy what's left of them."

"Then the Qarakhanids have a motive to ensure that you are not successful. Who else has a motive? Is there any other fighting going on?"

"I sent a small detachment to besiege the Sheikh of the Mountain in Alamut. They broke off for the winter too. The men pulled back to Qazvin."

Omar Khayyam and Malik-shah continued along these lines for some time, cataloging the various threats to the empire—the Byzantine Emperor of Rum, the Fatimid Caliph of Egypt, the Arab bandits on the hajj route. But the threats all seemed distant and tractable. Under the Seljuq Empire, for the first time in centuries, peace and stability reigned from the Sea of Rum to the Indus River.

At last it became time for them to exchange their farewells. Omar wanted to revisit one point before he left. "You told me you wanted me to investigate this because I was one of the *two* smartest people you know," he said. "Who's the other one?"

"That's the best part. You don't have to do this alone. When you get to Baghdad, you're going to have a partner."

Omar had a bad feeling about this. "Who?" he asked again.

"The first scholar in all my lands. Abu Hamid Ghazali."

*   *   *

The sultan's brother, Taj al-Mulk, was all business. "First," he said, "the sultan instructed me to prepare this." He handed Omar a scroll tied with ribbon.

"What is it?" Omar asked.

"It's a safe-conduct," Taj al-Mulk replied.

When Omar opened it, he found an official document commanding any and all who read it to provide him with safe passage through their territories, along with whatever assistance he demanded, including but not limited to information, cash, provisions, and immediate clearance through military checkpoints. The page was signed by Malik-shah and sealed with his signet.

"It's not every day that someone gets all the resources of the Great Seljuq Empire placed at his disposal," Taj al-Mulk said.

"I'll try not to use too many of them," Omar replied humbly.

"This isn't the time to be frugal. Malik-shah made these resources available to you for a reason. Use them."

"There is one thing I want to use," Omar said. "I want to get to Baghdad as soon as possible, but at the rate the sultan moves, with his whole camp with him, it will take at least ten days. Can I use the imperial post horses to go on ahead?"

"Take what you need. I'm in a hurry to get to Baghdad myself, and so is Yalbard. We can leave together, first thing in the morning."

They walked side by side along the main street of the encampment. Even in the midst of the Seljuq army, Taj al-Mulk was an imposing presence in his leather cuirass and metal helmet. Lower-ranking troops hastened to get out of his path. Preparations for the next day's departure were well under way. Slaves and soldiers scurried about on a variety of errands. Sacks of victuals and chests of weapons lined the street, ready to be loaded onto donkeys when the time came. Nonessential structures had already been dismantled, leaving gaps in the rows of tents like missing teeth.

"Were you with the sultan on Friday night?" Omar asked. "He told me he had a ruckus with the Nizam."

"He tried to start one," Taj al-Mulk replied, "but he didn't succeed."

"Why not?"

"He counted on me to take sides and I wouldn't do it."

"I'm surprised. From what I hear, you would have welcomed a chance to egg them on."

"Don't believe everything you hear, my friend. Yes, there was talk about a 'rivalry' between the Nizam and me. People like to invent factions. They said we had 'policy differences.' What a load of *sachmalik*! We agreed on every important issue. When you work with someone for twenty years, you gel as a team. They said I wanted his job. That was *sachmalik* too."

"But now you might get the job."

For a moment, Taj al-Mulk was stunned by Omar's impertinence. Then he burst out laughing. "Casting suspicions already, Khayyam?" he asked. "Good. My brother got the right man. Don't be afraid to suspect anybody, including me."

"I'm astonished by your disinterestedness."

"I want you to find out who did this. Nizam al-Mulk was an honorable man who wanted nothing more than to serve Allah, the empire, and my brother."

They turned down a side street and entered an open area where preparations for tonight's *iftar* were in full swing. Dozens of slaves sat on the ground as they chopped leeks, crushed spices, and plucked chickens. A cook cussed out a kitchen boy over a spilled bowl of carrots. Over the heat of open fires, stews bubbled in enormous cauldrons; steam and smoke mingled as they lazily escaped into the sky.

But Omar and Taj al-Mulk were just passing through. Beyond the cook fires, a cave was hollowed out of a hillside. Two soldiers guarded the entrance; they saluted Taj al-Mulk smartly as he and Omar passed between them.

Once inside, Omar noticed the drop in temperature immediately. The air was cool and refreshingly clean after the clammy and smelly cooking area.

"The local ice house," Taj al-Mulk explained. "It seemed like the logical place to put the two bodies until you got here. Although the imams are squawking because we haven't buried them yet."

They walked down a set of wooden steps into the chamber. All around them, blocks of ice, hauled down from the Zagros Mountains, were stacked four high. The blocks were arranged so that cubbyholes appeared every few feet; basins of sherbet chilled inside them. The thick earthen walls shut out the noise of the camp and combined with the dim light of the oil lamps to give the cave a solemn atmosphere.

In the center of the room, two stacks of ice, each about the size and shape of a coffin, had no cubbyholes. Two bodies, washed and dressed in white linen shrouds, lay lifeless on top of them.

"You did the right thing," Omar said. Not that he actually knew it *was* the right thing; he was making it up as he went along.

Omar knew it would be heartbreaking to examine the corpse of Nizam al-Mulk, so he got it over with. Despite his seventy-six years, the Nizam always seemed wise and energetic to Omar. So it was a shock to see his frail body and vacant face. He even seemed shorter than Omar remembered. It had been years since Omar had seen the Nizam without a turban; he hadn't realized the old man was almost completely bald.

Omar told himself that the Nizam would expect him to remember he had a job to do and to do it professionally. "Help me with the shroud here," Omar said to Taj al-Mulk, choking down a sob. After they tugged and lifted for a minute or two, the corpse lay naked on the ice.

The wrinkled cadaver didn't tell Omar anything he didn't already know. A single wound over the heart. Expertly inflicted and expertly cleaned, it was now a neat, almost surgical incision. No other wounds, no skin discoloration that could indicate poisoning, no clue of any sort that the cause of death was anything other than what a hundred witnesses said it was: a single thrust of a killer's knife.

The other corpse was that of a young man, nineteen or twenty years old, probably Persian. When they removed the shroud, Omar saw that the murderer had a muscular build.

"He would have made a good soldier," Taj al-Mulk said.

"He doesn't look like any Sufi I ever met, that's for sure," Omar replied. "Unless the Sufis have started branching out into militant orders."

Taj al-Mulk pointed to the murderer's chest. "Look at that scar," he said. "This wasn't his first fight."

Frustration welled inside Omar. "I love your brother," he said, "but I don't know what he was thinking when he ordered the killer executed before anyone could question him. Muhammad's tomb! We don't know who he is, where he came from, what his motive was. '*Their Mouths are stopt with Dust.*'"[15]

Taj al-Mulk didn't argue. "Perhaps this will help," he said. He handed Omar a basket that had been sitting on the floor next to the makeshift bier. "That's everything he had on him."

Omar set the basket on a block of ice, examined each item, and placed it next to the basket.

A dagger lay on top. "The murder weapon?" Omar asked.

Taj al-Mulk nodded.

It was identical to the one Malik-shah had shown him, down to the sapphire embedded in the handle. But this one had dark stains on the blade. The blood of Nizam al-Mulk. Someone he knew. He tried not to think about it.

Pointing to the gemstone, Omar said, "The killer had money."

"Or someone with money funded him. And there's more. Look in the purse."

Omar pulled a leather pouch out of the basket. It was heavy. He dumped the contents; dozens of gold dinars, each a little larger than a fingernail, clattered onto the ice.

"We counted them," Taj al-Mulk said. "Eighty-five."

"So about a month's pay for a minor official. They wanted him to easily cover any expenses that might crop up on the road but not have so much that he would be tempted to scamper off with it."

"Or so much that it would be a great loss if he didn't survive."

Omar held up one of the coins and examined it. "No wear," he said. "Newly minted."

"Read the inscriptions."

One side carried the standard dedication to the sultan Malik-shah, the other to the caliph al-Muqtadi. Nothing unusual there. The mint mark was Hamadan.

"That's only twenty farasangs from here," Taj al-Mulk said. "So he was local."

"Or someone gave him the money when he got there," Omar replied. "Or he had money when he got there but exchanged it to cover his tracks." There were too many *or*'s. Retracing the killer's steps wasn't going to be easy. "Is there an artist in the camp?"

"What kind of artist?" Taj al-Mulk asked.

"A wanted poster artist. The kind that draws wanted posters . . . a portrait artist."

"The military *shurat* have one."

"I suppose the imams squawk about that too. Graven images or something."

"They do, but they don't have any say in the matter. He's a Christian."

"Get him. Get some portraits drawn of the murderer and strew them around Hamadan."

"We already caught him. Why do we need wanted posters?"

"To find out if anyone knows who he is."

"Oh. Good thinking."

Omar started to examine the empty purse.

"Don't bother with that," Taj al-Mulk said. "It's mine. Merely a place to put the coins. When we found them, they were sewn into the hem of his robe. Whoever he was, he was a professional."

The robe was the last item in the basket. Omar examined it slowly, viewing a few inches of fabric at a time. But aside from the torn seams where the coins had been removed, he could find nothing unusual. It was just a patched woolen robe, the sort that any Sufi mystic might wear. For the first time, Omar was glad that Ghazali would be on the case. Perhaps he could make something of it.

"Can I steal this?" Omar asked.

"It's your investigation," Taj al-Mulk replied. "Steal the whole basket if you want. Except for the cash. If you want that, you have to sign a receipt."

They had just finished repacking the evidence and re-dressing the corpses when a soldier arrived with a message. "There has been a change in plans," Taj al-Mulk said when he had read it. "We're going to have to stick with the camp tomorrow. We won't be able to rush on ahead for another day."

"What is it?" Omar asked.

"You're in trouble now. The sultan's wife wants to see you."

"Which one?"

"The first one. Terken Khatun. The Bitch of Samarqand."

*   *   *

The lamp flame was just bright enough to light the page in front of him. The rest of the tent was in shadow.

Fakhr al-Mulk had taken the liberty of moving into his father's pavilion. *Iftar* in the sultan's tent had ended hours ago. Malik-shah put in an appearance, his first since the death of the Nizam. Nevertheless, it was a subdued affair that broke up early. Fakhr al-Mulk wasn't too disappointed; he had work to do.

He got straight to it, not bothering to change out of his robe of honor into something more practical. He sat cross-legged on a cushion. A sheet of pasteboard, resting on his lap, served as a writing surface. The diamond in his ring flashed in the lamplight as his pen shuttled across page after page. The stack of completed letters grew as the hours passed, all inscribed with his elegant handwriting. *To Muhammad Nasikh, Isfahan. To Abu Hamid Ghazali, Baghdad. To Ahmad Ghazali, Baghdad. To the Commander of the Faithful, Caliph Abu'l-Qasim al-Muqtadi, Baghdad.* But the letter in front of him was the most sensitive.

To Mu'ayyad al-Mulk, Baghdad
In the Name of Allah, the Merciful and the Compassionate.

Dear Brother:

By the time you read this, you will have heard about the death of our father, struck down by a murderer's dagger.

53

I leave Sahneh tomorrow to accompany the body back to Isfahan, where I will arrange for the funeral and the official mourning.

I would suggest that you join me, but we both grew up in our father's household and we know how things work. Our enemies will not be idle—we do not have the luxury of immersing ourselves in grief. You and I have not always seen eye-to-eye, but these are dangerous times. We need to put aside our differences and work together to look after our common interests—and our primary interest is to see that the Office of the Vizier stays in our family. Our fortune depends on the vizierate going to one of the sons of the Nizam, and not to a certain person whose name may be similar to ours but who is no relation to us. We must see to it that Taj al-Mulk is not appointed vizier or, failing that, that his term of office is a short one.

And so I ask you to remain in Baghdad. The sultan intends to resume his journey west. When he arrives, stay close to him. Do not let him forget our years of experience in his service, but do so humbly. I realize humility is not your strong suit, but I assure you it is the best course with Malik-shah. Also, miss no opportunity to sow the seeds of suspicion in the sultan's mind concerning Taj al-Mulk. As for the rest of the sultan's intimates, I'm sure I don't need to tell you how to spread the dinars around.

I will join you as soon as possible, but be assured I continue to work for the success of our cause.

Your loyal brother,
Fakhr al-Mulk

He translated the letter into code himself; it wasn't the sort of message that he could trust to a secretary. He had just finished, and was burning the original in the brazier, when a visitor arrived.

"Is it too late for a condolence call?" Omar Khayyam asked.

"It's never too late to receive an old friend," Fakhr al-Mulk replied.

Omar had known Fakhr al-Mulk since the two had been children. He didn't need words to express how sincerely he shared his grief. All he needed was to hold Fakhr al-Mulk's embrace a little longer than usual.

Fakhr al-Mulk unstopped a jug of wine and poured. It wasn't until they had finished their second cup that either of them said anything further.

"How are you faring?" Omar asked.

"I'm too busy to think about it," Fakhr al-Mulk replied. "And you?"

"The same. But you know me. Once I stop being busy, it will hit me like an arrow barrage from the Turkish cavalry."

"Then you'll drain the cups, scribble about the short time we have on earth and the void that awaits beyond, but find no relief except unconsciousness in the arms of a tavern wench—"

"You know me too well," said Omar.

"I even know why you're here."

"I tried to turn Malik-shah down. But he wouldn't take no for an answer."

"So go ahead, Omar."

"What?"

"Ask your questions."

Omar was caught off guard. He had been struggling to find a tactful way to interrogate his oldest friend without sounding like he was accusing him of something. He hadn't expected Fakhr al-Mulk to volunteer. He didn't know where to begin.

Seeing Omar's hesitation, Fakhr al-Mulk said, "I'll start you off. Yes, I had a motive to kill my father. His estate is worth millions in dinars and jewels and lands. Because of his death, I am a wealthy man. In addition, I now command his private army of twenty thousand Turkish mamelukes. And if the sultan appoints me to be his vizier, I'll become even richer and more powerful. So add me to your list of suspects."

"Who else do I inscribe in the Book of Badness? Malik-shah?"

"No. He needed my father and he knew it."

"Maybe he resented that."

"He's weak. Not insane."

"What about Taj al-Mulk?"

"Guilty as sin. But, then, I'm biased."

"Did your father have any enemies among the sultan's other officials?"

"If you had asked me that question a week ago, I would have told you that my father defeated all of his enemies long ago. I wouldn't have been able to think of anyone who would dare to oppose him. But obviously someone wanted him dead. And, what's more, he knew it."

The revelation shook Omar's faith in his longtime mentor. If the Nizam al-Mulk he knew had uncovered a plot against his life, he would have quashed it without mercy and dispatched the conspirators to an early death. Besides, ever since Omar had arrived in Sahneh, numerous people had recounted to him how Nizam al-Mulk had bested Malik-shah at his last *iftar*. The relaxed, confident, in-control elder statesman that they described didn't square with someone who feared his own murder.

"What did he tell you?" Omar asked.

"It wasn't anything he said," Fakhr al-Mulk replied. "It was something he wrote." The guileless, questioning look on Omar's face invited an explanation. "Since my father was killed, I've been going through his papers," Fakhr al-Mulk said. "Mostly they're run-of-the-mill government reports. Ledger sheets, troop dispositions, surveillance reports on minor officials suspected of diddling farm animals. It's all rather tedious, really. But then I found this . . ."

He picked up a manuscript from a table and handed it to Omar.

There were about a hundred pages. "What is it?" Omar asked.

"*The Book of Politics*. Volume two."

"*The Book of Politics* has only one volume."

"Your memory never ceases to astound me. In any case, the book was so popular, my father was writing a sequel."

Omar started to thumb through the pages.

"Here's the important part," Fakhr al-Mulk said. Reaching over, he flipped to the page of interest. "About a third of the way down."

The most damaging and odious enemies to the religion of Muhammad, Omar read to himself, *are also the worst enemies of the Master of the World.*

These people who, today, have power in the government, and who make propaganda for the Shiite creed, belonging to this sect: they carry out their affairs in secret, they employ violence, they indulge in proselytism, and they talk the Master of the World into the idea of annihilating the Abbasid dynasty.

If I wanted to lift the lid that covers this pot, what evils would come out! By their machinations, these people have procured the silver of the Master of the World; they have had their way because of economies they have shown him, and they have made him avid and greedy. As for me, they represented me like a spirit of evil intentions, so that now the advice I give under the circumstances is not well received. One will not know the extent of their intrigues and their ruses until I am gone, and only then will one know the extent of my loyalty to this victorious government, and the worry that the existence and the projects of this sect have given me. I have constantly submitted this situation to the lofty judgment of the prince, and I have not hidden anything.

Although I see my words are not pleasing, I will dedicate a short chapter on the history of these heretics, because it is important to understand this sect, its origins, its beliefs and religious opinions, the number of times they have rebelled, and how the rulers of the world have defeated them up to now.

I write this that it may remain, after my death, to be a memorial in the hands of him who is the sovereign of the world and of the faith.[16]

When he finished reading the passage, Omar was too dumbfounded to say anything. It was as if death had not merely stolen the Nizam from the nation but had stolen the *idea* of the Nizam as well.

Everyone knew that Nizam al-Mulk was the undisputed ruler of the sultan's realm—and of the sultan himself. It was inconceivable that he would lose control to the point that Shiite heretics could infiltrate the government and turn the sultan against him. It was absurd that these interlopers could talk the sultan—the orthodox Sunni Malik-shah—into the stunningly wicked idea of "annihilating" the Abbasid dynasty of caliphs. Sure, sultans had had their share of friction with caliphs for as long as there had been sultans. They had interfered in the caliph's affairs, kept them virtual prisoners, and occasionally flung armies at them. But the caliph was still the sultan's lord and master, the Commander of the Faithful, the scion of the sacred bloodline of Abbas, uncle to the Messenger. To cut that bloodline short would be an act of wickedness that would heap shame and scorn upon the perpetrator down to the end of time.

Almost as inconceivable was the idea that the Nizam had grown too feeble to do anything about it other than warn cryptically of "machinations" and "intrigues" in an unpublished manuscript, or whimper that the sultan would be sorry—after the Nizam was dead. Omar had known Nizam al-Mulk his whole life. He had watched him command, celebrate, mourn, and impart wisdom. But—Muhammad's tomb!—in forty years, Omar had never heard him whine.

Fakhr al-Mulk gave Omar time to let what he'd read sink in. When he finally spoke, he said, "I know. I couldn't believe it either."

"I took this job out of a sense of duty to Malik-shah," Omar replied. "But now it's starting to get interesting."

"You never could resist a puzzle."

"Who knew that your father was working on a second volume?"

"Most of his immediate family and his inner circle. Of course, we had no idea it was going to say this."

"Did you tell the sultan?"

"I tried to."

"What did he say?"

"Nothing. He laughed."

Omar pressed his lips together. He wondered whether the sultan's peculiar reaction had been because he believed the Nizam's warnings or because he didn't.

"Who are these heretics?" Omar asked.

"Believe me, I've been cudgeling my brains about it for days, trying to figure it out. As far as I knew, the sultan's officials were all completely loyal to my father. Any enemies he had were reconciled years ago."

"No arguments at all?"

"None."

"That's not normal," Omar replied. "Someone always disagrees about something."

"Not with this team."

"Not even Taj al-Mulk?"

"The sultan's brother is loyal and hardworking." Fakhr al-Mulk hesitated. "Well, there was one incident."

"What was that?"

"It's probably nothing."

"Tell me."

"A couple of months ago I was headed into my father's office and I heard raised voices inside. Then the door opened and Taj al-Mulk came out, looking furious."

"What did they argue about?"

"I don't know and my father wouldn't tell me. But I'm pretty sure I heard the word 'caliph.'"

"What about the caliph?"

"I don't know. All I heard was 'caliph.' Anyway, it only happened once. After that my father and Taj al-Mulk got along fine." He paused and then added darkly, "As far as I know." He quickly changed the subject. "Is there anyone else you'd like to know about?"

"No, that was all."

"That wasn't so bad. Now have another drink with me and let's reminisce about the old days."

But Omar was still thinking about the manuscript. "I need to hold on to this, of course," he said.

"You can have it for tonight," Fakhr al-Mulk replied. "But it's part of my father's estate and I want to take it back to Isfahan with me. I'm going to talk to Muhammad Nasikh about publication."

"Talking to a scribe about publication is fine. But promise me you won't actually publish without consulting with me first. If this manuscript wanders into the hands of the public, it will cause such a conflagration of outrage as to send this whole investigation veering into a ditch."

"I'll do my best."

Omar flipped absentmindedly through the pages. "You know, that was a clever thing you did there," he said.

"What?"

"Pretending that you were reluctant to tell me about Taj al-Mulk and thereby allaying any suspicions I might have that you're telling me this out of self-interest. And, of course, telling me that Taj al-Mulk and your father were arguing about the caliph instantly cast suspicion on Taj al-Mulk. It guided the mare of my mind to the passage in the manuscript about annihilating the Abbasids. But you let me tie up the tether on my own so that I would think I was brilliant."

"You know me too well, Omar. It works on most people. Of course, just because I'm devious doesn't mean I'm not telling the truth."

"And are you?"

"To quote a certain astronomer-poet, '*A Hair, they say, divides the False and True.*'[17] Now, how about those reminiscences of the old days?"

Omar shrugged and held out his cup. While Fakhr al-Mulk poured, Omar said, "As a matter of fact, I *have* been reminiscing about the old days. Mostly I have been thinking about those discussions we had at your house after school. You, me, and Hasan-i Sabbah swapping stories from the *Shahnama* until late at night, or locking horns over whether Islam was compatible with Aristotle."

"I remember the Aristotle debate. It lasted a whole summer. We had to break it off every night and pick up where we left off the next day, like the tales of Scheherazade."

"Your father gave us a nickname: the Three Professors."

"That was mainly because of you. You kept lecturing him about how to run the government."

"I can't believe I did that," Omar said. He hid his face in his hands in genuine embarrassment. "Like some kid from Nishapur with the taste of his mother's milk still on his breath could have told Nizam al-Mulk anything he didn't already know. I was so serious."

"The imam at school didn't think so. Or have you forgotten the infamous 'Name of Allah' question?"

Although thirty years had passed, Omar had not only not forgotten it, but it was still a sore point. "It was a perfectly serious question," he insisted. "The imam had no right to call me a blasphemer."

"Look at it from his point of view."

"All I wanted to know was, if Allah wrote the Quran, how come every chapter starts with 'In the Name of Allah'? Muhammad's tomb! You have to admit, for an author to start every chapter with his own name is an outlandish way to start a chapter."

"The important thing is that you learned from the experience."

Fakhr al-Mulk's tone was sarcastic, but Omar was still the serious one. "I learned nothing," he said. "To this day, I don't know the answer."

"You learned to put your blasphemous questions into your poems, where small minds can't understand them."

"What are you trying to say? That the imam had a small mind?"

"No. Hasan said that. I was too busy laughing."

"That's right. *W'allah!* You laughed the whole time the imam beat me with his cane! I ask a legitimate question about the Quran and get beat, and Hasan insults the teacher and gets away without any punishment at all. He always got away with everything."

"I didn't notice you complaining when he stole wine from the market. Hasan and I each drank a cup, and you polished off the jug."

"That's a lie."

"Oh?"

"You and Hasan each drank *half* a cup—and I polished off the jug."

Omar sighed. Coincidentally, half a cup waited in front of him now. He polished it off and poured some more. He offered the jug to Fakhr al-Mulk, who turned it down; his cup was still full. "Whatever happened to Hasan?" Omar asked.

"I don't know."

"Yes, you do."

"Why do you say that?"

"Because, old friend, Hasan left the government on bad terms with your father. I have to think your spies keep a close eye on him."

Fakhr al-Mulk walked to the entrance of his pavilion and looked through the flap to make sure no one was listening. Returning to his guest, he said, "Promise you won't tell anyone about this. I don't want word to get out that we dropped the ball—especially where a potential enemy of the state is concerned."

"I promise. What happened?"

"He escaped. About ten years ago he fled to Egypt and offered his services to the Fatimids. He betrayed his religion and his king."

"Is he still down there? I heard the politics of the Egyptian court has become suffused with peril."

"That's an understatement. I won't bore you with the details. Suffice to say there are two factions. Hasan joined one; the other arrested him. The first sprang him from jail and, eager to get him to safety, put him on a ship to Morocco."

"So he's all right, then—and far away from here."

"Here's the thing: the ship never arrived. We don't know if it was lost at sea or made landfall somewhere else. Our spies disappointed us. Whatever the case, Hasan-i Sabbah has dropped off the face of the earth."

*　　*　　*

Omar wanted nothing more than to close his eyes and drop off. He hadn't slept since Sunday—or was it Saturday?—but there was one more thing he had to do before he could get some sleep: read Nizam al-Mulk's manuscript. If the Nizam really did know that he had enemies who conspired to kill him, perhaps he had left clues in the book as to their identity.

Omar lay on his mattress, in the shelter of the tent assigned to him, and skimmed the manuscript by the light of an oil lamp. The overall flow of the text was intriguing. There were eleven new chapters, all unnumbered. Apparently Nizam al-Mulk had not settled on the final order. Still it appeared that when he set out to write a sequel to *The Book of Politics*, he had not intended to use it as a vehicle to warn against enemies of Islam infiltrating the court. He must have discovered their plots later on, because the second volume started out much in the same vein as the first, with anecdote-laden essays on various facets of good government.

Authors who dedicate books to kings are keen on generosity. So it was no surprise that the Nizam had chosen that topic to begin his new volume. He illustrated it with a story about the caliph Harun ar-Rashid. Thanks to a nightmare about the Day of Judgment, and the wise counsel of his principal wife, Harun had come to the realization that his vast treasury had been entrusted to him not for his own luxury and pleasure but for the benefit of the Muslim people. After that he set out on a lifetime of charity and public works; his generosity was said to extend into the millions of dinars. As for his wife, she did the same in her own right. Indeed, many of the wells she had dug and the khans she had constructed still existed.[18]

In the next chapter, Nizam al-Mulk complained that so many officials wasted their time trying to obtain honorific titles like So-and-so al-Mulk and Such-and-such ad-Dawla, resulting inevitably in title inflation. The catalog of appropriate uses of various classes of titles was pedantic, Omar thought, but the Nizam made up for it with a humorous story about Sultan Mahmud of Ghazna. Eager to obtain additional titles from the caliph of his time, the sultan went to absurd lengths, going so far as sending a spy to steal a diploma of title from the king of Samarqand. Alas, despite an otherwise distinguished career—in many ways he was Nizam al-Mulk's ideal ruler—

Mahmud's attempts to build a collection of honorifics were in vain. He died with a mere two: Right Hand of the State and Custodian of the Nation.

It was in the following chapter that things took a bizarre turn. In the midst of a typical discussion—this one about the inadvisability of assigning more than one post to a single individual—the Nizam plunged into despair: *"The dynasty has arrived at its peak,"* he lamented. *"I fear the influence of the Evil Eye and I don't know how things will end."*[19]

It wasn't merely that he was unappreciated, although that was a factor. He beat that point to death by inserting a long list of great kings whose reliance on their viziers set them on the path to glory:

> Solomon had for his minister Asif ibn Barkhiya; Moses, his brother Aaron; Jesus, Simon; and Muhammad the Chosen One, Abu Bakr the Truthful. Kai Khosrau had Goudarz and Manuchehr had Sam . . . Sultan Mahmud had for his minister Ahmad ibn Hasan; Fakhr ad-Dawla, Sahib Ismail ibn Abbad; Sultan Toghril had Abu Nasir Kundari; Alp Arslan and Malik-shah had Nizam al-Mulk, and there were a great many others.[20]

But the real problem was that the government had been infiltrated by the enemies of Islam. The passage Omar had read in Fakhr al-Mulk's pavilion merely scratched the surface. The Nizam longed for the days when *"no Jew, Christian, or heretic would have the audacity even to enter a Turkish camp, much less serve a great lord."*[21] He cautioned against allowing such people to obtain official posts, especially as tax collectors. They *"will harass the Muslims over the amounts of the imposts and the settling of accounts, treat them with contempt, and impoverish them."*[22]

He singled out the Jews in particular, telling a long story about the caliph Omar and a Jewish assessor:

> When the Muslims complain against the actions of an unbeliever, don't confer on him any situation that allows him to tyrannize the people. Don't let anyone tell you that one can't find, in the entire world, a scribe and an accountant like him in that if he came to disappear, no one would be capable of performing his job. These words are lies; don't give hearing to words like these;

63

replace this official, as did Omar, Commander of the Faithful. (May Allah be satisfied with him!)

It happened in the time of Saad ibn Abu Waqqas that a Jew was in charge of levying the imposts in the area around Baghdad—from Wasit and Anbar to Khuzestan and Basra. The inhabitants of these districts sent a petition to the Commander of the Faithful, Omar, to complain about the tyrannical proceedings of this agent. "Under pretext of performing his duties," they said, "this Jew mistreats us. We are oppressed by his mockery and the signs of his contempt. We are at the end of our resources, and if there is no other remedy, put an agent who is Muslim in charge of us. It could be that if he is our coreligionist, his conduct will be better and he will not violate our regard. But if he doesn't behave otherwise, we still prefer to be violated and scorned by a Muslim, rather than a Jew."

The Commander of the Faithful read this request. "This Jew," he said, "lives in security in this world, that is well; but he must not conduct himself in this manner, crushing the Muslims and oppressing them." He immediately sent a response to Saad ibn Abu Waqqas, responding in these terms: "Dismiss this Jew and confer his job on a Muslim." After having read these lines, Saad ibn Abu Waqqas appointed a horseman who he charged with bringing this Jew to Kufa, wherever he found him; other horsemen he sent as envoys to all coasts, to conduct to Kufa the Muslim tax collectors established in western Persia. He made comparison of this Jew in the presence of all the agents of finance; he found no one among the Arabs who could be charged with this employment, and among the Persian functionaries also was not found anyone as capable as this Jew. None knew better than he how to carry on business, levy the imposts, and construct public buildings. None were more familiar with dealing with the people, and no one knew the growth in revenue or the amount of arrears better than he did.

Saad, unable to replace him, kept him in his employ and explained to the Commander of the Faithful, "I had the Jew come before me. There is not, among the Arabs, anyone who knows like him how to carry out business and the way to administer it. I have been forced to leave him in his employment in order to prevent any problems in the conduct of affairs."

This letter caused the Commander of the Faithful the greatest astonishment. "What is most singular in all this," he said, "is that he substituted his own will for mine and that he found something better than what I found good." He took a pen and wrote four words at the top of the letter—The Jew is dead—and sent it back to Saad ibn Abu Waqqas. What he meant by these words was this: "Every man is subject to death, and for an official, dismissal is the same as death. For whether an official dies or is dismissed, his place is not left vacant; his replacement is immediately designated. Why have you been so weak and unable to act? Suppose the Jew is dead." When this letter reached Saad ibn Abu Waqqas, he immediately recalled the Jew, dismissed him from his post, and put a Muslim in his place.

After a year, it was clear that the Jew's functions were better fulfilled by the Muslim, the imposts were brought in, the people were satisfied, and prosperity was higher than ever. Saad ibn Abu Waqqas said, in consequence, to the Arab emirs, "Omar is a personage of genuine eminence. We had written, on the subject of the Jew, a long chapter. He responded in four words."[23]

But apparently Jews weren't the only ones who conspired against Nizam al-Mulk, because after the story of Omar and the tax collector, he covered the dangers posed by women interfering in the government. *"They live in a state of seclusion,"* he wrote,

and therefore don't enjoy complete information. One demands of them to perpetuate the nobility of the race; the higher their birth, the more they are worthy of the favors of the king; the more they live in retirement, the more they are worthy of praise.

But every time royal women offer their counsel, it is counsel that was suggested to them by people with bad intentions, who give them an account of what happens outside because they can't see anything with their own eyes. They follow the advice given by persons who are attached to their service, such as the lady-in-waiting, the eunuch, and the chambermaid, and the orders they give are necessarily contrary to justice and truth and give birth (in the state) to misunderstanding and sedition. The prestige of the prince will be harmed, the people will suffer, government and religion will be enfeebled, the public finances will be ruined, and the nobles will be persecuted.

There were times in the past when the king's women took as high a rank as his: this never resulted in anything but destruction, disaster, and discord.

We will say a little on this subject so that one can understand many similar cases.

The first man who obeyed a woman, and didn't collect anything for his submission but damage, chagrin, and bad luck, was Adam, who ate the wheat at the suggestion of Eve. He was chased from the Garden and spent two hundred years lamenting before Allah took pity on him and felt for his repentance.[24]

Apparently even children were a threat. *"On the final Day of Judgment,"* the Nizam wrote, *"the sultan will be accountable for the way he governed his subjects. He does not elevate underage persons to high office; but he must rule his affairs, and consult the sheikhs and the persons who have experience."*[25]

But the biggest danger to the House of Islam, according to the Nizam, was the Shiites, and he reserved his harshest words for them. That *"short chapter on the history of these heretics"* that he promised swelled to five—almost half the new volume. As far as Nizam al-Mulk was concerned, the history of Shiism was a plot to destroy Islam and enslave the Muslim people. Over the years, Shiites had gone by many names: Twelvers and Ismailis, Fatimids and Qarmatians. But each generation's rebranding only served to conceal that it was all the same thing: a conspiracy that spanned centuries. Even the Mazdak rebels were in on it—back when the priests of Zoroaster still ruled Persia and Islam was a hundred years in the future. In the Nizam's mind, that proved that Shiites weren't Muslims at all. They were discontented Zoroastrians who wouldn't even submit to their own religion, much less the true faith of the Messenger. Left unchecked, they would sap the foundations of society, redistribute wealth, subvert government and religion, and replace them with violence, destruction, and perversion. *"All they have ever wanted,"* Nizam al-Mulk wrote, *"was to destroy Islam. They are the enemies of religion and of the family of the Messenger. They turn the people away from the correct path. May Allah crush them with His curses!"*[26]

Having completed his survey of threats to the regime—and to himself—he returned to his main topic: the art of governance. In the reasonable tones of the first two chapters, he provided advice on proper bookkeeping and the necessity of subdividing the treasury between capital and expense accounts.

The Nizam saved one last bit of sage advice for the end: he implored the sultan always to take the middle course—between luxury and austerity, between pleasure and labor, and between drunkenness and abstinence. If the Master of the World were but to heed this counsel, then *"Allah Most High would give him the necessary capacity to conduct his affairs well, both temporal and spiritual, and grant him all his desires, both in this world and the next."*[27] It was a good, Aristotelian sentiment, Omar thought, albeit Nizam al-Mulk, following the Hadith,[28] attributed it to the Messenger—may the prayer and peace of Allah be upon him.

When he finished reading, Omar blew out the lamp but couldn't fall asleep. He lay on his mattress, too tired for sweet unconsciousness, the words of the Nizam racing in circles. He had hoped to find out who Nizam al-Mulk's enemy was and discovered that the Nizam considered himself surrounded by them: ministry rivals, Shiites, women, Jews—even children— all conspiring to undermine the regime and destroy the lives of good Muslims everywhere.

Gradually the sounds of the camp coming to life around him dribbled through the horsehide walls of the tent: cooks trudged to the kitchens to prepare the *suhur*, post riders dashed in with messages from every corner of the empire, porters shouted instructions to one another as they stacked trunks in preparation for departure. If Omar were to get any sleep, he'd better shift his mind to another track. He tried to relive his journey—the picturesque villages, the spectacular mountain vistas. Before long he was on his horse again, galloping out of Isfahan. As he glanced back over his shoulder, he saw the tower of his observatory. Up top, the graceful metallic curves of the armillary sphere shined in the moonlight. They spun around the ersatz Earth, growing ever smaller as they retreated from Omar at breakneck speed.

CHAPTER 3

ON THE ROAD, KERMANSHAH PROVINCE
WEDNESDAY, 15 RAMADAN 485
4 Abán 471

20 October 1092

O mar's instructions were to join Terken Khatun in her palanquin as soon as the army broke camp and resumed its journey to Baghdad.

The vehicle was quite large. It was suspended high up on a pair of poles between two camels, one in front and one in back. The frame and roof were made from gilded teak. Its columns were carved in spirals. A miniature onion-shaped cupola decorated the roof. All around the palanquin, pink curtains made from silk hid the occupants from a curious world.

Inside, another curtain divided the passenger compartment in two. It separated Omar from Terken Khatun. He heard her voice, softened by the singsong accent of the Land beyond the River, but he couldn't see her. From time to time, he heard her interrupt their conversation to quiet the child who traveled with her. When Omar offered his condolences for the death of Nizam al-Mulk, he even heard her sigh.

But not once did he hear her bark, howl, or yelp. Taj al-Mulk obviously had been joking when he called her "the Bitch of Samarqand"; there was nothing bitch-like about her. Before anything else, she saw to Omar's needs, verifying that his seat was comfortable and offering him refreshment. "I normally provide fruit drinks to my guests," Terken Khatun explained. "But your preference for something stronger is legendary. There is a pitcher next to your seat. Please help yourself."

The pitcher was made of gold and accompanied by a matching goblet. Omar filled it only halfway; he didn't want to spill any on the cushions due to the jostling of the cabin. He was about to taste the maroon liquid when he remembered something.

"I shouldn't," he said. "Ramadan. The sun still hangs in the sky."

"Wine is forbidden, isn't it?" Terken Khatun asked.

"Yes."

"Then how can it be more forbidden during Ramadan? A thing is forbidden or it isn't. It can't be forbidden more or less."

"Now you're speaking like a philosopher," Omar said. He was beginning to like Terken Khatun. He liked the wine too; it was on the sweet side—a good pairing for the plate of small, sticky pastries that came with it—and far smoother than the lamp oil served in his usual Isfahan haunts. There were benefits to being on special assignment to the sultan.

She asked how his journey from Isfahan had been.

"Fast," Omar replied.

"Traveling by post horses can be quite unsettling if done at full speed. I promise this leg of your journey will be more leisurely, although we'll still move at a good clip." A sharper than average bump jarred the cabin. "We'll get past Bisotun today. Have you been there before?"

"No, this is my first trip west of Isfahan."

"It's too bad we're only passing through. You'll miss the ruins. I'm sure they would appeal to someone with your philosophical outlook."

"Perhaps I'll explore them on my way back."

"I'm afraid seeing the sights can be a casualty when you travel quickly," she said. "On the upside, news travels quickly with you. And that's why I wanted to speak with you. You'll probably think my concerns are mundane. I apologize for bothering you with them. But, please, help yourself to more wine."

Omar poured another goblet. "I'm sure your concerns are justified. What are they?"

"I know that you were in Isfahan recently. Is there any news about the princes? I worry so when I'm away from them."

"There's nothing to worry about, Sahiba al-Jalala. Berk-yaruq is fine. As a matter of fact, he was with me when the sultan's summons arrived."

The conversation was abruptly interrupted by a shout from Terken Khatun. "Mahmud, sit still." The intended recipient of her shout was a small child who had crawled out from under the curtain. He was dressed in a colorful traveling coat and a matching Turkish hat, both made of heavy padded cotton. The palanquin wobbled slightly as the camels adjusted to the redistribution of weight.

"Did you see Uncle Berk-yaruq?" the boy asked excitedly.

"I did, and only three nights ago," Omar replied.

"Tell him to come and play with me."

"I will, as soon as I get back," Omar promised.

Having gotten what he wanted, the boy crawled back under the curtain to Terken Khatun's side of the compartment.

"Your grandson?" Omar asked.

"My one and only."

"He looks like the sultan. Except for the complexion. That came from his father."

"My son-in-law the caliph." She didn't say it with pride. "Al-Muqtadi, Commander of the Faithful. His ancestors married captured Rumi women for so many generations that the whole family looks like watered-down milk."

Omar realized he had picked at a scab. "Now it's my turn to apologize," he said. "I didn't intend to offend you by bringing up the Commander of the Faithful. I know that wasn't a happy marriage."

"It's been three years since Fulana left the caliph. Two years since she died. We're moving on. Mahmud is with us. He's a bright child. Mahmud, tell Khwaja Omar how old you are."

"Four!" Mahmud shouted gleefully from behind the curtain.

"And what comes after four?" Omar asked.

"Five!"

"And what comes after five?"

This time the boy poked his face out from under the curtain. "Six!" Then he disappeared again.

"He's turning into a scholar," Omar said.

"He misses his uncles, of course," Terken Khatun said. "We all do, but I thought it was important for Berk-yaruq and the other boys to remain in

Isfahan and focus on their studies. How did you happen to see Berk-yaruq? Were you at the palace?"

"No, he was up at the observatory. He's also turning into a scholar. I put him to work taking a reading of Saturn."

"How did he take the news of the Nizam?"

"Like a king, Sahiba al-Jalala. You would have been proud of him. His first concern was that justice be done."

"And his brothers?"

"I didn't see Sanjar or Tapar, but I'm sure if anything was wrong I would have heard about it—either from Berk-yaruq or through word around the palace."

"May Allah continue to preserve them."

He wanted to ask Terken Khatun a personal question. Too personal, really, but he was curious. "I'm surprised you're so solicitous," he said. "They're not your children, after all: that honor belongs to Safariyya and Zubayda. I always heard that the rivalries among a sultan's wives are terrifying."

"You've been reading too many stories in the *Shah-nama*, Khwaja Omar. I care about Malik-shah. Malik-shah cares about his children. Therefore . . . I believe that's what we philosophers call a syllogism. The family is my life."

"What about your other family?"

"What other family?"

"Your father's family. The Qarakhanids. Your husband is at war with your brothers and your cousins. Don't you ever feel conflicted about that?"

"The Seljuqs are the only family I have now. When I entered the harem of Malik-shah, it became my whole world."

"I'm sorry for my ignorance about the dynamics of a harem, Sahiba al-Jalala. I only had one wife myself."

"Yes, Malik-shah and I were both saddened when she died. '*For some we loved, the loveliest and the best,*

"'That from his Vintage rolling Time has prest,
Have drunk their Cup a Round or two before,
And one by one crept silently to rest.'"[29]

71

"She crept silently to rest a long time ago," Omar replied. "But it's kind of you to remember my wife. And my poem."

"It's curious how when tragedy intrudes in our lives and takes from us those we love, like the Nizam, it makes us think of all the other loved ones who have left us over the years."

She and Omar were silent for a moment; the only sound was the tramping of the boots of the guards who accompanied the palanquin. Finally Terken Khatun said, "My husband told me that it's because of the Nizam that you are here," she said. "Is there anything I can do to assist you with your investigation?"

"I just started," Omar replied. "Taj al-Mulk and I examined the body of the murderer and the items he had on him for clues."

"Did you find anything?"

"Not much. Some coins. A Sufi robe. A dagger with a sapphire in it. I'm going to ask around and try to find out where they came from."

"And then what?"

"Malik-shah wants me to work with Abu Hamid Ghazali. I suppose we'll start by putting together a list of people who might benefit from the Nizam's death. So far all I have are the same suspects everyone is already gossiping about."

"My husband."

"And Taj al-Mulk. But there's got to be others. Do you know anyone else who might have had a conflict or an antagonism with the Nizam?"

"Not a soul. Nizam al-Mulk was pious and charitable. He never missed the time of prayer and gave lavishly to the poor, the Sufi, and the scholar. Everyone always spoke so well of him."

"Surely not everyone. Someone that high up always has enemies. Was there anyone who wanted his job or disagreed with him about this policy or that policy?"

"This curtain puts me at something of a disadvantage." Metal bracelets jingled as she prodded the silk with her finger. "I don't hear about intrigues or policies, and Malik-shah doesn't enlighten me. But he makes up for it with a steady stream of jewels, and that's something I might be able to help you with: the sapphire you mentioned."

As he refilled his goblet, Omar expressed gratitude for any help she could provide.

"Do you know Abba Saad ben Samha?" Terken Khatun asked.

"He's a banker, isn't he?" Omar replied.

"That's like saying Avicenna was a doctor. Technically correct, and yet a vast understatement. The House of Samha is the biggest merchant house in all the Seljuq realm. Ben Samha has a hand in lending, caravans, ships, and workshops of every description—including jewelers' workshops. He is, in fact, *my* jeweler. If anyone can trace the origin of that sapphire, he can."

"And where do I find ben Samha?"

"Baghdad. The Mother of All Cities."

*   *   *

Motherly. If Omar had to sum up Terken Khatun in one word, it would be *motherly*. He stood in the road and watched the camels trot away with Terken Khatun's palanquin. In his imagination he pictured her as being a couple of years older than her husband; not plump exactly, but on the way there; a handful of gray hairs nestling among the black. She wore a simple padded traveling coat and no more than a piece or two of jewelry, too chunky to be fashionable but of great sentimental value. Her hands were industrious with embroidery or some such domestic art, which she would occasionally drop in her lap as a new worry about the widely scattered children of her household eroded her forehead, leaving the wrinkles ever so slightly deeper.

And while that may have been a perfect description of the tent maker's wife who was his own mother, Omar would have been surprised to see the Terken Khatun who awaited Malik-shah when the sultan arrived in her pavilion late that afternoon. She sat in a Rumi-style straight-backed chair, her elbows resting on a tabletop, her chin on her folded hands. It was the posture of a chess player conjuring an altered board from the manipulation of a single pawn. Her traveling coat—embroidered and colorful—hung on the back of her chair; with three braziers in the pavilion, she was quite comfortable in a chemise and an open robe. The loose sleeves had slipped off her forearms, uncovering stacks of golden bracelets that made her golden arms look slender but by no means delicate. They had the tautness of a bowstring, ready to propel a fatal sting at an outmaneuvered target.

When her husband pushed through the curtain into the interior of her pavilion, she did not acknowledge him at first, and when she did it was with a tart "Look who's finally dressed." But despite the curt greeting, she rose to embrace her Malik-shah, her slender body coiling around his stocky frame.

"I suppose Khwaja Omar's visit had something to do with your transfiguration," she said.

Malik-shah had long become inured to his wife's snippiness; it didn't generally get a rise out of him. He answered simply, "Omar helped put things in perspective."

"Oh," she replied, noncommittally. She returned to her chair, her back to her husband, picked up a letter from her worktable, and started reading it silently.

"What's wrong?" Malik-shah asked.

"I didn't say anything."

"Your silence says plenty. Do you have a problem with Omar Khayyam?"

"How would I have a problem? I hardly know him."

"I didn't realize you knew him at all."

"When a mother is traveling, is it wrong for her to ask for news about the children she left behind?"

"They're not your children. What the *sik* did you and Omar really talk about? The murder of the Nizam, maybe?"

"It might have come up."

"And?"

"And he's no friend of yours. He thinks you might have had a hand in it."

"I see." The sultan sat down in a chair with a wooden latticework back. The furnishings in Terken Khatun's pavilion were starkly different from his own. There were fewer cushions and sofas; more wooden chairs and metal tables, all carefully arranged in evenly spaced groupings.

"You have nothing to worry about," Terken Khatun continued. "I got Omar off your trail."

Malik-shah did not find that reassuring. "And how the hell did you do that?" he asked.

"I gave him a new trail to follow. I told him to go see ben Samha in Baghdad. Who will almost certainly lead him to Abu Shuja. Who will lead him to the caliph. And anything that puts the caliph under a cloud is good for us."

"I don't know that I like that. I didn't bring Omar all the way from Isfahan and put the resources of the empire at his disposal because I wanted to put on a *sikking* show for the public. This is a serious investigation. I intend to treat the death of the Nizam as if it were my own father who died. I want to know who killed him. You're not helping if you send Omar off in the wrong direction."

"I did nothing of the sort. Omar wanted an expert to look at the murder weapon and I sent him to ben Samha. There's nobody better."

"What a load of *sachmalik*. You knew perfectly well it would falsely implicate Abu Shuja and the caliph."

"I'm just a concerned mother confined in the harem. How do I know what's false?"

Malik-shah tried to argue, but she changed the subject. "I'm glad to see you finally ceased your weeping long enough to venture out of your tent," she said. "Things have been piling up. It's about time you made some decisions."

"That's why I'm here. I want your opinion on who should replace Nizam al-Mulk as vizier."

"Who are the candidates?" Terken Khatun asked disingenuously. She already knew the candidates. Everybody knew the candidates.

"Taj al-Mulk and Fakhr al-Mulk."

"Taj al-Mulk."

"Why?"

"You asked for my opinion, I gave you my opinion."

"You must have a reason."

She turned it around on him. "Is there a reason you're considering Fakhr al-Mulk?"

"His father served me well. Why shouldn't I choose someone from his family?"

"I don't think you should choose someone from his nation."

"What do you mean, his nation?"

"The *Persian* nation."

If Terken Khatun's objective was to throw her husband off guard, she succeeded. Excluding Fakhr al-Mulk from consideration on the grounds that he was Persian was absurd. "The vizier has always been Persian," Malik-shah said. "Ever since my grandfather and his brother defeated that *peech* Mas'ud and started the empire."

"Your grandfather and granduncle knew the camp and the saddle and the bow. But when they rode across the river and into Persia, they didn't know camphor from salt. They certainly didn't know how to govern a land of farms and cities. So they needed those Persian viziers. But that was fifty years ago. Fifty years of daily working side by side with the Persians. That's long enough for schooling. It's time to graduate. A Turkish sultan should have a Turkish vizier."

Malik-shah didn't say anything; clearly he was taking the idea seriously. Standing behind his chair, Terken Khatun leaned over his shoulder and whispered in his ear. "Imagine the scene when you give Taj al-Mulk his diploma of office. A bright sunny day, a military band playing, your emirs gathered in a circle, watching proudly as the Turks finally step out of the Persian shadow. The sons of Alp Arslan moving forward side by side."

The sultan could picture it. But he still said no.

"Why not?" Terken Khatun demanded.

"Fakhr al-Mulk knows the job better. He has been at his father's side all of his life. Practically the last thing the Nizam said to me was always to hire the most capable man. Persian, Arab, or Turk; Christian, Muslim, or Jew—it doesn't matter."

Terken Khatun threw up her hands in exasperation. "The Nizam," she exclaimed. "Since when did you listen so carefully to his lectures?"

"I decided it's the best tribute I can offer, in the wake of his passing."

"A week ago you were giddy in your fantasies of getting rid of him. Now you want to offer him a tribute?"

"A week ago I was angry and he was alive."

"You need to get angry more often. Dispatching the Nizam to his oft-threatened retirement would have been the most sensible thing you've done in years."

Malik-shah scowled. "I can get angry right now if you think it's such a good idea."

Terken Khatun abruptly softened her demeanor, if only long enough to cue up the next blow. "Okay," she said. "Fakhr al-Mulk. Son of Nizam al-Mulk. What does he have going for him? Besides thirty years of sharpening his father's pens."

"He's a good Muslim."

"Who says so?"

"Omar Khayyam."

"Fakhr al-Mulk's best friend!"

"He pointed out to me that instead of staying here to lobby for the job, Fakhr al-Mulk did the right thing. He went back to Isfahan to bury his father."

"I don't suppose it occurred to you that's why he did it."

It was clear from the sultan's face that it hadn't.

Terken Khatun elaborated. "By spending a few days away from you, he swayed you far more effectively than anything he could have said if he were here. But I'll bet you this—Fakhr al-Mulk won't waste any time finishing his business and coming back. I'll wager a hundred dinars that he won't be far behind us when we arrive in Baghdad."

The sultan lowered his brow in anger. "That *amm*! If he thinks he can—"

"Manipulate you? Why not? He obviously manipulated Omar—who you keep saying is one of the smartest men you know."

Malik-shah rested his chin in his hands and looked up at his wife. "So. Taj al-Mulk."

"At least you can trust him. Has *he* ever tried to manipulate you?"

"My brother is too *sikking* noble for that."

"Then it's settled. Taj al-Mulk will be the new vizier."

Afterward, Malik-shah couldn't remember agreeing that it was settled, but apparently it was, and, in any case, he didn't get an opportunity to argue. As if on a prearranged cue, young Mahmud charged into the room like a hero from the *Shah-nama* rescuing his comrades from a demon-infested castle. Albeit Mahmud differed from the heroes of old in that their swords were made of steel instead of wood, and they usually didn't nearly knock over an end table when they made an entrance.

"Who are you supposed to be?" the sultan asked, steadying the table.

77

"I am Rostam, the greatest hero *ever!*" Mahmud replied, beaming beneath his tiny leather helmet; it could barely contain his abundant black curls.

"Die!" Mahmud yelled as he poked his grandfather in the belly with the blunted tip of his wooden sword.

"AAAAAARRRRRGH!" Malik-shah clasped his hands over the pretend wound and flopped in his chair in make-believe death throes. "I die! All my plans at an end!"

"Rostam always wins!" Mahmud shouted. He pumped his sword in the air. But when several moments passed and Malik-shah didn't move, the boy became concerned. "Grandpa?" He prodded his grandfather's knee with a tiny index finger. Receiving no response, he let his sword drop and climbed into his grandfather's lap. "Grandpa?" he asked again, this time poking him gently in the nose.

"Gotcha!" the sultan yelled. He grabbed the boy around the waist and swung him into the air. Mahmud laughed in delight.

"Mahmud, don't bother your grandfather," Terken Khatun scolded.

"Oh, let him be," the sultan replied, positioning the boy in his lap. "I deserve some grandfather time after making decisions all day."

"You made one decision. You're not finished yet. Mahmud, go find your nurse."

Mahmud clambered down from his grandfather's lap and ran behind the curtain into another compartment.

"That boy has become quite fearless," Terken Khatun said.

"As befits a Seljuq."

"He's a promising little Seljuq, isn't he?" Terken Khatun looked around to make sure no one was in earshot. "There's something else you need to decide about," she said.

"I thought you were kidding about that," the sultan replied testily. *Wasn't one decision enough for an afternoon?*

"Your successor."

Relief washed over the sultan. This was an easy one. "Berk-yaruq," he said.

"You need to make it official. Name him crown prince."

"We talked about that. You advised me to wait a couple more years to keep him on his toes."

"But things are different now."

"What's different?"

"The Nizam is dead."

"So?"

"When he was alive, we knew that if anything happened to you, we could count on Nizam al-Mulk to ensure there would be smooth transition of power."

Malik-shah inflated his cheeks in frustration. "Of all the . . . a minute ago you said getting rid of the Nizam would have been the most sensible thing I ever did."

"I didn't say it would be the most sensible thing you ever did."

"Yes, you did. You said, 'it would be the most sensible thing you ever did.'"

"No, I said, 'it would be the most sensible thing you did in years.'"

"Either way, you thought I should get rid of the Nizam. Now all of sudden he's indispensable to the continuation of the *sikking* regime. You always do this."

"And you always ignore context. I was speaking in a completely different context before."

"Fine. I'll send for Berk-yaruq and we can have a ceremony for him in Baghdad."

"Are you sure Berk-yaruq is the right choice?"

A moment of stunned silence passed. Then the sultan jumped up and kicked over his chair. "Do you live to torment me, wife?"

"If you're going to get angry . . ."

"I'm not angry."

"My mistake. I thought when people kick over their chairs it's because they're angry. You're in my tent, not sacking a city."

He righted the chair and sat on the edge of the seat. "And this wouldn't have anything to do with Zubayda being Berk-yaruq's mother instead of you?" he asked.

"You're still angry."

He took a couple deep breaths and rephrased the question. "What's wrong with Berk-yaruq?"

Terken Khatun sat in the chair opposite him and leaned forward, putting her hands on her husband's knees. He glimpsed the curve of her breast through the opening in her chemise.

"Berk-yaruq is a wonderful boy," she said sweetly. "He's very thoughtful and always has time for his brothers. His nephew adores him. He's intelligent and applies himself to his studies. Someday he'll make an excellent scholar."

"But not a king."

"I didn't say that. Don't put words in my mouth. I'm just saying that he might be happier doing something else."

"He'll grow into the role."

"I wouldn't bet the empire on it. The boy has his head in the stars. Did you know that he was at that observatory of yours when your messenger arrived for Omar Khayyam, instead of tending to his responsibilities at the palace?"

"How do you know that?"

"Because I asked Omar Khayyam. Which you should have done."

"I'm glad the next sultan is showing interest in the observatory. It is part of my legacy; I'm heartened it will continue. Besides, who else would you put on the throne? Tapar? Sanjar?"

"I'm sure they would be fine kings. But unlike Berk-yaruq, they're underage. There would have to be a regent, and you need to consider who that would be."

"Their mother, Safariyya."

"Who's dumber than a brick."

"But shaped much better." A hint of anger crossed Terken Khatun's face, but Malik-shah plowed on before she could say anything. "Your sons died. Zubayda and Safariyya's sons are all I have left. Berk-yaruq, Tapar, Sanjar. Pick one."

"They're *not* all you have left. You don't even bother to consider who *I* have left."

The sultan looked puzzled for a moment. Then he said, "Oh."

Terken Khatun smiled demurely.

"That will never happen," the sultan said. "We have other plans for Mahmud. You know that. If he were crown prince, too, he would be too powerful. Which means, until he grew up, *you* would be too powerful."

Terken Khatun rose and walked around the back of her husband's chair. She leaned over and wrapped her arms around him, slipping her hands inside the neckline of his robe. He inhaled her musky perfume mixed with the charcoal smoke of the braziers. He felt her breath in his ear as she whispered, "But you *like* powerful women, don't you?"

The look in his eye was all the answer she needed. He turned his head toward hers; they made eye contact. She kissed him on the mouth with her soft lips. Malik-shah felt the warmth of her hands against his skin; it seemed to radiate from her palms and seep into his chest. "You might be right about some things," he said.

She kissed him again, with more feeling this time. "Only some things?"

"You're right that we can no longer wait. After we finish our other business in Baghdad, we could have a ceremony to invest the crown prince. Gather the emirs, have them pledge their allegiance—"

"I thought you would see things my way."

"—to Berk-yaruq."

"No! You mean Mahmud."

"I mean Berk-yaruq. If I meant Mahmud, I would have *sikking* said Mahmud!"

She tore herself away from him so forcefully that she ripped a seam in his robe. Seeing Mahmud's wooden sword on the floor, she grabbed it and swung at his head.

It was a skillful move, but a wooden sword is no match for a steel one. Malik-shah leaped from his chair and drew his sword swiftly enough to knock the toy from his wife's hand in time; the wooden weapon dropped harmlessly to the carpet.

"We'll get the caliph to present Berk-yaruq with the diploma personally," the sultan said.

"You wouldn't."

"It would be a good joke."

She started to argue, but the hollow rumble of kettledrums interrupted her; it came from outside the pavilion. The metallic clash of cymbals joined in. Together they kept the rhythm while the nasal whine of oboes took up a repetitive but cheerful melody. A chorus of a half dozen chanting men rounded out the military band.

81

"The call to prayer," said the sultan. "Then *iftar*. But first I better put on another robe." He poked a finger through the ripped seam and chuckled. Then he strutted to the entrance of the pavilion in time with the music.

"You're making a mistake," Terken Khatun called after him. "What makes you so sure Berk-yaruq can grow into the role?"

The sultan halted in the entryway, holding the curtain half open. He looked over his shoulder at his wife. "Because," he said, "today I think even *I* may grow into it."

With that, he left her pavilion.

*   *   *

Well after midnight, Terken Khatun's pavilion saw a different visitor.

"This better be important," he whispered. "If Malik-shah catches me here, he'll string me up alive and leave my body to be pecked to death by crows. What do you want?"

Terken Khatun looked up at him, her brown eyes laughing, her lips parted slightly in expectation. She lounged on the bed, propped up on one elbow, a thin sheet covering her body. Judging from its contours and the bare skin of her arms and shoulders, she had nothing on underneath.

"What do you think I want?" she asked, a challenge in her voice.

"I didn't think you wanted *that*!" he replied. "Seriously? Now?"

"Of course not," she said with angry sarcasm. She sat up with a jerk, wrapping the sheet around her. "I sent you a message in the middle of the night, arranged for my eunuchs to momentarily leave the entrance to my bedchamber unguarded, and posed like a reclining Venus because I wanted to discuss the cost of soldier's rations in Balkh."

A part of him wanted it. He had been riding all day. The fresh air pumping in and out of his lungs and the rhythmic bouncing of his horse had left him invigorated and aroused, yet somehow mellow at the same time. Fresh air did that to him. But this was insane.

"We're in a *sikking* tent," he said, clearly angry, but still whispering. "Malik-shah is right next door. There's nothing between him and us but two layers of horsehide. Can't you wait until we get to Baghdad? Once we're safely entrenched behind the security of brick walls, we can hump each other until we're so exhausted we can't think straight." He turned and headed to the exit. "I'm going back to my tent," he said.

"You say that like you think you have a choice," she replied. "That's cute."

He spun around and glared at her impudence.

Getting up from the bed, still holding the sheet wrapped around her, she planted herself right in front of him and defiantly returned his glare. "You know that you don't," she said.

"We'll see about that," he replied.

She walked in a circle around him as if she were casting a spell. The clean scent of her just-washed hair surrounded him and filled him. She brushed her hand across his chest and shoulders and the bare skin of the nape of his neck. The sensation of her practiced fingers on his body sent a jolt of excitement through him.

She taunted him. "You know that you can't live without me. So let's not hear any more foolish talk about you going back to your tent."

The circle complete, she faced him again and let the sheet drop to the floor. She stood proudly naked in the lamplight, her only adornment the gold bangles on her arms.

He looked her up and down helplessly. His eyes were drawn to her pert breasts and the dark patch of the *amm* between her legs. He ached to wrap his hands around her slender waist and stroke the smooth skin over her flat stomach. He felt his *huyar* begin to stir.

"Now, that's more like it," she said as she placed one hand over the bulge in his robe to help things along. "I told you that you weren't going to leave."

Furious with himself, he grabbed her by her upper arms and dug his fingers into the sinews.

"You're hurting me," she said. She wasn't complaining.

He planted his mouth violently over hers. The sensation of her moist tongue intertwining with his was pure ecstasy. He held her like that for what seemed like an eternity.

She was the one who broke it off. "Do you hear something?" she asked.

"What?" he replied, confused and unsatisfied.

"I thought I heard something."

He couldn't hear anything but the sound of his own heavy breathing. With disciplined effort, he got it under control.

"Maybe it's nothing," Terken Khatun said.

"Be quiet," he ordered. He stood very still and listened carefully, and, sure enough, someone was moving around in the next tent—the sultan's tent. He thought he heard the splatter of piss streaming into a chamber pot, the swish of footsteps on the carpet, and the creaking of a bed frame as someone lay down and tried to find a comfortable position.

As he tracked the movements of the person in the neighboring tent, he felt himself paralyzed with fear. Sweat oozed from every pore in his scalp. And then he noticed the pain in his *huyar* as it swelled beyond anything he had ever experienced. Until this moment, he had never realized that fear could be such a turn-on.

Terken Khatun read it all in his face and laughed at him. She had planned this, knowing exactly what it would do to him. He pushed her roughly onto the bed. Lying back against the pillows, she waited for him, her long black hair splayed around her, her tongue moistening her smirking lips.

He hiked up his robe and lowered his trousers.

CHAPTER 4

*T*he journey from Bisotun to Baghdad was much like the journey from Isfahan to Sahneh. A blur. Taj al-Mulk woke Omar well before sunrise, they mounted their post horses, and galloped off to the west. Emir Yalbard joined them. The mood was glum at first; it's hard to be cheerful when your fingers and toes burn with cold and you can hardly move in your bulky padded coat. But once the travelers descended from the mountains and began to cross the lush—and warm—farmlands of eastern Iraq, the mood improved.

After a solid twenty-four hours of hard riding—the three men stopped only to change their mounts—they arrived in Baghdad in the early hours of Friday. Since they were the advance party, the Dar Saltanah—the palace of the sultan—was nearly deserted. A lone stable boy was on duty to take their horses. Once that was taken care of, they went their separate ways—Taj al-Mulk to the vizier's suite and Yalbard to the guards' barracks—while Omar navigated deserted corridors and unlit staircases until he found the guest quarters.

Being the first to arrive, he had his pick of the accommodations. He chose a corner room on the top floor and immediately dropped onto the bed, his energy too depleted to burrow under covers or close the shutters. He went right on sleeping when the palace musicians beat their drums to wake the faithful for the *suhur*. But when his windows grew bright with morning, the light awakened him and further sleep proved elusive.

He stomped across the room with half-closed eyes and was about to yank the shutters closed on the side window when the spectacular view jolted him into amazement.

The city of Baghdad was laid out beneath him, all green trees and sand-colored buildings. They spread to the horizon under the sort of crystal-blue sky seen only a few times a year in a metropolis that two million inhabitants shared with cook fires, brick kilns, and mill dust.

The palace gardens grew directly below him. Irrigated by the waters of the Tigris River, the landscape was a forest of palm and cedar, the trunk of each tree sprouting from a square of roses bordered by painstakingly groomed shrubs. When the breeze blew just so, the flowers' scent wafted up to Omar's window. Here and there, goldfish maneuvered lazily among the roots of lily pads that floated on the surface of tiled pools. Sandy pathways converged on charming gazebos, where clusters of potted plants covered mosaic floors and decorated pointed archways. Fountains shot their spray into the air in ever changing patterns—sometimes a single tall column of water, a moment later four short ones. Omar made a mental note to find out how the mechanism worked.

Beyond the gardens, a pontoon bridge, the Main Bridge of Boats, crossed the Tigris. The river was so wide at that point, it took over two hundred boats to complete the span. Iron chains linked them to one another and anchored them to pylons on each shore. It seemed like all of humanity, and some pack animals to boot, jammed the causeway that stretched across the top: merchants led camels on the last leg of their journey to market; scholars, lost in debate about some point of shari'ah, bumped into passersby; Jewish youths hurried to study, fringed tallithim over their shoulders and beautifully bound books under their arms; wealthy women with fashionable shawls over their heads and veils over their faces returned from early morning shopping with tired chaperones and porters in tow; tourists out for a stroll admired the view from the railings.

The bridge led to the western shore, a curvy strip of land interrupted at intervals by the mouths of canals that carried fresh water and commerce through the precincts of Harbiyah, Attabiyah, Karkh, and a dozen other neighborhoods, each with its own "city" wall. Within them were sturdy houses and flourishing markets, no doubt stocked with the output of the sprawling workshops on the horizon.

At the center of West Baghdad, the tide of citizens in secular pursuits washed up against a sacred mosque but could not erode its solid walls. Its silvery teak roof capped a sapphire-blue façade, which bore the seams of centuries of expansion and renovation. The edifice had to be the Mosque of Mansur, located as it was at the intersection of four main arteries: the Khorasan Highway headed northeast; the Basra Highway, southeast; the Kufa Highway, southwest; and the Damascus Highway, northwest. The Mosque of Mansur was literally at the crossroads of the world.

And yet, the timeless vista from the side window turned out to be poor and dusty compared to what awaited Omar when, eager for more, he hurried over to the front window.

Granted, the view *immediately* below the window wasn't much to look at. A construction zone had driven everything else away. Porters carried baskets of kiln-burnt bricks on their heads and stirred up a cloud of dust each time they dumped them in sand-colored piles. Nearby, bricklayers filled large tubs with water and mixed in lime for mortar. Carpenters hammered wooden roofs onto houses of considerable size; clearly this was going to be a neighborhood for wealthy merchants or senior officials. At the center of activity, a newly completed foundation marked the future home of a building larger than any other in the neighborhood. Its footprint traced the outline of a massive court and four minarets: construction on the Mosque of the Sultan was well under way. In the central court, an elephant stamped the soil flat.

A farasang downriver, the view improved spectacularly: the spires of the Dar Calipha—the House of the Caliph—gleamed in the sunshine. The term "House" was figurative; the Dar Calipha was not so much a single dwelling as a complex, made up of not so much houses as palaces. For the last hundred years, held captive by one dynasty of sultans after another, the caliphs had had little to do other than build, and they applied themselves to it with all the zeal that their ancestors had applied to conquest. At this distance it was difficult to distinguish the dozens of buildings that comprised the complex or to guess their various purposes. Some were constructed with towers shooting up toward heaven; others were barely visible beneath thousands of shade-giving trees. The complex was enormous. Its open spaces looked like parkland and even included a pond. And yet it wasn't big enough: some edifices burst the seams of the precinct and cantilevered out over the Tigris.

Alas, with the whole city spread out beneath him, Omar was unable to see the one building that interested him most, his destination for today. He knew that the Baghdad branch of the Nizamiyya—the system of universities founded by Nizam al-Mulk—was also on the waterfront, just beyond the Dar Calipha. But the palaces of the caliph blocked his view. Omar would have to wait until he got there to see how it compared to its little brother in Isfahan.

*   *   *

The Gate of the Arch stood at the head of the Main Bridge of Boats. It was a stand-alone structure whose beauty belied its enormous size. Elegant stone vines climbed its slender legs and twisted along the curve of the arch to the point at the top.

In the shadow of the arch, a row of water taxis, rafts lashed together from reeds, bobbed in the water. Omar selected a pilot who didn't look too much like he planned to cut a customer's throat and gave him three silver dirhams in payment. They cast off for the trip downriver, the ferryman standing at the back of the vessel with a long, double-headed oar, and Omar seated on a cushion in the middle, a neatly wrapped parcel resting on his lap.

Traffic was heavy on the Tigris. Passenger ferries and pleasure yachts dodged barges laden with fresh vegetables, building materials, and soap to gain a few boat lengths' advantage. Omar's pilot had to ship his oar several times to allow traffic ahead to clear. But after four or five near collisions, and one heated argument between Omar's pilot and the custodian of a boatload of pomegranates, they reached the Dar Calipha, where a second bridge of boats, the Later Bridge, blocked further progress. Pulling up to a wharf, the pilot explained that Omar would be able to cut across the bridge on foot and board another ferry on the other side to complete his journey.

But it was a fine day. The warmth of Baghdad rejuvenated Omar after days spent traveling through the chilly mountains; he decided to walk the last leg. Beyond the bridge a market was jammed with dozens of stalls, all carrying the same product. "Fresh dates!" shouted a hawker. "Get your dates! Break your fast tonight like Muhammad, the Messenger of Allah. Fresh from the caliph's garden!"

Omar was sure that somewhere in this market, dates from the caliph's garden could be had—the orchards of the Dar Calipha were extensive—but he couldn't help noticing that all along the quay, porters unloaded basket after basket of the shiny fruit from barges issuing from more distant locations. They reminded him that he had missed the *suhur* and was hungry.

Omar had never given much thought to the Ramadan fast, at least not since he had been a child. He had spent his adult life working nights in the observatory and sleeping during the day. So the monthlong ban on daytime eating didn't have much effect on his routine. Nighttime eating was permitted, which is what he did anyway. But now that his routine had been disrupted, he had slept through the predawn meal at the palace and couldn't get his mind off the hollow feeling in his belly. *Well*, he thought, *Allah put the temptation of a date market in my path. He can't be too upset with me if I give in to it.* He risked the price of a quarter maund and resumed his course to the Nizamiyya, munching dates while attempting to balance the small bag of fruit with the parcel he had brought from the palace.

Walking the length of the Dar Calipha impressed on Omar once again the massive scale of the caliph's building program. It took him a good twenty minutes to get from one end to the other. The cantilevered buildings he had seen from the sultan's palace loomed above him and provided shelter from the sun.

On reaching the university's wharf, he looked around for the best way up into the building itself.

Someone called out, "Omar Khayyam?"

Omar turned and saw a man about sixty years old wearing a plain black robe over his shoulders and a look of disapproval on his face. "Chief Professor Ghazali sent me to welcome you to the Nizamiyya," the man said with a trace of a Spanish accent and a tone that was anything but welcoming. As an afterthought he introduced himself. "I'm the chief professor's deputy. Abu Abdullah Humaydi."

Omar recognized the name. "You're too modest," he said. "You're much more than Ghazali's deputy. I'm honored to meet the author of the *Al-Jama bain as-Sahihain*. Perhaps while I'm here we can discuss your insights into the chronology of the Hadith." He bit into another date and, remembering his manners, offered one to Humaydi.

"I doubt that someone who eats dates during the Ramadan fast would get much out of my insights," Humaydi replied.

"Oh, sorry," Omar said sheepishly. "It just seems to me that a tiny, tiny bit of cheating helps me get my mind off how hungry I am. Then I can better observe the fast for the rest of the day. Do you know what I mean?"

"No, I'm certain I don't know what you mean. I have no experience with cheating to enable me to have an opinion on the subject one way or another."

"No, I doubt that you would," Omar muttered under his breath.

"What's that?"

"I said that discipline is good."

Humaydi grunted. "Perhaps Chief Professor Ghazali can instill some in you." He pointed to a stairway leading up off the wharf. "This way, Khwaja."

Omar slipped the package of dates back into his pocket and followed Humaydi up the stairs. A market was spread out in front of them, with the buildings of the Nizamiyya looming beyond. The stalls catered to the special needs of the neighborhood: books, paper, pen sets, and scholars' robes filled their shelves. Here and there, acrobats gyrated on hanging ropes and storytellers offered dramatic renderings of tales from *The Thousand and One Nights*, bringing the various kings and slaves, merchants and whores to life with unique voices for each.

Beyond the market, they passed through the gate of the Nizamiyya and crossed its vast courtyard. "Chief Professor Ghazali is giving a lecture now," Humaydi explained as they approached a large pair of carved wooden doors. "He'll join us as soon as he's finished."

*   *   *

Over three hundred students crammed the lecture hall. They sat on prayer rugs in perfectly straight, evenly spaced rows and columns, as if they had been placed there by Euclid or some such ancient Greek master of geometry.

Chief Professor Ghazali also sat cross-legged, but he enjoyed the comfort of a luxurious cushion on a raised platform topped by a small wooden cupola. He was in his early thirties—young for a professor, and even younger for a chief professor. Heavy-set, with a low center of mass and a large round head, he looked more like a boxer than an intellectual. His small eyes challenged the world suspiciously from beneath a thick, dark brow. His fat lower lip jutted out, spoiling for a fight. But the force with which he spoke and the dramatic sweep of his hands with which he punctuated each point inspired confidence in his qualifications to lead an institution as eminent as the Baghdad Nizamiyya.

"The next text I want to cover today," Ghazali said, "also bears on this question of the origin of authority in Islam. It is chapter four, verse fifty-nine of Allah's Holy Quran: *'O ye who believe! Obey Allah, and obey the Messenger and those in authority amongst you.'*

"The obvious question is, who is the legitimate 'authority amongst you' whom we are enjoined to obey? Arguably, this is the most disputed question in all of Islam in that the death of the Messenger—may the prayer and peace of Allah be upon him—has been followed by centuries of warfare over who is to be his successor. There have been many so-called scholars who, in order to demonstrate the originality of their intelligence, have advanced novel theories about legitimacy. Quite conveniently these theories have obtained for them the profitable but tainted patronage of Shiite usurpers, like the so-called Fatimids of Egypt, whose legitimacy has no basis in the genuine teachings of the Messenger."

Two assistants flanked the chief professor. After each sentence, Ghazali paused to allow them to echo his words loudly enough for those at the back of the hall to hear. It gave him the opportunity to survey his audience. Few held his gaze for long.

"No," Ghazali continued, "the authority amongst you is not the false caliph in Cairo. There is only one legitimate authority amongst you, and he is here in Baghdad: the most orthodox Sunni leader, the caliph Abu'l-Qasim al-Muqtadi B'illah, Commander of the Faithful and Scion of the House of Abbas. Indeed, the very word 'caliph' testifies to the divine origin of his appointment, coming as it does from *calapha*, meaning 'to follow or succeed.' The caliph, thus, is the successor to the Messenger Muhammad, may the prayer and peace of Allah be upon him, and hence the deputy of Allah on earth. The caliph is chosen by Allah Himself, through the acclamation of His people. All subordinate officials, whether they be the imams who lead the prayer in the mosque or the qadis who judge the fate of accused thieves in the local court, derive their authority from their appointment by the caliph. So the next time you hear some smug pseudo-intellectual questioning the legitimacy of the caliph, you can destroy him utterly by pointing out the incoherence of his arguments: without the caliph there are no imams and no qadis, which means no settlements of contract disputes and no punishment for criminals—society would crumble into chaos, which is and has always been the true motive of heretics and unbelievers."

Standing at the back of the hall, Omar glanced at Humaydi. As Ghazali's deputy, and a scholar in his own right, Humaydi must have heard this lecture many times, both from Ghazali and from others. And yet Humaydi fixed his gaze on Ghazali in a glow of stunned admiration, as if marveling at a new discovery that only the genius of Ghazali could uncover. It was an expression of mindless acceptance.

Ghazali, for his part, intensified his attack on heretics and unbelievers. "In every generation," he said, "Allah sends these fools to us as a test. It is therefore necessary for the caliph to have a strong right arm, to crush their rebellions and force their submission to the will of Allah. And thus Allah has placed the Turks, under the command of the sultan, at the disposal of the caliph.

"The authority of the sultan is a gift from Allah, via the caliph; the sultan must show appreciation for this gift. There are many ways for him to do this: he should seek the guidance of the ulama—the scholars learned in shari'ah; he should live a frugal life and be a careful steward of the public purse. For the treasury belongs not to him but to the Muslim people. Indeed he could profit from the example of the caliph Omar ibn Abd al-Aziz, who, when working at night, occasionally needed to divert his attention from the public business and attend to some personal matter. When this occurred, he conscientiously doused the publicly funded lamp.

"The sultan should not waste funds on robes of silk or brocades or richly embroidered fabrics. Self-adornment and silliness are the realm of women. A sultan who indulges in them is a woman in a man's body and is therefore unfit to be sultan.

"Of course, the sultan should abstain from alcohol entirely and be moderate in indulging the other pleasures of this world. For the world is a dirty and toothless old hag who has had thousands of husbands and killed them all. Death is inevitable for all of us. Our lives in this world last but a moment; the World to Come is eternal. It is a foolish man, therefore, who jeopardizes his chances of entering the Garden for the transitory pleasures of the flesh.

"But the highest priority of the sultan is the administration of justice. As the Messenger says in the Hadith, '*A single day of honest government by a just sultan is dearer to Allah than sixty years of continuous prayer.*'

"Like the imam and the qadi, the sultan derives his authority from the Commander of the Faithful and therefore must be obeyed. But if he fails to rule justly, he forfeits the authority that has been entrusted to him.

"Thus, in questions of authority, as in all questions, Allah is great: He pushes us to discern true authority from false that we may obey the first and destroy the second."[30]

*   *   *

Humaydi and Omar pushed their way upstream against the current of chattering students surging toward the exit. Wielding the authority of deputy head of the Nizamiyya, Humaydi easily breached the large circle of admirers bubbling around Ghazali, dragging Omar in his wake. "Chief Professor," Humaydi said, "Omar Khayyam is here."

Ghazali approached and embraced Omar warmly. "My old friend," he said. "What a pleasure to finally see another intelligent face. They are few and far between around here. Welcome to Baghdad."

"I wish I were here under happier circumstances."

"Yes, I received your message about Nizam al-Mulk. But death is a tragedy only to those who love the mortal world." The crowd around Ghazali was silent for a moment, and then Ghazali, remembering his manners, saw to some introductions. "This is Abu Muhammad Tamimi, one of our professors of shari'ah," he said, indicating a wizened man who was well into his eighties. "And this is one of your fellow poets, Abu Ishaq Ghazi. And do you know Shihab al-Islam?"

"I know the name, but we never met," Omar replied. Turning to the man Ghazali indicated, Omar said, "I believe Nizam al-Mulk was your uncle." Shihab al-Islam nodded. "Please accept my condolences," Omar said.

Ghazali finished the introductions and then said, "Your arrival is opportune, Omar. Shihab al-Islam and I were having the most interesting dispute."

"What about?" Omar asked.

"I agree with the chief professor when he says that an unjust ruler forfeits the authority that Allah entrusted to him," Shihab al-Islam explained. "Where we part company is on the question of what should be done about it."

"In other words, you're asking if it's allowed to overthrow an unjust ruler, or maybe even kill an unjust ruler," Omar said.

"Exactly. I say it's forbidden in the Hadith, but I can't remember where. Chief Professor Ghazali says I'm in error."

"You're thinking of the collection by Bukhari. Volume nine, book eighty-eight, numbers . . ." He stopped to think. "Numbers one seventy-six and one seventy-seven. It says to be patient if your ruler does something unjust or—"

"Say it right," Humaydi interjected.

Omar had left out the chain of transmission. He began again. "Ibn Abbas said that the Messenger said to be patient if your ruler does something unjust or tyrannical. Disobeying the ruler is like dying in the Time of Ignorance, before the teachings of Islam were around to ease your path into the Garden."

Shihab al-Islam glanced at Humaydi, who nodded reluctantly. As usual, Omar's memory was spot on. "So then I'm right!" Shihab al-Islam crowed.

Ghazali started to interrupt, but Omar raised a hand to let him know he had the situation under control. "The only trouble with that is this other hadith—it happens to be the next one—says something different," Omar said. "Number one seventy-eight: Ubada ibn as-Samit said that when he pledged his loyalty to Islam, the Messenger made him promise to obey his rulers, *unless the rulers were openly unbelievers.* So we can conclude that you and Professor Ghazali are both right: it is not permissible to kill a bad ruler—*normally*—but there is a special exception for the case of an unbeliever on the throne. And we can thank Allah that we live in a time of good government, under rulers who are loyal in their belief, and that those circumstances are not relevant."

Ghazali smiled with genuine happiness and patted Omar on the back. "If only we had a hundred men like you!" he exclaimed. "There are so few scholars who know the Hadith this well by heart." But even in delivering a compliment, he had to be argumentative. "And even fewer philosophers," he added.

Before Omar could thank Ghazali for his semi-kind words, a student jostled past him on an urgent mission.

"Chief Professor!" the student called insistently. "Chief Professor!" He had the slender build of youth—he was perhaps sixteen or seventeen— and wore the befuddled facial expression that accompanies an earnest quest to understand the clash between the ideals of his professors and the world of men. But neither bewilderment nor failure to attract Ghazali's attention deflated him. "Chief Professor!" he shouted one more time, with greater success. "You said in your lecture that the sultan is subordinate to the caliph. But these days isn't it the other way around?"

"That's exactly the sort of false innovation I tried to warn against in my lecture. What could possibly make you think that?" Ghazali replied.

"The sultan has the army," the student explained. "He can *make* the caliph do his bidding. We saw that last year with what happened between Abu Shuja and ben Samha."

"What of it?"

"What of it! Nizam al-Mulk, who was the sultan's vizier, fired Abu Shuja, who was the caliph's vizier. Surely that means the sultan is more senior than the caliph now."

"You have fallen into error, young man. If you have any doubt that the caliph is more senior, listen to the Friday sermon in the mosque. The caliph's name is always invoked before the sultan's. But in any case, suppose it is as you say, and Malik-shah, through his vizier, succeeded in exerting authority over al-Muqtadi. It would only mean that the world is not as it should be and you are confusing categories, confounding the normative with the positive."

That was merely the student's first question. He consulted a scrap of paper he was holding for the next one. It appeared to be a long list; Humaydi intervened. He clapped the student on the shoulder and guided him away from Ghazali. "The chief professor has a full schedule," he explained with irritation. "I'm sure one of the assistants will be able to correct any misconceptions you have regarding today's lecture." Then, to prevent any further challenges, he suggested that he and Omar accompany Ghazali to a less public place, where they could discuss Omar's business in Baghdad.

Omar said his farewells to Shihab al-Islam and the others and followed Ghazali and Humaydi to Ghazali's office.

*   *   *

The office was bright and spacious, dotted with potted palms and open on one side to a courtyard. Books filled the shelves that lined the other three walls. On the surface of the ornate worktable, more books were stacked precariously. Ghazali indicated for Omar to make himself comfortable on the divan. Humaydi opted to sit cross-legged on the carpet. Standing behind the worktable, Ghazali reviewed several messages. Then, settling next to Omar, he said, "Nizam al-Mulk was a generous patron." Though Persian himself, he spoke Arabic for Humaydi's benefit.

"Isn't that the truth?" Omar replied. "Nine universities, all living off his purse."

"This is actually something of a problem." A handful of stragglers remained in the assembly hall. Their murmurs filtered into the office. Ghazali gestured for Humaydi to close the door.

"I realize that it is unseemly to bring this up so soon after his death," Ghazali continued. "But a university is an expensive undertaking and the bills come due even during times of mourning. Large sums of money are needed to pay the professors' salaries, maintain the buildings, and provide stipends to three hundred students. We own the market that you walked through on the way up from the quay, and we charge rent to the merchants, but it is not enough. If we don't replace the Nizam's contribution, we might have to slash the number of professors and reduce the students' stipends substantially. You are friends with Fakhr al-Mulk. Does he plan to follow in his father's charitable footsteps?"

"I saw him in the sultan's camp. But we didn't discuss any financial matters. His father had just died."

"Of course, of course. It was not the right time. What about Taj al-Mulk? Did he say anything to you about the future of the Nizamiyya?"

"I wouldn't count on help from that quarter. Taj al-Mulk has a university of his own to support. You might get something out of Malik-shah, but at the moment his most important concern is how to make sure everything the Nizam used to do *for him* still gets done. That and bringing the murderer to justice."

"Which according to your message, he delegated to you and me. What do we know so far?"

Omar filled in Ghazali on what he had learned in the sultan's camp. "The killing was well planned," he concluded, "and the killer was well trained and well funded. He had to be a stooge for someone important."

"Who?" Ghazali asked.

"That's what you and I've got to figure out."

"Do you have any thoughts about where we should start?"

"We have two pieces of physical evidence," Omar said. "The first is the murder weapon. I want to bring the dagger to the banker ben Samha to see what he can tell me about the workmanship and the bauble in the handle. I made an appointment for tomorrow night. You're welcome to come with me."

"Nighttime is not convenient," Ghazali replied. "I have extra prayers for Ramadan.[31] Why can't we visit him during the day?"

"It is the Jewish Sabbath," Omar explained. "Ben Samha won't conduct any business until sunset."

"I don't understand why the Jews' ritual should have precedence over ours," Humaydi interjected. "We have no obligation to respect a *dhimmi's* worthless practices."

"That *dhimmi* has information we need," Omar said.

"Then get the qadi to order him brought in for questioning."

"Don't worry about it," Omar said. "If Professor Ghazali doesn't want to come, I'm a grown man; I can go out without a chaperone."

"I never said I didn't want to come," Ghazali objected. "I said it's not convenient. But if it's all arranged for tomorrow night, then I'll see you tomorrow night. Now, what's the other piece of evidence?"

"This," Omar replied. He stood and placed the package he'd brought downriver on the table. Ghazali moved some books and papers to make more room for it. Omar unknotted the string and unfolded the paper wrapping. "The murderer's robe."

Ghazali glanced at the coarse blue wool. "Our murderer was a Sufi," he said with distaste.

"He dressed like one, anyway," Omar replied. "I'm hoping his garment holds some clue for you that I overlooked."

Ghazali picked the garment up by the shoulders and shook out the folds. He scanned it up and down and then up again, but his normally intelligent face had a blank expression. "If you want to know about Sufism," he said, "you're talking to the wrong Ghazali. Ahmad is the Sufi in the family. Can you believe I have a brother who sits on his ass all day? Meditation, he calls it."

"Where is he these days?"

"He has his own lodge now. The Lodge of the Sufic Brotherhood."

"Then that should be my next stop."

*   *   *

When Omar announced his intention to visit the Lodge of the Sufic Brotherhood, Ghazali was relieved. Ghazali himself was headed to the Mosque of Mansur and was at a loss as to how he could avoid inviting Omar to come with him. The chief qadi, Abu Bakr Shami, was going to be there and what Ghazali had to say to him wasn't for Omar's ears.

He found Shami in the courtyard of the mosque, talking to Abu Muhammad Emir, the chief imam. Although Shami spoke with great animation, his hand waving was lost on Abu Muhammad: the imam was blind. The two old men held their ground on the paving stones, two immovable rocks in the stream of people who made their way to Friday worship. When Ghazali arrived, Humaydi in his wake, Shami acknowledged them with greetings of *Ramadan Mubarak* and continued his story.

"Completely ignorant of the words of the Messenger, may the prayer and peace of Allah be upon him. He must have said it a dozen times: the man who wears a silk cloak will have no place in the Garden. But this fool shows up in silk anyway—for court. Proud of it, too, all puffed up holding on to his lapels as he orates."

"What did you do?" the Blind Imam asked.

"I sent him away. I told him I wouldn't accept his testimony. Not in my court. It's un-Islamic."

Needless to say, neither the qadi nor the imam wore silk. Their clothes were mirror images of each other, black woolen robes, the fabric as free of wrinkles as it was of embroidery. Their white turbans were wound tightly and precisely, as flawless as their robes.

"Then what happened?" the imam asked, his sightless eyes unfocused and unmoving.

"The fool had the bad sense to argue with me." Shami's beak-like nose wrinkled as he snorted, and the small eyes on either side of it narrowed under his heavy gray eyebrows. "He said, 'I don't see the problem. Malik-shah and Nizam al-Mulk wear silk all the time.'"

"I can't imagine that going well."

"It didn't. I told him, 'I wouldn't take testimony from Malik-shah or Nizam al-Mulk about a donkey-load of vegetables.'" Shami's laugh sounded like the cawing of a crow. "That took him down a notch."

Ghazali shifted uncomfortably. Clearly Shami hadn't heard yet. Seeing the expression on Ghazali's face, Shami asked, "What's the matter?"

"Nizam al-Mulk is dead."

The silence would have been less uncomfortable if Shami had not just been making fun of the deceased. But eventually, the Blind Imam said, "*Inna lillahi wa inna ilayhi raji'un.*" We belong to Allah and to Him we shall return. He shook his head sadly. "The Nizam was old. It had to happen sooner or later."

"It wasn't old age that killed him," Ghazali replied. "He was murdered." He shared the details that Omar had given him about the tragedy at Sahneh.

Another silence. Then Shami said, "I never thought he was a great Muslim. But he knew his Hadith and he was a good patron of the ulama. He deserved better."

"I'll say a few words during the sermon," the Blind Imam said.

*   *   *

Shami and Ghazali remained in the courtyard long after the imam's assistant, a boy of ten in a striped robe, arrived to guide the Blind Imam into the mosque. The professor and the qadi spoke in hushed tones, even though the crowd had moved inside and they now had the courtyard to themselves.

By the time they finished and slipped into the mosque, unrolling their prayer rugs at the back of the congregation, the Blind Imam was wrapping up his sermon. "Do not wait until the Day of Judgment," he projected into the massive hall. "By then it will be too late to learn that Allah is not a merchant. He will not count the number of days that you fast and the number of extra *raka'a* that you pray, and when the accounts balance, declare your transaction with Him to be complete. Rather, when the Day of Judgment comes, Allah will look within your heart. When you fast your fast, is there love for Allah in your heart? When you pray your prayer, are there submission and gratitude? During this most holy month, look within your heart. For if you find love, submission, and gratitude, then it will truly be a blessed Ramadan—a Ramadan Mubarak."

The Blind Imam stood at the top of the long wooden staircase that led to the pulpit. Unable to see the edge of the step, he held tightly to the banister with one hand to ensure that he didn't lose his footing. He used the other to punctuate his sermon. Behind him, the pulpit cupola sat like a crown upon four Corinthian columns. Down below, the members of the congregation nodded their approval to one another. The Blind Imam's Ramadan sermons were always outstanding.

"Before I conclude," he said, "I have a painful duty to perform." Members of the congregation looked at each other, puzzled. The lesson did not usually end with painful duties. "It saddens me to be the bearer of bad news," he explained. "Some of you already know this, but most of you do not. Nizam al-Mulk is dead. He was struck down by a murderer's blade."

A rumble of disbelief, indignation, and fear surged through the crowd. The ushers' calls for silence were ignored amid cries of "We belong to Allah and to Him we shall return" and "Someone will be sorry they interfered with our government." A couple of men muttered, "He had it coming," but they were quickly silenced by their neighbors.

It was several minutes before silence was restored and the Blind Imam was able to chant the blessings that marked the conclusion of the sermon. "May Allah bestow continued good health and victory to our most orthodox Sunni leader, the caliph Abu'l-Qasim al-Muqtadi B'illah, Commander of the Faithful and Scion of the House of Abbas, along with his honored vizier, Amid ad-Dawla Jahir. And may Allah guarantee victory to the caliph's strong right arm, Sahib al-Jalal, the Sultan Malik-shah, King of the East and the West, Glory of the Nation, Master of the World, Builder of

Bridges, and Slasher of Taxes, along with his honored vizier Taj al-Mulk Abu'l-Ghana'im Tutush ibn Alp Arslan.

"Verily, Allah bids you do justice and good, and give to kindred their due, and He forbids you to sin, and do wrong, and oppress; He admonishes you, haply ye may be mindful!

"Be steadfast in prayer; verily, prayer forbids sin and wrong."

At the mention of forbidding sin and wrong, Chief Professor Ghazali and Chief Qadi Shami, still at the back of the hall, exchanged meaningful glances. Their gazes went unnoticed by their neighbors, who were absorbed in fixing submission and gratitude in their hearts as they prepared to pray.

CHAPTER 5

*O*mar never made it to the Lodge of the Sufic Brotherhood on Friday. He left the Nizamiyya with the best of intentions. But five days of nearly continuous travel with little sleep suddenly caught up with him. He was too exhausted to move. Every part of him hurt. Even his hair hurt. He decided to save the lodge for Saturday and return to the Dar Saltanah by sedan chair for a nap. This had the side benefit of easing the rest of the day's fast. It's hard to be hungry when you're unconscious. After *iftar*, he went for a walk in the sultan's gardens and then made an early night of it—easy to do in the quiet of the nearly deserted palace.

So he had plenty of sleep and was up well before sunrise for *suhur*. He wasn't hungry, though, and stuck to a light meal of bread and fruit, a decision that he soon regretted. Before he even got to the Lodge of the Sufic Brotherhood, he felt lightheaded with hunger.

Nizam al-Mulk had donated generously to the lodge. That was obvious from the façade. The Brotherhood had lavished a fortune on carving chains of calligraphy into the stone. When Omar inspected them closely, he saw a single phrase repeated over and over, a mantra to drive worldly thoughts from the mind, leaving holiness and peace behind: *la ilaha illa-llah*—There is no god but Allah. Omar had seen similar adornments on hundreds of mosques, yet in this case something was off. The carvings made him think of snakes, slithering across the walls and coiling around the columns. They reminded him of travelers' accounts of the temples of India, a country that bordered the Seljuq Empire and yet was alien.

An initiate greeted Omar at the entrance, requested he leave his sandals behind, and insisted on carrying the bundle that Omar had dragged all over Baghdad. Silently, he conducted Omar through the main hall and out into a garden where meditating Sufis in patched robes—black for initiates, blue for the full-fledged—dotted the landscape like proto-Buddhas in an Indian painting. The garden was enclosed by a colonnade that connected the cells of the mystics-in-residence.

The cell housing Ahmad Ghazali was surprisingly humble, given his position as founder and administrator of such a richly funded institution. The room was dimly lit and saturated with the fragrance of straw that had baked for numerous summers within the brick walls. When Omar's eyes adjusted to the light, he saw that the straw was a mattress lying on the floor. The only other furnishing was a well-worn prayer rug. No decoration covered the walls. On the way here, Omar had passed the cells of Ahmad's less exalted neighbors and glanced through the doors. Ahmad's cell was identical to theirs, one of many.

Ahmad wore the white robe of a Sufi master. He kneeled on the prayer rug, motionless in his meditation. The guide signaled for Omar not to interrupt, but they didn't have long to wait. Their figures in the doorway further darkened the already dark room; the change in the light level was visible even to closed eyes. Blinking his way back to his surroundings, Ahmad recognized his visitor and smiled. It was the smile of a jackal—two parts loyalty, one part craft.

"Omar Khayyam!" he said. He stood and stretched his arms to embrace his guest. *"Ramadan Mubarak!"*

As the two men hugged, the initiate who had been Omar's guide and porter placed Omar's bundle on the mattress and left discreetly.

"Have you finally admitted you're secretly a Sufi and come to join us?" Ahmad asked.

"What could possibly make you think that?" Omar replied.

"Your poems."

Omar was visibly surprised. "Sufic" was not the adjective he would use to describe his alcohol-soaked, vaguely racy, and undoubtedly heretical verses. But Ahmad was determined to win the point. "A Book of Verses underneath the Bough," he quoted,

> "A Jug of Wine, a Loaf of Bread—and Thou
> Beside me singing in the Wilderness—
> Oh, Wilderness were Paradise enow!"[32]

"All the elements are there," he explained. "The wilderness is the dwelling of the holy man. Ishmael, Moses, Jesus—they all found Allah in the desert. The loaf of bread is the simple diet of the Sufi. The book of verses is his song. As for the jug of wine, it's the ecstasy of communion with Allah, the 'Thou,' singing beside the 'me.'"

Omar smiled inwardly at how much Ahmad had gotten wrong. "I am sorry, friend," he said. "But in this case 'thou' isn't Allah."

"Then who is it?"

"Well, there was this barmaid in Balkh," Omar began. Then he thought better of it. The cell of a holy man was not an appropriate venue for *that* story.

"You underestimate the significance of your own poem," Ahmad insisted. "For example, you can't tell me that wine doesn't represent communion with Allah."

"It doesn't."

"So what does it represent?"

"It represents wine."

"Of course, but what does that *mean* to you?"

"Sin."

That wasn't the answer Ahmad was expecting. "If wine is so sinful," he asked, "why do you drink it?"

"To forget."

A moment of silence passed between the two men. Then Ahmad said, "I never knew you were that unhappy. You certainly don't show it."

"I'm *not* unhappy. Not usually. I have the observatory, friends . . . ten thousand a year to spend on wine and barmaids. My life is blessed. And yet, I can't shake this feeling that none of it matters. We die, our friends die, our bodies rot in the earth, and everything we have built crumbles to dust."

Ahmad gave Omar a look of sympathy. "Did the death of Nizam al-Mulk affect you that deeply?"

Omar didn't answer. *I didn't mean to open up this much*, he thought. Ahmad's easygoing manner and handsome face and way of making eye contact had made Omar want to talk. But something about Ahmad didn't sit right with him.

Ahmad pointed through the open doorway. It was a beautiful day. The chirps of birds and the scent of dried grass wafted into the cell. The clear blue sky seemed even bluer when viewed from within the dim light inside.

"Do you see the Sufi meditating under the acacia tree?" Ahmad asked. "His wife and three children were killed by smallpox. When he came here, he sounded very much like you. Lamenting the tragedies of this world and doubtful about the world to come. Now look at him. Do you see how serene his expression is?"

Omar thought his expression was more blank than serene, but he nodded.

"He found a better way than unconsciousness in the arms of a tavern maid," Ahmad said.

Omar looked dubious.

"You're spared the expense," Ahmad remarked. "And the hangover. But I assume you didn't come here merely to discuss the meaning of your poetry. What can I do for you?"

Omar opened the bundle on the mattress. "It's the robe that Nizam al-Mulk's killer wore. I hoped it held some clues to his identity and his background. But I don't know what to look for. I thought you could take a look."

Ahmad studied the blue fabric carefully, inching it through his fingers. He spent extra time on the patches, frowning as he examined them. "Take a look at this," he said to Omar. "Do you see the way the patch is sewn on, with these flourishes in the stitches?"

"It's like a poor man's needlework."

"An apt analogy. Just as every seamstress has her unique style, so every order of Sufis has its unique stitch. Like the seal ring of a king. His signature. You can identify which order of Sufis the wearer belonged to by the way he sews the patches onto his robe."

Omar was excited by the prospect of a break in the case. "And which order is this?" he asked.

"That's the problem," Ahmad replied.

"What?"

"Brother Omar, I studied under many sheikhs. I traveled to the farthest borders of the House of Islam to seek them out and learn from them the hidden meanings of the Quran. As I journeyed across the land, there were always lodges along the road where I could get a few bits of bread and a shelter for the night. I thought I had encountered every mystic order there is. But I have never seen this stitch before. The owner of this robe belonged to no order of Sufis that I know."

*　　　*　　　*

Omar was disappointed by the dead end with the robe but was optimistic he would have better luck with the dagger. He set off for the House of Samha right after evening prayers. He picked his way through the crowds in the Square of the Arch, a large open space adjacent to the gate from which it took its name. The wine shops that lined the square had been the gathering places of poets for centuries. Perhaps it was the view through the arch that drew them here: the outline of the Main Bridge of Boats, traced in light by hundreds of lanterns, inspired even the most practical of merchants and bureaucrats to pen a few verses. Or perhaps their imaginations were captured by its location on the Khorasan Highway, which began at the Mosque of Mansur, crossed the Main Bridge, and traveled under the arch into the square. Beyond that, it seemed like a wider than average urban street as it crossed East Baghdad. But then the highway burst through the city limits and raced across an empire. It passed through mysterious and exotic cities before reaching its end, exhausted, in the Land beyond the River.

Whatever attracted the poets here—the beautiful view, the lure of travel, or just the cheap wine—the rhymes flowed freely tonight. Boisterous and occasionally obscene verses celebrated the end of another day's fast. Omar was tempted to join them, but business dragged him elsewhere. He headed down the Khorasan Highway, away from the river, but stopped well short of any mysterious and exotic villages; he merely walked a few blocks, to the point where the road was swallowed by the Market of the Goldsmiths.

When he arrived at ben Samha's door, Ghazali was waiting for him. "I knocked several times," Ghazali said. "But the Jew didn't answer."

"They must still be closed for the Sabbath," Omar replied. "Give them a few minutes."

While they waited, a cat approached cautiously. She sniffed the hem of Omar's robe and brushed against his legs, but when Omar bent to pick her up, she darted into the night. Ghazali knocked again and suggested they should look for another entrance when an elderly servant shambled to the door from somewhere in the interior. The servant apologized for the wait; he explained that ben Samha was preparing to conduct the Havdalah ceremony. Omar and Ghazali were welcome to join the family in marking the end of the Day of Rest.

Ghazali objected. "We're here on official business concerning the murder of Nizam al-Mulk," he said. "Tell your sahib that we will not be kept waiting."

"I'll tell him," the servant replied, "but it won't do any good. I've served him for thirty years, and he has never once chosen an official summons over the rituals of his people."

After some back-and-forth between Ghazali and the servant, Omar asked, "What is the nature of this ceremony?"

"It is a series of four blessings—over spices, over fire, over wine, and—"

"I'm honored to participate," Omar said.

More arguing followed, with Omar pointing out that it would be bad manners to turn down hospitality when it was offered and Ghazali reminding Omar of a verse in the Quran that prohibited friendship with unbelievers.[33]

In the end, they split up. Omar followed the servant through a curtain in the back of the shop; Ghazali remained behind. The storefront was deceptively small. Navigating a tangle of hallways, the servant shepherded Omar past offices and workrooms before emerging into a courtyard behind the building. They passed a cold stone forge, which sat stolidly under the shelter of a tin roof.

On the far side of the courtyard, they entered the residence, where they found themselves in a receiving room crowded with noisy people and gold bric-a-brac.

Their arrival interrupted a minor family drama. In the middle of the room, ben Samha's wife held her husband's arm in a death grip as she tried to jam it into the sleeve of a beautifully embroidered caftan. She countered his resistance with surprising agility, given the weight of the gold jewelry that coiled around her arms and dangled from her neck. Omar's Aramaic was good enough to follow her protests.

"Stop squirming," she insisted. "You can't receive the Astronomer Royal looking like a beggar."

"It's my house," ben Samha protested. "I don't see why I can't wear one of my regular robes."

"You have to look respectable."

"Omar Khayyam is a scientist. He's not going to be swayed by a few yards of brocade and some gold thread. Besides, you're respectable enough for the both of us."

But the lady of the house was undeterred. She gave the coat one more powerful yank and it was on. Ben Samha started to protest further, but just then the servant cleared his throat to signal that the family was no longer alone. As his wife fastened the laces of his caftan, Ben Samha greeted Omar warmly. "Shalom!"

He was short, with the round midsection of a man who loved to indulge in good food and the good-natured grin of a man who loved to meet new people. His caftan was cut generously to leave room for his paunch, and his embroidered skullcap didn't quite conceal his baldness. Were it not for the traditional fringed shawl that his wife draped over his shoulders, anyone looking at him would have mistaken him for a Muslim.

Switching to Arabic, he said, "I am honored to receive such an eminent scientist and poet in my home."

"And I am humbled to be received by one of the leaders of a People of the Book."

"I wish I were receiving you under happier circumstances. The Nizam was my patron and my protector."

He introduced Omar to his family. In addition to his wife, he rejoiced in three sons and a daughter. The oldest, Saad, had a wife of his own. Ben Samha was especially proud of the baby boy she held in her arms. "My first grandchild," he said.

He also rejoiced that his new friend had arrived in time to join him for Havdalah. "The ritual goes back quite a way," he explained. "Over a thousand years. It comes from a time when the temple still stood in Jerusalem."

It was a beautiful ceremony. A goblet of wine and a bottle of rosewater were passed from hand to hand; the participants sipped from the former and inhaled the flowery scent of the latter. The gloomy light of the candle and the mournful tones of the prayers tinged the air with sadness. When Omar commented about it afterward, ben Samha explained that the Jews were sad to be separated from the joys of the Sabbath—and from the home of their ancestors in Palestine.

Ben Samha doused the candle in the remaining wine; the death hiss of the flame signified the end of the ceremony and the start of a new workweek. The host led Omar back to his place of business, accompanied by Saad and the servant. They found Ghazali sitting stonily on the floor. "A Jewish ritual doesn't need to take that long," he insisted.

There was another exchange of greetings. Ben Samha ushered the guests into his office, a large room lined with beautifully polished wooden cabinets. Luxurious furnishings adorned the chamber: a carved Rumi-style worktable with a matching chair and a second table, low to the ground, for entertaining visitors. An embroidered hanging decorated one wall. It depicted a tree with a lush crop of colorful leaves. Birds flitted among the branches, which were weighed down by ripe pomegranates. The design was circular, formed by the curved tree top and the roots at the bottom. Surrounding the image was a circular Hebrew inscription. "The Tree of Life," ben Samha explained when he noticed Omar admiring it. "It represents—"

"—wisdom," Omar interjected. He quoted Proverbs: "'*She is a* Tree of Life *to them that lay hold upon her: and happy is every one that retaineth her.*'"[34]

"Words to live by."

"I have always tried to. But I didn't expect to find that sentiment in the lair of a banker."

"In life it is important to have priorities," ben Samha replied. "Wisdom, faith, family, friendship. And hospitality. Speaking of which, may I offer you some refreshment?"

Ghazali declined, but Omar said, "If it's allowed, because, of course, if you use it only for sacramental reasons, I wouldn't dream of asking—"

Ben Samha knew what Omar wanted before the sentence was completed and gave the necessary orders to his servant. "Daniel, bring some wine for my guest," he said. "Some of the vintage we used for Havdalah."

The servant disappeared back into the house and the others got down to business. Omar removed a roll of cloth from inside his robe and unfurled it on the worktable to reveal the dagger that had taken the life of Nizam al-Mulk. "Where did it come from?" he asked.

Ben Samha moved an oil lamp closer to the dagger. His affable grin morphed into an expression of concentration.

"Does the design look familiar to you?" Omar asked. "The handiwork of anyone in particular?"

Ben Samha shook his head. "No one I know. The craftsmanship is of high quality, but there's nothing unique about it. It could have come from anywhere."

"I thought the sapphire might tell us something."

"Hmmm." Ben Samha opened a drawer and removed a small glass disk. Viewing the sapphire through the disk, he once again said, "Hmmm."

"What is that?" Omar asked, pointing to the glass.

"What? Oh, see for yourself. The curved surface is what causes the object to appear larger." He handed the glass to Omar, who examined it and then peered through it at the sapphire. "Hold it a little closer," ben Samha suggested.

The sapphire burst into focus. In the light of the oil lamp, each facet sparkled with cobalt-blue flame, its boundaries as sharp as a knife edge. When Omar was finished examining the sapphire, he moved on to the grain of the wood tabletop, the leather cover of an account book, and his own fingerprints. "This is remarkable!" he said, excited. "Where did you get it?"

"From a great Muslim scientist, of course. One of your predecessors in the world of astronomy, who died half a century ago."

Omar's eyes grew wide as it dawned on him who ben Samha meant. "You mean ibn Haytham!" he exclaimed. "You've got a copy of *The Book of Optics*! Where'd you dig that up? Finding anything by him is like finding a flying horse. I have the *Treatise on Light*, but I've been searching for *The Book of Optics* for years. I ransacked every bookseller from Tus to Isfahan and got nothing for my trouble. What about *The Model of the Motions of Each of the Seven Planets*? Do you have that?"

Omar was too excited to wait for the answer. He handed the glass to Ghazali. "You've got to see this!"

Ghazali let the glass lie in the palm of his hand like something cleaned out of a drain. Then he shrugged. "Like everything else in science," he said scornfully. "It appeals to a certain kind of mind but gets us no closer to truth."

"Perhaps it will tell us more than you think," said ben Samha. He took the glass back and examined the sapphire again. This time he took longer, uttered even more "hmmm's," and viewed the gem from a dozen different angles. He grew thoughtful, as if his mind were elsewhere and he was no longer seeing the stone. Finally he said, "Yes, I've seen this before." He let Omar take another look.

"Do you see the dark spots?" ben Samha asked. "They look like pinpricks."

"Yes," Omar said. The spots were tiny but definitely there. "They're like bubbles in a piece of glass."

"We call them 'inclusions,'" ben Samha explained. "Tiny impurities. Bits of calcite, mica . . . these look like pyrite—common enough in gems from the Khazar Sea region. This sapphire was mined somewhere in the Alborz Mountains. Near Qazvin. I'd swear it. That's where you should start if you want to know where the dagger came from."

Omar returned the glass to ben Samha. Saad asked if he could take a look, but his father had other plans: he folded the glass into Omar's hand. "Keep it," he said. "I can have another one made easily enough."

"I couldn't," Omar replied. "It would be too much trouble."

"Don't worry about it. I'm almost certain I own a glassblower's workshop somewhere." Yet for all his generosity and good humor, something was bothering ben Samha.

While he had been extracting the secrets of the dagger, the shop had gradually awakened from its Sabbath rest, the staff intent on getting in a few hours' work before closing time. Various assistants filtered in from their respective homes. Through the open door of the office, Omar spied two accountants taking their places on cushions in an adjoining room, laying out their ledger books on the floor in front of them and sharpening their pens. A servant rushed through the hallway carrying an armload of kindling to the forge out back. Soon the pleasant scent of wood smoke wafted into the office. Customers could be heard in the front room, arguing with the clerks about the cost of a necklace or inquiring as to the lead time for transferring funds to Cairo. From the workshops, the pinging of jewelers' hammers provided a musical beat for the evening's labors.

The servant Daniel, who ben Samha had sent for wine, returned fully laden. The tray he carried was heavy, but he balanced it expertly: thirty years of experience with the Samha hospitality had paid off. It held a pitcher of wine and two matching goblets; a second pitcher was filled with a concoction of apricot syrup and water, in case Ghazali changed his mind.

"I didn't know if you had a chance to break your fast, so I brought something to eat as well," Daniel explained as he tiled a low table with dishes of olives, apples, dates, figs, raisins, savory little pastries filled with ground lamb, a whole roast chicken, and pistachio nuts. Ben Samha invited his guests to be seated around the table and partake.

He didn't do a lot of partaking himself, however: after he poured the wine, one of the accountants approached with a stack of papers for his approval. After carefully reviewing each document, ben Samha dribbled a little wax on it and sealed it with his signet ring. He stopped only occasionally to absentmindedly sip his wine or challenge the accountant with a question.

One paper in particular got his attention. "What's this?" he asked.

"The *jizyah* is due on the first of Shawwal," the accountant said. "That document is an authorization to move cash from your personal account to the sultan's account to cover you and your family."

Ghazali scowled as ben Samha approved the transfer. "You're supposed to pay the *jizyah* in person," Ghazali said.

"Pardon me?"

"You're supposed to go to the Registry of Taxation and remit the tax in person."

"Let me get this straight," ben Samha said. He walked across the room, removed a set of keys from his pocket, and opened a cabinet door to reveal dozens of strongboxes stacked on shelves. They were formidable repositories: solid oak reinforced with iron. Pointing to one of them, he said, "You want me to take some coins out of this box, bring them to the Dar

Saltanah, and submit them to an official. Then, a little while later, someone from the registry will bring the coins back here and give them back to me so that I can put them in this other box."

"It's the law," Ghazali replied.

"We never enforced that in Baghdad. Why should we?"

"Because the Shari'ah says that after you pay your tax, the official is supposed to strike you on the side of the head."

"It's bad enough that I have to pay higher taxes because I'm a Jew. Are you telling me I have to be humiliated while I pay it?"

"Legal scholars are quite unified on this point."

"The tax collector can try to start a fight with me if he wants. Abu Shuja tried it, and you know how it ended for him."

"That's because Nizam al-Mulk intervened. Things are going to be different from now on."

Omar tried to restore peace. "We heard about that at the Nizamiyya yesterday. Remember, Ghazali? That student besieged you about it." He turned to ben Samha. "What happened between you and Abu Shuja? All I could understand was that he was dispatched to an early retirement."

"Have some more wine and I'll tell you the whole story," ben Samha replied. He chopped the last of the receipts and returned the pile to the accountant, who hurried back to his own office. Ben Samha saw to the refilling of the goblets and then began.

"It was about a year and a half ago. The sultan had written me concerning the condition of his palace. His father had not spent much time in Baghdad, and the Dar Saltanah had fallen into disrepair. When Malik-shah had visited previously, to attend the wedding of his daughter to the caliph, he was unhappy with the state of things. He ordered me to oversee renovations and to complete them in time for his next visit, which he planned for the fall.

"It was a big job and completing it in six months was going to be a challenge. Leaky roofs had to be repaired. Plaster had to be removed and replaced. Mosaics had to be restored. All the rooms needed new furniture. And every bit of carpet in the place needed to be scrapped.

"So one day I went with Saad and two assistants to the Suq of the Rug Merchants to search for a carpet seller whose wares were luxurious enough for a king and who carried on a large enough trade to handle a project of this size. Word of my errand got around quickly, and soon every merchant in the place had attached himself to my entourage, following me from shop to shop, each man jostling his neighbor to try to get close to me and convince me that his shop should be the next one I visit.

"One man was particularly insistent, grabbing my sleeve, and shouting, 'Come see my rugs! They're the best!' What was his name? Ibn Tariq?"

"Ibn Yasir," Saad interjected.

"That's right," his father continued. "Ibn Yasir. Ibn Yasir the Rug Seller. His appearance was not promising. His robe was dirty and patched, and his beard was poorly trimmed. But appearances can be deceiving, and I had already visited and rejected several of the better-known establishments. I figured there was no harm in seeing what he had. When I told him to lead the way, ibn Yasir became giddy. 'You show excellent taste. You won't be sorry!'

"But I was sorry the minute I saw his shop. Actually, the word 'shop' is rather grand: it was little more than a stall. A sad collection of perhaps twenty rugs, rolled up and leaning against the walls at various angles. When I moistened my handkerchief and rubbed one of the carpets with it, the dye came right off. One carpet was actually sitting in a puddle and reeked of mildew. But ibn Yasir the Rug Seller beamed with pride. 'What did I tell you? The best!' he said. 'Every rug imported from Armenia. The sultan can have the whole lot for five hundred dinars.'

"The style of rug was quite familiar to me, and they weren't from Armenia. They were manufactured on the outskirts of Baghdad and wholesaled for a dinar apiece. And if you wanted them to last, it was best to put them in places where no one would walk on them.

"I politely thanked ibn Yasir and started to leave. 'You got me!' he laughed. 'I was kidding about five hundred dinars. I didn't realize I was dealing with a man who possesses a sophisticated knowledge of carpets. Four hundred dinars, and that includes delivery. When should I send them over to the palace?'

"But I kept going. He ran after me and grabbed my sleeve again. Earnestly looking in my eye, he said, 'Please, I have to sell these carpets. My children need food. Three hundred dinars.'

"When they're haggling, most merchants will invent a starving child or two, but I suspected this man really had some. I gave him a dinar for their benefit. And then I turned around and started walking again. And that was the moment he realized that I wasn't going to buy. Until then, he thought I was simply engaging in a negotiating tactic. Pride and giddiness turned to hate. I heard the dinar clatter on the cobblestones. Then he yelled, 'Jew!'

"I don't know why I stopped and turned around. It's not as if I wanted to say anything. I think I just needed to see his face. It was contorted in an expression of anger. His eyes were crazed.

"'You think that being rich makes you better than us?' he shouted. 'You think you're the caliph himself and can look down on us and that I'm an object for your charity? You could be ten times as rich and you'd still be a stinking Jew, not worthy to lick the asshole of the poorest Muslim. Come the Day of Judgment, Allah will cast you and every other member of your cursed tribe into the fire.'

"I stood there looking at him. I didn't say anything. It was like I was studying him. I think that made him madder. The obscenities and threats of hellfire escalated. The crowd grew ugly. Some just laughed at the pathetic figure of a merchant. But others took his side, and egged him on with cries of 'You tell him, brother!' and 'Death to all Jews!' I whispered to Saad to find the *muhtasib* and get help. He managed to squeeze through the ring of onlookers and slip away. My assistants stepped between me and the crazed man, but that only made things worse. 'Coward! Hiding behind other people! Like every other member of your miserable tribe. You had the favor of Allah and you scorned it. Now He has cursed you.'

"Then, with the curses of Allah on his lips, he charged. He shoved my assistants out of the way and lunged at me. I thought that I was in real trouble. But by then Saad had returned with the *muhtasib*, who brought five of his men armed with truncheons. They shoved their way through the crowd and pulled my attacker off of me. The only harm he was able to do was knock the turban off my head.

"The *muhtasib*'s men arrested my assailant and dispersed the crowd. One of the wealthier merchants helped me with my turban and brought me to his shop, which was nearby. He served me date juice and pastry and all the while apologized profusely for the behavior of his fellow merchant. I sampled the refreshments, went home, and shopped for rugs another day."

Omar tried to imagine what it was like to come face-to-face with hatred and unreason, but he couldn't. It didn't seem to belong in the same world as accountants scribbling industriously in their ledgers and goldsmiths hammering scraps of metal into works of art. "That must have been a harrowing experience," he said. "How did Abu Shuja get involved?"

"The *muhtasib* brought ibn Yasir in for questioning and wrote a report about the incident. Since Abu Shuja was the caliph's vizier, the report came to him in the normal routine of official life. And he made a decision: the response to the incident was *not* going to be routine.

"He drew up an order of expulsion and brought it before Caliph al-Muqtadi, who signed it. I was given ten days to gather my family, pack my belongings, and leave Baghdad.

"I moved my family to our summer house in the mountains. From there I needed to report back to Nizam al-Mulk and Malik-shah. They were campaigning around Samarqand at the time, so I had a long journey ahead of me, across the Amu Darya, to the Land beyond the River."

"While I was gone, evil possessed al-Muqtadi and Abu Shuja. They committed an act so wicked that their names will certainly be united with those of Pharaoh and Haman in the annals of the Jews."

"What did they do?" Omar asked.

"They restored the Ordinance of Omar."

Ben Samha paused to let that sink in. The significance was not lost on a scholar as learned as Omar Khayyam. Hundreds of years ago, when the caliph who shared his name had led the armies of Islam out of the Arabian Peninsula and forged an empire that stretched from Persia to Egypt, he concluded a series of treaties with the Jewish and Christian communities he vanquished. In exchange for the protection of the Muslims, the conquered peoples agreed to certain restrictions. They were the first *dhimmis*. In addition to paying the *jizyah*, they were required to wear distinctive clothing as a badge of their inferior status. They could not build their homes or houses of worship higher than the Muslim buildings. They were prohibited from riding horses, and they could ride a donkey only if they used a wooden saddle. They were required to make way for a Muslim if they were to meet him on the road, and were banned from ringing church bells or otherwise making noise during their religious ceremonies. Collectively these treaties became known as the Ordinance of Omar.

Observing the look of disgust on Omar's face, Ghazali reminded him, "The *dhimmis* signed these treaties voluntarily."

116

"Or as voluntary as it gets when there's a Muslim army standing by to kill you if you don't," ben Samha pointed out.

"It's still shari'ah," said Ghazali. "The law of the land.[35] I had just arrived in Baghdad and was blessed that the Commander of the Faithful consulted me on the matter."

"It was a sad summer for the Jews of Iraq," ben Samha said. "Along the road, I received letters about hundreds of Baghdad Jews fleeing the city. Hundreds more converted to Islam. Al-Muqtadi personally officiated at conversion ceremonies. Even some of my best friends gave in, leaders in our community. When ben Musilaya the Scribe converted, and his nephew Abba Nasir ben Ali, it broke my heart."

"I heard Fakhr al-Mulk mention Abba Nasir once," Omar said. "He's a government official, isn't he?"

"Yes, he's the sultan's chief intelligence officer. We're proud of how many Jews play such a prominent role in serving our Muslim rulers. When al-Muqtadi and Abu Shuja betrayed us, it cast a pall over the synagogues. The numbers of worshippers dwindled. Those who remained dressed in drab-colored robes, the only colors allowed now, with a yellow cord on the shoulder, their badge of their *dhimmi* status. They chanted their prayers in hushed tones—in part because they felt subdued, in part because the new edict required it.

"In the meantime, I reached the sultan's camp and reported to Malik-shah and Nizam al-Mulk. I told them about what had happened to me and the oppression that had befallen the Jews of Baghdad. I was a little apprehensive; although they had always treated me well, I did not know whose side they would take in a dispute between a Jew and a Muslim. But when they heard my story, they were furious with Abu Shuja and al-Muqtadi. They promised me that this interference with an official carrying out the plans of the regime would be punished."

Ghazali interrupted. "It's getting late," he said, rising from his cushion with a groan. "And I have extra prayers to recite. We should take our leave."

"Now?" Omar asked. "He's right at the climactic moment in the story."

"The Jew examined the dagger. We've done what we came for. Let's go."

117

"You go. I'm staying here." In case there was any doubt about Omar's commitment to hearing ben Samha's account to the end, he sliced a few pieces of chicken and put them on his plate.

Ghazali gave in and returned to his cushion. Ben Samha resumed narrating the events of the previous year.

"In the fall, Malik-shah and Nizam al-Mulk arrived in Baghdad at the head of their armies, as they had planned. As they approached the city, they sent a message to the caliph, berating him and Abu Shuja for interfering with the sultan's business. They demanded the caliph suspend enforcement of the Ordinance of Omar and oust Abu Shuja. They even handpicked Abu Shuja's replacement: they brought back his predecessor, Amid ad-Dawla Jahir."

"Oh, I know him," Omar said. "I was at his wedding. That was a *long* time ago. I must have been twenty years old. He married one of Fakhr al-Mulk's sisters. I was jealous actually. I had a crush on her."

"Convenient for the Nizam, wasn't it?" ben Samha replied. "To have a son-in-law so highly placed in the Dar Calipha. In any case, by now the sultan's armies had pitched their tents outside the city. Al-Muqtadi didn't have a choice. He suspended enforcement of the Ordinance of Omar, fired Abu Shuja, and appointed Amid ad-Dawla.

"It's a cutthroat world. A fallen vizier can usually look forward to a short life. But Nizam al-Mulk was merciful to Abu Shuja: the Nizam placed him under house arrest, where he remains to this day.

"As for the sultan and his officials, they went about their business in Baghdad. Malik-shah laid the cornerstone for the Mosque of the Sultan. Nizam al-Mulk, Taj al-Mulk, and many other senior officials arranged to have houses built—perhaps you saw the construction going on outside the Dar Saltanah. But none of them called on the caliph—not even once—an intolerable rudeness in the caliph's own city. As for my family and I, we returned to our home. I resumed work on the palace renovations; you've seen the results for yourself. And the Jews of Baghdad declared a special day of prayer. We went out into the countryside and gathered at the Tomb of Ezekiel, where we gave thanks to ha-Shem and celebrated our deliverance."

*　　　*　　　*

Ben Samha escorted Omar and Ghazali to the gate. Ghazali couldn't get out of there fast enough and started up the Khorasan Highway toward the ferry landing without even bothering with the usual pleasantries. But when Omar went to follow him, ben Samha detained him. Taking Omar by the arm, ben Samha said, "Don't trust Ghazali."

Omar's first reaction was that ben Samha was kidding. But the banker's face was a study in sincerity. So Omar set him straight. "I've known Abu Hamid for years," he said. "I can assure you that he's never been anything but an honest man and a good friend."

"But you've never worked with him," ben Samha replied. "The chief professor has a tendency to twist things to serve his own agenda."

"What are you talking about, 'agenda'?"

But ben Samha was unable to answer. Ghazali had already doubled back to see what was keeping Omar.

*   *   *

"That's really not necessary."

Ghazali's reluctance took Omar by surprise. Omar rather liked ben Samha. But he knew from Nizam al-Mulk's manuscript that a Jew might be involved in the murder. That put ben Samha under suspicion, and Omar had a job to do. Logically, the next step was to check on his story by visiting Abu Shuja and hearing the other side. In view of Ghazali's attitude toward the Chosen People, Omar would have thought that he would be only too eager to follow that line of inquiry. But when Omar asked him to arrange an introduction, Ghazali refused.

The two men walked down the Khorasan Highway, back the way they had come. It was late, but as they neared the Square of the Arch, the street was still crowded with partygoers. Omar and Ghazali passed a wine shop where a poet recited some off-color verses and a crowd of patrons cheered loudly. Omar would have liked to join them, but of course Ghazali would never enter such a place.

"Why can't we see Abu Shuja?" Omar asked.

"It's a good thing actually," Ghazali replied. "From now on, we don't have to run all over town chasing down witnesses. The witnesses are going to come to us."

"What are you orating about?"

"Simple. I've been hard at work for our cause. I found some help for us."

Five minutes earlier Omar would have welcomed any help he could get. But now ben Samha had planted suspicions in his mind. "Who?" he asked cautiously.

"For you, Omar, I went straight to the top. The number one crime fighter in Iraq. Not some stupid *shurta* or low-level magistrate. I recruited Abu Bakr Shami, chief qadi of the city of Baghdad."

"Oh," Omar said. "What sort of man is he?"

Ghazali hastened to reassure him. "I know the qadi quite well," he said. "He attends my lectures frequently. He is absolutely incorruptible, a pious Muslim, and completely unintimidated by the sultan and his officials. Why, just yesterday he told me that he wouldn't take testimony from Malik-shah or Nizam al-Mulk over a donkey-load of vegetables."

"It doesn't sound like he was very well disposed toward the Nizam. Is he going to really put an effort into the investigation?"

"He's already busy on our behalf, setting up hearings. We start the day after tomorrow."

"You shouldn't have done that. I'm your equal partner in this. You should have checked with me."

Ghazali looked surprised. And a little hurt. "I assumed you would be eager to have someone on board with experience in these matters," he said. "A professional."

Omar had to concede the merit of that. Ever since the sultan had given him this assignment, he had been all too conscious that crime wasn't his field of expertise. "I suppose Shami does have the right sort of background," he conceded.

"You won't regret it," Ghazali exclaimed.

They walked in silence until they got to the ferry landing. Ghazali found a pilot who was patiently hoping for one last fare before he called it a night. Ghazali handed him three silver dirhams for the journey downstream to the Nizamiyya. He was about to step onto the raft when Omar stopped him.

"I still want to see Abu Shuja," Omar said.

"Of course," Ghazali replied. "You can see anyone you want. At the hearing. Give me a list of who you want to have testify, and Shami will issue the necessary summonses. Now, how are your accommodations? I know the Dar Saltanah can seem impersonal. If you're not satisfied there, you're welcome to stay with us at the Nizamiyya. The company is more intelligent and we have comfortable guest quarters. Come by tomorrow and I'll show them to you."

"Abu Hamid, I appreciate your concern for my comfort and convenience. I really do. But I want to keep up my inquiries. Informally. Especially since the hearings aren't going to start for a couple of days."

Ghazali frowned. "I think it would be better to wait until then. I'm sorry, but—"

"Hey, buddy!" the boatman interjected. "You coming or ain't you?"

Ghazali gestured for the boatman to wait a minute. "Like I said, I'm sorry, Omar. This is a government investigation. We have to do things in the proper way."

Omar started to argue, but Ghazali cut him off. The crease in his forehead betrayed his worry. He held Omar by the shoulders, looked him in the eye, and said, "Be careful. I know you're eager to get to the truth. I know that you value truth above all things. But this is different from the truths you're used to. It's not a mathematics problem. When you find the roots of a cubic equation, no one is threatened. But the truth of the murder of Nizam al-Mulk is dangerous. I don't know who's behind it, but when he realizes you're on his trail, he'll fight back. Whoever he is, he's rich, he's powerful, and he doesn't care that the Quran forbids him from killing a fellow Muslim. Tread carefully, my friend."

With that, he climbed onto the raft. The pilot pushed off and rowed the slender vessel out into the Tigris. Soon it was barely a dark outline in the murky night, the lantern, no bigger than a dinar, floating above the black surface of the water.

*   *   *

Omar stood alone at the edge of the landing for some time, frustrated and wondering what to do next. A friendly voice behind him, speaking in Arabic, supplied the answer. "The gentleman wants a drink."

Omar turned to see a portly man with a clean chin and impressive mustache.

"Yes," Omar replied, surprised that he hadn't thought of it himself. "A drink is exactly what I want."

"Then you've come to the right place, my friend. Welcome to the home of the best wine in the Square of the Arch. My name is Hujayya and this is Hujayya's Tavern."

He pointed to a large establishment close to the ferry landing. It was clearly trendy, especially with the poets who loitered in the square. It had a patio on the quay for outdoor dining and river views. Omar could see the interior was crowded with people celebrating *iftar* out on the town. Men stood in groups and toasted the end of another day's fast. Above their turbans, gold and blue pendants shaped like stars and crescent moons hung from colorful streamers. Other groups, not content merely to toast full stomachs, sat in circles and did something about it. They feasted on roasted goat with all the trimmings. Some were joined by barmaids with lutes; the lyrics of their songs ranged from the literary to the obscene. Other customers sat by themselves, quietly reading. Hujayya apparently sought to cultivate their patronage: the tavern was filled with lamps and bookcases. The bookcases were against the walls, the lamps were everywhere—sitting on tables, hanging from the ceiling, and mounted on poles on the patio. The staff bustled to keep customers happy—taking food orders, refilling goblets of wine, and clearing off an outdoor table that, luckily for Omar, had just been vacated.

Hujayya led the way and Omar was barely seated on a cushion when a cute barmaid brought a goblet of wine and an ornate bronze lantern with multiple wicks—more than enough to read by. "You're welcome to browse any of the books," she explained.

Omar assayed the wine before the literature and concluded that Hujayya's claim, "best wine in the square," was exaggerated for advertising purposes. The palate of the connoisseur would detect no hints of cherries or tinges of pastry filling at Hujayya's, just honest fermented grapes—bitter, sour, and familiar—but that's saying something. Much as he had savored the vintages that graced the tables of Malik-shah and Abba Saad ben Samha, Omar was glad they hadn't spoiled his taste for standard tavern-issue lamp oil.

A disturbance at the back of the tavern cut short Omar's contemplation of his wine goblet. A group of soldiers had taken over a corner and were egging on a young recruit as he tasted wine for the first time. He grimaced at the sour taste, sending his companions into raucous cheers. A scholar sitting near Omar looked up in disgust. "More of them every day," he complained to his companion.

"Advance guard for the sultan," his friend replied. "Wait 'til the Master of the World gets here with the rest of them."

"There are plenty of taverns down by the docks. Why do they have to come here and ruin a classy place? I'm surprised Hujayya lets them in."

Like all noisesome people, the soldiers were impervious to the idea that no one wanted them around. They emptied their cups and shouted for the barmaid. She approached their corner with a jug and asked indifferently, "What do you want?"

"Your tits in my face," the captain replied and laughed. "Those things are huge. How did a little girl like you get to have such big, round tits?" His men joined the laughter, but the barmaid rolled her kohl-lined eyes.

"Well, then, sweetheart, how about a screw?" the captain said. "Let me build up a thirst for more wine." The other soldiers jeered and hooted.

The barmaid scanned their stupid faces wearily, then smirked. "Okay," she said. "Take off your cuirass."

The jeering and hooting stopped abruptly. The captain looked confused. "What's that now?" he asked.

"Take off your cuirass," the barmaid repeated patiently.

"What, here?"

"You don't expect to screw with your armor on."

"But in front of all these people?"

"If you changed your mind . . ."

"But aren't you going to give me a smart answer that puts me in my place?"

"Why?"

"You're supposed to give me a smart answer that puts me in my place." The captain didn't know what to do. He looked to his men for support, but they just grumbled. This barmaid wasn't doing it right. "Well," the captain muttered, "the thing is, I didn't think you were actually going to...I only have a few dirhams..."

"Don't waste my time if you can't afford it, buddy."

The captain made a last-ditch effort to save face. "I don't suppose you'd give a freebie to a loyal soldier in the service of our glorious sultan?"

She planted the jug firmly on the table. "Pour your own wine." Then she turned around to tend to her other customers.

Everyone in the tavern was looking at her. For a good five or six seconds—which is a long time when no one says anything—they stared at her and she stared at them. Then she gave them a pretty smile and an exaggerated curtsy and they got to their feet and applauded. As she fetched another jug and made her rounds of the tables, customers grinned and congratulated her. "It's about time someone shut those assholes up" was the common refrain. Omar exchanged a nod with her when she refilled his cup.

He made his own rounds—of the bookcases—and picked out a worn copy of the *Shah-nama*; passing through Bisotun had put him in the mood to relive the reign of King Khosrau. He had reached the part where Khosrau, driven temporarily from the throne, appealed to the emperor of Rum for aid when someone jostled his elbow. Startled, he glanced up and saw the soldiers skulking past him on their way out of the tavern. After their altercation with the barmaid, they had sat in the corner for a while, their heads lowered and their voices subdued; they even seemed to shrink into a smaller space. Now that enough time had passed that they could leave without appearing to have been chased out, they were on their way.

Omar made eye contact with the soldier who had bumped him. "I'm very sorry, sir," the soldier said softly. No doubt about it, the little barmaid had taken the fight out of them.

The story of Khosrau ended sadly. After regaining his throne and reigning for thirty-eight glorious years, he had been betrayed by the people around him and stabbed by an ugly, blue-eyed vagabond who volunteered for the job in exchange for a hot dinner. The tale of the murder of a king reminded Omar of the dagger left on Malik-shah's pillow; the threat it represented wasn't getting any less serious while Omar sat here drinking wine and reading stories. He had to get to Abu Shuja, but there was no way a former vizier would see a lowly astronomer without a proper introduction. Without Ghazali's help, Omar didn't know what to do.

It happened exactly the way he had predicted to Fakhr al-Mulk. The moment Omar had nothing else to think about, the enormity of the loss to himself and the nation hit him hard.

It was strange how everyone talked about the Nizam. The great minister who kept an empire—and two emperors—under his thumb for thirty years. The patron of scholars who employed a small fraction of his great wealth to build nine universities. The holy man who had been permitted to sit at the caliph's right hand. In the past few days, Omar had heard a lot of tributes to Nizam al-Mulk the vizier. But the man Omar remembered was Nizam al-Mulk his friend's dad.

Buried under almost thirty years of memory was a journey. The Nizam and his family had led a caravan to the Shrine of Imam Reza, near Tus. As friends of Fakhr al-Mulk, Omar and Hasan-i Sabbah had tagged along. The boys were sixteen at the time. Omar was sure of the year because it was right after the Seljuq victory in the Caucasus. Nizam al-Mulk had returned from jihad married to a captured Georgian princess. Riding in her palanquin, the proud Christian woman accompanied her new family on its Muslim pilgrimage.

Nizam al-Mulk's beard was still brown in those days with just a few gray hairs. *I thought he was ancient*, Omar recalled. *But he was the same age I am now*. It must have been late summer or early fall, because the wheat was tall. An old widow was peddling cantaloupes by the side of the road, and when Nizam al-Mulk walked over to her, the hem of his robe raised a small cloud of dust. Gingerly, he lifted a melon up to his ear and shook it, a tentative grin on his face, as if he were shy about meeting new fruit.

The boys meanwhile milled about on their horses near Fakhr al-Mulk's stepmother. "I bet when he comes back he tells us the story about the caliph Omar and the impoverished widow," Hasan-i Sabbah said impishly. "For the thousandth time."

From behind the curtain of the palanquin, an angry voice erupted. "Hasan-i Sabbah!" Nizam al-Mulk's latest wife was the daughter of a king; she had been raised to give orders. "You *will* be respectful when you talk about the Nizam. Making fun of him is *my* job." Even her jokes sounded like commands.

During this exchange, Nizam al-Mulk stood by the fruit stand, waving a pair of cantaloupes over his head. "He's trying to get your attention," Fakhr al-Mulk said to his stepmother.

She parted the curtain slightly to see what her husband wanted. He held the two melons out in front of him for her approval.

"Jesus Christ," she said, without any awe at her husband. "He can run an empire, but he can't buy cantaloupes."

The Nizam might not have known melons, but he knew the Hadith. He proved that the following day. After completing his prayers at the tomb of the Imam, he emerged from the colossal pointed arch to find Omar sitting by himself at a fountain in the courtyard.

"Have you been inside?" the Nizam asked.

"No. I'm not going in."

"Why not?"

"Visiting the tombs of saints is a Shiite thing. As a Sunni, I know better."

The Nizam smiled, but so slightly that the only clue was a slight lift of the corners of his mustache. "Instruct me, Professor," he said, sitting next to Omar on the rim of the fountain. "Where does the Messenger—may the prayer and peace of Allah be upon him—prohibit visiting the tomb of a saint?"

"In the Hadith," Omar replied, self-importantly. "When he was on his deathbed, the Messenger said that Jews and Christians were damned because they perverted the final resting places of their saints and turned them into houses of worship. His wife Aisha, who was there, said that's why Muhammad's grave was obscure—so that we wouldn't pervert the final resting places of *our* saints." Nizam al-Mulk started to reply, but Omar wouldn't let him interrupt until he got the citation in. "*Sahih Muslim*, book four, number one thousand seventy-nine."

Looking back across the decades, all Omar could think was *I was so damn pompous*. But if the Nizam felt that way at the time, he didn't let on. Instead he welcomed the opportunity for debate. His skill at citation was as good as Omar's. "But what about number two thousand, one hundred twenty-nine?" he asked.

"I know. That's the one where the Messenger prayed for permission to visit the grave of his mother and Allah granted him his permission."

"So visiting graves is permitted."

"Allah granted permission to the Messenger for many things He forbade the rest of us. Like having more than four wives. Chapter thirty-three, verse fifty of the Quran."

Omar and the Nizam exchanged chapters and verses for some time. It struck him that at school the imam never debated like this; he just beat Omar with his cane whenever he couldn't answer Omar's questions. The Nizam treated him like an adult.

In the end, Nizam al-Mulk conjured a verse that Omar had overlooked. It was so obvious, it was clear the Nizam had been holding it in reserve. He had been playing with Omar the whole time. "*Sahih Muslim*, book four, number two thousand, one hundred thirty-one. '*I forbade you to visit graves, but you may now visit them*.' That settles things, doesn't it?"

Omar didn't want to admit he had lost. But the best he could come up with was "Then the hadith contradict each other."

"And when the hadith *appear* to contradict each other, what do you do?"

"Find a way to reconcile them."

"So what's the reconciliation in this case?"

Omar suddenly realized there was a crowd gathered around them. Of course there was; anything the grand vizier did was newsworthy. Amid the beards and turbaned heads, some of the weather-lined faces were laughing. Looking back on the situation, Omar was amazed that he had kept his head well enough to come up with a sensible answer. "The Hadith says it's permitted to *visit* a grave, but not to turn it into a house of worship. So it's permissible to remember the departed, and to reflect on his good example, so long as you don't *pray* to him. That way it's not idolatry."

"So you can go inside. And while you're in there, reflecting on the good example of Imam Reza, you may of course pray to Allah," the Nizam said. "And when you come out, bring Hasan-i Sabbah with you. He's been in there a long time. I've never seen him so reverent." With a smile, he added, "He must be a secret Shiite."

Under the dome of the shrine, the Imam rested inside an ornate rectangular enclosure, a little taller than a man and covered in gold. As Omar stood solemnly in front of the tomb, he neither reflected on the lives of the saints nor offered his prayers to Allah. Instead he kicked himself for debating so badly. *I'm a dullard*, he lamented. *How did that hadith escape me? It was on the same page as the one about Muhammad and his mother's grave. From now on I'm going to study twice as hard.* It surprised him how much he cared about what the Nizam thought of him; he had never cared about what the imam at school thought of him.

In any case, the Nizam didn't seem to share Omar's low opinion of his performance. As they were leaving the shrine, the Nizam said, "Omar, I'm impressed with how well you've memorized the Hadith. In the spring I'm leaving with the army for the Land beyond the River. While I'm away, I'd like you to think about your future, and we can discuss it when I get back. I may have a position for you in the government."

And so everything Omar had achieved was because Nizam al-Mulk was impressed with his memory. All his life, people had told Omar that his ability to remember was a blessing from Allah. They didn't understand what a curse it was. Sitting on the patio of Hujayya's, Omar could look across a span of almost three decades and see the gold dome and turquoise tile of the Imam Reza shrine, the pilgrims scattered about the vast courtyard, the splashing of water in the fountain, and the fatherly expression on the face of the Nizam. He saw these things as clearly as he had seen the naked and mutilated corpse of the same man laid out on a block of ice last week, never again to be proud of a protégé or dumbfounded by melons.

Memory fueled despair as Omar toasted the dead. Holding the goblet the full length of his arm, he said, "To Nizam al-Mulk. Never did an astronomer lose a brighter guide star." Then he remembered that so far he had failed to find the culprit who had extinguished that star. "I let you down," he added. The wine sloshed as he spoke. By the time he brought the cup to his lips, it was half empty. He gulped what was left and slammed the cup back down on the table.

A sob welled up like the first bubble in a pot of boiling water. Once it broke the surface, Omar was helpless to hold back its brothers. He clutched his head in his hands and convulsed silently. His mustache grew soggy with tears; the taste of salt dripped into his mouth.

When he had nearly cried himself out, he felt a comforting hand on his shoulder and heard a gentle voice in his ear. "Are you all right?" it asked.

Omar looked up to see the barmaid standing behind him. "I'm all right," he said, unconvincingly.

"Can I get you anything?"

Omar ordered more wine. "Leave the jug," he said.

He fished in his pocket for a piece of paper and began to scrawl furiously. The tavern faded as he brainstormed metaphors, struggled with meter, ex'ed out lines, and re-scribbled them. He sipped absentmindedly as he worked. Two goblets later, the verse was perfect. He wrote it out in its final form and was shaking dust on the page to blot the ink when he was startled by the barmaid, who had returned to check on him.

"What are you writing?" she asked.

"A poem," he replied indifferently.

"May I read it?"

He shrugged and handed her the page.

"'*Khayyam, who stitched the tents of science*,'" she read aloud. "Is that Omar Khayyam the astronomer?"

"Yes. Have you heard of him?"

"People have been talking about him. They say that he arrived in town a couple of nights ago to investigate the death of Nizam al-Mulk."

"What else do they say?"

"They say he's from a poor family. His father was a tent maker. I heard some people arguing over how, from those beginnings, he got to be the Astronomer Royal."

"And what are the leading hypotheses?"

"One man said it was because he was such an outstanding student at the madrasa. But the other said it was because he was friends with Fakhr al-Mulk."

Omar laughed. "They're both right."

"But they did agree on one thing."

"What was that?"

"They said he has the most atrocious accent. One of them even did an imitation."

"What did it sound like?"

"It sounded kind of like you." It took her a moment, but she figured it out. "We're honored to have you, Khwaja Omar," she said with a curtsy.

She resumed reading his latest creation but now with reverence in her voice. "'*Khayyam, who stitched the tents of science*.' I understand.

Because *khayyam* means 'tent maker.' Why do you refer to yourself by your own name?"

"Inside joke. If Allah can do it . . ."

The barmaid had a nice smile.

"What's *your* name?" Omar asked.

"I'm Lina."

"Of course you are."

"Why do you say that?"

"It means kindhearted."

Lina rewarded the compliment with another smile.

"That's a beautiful outfit you are wearing," Omar said.

"I made it myself."

"The bodice is exquisite." Suddenly flustered, he explained, "I mean the embroidery on the bodice."

"Embroidery is my specialty." With a sinful grin she added, "One of them."

"I like the pants too. Especially the slits."

"I like to show off my legs." She thrust one of them through the slit to demonstrate. It was a shapely leg, with strong thighs and a beautifully curved calf.

"They're worth showing," Omar said. "Being on your feet all night pays off."

"I'm not always on my feet when I'm working," Lina replied.

Omar thought he knew what she meant by that, but then she helped herself to a cushion at his table, and he was left wondering.

"Now, be quiet," she insisted, "or I'll never get through this poem."

"Khayyam, who stitched the tents of science,
Has fallen in grief's furnace and been suddenly burned;
     The shears of Fate have cut the tent ropes of his life,
And the broker of Hope has sold him for nothing![36]

"I can't tell if it's sad or angry," she said when she finished reading.

"Neither," he replied, emptying his goblet again. "Both."

"But why?"

"The Nizam was my friend and my benefactor."

"I'm so sorry. Let me pour you another cup."

She reached for the jug, but Omar took her hand to stop her. "Don't bother," he said. "I've had six already. I just don't feel it tonight."

She raised his fingers to her mouth and kissed them. "Do you feel this?" she asked. He did.

She stood up, still holding his hand. Following her lead, he stood and faced her. Encouraged by her dark eyes, filled with liquid kindness, he wrapped his arms around her waist. The exposed skin of the small of her back felt cool and smooth beneath his hands. She belonged on this beautiful terrace, where reflections of a hundred lamps flickered on the black waters of the Tigris. The lapping of waves against the quay gave Omar a sense of peace for the first time since a soldier had galloped up to his observatory and turned his well-ordered life upside down.

A small sailboat glided by and disappeared into a canal. Bending to kiss the top of Lina's head—she was very short—Omar drowned in her perfume, but, then, roses were his favorite. Her black tresses splashed over her shoulders and came to rest on her breasts, drawing Omar's gaze into the deep shadow between them.

"Is that all you want to do?" she asked. "Just look?"

She guided his hand under her bodice. Her breast was heavy and round. The nipple felt quite large under his grasp. She stood on her toes and whispered in his ear. "I have a room nearby." Her breath caressed his skin like a massage from gentle fingers.

Well, there were other ways to forget besides wine.

CHAPTER 6

BAGHDAD
SUNDAY, 19 RAMADAN 485
8 Abán 471
24 October 1092

*A*t first he thought it was a hangover. Perhaps he was feeling those six cups of wine after all. But then he realized the pounding wasn't inside his head; it was next to it. Someone was making the bed while he was still in it. He knew only one person who could fluff a pillow quite so violently. But she couldn't possibly be here. Allah wasn't that cruel.

He opened his eyes and, sure enough, it was her. "You're finally awake," she said, yanking the second pillow away from him; his head hit the mattress. She was tall and stout, around twenty years old, wearing a practical dress with an apron over it. Her frizzy hair was tied neatly with a scarf. Or as neatly as frizzy hair ever gets.

"Where's Lina?" Omar asked.

"Who?"

"Lina. The woman who was with me."

"She probably went to the bath to wash the sin away. You were alone when I got here." She finished with the pillow. "Get up. I have to straighten the sheets."

"No, you don't. They have servants for that."

"And when will they show up? Sunrise was two hours ago. Probably still in bed like everyone else in this den of vice. Allah only knows what goes on here. Fornication. Fellatio. Back-door hijinks. It's disgusting."

"You seem to have given it a lot of thought."

She pointed to a long-shirt draped over a chest. "Is that yours?"

132

Omar nodded.

"Put it on," she said, tossing it to him. "I won't fall prey to the curse of Ham."

Omar wiggled into his long-shirt under the sheets. "How did you find me, Khuld?" he asked.

"How do I ever? I go to where the poets gather and ask around. 'I'm looking for my father. Where's the nearest whorehouse?' I blush to be your daughter."

"You shouldn't be out in the streets without a chaperone."

"Neither should you."

Omar let that pass. Instead, he asked, "And what satanic magic whisked you from Isfahan to Baghdad? I suppose some evil jinn was scheming to do me a bad turn."

"Don't be childish," Khuld replied. "You don't believe in jinns."

"Oh, I forgot. So how did you get here?"

Before Khuld could answer, Lina returned. The little barmaid didn't see Khuld at first. Her hands were full with a breakfast tray, and she had to push the door open with her shapely bottom and enter the room backward. She placed the tray on the nightstand and busied herself with pouring a mango drink into cups and spreading sweet poppy-seed paste on the flatbread. She hummed as she worked. It wasn't until she was kneeling in bed beside Omar, feeding him a piece of flatbread, that she noticed they weren't alone.

"Oh," Lina said, surprised. "A threesome costs extra."

"*And* the shame continues," Khuld said, rolling her eyes. "He's my *father*."

"Don't be ashamed," Lina replied sympathetically. "Some of *my* clients want me to call them 'Daddy,' too. You'd be surprised how many respectable people like to play games like that. Famous people. People you've heard of."

"You're confused. He's my *actual* father. Being Omar Khayyam's daughter is no game."

Lina looked quizzically at Omar, who had a wedge of flatbread sticking out of his mouth; it flapped as he nodded. Taking the bread in his hand he said, "It's the truth, Lina. Meet my daughter, Khuld. Khuld, this is Lina."

"What a gentleman," Khuld said. "Always gives me a proper introduction to his whores. Stop eating. It's Ramadan."

Omar obeyed—as soon as he finished the piece of bread he had already started and washed it down with some of the mango drink. Finally ready to leave, he put on his robe, pulled a sheet of paper out of the pocket, and handed it to Lina. "After you nodded off," he explained, "I scribbled out a new poem."

Lina unfolded the page and read:

> "Submit not to this World's Iniquities.
> Pine not for whom the last Embrace did seize.
>   Love one jasmine-bosomed and fairy-born,
> Drink Wine—and cast not thy Life to the Breeze![37]

"That's so sweet," she said. "Do you really think I'm '*jasmine-bosomed and fairy-born*'?"

"Yes. Also ebony-haired, rose-scented, and houri-curved."

Khuld rolled her eyes.

Lina tried to give the poem back to Omar, but he insisted she keep it. "It's a gift," he said. "Gratitude for last night."

She read the poem again, but as she had exhausted the compliments, she considered its other aspects. "It's a lot more optimistic than the other one," she said. "'*Fallen in grief's furnace*' has been replaced by '*pine not*,'" she said.

"I've got you to thank for that," Omar replied.

The hug that Lina gave him was genuinely warm and friendly.

Khuld crossed her arms and waited not so patiently for it to be over so that she could extract her father from this place of sin.

*   *   *

The clouds had massed during the night; now a patchwork of light and dark gray suffocated the city. In general, Omar was reluctant to forecast the weather—it was far from the realm of science—but in this case he was willing to roll the bones, or spin the astrolabe, or whatever it was weather forecasters did: before the morning was over, a cloudburst would send Baghdadis scampering for cover.

Father and daughter passed through the palace gate and traversed a vaulted corridor that opened onto the gardens.

"Here we are," Omar said. "I'm sure you can find your way from here."

"We need to talk," Khuld replied. "What were you thinking? Running off two hundred farasangs in the middle of the night. No luggage, no money?"

"I didn't have a choice," Omar replied. "Sultan's orders."

"Did the sultan order you to spend the night with some cheap prostitute?"

"She happens to be a very expensive prostitute."

"I would think you wouldn't be so foolish with your money."

"*'Blame me not if I act the fool,'*" Omar replied, "*'for once more am I drunken with the wine of love.'*"[38]

"Enough with poems," Khuld said. "You won't turn my head with shiny words. I'm not little Lina. So you're in love now? Do I have to spell out how ridiculous that is at your age? In the first place—"

Omar was literally saved by the bell. A church bell, to be precise, whose solemn clang summoned the Christians of Baghdad to Sunday mass. Omar took off across the garden in the direction of the tolling.

"Where are you going?" Khuld yelled, chasing after him.

"Sanctuary," Omar replied, exiting the palace through a back gate and disappearing into the streets of the Christian Quarter.

By the time she caught up with him, he had arrived at the Monastery of Rum and was admiring the architecture, or pretending to. In order to reach him, Khuld had to shove her way across a line of people filing through the main gate. It was a graceful structure of gold-colored brick with a large central arch and pairs of smaller arches stacked on each side, the whole arrangement crowned with a crenellated roofline and an ornate bronze cross.

"See how the center arch frames the entrance to the cloisters?" Omar said, pointing through the gate and across the courtyard to the building beyond.

"I didn't chase after you for a lesson on architecture," Khuld replied.

"Why did you chase after me?"

"If you can go to a church, I can go to a church."

"I don't mean the church. Why did you chase me to Baghdad? You didn't need to do that."

"Yes, I did," Khuld replied. "Who's going to look after you?"

"I can look after myself—"

"—said the man who woke up this morning in a whorehouse with a hangover."

"I don't have a hangover."

"I stand corrected. The man who woke up this morning in a whorehouse *without* a hangover."

At that moment a family—husband, wife, and two daughters— passed Omar and Khuld. The husband, who carried a prayer book, gave Omar a dirty look.

"Keep your voice down," Omar implored Khuld. "If we have to squabble, let's squabble someplace where we don't startle the Christians. There must be a garden around here somewhere."

There was. It was tucked into a quiet corner between the monastery and the church.

"Now, isn't this better?" Omar asked as father and daughter strolled between rows of cedar trees.

But Khuld picked up where she left off. "Have you even been eating properly?"

"Stuffing myself. All night long. I'm a Ramadan glutton."

"Liar. They told me at Hujayya's that all you ordered was wine and prostitutes."

"Muhammad's tomb! What did you do? Interrogate everyone I met last night? Because there was a poor, disheveled beggar on the way to Lina's who you might have missed. I gave him a dinar."

"Someone needs to check up on you. Because wine and prostitutes. And giving away a dinar when a dirham would do."

Omar stopped to appreciate a rosebush. He bent over to savor the sweet scent of the blossoms. "There was only one prostitute," he said. "And it was an after-dinner drink."

"I heard it was six after-dinner drinks. And what was dinner exactly? A handful of dates?"

"I had a veritable feast at the home of my new friend, ben Samha. He served these delicious lamb pastries . . ."

Out of the corner of his eye, Omar saw Khuld folding her arms skeptically. He straightened and faced her.

"Khuld, Khuld," he said. "You don't need to babysit an old, broken-down astronomer. You should babysit a husband. That's what other women your age do."

"Other women my age don't have you for a father. How can I look after a husband? You're a full-time job."

"I fended for myself for a long time before you were born."

"To the enrichment of vintners and whores everywhere."

From inside the church, the song of a choir drifted into the garden. "If you're so fired up to get me married," Khuld said, "how come you've never found a proper match for me?"

"*W'allah!* I've found dozens of proper matches."

"Name one."

"Maymun ibn al-Najib."

"From the observatory? An old broken-down astronomer."

"Touché. What about Abu'l-Muzaffar al-Asfizari?"

"Too stupid."

"Muhammad Nasikh."

"Too short."

"He's not too short. You're too tall."

"I knew it was my fault."

"Fakhr al-Mulk."

"And we're back to old."

"He's the same age I am."

"Like I said . . ."

"Abu Hamid Ghazali, then. Brilliant, successful, decent height, never married, and only thirty-four. Thirty-four isn't too old, right?"

"No, I can do thirty-four. Ghazali is a perfect match. Except for one thing."

"What's that?"

"He thinks women are evil." She stomped away angrily along the garden path.

"Picky, picky, picky." It was Omar's turn to chase after *her*. "How *did* you get to Baghdad?" he asked.

"After you galloped off, Berk-yaruq came to the house with your ridiculous message," Khuld replied. "You know you left him standing all alone like an idiot on the platform of your observatory. And what's the deal using the Prince of the Realm as your errand boy?"

"I assumed he would send somebody. He didn't have to deliver my message in person. Why did he do that?"

"I don't know. I think he has a crush on me."

"There you go. Marry Berk-yaruq."

"What am I, a princess? The best I can hope for with Berk-yaruq is to be his concubine. A slave. Is that the life you want for me?"

"Concubines have risen to rule empires. That's the life you were born for."

"Don't be absurd. Selling me into slavery. It's disgusting."

"You have no sense of humor. You never know when I'm joking," Omar muttered.

"What was that?" Khuld demanded.

"I said, let's go inside. We're going to get a soaking."

Indeed as they were arguing, the clouds had thickened; now fat drops of rain were beginning to fall. They set off tiny bursts of dust as they hit the dirt path.

"There's the door over there," Omar said. He held it open for her and they found themselves inside the church.

They stayed in the vestibule. The room was cool and dimly lit. The scent of candles and incense and the chanting in Syriac that drifted in from the sanctuary had a soothing effect on them; their conversation actually became cordial, or as cordial as they ever got.

"You never did tell me how you got to Baghdad," Omar whispered. The peaceful vestibule seemed like a place where whispering was mandatory.

"Berk-yaruq," Khuld whispered back. "I told him to get me to his father's camp. He was reluctant, so I pointed out that as sultan he would have to move large armies over huge distances. Surely he could move one young girl. It would be good practice."

"Yes, that would convince him, all right."

138

"He came through with style. By midday I was riding top speed on a fine horse. Two guards escorted me and there were fresh horses at every post station."

"Since when do you know how to ride a horse?"

"Since I was nine. You pay no attention to me or you'd know that. Anyway, Berk-yaruq arranged lodging too. Most nights I had a private room in a khan. But one night I stayed at the camp of Fakhr al-Mulk—he's taking his father's body back to Isfahan. Two nights ago I got to the sultan's camp and they told me you had moved on to Baghdad."

"Where were they?"

"Still in the mountains. Terken Khatun expects they'll be here by Friday."

"You talked to Terken Khatun?"

"Yes. She insisted I have an audience with her."

"How did she receive you?"

"She was very formal and haughty. But hospitable. She gave me a hot meal and a bed for the night."

"What did you and she discourse on—other than sleeping arrangements?"

"She questioned me about where I was going and why. It felt like an interrogation, but one of her ladies-in-waiting assured me that she treated everyone the same way. Although, Terken Khatun did seem upset when I told her how efficiently Berk-yaruq had arranged my travel."

This surprised Omar. His impression of Terken Khatun's attitude toward Berk-yaruq was that she would be proud of his skill at logistics. He wondered what else he had gotten wrong.

"What does she look like?" he asked.

"Terken Khatun?"

Omar nodded.

"Thin as a steel blade and twice as tough," Khuld replied.

Not the motherly type after all. Omar realized—not for the first time in his life—that he was at a disadvantage, talking to women through a curtain, unable to observe body language or facial expressions. Perhaps it *was* a bit of luck that Khuld followed him to Baghdad. The information she could provide might prove valuable.

When they emerged from the church, the rain had stopped and the sky was once again a crystalline blue. The air was noticeably more pleasant because of the cold front that had passed through. Groups of tourists had come out with the sun and strolled the garden paths. Many of them Muslim, they enjoyed the roses and the cedars, the jasmine and the narcissus, undeterred by the crosses atop the towers or the bells swinging noisily in their rectangular frames.

Omar and Khuld navigated the narrow streets of the Christian Quarter back to the Dar Saltanah. When he got to the foot of the stairs that led to his room, Omar realized he had no idea whether Khuld had accommodations in Baghdad.

"I don't suppose Terken Khatun arranged a place to stay here as well," he said.

"She did," Khuld replied. "Women *can* take care of these things. When I left camp, she gave me a letter to arrange things. Last night I showed it to the eunuchs and they set me up in a room in her apartments. It's a beautiful room. But the rest of the harem is deserted. Until the court gets here, I'll be roaming empty halls by myself."

*　　　*　　　*

The anteroom to Taj al-Mulk's office was packed. It seemed everyone who could wield a pen was eager to secure a place in the new administration. They crowded the door of the inner office every time it opened, in the hope of being next to be interviewed by the new vizier. Couriers rushed in and out with messages. In one corner six frazzled secretaries sorted through boxes of papers that had belonged to Nizam al-Mulk. They would no sooner finish with one box when a porter would lug in two more.

"This report is five years old," one of the secretaries complained. "Someone get me the *current* state of Rumish defenses."

"I'll take care of it," a colleague replied impatiently. "Just as soon as I find the list of canal-dredging projects."

Omar was grateful when Taj al-Mulk spotted him in the crowd and insisted on seeing him right away.

The inner office was only marginally less chaotic. "Be careful what you wish for," said Taj al-Mulk, with a weak smile. "Or someday you might end up as the sultan's vizier."

"Did the Nizam leave things in a state of disarray?" Omar asked in reply.

"It's a horrible mess. It turns out that when the grand vizier dies, every government official's term automatically comes to an end. We have to reappoint everybody from scratch. We have to decide who to keep and who to let go. The entire government. And no one is sure of the procedure, because we haven't been through this in thirty years."

A secretary scurried in with a report. "Thank you, Raqim," Taj al-Mulk said. He scanned it and frowned. "There should have been twice as much tax revenue from Khorasan. See if this report has another part. Is there anything else?"

"Yes," Raqim replied. "Amid ad-Dawla Jahir sent a message from the caliph's palace. He wants to know when you can come over and review the plans for Eid al-Fitr."

"I'm sure they're fine. Tell him I'll talk to him when we go out to greet the sultan. And as soon as I'm finished speaking with Khwaja Omar, start sending in the candidates for finance minister. The sooner I can stop doing both jobs, the sooner things will calm down."

Raqim hurried out and Taj al-Mulk said to Omar, "I don't suppose you want to be finance minister."

"Muhammad's tomb! What did I ever do to you?"

"I know you can handle the math."

"No, math doesn't scare me. But the court politics . . ."

"There are other offices open. Offices far away from the court. There's the qadi in Borujerd that Nizam al-Mulk fired. And I don't plan to reappoint the governor of Nishapur. You're from Nishapur. How would you like to be governor?"

"Nizam al-Mulk tried to inflict that position on me eighteen years ago," Omar replied. "'No, thank you,' I told him. 'Build me a tower to study the stars.'"

"Eighteen years? You must be wishing for a change by now."

"Sometimes. But someone told me to be careful what I wish for. Besides, I can't take on anything new until I solve this murder. And on that topic, you know the wanted posters we sent to Hamadan?"

"It's too early to have any response yet. It will probably be the better part of a week before we hear anything."

"Yes, I know. That isn't what I'm asking. Can you get some more copies made and sent up to Qazvin?"

"Sure. Whatever you want, Khwaja Omar. Why Qazvin?"

Omar told Taj al-Mulk about the meeting with ben Samha. He showed him the magnifying glass and explained how ben Samha determined that the murder weapon came from the Khazar region.

"The posters will be drawn up today," Taj al-Mulk promised.

*   *   *

Three dirhams to the ferryman and Omar was gliding downriver toward his next stop, the Nizamiyya.

It turned out that Ghazali was tied up with some sort of financial crisis and didn't have time for him. "Humaydi can help you," he told Omar. "Tell him I said to give you whatever you need."

The deputy director's office was lined with bookcases. The volumes of hadith, commentary, and jurisprudence were stacked horizontally on the shelves, each snugly in its place in accord with Humaydi's meticulous system of organization. Seating was austere, however. No divans or cushions. Merely a pair of prayer rugs. Evidently Humaydi found comfort un-Islamic.

"I need an assistant," Omar explained when he got settled. "Someone to schedule my appointments while I'm in Baghdad, run my errands, keep my inkwells full and my pens sharp. But more important, I need someone I can discuss the case with. Someone who can come up with ideas I didn't think of and who isn't afraid to follow those ideas, even if they lead to powerful and seemingly pious individuals."

Humaydi grunted. "I suppose we can get you someone," he said. After a moment of thought he added, "I know exactly the person."

"Thank you."

"You two deserve each other. I'll send him to you this evening. If I can find him."

"If it's too much of a burden . . ."

"No burden. Anything to keep you from bothering Chief Professor Ghazali every time you need something. He has important work of his own, you know."

"Yes, because finding out who murdered Nizam al-Mulk is such a waste of time."

"It is. We know who did this."

"That's news to me."

"Who is the one person who hated Nizam al-Mulk the most?" In his enthusiasm, Humaydi spoke rapidly, his al-Andalus accent thicker than usual. "Who is the one person who spent his entire life submitting to the Nizam's 'guidance'? What does it do to a man to always be in the shadow of another, lose every argument, and constantly be manipulated and lectured to?"

Omar saw where Humaydi was going with this and tried to head him off. "Recently I had some experience with the being lectured to part," he said. "Very recently."

But Humaydi was undeterred. "The truth is undeniable," he replied. "Nizam al-Mulk was murdered by the sultan. Malik-shah of the House of Seljuq."

"If we accuse Malik-shah of anything, then our accusation better have damn good proof behind it."

"It does," Humaydi replied. "Who ordered the murderer killed before anyone could question him?" he asked.

"Malik-shah," Omar conceded.

"And who ordered the guards to allow the murderer to approach Nizam al-Mulk's litter?"

"Not Malik-shah. That was Yalbard."

"But who does Yalbard work for?"

"Malik-shah." Omar pressed his lips together in frustration. These were valid points.

"And who—"

"I understand what you're trying to tell me. The only problem is that it's completely ludicrous."

"Is there anything I said that isn't the truth?" Humaydi asked indignantly.

"Yes, it's the truth," Omar replied. "But it isn't the whole truth. You left important stuff out. Like the sultan didn't have to employ a killer to step out of Nizam al-Mulk's shadow. He could have stepped out of it anytime by giving the Nizam the sack. So why didn't he? He didn't want to. On the night of the murder, five hundred dinner guests observed the sultan go to the brink of accepting Nizam al-Mulk's resignation, only to back down because he didn't want to work too hard."

"Playacting to divert suspicion from himself." Humaydi's smile was half satisfaction with his cleverness for seeing through the sultan's ruse and half challenge to Omar to contradict him. "Anyway, you're wrong about the sultan being able to fire the Nizam," he said. "Nizam al-Mulk controlled the treasury. He controlled the bureaucracy. He controlled a private army of twenty thousand mamelukes, loyal to him, not the sultan. The Nizam was too powerful to fire."

"No, no, no. You didn't see Malik-shah in Sahneh. I did. He was seriously grieving. As if he had lost a father."

"More playacting. He fooled you completely."

"If Malik-shah was behind it, then why was he threatened too? The killer left a knife in his bed."

"Did anyone see the murderer plant the knife in the sultan's pavilion?" he asked.

"Well, no, because he lured the guards away with a jug of wine," Omar replied. "But obviously the guards saw him when he lured them away."

"That's right. The two guards. The ones that Malik-shah conveniently beheaded. Clearly no one planted the knife. Malik-shah had it all along. Yet another attempt to divert suspicion from himself. And isn't it interesting that he had a knife that was identical to the murder weapon?"

"*W'allah!*" Omar swore in frustration. "According to you, every point against the sultan is proof of his guilt, and every point in favor of the sultan is proof of a cover-up. In logic, a proof where any premise leads to the same conclusion isn't any proof at all."

"Perhaps it would be better if you set aside your faith in logic and put your faith in the Quran. If you did, none of this would surprise you.

Malik-shah was never a good Muslim, with his silk robes and his drinking parties and his wars against other Muslims. He's guilty . . . I believe the phrase you philosophers use is *a priori*."

With hindsight, Omar realized he should have left well enough alone and ended the interview right there. But now he was determined to make one more point.

"If Malik-shah was so enthusiastic to cover up the crime, why did he appoint me to investigate it?"

"Why indeed? Don't you think it's strange that the sultan appointed an astronomer? Someone who spent eighteen years shut up in an observatory, with no experience in *shurat* business or court intrigue?"

Omar had to concede that Humaydi had a point; Omar had raised the same objections when the sultan appointed him.

"Face it, Omar Khayyam," Humaydi said. "You were meant to fail."

*   *   *

Badly shaken by the conversation with Humaydi, and unsure what to do next, Omar went shopping. It was just as well. He badly needed a change of robes.

It was after sunset when he arrived back at the palace. The corridor outside his room wasn't quite deserted. A young man with a student's yellow stole across his shoulders sat by the door, a satchel resting on his lap. Omar recognized the visitor; he was the student who had waylaid Ghazali after his lecture at the Nizamiyya. When Omar approached, he scrambled to his feet, causing the satchel to tumble onto the marble floor.

After Omar helped him pick it up and asked him what he was doing there, the young man explained, "Deputy Director Humaydi sent me."

"Oh, you must be my new assistant," Omar replied. "I've been expecting you. What's your name?"

"Muhammad Baghdadi."

"A pleasure to meet you, Baghdadi, I hope I haven't kept you waiting too long."

"That's all right; I only got here a moment ago," Baghdadi said. "I'm sorry I wasn't here earlier. I wanted to attend my evening lecture. I don't like to miss one. Learning is very important to me."

145

"That's a fine characteristic in a student."

"It's why I was so happy that Chief Professor Ghazali assigned me to work with such an illustrious scholar. I'm sure I'll learn a great deal, in view of your accomplishments in the science of astronomy, the science of mathematics—"

"At the moment, it's the science of cooking that interests me. Have you eaten, Baghdadi?"

"I'm not hungry."

Omar took that as a no. "I am," he said. He had been planning to raid the palace kitchen. But now that he had company . . .

"Let's go out and get something," he said.

*   *   *

"Something" turned out to be dinner at Hujayya's. But when they arrived and Baghdadi glanced through the open door, he said, "Oh. Do they serve wine here?"

"'*That ruby in a clear glass!*'"[39] Omar replied. "'*The juice that frees thy heart from a hundred pains!*'"[40]

"I beg your pardon, Khwaja, but I do not follow you."

Omar sighed. "Yes, they serve wine here."

Hujayya noticed them standing at his front door and hustled to greet them. "Omar Khayyam!" he said. "I am honored that you have returned. I have an excellent outdoor table for you."

"If you've got something a little more secluded," Omar replied, "my friend and I have affairs of state on which to converse."

"Of course, of course," Hujayya said affably, gesturing for Omar and Baghdadi to follow him inside.

Baghdadi hesitated. "I am no longer hungry," he said. "I'll just wait by the quay." He reminded Omar of another teenage boy who had insisted on waiting outside while the rest of his party visited an un-Islamic place.

Omar decided to lure Baghdadi into the tavern the same way Nizam al-Mulk had lured him into the Shrine of Imam Reza: by means of the Hadith. Granted, Omar had the more difficult task: the Shari'ah had been on Nizam al-Mulk's side. It was not on Omar's. Still, he gave it a try.

146

"The Quran says no drinking alcohol. But there's no prohibition against going into an establishment where *others* are drinking alcohol."

"True," Baghdadi replied. "Not in the Quran. But in the Hadith, At-Tirmidhi, book forty-three, number three thousand thirty-one. '*Whosoever believes in Allah and the Last Day, then he is not to sit at a table where wine is served.*'"[41]

"Aha!" Omar exclaimed. "You can't sit 'at a table' where wine is served. Now brace yourself for my brilliant solution." He turned to Hujayya. "Sir," he said, "we would like two tables pushed together. And serve wine at only one of them."

Hujayya ducked inside to make the necessary arrangements. Baghdadi was still reluctant to enter, though. "But *you'll* be drinking, Khwaja Omar," he said. "And the Quran commands me to enjoin good and forbid evil."[42]

"Go ahead, then," Omar replied.

"Huh?"

"Forbid evil."

"I couldn't. You're my *khwaja*."

"The Quran commands it."

Baghdadi continued to hesitate, but after some more cajoling from Omar, he said, "Very well, Khwaja Omar. I forbid you to drink wine."

"Well said," Omar replied. "Ghazali himself couldn't have said it better. You've done your duty. In fact, you've done it admirably."

Baghdadi smiled at receiving a compliment from such an illustrious scholar.

"Now, let's go into the tavern," Omar said.

Hujayya had arranged a private room for them. No sooner had Omar and Baghdadi been seated when Lina ran in and jumped into Omar's lap. She landed so abruptly that she nearly fell over backward; she had to throw an arm over his shoulder to steady herself and avoid spilling the jug of wine in her other hand.

"I missed you!" she said, giving him a quick kiss on the cheek.

"You don't say that like you mean it," Omar replied.

"How about now?" She tilted her head, letting a tousle of black hair fall to one side, and kissed him slowly on the mouth.

"Now I believe it," Omar said.

"Oh, I've barely started." She pressed her cheek against his and saw Baghdadi sitting at the adjoining table with his gaze fixed on his folded hands. "Who is your shy friend?" she asked.

"Lina, this is Muhammad Baghdadi."

"Any friend of Omar Khayyam is welcome in Hujayya's," Lina said. "May I pour you some wine?"

Baghdadi mumbled something unintelligible, so Omar stepped in. "Baghdadi's table is free of alcohol."

"You need to corrupt this youth, Socrates," Lina replied.

"I'm working on it. Excessive virtue is a decidedly unattractive quality in the young." By now Baghdadi was blushing.

No need to ask if Omar wanted wine. Still seated in his lap, Lina filled his goblet to the brim.

Fortunately (from Baghdadi's point of view), the business of pouring wine and sitting in laps was dispensed with quickly, Lina went on her way, and Omar turned to a topic of conversation Baghdadi was more comfortable with: murder.

"How much did Humaydi tell you?" he asked.

"He said only that you're investigating the murder of the Nizam and that you need an assistant," Baghdadi replied.

Omar explained the details of Baghdadi's assignment to him and then filled him in on the progress of the investigation to date. As they conversed, Lina returned with two plates of the night's special and left to tend her other customers.

Omar plunged heartily into the charcoal-broiled lamb kabobs—they came with onions, peppers, and pilaf—while Baghdadi politely tasted his.

When Omar had finally answered all Baghdadi's questions about the murder, Baghdadi said, "There was something else I wanted to ask for your help with. Not for the case. Just for my own interest."

"If there's anything I can do to aid and abet," Omar replied.

"Never mind, it's not important. Deputy Director Humaydi said I shouldn't bother you with it."

"Too late now."

"It's just that I was wondering, if we have some spare time in between working on the investigation, I was wondering if you could teach me some philosophy."

"Ordinarily, I don't take on students—" Omar began.

Baghdadi looked down at his plate, embarrassed that he was proving a nuisance.

"Hang on," Omar said. "You didn't let me finish. What I was going to say was that seeing as we'll be spending time together, we ought to put the odd free moment to productive use. What have you studied so far?"

Baghdadi opened his satchel, removed a book, and handed it to Omar, who read the title page out loud. "'Aristotle. *The Prior Analytics.*' An excellent place to start. How far have you read?"

"Not very," Baghdadi replied, lowering his head again. His voice was thick with disappointment in himself. "I'm still on chapter one. I understood the first section, where he defines premises and syllogisms. But then I got stuck on section two. What does it mean for a premise to be convertible?"

*   *   *

The lesson on convertible and inconvertible premises took long enough for Omar to enjoy several refills of his goblet. When they got back to Omar's room, he opened the door and held it open for Baghdadi. But the minute Baghdadi got inside, he yelped, "Oh, I'm so sorry," and fled back to the hall, pushing past Omar in the doorway.

As an agitated Baghdadi paced the corridor, Omar went into the room to see what had terrified him so. It turned out Khuld was in there, her head uncovered, her curly hair settled on her shoulders, her scarf in a heap on a table. She was unpacking a pair of saddlebags.

"The porters *finally* brought the bags up," she said as she refolded a green robe and placed it in a wardrobe. "I brought some of your things from Isfahan."

"You didn't need to do that."

"Yes, I did. You ran off without luggage."

"Baghdad is the greatest metropolis in the world. They have tailors. I bought a half dozen new robes this afternoon. Beautiful robes. One has tassels."

"Well, it's done," Khuld said, placing the empty saddlebags in a cabinet and shutting the doors firmly. Her parting words, as she retied her headscarf, were "Your robe of honor is in that chest, on the top—in case you have any formal occasions."

It occurred to Omar that the room seemed darker than previously. It took him a moment to realize why. "What happened to the candles?" he asked.

"I had them taken away," Khuld replied.

"Why?" Omar asked patiently.

"Who do you think you are? The grand vizier? Oil lamps are good enough for you. And much cheaper."

"This is the Palace of the Seljuqs. Malik-shah can afford candles. Bring them back."

Khuld marched out of the room, her head high despite her father's lack of appreciation.

She passed Baghdadi in the hallway, who stopped his pacing and watched her leave. With the risk of contact with the opposite sex eliminated, Baghdadi reentered the room. "Who was that?" he asked.

"That was Khuld, my little girl," Omar explained. "I'm sorry, I should have introduced you."

"That would be inappropriate. Although I *would* like to meet her. But I'm not in the family." Baghdadi helped himself to a cushion at Omar's table and scowled as he tried to think of a solution. "Of course if I were in the family . . ." Suddenly his face lit up. He stood and with great formality said, "Khwaja Omar, sir, I wish to marry your daughter."

Omar laughed. "You're a little impulsive, aren't you, Baghdadi?"

"What do you mean?"

"You just met her. Actually, you haven't even done that. You don't know what you're getting yourself into."

"I see that she's beautiful. And obviously from a good family."

"Not that good a family. I'm in it. But in any event, it isn't up to me."

"Oh, yes, of course. Khuld's mother is the one who should make the arrangements. But I'm sure if you're in agreement, that's merely a formality. I'll have my mother get in touch with her and—"

"No, that isn't it. Khuld's mother has passed behind the Door of Darkness."

"I'm so sorry. My sincere condolences. I didn't mean to—"

"It was a long time ago. But as far as marriage is concerned, it's Khuld herself we need to convince."

"But I never heard of a woman having a say in these matters."

"You don't know Khuld."

"But I don't know how to . . ." Baghdadi said. He slumped on his cushion. "Alas, all is lost," he said, as if the trumpet had just sounded the Day of Judgment and he was halfway through a pork chop.

Omar smiled. "Oh, to be young," he said.

"Khwaja Omar, you have a way with women. How do you get them to like you?"

"I pay them."

"No, that's not it. I saw you with Lina. Maybe you do pay her, but her affection for you is real."

"I wrote her a poem."

"I'd like to hear it . . . if it's not too personal."

Omar recited the poem he had penned in Lina's bed early that morning, the one about loving someone "jasmine-bosomed and fairy-born." On reflection, it wasn't one of his best efforts, but Baghdadi loved it.

"Oh, that's wonderful!" he exclaimed. "Are women really like that? Is poetry the way to their hearts?"

"It's *one* way to their hearts. The point is, poetry is romantic, and women like to be romanced. Read the great love epics. The man always does something romantic. He makes a grand gesture or takes on an impossible task to show how mad he's been driven by love. Farhad carving steps into the mountain of Bisotun in the hopes of one day being reunited with Shirin. Or Majnun sneaking into the enemy camp for one glimpse of his beloved Layla through a tent flap."[43]

Jumping from his cushion and hugging his prospective father-in-law, Baghdadi exulted, "Yes, that's it! Thank you, Khwaja Omar. Oh, thank you. Thank you!"

Then he ran out of the room. Left alone, Omar wondered what he had started.

CHAPTER 7

BAGHDAD
MONDAY, 20 RAMADAN 485
9 Abán 471
25 October 1092

*O*mar didn't sleep well. He had been out late at Hujayya's with Baghdadi, and he knew he had to get up early for the *suhur*. He awoke every hour or two and glanced at the window to see if there were signs of light yet.

Morning came too soon and found him forcing down breakfast in his room in the palace. While he was eating, a message arrived from Ghazali. Omar read it in the predawn light that filtered through the shutters. To his surprise, it said, *Come by my office. I'll take you to Abu Shuja.*

He ladled out a second helping of lamb stewed with spices and dried figs. He had learned his lesson the other day: the *suhur* was no time for a light meal. It had to be substantial enough to last him until sunset. Alas, before he was half finished, Khuld took his plate away with a brusque movement.

"*W'allah!*" he protested.

"Don't swear," she scolded.

"I'm not finished with that."

Khuld nodded in the direction of the window. The sky outside was bright. He had lost track of time and the *suhur* had slipped past sunrise. Before his daughter got out of range with the plate, he managed to grab a few wedges of flatbread, which he stuffed into his pocket. Not that he planned to eat them, but if he did get hungry, and he somehow managed to get a

152

moment free from the watchful eyes of Abu Hamid Ghazali and Abu Shuja Rudhrawari, it would be handy to have some emergency rations.

Khuld left to bring the dirty dishes back to the kitchen just as Baghdadi arrived. He looked like he had gotten even less sleep than Omar. No doubt he had been tossing and turning all night in the throes of new love. Omar decided to help him out.

"I don't know how long I'll be stranded at Abu Shuja's home," he said. "What do you have for lectures today?"

"Only the morning," Baghdadi replied.

"Good. This afternoon I want you to escort Khuld while she shops for some new clothes."

Baghdadi was delighted with this assignment. "I will see to Miss Khuld's every need," he said, a big grin on his face. "Is she dressing for some special occasion?"

"We live in a world where there are places she can go and people she can talk to who are off limits to you and me," Omar explained. "In a few days, Terken Khatun will arrive in Baghdad with all her ladies. I'm convinced they have information about the murder of Nizam al-Mulk, and I want Khuld to find out what they know."

"You mean you want Miss Khuld to spy on them?"

"No, no, no. You make it sound so sordid. There will be *iftar* dinners and Eid al-Fitr celebrations. Perfect opportunities to talk casually with the women of the court when their guard is down. But she's going to need to fit in, and that means dressing appropriately."

"I don't know if I like this plan," Baghdadi protested, as if he were already Khuld's husband. "Miss Khuld is a delicate flower. She should not be sullied with a criminal inquiry."

"Let's leave that up to her."

Khuld returned and Omar broached the subject. But perhaps it was a mistake to lead with the shopping angle. "I don't need more clothes," she insisted.

Baghdadi tried to help. "Surely a woman such as Miss Khuld should have many, many different gowns," he said, "so that she has that many more ways to display her loveliness." He thought it was a rather fine thing for him to say, but Khuld simply rolled her eyes.

Fortunately, Khwaja Omar came to Baghdadi's rescue. "Khuld, your dresses are very practical," he said. "Both of them."

"Don't be ridiculous. I have more than two dresses."

"Okay, three, then." Before Khuld could interrupt with the correct dress count, he continued. "That's not the point. I need your assistance with something and it requires a different sort of apparel."

"So you admit you need my help," Khuld replied. "It's about time."

"Khuld! I couldn't live without your help. Not just now, but anytime. Although, as it happens there's a particular undertaking I have in mind that requires your peculiar talents."

"And what talents would those be?" Khuld asked with suspicion.

"Well, your talents as a woman."

Khuld's shock was manifest on her face—followed by anger. "I see," she said. It's *that* kind of help. Forget it. Get little Lina to do it. Sounds like something better suited for her 'talents.' Of course, I knew that's what you thought of me. Ever since you suggested I become Berk-yaruq's concubine. It's disgusting."

"Am I ever going to live that down?" Omar asked. "That was ages ago."

"It was yesterday."

Omar became serious. He took his daughter's hand and said, "Khuld, you misunderstood me. It isn't like that at all. Sit down next to me and let me enlighten you. You know I care about you. Listen for once in your life."

"Fine," she replied. She plopped onto a cushion next to Omar and folded her arms.

When Omar finished explaining his plan, Khuld was noticeably calmer. "And you really need my help?" she asked.

"It's indispensable."

"Then I'll do it. I'm your spy," she said, her brown eyes sparkling with excitement.

"But a spy needs to blend in," her father explained. "And the others won't be wearing house dresses and aprons."

"I'll buy new dresses."

"And I will take her!" Baghdadi chimed in. Then a frown crossed his face as something occurred to him. "I'm not a proper chaperone," he said sullenly. "I'm not actually related to Miss Khuld."

"Well," Omar replied, "the shopkeepers don't know that. And, Khuld, wear a veil over your face."

Khuld became indignant again. "Veil," she scoffed. "Who do you think I am? The wife of the grand vizier? As someone keeps telling me, I'm a tent maker's granddaughter. I'll do what you ask. I'll let Baghdadi escort me. I'll buy some fine gowns. But I don't need a veil to go shopping."

*   *   *

An hour later, Omar was at the Nizamiyya. Seeing the Astronomer Royal in the doorway of his office, Ghazali cut short a meeting with Humaydi and proposed an immediate departure for the Dar Calipha. He whisked Omar through the empty assembly hall; in moments they reached the far end with the carved wooden doors that led outside. In the doorway a couple of deferential students, arriving early for the day, stepped out of the path of the two famous and fast-moving scholars. They were halfway across the courtyard when Omar stopped short to confront Ghazali.

"I was surprised to get your note," he said. "I thought you wanted me to wait for the hearings before I interrogate more witnesses. What made you change your mind?"

"Abu Shuja changed it for me," Ghazali replied. "He sent me a message last night asking to see you."

"What does he want?"

"He didn't say."

They didn't have far to go. The former vizier to the Commander of the Faithful still lived on the grounds of the Dar Calipha, near the Gate of Degrees, which connected the sacred precincts with the Nizamiyya. Omar spotted the house right away: the two Turkish soldiers on guard to enforce the owner's house arrest made it unmistakable.

Once inside, a servant greeted them. "My sahib will be with you two gentlemen in a moment," he said. "May I suggest you enjoy the garden while you wait?"

He led Omar and Ghazali through a reception room. One wall had a row of windows that looked out over the river. Opposite them, a latticework door opened onto a tableau of fountains and roses. There were guards at this door too. Evidently the terms of Abu Shuja's home confinement didn't permit him to wander amid the greenery. Perhaps the garden wall was too low.

Approaching a bench, Omar was about to sit, but Ghazali insisted they walk instead. The effects of yesterday's cold front still lingered; the autumn chill incited Ghazali to keep moving. Ghazali was in a good mood; his insults for the "dimmer candles of Islamic scholarship" were particularly humorous.

After they had been walking for a quarter of an hour or so, Abu Shuja's servant appeared at the door to the house. "Chief Professor?" he called deferentially, and with a hint of anxiety. "May I have a word with you, sir?"

Omar remained on the garden path while Ghazali jogged back to the house to speak with the servant. It was a whispered conversation that took several minutes. The servant bowed his head as if something embarrassed him; Ghazali patted his shoulder reassuringly. Then the servant slipped back into the house and Ghazali returned to Omar.

"Is there a difficulty?" Omar asked as he and Ghazali resumed their walk.

"Not really," Ghazali replied.

"Then why this pleasant interval in the garden?"

Ghazali reached for a diplomatic way to explain. "Abu Shuja Rudhrawari takes his responsibilities to Islam very seriously."

"So I'm told," Omar replied. "Ben Samha seems to have been on the receiving end of those responsibilities."

"He's compunctuously observant of the Shari'ah, extremely charitable . . ."

"And?"

"And he refuses to get dressed."

"So? It isn't like we never saw a man in his long-shirt. It doesn't bother me."

"He's not wearing his long-shirt. He's naked."

This turn of events was so unexpected that without thinking, Omar blurted out, "On such a cold morning? He'll freeze his thingy off."

"He's positively shivering. His wives and son are trying to get him to put something on, or at least allow a servant to light a fire, but he won't budge."

"But why not? I don't recollect any hadith enjoining us to be cold and naked."

"There are many hadith enjoining us to be charitable. Apparently Abu Shuja heard that there's a widow in the Street of the Pitch Workers who can't afford clothing for her four children. He sent his secretary over this morning with a hundred dinars, but he says he won't get dressed until the children can do the same."

Omar wondered what to do now. "Where is the Street of the Pitch Workers?" he asked.

"In Karkh," Ghazali replied. "On the other side of the river."

"That's a good hike from here. Might be awhile. Should we reconvene this symposium later?"

"Abu Shuja's secretary has already been gone awhile. It shouldn't be long now."

"Then we'll wait."

"I hope this doesn't give you the wrong impression about Abu Shuja," Ghazali said. "When matters of religion aren't involved, he's quite easygoing."

"You know him pretty well?"

"We connect at his weekly salons," Ghazali replied. "Scholars gather to discuss different subjects. Sometimes there's a speaker. They're always interesting, not like some of the fools who roam about claiming to be scholars. In fact, Abu Shuja has invited me to give several talks."

"What did you talk about?"

"Various topics," Ghazali replied. "He particularly liked the lecture you heard the other day at the Nizamiyya—the one about the sultan being subordinate to the caliph. He asked me to present it several times to different groups of guests."

They explored the garden for a while longer, at one point stopping at a fountain and watching the water splash in the basin. It made Omar realize he was thirsty. He had taken pains to eat an ample breakfast, but the food had been heavily salted, and he hadn't had enough to drink with it.

Eventually the servant reappeared. "Abu Shuja will see you now," he said.

Abu Shuja awaited them in his receiving room—fully clothed. His appearance surprised Omar. The pillars of orthodoxy in Baghdad favored austere, black robes made from linen, cotton, or wool. In view of Abu Shuja's reputation, Omar expected him to be wearing the same. But it seemed the former vizier was vain. The gray silk caftan he wore shimmered silver in the morning sunlight that streamed through the garden doors. It was well-tailored and a little on the tight side, emphasizing his tall, elegant figure. His long face was sullen with disapproval, as if he had heard someone mispronounce a word in the Quran. He would certainly never mispronounce a word himself; his mouth was precisely sculpted for only the most elegant of speech. But when he saw Ghazali, he broke into a smile. It was a nice smile—all traces of disapproval vanished—and Omar understood the man's popularity.

"*Ramadan Mubarak*," he said, hurrying toward his visitors to greet them. He carried a walking stick with a handle made of carved ivory, but since he moved quite nimbly, Omar concluded it was not so much for support as for making a fashion statement. It seemed a shame that such an energetic man had been deprived of employment at the relatively young age of forty-six. When he reached Ghazali, he opened his arms wide—still holding the stick—to embrace him.

"*Ramadan Mubarak*," Ghazali replied, returning Abu Shuja's embrace.

"It is quite sad about Nizam al-Mulk. I grieve for him."

"We all do."

"Do you know if the sultan still intends to come to Baghdad?"

"My good friend Omar here was with him a few days ago. He tells me that the court is on its way. They should be here by Friday. But where are my manners? Allow me to introduce Khwaja Omar Khayyam."

"I am honored to have the honor of your acquaintance," Abu Shuja replied, bowing to Omar.

At the center of the room, three cushions were arranged in a circle. Abu Shuja invited his guests to be seated. Joining them, he sat down and laid his walking stick across his knees.

"Now, tell me about this widow in the Street of the Pitch Workers," Ghazali said.

"The family was naked and starving," Abu Shuja replied. "I sent some money to get them back on their feet."

"You can't afford it."

"'*Spend your money both in prosperity and adversity,*'" Abu Shuja quoted. "'*Spending it in times of prosperity will not reduce it, whereas hoarding it in times of adversity will not save it.*'"[44]

"From your book," Ghazali said. Turning to Omar, he explained. "I'm afraid my friend Abu Shuja's circumstances are much reduced since Nizam al-Mulk ousted him from office so egregiously. The regime confiscated everything."

"The confiscators didn't confiscate everything," Abu Shuja insisted proudly. "I still have my family lands in Rudhrawar. I receive quite a regular income from that."

"It's not enough. You had to borrow money."

"That was a one-time thing."

"And what one-time calamity befell you?" Omar asked.

"The lands of Rudhrawar have not bestowed a good harvest this year," Abu Shuja explained. "There is not enough income to cover my expenses. It is a time of adversity. I am sure prosperity will return next year."

Omar raised an eyebrow. "I just traveled through there. The countryside is beautiful. Rife with color this time of year."

"Yes, I would rather like to return there someday," Abu Shuja replied. "I—" But something in the garden distracted him. Omar followed his gaze through the open door just in time to see a pigeon in flight escape over the garden wall.

Abu Shuja's mood switched abruptly. The self-importance vanished and he deflated like a tent that had its center pole yanked away. After an uncomfortable silence, he muttered, "Of course, at the moment I cannot go anywhere."

"Yes," Omar replied. "Your unfortunate confinement here. How did that happen?"

When Omar had heard about the events of the previous year from ben Samha, he had assumed there was another side to the story—one not so favorable to the banker. But although Abu Shuja was able to add some details, for the most part he merely confirmed ben Samha's account: the altercation in the rug market, the reissuance of the Ordinance of Omar, the sultan's interference, and Abu Shuja's forced retirement.

"I went into the ministry without an enemy," he concluded. "I left without a friend."

"Now, you *know* that's not true," Ghazali interjected. "You have literally thousands of friends, and they stand by you. Tell Khwaja Omar what happened the day after you were forced out."

Abu Shuja smiled at the memory of how that day began. "It was a Friday," he said. "The tenth of Ramadan. I went to the mosque as usual. You were there, Abu Hamid, and so was your brother. You both showed your support. Abu Abdullah Humaydi and dozens of other supporters from the Nizamiyya supported me as well. It cheered me considerably."

He pointed through a window to a minaret that jutted above a cluster of palm trees. "As you can see, the Mosque of the Caliph is not far away. Still, by the time we got there, thousands of well-wishers had joined the procession. I remember thinking that if only Nizam al-Mulk were to hear about this vigorous display of love and support by the Muslim community, he would certainly reinstate me. I was already planning new policies for when I got back to ministry. The crowd made me believe. They were well-behaved. There were no chants against the government and no rock-throwing.

"But the peaceful mob was not peaceful enough, apparently. A squadron of Turks arrived and ordered the crowd to disperse. As I said, it was a peaceful mob and they obeyed. The Turks quite politely escorted me back to my house. They haven't let me out since. And so my confinement began on a day that started so well and ended so badly. It was a day I will never forget. Exactly one year ago, one year and—what is today? The nineteenth?"

"The twentieth," said Ghazali.

Abu Shuja smiled bashfully. "I lost a day. That happens to me quite a lot lately. Exactly one year and ten days ago I was confined to my confinement."

"What do you do to pass the time now?" Omar asked.

Abu Shuja shrugged. "Since I can no longer make history," he said, "I have to be satisfied with writing it."

"Don't be so modest," Ghazali interjected. "It's an important book. To those intelligent enough to appreciate it." To Omar, he explained, "Abu Shuja is writing a second volume to his history of the caliphs."

"I heard about volume one," Omar said. "It covers the reigns of at-Tai and al-Qadir, doesn't it?"

Ghazali corrected him. "Only part of al-Qadir."

"I had to give up writing when I entered public life," Abu Shuja explained. "In the new volume I pick up where I left off, and I plan to bring it up to the present."

"That should be an invaluable resource."

"Have you read the first volume?" Ghazali asked. "It's quite unique."

Omar apologized; he hadn't. Ghazali laughed. "I'm shocked to discover there's a book Omar Khayyam hasn't read and memorized."

"We will rectify that," Abu Shuja said. He stood and called for his servant. "Bring a copy of *The Experiences of the Nations* for my good friend Omar Khayyam."

The servant approached and whispered something into Abu Shuja's ear. "What do you mean, we don't have any?" Abu Shuja replied angrily.

"I mean we're fresh out," the servant replied. "You gave away your last copy."

"Did you not order more?"

"I did. The bookseller refused the order. He said you haven't paid him in months, and he won't give you credit until you do."

Abu Shuja's large ears turned crimson with anger. "So pay the bill!" he shouted. "I don't pay you for excuses. I pay you to get things done."

"You don't pay me at all!" the servant replied. "I've been waiting to be paid longer than the bookseller."

"You insolent worm! Insulting me in front of my guests!" He raised his stick to strike the offending servant, who fled into the garden. Abu Shuja tried to follow him, but when he reached the door, the two Turkish guards stepped in front of the threshold to block his progress. "Do not come back!" he yelled after the servant. "You are fired!"

Ghazali leaned over and whispered to Omar, "Don't be concerned. He does this at least once a week. His servant will be back on the job before the muezzin calls noon prayers." But despite Ghazali's reassurances, Omar was stunned by the venom Abu Shuja spat at a loyal employee—and the speed with which he recovered his temper. The retired vizier resumed his spot on his cushion, smiling pleasantly. He arranged the skirts of his caftan and apologized for his outburst.

Ghazali changed the subject. "We're starting hearings tomorrow into the killing of the Nizam. Qadi Shami, Khwaja Omar, and myself."

"I heard," Abu Shuja replied. "Who will you call as witnesses?"

"We're still working on that. Certainly the eyewitnesses will be well-represented. Yalbard. Fakhr al-Mulk when he gets back."

"Anyone else?"

"We'll try to get as many of Malik-shah's intimates as we can. Taj al-Mulk, ben Samha, Nush-tegin—"

"I never liked him," Abu Shuja said. "Cupbearer to the sultan is no job for a Muslim." He suggested a couple other names and then said, "It's quite civic-minded of you to do this, Chief Professor. No one wants to see Nizam al-Mulk's killer captured and executed more than I do."

"I have to say, I'm surprised," Omar piped in. "After everything that happened, it'd be understandable if you had some hostility toward Nizam al-Mulk. Instead you mourn with the rest of us."

If Abu Shuja was antagonized by Omar's words, he didn't show it. "It is rather amusing," he responded. "In spite of all the hostility I received, I do not feel hostile toward anyone. Not Nizam al-Mulk. Not Malik-shah. Not even Abba Saad ben Samha. I even do some banking with him."

"Is that right?"

"I know what you've heard: 'Abu Shuja Rudhrawari brought back the Ordinance of Omar.' 'He is against the Jews.' But it was my job to enforce the law, and that is what I tried to do. I do not have anything against Jews personally. There are some who are rather splendid. Ben Samha's firm is one of the few in Baghdad with a branch in Rudhrawar. So he is the most competent person to transfer funds for me—when there are funds to transfer. And when there aren't, and I need to borrow, I'd prefer a Jew commit the sin of usury than lead a Muslim into wickedness. The Jew is going to be consumed in the Fire anyway."

Clearly Abu Shuja had a peculiar notion of the meaning of "I do not feel hostile toward anyone."

"Getting back to the Nizam," Omar said, "have you had any dealings with him since last year?"

"We remained good friends. A few months ago he wrote to me and told me that he wanted to do me good. He raised the possibility of another position in the government. He mentioned several openings, but I told him I had closed my pen case. Between us, I did not think any of the postings he proposed were suitable."

"So you do want to return to public life—for a suitable posting?" Omar asked.

Abu Shuja hesitated. He looked at Ghazali, who looked back, puzzled, unsure where Abu Shuja was going with this.

Leaning forward and putting both hands on Omar's shoulders, Abu Shuja said, "My friend tells me you are friends with Malik-shah. Perhaps when the time comes, you can plead my cause before him."

"When what time comes?"

"Abu Bakr Shami is seventy-two years old. Someday soon he is going to retire," Abu Shuja explained. "Or he will receive the summons that no man can turn down. And then there will be an opening. I am sure a good Muslim like yourself would appreciate it if Malik-shah appointed a qadi who will see to it that the Ordinance of Omar is enforced, that usurers are banished, and that wine shops are shut down."

Ghazali flinched at the mention of wine shops. If Abu Shuja was hoping to enlist Omar's support, he should have found out something about the man first. As for Omar, it was now clear to him why Abu Shuja wanted to see him. And yet, despite Abu Shuja's blatant attempt to use Omar's friendship with the sultan for his own ends, and despite the threat to Omar's beverage supply, Omar felt sorry for Abu Shuja. He had not expected to, certainly not after seeing how Abu Shuja treated his servant, or discovering there was no other side to ben Samha's story. But it was hard not to empathize with this charismatic yet broken man who had had everything taken away from him. Pathos incarnate. He lived in denial as he enthusiastically plotted his comeback—a comeback that couldn't possibly happen. Malik-shah would never allow it.

Even before the altercation with ben Samha, Abu Shuja had found his way into the sultan's disfavor. In his eight years as the caliph's vizier, the most celebrated event had been the marriage between the caliph and Fulana, daughter to Malik-shah. The bond between the Houses of Seljuq and Abbas had been negotiated years before between Terken Khatun and Amid ad-Dawla Jahir, Abu Shuja's predecessor. Terken Khatun drove a hard bargain. The caliph was required to divorce all other wives. Their sons would come after any sons of Fulana in the line of succession.

But the twists and turns of the negotiations were soon forgotten as they were overshadowed by the event itself. With the subjects of the Seljuq Empire talking of little else for months afterward, tales of the royal wedding had even penetrated to Omar in his observatory. A hundred and thirty camels had carried the bridal party from Isfahan to Baghdad; seventy-four mules carried the dowry, their gold bells tinkling festively. A candlelight procession escorted Fulana from the Dar Saltanah to the Dar Calipha, where she appeared before her husband-to-be seven times, showing off a different gown each time. Her trousseau was a treasure trove of satin, brocade, and gold. The crowd oohed and aahed; each successive gown was sewn from more luxurious fabrics and more ornately adorned than the one before.

The Commander of the Faithful, then thirty-one years old, sat proudly on his throne as his teenage bride twirled for his guests. Flanking the throne were Abu Shuja on the left and al-Muqtadi's oldest son, Abu'l-Abbas, on the right, dressed in a suit of shimmering silver with a matching turban. Abu'l-Abbas had as little interest as any eight-year-old boy at a display of women's dresses, but he did his best to pay attention without fidgeting.

Out in the city streets, boys might not have been as well-dressed, but they definitely had more fun. Brightly lit shops catered to partygoers all night, and the entire population was treated to lavish banquets. Thirty thousand lambs and goats were slaughtered and cooked on spits; the aromas of charcoal and roasting meat permeated the city. Forty thousand maunds of sugar sweetened the desserts. When it was all over, Malik-shah and Terken Khatun returned to Isfahan, tired but confident that they had laid the foundation for a happy life for their daughter and a shrewd alliance for themselves. The birth of Mahmud the following year seemed to seal the deal. But then the post began to bring disturbing letters from Baghdad.

Perhaps a letdown was inevitable. After such a grand beginning, to carry out the myriad chores of daily life—even life in a palace—was like the disappointment of biting into a shiny, red, perfectly formed apple and discovering it was mealy inside. Fulana was unhappy with her husband: he spurned and neglected her. In addition, there was friction between the Turks in her entourage and the citizens of Baghdad. After one Turkish soldier bashed in the head of a fruit merchant in a dispute over the price of a quince, al-Muqtadi banished Fulana's Turkish attendants from the city, leaving her demeaned and isolated. As the unhappy couple approached their second anniversary, Malik-shah demanded that his daughter be returned to him; the disheartened al-Muqtadi complied and dispatched his wife to Isfahan with their infant son without saying good-bye. She soon became sick and weakened steadily. When the life finally slipped from her body, eight months later, the change in her was so slight as to be barely worth a mention. The friendship between sultan and caliph died with her.

It was bad luck for Abu Shuja. It wasn't he who had negotiated the deal. But after things imploded, it fell to him to pick up the pieces. He advised al-Muqtadi to disinherit Mahmud and rename Abu'l-Abbas as his successor, earning the enmity of Malik-shah. Under the circumstances, Omar was surprised that Abu Shuja lasted as long as he did. Perhaps he had a chance for a new assignment while Nizam al-Mulk was alive—the Nizam was always on the lookout for talent. But there was no chance that Malik-shah would ever let Abu Shuja's bottom anywhere near a judge's throne now that the Nizam was dead. And speaking of Nizam al-Mulk . . .

"Abu Shuja, something doesn't add up," Omar said. "If the Nizam didn't bear any ill will toward you, why did he dismiss you?"

"I have had a year of house arrest to puzzle over that puzzle," Abu Shuja replied. "And I am still puzzled."

"He must have given you *some* explanation?"

"He said I was interfering with the plans of the regime."

"What plans were those?"

Abu Shuja seemed irritated by the question. Omar feared there would be a repeat of the display of temper the former vizier showed his servant. But Abu Shuja managed to keep himself in check, merely complaining, "That was the problem, was it not? He never confided his plans to me. And then when I inadvertently interfered with them, somehow it was *my* fault."

*   *   *

Baghdadi was completely at fault. He should have watched where he was going. If he insisted on reading while he navigated the arcades of the Nizamiyya, the least he could do was slow down. Instead he crashed into someone; the stack of books under his arm scattered all over the floor. It wasn't a particularly busy time of day, but there were still several groups of students huddling under the arches and arguing the fine points of the Hadith.

Distracted by the swish of fine leather bindings skidding across marble, several peered over their shoulders to see what happened. A few snickered before returning to their debates. To Baghdadi's horror, it turned out the man he had nearly knocked over was someone whose approval actually was important to him—both because Baghdadi respected him and because he could expel Baghdadi from school with a cross word.

Ghazali was angry, but only for a moment. "Why don't you watch where you're going, you stupid . . . oh, it's you, Baghdadi," he said. "You look terrible. Didn't you sleep? Hard at work for your new *khwaja*, no doubt. Good. You represent the Nizamiyya, so I want you to make a good impression. Actually, I just left him, and he seems pretty happy with you. How do things look from your point of view?"

"We have barely started. He apprised me of his progress, but that's all we had time for."

"Is he inclined toward any particular suspect?"

"Not yet." Baghdadi leaned over to pick up one of the books he had dropped.

"Let me help you with that," Ghazali said.

"I appreciate that," an astonished Baghdadi replied. It wasn't like Ghazali to be so friendly to a student. Especially one who had nearly knocked him over. "I'm sure you have more important things to do."

"It will only take a moment." Ghazali picked up the closest book and, like any good intellectual, checked out the title page. "*The Experiences of the Nations*," he read.

"I want to learn as much about the people associated with the case as possible."

"'*Whoever takes a path upon which to obtain knowledge, Allah makes the path to Paradise easy for him.*'"[45] Ghazali picked up several more books and read their titles. "The *Malik-nama* . . ."

"For background on the Seljuqs."

"*The Book of Politics*. Of course. Nizam al-Mulk's book."

"Maybe there's a clue on who he might have had disagreements with."

Ghazali frowned at the next title. "*A Compendium of the Jurisprudence of the Imam Shaf'i*. By Abu Hamid Ghazali."

Baghdadi could feel his face turn red. "That's just for me," he muttered, grabbing the book from Ghazali. "It's not for the case."

"Hmmm," Ghazali replied, skeptically. And yet he continued to be friendly. He picked up the last item on the floor—a loose sheet of paper. He was about to hand it back to Baghdadi when the lines of text scribbled on it caught his attention. "'*Your eyes are like the stars, twinkling at night,*'" he read.

"They are indeed a heavenly sight.
    I'll never forget the first time I saw them.
Fixed in your face, at such a great height."

Baghdadi was blushing purple now. "Khwaja Omar thought poetry would help get a woman to like me."

More serious now, Ghazali said, "Better for you to put your efforts into assisting him with his investigation."

"It's just that I want to take a wife. The Messenger—may the prayer and peace of Allah be upon him—instructs us to marry, doesn't he?"

"It depends on the circumstances. Every man needs to weigh the advantages and disadvantages for his particular situation. It was right for the Messenger—may the prayer and peace of Allah be upon him—but not right for Jesus."

They were interrupted by one of the junior professors, who bowed low to Ghazali, apologized for disturbing him, and explained that he had a concern about lecture hall assignments. The intruder was older than Ghazali, but Baghdadi couldn't help noticing the excessively polite and deferential tone of voice in which he addressed the head of the Nizamiyya.

Baghdadi grew thoughtful. He wanted to marry Khuld. But he had to admit that his poem was pretty bad. Khwaja Omar's advice obviously wasn't going to work out. Chief Professor Ghazali seemed to have given the subject of marriage some thought, though. Baghdadi wondered what advice *he* had.

"You're not married, are you, Chief Professor?" he asked as soon as the junior professor had gotten his issue taken care of and gone on his way.

"No," Ghazali replied. "A wife would be too much of a distraction from my studies. Although sometimes I wonder if having someone to manage my household would offset that. So I haven't ruled it out."

"I think I could handle it. I'd like to try."

"Then be prepared to assert your authority daily. Because that's how often your wife will test it. Women are so contrary that if you show them any leniency, they'll take advantage of you. Arab women used to teach their daughters, 'Break the tip off your husband's spear. If he doesn't complain, use his sword to cut up bones. If he still doesn't complain, he's ready. Put a saddle on him and mount him like an ass.'"

"Allah is great, and so are you, Professor!" the impulsive youth gushed feverishly. "Thank you! I know exactly what I have to do now. Thank you so much! I can't wait until I see Miss Khuld again so I can assert my masculine authority."

"You're welcome," Ghazali replied. "I'm glad I could . . . wait . . . Khuld? Khwaja Omar's Khuld?"

"Yes. I want to marry her."

"If you have to marry, I can't recommend Khuld."

"Why not?" Baghdadi sounded hurt.

"I heard she's rather tall."

"Oh, yes! Like the cedars of Lebanon!"

"Marry a short woman."

"But why?"

"If you insist on having evil in your house, it's better to have less of it."[46]

*   *   *

He commissioned Abu Tahir Daridah Shiri to go to Ahwaz with a troop of Dailamites and dispatched Abu Harb Shirzil to Basra. News arriving that the army of Fars had left Arrajan, Baha ad-Dawla ordered his tents to be brought out. It was presently reported that they had got to Ramhurmuz. He commissioned Tughan the Chamberlain under whom he placed a number of retainers, and on whom he bestowed a robe of honor. He sent out with him Isa b. Masarjis to act as vice-vizier.[47]

Omar yawned, closed the book, and placed it on the table.

The Experiences of the Nations had been easy to find. Which didn't prevent Omar from making an afternoon of it. Unaware that Baghdadi had already obtained a copy, Omar mentioned, upon saying good-bye to Abu Shuja and Ghazali, that his next stop was the Suq of the Booksellers. Abu Shuja insisted that Omar travel in style, if only partially in comfort. Since the temporarily discharged servant had not yet returned, the task of arranging transportation fell to Abu Shuja's secretary. Within minutes, Omar was jostling in the seat of a litter while the bearers hustled him to the Later Bridge of Boats. Fortunately the litter had an awning over the seat. After the cold start, the day had become hot and sunny; Omar welcomed the shade. From the litter, he transferred to a water taxi. Between the wakes of the larger boats, the need to dodge between them, and a strong breeze, the crossing of the Tigris was choppy; for the first time that day, Omar was grateful for his empty stomach.

But about a quarter farasang upstream, the pilot turned off into the Sarat Canal and the mood changed. The water calmed and the traffic thinned out; only the smallest boats and rafts could navigate the narrow and shallow channel. The canal curved gently; it had once followed the round wall that the caliph Mansur had built around his city hundreds of years ago. But Baghdad had long since overflowed those walls, and the wars that had made them necessary were over. As long as Turkish armies marched under the banner of the Seljuqs, the noise of the siege would remain far away. On the Sarat Canal, the drums and trumpets, the shouts of the attackers, and the screams of the dying were mere whispers on the pages of history books. Having outlived their usefulness, what was left of the walls was demolished, leaving only a charming, cool, tree-lined canal, with a new vista waiting beyond each curve: at first the workshops of textile manufacturers, then the blue-green domes that marked the tombs of saints in the Maruf Karkhi cemetery, and finally the stone arch of the New Bridge, where Omar disembarked.

More than a hundred stalls were crammed into the Suq of the Booksellers. They lined the canal and spilled over the bridge to the other bank. Each had a display case of colorful merchandise out front to draw in the customers and a striped awning overhead to keep them comfortable once inside. Nearly every establishment had a copy or two of *The Experiences of the Nations* on some back shelf, mostly used. Omar suspected that many

Baghdadis bought them simply because of the popularity of the author and, having never read them, eventually cashed them in for a few dirhams. With so many choices, he was determined to be selective and find the perfect copy at a bargain price. And if, while investigating Abu Shuja for the sultan, he happened to find some science books for himself—books that he'd been unable to obtain in Isfahan—then everybody won. He therefore enjoyed a pleasant afternoon, strolling along the canal and browsing.

At the Lodge of the Sufic Brotherhood, Ahmad Ghazali had spoken of the serenity of the mystic. Omar had never experienced serenity in a mosque or a lodge. A bookshop was another matter. There were no Ramadan hunger pangs, irritating legalists, or threats to the life of Malik-shah among wooden shelves sagging under leather-bound volumes. The soothing smell of musty pages was Omar's incense, the easy concentration of leafing through them his meditation. By the time the sun set and the muezzin chanted the call to evening prayer, Omar had splurged on a dozen science texts (alas, nothing by ibn Haytham was among them) and an insanely cheap, like-new copy of *The Experiences of the Nations*. He paid a porter to haul the science books to the Dar Saltanah and, with the copy of Abu Shuja's book under his arm, made his own return journey by boat. It was late afternoon when he arrived at the palace, returned to his room, and began to read.

Omar didn't have to dive very deep to understand why so few people who bought *The Experiences of the Nations* actually read it: the book was *dull*. It takes skill to recount tales of battles, palace intrigue, and high finance with all the excitement and humor of an accountant's ledger, but somehow Abu Shuja had pulled it off. There were moments when Omar wanted to wander over to the construction site next door and filch a hammer so that he could determine scientifically which was less painful: smashing one of his fingers or reading another paragraph. When he managed to win the struggle to make it to the end of a particular episode without shattering an appendage, Abu Shuja "rewarded" him by imposing a moral on the story:

Thus is every slayer slain and every betrayer betrayed . . .[48]

Such is the reward of a man who betrays his master and sells his religion for this world's goods. He loses both . . .[49]

When women interfere in politics, an unhealthy state of affairs results, disintegration begins, and success departs. When they control affairs, the consequences are disastrous; the edifice is ruined. When they have a voice in the council, wrong measures are adopted. Destruction hastens upon the state as fast as a torrent descending.[50]

That must have been what Ghazali meant when he said the book was unique. Unlike most historians, who merely chronicled facts, Abu Shuja interpreted each incident as a teachable moment, an educational fable like *Kalila and Dimna*—but without charm, irony, or furry animals.[51] It wasn't Omar's sort of thing. What fun is it to read about the wicked men of the past if one can't participate (vicariously, at least) in their wickedness?

As for the men of the present, Abu Shuja expressed a great deal of admiration for Malik-shah and Nizam al-Mulk. "*What would an author living ninety years ago have said,*" he asked,

had he lived to our time and beheld this victorious dynasty (the Seljuqs), whose armies career through all quarters of the globe, carrying out their sovereign's orders, entering the waters of the Gulf as they do those of the Syr Darya, whose raiders are at this moment in the Sinai approaching the waters of the Nile? And how many a vast country stretches in length and breadth between these three waters! The orders of his vizier are executed in all of them, positive and negative alike. By his wisdom and counsel the peoples through them are in tranquility; all are kept in awe by his control and repression.[52]

But not everyone earned his admiration. For bankers and merchants, he had nothing but loathing:

What glory is there in a bill drawn on a commercial house being accepted in enemies' country? If this is to be considered a source of pride, then the merchants are more powerful than the viziers in East and West, as they draw bills for vast sums on their correspondents and they are taken more readily than tribute and land-tax. Real glory lies in enforcing laws in countries which the sword has subjected to the pen, and a dominion is that over the

conquest whereof blood has dripped from the blade, after which
ink has flowed over the leaves in the assignation of its revenues.[53]

In addition to the attack on the useful profession of banking, there
was another aspect of the paragraph that disturbed Omar. Like many
intellectuals, Abu Shuja had an unhealthy obsession with men of action—
especially those annoyingly virtuous warriors who, in the name of virtue,
spilled far more blood than the wicked ever did.

*   *   *

Baghdadi stood alone in the hallway outside Terken Khatun's
apartments. The eunuch had closed the door in a normal fashion. He didn't
slam it. He certainly didn't slam it in Baghdadi's face. But that's how it felt
to Baghdadi. For a moment he stared at the solid wood, iron-reinforced door.
Then he turned around to go back the way he came. A long, empty, gloomy
corridor stretched in front of him.

Today had not gone well. Baghdadi had to be honest with himself
about that. When Khwaja Omar had assigned him to accompany Khuld while
she shopped for clothes, Baghdadi had been thrilled by the prospect of
spending time with the woman he intended to marry. He was determined to
take advantage of the opportunity to put Ghazali's advice into practice.

As for Khuld, now that she had been sold on her mission, she took to
it with the efficiency of a blunt instrument. As they crossed the Main Bridge
of Boats to West Baghdad, Baghdadi had to admonish her several times to
slow down. "It's not appropriate for a woman to get too far ahead of her
chaperone," he insisted.

"If you don't like the way I walk," Khuld replied, "go home."

The arguments began in earnest when they got to the Suq of the
Dressmakers. They disagreed about which shops to enter, which fabrics to
buy, and how to haggle. On more than one occasion, a store owner discreetly
remembered a task in the back room, thereby giving the unhappy couple a
moment of privacy. Each time that happened, Baghdadi admonished Khuld
for driving the store owner away.

But this was merely a preamble to the blow-up that erupted over a
burqa. Baghdadi found it in a store whose walls were covered with stylish,

colorful dresses. The garment was hiding in a corner, behind two gowns of blue-and-green-striped silk.

"Here's what you need," he announced, grinning as he pulled it off the hook and held it up for Khuld to see.

It was a shapeless, head-to-toe coverall of scratchy wool. The crown of the headpiece bulged in an unflattering way, and the mesh grill over the eyes had all the elegance of a livestock fence.

"It's beautiful!" Baghdadi declared with enthusiasm.

Khuld was more skeptical. "What color is that?" she asked. "It looks like a cross between bile and vomit. Or is it just moldy?"

"The perfect eveningwear for the Muslim woman. It covers the bosom, as required by the Quran."[54]

"Do you even know where a woman's bosom is? Or did you figure with this ridiculous thing you don't have to? Because I assure you, my bosom isn't on my face."

"Don't be perverse. Your father sent me to supervise you while you buy dresses, and I say you're buying this one."

"Fine. If we're here to buy dresses, buy dresses. That thing isn't a dress. It's a tent. What will my father say when he learns his assistant is too stupid to know the difference between a dress and a tent?"

The argument went on for some time and involved a great deal of insult hurling by both parties. In the end, Khuld bought what she wanted: half a dozen dresses fashioned from stylish, colorful silk; an equal number of silk shawls to wear over them; several hijabs; but no burqas.

Baghdadi had little cause to admonish Khuld during the return journey, if only because she didn't talk to him until they got back to the palace. And then all she said was "Thank you for a fascinating day. I'll let you know if there's anything else I can't do without a man's help. So you'll hear from me—never. Tell my father that I'm going to wash up. Then I'll bring him some dinner." With that she disappeared into the shadowy interior of the apartment and the eunuch closed the door behind her.

The hopes with which Baghdadi had started the day were unfulfilled. He relived every humiliating moment as he traversed the darkened corridors and crossed moonlit courtyards on his way to Khwaja Omar's room.

*   *   *

That was a waste of time, Omar fretted when he finished reading *The Experiences of the Nations*. He lay down on the bed to think through what to do next. He had been in Baghdad for a few days now, following the trail from one person to another, but he didn't feel like he was getting anywhere. He needed a more systematic approach. Perhaps an organized list of suspects. Who had the means to pay for a murder? Who had a motive? Also he needed to take into account the accusations that Nizam al-Mulk made in the new volume of *The Book of Politics*. The culprit had to be someone close to the sultan. Most likely a Shiite, a woman, or a Jew. But possibly the sultan himself.

He got up and moved over to the table. Taking a fresh sheet of paper from his writing kit and dipping his pen in the inkwell, he noted with approval that it was sharp—Baghdadi was carrying out his work with little need for direction. Omar was about to jot down the first entry when a knock on the door interrupted him. "Come in," he called.

The door creaked open just wide enough for Baghdadi to slink through; he entered in a pitiful state. He looked like a soldier on forced march in a freezing drizzle—bedraggled and shivering but still expected to maintain a brave façade. As commanding officer, Omar decided the most compassionate thing he could do was let Baghdadi succeed at that. So he didn't ask any questions. Instead, he said, "You're just in time. I was about to make a list of suspects." He passed Baghdadi the pen. "I'll dictate, you write."

Baghdadi seated himself on a cushion.

"First—" Omar said.

"Taj al-Mulk?" Baghdadi asked.

"Everyone's top suspect. Word is he wanted the Nizam's job. Plus, he has power in the government, so he'd seem to be one of the people Nizam al-Mulk warned us about in his manuscript. And as minister of finance he had access to ample funds to hire the killer."

Baghdadi wrote:

1. Taj al-Mulk. Means: Yes. Motive: Wanted to replace Nizam al-Mulk as vizier.

Looking up, Baghdadi saw that Omar was reading over his shoulder and shaking his head. "What's the matter?" Baghdadi asked.

"I don't believe it," Omar replied. "Taj al-Mulk seems to have a lot of nobility. A soldier through and through."

"Should I cross him out?"

"No, we have to consider every possibility. Keep him. Next—what to do about Malik-shah. Humaydi is sure the sultan is behind it. Granted, his logic is insane." Omar winced as he recalled the painful discussion at the Nizamiyya.

"Professor Humaydi's argument is flawed," Baghdadi pointed out, "but that doesn't mean his conclusion is incorrect."

"Good point. Inscribe Malik-shah on the roll of honor."

"Who else has power in the government?" Baghdadi asked when he finished writing.

They considered the members of the sultan's inner circle. Fakhr al-Mulk and his brother, Mu'ayyad al-Mulk, certainly had the means to hire a murderer and also stood to benefit from their father's inheritance. The intelligence chief, Abu Nasir ibn Ali, had come up in the meeting with ben Samha. And he was a Jew. Or a former Jew anyway. They wrote down his name. They spent some time discussing Amid ad-Dawla. As al-Muqtadi's vizier, he was technically part of the caliph's government and not the sultan's. But he was also the son-in-law of Nizam al-Mulk, who had handpicked him for the job. That put him in the sultan's camp.

"I wish I knew who he was really loyal to," Omar said.

Baghdadi added him to the list. "Who's next?" he asked.

"Women. *The Book of Politics* pontificated that women sow 'discord, trouble, and sedition.' Which brings us to—"

"Terken Khatun."

"She went to a lot of trouble to put on the concerned mother act for my benefit. I found out only later—thanks to Khuld—that she fooled me completely. The sultana is tough, devious, and has a hand in everything that transpires."

Baghdadi didn't reply.

Forgetting his resolve to be compassionate, Omar shouted, "Muhammad's tomb, Baghdadi! Wake up! You're no use to me if you go into a lovesick daze every time someone alludes to Khuld."

"Sorry," Baghdadi replied, snapping out of his reverie. "Number six, Terken Khatun."

Baghdadi started to write, but Omar stopped him. "Hold on, Baghdadi," he said. "What's her motive?"

Baghdadi thought for a moment. "Malik-shah and Nizam al-Mulk are at war with the Qarakhanids," he said. "That's Terken Khatun's family."

"Does she still have an emotional attachment there?" Omar wondered. "She insists she doesn't. She was twelve years old when she and Malik-shah celebrated their nuptials and she left her family behind. Still, I wonder . . ."

"What about Mahmud then?"

"Her grandson? Four years old is much too young to perpetrate a killing of this magnitude."

"Not as a suspect, Khwaja. As a motive. There's a rumor that Terken Khatun wants him to be the next sultan. Maybe Nizam al-Mulk was standing in her way."

"Hmmm. That could be the case. It would definitely explain the part in *The Book of Politics* about elevating underage persons to high office. And it would explain why Berk-yaruq is so concerned that he hasn't been named the official heir. Write her down."

When Baghdadi finished writing he said, "If you're following the leads in *The Book of Politics*, your next suspect will be a Jew. Should I write down ben Samha?"

"I don't know," Omar said, throwing up his hands.

"He's the most prominent Jew in the sultan's employ. And he definitely has the means."

"I know, it's just that—"

"What?"

"I kind of like ben Samha."

"You're the one who said we have to consider every possibility."

Omar sighed. "You're right, of course. Put him down. What's his motive?"

"How did your conversation with Abu Shuja go this morning? Is there any possible motive there?"

"Somehow my conversation with Abu Shuja ended up being about Abu Shuja." He gave Baghdadi an account of the morning's meeting.

When he finished, Baghdadi observed, "Ben Samha and Abu Shuja both told you the same thing in the same words."

"What thing was that?" Omar asked.

"They both said that Nizam al-Mulk fired Abu Shuja for 'interfering with the plans of the regime.' I wonder what plans he meant."

"I don't know. I wish I did. It may be important. I asked Abu Shuja and he doesn't know anything. At least he says he doesn't. If he does, he sure put on a good show of bitterness over Nizam al-Mulk keeping him in the dark."

"Does ben Samha know the plans?"

"He must. Whatever these plans are, he's apparently indispensable to them. I should pay him another visit." He asked Baghdadi to set up an appointment. "See if he'll receive me tomorrow night, after the hearing."

They continued to brainstorm, Omar pacing the room, Baghdadi seated. Whenever they seemed to run out of ideas, Omar insisted, "We have to be more creative." But although they kept at it for some time and considered numerous suspects, none of them seemed likely enough to make the list. By the time Khuld arrived with their dinner, they still had the same seven entries:

1. Taj al-Mulk. Means: Yes. Motive: Wanted to replace Nizam al-Mulk as vizier.
2. Sultan Malik-shah. Means: Yes. Motive: Wanted to rule on his own behalf instead of serving as a figurehead.
3. Fakhr al-Mulk (possibly in collusion with his brother, Mu'ayyad al-Mulk). Means: Yes. Motive: Inheritance.
4. Abu Nasir ibn Ali. Means: Yes. Motive: Unknown.
5. Amid ad-Dawla Jahir. Means: Yes. Motive: Unknown.
6. Terken Khatun. Means: Yes. Motive (tentative): (a) Revenge for Nizam al-Mulk and Malik-shah's war on her family, (b) Make Mahmud the next sultan.
7. Abba Saad ben Samha. Means: Yes. Motive: Unknown.

It pained Omar that two of the suspects—Malik-shah and Fakhr al-Mulk—had long been friends of his. And even though he had just met ben Samha, he was beginning to think of him as a friend as well. Omar had to keep reminding himself what Aristotle had said concerning his philosophical wrangling with Plato, his one-time mentor: "The truth is a friend and Plato is a friend. But the truth is a truer friend."

"There's stewed chicken," Khuld said as she entered, carrying a tray.

The aroma of a lemon-pomegranate sauce filled the room. Khuld seized the papers from the table and banished them to the nightstand to make room for dinner, ignoring her father's protests that she was getting them all mixed up.

He noticed that Khuld and Baghdadi didn't greet each other, and when she queried Baghdadi, far too politely, whether he would join them for the meal, he didn't reply. He appeared to be lost in a sheet of paper that he had rescued from the table before she could get ahold of it. The exchange between daughter and assistant, or to be precise, the lack of exchange, confirmed what Omar had suspected earlier: Baghdadi's courtship of Khuld was not going well. It was too bad; Omar had hoped there might be a match there.

CHAPTER 8

CASTLE OF SHIRIN, KERMANSHAH PROVINCE
MONDAY, 20 RAMADAN 485
9 Abán 471
25 October 1092

*W*hile Omar was following clues and trying to get his daughter married off, the sultan's caravan had continued plodding west. It was only today that the procession finally descended from the Zagros Mountains and pitched its tents at the base of the Castle of Shirin, on the edge of the Iraqi plain. The change in climate was abrupt, and many in the camp found it too hot to sleep.

But it wasn't the heat that kept Terken Khatun awake; she merely had a lot to think about.

She sat in her straight-backed chair at the worktable in her pavilion. In the corner, a giant of a eunuch stood and operated a reed punkah. The hanging fan oscillated over a tub of ice, setting a stream of cool air into motion. Alas, the eunuch himself wasn't in the stream, so his bare chest shined with perspiration. But where Terken Khatun sat it was delightfully cold. Too cold, really—she should tell the eunuch to take a break. But it was important to make servants sweat. Otherwise they start putting on airs and become useless. Instead she put on an embroidered jacket and remained where she was as she contemplated a sequence of questions: How were Taj al-Mulk and Omar Khayyam getting on in Baghdad? Had she considered every scenario as to how things would play out when the sultan got there? What should her next step be to secure the succession for Mahmud? She covered each topic with the precision of the pulleys and cords that constituted the punkah mechanism.

The arrival of the mail was a welcome development at first. New data for her calculations. She sorted the stack, setting most of the letters aside, until she came to a longish missive from Taj al-Mulk. She started swearing even before she began to read—she had told that brainless *peech* a thousand times not to send a message without encrypting it. As she absorbed the lines of text, her humor worsened. Sensing the gathering storm, the eunuch suddenly remembered a task he had to perform in another compartment, but Terken Khatun ordered the giant back to his post before he could tiptoe out.

When she finished reading, there were more orders. "Bring me the courier who brought this letter," she demanded. "Then fetch a brazier."

"I don't understand," the frightened giant whimpered, wiping perspiration off his brow. "Do you want charcoal as well?"

"If I wanted charcoal, I would ask for charcoal, you ball-less moron."

While the eunuch scurried off to carry out her orders, Terken Khatun scribbled a reply to Taj al-Mulk. The letter was only a few lines but encryption was still painstaking. By the time she finished, the eunuch had long since returned with the empty brazier, and the courier was bored with waiting in the anteroom.

"You are carrying a package to Qazvin," she said to him through a curtain, with no greeting of any sort.

"Yes, Sahiba al-Jalala," he replied.

"Give it to me."

He removed a package the size of a large book from his pouch and slid it through an opening in the curtain. Terken Khatun took it and handed him a letter in exchange. "Go back to Baghdad and give that to Taj al-Mulk." The pad of her footsteps on a carpet was the only clue the courier had that the interview was over.

Back at her worktable, Terken Khatun grabbed a knife and sliced through the string that bound the package. She tore off the wrapping, releasing the odor of fresh ink. As expected, there were fifty copies of a wanted poster inside. It featured a drawing of a young man and instructions for anyone who recognized him to report to the military governor. The young man sported a tapered beard and a ragged turban.

She dumped the posters into the brazier, spreading some out and crumpling others. Then, with a candle, she lit the corner of one of the pages. She watched as the fire spread; occasionally she stirred it up with the tip of her knife. Eventually, all she could see was the killer's angry face glaring at her from a ring of flame and smoke.

"That's right," she said. "Burn in hell."

CHAPTER 9

BAGHDAD
TUESDAY, 21 RAMADAN 485
10 Abán 471
26 October 1092

*T*he line of sedan chairs and palanquins outside the Mosque of Mansur was two blocks long. One at a time, they pulled up to the entrance and discharged some leading citizen of Baghdad, dressed in his finest silk caftan, or perhaps a colorful robe of honor that the powers that be had bestowed on him for some service or other. Two lines of Turkish mamelukes kept the path to the entrance clear. Behind the soldiers a noisy jumble of onlookers shouted greetings and attempted to thrust petitions into the hands of the powerful. But the Turks were far too conscious of the fate of Nizam al-Mulk to allow them to get close; the rich and powerful proceeded deliberately to the door, unmolested and with great dignity. Two more lines of soldiers guarded the route to the women's entrance. Rings, necklaces, and headdresses sparkled with colorful jewels as the fair sex flitted to the door in a flurry of silk and disappeared up a flight of steps. They all wore veils. Most of the women weren't high enough into the upper classes to require them, but they all wanted their peers to think they were.

The size of the crowd didn't surprise Omar. If you were under thirty, the death of a sultan's vizier was a first-in-a-lifetime occurrence. Regardless of your age, an investigation into his murder was an *event*. Inside the mosque, the spectators milled about, looking for places or greeting friends, transforming the sanctuary into a colorful ocean of bobbing turbans, the excitement evident in their animated voices. Wooden screens had been installed along a portion of the balcony to hide the occupants, but through the gaps in the latticework colorful women's garments could be seen moving about. The animated female voices in the balcony mixed with the male ones on the main floor, amplifying the general noise.

The carpenters and upholsterers had plugged away all night to finish the two extra thrones in time for the hearing. They installed them in the mosque early that morning on wooden platforms that flanked the qadi's throne. Not as high, of course—the new platforms boasted a mere three steps compared to the qadi's five—but the same gold-bordered brocade was draped over the high backs, and the designs embroidered on the cushions were identical. When Omar saw them, he whispered to Ghazali, "They needn't have bothered. That center throne is wide enough for all three of us."

More mamelukes held the crowd back from the center aisle. They stood at attention, helmets straight, eyes forward, spears held perfectly vertical at their sides as Omar and Ghazali passed between them. Omar wore a plain, black, woolen caftan. Ordinarily he would have donned his robe of honor for a state occasion such as this, but it was made of silk, and Ghazali had warned him of Shami's disapproval.

They reached the front of the hall and took their places standing in front of the judge's thrones. Back at the entrance, an usher called for silence and announced the arrival of Abu Bakr Shami, chief qadi of the city of Baghdad. Shami slowly shuffled down the aisle with all the dignity of his seventy-two years, leaning on his long staff. He dressed as he always did: black robe and long-shirt flawlessly pressed, with the addition of a black shawl of office over his turban.

Shami banged the end of his staff on the platform to call the proceedings to order. "The Commission of Inquiry and Justice in the Murder of Nizam al-Mulk is hereby convened," he said. The spectators took their seats on the Armenian prayer rugs scattered about the floor. A low bench in front of the qadi's throne served as a clerk's table. Seated on a prayer rug behind it, the clerk of the court shuffled some papers and then rose to read a pair of diplomas. The gist was that Omar Khayyam of Nishapur and Abu Hamid Ghazali of Tus were deputized to serve as assistant qadis for the duration of the investigation into the murder of Nizam al-Mulk; the actual diplomas used a lot more words than that and had to be read one at a time, even though, except for the names, they were identical. Omar shifted impatiently from foot to foot, tired from having to stand so long with nothing to take his mind off his discomfort other than the thought that the day had barely begun and he was already lightheaded from fasting. Eventually the clerk stopped his droning, and Omar and Ghazali were permitted to ascend their thrones on either side of Shami.

"Call the emir Yalbard," Shami ordered.

The clerk shouted, "Emir Yalbard," and Yalbard advanced down the center aisle and stood with military posture in front of the judges. Omar hadn't seen him since the night they had limped into Baghdad, coated with dust and exhausted from twenty-four hours straight of nonstop riding. Now the emir was all discipline and polish. The leather plates of his cuirass had been cleaned and buffed, and his pointed steel helmet sparkled in the sunlight that poured through the windows.

"Khwaja Omar," Shami said. "You're our guest in Baghdad. We would be honored if you took the first round of questions."

"Thank you, Qadi," Omar replied.

He didn't actually have any questions for Yalbard—they had had plenty of time to talk on the road—but he reenacted the highlights for the benefit of Shami and Ghazali. Yalbard recounted how the Nizam had joined the sultan for *iftar* in the sultan's pavilion. The meal was tense, as the sultan had told several people of his intention to relieve the Nizam of office. However, he didn't go through with it. Afterward, the Nizam had mounted his litter, ordered the bearers to carry him to his wives' pavilion, received several petitioners along the way, and was attacked by the killer dressed as a Sufi. The emir went on to describe the chase after the killer, his capture, and his immediate execution on the orders of the sultan. He spoke in his normal voice, but it was loud enough to fill the large mosque. His words were plain, as if he were reporting troop movements to a commanding officer.

"Who decided which petitioners were permitted to approach the Nizam?" Omar asked.

"I did."

"You alone? Wasn't there someone else involved in the decisions?"

"I was in charge of security."

"Your sense of responsibility is praiseworthy, Emir. But isn't it true that Fakhr al-Mulk was also involved?"

"He did suggest that we let through a qadi and a doctor, because he thought they would be entertaining." Laughter erupted in the courtroom.

Qadi Shami banged his staff on the platform for silence. "I heard of this case," he said sternly. "It's no laughing matter to my brother judge in the city of Borujerd." He nodded to Omar to continue.

"And which of you were first to spot the Sufi in the crowd?" Omar asked the emir.

"Fakhr al-Mulk and I saw him at the same time and simultaneously agreed to let him through."

"Had you ever seen him in the camp prior to that moment?"

"No, but it was a large camp."

"Do you have any idea how he got in?"

"There's always a steady stream of civilians coming and going to meet the needs of the army. Farmers bringing food. Armorers bringing weapons. Whores bringing . . . well, you know." Again there was laughter in the courtroom. "The guards stop some people for questioning, but they can't interrogate everyone," he added, but these words were drowned out by the banging of Shami's staff.

"Thank you, Emir," Omar said.

"Chief Professor," Shami said, "do you have any questions for this witness?"

"A few, Qadi," Ghazali replied. He turned to Yalbard and said, "Emir, you testified that the sultan intended to remove Nizam al-Mulk from office. My sources in the sultan's court tell me that this was the result of an incident some weeks ago, when Malik-shah sent you and Taj al-Mulk to the Nizam. What was the purpose of this visit?"

"The sultan was angry with one of Nizam al-Mulk's grandchildren. He wanted us to tell the Nizam that the young man needed to learn his place."

"So you were delivering a message. A page boy could have done that. Why did the sultan send an experienced combat veteran like yourself?"

"I didn't ask."

"He must have had a reason."

"I suppose he thought I would be more intimidating."

When the laughter died down, Ghazali moved on. "What was Nizam al-Mulk's response to the sultan's complaint?"

"He said, 'The sultan's crown rests on the vizier's inkwell.'"

"What did you think that meant?"

"I asked Taj al-Mulk that on the way back. He said it meant that if it weren't for Nizam al-Mulk, the reign of Malik-shah would have come to nothing."

"Did you report this remark to the sultan?"

"I accompanied Taj al-Mulk when he reported it," Yalbard replied.

"And how did the sultan respond?"

"He was furious."

"What did he say?"

"It was a barrage of insults. I'm sure he didn't mean them."

"We'll be the judges of what he meant. Just tell us exactly what he said."

"It would be better if I didn't."

Ghazali would have none of it. "'*Conceal not testimony,*'" he quoted. "'*For he who conceals it, verily, sinful is his heart: Allah knows what ye do.*'"[55]

"It's a lie!" Yalbard said. "Let no one say the emir Yalbard is sinful in his heart. The sultan called Nizam al-Mulk a dog and a son of a whore."

"Was that all?" Ghazali asked.

"No, there was more."

"What did he say?"

Yalbard glanced at Shami.

"Go on!" Shami snapped.

"He said that Nizam al-Mulk was the *sikker* of an infidel *amm*."

Omar winced at the vulgar term for the private parts of the woman he had come to know as his friend's stepmother. Everyone else laughed.

It took Shami several minutes to restore order to the courtroom this time. When the spectators finally settled down, Ghazali resumed: "So clearly the sultan was angry. Did he threaten the Nizam?"

"Well, you know how people are when they're mad."

"Tell us what he said."

"He said he would run his sword through the Nizam's liver and feed it to his dogs."

Omar was becoming impatient with Ghazali's interrogation of Yalbard. He knew where this line of questioning was coming from, and indeed he had noticed Ghazali exchange several glances with Humaydi, who was seated at the clerk's bench.

Omar couldn't resist asking, "And did Malik-shah run a sword through the Nizam's liver and feed it to his dogs?"

Shami looked down at Omar from his more elevated throne like a bird perched in a tree. "Khwaja Omar," he said. "I realize you've spent most of your career in academia, so it's understandable that you're not familiar with courtroom procedure. However, part of that procedure is that you do not interrupt when someone else is questioning a witness—especially if you've already had your turn. I trust that now that this has been explained to you, there will be no further breaches."

Omar had every right to be indignant at the qadi's tone, but it didn't occur to him. He was too embarrassed that he hadn't followed the correct procedure. *What the hell am I doing up on this throne?* he wondered.

Ghazali, meanwhile, had moved on to the night of the murder. "Was it the sultan who assigned you to Nizam al-Mulk's security detail?" he asked.

"No, sir," Yalbard replied.

"Then who did?"

"No one assigned me."

"Then you just happened to be on hand when the murder was committed?"

"I know my job. I don't need the sultan or anyone else to tell me where to be."

"And what is your job exactly?"

"I'm responsible for the security of the sultan and his senior officials."

"You didn't do that job very well," Shami snorted. Apparently the rule about not interrupting didn't apply to the chief qadi.

"I did the best I could," Yalbard replied. "The Nizam always insisted on receiving petitioners. That tied my hands somewhat. Still, sir, I take full responsibility for my role in the events of the tenth of Ramadan."

"And in that role, you allowed a murderer dressed as a Sufi to approach the Nizam," Ghazali said. "That wasn't very bright of you. Did the sultan tell you to do that?"

"I thought the Nizam would want to talk to the Sufi."

Fakhr al-Mulk thought so too, Omar thought. *Don't be so noble, Yalbard. Point that out. You don't have to take* all *the responsibility yourself.* Omar considered pointing it out for him, but Shami appeared to be in no mood for another interruption. In fact, the qadi was making impatient gestures for Ghazali to wrap up.

Ghazali could read the qadi's body language too. "I think I've taken this line of inquiry as far as I can," he said. "I have no further questions. But I have to say, Emir, I'm not satisfied with your answers. Perhaps the qadi can make something of you."

Shami took that as his cue to begin. "Emir," he said. "You testified that you were responsible for taking charge of the Nizam's security and determining which petitioners to allow through. And you said that you were not acting under specific orders from the sultan. Now, part of the job of this court is to decide whether or not to believe you. So tell me, what sort of a man are you?"

"I'm a soldier, sir," Yalbard replied.

"And are you a Muslim?"

"Of course."

"Have you eaten today?"

"No, sir. Not since sunrise. It's the fast of Ramadan."

Omar wished the qadi had not brought up food. He felt his belly protest its emptiness. He had eaten a generous breakfast and, unlike the previous day, remembered to drink enough water. But that was before sunrise and now it was after noon. He felt drained. On top of that, his woolen caftan was hot and scratchy, irritating him through his longshirt. *W'allah!* he thought with annoyance. *What does this line of interrogation have to do with anything?* Yet the audience seemed to like it. With each question, Omar saw spectators glance at each other and nod in approval. He began to suspect that some of them had not come out of mere curiosity. The house had been packed according to some criteria decreed by Shami.

"Have you observed the fast the entire month?" Shami continued.

"Except while I was traveling up from Isfahan. The Quran says we don't have to fast when we're traveling."[56]

"Quite right. Don't forget to make up the days afterward. Now, what about prayer?"

"Five times a day. And I require the same for the men under my command."

Enough of this, Omar thought. "Qadi," he interjected, "I don't see how these questions advance our quest for truth."

188

The audience reacted before Shami did. There were hisses and Omar was pretty sure he distinguished the word "amateur."

Shami jerked his head in Omar's direction and scolded him. "Khwaja Omar, I've already warned you once about interrupting. I hope it won't be necessary for me to warn you again." Omar slumped impatiently on his throne.

"Now, Emir," Shami said. "We've addressed what sort of Muslim you are. What sort of soldier are you?"

"I fight for my king."

"Do you fight well?"

"The unbelievers at Manzikert thought so. The few who survived."

"But I'm sure you're not quite so ferocious after the battle is over."

"What do you mean?" Suspicion tinged Yalbard's voice.

"For example, I'm sure you would never fight against one of your fellow Muslims," Shami explained.

"As long as he doesn't insult me."

"And you stay away from the whorehouse."

"I have needs."

"And you eat moderately."

"It's not true! I once ate four roast chickens in one sitting—with bread and roasted vegetables."

"All washed down with water, of course."

"Who told you this lie? Do you think I have no head for wine?"

"Some men find it's more than they can handle."

"I can handle it! Anyone who says otherwise will be introduced to the bronze head of my mace!"

In his wounded pride, Yalbard failed to notice that the crowd—which had laughed at his jokes earlier—was beginning to turn on him. There were boos and cries of "*Haram!*"

"So," Shami continued, "we've established that you can handle your wine. How often would you say you handle it?"

"I don't know," Yalbard said, visibly less sure of himself. "A couple of times a week maybe. Of course this month, with *iftar* every night . . ."

"Every night," Shami screeched from his perch. Then, replacing indignation with piety, he intoned, "And during this most holy month of Ramadan."

He then rattled off questions about who participated in these drinking parties, where the wine came from, whether singing girls were present, and how much cleavage they displayed. He seemed particularly interested in the last question. Yalbard managed to keep Malik-shah's name out of his responses but otherwise fulfilled his responsibility to tell the whole truth. There were frequent interruptions as the mob applauded the questions and jeered the answers.

Omar could distinguish a man in the front row saying to his neighbor, "I'm not a fan of Abu Bakr Shami, but it's about time someone stood up for the Shari'ah." Now that the spectators were underscoring his points for him, Shami wasn't as quick to shush them.

Omar squirmed on his throne. He was starving, bored, and every minute he sat there listening to Shami inquire into the sale and consumption of alcoholic beverages was a minute he wasn't doing anything actually useful to find out who was behind the murder of Nizam al-Mulk. Twice he tried courteously to nudge Shami into a more productive line of questioning. Both times the spectators shouted him down, and Shami let them.

By the time the cross-examination wound down and Shami began his summation, the sky beyond the windows was turning dark. A custodian silently passed through the mosque, lighting the lamps. In the flicker of the oil light, the judges' three thrones cast long shadows across the hall.

"Emir Yalbard," the qadi said authoritatively. "This court finds that you were careless in the exercise of your duty to protect the sultan's top officials. It was your sacred obligation to prevent those who would harm the Nizam from getting close to him. Instead, you let a murderer through.

"However, this court is not in the business of punishing incompetence. We're concerned with crime here, and as far as I can find, you committed no crime with respect to the murder of the Nizam. But your use of wine is another matter. By your own admission, you violated the Quran on a regular basis. Indeed, your attitude on the subject is so cavalier that you made this admission quite casually, as if it were of no consequence. This court takes the most severe view of your offense. I sentence you to be taken to the Thirst Market at noon tomorrow, where you will receive forty lashes with a palm branch."

Shami let the spectators cheer freely this time. Omar waited patiently for them to settle down. This time he was determined to be heard. He stood on his platform, which brought him eye level with Shami. "Qadi," he said, as authoritatively as his working-class accent would allow, "I wish to appeal for leniency for this witness."

The crowd grumbled, but Shami silenced them with a single strike of his staff against the platform. "An appeal for leniency is sweet to the ears of Allah. Please go ahead, Khwaja Omar. Let no one say that this court is deaf to voices of mercy."

"I thank the qadi. Mercy is indeed the best course in this case," Omar said. "I implore the qadi to take into account that the witness cooperated with the commission in every respect today. He answered all of our questions. He answered them freely and he answered them without evasion. I also implore the qadi to take into account the witness's years of service in the armies of the King of the East and the West, spending months at a time living in the most Spartan of conditions as he traveled to the ends of the earth, in order to expose himself to spear and arrow for the glory of Islam."

"The court recognizes the witness's record," Shami replied sternly. "But it must also take into account the witness's offense."

"Indeed. The offense of the consumption of alcohol. I submit that the emir Yalbard committed no offense other than the offense of weakness in the face of temptation. But surely the Shari'ah exists to punish the wicked, not the weak. Forbearance becomes this court far better than the lashes of a palm branch."

It was fortunate that Omar stopped when he did; the crowd was about to boil over again.

"Khwaja Omar, you are to be commended for requesting clemency," Shami said. Omar was hopeful about the direction this was taking. But the next word from Shami was "however," and Omar's hopes crumbled. "However," Shami said, "this court does not share your willingness to dismiss weakness on the part of the witness. The weakness of one man weakens the Muslim community—especially when the one man is a leader of men, from whom others draw their example. Furthermore, it is the opinion of this court that we *have* been lenient. Surely someone with Khwaja Omar's reputation for memorizing the Hadith knows that the Messenger—may the prayer and peace of Allah be upon him—sentenced those who drank to forty lashes with a palm branch, as did his successor, the caliph Abu Bakr. But *his* successor, the caliph Omar, raised the penalty to eighty lashes.[57] By embracing the more moderate sentence imposed by the Messenger and Abu Bakr, this court has already given every consideration to the emir Yalbard's cooperation and years of service. Now take him away."

*   *   *

The qadi instructed the bailiffs that, despite the rank of emir, Yalbard would receive no special treatment. Until his sentence could be carried out, he was to be imprisoned in the city jail with an assortment of drunks and pickpockets. "This court is committed to equality in the administration of justice," Shami asserted.

Omar felt as though he owed Yalbard some sort of apology. He found the emir in a crowded underground cell. The place was damp with moisture dripping from a nearby canal and reeked of urine, body odor, and feces. Omar held the ends of his turban over his nose and mouth to filter out the stink but let them drop when the bailiff laughed at his daintiness. It didn't help anyway.

The emir bore his fate with dignity. He stood at attention behind the iron bars, his cellmates crowded around him. The steel helmet that some aide-de-camp had polished so carefully for his court appearance still gleamed, out of place in the gloomy surroundings. "I appreciate what you did for me back there," he told Omar.

"I wish it had done some good," Omar replied. "Shami had no right to talk to you the way he did." In frustration he added, "But, Muhammad's tomb! Whatever possessed you to blurt out a confession like that?"

"It was the truth." The emir's face seemed to be carved out of wood, the small brown eyes expressionless, his long white mustache hanging impassively.

"You're taking all of this calmly," Omar observed.

Yalbard shrugged. "I have been whipped before. I came up through the ranks like any good Turk. I have had my share of discipline."

"Was your share of discipline ever forty lashes?"

"No, never that many."

"And you were probably a young man then. Not so much now. At your age, forty lashes could prove fatal."

"If it's my time to go, it's my time. I can't control that. But I can try to control whether I cry out. If I can do that, if I can show Shami and Ghazali that they're not really hurting me, then I win."

"And *can* you control that?"

"We'll find out tomorrow. You wait and see. I'm going to walk away from this."

*   *   *

Arriving back at the palace, Omar went straight to Taj al-Mulk's office and pleaded with him to intervene on Yalbard's behalf. But the vizier refused to interfere with the judgment of the court. Omar argued with him for some time, but he wouldn't budge.

Dejected, Omar dragged himself through the Square of the Arch on the way to the Suq of the Goldsmiths. There had to be something he could do for Yalbard. When he passed Hujayya's Tavern, an idea came to him. He sought out the proprietor and ordered *iftar* for two dozen people.

"All the trimmings," he said. "Get a porter—two if you need—and send it over to the jail for Yalbard and his cellmates. Come to think of it, make it thirty people. We might as well treat the bailiffs to a spread as well. And water—brings jugs of clean water. And if you can conceal a jug or two of wine among them, so much the better."

He entered ben Samha's shop as a clerk was escorting the last customer to the door. Hoping that ben Samha's hospitality would be as generous as last time, Omar had held off breaking his fast and arrived hungry. Ben Samha didn't disappoint. A dozen hot dishes had been laid out on the low table. The steam from the various sauces mingled, saturating the office with a savory aroma. "I made certain that we had some of those lamb pastries you liked," ben Samha said. The wine—ben Samha imported it from Italy—didn't disappoint either. He described it as "fruity," but that was an understatement; the first sip was like biting into a juicy, ripe peach. Ben Samha invited Omar to take a cushion at the table and took the adjacent cushion for himself.

"Where is your assistant tonight?" ben Samha asked. "He seemed like a bright young man. Saad thought so too."

"He has a lecture," Omar replied. "He'll swing by when he's finished."

"I'm glad you sent him to arrange an appointment with me. As it happens, I have a gift for you." He stood, retrieved three books from his worktable, and resumed his seat next to Omar. "Perhaps they will help you make some breakthrough at your observatory," he said as he handed them to his friend.

The books were works of art. Gilt-edged pages of the highest-quality paper, bound in polished, chestnut-colored leather. Ben Samha must have mobilized an army of book dealers in order to find these rare jewels in three days. But what excited Omar most was the titles inscribed on the first page of each volume: *The Book of Optics*, *Doubts Concerning Ptolemy*, and *The Model of the Motions of Each of the Seven Planets*. All by Abu Ali ibn Haytham.

He opened *The Model of the Motions* first. Laying it down on the low table, Omar leafed through its pages. He stopped at a colorful illustration consisting of a series of concentric circles. "The sun and planets rotating around the earth," he explained. "Ptolemy's model of the universe. From the time of the ancient Greeks." But after closer examination, he realized it wasn't quite Ptolemy's model. "*W'allah!*" he exclaimed. "Ibn Haytham improved it! There's no equant point!"

Ben Samha smiled tolerantly. The equant point might have been a source of great excitement to astronomers, but it was a mystery to bankers.

Indeed, Omar was far too excited to spend long on one book. Soon he thrust *The Model of the Motions* aside and feverishly flipped the pages of *The Book of Optics*. Moments later he swapped that for *Doubts Concerning Ptolemy*. One passage struck a chord with him; he took a deep breath and read it out loud: "'*The scientist, if the pursuit of truth is his aim, harshly judges everything he reads, and uses his reason to the utmost to scrutinize it from all sides. He should doubt the results of his own research too, in order to avoid being too narrow-minded or too lenient.*'"[58] He paused to let that sink in and then stacked the books in perfect alignment on the table. "Thank you, Abba Saad," he said. He meant it. "Ibn Haytham. His words are just what I needed."

"My scientist friends tell me no library is complete without his works," ben Samha replied.

"True, but that isn't what I meant. Of course I'm grateful to fill a gap in my collection. But right now what I need most is a reminder that ten days ago I lived in a different world than I do now. A world that I hope to return to soon."

Ben Samha nodded his head knowingly. "The hearing didn't go well today."

"How did you know?"

"I had a man in the audience."

"I have no idea what happened in there."

"What happened is that you have walked into the middle of a war."

Omar gave ben Samha a blank look.

"Let me explain," ben Samha said. "For thirty years Nizam al-Mulk united the country. Everyone served the regime. Of course, the caliph sometimes got out of line, and there was friction with Taj al-Mulk, but it was nothing the Nizam couldn't handle. With his death the old alliances fell apart. Now all the rivalries are breaking out into the open again, with every faction scrambling for advantage: the caliph versus the sultan, the friends of Taj al-Mulk versus the sons of Nizam al-Mulk, hardliners like Qadi Shami who want to strictly enforce the Shari'ah versus moderates like yourself who don't mind winking at a few sins in a spirit of forgiveness."

"I lost control of my investigation completely. Shami transformed it into his own personal tribunal of public morality."

"Yes. My man told me what happened to Yalbard. He also told me you tried to stop it."

"For all the good it did. The flogging begins at noon."

"You stood up for what's right. You may have been shouted down, but now people know that Shami doesn't speak for all Muslims. That does more good than you think."

"He plans to call you to testify, you know."

"I know. As a Jew, I doubt I live up to his standards of public morality. I'd prefer not to be flogged. I'm funny that way."

"What can you do? The bailiff will be over here with a summons as soon as the clerk completes the paperwork. You'll have to obey."

"Only if I receive it." Ben Samha grinned. "Interesting thing about that bailiff," he said, rubbing his hands together. "On the way over here, he's going to run into an old friend who he only vaguely remembers. The friend will insist on buying him dinner, and who is he to turn down a free meal? Wine will be poured, goblets will be drained, and by the time the bailiff staggers over here with his summons, I'll be nowhere to be found."

"And where will you be?"

"Three or four farasangs east of here, on my way to the protection and security of the sultan's camp. But enough about my problems. Baghdadi said you had questions for me."

"There are three things I want to ask you about, but maybe I should wait. You need to pack for your trip."

"That's what servants are for. They're making all the preparations as we speak. There's nothing I need to do but enjoy this meal and answer your questions." He picked up a sweet pastry as if to emphasize the point. "What did you want to ask?"

"My first interrogatory is completely personal," Omar replied. "It has nothing to do with the investigation. At least not directly."

"Not a problem."

"The death of Nizam al-Mulk—in fact everything that transpired in the last week or so—has rendered me nostalgic."

"That's common when someone dies."

"I think you know that I grew up with Fakhr al-Mulk. But there was a third 'professor' in our little university. We lost track of him. Can you help me find him? I thought with your connections . . ."

"Of course. I'll do everything I can. What's his name?"

"Hasan-i Sabbah."

Ben Samha frowned. "He's a friend of yours?" he asked, not quite hiding the surprise in his voice.

"He was."

"I know he was in government service and left under a cloud. Where was he last seen?"

"That's the thing that's peculiar. He *was* in Egypt, but he boarded a ship for Morocco. It never reached its destination. No one knows if it sank or if it landed somewhere else."

"That sounds vaguely familiar," ben Samha said. "If it did survive, then someone bought the cargo. It could have been me. How long ago was this?"

"About ten years ago."

"I'll look into it. Give me a few days." Ben Samha went over to his worktable and scribbled a note. Returning to his cushion next to Omar, he asked, "What's your next question?"

"Abu Shuja told me he does his banking here. I was surprised that you transact business with him, given your history."

"I'm a sedan chair for hire, required to carry any passenger who wants a ride."

"What business do you two transact? And how hard up is he?"

Ben Samha took a long time to reply. He ran his fingers through his beard several times, not in a thoughtful way, but as if he were struggling to comb out the tangles. He challenged Omar with an intrusive stare and then combed out his beard again. When he finally spoke, the effort to sound friendly, in spite of his words, was obvious.

"Khwaja Omar, you know I am honored to have you in my house. But I can't answer those questions."

"Why not?"

"Every client who does business with the House of Samha knows that he can rely on the complete confidentiality of his transactions. I would no more violate that trust than I would turn my back on the Laws of Moses."

"Not even for a duly-appointed representative of the sultan delving into an odious crime?"

"Not even if you had me arrested and tortured."

"I've had enough of arrests and tortures."

Omar got the distinct sense that in spite of his protests to the contrary, ben Samha was itching to answer without Abu Shuja's permission. But the rotund ben Samha merely sat there. Normally jovial, he seemed to deflate, sinking into his cushion, a miserable expression on his face.

Omar decided to press the point. "You promised to tell me about Hasan-i Sabbah. Why do you refuse to tell me about Abu Shuja?" he asked.

"Hasan-i Sabbah wasn't my client," ben Samha replied.

"*W'allah!* If you won't do it for me, then do it for Nizam al-Mulk. When you needed help, he was steadfast in your cause. He—"

Ben Samha cut him off. "Your time would be better spent investigating the Qazvin lead," he said. "That's where the dagger came from; that's where you need to go."

"That's already being addressed," Omar replied.

"No it's not. Your wanted posters will never reach their destination."

"Taj al-Mulk sent them out yesterday morning."

"And Terken Khatun burned them last night."

Omar slammed his fist on the table. The little copper serving dishes rattled with the impact. "Muhammad's tomb!" he exclaimed.

He got up from his cushion and paced the room in agitation. "How could you possibly know such a thing?"

Ben Samha shrugged. "Spies," he said.

"And did these spies of yours enlighten you as to her reason?"

"No."

"What should I do?"

"Go to Qazvin yourself."

Omar stopped pacing. "How can I go to Qazvin? We're in the middle of hearings."

"Did today's hearing get you any closer to the truth?"

"No, but maybe going forward I could influence them onto a more positive trajectory."

"Do you think Shami and Ghazali are going to permit any change in trajectory that distracts from their own agenda?"

"Well, no—"

"Then what are you loitering in Baghdad for?" When Omar didn't respond, ben Samha pressed the point. "You just quoted ibn Haytham to me: a scientist scrutinizes a problem from all sides. Baghdad is one side of the problem. Qazvin is another. So what would ibn Haytham do?"

"Scrutinize the Qazvin side. But there's no rule I have to do it in person. Don't you have any espionage capabilities in Qazvin?"

"Not for this mission."

"Why not?"

Ben Samha didn't answer. His face wore the same unhappy expression that it had when he refused to talk about Abu Shuja.

Omar gave up. He grabbed his goblet from the table and drained the Italian wine. "Do you really think I should go myself?" he asked.

"Omar—you can stay here and attend hearings, and there will be three of you all listening to the same witnesses and hearing the same testimony. And if anything useful comes out of it—which I doubt—you won't hear anything that Ghazali and Shami haven't heard as well. Or you can go to Qazvin, and there will be two people sitting in the Mosque of Mansur and a third person running around scrutinizing the problem from every side and following leads that Ghazali and Shami would never think of. If you're serious about solving this case, doing justice for Nizam al-Mulk, and possibly saving the life of Malik-shah, it's clear what you need to do."

Before Omar could give him an answer, there was a knock at the door, and Saad poked his head inside. "Someone wants to say good night," he said.

"Come in, come in," ben Samha replied. "Omar, you remember my son Saad."

"Of course," Omar replied.

"And this is my grandson," ben Samha said, reaching out to take the baby that Saad carried in his arms. The baby was dressed in swaddling clothes; only his little head peeped out from the linen strips wrapped around him. The tiny, round face looked like a miniature version of ben Samha.

"There's my little Mordecai," ben Samha said. "Can you say good night to Papa? . . . Good night, Papa . . . Good night, Papa." But the baby merely opened his little mouth to yawn. The infant's lack of language skills didn't bother his grandfather. It was clear from the look on ben Samha's face that he adored his grandson.

Indeed, he protested when Saad insisted on bringing Mordecai back to the house and putting him to bed. "What's your hurry?" he asked. But Saad was firm about enforcing bedtime. Before he left, ben Samha asked him, "How are the preparations for my trip coming along?"

"They're almost finished with packing."

"Is anyone left in the shop?"

"Just the three of us."

"Make sure everything's locked up before you go back to the house."

After Saad and Mordecai left, ben Samha sat and beamed for a moment. Then he asked, "Do you have children, Omar?"

"A daughter," Omar replied.

"Is she married?"

"I'm working on it."

"See that she gets married and gives you grandchildren. At the end of the day, that's far more important than how the planets move or even who killed the grand vizier."

"In Khuld's case, it's more easily said than done."

"You know, Omar, Nizam al-Mulk once showed me a poem you wrote.

> "Ah, make the most of what we yet may spend,
> Before we too into the Dust descend;
> > Dust into Dust, and under Dust, to lie,
> Sans Wine, sans Song, sans Singer, and—sans End!"[59]

"I see the study of Talmud sharpens the memory," Omar said.

"As effectively as the study of the Hadith," ben Samha replied.

"I assume you've got some rationale for reciting this particular verse of mine."

"You're skilled at stringing words together in beautiful combinations, Omar. '*Dust into Dust, and under Dust, to lie.*' It rolls off the tongue. But I don't agree with it. Death isn't the end; there's more than simply lying under the dust, sans wine, sans song, sans singer, sans end. I don't mean heaven and hell—what I mean is we're part of history. My father passed the Torah to me, and I passed it on to my children. It's a tradition that goes back thousands of years—past the time when Caesar crossed the Rubicon, past the time when Alexander wept that he had no more worlds to conquer, even past the time when Nebuchadnezzar built hanging gardens for his beloved Amytis. The tradition goes back nearly to the Creation. And yet this long tradition was built one generation at a time."

"Perhaps you would get more gratification from a different verse," Omar said.

> "For let Philosopher and Doctor preach
> Of what they will, and what they will not—each
> > Is but one Link in an eternal Chain
> That none can slip, nor break, nor over-reach."[60]

"That's more like it," ben Samha replied. "When my grandson, Mordecai, was born, I was proud of him and proud of his father. But they're not merely my grandson and son. They're also the next two links in the eternal chain."

Omar stood and refilled the goblets. He handed one to ben Samha and said, "To more links." They both drank to that.

When Omar resumed his seat, ben Samha apologized for getting them off track. "You said there were three things you wanted to discuss with me. Hasan-i Sabbah was one. Abu Shuja was another. I'm sorry I couldn't help with that. But what was the third? I'd like to help if it's something about which I can be more cooperative."

"I think you'll have the same difficulty," Omar replied. "I wanted you to tell me your responsibilities for Sultan Malik-shah."

"Some of it is public information. I can tell you that much. I'm his banker. He deposits tax revenue with me, and I issue letters of credit to cover expenses anyplace in the empire where they need to be paid. But revenue and expenses don't always line up in the calendar. If bills need to be paid before revenue comes in, I loan the sultan money to fill the gap. I'm also in the jewelry trade, and if I come across a stone that I think might interest Terken Khatun, I'll give her right of first refusal."

"And you also manage Malik-shah's properties here in Baghdad."

"That's right. Last year I oversaw the renovation of the palace. After that I acquired the land for the Mosque of the Sultan, and now I'm overseeing construction. I do the same for several houses that we're building. One is for Taj al-Mulk. Another was for Nizam al-Mulk—I need to talk to Mu'ayyad al-Mulk and see what he wants to do with it. Of course I don't do all of this myself. Almost half my staff is assigned to Malik-shah. There's no secret about any of this. Why do you ask, Omar?"

"I have reason to believe that what you're doing is part of a bigger plan. A very important and very secret plan. Maybe a plan that has to do with 'the annihilation of the Abbasids.' That's the phrase Nizam al-Mulk used in his manuscript. Can you enlighten me?"

Ben Samha shook his head. "Not without the client's permission. We've left the realm of public information."

Omar pressed his lips together in frustration. He was certain Malik-shah would give permission, but it would be a couple of days before Omar could receive it. The sultan was camped somewhere near the eastern edge of the Iraqi plain. Suddenly a smile popped onto Omar's face as he remembered something. He pulled a jumble of papers out of a pocket in his robe; some were folded, others rolled and tied with ribbon. Omar sorted through notes and half-written verses until he found what he was looking for. He unfurled it on the table to reveal an official document with the royal seal—the safe-conduct Taj al-Mulk had given him. He slid the page across the table to ben Samha.

"Does this constitute permission?" he asked.

The edges of the page kept curling, and ben Samha had to pick it up and hold it open to read the preamble: "'*Sahib al-Jalal, the Sultan Malik-shah, Son of Alp Arslan the Seljuq, King of the East and the West, Glory of the Nation, Master of the World, Builder of Bridges, and Slasher of Taxes doth hereby command all emirs, governors, and other officials within his realm to permit the bearer, Khwaja Abu'l-Fath Omar ibn Ibrahim Khayyam, to safely traverse the territories under their control without delay, annoyance, or harm. The Master of the World doth further command all officials to render to said Khayyam any and all assistance, upon demand, including, but not limited to . . .* '"

Ben Samha smiled and once again Omar got the impression that his host really did want to tell him everything.

"Yes, I'll count this as permission," ben Samha said, returning the document to Omar. "You're going to find out anyway at the end of the month, when everybody else does. But until then you can't breathe a word. Swear to it."

"I swear upon Muhammad's tomb. Not a syllable shall escape my lips."

"Not here," ben Samha said. "These offices are a maze; it's too easy for someone to listen in."

Ben Samha routinely held confidential interviews with clients, and Omar figured he must have measures in place to prevent eavesdropping in his offices. On top of that, Saad had already told him there was no one else there. The precaution of going elsewhere, on top of the oath ben Samha made him swear, convinced Omar that the plan must be something big, the kind of plan that would change the course of Islam and, if leaked prematurely, have drastic consequences.

"You've aroused my curiosity," Omar said, conscious of the understatement. "But if we can't talk here, where *can* we talk?"

"Come with me to the sultan's camp," ben Samha replied. "He's only eight hours away by post horse. There will be wide stretches of open road where we can talk freely. When you get there you can ask Malik-shah to intercede on Yalbard's behalf. There's still enough time—barely—to get a message back to Baghdad before the sentence is carried out tomorrow. And then if you decide to go to Qazvin, you'll have a head start. If not, just turn around and come back to Baghdad."

Omar had to admit it made sense. "I must talk to my daughter," he said. "She'll shove me through the Door of Darkness if I skip town in the middle of the night again without telling her. Have I got time to go back to the palace?"

"I'm not leaving for another hour. Make whatever preparations you need."

"Baghdadi should be here by then. Tell him to stay here until I return."

Omar was so absorbed in making plans that he almost forgot his books. He rose to leave for the Dar Saltanah and started heading to the door but then turned around abruptly to gather them from the table.

"Thank you again for these," he said. "I'm humbled by your generosity. They're beautiful."

Ben Samha rose to escort Omar to the front door. Clasping Omar's arm warmly, he said, "I'm happy to do it—for a friend." He held the office door open for Omar. "After you," he said. Carrying the books under his arm, Omar stepped into the corridor.

The punch in the mouth slammed his jaw shut. Omar felt the hard surfaces of his teeth gnash together and force the impact into his skull, where a universe was born in a burst of stars and color. What happened after that was hazy. Omar knew he was on the floor gasping. He choked on the body odor of someone who had not been to the baths for a week. The pain in his ribs made breathing painful; someone was kicking him hard with pointy-toed boots. He heard a shuffle of papers in the office, but Omar wasn't sure if that had started right away or some time had passed. Then he smelled smoke. The stars faded, but instead of giving way to dawn, there was only night.

*   *   *

Baghdadi's classmates clearly valued their nightly Ramadan celebrations far more than Professor Tamimi's course on commercial law;

the class in the dimly lit hall was sparsely attended. But Baghdadi was grateful to be there, as it took his mind off Khuld for an hour. He was particularly fascinated by the discussion of whether a contract is valid if one party undertakes excessive risk. But all too soon the octogenarian scholar of shari'ah finished his lecture and, with the help of an assistant, hobbled down from the speaker's platform. Once again, Baghdadi was free to torture himself with the definitive dilemma of his existence—well, not his whole existence, obviously, but the last two days of it anyway: *how do I win her heart?*

He thought of little else in the water taxi headed upstream, bucking and gliding across the black waters. Khwaja Omar had meant well, but his advice wasn't really for Baghdadi. Ghazali's advice hadn't worked either. Baghdadi was out of ideas. Maybe that was a blessing. It wasn't by chance that the only serenity he had found in the last forty-eight hours was in listening to Professor Tamimi define "excessive" in the context of contract risk. *That's what Allah destined me for*, he thought. *From now on, I'll fulfill His plan for me and devote myself entirely to intellectual development. That's what Chief Professor Ghazali did, and he took the reins of the Baghdad Nizamiyya when he was thirty-three. If I learn from his example, I could do even better: a university of my own by age thirty.*

"Hey, kid! What's the matter with you?"

Baghdadi jerked his head up to find the source of this question and was startled to find the boatman yelling at him. "I told you twice already, we're here."

Sure enough, the Gate of the Arch loomed above them. Lit from behind by the lanterns of a dozen restaurants and taverns, its curved façade appeared dark and isolated. Baghdadi stumbled off of the raft and mumbled something apologetic to the boatman.

He passed through the gate into the Square of the Arch and pushed his way through the Ramadan partygoers as quickly as possible, not pausing for breath until he reached the murky shelter of the Suq of the Goldsmiths on the far side of the square. The shops were shuttered for the night. Other than the occasional passerby rushing past him in the opposite direction, Baghdadi was alone on the Khorasan Highway. When he glanced behind him, the crowded square was still visible at the head of the street, but the little rectangle of light got smaller each time he looked.

Many jewelers conducted their trade in this neighborhood. When Baghdadi had visited earlier in the day, to arrange an appointment for Khwaja Omar, the forges had all been fired up. So now he didn't think anything of it when he smelled smoke. Not at first. But as he got closer to the House of Samha, he sensed something was wrong. When the building came into sight, he was certain of it.

"No, no, no," he said as he sprinted the last half block. Smoke poured out the open door and curled over the lintel. Flames roared in most of the windows. The building lit up the street like an oversize lantern.

Like Baghdadi, the neighbors must have assumed the smoky odor was one of the local forges; they were only now coming to investigate. Some merely poked their heads out doors and windows; others jogged toward ben Samha's and called for help.

As Baghdadi sped toward the entrance, a man grabbed his robe. "Don't go in!" he shouted. "It's too dangerous."

"My *khwaja* is in there!" Baghdadi yelled back, tearing himself free.

The front room was a funnel for smoke. Baghdadi coughed violently as he passed through. He pulled the loose ends of his turban over his mouth for protection. At least there were no flames.

The situation was different in the hallway that led to the workrooms and offices. Pillars of fire were strewn along its length; their flames flowed upward like the spray of some hellish fountain. Baghdadi peered through the turbulent smoke; there didn't seem to be anybody there. He knew he should search the offices, but when he tried to enter the corridor—and he tried three times—the heat slingshotted him back. Out in the street, the neighbors were organizing a bucket brigade; their shouts carried over the crackling flames. Perhaps the best way to help Khwaja Omar was to join them. Torn, he took one more look down the hallway. The smoke churned in an ever shifting pattern. Baghdadi was about to return to the street when a chance clearing near ben Samha's office afforded him a glimpse of his *khwaja*.

Omar lay on his back, just outside the office door. His turban had been knocked off his head and lay on the floor behind him; several books were scattered nearby. This time Baghdadi smashed through the barrier of heat without hesitation. He dodged the plumes of flame; a chunk of falling debris nearly hit him. As he sped toward his *khwaja*, he saw the shadowy figure of a man approach through the smoke from the other end of the hallway.

"Help!" Baghdadi shouted. "Khwaja Omar is unconscious."

The other man picked up his pace. "Is that you, Baghdadi?" he shouted.

"Yes," Baghdadi replied. "Who's that?"

"It's Saad. Have you seen my father?"

Baghdadi reached the office door. Inside, the flames were high. They climbed up curtains and devoured furniture. Clearly this was the epicenter of the conflagration. In a shadowy corner, beyond a wall of fire, the inconstant light revealed a mound on the floor that may or may not have been ben Samha.

"I think he's in the office," Baghdadi yelled. "Khwaja Omar is blocking the door. Help me move him."

Baghdadi lifted Omar under the arms and Saad snatched his legs. They lugged him a little way down the hall, away from the worst of the blaze. Then they ran back to the office, Baghdadi leading the way. The heat was unbearable; Baghdadi had to force himself through the door. Saad was right behind him. They struggled to get through the wall of flame that separated them from ben Samha, but it was too hot. The heat seared their hands and faces with a pain like a thousand wasps stinging at once. Saad stared, helpless and horrified, as his father's robe began to smolder; bubbles of fire, no bigger than a lamp flame, puffed to life at the hems. Baghdadi looked desperately around the office until he saw something he could use— the tapestry of the Tree of Life was still intact. Baghdadi tore it off the wall and threw it over a portion of the fire, suffocating the flames and clearing a path to ben Samha.

As Baghdadi and Saad dragged ben Samha's limp mass out of the office, a groan above them grabbed their attention. "Hurry!" Saad shouted. "The ceiling's about to collapse."

*   *   *

The voices were jumbled. Something about buckets. And dousing the hot spots. And transporting the strongboxes to a safe location that might have been another bank. There was smoke and Omar was floating in the smoke, and then his jaw ached and everything crystallized into solid objects. His body lay on the hard pavement, and his head lay on a piece of cloth that wasn't much softer. But he could still smell smoke. It wafted into his nostrils and carried his last memories with it: Leaving ben Samha's office to go to the palace. Then someone hit him.

He blinked his eyes open and found himself looking into the earnest—and relieved—face of Muhammad Baghdadi. "*Al-hamdu li-llah*," Baghdadi said softly. Praise be to Allah.

Omar raised his head, but his body wouldn't follow. "Help me up," he said with more breath than voice. With Baghdadi's support, Omar struggled to a sitting position. Besieged by dizziness, he rested his forehead in his hands until it passed and then pushed his fingers back through the stubble of his shaved head. *Where's my turban?*

Baghdadi guessed what he was looking for. "We used it as a pillow for you," he explained, handing Omar the long strip of cloth.

Compulsively winding and unwinding the cloth around his fingers, Omar gaped at the desolation in front of him. He sat in the road, across the street from ben Samha's shop. Except it wasn't ben Samha's shop. Not anymore. The residence behind the house was still standing, if a bit charred, as was the forge in the courtyard. But all that remained of the shop—and three neighboring buildings—was burned rubble and an occasional section of broken wall whose empty window holes had recently held beautifully carved wooden screens. As Omar watched, one wall gave up; it crumpled silently into a pile, too exhausted to cry out in protest. Fresh flames spurted from its corpse. Volunteer firefighters—mostly neighbors with soot-smeared faces—rushed over to put them out. Steam hissed as they dumped their buckets on the rubble. Along the Khorasan Highway, more volunteers formed a human chain stretching as far as Omar could see. They passed buckets of water, drawn from the Tigris, from one person to the next.

In the center of this scene of ruin, a heavy-set man on horseback directed the firefighters. Omar recognized Amid ad-Dawla Jahir, Abu Shuja's replacement as the caliph's vizier.

Amid ad-Dawla pointed the volunteers toward gaps in the bucket brigade, withering flames, and still smoking patches of debris. Indeed, he commanded more by gesture than by words. Having read in the Quran that "*man is an evidence against himself*,"[61] he was determined to provide the world with as little evidence as possible. His reticence bestowed on him a gravity that had caused him to stand out when he was young. As the years passed, his beard had grown grayer, the wrinkles on his forehead burrowed ever deeper, and he only became that much more dignified.

Satisfied that the fire was under control, he glanced in Omar's direction and, seeing that the Astronomer Royal was conscious, picked up the reins and trotted over to him.

Omar attempted to stand in order to honor the vizier with a proper bow, but since he was clearly struggling, Amid ad-Dawla urged him to stay seated. "How do you feel?" he asked Omar.

Omar's first attempt at a reply was cut short by a fit of coughing, but on the second attempt he managed to say, "It's an epic hangover, but I've had worse."

If Amid ad-Dawla thought the joke was funny, he didn't let on. He merely said, "I'm happy you came through," and rode off again.

"I found some books near you and rescued them," Baghdadi said, pointing to the three volumes by ibn Haytham, stacked on the pavement next to Omar. Their covers were blackened but the pages were intact.

"The books," Omar muttered, remembering. "Ben Samha—where is he?"

Baghdadi shook his head, a pitiful expression on his face. He nodded in the direction of ben Samha's body, which was decorously covered with a blanket. Kneeling by his father, Saad buried his face in his hands and sobbed.

Omar held out a hand to Baghdadi, who helped him stand. "We thought we reached him in time, Saad and I," the younger man said as they made their way to the grieving son. Omar leaned on Baghdadi as they walked. "We pulled him out of the office an instant before the ceiling collapsed. But when we got him out to the street, he was no longer breathing." As the significance of "no longer breathing" sunk in, Omar shuffled to a stop.

"Another hour and he would have been safely away from here," Omar said, shaking his head. When Baghdadi looked at him with a puzzled expression, Omar explained. "We were going to the sultan and—" It was coming back to him. "Baghdadi," he said, agitated. "You have to go to Malik-shah right away. He has to intercede for Yalbard. But you must hurry. The sentence will be carried out at noon tomorrow. That gives you only . . ."

Omar suddenly realized he had no idea how long he had been unconscious. "What time is it?" he asked.

"A couple of hours after midnight," Baghdadi replied.

"So late?" Omar shook his head as the disappointment swelled inside him. No way a rider could get to the sultan's camp and back in time.

Baghdadi soon had Omar on his way again. When they reached Saad, who still kneeled by his father's corpse, Omar laid a hand on his shoulder. Looking up and recognizing his comforter, Saad managed a weak smile, the way people do when they try to be brave despite their tears. He clasped his own hand over Omar's and they remained like that for several minutes without the need to talk—their silence was their tribute to the life of Abba Saad ben Samha.

When the time came, Omar spoke first. "It's a crime that the sword of destiny has cut your father down so suddenly.[62] It was only for a few days that I had the privilege of knowing him. But I was honored that he numbered me among his friends."

Saad gave Omar's hand a squeeze. "Thank you, Khwaja Omar. My father spoke highly of you. It means a lot to me that the regard was mutual."

"I have had to feel my way since I arrived here in Baghdad, but even I know that most people don't want the sultan's special investigator investigating their affairs. Your father was the one person I met who was always genuinely happy to see me. It was that big grin of his; I'll never forget it.

"Today I walked into what I thought was a court of justice without a clue that it was in fact a nest of vipers. I needed a guide and didn't even know it. But your father became my guide without my having to ask. If it hadn't been for him, I would still be a pawn of Abu Bakr Shami in a game I didn't know was being played. Your father's friendship and generosity were a shining example to all of us."

"I worry I won't live up to his example," Saad replied. "His expectations were always so high for me, I live in fear of disappointing him."

"There's no danger of that, Saad. Practically the last thing he said to me before we were attacked tonight was how proud he was of you and your son. Proud of who you are, but also proud that you and your son are the next links in the eternal chain of the Jewish people. The thing he wanted you to do, above all else, was keep the chain going. You did."

CHAPTER 10

BAGHDAD
WEDNESDAY, 22 RAMADAN 485
11 Abán 471
27 October 1092

*B*aghdadi arranged for Omar to be carried back to the Dar Saltanah in a sedan chair. The *khwaja* was in rough shape: he was exhausted, his eyes were bloodshot, and he complained of a headache. Khuld helped him wash and put him to bed, but before he nodded off, he called for Baghdadi. "Look for clues in the death of ben Samha," he wheezed. "Before the trail goes cold."

Back in the Suq of the Goldsmiths, Baghdadi surveyed the expanse of charred rubble in front of him and wondered how to go about his assignment. Anything out of the ordinary could be significant. But what was ordinary in the ashes of a bank?

Maybe Saad can help, he thought. He crossed the courtyard to the residence, but as he approached, he heard the mourners wailing their lamentations over the corpse of ben Samha and realized Saad must be getting ready for the funeral. Reluctant to bother him, Baghdadi headed back to the shop.

For twenty minutes he combed through piles of brick, partially burned scraps of paper, sticks of furniture, and twisted bits of iron, uncertain what he was searching for. He trudged through debris; still damp from the bucket brigade's labors, it felt squishy under his sandals. Occasionally he would pick up some soot-encrusted object—an ink bottle from one of the clerk's offices or a cracked dish from the supper Omar had shared with ben Samha—which he examined carefully before letting it fall back where he

210

found it, no closer to reconstructing the crime than he had been before. But beneath a collapsed wall in what had been ben Samha's office, he uncovered something that might be significant: the charred leather cover of a ledger book. It appeared the pages had been torn out.

Working through the ramifications of his find, Baghdadi didn't notice Saad approach. "Oh, it's you, Baghdadi," Saad said. "I saw that someone was out here and came to investigate."

"I hope it's all right," Baghdadi replied. "Khwaja Omar asked me to do some investigating of my own."

"I'm grateful for your support. Let me help."

"I'm sure you have a lot you need to do, with the funeral and all."

"I have *nothing* to do. The funeral isn't until noon, and the mourning week doesn't officially begin until after. For now I'm in limbo." He smiled weakly. "I welcome the distraction."

"What do you make of this?" Baghdadi handed Saad the ledger book cover.

"I found a couple of others like that," Saad replied. "I think whoever set the fire tore the pages out to start it."

"The loss of the records must be a big problem for you."

"It's not a catastrophe. The clerks and I can plumb our memories and reconstruct some of it. And our clients have their own copies of their . . . yes, it's a catastrophe."

"How much information did you lose?"

"Most of the last six months. The older records were still on the shelf, damaged but salvageable. We moved them to the house for safekeeping."

"From what you know of the business," Baghdadi asked, "could there have been some transaction in the last year that someone wanted to hide?"

Saad thought for a moment. He had assumed that the culprit had taken the ledgers on the top of the stack to use as kindling. It hadn't occurred to him that the object was to destroy *particular* records. "We run a confidential operation," he said. "Half of our transactions are something *someone* wants to hide. But I can't think of any that stand out enough that someone might kill for them." As an afterthought, he added, "Granted, my father didn't tell me everything." He tossed the ledger cover back into the rubble.

Baghdadi retrieved it to keep as evidence. He suspected he was on to something with the missing pages. "Is anything else missing?" he asked.

"All the strongboxes are accounted for," Saad replied. "Only one of them was even opened."

"What was in it?"

Saad shrugged. "Some cash. Most of it was still there. He took a couple hundred dinars. Two hundred and eight. So basically as much as he could shove into his pockets."

"Not much of a robber if that's all he took," Baghdadi said. "I would have brought a mule and loaded him with as many strongboxes as he could carry. And I wouldn't have wasted time opening the boxes here. Not with two unconscious men on the floor who could come to at any moment." Baghdadi had seen the strongboxes when he visited ben Samha the day before and been impressed by their intimidating rivets. Breaking into one would be no easy matter.

"How did he get it open?" Baghdadi asked.

"With the key, apparently," Saad replied. "When we prepared my father for burial, his key ring was gone."

"Did your father always have his keys with him?"

"From the time he got up to the time he went to bed."

"What else did they open?"

"The cabinets where the boxes and the ledgers were kept. And the doors to the shop."

"Are the doors normally locked after quitting time?"

"The front door was. I checked it myself after I said good night to my father."

"How did the culprit get in, then? Could he have crawled through a window?"

"They were too small. And they were blocked with iron bars."

"What about the back door?"

"That was unlocked. My father would have locked it behind him when he finished with Khwaja Omar and returned to the residence. But it only goes to the courtyard."

"Let's take another look."

They retraced their steps back to the courtyard. Baghdadi tried to imagine how it had looked before the fire. As best he could remember, it was hemmed in by neighboring buildings four stories high—before they burned down. There had been no access from the outside.

"Why bother to lock the back door at all?" Baghdadi asked.

"To keep the servants out of the shop," Saad replied.

"Didn't your father trust them?"

"He did. But he was a cautious man."

"Let's check the street side."

The front wall of the shop was gone, but the arch of the doorway stood alone and defiant at the edge of the rubble. The double doors were still mounted on their axles, although one fell off when Baghdadi tried to push it open. Saad and Baghdadi spent some time examining the doors but found no gouges in the wood nor other evidence that someone had forced them open. Granted, it was hard to be sure with the fire damage.

"So how did he get in?" Baghdadi wondered out loud.

Something occurred to Saad. "*You* got in," he said. "During the fire. How did you do it?"

"The front door was open. I walked in."

"That doesn't make any sense," Saad replied.

"Why not?

"As I said, I checked that door myself. It was locked."

Baghdadi tried to think it through. *Locked from the inside. No sign of forced entry. No other way in.* He tried to imagine some syllogism that Khwaja Omar would apply to the dilemma. "The culprit was inside the building. He couldn't have entered after the door was locked, therefore . . . he entered before the door was locked."

"I don't understand," Saad replied.

Baghdadi was excited. "Don't you see?" he said. "He came in during business hours. The clerks probably thought he was just another customer. Or maybe he was dressed as a workman or something. Then he hid somewhere—"

"He could have used one of the storerooms," Saad offered.

"—he hid in one of the storerooms until everyone left except your father and Khwaja Omar."

"Of course! Then after he started the fire, he simply strolled to the front door, inserted the key that he stole from my father, and let himself out."

The two of them basked for a moment in the knowledge that they had figured out how the crime was committed. But then they realized they were no closer to figuring out who had committed it or why.

*   *   *

Saad and Baghdadi combed the rubble for another couple of hours but found nothing of further significance. Their investigations were cut short by the appearance of several neighbors, early arrivals for the funeral. Baghdadi nodded to those he recognized from the previous night's bucket brigade. Before long, a crowd bustled in front of the burned-out shop. Ben Samha clearly was beloved in Baghdad. Jews, Christians, and Muslims put their busy lives aside for a few hours to honor him and accompany his remains to the cemetery. Baghdadi stayed by the doorway, close to Saad, who greeted friends and relatives and quietly acknowledged their messages of condolence.

A man who was apparently a secretary in the Office of the Vizier conveyed Taj al-Mulk's regrets that he was unable to attend in person. "Official business," he explained. "He'll try to come by during the mourning week."

"Thank you, Raqim," Saad replied. "Please tell him it means a lot that he's thinking of me."

Raqim carved out a place next to Baghdadi in order to make way for an elderly man who was covered by a high-collared black robe and wore a shaggy white beard. Evidently he was someone important: a large entourage churned around him, and when he approached Saad, the voices of the crowd were suddenly cut off.

"Who's that?" Baghdadi whispered to Raqim.

"Isaac ben Moses," Raqim replied. "The Baghdad Gaon." When Baghdadi responded with a blank look, Raqim explained, "The head of the Yeshiva."

At the mention of the Jewish academy, it occurred to Baghdadi that no one had ventured from the *Muslim* academy—the Nizamiyya—to honor the city's leading Jewish banker. No one except Baghdadi himself, that is.

Come to think of it, no one from the caliph's government had either. Ben Samha's friends may have been numerous, but they were drawn overwhelmingly from among the Jews, the merchants, and the sultan's bureaucrats.

Clearly, Saad was touched that so many had come out to honor his father. Yet there was one visitor whose words of sympathy he spurned. This unwelcome comforter's small eyes were a nondescript brown, as was his robe—neither too dark nor too light, as if he wanted to blend in with the crowd. Saad was doing his best to make sure he failed.

"You're not welcome here," Saad shouted as the man approached.

Baghdadi, who had watched Saad keep his cool inside a burning building, was stunned to see him angry now. "What's that about?" Baghdadi asked his neighbor.

"That's Abba Nasir," Raqim replied. "I suppose it's *Abu* Nasir now. The sultan's intelligence chief."

For a man who was supposed to know everything going on in Baghdad, Abu Nasir was clearly perplexed by the hostile reception. He tried to explain himself. "Your father and I were friends. I want to honor him one last time."

"My father wouldn't want to be honored by you," Saad yelled in reply. "He said you were a traitor."

"What did he do?" Baghdadi whispered.

"He converted to Islam," Raqim replied.

Abu Nasir tried to explain. "I did what I thought I had to do," he said. "I know it made me unpopular with your father. But I'd like to make it up to his son."

"It sounds like Saad's approval is important to him," Baghdadi observed.

"I wish *my* approval were important to him," Raqim replied. "As our Turkish friends would say, he's a real *huyar* to me. But, then, I'm not the heir to the House of Samha."

By this time Abu Nasir's friends were separating him from Saad. They took him by the shoulders and guided him away from the crowd. "We can find some other way to honor ben Samha," one of them said.

*   *   *

A few blocks away, at the head of the street, not everyone passing through the Square of the Arch was on his way to honor another human being. Some were on their way to watch another human being suffer, and they intended to enjoy it. Many of those who left their bakeries, paper mills, and libraries to watch Yalbard get flogged came from the neighborhoods of West Baghdad. Their route took them across the Main Bridge of Boats and through the Gate of the Arch. They emerged into the square side by side with mourners on their way to the Samha funeral.

On the west edge of the square, Hujayya and Lina sat on a stone block in front of Hujayya's Tavern and watched the crowds go by. It was pleasant loafing in the sun, and they had nothing better to do anyway. Because of Ramadan, the tavern would stay closed until sunset. They even made a game of it: as new people entered the square, Hujayya and Lina tried to guess which way they would go—straight ahead to the Khorasan Highway and the funeral, or to the right to the Great Road and the flogging.

"Definitely funeral," Hujayya said as he pointed to a well-dressed man wearing a fine silk robe; it was decorated with pictures of birds. Sure enough, the man crossed the square and disappeared down the Khorasan Highway.

A student, easily identified by the yellow stole over his shoulders, went by. "Flogging!" Lina chirped cheerfully.

Four bearers carried a litter with its curtains drawn into the square. Hujayya and Lina looked at each other and laughed. Obviously funeral.

It was the working class that gave them the most trouble. They were certain that a party of construction workers, covered with brick dust, was headed to the flogging, but to their surprise, the laborers headed down the Khorasan Highway instead.

Suddenly a heavy object shot past Hujayya. It missed his head by a finger's breadth, ricocheted off the tavern wall, and came down onto the pavement with the distinctive clack of stone on stone. Hujayya spun around to see where it had come from and saw a man with a ragged woolen robe and unkempt beard getting ready to chuck another.

"I know you, ibn Yasir," Hujayya shouted. "You put that rock down now!"

"You think you can tell me what to do?" ibn Yasir yelled back as he waved the rock around. "Just because you're rich and I'm poor. Things change. Maybe I'll tell *you* what to do."

Lina joined in. "Go back to selling your moldy carpets, ibn Yasir!"

"Carpets are something a Muslim *should* sell. I can't say the same for wine. But your turn will come."

"What's that supposed to mean?" Hujayya demanded.

"The real Muslims are fighting back, that's what it means. Today we flog the drinkers of wine. Tomorrow we flog the sellers." He cackled at what he seemed to think was a clever play on words.

On the other side of the square, Abu Nasir and his friends were passing through on their way back to the palace. Already smoldering at the way Saad had embarrassed him, the disturbance in front of Hujayya's didn't improve Abu Nasir's mood.

"Now what?" he grumbled. He told his friends to go ahead. "I'll catch up with you," he said.

Spying a couple of Turkish soldiers nearby, he identified himself and ordered them to follow him. When they arrived at Hujayya's, the Turks cleared a path for him through the gathering crowd.

"What's the problem here?" Abu Nasir demanded.

"Oooh, it's the big, scary Turks," ibn Yasir taunted. With less humor, he added, "And they're taking orders from a stinking Jew."

"Ibn Yasir. I should have known."

"So you know my name. Am I supposed to be flattered?"

"We've had our eye on you. But I wouldn't be flattered. If I were you, I'd stay out of trouble."

"Listen to Abba Nasir. Thinks he can order me around because the sultan gave him a job. Like that's something special. The Turks give the Jews *all* the good jobs. They make it impossible for a Muslim to get ahead. But that's going to change. Shami and Ghazali are bringing back the Shari'ah. They'll *make* the Turks enforce the Ordinance of Omar. And don't think you can get around it by pretending to be Muslim, Abba Nasir."

With that he aimed the rock he was holding at the intelligence chief and let it loose. But the Turks were ready for him. They stepped between him and Abu Nasir before the rock even left his hand; it clattered harmlessly off one of their round shields. "You better come with us," the other one said, putting a hand on the carpet seller's shoulder. Ibn Yasir twisted free and dived into the crowd. The soldiers ran after him.

*   *   *

"It's getting dangerous out there."

Taj al-Mulk looked up from his worktable to the visitor in the doorway. "Abu Nasir," he said. "I thought you were going to the funeral."

"Something came up," Abu Nasir mumbled, looking at his sandals.

"What happened?"

"I just broke up a disturbance in the Square of the Arch. It was that rug seller again. Ibn Yasir. He threw rocks at Hujayya—you know, Hujayya's Tavern Hujayya. When I brought over a couple of Turks and intervened, he tried to throw rocks at *us*."

"Did you arrest him?"

"He escaped into the crowd. But there's more. When I got back to my office, four reports were waiting for me about similar incidents."

Taj al-Mulk grunted. "What's your professional assessment? How volatile is the situation?"

"When is Baghdad ever *not* volatile? If this keeps up we'll have a full-scale riot on our hands."

"Don't exaggerate, Intelligence Chief."

"I apologize, Vizier. I don't mean to argue. But when it comes to this city and civil unrest, exaggeration is impossible."

"It can't be that bad."

"Fifteen years ago, Abu'l-Qasim Qushayri came to Baghdad to give a lecture at the Nizamiyya. He was an adherent of the Ashari School of interpreting the Shari'ah. The adherents of the Hanbali School got so upset they started a riot in the Suq of the Nizamiyya. Several people were killed."

"That was a long time ago."

"Five years ago a woman started selling iced fruit drinks down by the river. Mobs chanting 'Water for free!' burned three neighborhoods. If the citizens of Baghdad get that destructive over being asked to pay for a beverage, you can bet that emotions run high when all the resentment of rich versus poor, Turk versus Arab, and Jew versus Muslim are in play."

Taj al-Mulk walked silently to the window and reconnoitered East Baghdad. His offices were on the top floor of the palace and provided an ideal vantage to assess the tactical situation. It was exactly as he feared. Below him, mourners jammed the Khorasan Highway, awaiting the start of ben Samha's funeral. And a few blocks south of the highway, off the Great Road, more crowds squeezed into the Thirst Market. They filled the central plaza and spilled into the narrow passages between the stalls.

Taj al-Mulk might have been wearing civilian robes now, but he was still a general. He spun on his heels and issued orders. "Go to the Sahib ash-Shurat, and request an escort for ben Samha's funeral procession. And have him post a few men in the Square of the Arch to make sure the funeral crowd and the flogging crowd don't mix."

"With all due respect, wouldn't it be better to send our own men?" Abu Nasir asked.

"No, there's too much resentment against the Turks. Sending our own men would only aggravate the situation. As a matter of fact, I want them off the street." Taj al-Mulk returned to his worktable and scribbled an order on a scrap of paper. "Bring this to the deputy commander. He'll know what to do."

*   *   *

Earlier that morning, before the sun had risen, two market guards arrived at the city jail with orders for the emir Yalbard to be released into their custody. The bailiffs turned him over, but not without a joke or two about market guards not being real *shurat*. The other prisoners were sorry to see him go; he was, after all, responsible for the feast they had enjoyed the previous night. Granted, he was also responsible for their hangovers this morning. But that was a small price to pay for the luxury of a deep, alcohol-fueled sleep that let them forget, for a few hours, their damp cage, filled with the scurry of rats and the stink of the shit bucket.

Yalbard's escorts conducted him to the *muhtasib*'s house, located at the edge of the Thirst Market. Honored to have a celebrity prisoner as his guest for a few hours, the *muhtasib* insisted that Yalbard relax on the most comfortable cushion in the house.

219

"I would bring you *suhur*," he said, "but it is better to be flogged on an empty stomach. A bruised backside is bad enough. No need to puke your guts out too."

Yalbard insisted he didn't deserve such consideration anyway. "I'm a convicted sinner," he reminded the *muhtasib*.

"There are sins and there are sins. Did you know we have three wine shops in the suq? Technically, it's my job to shut them down. But, well, they aren't the worst tenants I have."

They spent the morning swapping stories. Yalbard told of his years on the battlefield, steeped in the blood of the enemies of two sultans; the *muhtasib* spoke of his own, less bloody battles against unruly shoppers.

At noon the muezzin of the Rusafa Mosque brought the exchange of war stories to an end. His nasal chant broadcast the articles of his faith across three city districts as he called the Muslims to prayer. "*Allahu akbar.*" He drew out the second *a* in "Allah" in a display of musical mountaineering, ascending the scale of a minor key and rappelling down again. "*Ash-hadu an la ilaha illa-llah.*" The melody was doleful; the words sang of heartache, and of ancient battles, and of ancestral longing to commune with Allah. "*Ash-hadu an la ilaha illa-llah.*"

"Shall we go?" the *muhtasib* asked his guest.

*　　*　　*

The citizens of Baghdad had little choice in who governed them. Maybe that's why they were so ingenious in thinking up random acts of defiance, each one too petty to merit punishment, but taken together a force to be reckoned with. Indeed, that was how the Thirst Market got its name. When city officials wanted to develop the east bank of the Tigris, they tried to lure people across the river by constructing a grand market, unlike any other. In a city of commercial hubs that each featured a single product—the Suq of the Rug Merchants, the Suq of the Booksellers, the Suq of the Poulterers, and so on—this new bazaar would sell every product that the Islamic world's armies of caravans and flotillas of merchant ships could bring home. Chinese silks would be found next to Basra glassware, Indian armor side by side with Persian dyes. Whatever you thirsted for, the new market would quench your thirst, and so the city fathers named it the Quench

Market. Alas the shoppers of the day were quite happy with their familiar markets on the west side of the river. Skeptical that the new establishment would live up to its hype, and certain that they would come away with their desires unfulfilled, they took to calling it the Thirst Market. And although East Baghdad eventually became home to the trendiest neighborhoods in the city, and the unique bazaar eventually did catch on, so did the disparaging name.

For the spectators who jammed the shop-lined alleys outside the *muhtasib*'s house, watching an emir—one of their rulers—being led to the place of punishment was another act of defiance. Shouts of "sinner," "unbeliever," and "Turk," greeted Yalbard as the *muhtasib* and the two market guards escorted him to the central plaza. He saw faces contorted in anger and fingers raised in obscene gestures. Ibn Yasir the Rug Seller actually spit on him, a big, viscous globule of hate that landed on Yalbard's leather cuirass. It did Yalbard no harm, but it earned ibn Yasir a whack from a truncheon wielded by one of the market guards. He wasn't the only one; the truncheons swung savagely as the market guards struggled to keep the path clear.

At the center of the market, Qadi Shami and Imam Ghazali sat atop a raised platform awaiting the prisoner, the qadi's claw-like fingers drumming impatiently on the arm of his chair. When Yalbard and his escorts arrived, the two market guards joined a half dozen of their colleagues in holding back the spectators and maintaining a rectangle of open space in front of the platform. "Take off your boots," the *muhtasib* told Yalbard as one of the market guards led them past the front of the crowd into the open area. The *muhtasib* allowed Yalbard to lean on him as the emir unfastened the garters and removed the stiff leather footwear. Yalbard returned the favor as the *muhtasib* removed his own sandals.

Up above them, Shami and Ghazali rose from their chairs, removed their shoes, and performed the ritual washing from a basin. The shouts of the crowd subsided to a solemn hush as they descended three steps to ground level. They took their places at prayer rugs that had been laid out ahead of time, Yalbard and the *muhtasib* behind them. The four men stood at the center of the open span of pavement, four corners of a square with their backs to the crowd.

Ghazali looked down for a moment to prepare his intentions. Then he lifted his head and chanted, "*Allahu akbar.*" Behind him, filling the plaza, a thousand worshippers raised their hands to either side of their faces and bowed slightly with head and hands. "*Bismi 'llahi 'r-Rahmani 'r-Rahim,*" Ghazali continued. "*Al-hamdu li-Ilahi Rabbi 'l-'alamin.*" In the name of Allah, the Compassionate and Merciful. Praise be to Allah, the Lord of the worlds.

Even the important business of punishing a sinner has to wait for noontime prayer.

*   *   *

Like their fellow citizens in the Thirst Market, the mourners who gathered outside the House of Samha heard the muezzin call the Muslims to noon prayers from the minaret of the Rusafa Mosque. Since his chant doubled as the municipal clock, and since ben Samha's funeral was scheduled for noon, the muezzin unknowingly called the Jews together as well. Congregating in the street, their Muslim and Christian friends by their sides, they silently witnessed the mournful chant, so like their own liturgy. When the final syllables faded, they turned expectantly to the residence on the far side of the field of rubble. The door to the house swung open and the pallbearers emerged, bearing the coffin on their shoulders. The wood was of high quality, sanded until it was as smooth as water, but without ornament or polish. Saad's brothers and a cluster of household servants followed in its train.

The pallbearers crossed the empty lot that the day before had been a hive of commerce. Slowly, they closed the gap between the house of the departed and the silent, motionless spectators that lined the street. The emergence of the coffin from the arch of the shop doorway was like a trumpet call, jolting the mourners to life and commanding them to charge. Each man jostled his neighbor to get as close to the departed as possible; the result was an erratic procession that moved along with the pallbearers and surrounded them. Yet amid the chaos, there were those who quietly remembered how ben Samha's life had touched their own.

Baghdadi had enough language study under his belt to get the gist of the mourners' chants. Most of it was Hebrew; some of it was Aramaic. Each little group within the crowd seemed to be singing its own song. The melodies were more boisterous than sad, but somehow it fit ben Samha to be seen off this way, surrounded by friends. Not that Baghdadi knew him well enough to know what was fitting. He had met him only the one time—when he had scheduled the previous night's appointment for Khwaja Omar. Baghdadi had assumed he would be meeting with one of ben Samha's assistants and was surprised when he was ushered into the office of the sahib himself. When he thanked ben Samha for taking the time to see him, even though he was just a student, ben Samha replied, "There is no such thing as 'just a student.' Study is the beginning of wisdom."

Saad and his brothers remained behind at the house. That was the custom. One of his brothers whispered in his ear about another custom. Reminded, Saad grabbed the lapel of his robe and ripped the fabric as a sign of grief.

His clothes grieved, but his thoughts didn't. He remembered how eagerly he had always looked forward to Passover when he was a young boy. His father's hospitality was legendary, but for that one week each spring, ben Samha outdid himself. A Seder in the House of Samha was a twelve-course feast for a hundred guests. But even after the Seders were over, the kitchen staff had to keep plenty of roast lamb and stewed fruit on hand for the stream of last-minute lunch guests that ben Samha dragged home from the shop. "What else are you going to do?" he asked customers and employees. "Eat a dry piece of matzah on a park bench?"

As an adult, Saad had occasion to be hospitable in his own right. He treated large groups of friends or business associates to Baghdad's kosher restaurants. Between the full bellies and the spirited conversations, everyone felt warm and jolly by the end of these evenings. When Saad paid the bill— he wouldn't let anyone else contribute a dirham—he often thought, *I bet this is what it feels like to be my father*.

By now Saad could barely see his father's coffin. The procession behind it stretched for several blocks, a congregation of dark-colored robes squeezed between the buildings on either side of the Khorasan Highway. Spectators leaned out of windows and crammed onto rooftops. The pallbearers reached the end of the street and proceeded into the Square of the Arch. Emerging suddenly from the shadow of four-story structures into the noontime sun, the blond wood of the coffin shined brightly for a moment. Then it vanished from Saad's view entirely.

*   *   *

Taj al-Mulk was back at the window, watching the scene in front of him unfold. Ben Samha's coffin was entering the Square of the Arch. Behind it, along the Khorasan Highway, the white trousers and greenish-tan palm frond cuirasses of city *shurat* stood out among the dark robes of the mourners; the chief had stationed his men there in time. The Square of the Arch itself was nearly deserted. Only a handful of stragglers hustled through on their way to the flogging. In the Thirst Market, noon prayers were wrapping up. The distinctive motion of several thousand people prostrating themselves as one could be detected even at this distance. And directly below Taj al-Mulk, at the palace gates, armored Turkish soldiers, following orders, were returning to the palace in groups of twos and threes. "Crisis averted," he muttered. He felt the tension drain away from himself as it drained away from the city.

*   *   *

"*As-salamu 'alaykum wa rahmatullah. As-salamu 'alaykum wa rahmatullah.*" Peace and the mercy of Allah upon you. Peace and the mercy of Allah upon you.

Upon completing the closing lines of the noon prayer, Ghazali and Shami returned to the platform, put their shoes back on, and took their seats. A market guard helped Yalbard remove his armor, taking his helmet from him and unfastening the leather laces on the back of his cuirass. Holding the cuirass and helmet in his arms, the guard was about to retreat to the edge of the open area, but Yalbard stopped him.

"Hold on a minute," Yalbard said as he raised his arms and began to remove his knee-length tunic.

"You don't have to," the *muhtasib* said. "It'll hurt less if you leave it on."

"Do your worst."

The *muhtasib* shrugged as Yalbard yanked the tunic over his head and handed it to the guard. The emir now stood stripped to the waist at the center of the plaza, his cotton trousers his only garment. The scars of youthful beatings crisscrossed his back. Knotty sinews snaked up his arms and across powerful shoulders. In the crowd, conversation dropped a notch; clearly some of the spectators were impressed.

"Not bad for an old guy," Yalbard joked.

The reading of the charges and sentence took some time. When Shami finally reached the end and gave his screechy voice a rest, one of the market guards handed the *muhtasib* a palm-branch switch. Over two cubits long, the greenish-brown leaflets were stained with blood; they had dried out enough to grow stiff and sharp, but not so much that they might crumble. The *muhtasib* tested the switch by whipping it through the air with a vicious swish—an inauspicious practice stroke. Then he raised it above his head and brought it down on Yalbard's shoulders.

Tap.

The sound was so hushed that the market guard who had been tasked with tallying the strokes mistook it for another practice swing. He didn't call out the count until one of his colleagues elbowed him in the ribs. Then, to cover his embarrassment, he puffed his chest in an exaggerated way and bellowed, "One!"

Tap. Tap. Tap.

"Two! Three! Four!"

Four strokes down and the *muhtasib* hadn't hit Yalbard hard enough to leave a bruise, much less break the skin. Yalbard looked over his shoulder at the *muhtasib*; his expression asked, *What the hell are you doing?*

"I told you before," the *muhtasib* explained, softly enough that only Yalbard heard. "There are sins and there are sins."

Tap. Tap. Tap. Tap. Eight.

Custom demanded silence during a flogging, but a grumble now welled up in the crowd. By the time Yalbard received another ten taps, the grumble had swelled to a clamor.

"Come on," ibn Yasir the Rug Seller shouted. "Give him a real blow."

"Smack him!" cried the man next to him; judging from his stench of rotting carcasses and chemicals, he must have been a tanner.

Up on the platform, Shami muttered to Ghazali, "It's supposed to be a punishment. Not a music lesson."

But the *muhtasib* kept right on as before. Tap. Tap. Tap. Tap. Tap. Tap. Tap. Twenty-five. More than halfway.

"At least make it *look* like you're trying," Yalbard whispered.

The *muhtasib* raised his arm higher than before and gave the switch a powerful swing. But at the last minute he pulled back imperceptibly. Tap. The sound betrayed him.

Shami slammed his fist on the arm of his chair. "This is unacceptable!" He leaped up and clambered down the steps in an instant. But the *muhtasib* still managed to get in six more taps before Shami reached him. Thirty-two.

"Is there a problem here?" Shami asked.

"You have to speak up," the *muhtasib* shouted. "I can't hear you over the crowd." Indeed, the crowd was in a frenzy by now.

Shami practically screamed. "I asked, is there a problem?"

"No. There is no problem," the *muhtasib* replied. He paused the flogging and stepped back from Yalbard as if stunned by such an off-the-wall question.

The chief judge did not intend to argue. "Hit him harder," he screeched. "We're here to set an example. Now, you've got eight more. Make them count."

He turned to go back to the platform. But before he got to the foot of the stairs, the *muhtasib* delivered eight more taps in rapid succession. "Forty!" the market guard yelled out.

"*Allahu akbar*," the spectators called out. But their hearts weren't in it. The cry was subdued, as if the neighborhood polo team had lost. "*Allahu akbar. Allahu akbar.*"

The skirts of Shami's black robe whirled around him as he spun and grabbed the switch from the *muhtasib*. He drew back his arm and whipped the bundle of palm blades across Yalbard's back with surprising strength for an old man. Stunned silence overwhelmed the plaza. Yalbard sucked in a mouthful of air; he felt like someone had sliced his back with a carving knife. After several seconds, warm blood began to ooze from the long gash. The market guard looked to the *muhtasib* for guidance. The *muhtasib* shrugged, but Shami barked, "Forty-one!"

"Forty-one," the guard repeated and a cheer went up from the crowd.

Shami brought the switch down with another savage blow. "Forty-two."

Ghazali scrambled down from the platform and approached his colleague. "What are you doing, Abu Bakr?" he asked loudly, trying to be heard over the feverish spectators.

"I'm increasing the sentence," the qadi shouted back, without pausing the stinging lashes that he now inflicted on Yalbard with a steady rhythm.

"You can't do that. You've fallen into error."

"The Shari'ah says I can condemn him to eighty lashes."

"But you didn't. You assigned only forty. You can't increase the sentence after it's been carried out. There's no precedent for it."

"There is now," Shami replied smugly. He smacked Yalbard's back even harder. Ghazali grabbed Shami's wrist, but the qadi twisted himself free. He jerked his head in the direction of the market guard and ordered, "If Professor Ghazali interferes again, arrest him."

By now Yalbard's back and sides and shoulders were a tangle of red strips, a garment woven from dripping, bloody threads. The beating was wearing him down. He dropped to one knee, but the blows kept coming. Between the speed of the lashes and the interruption by Ghazali, the market guard lost count, but Shami didn't care. He just kept swinging the scourge wildly.

In the crowd, something strange was happening. The noise was petering out. Only a few spectators were still cheering, and then they stopped too. The vast plaza was silent, except for the whistle of the switch and the slap of palm blades against skin. Whoosh, slap. Whoosh, slap. Whoosh, slap. Again, and again, and again.

At last Yalbard was too wrung out even to kneel. He collapsed facedown and lay panting on the blood-spattered paving stones. Shami gave him two more lashes for good measure and then stopped, out of breath, his turban coming undone, his heavy gray eyebrows soaked with sweat. He turned to the crowd, pumped the slender switch in the air with his closed fist, and exclaimed, *"Allahu akbar!"*

The spectators replied with silence. They merely stared at the judge, disapproval in their eyes. A few of them, ibn Yasir among them, looked down at the paving stones.

"*Allahu akbar!*" Shami shouted again.

Still no response. Shami didn't try a third time.

Then a figure rose up behind him. The hushed spectators watched as Yalbard slowly pulled himself to his feet. The emir's whole body trembled, but eventually he reached his full height, his bulk looming up behind Shami. Wondering what the spectators were gawking at, Shami turned to see the emir glowering down at him.

"Seventy-nine," Yalbard said.

"What?" Shami replied in surprise.

"That was only seventy-nine stripes. You owe me one more."

"Fine." Shami circled around the emir and flicked the palm switch against Yalbard's back one last time, but it was a weak blow; the old man's strength was spent. He dropped the switch on the pavement and shuffled away. Rounding the corner of the platform, he disappeared from the view of the still silent crowd.

A soup stall bordered the plaza. The cook fetched a basin of water and a rag and did his best to mop the blood from Yalbard's wounds. Yalbard winced at each touch of the rough cloth. The spectators did not disperse; they stood by and watched while the cook tended to the emir. The only sound was a gentle splash each time the cook dunked the rag in the basin. By the time he was finished, the water was saturated crimson.

The *muhtasib* brought Yalbard's clothes and armor. Pulling his tunic over his shredded back was a slow process; it had to be done a few finger-widths at a time. One of the market guards helped with his boots, and Ghazali laced his cuirass for him—loosely at first, but then Yalbard insisted he tie it normally. Finally, the emir pulled his helmet down over his braids and pivoted on his heels to leave.

In contrast to the way in, on the way out there was no need for the guards to clear a path. The crowd parted on its own. Yalbard saw no angry expressions or obscene gestures as he left the market. He walked slowly and stiffly between two lines of ordinary citizens with weathered faces and coarse woolen robes, a silent honor guard to witness his passage.

*   *   *

Khuld insisted her father stay in bed. "You have to rest," she said.

"No," he protested. "I have to pay my last respects to ben Samha."

"Don't be ridiculous. You almost died."

"In death, as in polo, almost doesn't count." He shuffled around the room, trying to get dressed. Alas, Khuld made this impossible. Every time he picked up an item of clothing, she pulled it out of his hands and put it away. At last a severe coughing fit, followed by a dizzy spell, settled the dispute. Omar returned to bed.

"Good," Khuld said. "Baghdadi can fill in for you at the funeral. And no visitors."

She meant it. When Abu Hamid Ghazali knocked at the door to inquire after Omar, Khuld sent him packing. She did the same to Taj al-Mulk. He had to settle for leaving a message through a gap three fingers wide; that was as far as Khuld would crack the door.

"Please tell Khwaja Omar that I am praying for his speedy recovery," he said. "And if he's up to it, I hope he will join me for a short journey tomorrow. The sultan has nearly reached Baghdad; a group of us will ride out to greet him."

The only exception she made was for Baghdadi. He was, after all, not merely an employee. He had pulled Omar out of the fire and was now a hero. When he came back to the palace after the funeral and announced himself at Omar's door, Khuld flung it open and hugged him like he was a long-lost kitty who had unexpectedly found his way home. Baghdadi, however, removed Khuld's arms from around his neck and, without saying a word to her, rushed to the bed.

"I brought the *Prior Analytics*," he said, waving the book with excitement. "We have the rest of the afternoon and all evening—I figured we can cover five sections!" But finding Omar lying with his eyes shut, dressed only in a long-shirt and skullcap, Baghdadi fell to his knees beside the mattress, raised his hands to heaven, and cried out, "O my *khwaja*! What have they done to you?"

Without opening his eyes, Omar replied. "Muhammad's tomb! No one has done a thing to me since you left this morning. Can't a man rest his eyes for a few minutes without inciting an outpouring of frenzy?"

"My apologies, Khwaja. I will be less outpouring."

"Just be useful," Omar said as he blinked his eyes open and pulled himself to a sitting position. He picked up a tray that was sitting on the mattress and handed it to Baghdadi. "I've completed my lunch," he said. "Help Khuld with the dishes."

"I'm sure she can manage," Baghdadi replied, handing the tray to Khuld. "I will study while you rest." He sat down on a cushion and carefully arranged his book, a notebook, a pen, and an inkwell on the floor in front of him.

Still holding the tray, Khuld smiled sweetly. "Can I get you something to eat, Muhammad?"

"No, thank you. I'm fasting."

"With all the smoke you breathed last night? You need to keep your strength up."

"I'm fine."

What's the matter with those two? Omar wondered. W'allah! *First he's in love with her and she couldn't care less. Now she's in love with him and he's in love with Aristotle. What a wasted opportunity on his part! Aristotle isn't going anywhere, but how often does he incur the gratitude of an eligible maiden for saving her father's life? Clearly lugging bodies out of the fire has dehydrated him. It has affected his brain.* "Drink some broth at least," Omar insisted. "It's chicken."

"I appreciate your hospitality, but—"

"This isn't hospitality. Your doctor orders it."

"I didn't know you were a doctor."

"I study the physical universe. The human body is *in* the physical universe."

Khuld inserted a small glass into a gold filigree holder and filled it from a kettle. "This just came up from the kitchen," she said as she handed it to Baghdadi. "Be careful. It's hot."

Baghdadi looked at her with a resigned expression, as if he was humoring her only because it would get him back to his book faster. He took the glass and emptied it in a single gulp.

The pain was apparent in his eyes; they narrowed enough to squeeze tears from the corners. His hands flailed as if he were running for his life while still sitting down. But he managed to hold the hot liquid in his mouth until it was cool enough to swallow. Khuld hastened to pour him a glass of cold water, but Omar was less sympathetic.

When Baghdadi seemed sufficiently recovered to carry on a conversation, Omar said, "Aristotle can wait, Mister Too-much-of-a-hurry-to-let-his-soup-cool. I want to talk about murder."

"Murder, indeed," Baghdadi said. He concealed his disappointment with a show of activity, laying out a fresh sheet of paper and sharpening his pen, but he fooled no one.

"How did things transpire at the House of Samha this morning?"

"Excellent, Khwaja. Clue after clue after clue." He recounted what he had found in the rubble—the charred account book covers, the missing coins and key ring, the absence of evidence that the front door had been forced.

"So it has to be someone with a familiarity with the bank," Omar said. "A customer, an employee . . ."

"Why is that, Khwaja?"

"He entered unnoticed. He knew where to conceal himself until he was ready to strike. He knew that ben Samha would have his keys with him. He knew where the strongboxes and ledgers were kept. And he knew to take the keys with him so that he could get out instead of trapping himself in the conflagration. Either he knew the place well or he was the luckiest thief in Baghdad."

"So what is the next step of our investigation?"

"Taj al-Mulk came to see me earlier," Omar said. "He wants us to ride out with him tomorrow to greet the sultan. That fits perfectly with my strategy for the next phase."

"Aha!" Baghdadi replied. "I knew you would have a plan! You wouldn't let a cowardly attack on you hold you back."

"Attack on him?" Khuld responded, concerned. "Surely the attack was on ben Samha. My father was merely caught in the crossfire."

Baghdadi's remark touched off a cascade of questions in Omar's mind. Like Khuld, he had assumed the intended victim of the attack was ben Samha. Did he really have any reason to think that? Could he, Omar, have been the target instead? Was the course of his investigation starting to worry someone? He tried to remember who knew he would be in the Suq of the Goldsmiths.

Baghdadi was eager to hear where Omar was going with this. "What is the strategy, Khwaja?" he asked.

"Baghdadi, we're going to make a little excursion," Omar replied. "To Qazvin."

"Qazvin!" Baghdadi exclaimed. He had never been more than ten farasangs from Baghdad in his life.

"Qazvin," Omar repeated. He recounted his conversation with ben Samha, the intelligence that Terken Khatun had burned the wanted posters, and the lack of leads in Baghdad. His coughs interrupted the narrative several times, and once he stopped to ask Khuld to pour him some water. But finally he concluded, "Ben Samha insisted that I go to Qazvin in person." He looked sadly at the ibn Haytham books, with their charred covers, stacked on his table. "Now I feel I owe it to him to follow through. I had hoped to leave today, but *someone* won't let me." He gave Khuld a mock dirty look. "So instead we'll ride out to greet the sultan tomorrow, and then, rather than reverse course to accompany him on the last leg of his journey, we'll keep going."

"Just as I thought," Khuld said sourly. "You never really intended for me to spy on Terken Khatun."

"Yes, I did."

"And how am I supposed to do that from Qazvin?"

"You can't. That's why you're not coming. You're going to remain right here and commit espionage like we planned."

Khuld was delighted that not only did she still have her mission, but she was going to be allowed to carry it out without supervision. In fact, she couldn't wait. She began yanking open cupboards and chests in order to start packing for her father.

Baghdadi, in contrast, was clearly uncomfortable with the plan. "Khwaja Omar," he said, "perhaps we should delay until you completely recover."

"I'll be fine by tomorrow," Omar replied.

"Then perhaps we should wait until we can arrange for an armed escort," Baghdadi said.

"Why?" Omar asked. "This is the Seljuq Empire. Brigands on the highway are a thing of the past."

"Should I pack everything?" Khuld asked, placing an empty set of saddlebags in the center of the room. "Or only what you'll need for Qazvin?"

"Good question. The trouble is I don't know if I'm going back to Isfahan afterward or returning to this locale."

"Like I can't look after your stuff for you."

"True. Pick out half the robes and hold on to the other half until you hear from me. And pack the murder weapon. I'll want to show that around the city while I make my inquiries."

"It's not so much security on the road that worries me," Baghdadi explained. "It's the situation when we get to Qazvin."

Khuld started pulling robes out of a chest and sorting them. She packed the Qazvin robes in the saddlebags and threw the rest on the bed, despite Omar's continued presence there.

"After you complete that, start on the books," Omar said. "I finished reading *The Experiences of the Nations*. Ship that to Isfahan. Ship the science books too."

Baghdadi persisted. "You know Qazvin is fewer than twenty farasangs from Alamut."

Khuld held up the three charred ibn Haytham volumes that had been saved from the fire. "Do these go to Isfahan as well?"

"No. They're too sick to travel. Find some establishment here in Baghdad and have them re-bound."

Baghdadi had had enough. "Everybody just slow down!" he shouted.

Omar and Khuld looked at him with surprise. "If there's something on your mind," Omar said, "say so. There's no necessity for shouting."

"Yes, there's something on my mind! You're planning to go to a very dangerous part of the country, and I think you should reconsider."

"What's so dangerous about Qazvin?"

"The Sheikh of the Mountain."

The name had the intended effect. Omar forgot his glass of water halfway to his mouth. Khuld gave up sorting clothes and waited for Baghdadi to elaborate, a long-shirt draped over her arm. From the nearby construction site, the hammering of iron tools penetrated Omar's window; paradoxically, it made him all that more aware of the sudden hush inside the room.

When Omar finally spoke, it was in measured tones. "The Sheikh of the Mountain," he echoed. "A name I hear spoken in the dark corners of government buildings. But it's always uttered in whispers. What do you know about him?"

"Only what the other students say around the Nizamiyya," Baghdadi replied. "That two years ago he appeared at the castle on Alamut Mountain and somehow convinced the governor to turn it over to him. He installed himself in the governor's house and no outsider has seen him since. They say he never comes out of the house. He stays indoors, praying, studying, and managing the cult's affairs. He told the governor his name was Deh-khoda, but since that means 'The Legions of Allah,' I assume it's a false name. No one knows his real name. Not that it matters. Since he became the lord of Alamut, friend and foe alike call him the Sheikh of the Mountain.

"Now he uses the castle as a base to terrorize the surrounding countryside. He launches raiding parties to exact tributes and pledges of allegiance for his own form of Islam. They say no one can defeat his warriors. They're incredibly fierce and fanatically loyal to him."

"But how does he inspire such devotion?" Khuld asked.

"Because they know his power. He uncovered the hidden meanings in the Quran and learned the secret to sending people to the Garden and bringing them back again."

Omar rolled his eyes.

"It's true," Baghdadi insisted. "He sends his scouts among the people to seek out the strongest and fiercest teenage boys. When they find a likely candidate, they drug him with hashish, he falls into a deep sleep, and when he wakes up, he's in the Garden. Paradise. Exactly as it's described in the Quran: '*Rivers of water without corruption, and rivers of milk, the taste whereof changes not, and rivers of wine delicious to those who drink; and rivers of honey clarified; and there shall they have all kinds of fruit and forgiveness from their Lord!*'[63] . . . '*A blissful place,—gardens and vineyards, and youthful girls with swelling breasts.*'"[64]

"The seventy-two houris," Omar said. "Every one a virgin."

"They don't remain virgins," Baghdadi replied. "The recruit is allowed to enjoy himself in the Garden with the girls for a few days—"

"Disgusting," said Khuld.

"—and then he's given hashish again and brought into the presence of the Sheikh of the Mountain. 'Now I have proven my power to you,' the sheikh says. 'I can bring you into Paradise. If you want to go back, here's who I want eliminated.'"

"It no doubt makes for some motivated killers," Omar said.

"They are. Because of the hashish, people call them *al-Hashasheen*. The Assassins."

It's a compelling idea, Omar thought. *To journey to the Garden while I still breathe and return to this vale of tears with certainty about what awaits me after I pass through the Door of Darkness. How much happier I would be if I knew that my fate was not merely to rot in the ground. How much easier it would be to bear the daily challenges and disappointed hopes of life. Plus*—"rivers of wine." He noticed his forgotten water glass, still in his hand. Sipping the cool liquid, he thought, *No, Baghdadi's story is too good to be true. You can't merely visit the afterlife.* 'Not one returns to tell us of the Road, which to discover we must travel too.'[65] *And then there's another difficulty.*

"Doesn't it spoil?" he asked out loud.

"What?" Baghdadi replied.

"The river of milk. Doesn't it spoil?"

"The Quran says '*the taste whereof changes not.*'"

"In the real Garden, cultivated by Allah, that may be miraculously true. But I think the Garden of the Assassins, if there is one, is a manmade garden, cultivated by a Khazar Sea warlord. The laws of nature are in full operation and milk spoils."

"How do you know it's not the real Garden? Maybe the Sheikh of the Mountain's hidden knowledge of the Quran reveals the secret of traveling to other realms."

"Or maybe it reveals the secret of extending the shelf life of milk," Omar said.

Petulance saturated Baghdadi's reply. "You don't take me seriously."

"Actually, I do," Omar replied. "You persuaded me that dangers exist in visiting Qazvin."

"So we're not going?"

"I didn't say that. Nizam al-Mulk's murderer is still at large and his trail leads to Qazvin. Dangerous as it may be, we have to go."

It was already late afternoon and there was much to do. Omar wanted Khuld to send him regular reports on her mission, but he needed to teach her how to encrypt her letters. He chose a simple code—one that he had made up when he was in his teens to carry on borderline heretical discussions with Fakhr al-Mulk and Hasan-i Sabbah. He insisted that Baghdadi sit in on the lesson as well so that the young man could decrypt the letters when they arrived at the other end. Then there were errands to be done. Omar gave Baghdadi a long list: Procure supplies. Arrange letters of credit with the House of Samha so that Omar could obtain cash on the road. Bring Yalbard some ointment from Omar's medical kit.

"Oh, and most important," Omar said, "take a wanted poster—there should be one on the table—and take it to the Suq of the Booksellers to procure some duplicates. Fifty ought to be enough. We'll take them to Qazvin to replace the ones that Terken Khatun burned. Tell them to mobilize every copyist in their employ. An armada of copyists. Tell them we'll pay any sort of premium if they're completed by morning."

Baghdadi glanced out the window and noticed that the shadow of the Dar Saltanah had grown quite long as it stretched across the palace gardens toward the river. "Can't you get them from Taj al-Mulk?" he asked. "He arranged the earlier batches for you."

"I don't want to alert anyone in the government that we intend to abscond from Iraq. If it gets back to Terken Khatun, she'll try to stop us. And that reminds me: Khuld, don't use the government post—Terken Khatun is monitoring that as well. Get Saad to send your letters through his own network."

As Baghdadi searched the stacks of paper on the table for the likeness of Nizam al-Mulk's killer, Khuld stepped out for a moment and returned with a steaming bowl of water and a washcloth. "Time to clean you up," she told Omar as she approached the bed.

"Please. I'm perfectly capable of performing my own ablutions. In fact, I think I'm well enough to go to the baths."

"I found it," Baghdadi said, holding up the wanted poster. He placed it in his satchel and headed toward the door.

"Don't be ridiculous," Khuld said. "You're in no shape to go to the baths. Now, let's get that shirt off."

"Hey, Baghdadi," Omar called.

Baghdadi stopped in the doorway and looked back at Omar. "What is it?" he asked.

"Take Khuld with you."

*   *   *

Baghdadi and Khuld had to run all over town. Yalbard's barracks and the House of Samha were nearby, but the Suq of the Booksellers was on the other side of the river. Haggling over the wanted posters took some time. "I'm going to have to make my people work all night," the proprietor kept complaining. But for a sufficient number of dinars he agreed to a rush job of fifty illustrated pages. Even then, the best he could promise was to finish by noon the following day. Baghdadi was going to have to remain behind when Omar rode out of the city and catch up later, after the posters were completed.

It had been a long day, Baghdadi and Khuld were both tired, and when Baghdadi suggested they hire a water taxi to return to the palace instead of hiking across the Main Bridge of Boats, Khuld didn't object to the unnecessary expense. They took their seats on the raft, their various purchases wrapped in banana leaves and stacked around them.

As they pushed off from the quay, Baghdadi said, "We worked well together today."

"We completed all of the tasks on my father's list," Khuld replied.

The shores of the Tigris were ribbons of light, decorated for another night of *iftar* festivities. But the palaces and taverns seemed far from Khuld and Baghdadi as they floated in the middle of the river. The sounds of celebration did not reach them here; there was only the lapping of water around them. The black surface of the river and the moonless black sky cut them off from the rest of the world. Except for the pilot, minding his own business at his oar, they were alone inside the luminous globe cast by the raft's lantern. The beauty of the night made Baghdadi regret that he had acted so distant toward Khuld. "I wish I didn't have to go away," he said. "I'll miss you while I'm gone."

The love poem setting must have worked its magic on Khuld as well, because she replied, "I'll miss you too. But it will be all right. You'll be back before we know it."

"Are you going to be all right all by yourself in Baghdad?"

"It has to be done. Besides, someone needs to look after my father. If it can't be me, I'm glad it's you."

It occurred to Baghdadi that the way Khuld looked at the world, this was the highest compliment she could give. He could feel the warmth of her body on the bench next to him. He turned to look at her. Her brown eyes drank the lamplight beneath the shade of her long lashes. Baghdadi realized that he was glad she wasn't wearing a burqa and hiding those eyes behind a mesh screen. He thought about what Chief Professor Ghazali had said about women being evil. *What does a bachelor academic know about being alone on a raft with a woman you love on a beautiful autumn night?*

Baghdadi reached over and took Khuld's hand in his. To Baghdadi's surprise, she didn't pull away. The two of them sat like that, hand in hand, in their little bubble of light, until the boat landed on the eastern shore. Then the boatmen tied up to the quay and reconnected the lovers to the crowded city.

CHAPTER 11

NAHRAWAN, DIYALA PROVINCE
THURSDAY, 23 RAMADAN 485

12 Abán 471

28 October 1092

*T*he following morning the Khorasan Highway witnessed another procession, this one far more jolly than yesterday's funeral and going in the opposite direction. Eager to greet the sultan, almost a thousand of the city's most prominent citizens jammed the road out of Baghdad. Abu'l-Abbas, oldest son of the caliph, led the way. Wearing an enormous sable-colored turban with a scarlet plume, he sat with rigid posture on the back of his white horse. Eyes forward, expression serious, it was an impressive display of gravitas by a thirteen-year-old boy.

His father's vizier, Amid ad-Dawla Jahir, rode behind him, accompanied by Taj al-Mulk, who looked almost regal in a satin robe of honor. It was an elaborate garment, with a hood and cape, designed to be worn over the shoulders, on top of his regular robe. Indeed the sleeves were far too long to actually put one's arms through. The two viziers were followed by the top thirty or so government officials. Next came the esteemed scholars of the Nizamiyya, led by Ghazali, Humaydi, and Omar.

When Omar had arrived in Baghdad the previous Friday, it had been night and he did not have an opportunity to get a look at the surrounding countryside. It turned out to be farmland crisscrossed by canals that brought the runoff from the Zagros Mountains to thirsty fields of wheat, albeit there wasn't much wheat at the moment. The summer harvest had long since been brought to market, and the farmers were hard at work planting the winter crop.

The travelers passed the time telling stories. Nizam al-Mulk obviously was on everybody's minds, and at first the stories were about him. Omar shared the incident of the great man's difficulties buying melons. True to form, Ghazali sought to draw a moral from the suddenness of the Nizam's tragic end. He told a story about a companion of King Solomon who, upon seeing the Angel of Death eyeing him, asked the king to use his magic to send him to India to escape his fate. Alas, fate cannot be escaped and the man died in India that very day. Afterward, the Angel of Death explained to Solomon that the reason he was eyeing the man was he was surprised to see in Jerusalem a man fated to die so soon in India.[66] That story opened the door to more general topics. The atmosphere became relaxed and informal. Even Humaydi joined in with an uncharacteristically exciting account of his long journey from Spain to Iraq.

By midafternoon, however, everyone in Omar's party was tired, and the conversation lagged. It was odd how riding slowly in a procession for half a day, with frequent stops for congestion ahead, was more exhausting than twenty-four hours at a gallop on the open road.

In an effort to perk up his companions, Omar said, "I don't know about the rest of you, but I'm looking forward to the sultan's *iftar* tonight. It's usually quite a feast."

"You've been eating all day," Humaydi said with disapproval, his head bobbing slowly with the motion of the horse beneath him.

"The Quran doesn't require one to fast while traveling."

"I know. But doesn't that make it utterly pointless to hold a feast to *break* your fast?"

"Purely business. Almost every one of our suspects will be in attendance. We'll have a terrific opportunity to observe them when they're relaxed and off guard."

"I suspect it's neither food nor business that interests you, my friend," Ghazali interjected. "Are you sure there isn't anything else?"

"There is one thing: the grape!" Omar replied enthusiastically.

"Oh. Will there be wine there?" Humaydi asked.

"The Sahib al-Jalal unfortunately wallows in error. He would no sooner entertain without wine than go into battle without armor," Ghazali replied.

"You would think that after what happened to Yalbard, he would be more circumspect."

"Speaking of the emir," Omar asked, "how's he doing?"

"He walked away from his flogging," Ghazali replied, "in spite of Shami's best efforts."

"Then I'm not going to *iftar*," Humaydi said. "Not if there's going to be wine. The Shari'ah is clear about that."

"It's also clear that we're required to enjoin good and forbid evil."

"What's your point, Chief Professor?"

"That with or without wine, we can't pass up an opportunity to remind the sultan that this world is merely a foul and wicked stop on our soul's journey, of no more substance than a shadow in the sun. He must consider what his place will be in the world to come if he continues on his current path. Especially now."

"Why now especially?" Omar asked.

"The sultan was soft on shari'ah, even when he had Nizam al-Mulk—may Allah have mercy upon him—to keep him in line. Not that Nizam al-Mulk was always so observant in his own life, but he was better than Malik-shah. Now it's up to us."

Omar didn't like the way this conversation was going. "Do you seriously intend to lecture Malik-shah in his own pavilion?"

"It's my duty," Ghazali replied.

"This is going to be an interesting dinner."

*   *   *

"Explain to me again why the *sik* I have to be humiliated like this."

Malik-shah stood on a low wooden box while the Keeper of the Wardrobe buzzed around him, arranging the folds of his robe. His dark eyes and black beard were intimidating as he looked down at Taj al-Mulk. *The privilege of being seated in my brother's presence is not always an advantage*, the vizier thought.

They were tucked away in the sultan's robing room, a narrow compartment partitioned off from the rest of the pavilion by a white curtain. On the other side of the divider, distinguished guests, arriving for *iftar*, cast a tangle of spindly silhouettes that flitted along the wall of silk. The hum of their voices grew louder as their numbers increased, irritating Taj al-Mulk like the whine of a mosquito. Spaced at regular intervals among the darting shadows, more stolid figures, a row of sentries, stood watch. Their swords were drawn to discourage any would-be eavesdroppers—or murderers—from straying too close to the curtain.

Inside the compartment, slaves came and went with various garments and accessories. But for the moment, Malik-shah wasn't interested in clothes.

"Answer the question, Vizier," he demanded. "Why does a king who spent his entire life on the battlefield, terrifying the enemies of Allah, have to kiss the ass of a boy who still has the smell of his mother's tit on his lips?"

"Because that boy is the heir apparent to the caliphate," Taj al-Mulk replied.

"'Apparent' is right. We both know Abu'l-Abbas will never sit on his daddy's throne."

Fortunately the slaves had momentarily left the compartment and the Keeper of the Wardrobe was preoccupied with attaching a fur collar to the sultan's robe. Taj al-Mulk was able to touch one finger to his lips—a warning to his brother to choose his words carefully. Choosing his own words carefully, he replied to the sultan in the most general terms he could think of.

"It's important to show respect to the institution," he said, "if we are to gain the support of the ulama."

"Haven't we got that yet?"

"These things take time."

Wrapped in a green silk robe of honor, Mu'ayyad al-Mulk, Fakhr al-Mulk's brother, lounged on a divan in the corner of the compartment, enjoying the sultan's dressing down of his vizier. "It does seem like you've already had a great deal of time," he said, a sly smile on his fat lips.

"He certainly did," Malik-shah agreed angrily. "He's been in Baghdad a whole *sikking* week. What the hell have you been doing all that time?" He yanked the collar off his robe, launching a barrage of pins against an unseen enemy. Flinging the fur onto the floor, he shouted at the Keeper of the Wardrobe, "Are we still in the mountains?"

"Sahib al-Jalal?"

"It's too hot for fur!" Rerouting some of his anger took the edge off his irritation with Taj al-Mulk. But only a little. "When are you going to close the damn deal?" he demanded.

Taj al-Mulk glanced over his shoulder at the silhouettes on the curtain. At a word from the sultan, the guards' drawn swords could be redirected to prodding him toward the stockade. He had better tell his brother what he wanted to hear. "Tonight," he said. "If all goes well at *iftar*, we close the deal tonight." Well, it *could* happen.

But Malik-shah was unappeased. "That's another thing," he replied. "*Iftar*. Nush-tegin tells me you ordered him to take the night off."

"That's right, I did."

"What the hell for?"

"No wine tonight."

"No wine," Mu'ayyad al-Mulk repeated. "What a dismal prospect."

"We need to show Ghazali and his adherents that you respect the Shari'ah," Taj al-Mulk explained.

"Respect. Respect!" Malik-shah shouted. He shoved the Keeper of the Wardrobe, who was attempting to wrap a satin collar around the sultan's neck in place of the fur one. "Respect the caliphate. Respect the Shari'ah. When the *sik* do *I* get respect?"

Taj al-Mulk was spared the need to answer by the arrival of Raqim, who pushed his way through the opening in the curtain and prostrated himself before the sultan—juggling an armload of papers. Malik-shah gestured for him to rise. Approaching Taj al-Mulk, Raqim turned the stack of letters and reports over to him. "Post from the east," he explained.

Raqim stood by, waiting for any instructions while Taj al-Mulk thumbed through the pages. "What is happening on the roads?" he asked absentmindedly.

"The post rider says everything's peaceful. He met Fakhr al-Mulk and his party south of Qom. It appears they'll arrive in Isfahan on Sunday, and the funeral for the Nizam will be the next day."

"Thank you," Taj al-Mulk muttered. His attention was absorbed by the report on the top of the pile.

"Anything important?" Malik-shah asked.

"The results of the wanted posters."

"What posters?"

"It was Omar Khayyam's idea. We sent some drawings of the Nizam's killer to Hamadan to find out if anyone had information about him."

"And did they?"

"There were quite a few sightings, but only going back to the middle of last month. He was seen in several markets and—"

The sound of the military band announcing evening prayers and the end of the day's fast interrupted him. "We should go into *iftar*," he said.

"No, keep going," Malik-shah replied. "I'm actually enjoying this. We're doing government."

Taj al-Mulk began discussing the report again, but the sultan wanted a bigger audience while he "did government." "Omar should hear this," he said. "Raqim, send Khwaja Omar to me."

Raqim hastened to carry out his orders, but Mu'ayyad al-Mulk told him to wait a moment. "The emir Yalbard should be here as well," he suggested helpfully.

The vizier looked worried. "Why Yalbard?" he asked.

"The murder of my father is a security matter. Anything related to security falls in Yalbard's domain."

"Yalbard has been apart from his troops for over a week. I'm sure he has a lot of things to do."

"He does," the sultan interjected. "And one of them is to see to security. Or did you forget there's still a *sikking* threat on my life?" He flicked his hand impatiently toward Raqim, who disappeared behind the curtain.

Mu'ayyad al-Mulk suppressed a triumphant smile.

"Now," Malik-shah said, "what's next on the doing government agenda?"

"I received a delegation of Turkish tribesmen newly arrived from the Land beyond the River," said Taj al-Mulk. "They want permission to settle in Seljuq territory."

"I don't want them. Between the raiding and the grazing they leave a *sikking* wasteland wherever they go."

"Then I should continue Nizam al-Mulk's policy?"

"Yes. Give them safe passage to Anatolia. Let the emperor of Rum deal with them."

"Agreed. The more Muslims we infiltrate into Christian lands—"

"—the sooner we defeat the unbelievers once and for all. Oh, Omar, you're here."

Omar was standing in the entry, looking uncertain as to whether this was something he was supposed to hear. "Yes, Sahib al-Jalal," he said, bowing his head. "I didn't know if you were ready for me."

"Yes, yes, come in," Malik-shah said. He stepped forward to embrace his friend. "We're doing government. You got here quickly."

"I was already in your pavilion. The orb of the sun has sunk beneath the horizon. Everyone's waiting on you to commence the *iftar*."

"They'll have to wait a while longer. We're doing government."

Omar tried to conceal his disappointment; the aromas of lemon and cinnamon, wafting in from the main compartment, were mouth-watering.

"Find a cushion for yourself," the sultan said. "Taj al-Mulk, give him yours. You can stand."

"With your permission," Omar replied, "I prefer not to sit. I've been riding all day." Omar was beginning to learn diplomacy.

The sultan looked down at his attire. "It needs a belt," he said to the Keeper of the Wardrobe.

Taj al-Mulk watched the sultan fuss over his clothes with distaste. Malik-shah had grown up in the camps of their father's soldiers. He was as skillful with a horse or a bow as any of his men. Where he had come by his obsession with Persian fashion mystified his brother.

Turning back to Taj al-Mulk the sultan said, "Now let's hear that report from Hamadan."

"I was telling the sultan before you came in that quite a few people saw the killer," Taj al-Mulk explained, "but only during the past few weeks. So you were right about him coming from somewhere else." He leafed through the pages and picked out some highlights. "The man seems to have spent a great deal of time walking around the city."

Taj al-Mulk droned on about sightings of the murderer in the bazaars, sightings near moneychangers' stalls, sightings in Jew Town. Despite the sultan's determination to do government, his attention wandered. Soon he was fussing over belts with the Keeper of the Wardrobe. "Let's try it with the robe open and the belt underneath," the sultan would say, and then the Keeper of the Wardrobe would reach under the layers of silk to wrap the embossed leather band around the sultan's long-shirt. Then the sultan would complain about the buckle and suggest that they use a square one, with more jewels.

Taj al-Mulk meanwhile was becoming irritated with how little useful information was in the report. "No one seems to have actually talked to the man at all . . . Wait a minute. Here's something important. Several people saw him entering and leaving a house near the Friday mosque. My men had it searched . . ." He tossed the report onto a nearby table in frustration. "Nothing. The house was empty. Completely cleaned out. Not an article of clothing or a crust of bread. No trace of the owner."

"It seems like your men didn't learn very much," Mu'ayyad al-Mulk said.

Taj al-Mulk jumped from his cushion and charged the son of the Nizam. "I've had about all the sniping from you I'm going to take," he shouted.

Mu'ayyad al-Mulk put up his hands to shield himself from the vizier. Omar stepped between them. "It's all right," he said. He guided Taj al-Mulk back to his cushion. Omar took the sheaf of papers and leafed through it. "This isn't a complete surprise," he said. "We knew these people were professionals. The house was expendable. And we learned a new fact."

Mu'ayyad al-Mulk looked incredulous. "We did?" he asked.

"Money changers. Jews. Our man had a fixation on bankers. Either he was a pious Muslim who was upset that the laws against usury aren't enforced. Or he was stricken with poverty and blamed bankers for it. Probably a little of each."

"It appears your men came up with very little information that's useful," Mu'ayyad al-Mulk said.

"It's a start," Taj al-Mulk replied. "They'll keep asking around."

"Yes, proceed with that," the sultan responded.

The Keeper of the Wardrobe signaled a slave, who kneeled in front of the sultan and held out a jewelry case with a dozen or so padded compartments. In each compartment a gold ring with a precious stone sparkled. Malik-shah browsed the selection, now and then picking one up, studying it, and putting it back. "What about you, Omar?" he asked as he held a ring with a larger than average ruby up to the lamp. "What's your next step?"

246

Omar was on the spot. He couldn't tell the sultan that his next step was to sneak off to Qazvin in the middle of the night. Fortunately, he didn't have to; the sultan unexpectedly burst out laughing and said, "What happened to *you*, you old *amm*-grabber?"

A startled Omar needed a moment to realize the question wasn't intended for him: behind him, Yalbard had pushed his way through the curtain into the compartment. The old emir walked haltingly, his back stiff, his expression stoic. When he reached the sultan, he began to bow, but the sultan insisted on embracing him instead. Omar could see Yalbard's shoulders flinch as Malik-shah wrapped his arms around the emir's back. The sultan must have felt the move, because he released his embrace, held Yalbard at arm's length, and asked, without laughter this time, "What *did* happen to you?"

Yalbard gave Taj al-Mulk a puzzled look and then, to the sultan, he said, "I thought you knew. Eighty lashes for drinking."

Malik-shah whirled toward Taj al-Mulk. "How could you let one of my emirs be flogged?"

"Circumstances made it impossible to prevent," Taj al-Mulk replied.

"Circumstances!" Malik-shah scoffed. He smashed his fist down on the jewelry case, which tumbled to the floor, scattering gold rings everywhere. The red and green and blue of their jewels were flashing lights, skidding across the Armenian carpet. "What circumstances? I expect you to have circumstances under control! Who the *sik* do you think you are?"

Once again Taj al-Mulk was on his feet. "I think I'm the front-line commander," he shouted back. "The man who had the facts on the ground and understood the tactical situation when you were three days away."

"Facts on the ground," Malik-shah scoffed. "I ought to strangle you with your own bowstring. How would that be for a 'fact on the ground'?"

"Maybe if the vizier told us what the facts were," Omar suggested.

"The crowds," Taj al-Mulk explained. "Thanks to ben Samha's funeral, the Square of the Arch was a solid mass of traffic. And another crowd filled the Thirst Market. Everywhere people were on edge: Abu Nasir was getting reports of fights breaking out all morning. If I tried to cross the square with a squad of troops, then push through the spectators at the Thirst Market and rob them of the spectacle they had come to see, a riot would have broken out. Only Allah knows how many of your subjects would have been

247

killed if I had to send the army in to put it down. If you were more involved in day-to-day affairs you would know these things."

Malik-shah crossed his arms in a huff. He snapped at Yalbard, "It was your damn back. What do you have to say?"

"It's not my place to say anything," Yalbard replied. "I serve the Sahib al-Jalal."

"Taj al-Mulk could take a lesson from your loyalty." The sultan cast about the compartment for an ally. His eye fell upon Omar. "You were in Baghdad," he said. "Was it really that bad?"

"I was laid up all day," Omar replied. "But on the way here, a lot of people were talking about it. They said yes, it was bad. Yalbard turned it around, though. He conducted himself so well that he earned the heartfelt respect of the people of Baghdad for himself. And for you. It seems to me that by respecting the judgment of the Shari'ah court and allowing the sentence to go forward, Taj al-Mulk showed the people of Baghdad that you are a pious Muslim, who does not allow anyone to be above the law."

The sultan grunted, still dissatisfied. He stood still long enough for the Keeper of the Wardrobe to reattach the satin cuff. Then he swept toward the entrance and peeked through the opening. But instead of continuing out into the main compartment, he spun around with a new complaint. "Why aren't Ghazali and the other representatives of the ulama seated at my table?"

Taj al-Mulk chose his words carefully. "I thought it might be best if I entertained them myself."

"Why? You're the one who said I need to be more involved in day-to-day affairs."

"While I wholeheartedly support the Sahib al-Jalal's intent to get more involved, perhaps we should wait for another opportunity. One with less riding on it."

The sultan had had it with his brother. "Are you saying I can't handle it?" he demanded.

"You don't have a lot of experience with the Nizamiyya."

"I *do* know how to get along with people. I've been a commander since I was in my teens."

"A scholar is not a soldier, O Sahib al-Jalal. He won't blindly follow orders."

A look of fury crossed the sultan's face. Omar and Taj al-Mulk braced themselves for the storm that was about to break. Mu'ayyad al-Mulk grinned in anticipation. But then Malik-shah surprised everyone. He took a couple of deep breaths and held up both hands in a gesture of surrender. But it wasn't the sultan who was giving in. It was his anger. "Ghazali is a proud man," he said. "He won't just roll over for me. I have to forge a relationship with him, build trust, and demonstrate my allegiance to Allah."

The others were so stunned to hear wisdom coming from Sahib al-Jalal, they had nothing further to say.

*　　　*　　　*

Iftar for five hundred people was an expensive undertaking, but as the Nizam wrote in *The Book of Politics*, the sultan is the Father of his People; it is his duty to feed them. Fortunately, the treasury was equal to the task, as was the pavilion of Malik-shah, which easily accommodated the crowd. It looked considerably more festive than the last time Omar had been there. Hundreds of hanging oil lamps filled the space under the canopy with light. The lamps brightened the colors of the elaborately patterned Armenian carpets that covered the walls and floors. Overstuffed cushions and low tables were scattered about. Slaves in belted tunics carried in platters of lamb stew, roasted quail, cucumbers, lentils, and rice. The earthy aroma of turmeric and the raisin-like scent of saffron filled the air. Hoisting trays of steaming dishes on their shoulders, slaves struggled to maneuver through narrow aisles without bumping into anyone. The combined noise of discussion, laughter, argument, and knives clinking on gold platters was overwhelming.

There had been a tussle over the last-minute seating change. The decision to move Ghazali and the other leaders of the Nizamiyya to the sultan's table meant several people had to be demoted to less prestigious locations, including Mu'ayyad al-Mulk, who had parked himself there the moment he left the sultan's robing room. When a slave politely requested that he move, Mu'ayyad al-Mulk had a few harsh things to say. These included "You miserable little worm," "Do you know who I am?" and "I'll flog you until you drown in your own blood." He remained stubbornly on his cushion until someone more intimidating—Yalbard—intervened.

But the question of *who* would dine with the sultan was easy compared to *where* everyone would sit around the table. Malik-shah seated Abu'l-Abbas on his right, of course—the caliph's heir was the guest of honor. They should have been flanked by their respective viziers, Taj al-Mulk and Amid ad-Dawla. But Taj al-Mulk insisted on sitting on the opposite side of the table, in the place of lowest precedence. The caliph's heir, Abu'l-Abbas, mentioned several times how taken he was by this show of humility. Amid ad-Dawla took the hint and joined Taj al-Mulk, leaving the boy virtually chaperone-free for the night. This freed up two cushions near the head of the table, and these went to Omar, who sat beside the sultan, and Ghazali, who sat beside Abu'l-Abbas.

"The rulers of the principality are seated between science and shari'ah," Omar remarked pleasantly as they settled on their cushions. Abu'l-Abbas liked that. He said he would try to remember it so he could share it with his father. But Ghazali had to turn Omar's pleasantry into something contentious by pointing out, "The Shari'ah is on the right—the place of honor. As it should be."

At last the seating arrangements were settled and everyone took a place at the table. A pitcher of water, a bowl, and a towel were passed around so that each guest could wash and dry his hands. Humaydi had the spot on Ghazali's other side. As he passed the pitcher, he whispered, "I didn't know there would be so many soldiers around. You should be careful what you say."

"Soldiers daunt only fools," Ghazali replied. "Men of understanding know that military might can harm us only in the mortal world—which is not our true home."

He certainly seemed undaunted himself. From the first course—a sweetened porridge of boiled grain and seasoned goat meat—Ghazali talked almost continuously, leaning across Abu'l-Abbas so that Malik-shah could hear him over the crowd. He paused only to scarf large mouthfuls of the various delicacies placed in front of him and noisily lick any stray sauce off his lips. Then the lecture went on as before.

The symposium commenced with comparing and contrasting shari'ah and science; it was mostly contrast. Next Ghazali enumerated the responsibilities of monarchy. It was the same crap Malik-shah had heard from a thousand other intellectuals, far less prestigious than Ghazali, who were so taken with the power of their own oratory that they seriously believed it could compel a king to repent from luxury and despotism. The sultan must submit to the caliph, they said. The sultan must administer justice. The sultan must take his shits in the manner prescribed by law. Malik-shah had to admit that sucking up to the ulama was a challenge after all. He hadn't realized how boring it would be. He managed to show interest for a while—Ghazali's frequent diatribes on the "incoherence" of "heretics" and "boneheads" made it entertaining at least—but eventually his attention wandered.

It soon became clear why Taj al-Mulk had positioned himself at the table the way he did. He wanted a clear line of sight to Malik-shah in order to coach him, by means of silent gestures, on how best to deal with Ghazali. The vizier had been doing a lot of this gesturing since the meal began. For the most part, Malik-shah couldn't tell what these gestures meant. Perhaps "say something," or "offer him another kabob," or, for all he knew, "piss on his shoes." At the moment, Taj al-Mulk was looking at his brother with an expression of disapproval and flicking his hand in Ghazali's direction. Malik-shah was pretty sure that meant "pay attention."

Malik-shah did his best. Ghazali had reached the part of the lecture where he nagged the sultan to listen to the ulama. *As if that's not self-serving*, he thought.

"Nizam al-Mulk—may Allah have mercy upon him—wrote about this in *The Book of Politics*," Ghazali said. "He said that you should hear lectures or debates between scholars once or twice a week, to avoid falling into error. And even though he is no longer with us, I hope you will follow his wise counsel."

The sultan gulped from his goblet and wondered why his wine lacked flavor. Then he remembered, for the tenth time tonight, that it was water. He peered into the cup, as if the evidence of his eyes and nose could somehow overturn the sad judgment of his taste buds if only he were forceful enough. But the beverage persisted in its contrariness and refused to take on color or scent. Water.

When the sultan looked up from his cup, Taj al-Mulk was gesturing again. No doubt he wanted his brother to say something. The sultan obliged. "Nizam al-Mulk indeed gave wise counsel," he said. "But whatever wisdom he had he learned from the ulama. I do not intend to change a policy that has served us so well."

He hated groveling before Ghazali, but Humaydi's reaction almost made it worthwhile. Sitting on the other side of his boss, the deputy director of the Nizamiyya scowled in disappointment. He had come to watch a fight, and the sultan wasn't giving him one. On top of that, Humaydi had let his cuff get too close to one of the stews, and now the fabric wilted with sauce.

But the lift in the sultan's spirits was momentary. Ghazali went on with his ode to the ulama for some time and then started a new topic: the sultan must not live extravagantly. *No one is living extravagantly at this meal*, Malik-shah thought as he forced down a mouthful of chicken stewed with prunes and onions. The chicken was overcooked—*How can something that's been stewed be so* sikking *dry?*—and as for spices, he could taste nothing more extravagant than salt. A slave stood by, awaiting the sultan's orders. "Take this away and bring something else," Malik-shah demanded. He didn't have to add "And fire whoever cooked it." Sending the dish back was enough to make that happen.

During the sultan's exchange with the slave, Ghazali didn't break his tedious pace. "The sultan should be modest in his attire. Also, avoid excessive chess-playing and hunting," he said. "This is time better spent on jihad against the heretic inside the borders of Islam, and pushing those borders ever farther into the lands of the unbelievers."

"Did you say something about hunting?" Malik-shah asked. At last, something he knew about.

"I said it's fine in moderation, but too much time spent on it distracts from more important pursuits."

"Have you ever been hunting?"

"No."

"Let me tell you something. Hunting is war in rehearsal. Every minute I spend in the chase furthers the cause of jihad."

It was a good argument, but Ghazali went on as if the sultan hadn't said anything. "The Shari'ah is clear," he said. "First of all, there's Bukhari, book seventy-two . . ."

Bukhari, book seventy-two, was merely the first in a list of relevant citations. As he enumerated the rest, Ghazali ticked off each point on his fingers, drawing the sultan's gaze to his hands. They were soft hands, milky and fattish, without calluses, scars, or visible sinew. They were hands that had spent their life in academic combat without ever knowing a real battlefield. The sultan hated Ghazali's hands, and the hatred surged through his being like molten iron. Jumping to his feet, he bellowed, "Enough!"

"If you just let me finish, it would be clear that the next hadith, from *Sahih Muslim*—"

"Send for Nush-tegin!" To punctuate this demand, Malik-shah thrust one arm out to the side, accidentally smacking a slave. It was the server who had taken away the chicken stew and was now hurrying back with a whole roast lamb on an enormous platter. The unfortunate ovine splattered on the carpet in a shamble of juices, garnish, vegetables, and cooked-to-perfection sheep parts. Slaves scurried in all directions, some to clean up the sticky mess, others to find the sultan's cupbearer.

While Omar and the others waited for Nush-tegin, a hush ruled the sultan's table. Because Malik-shah's outburst was the last thing they heard, it echoed in their minds, over and over, like an unsolved problem in a bad dream. Their silence and discomfort rippled to other parts of the pavilion as other guests sensed something unpleasant had happened.

At last Nush-tegin appeared. Accomplished servant that he was, no one actually noticed him enter. He was just sort of there, passing out ruby-studded goblets from a tray, which also held a matching carafe.

As the cupbearer went about his business—unobtrusively, of course—Malik-shah tried to restore good humor by pretending that no disturbance had taken place. "This is a particularly fine vintage from Mosul," he said. "The monks at Saint Elijah's ferment it for communion, but they discovered a flourishing market for their surplus. Nush-tegin, see that everybody gets some."

Protests erupted around the table. Ghazali recited three verses from the Quran that prohibited drinking alcohol. Humaydi tried to throw in some citations of his own, but he was interrupted by the old professor of shari'ah, Abu Muhammad Tamimi, who quoted a hadith that prohibited buying, selling, and transporting the products of the vintner's art. Omar really wanted a drink, if only to get him through tonight's social fiasco, but he still tried to talk his royal friend out of damaging the reputation of the House of Seljuq. Alas, Omar's pleas bounced ineffectively off the sultan's resolve.

"I insist," the sultan said, the expression on his face like he was about to utter a sentence of death. To his satisfaction, most of the table gave in. Only three people had the strength of character to hold out: Abu'l-Abbas, Abu Hamid Ghazali, and Abu Abdullah Humaydi. It was no surprise that the sycophantic Humaydi aped Ghazali. As for the other two, perhaps the power of their faith compelled them to fear Allah more than they feared the sultan. Or perhaps they gambled that even in his ornery mood, Malik-shah would not harm the heir to the caliphate or the foremost scholar in Islam. The repercussions would be too spectacular.

Abu'l-Abbas spoke formally but sincerely. "This is my first time as a guest in a sultan's pavilion," he said. "May I request your guidance about something?" In one sentence he had put Malik-shah in his place by reminding the sultan that he was a host and, at the moment, not a very good one. And yet Abu'l-Abbas rebuked the sultan so gently that the sultan was utterly charmed.

"I'll guide you if I can," he replied. "What is your question?"

"I understand you have a son, Berk-yaruq, and that he is my age."

"Your grace honors our family by taking the time to learn about us," Taj al-Mulk said from across the table.

"I cannot claim any special credit for that," Abu'l-Abbas said. "From the Indus River to the Sea of Rum, everyone knows the House of Seljuq." He turned back to the sultan. "Whatever rules you lay down for Berk-yaruq, I will abide by them as well."

"Well, of course, he's only thirteen," Malik-shah hemmed. "I don't let him—"

"Then it's settled. I shall not drink either. The wishes of fathers shall always be respected in the Abbasid caliphate."

Was I outwitted by a thirteen-year-old boy? Malik-shah asked himself.

Abu'l-Abbas didn't give him time to consider the answer; the boy changed the subject. "I was quite interested in what you said about hunting," he said. "My father never took me on the chase. Perhaps during your stay in Baghdad you could teach me the basics."

No doubt about it, at thirteen Abu'l-Abbas was a skilled courtier. The guests around the table were so impressed they were speechless. Most of them anyway; Humaydi took advantage of the gap in conversation to get in a few words. "What a polite young man," he said. "It's a shame so few young people are brought up that way."

"What about you two?" the sultan asked Ghazali and Humaydi. "Will you drink with me?"

"We will not," Ghazali replied. He slapped both hands flat on the table to show his resolve. The dishes rattled faintly with the impact. "It is *haram*."

"Very well, then," Malik-shah said with finality. "But it won't do for you to do nothing while the rest of us drink. And therefore, by the grace of Allah, I, Malik-shah, son of Alp Arslan the Seljuq, King of the East and the West, Glory of the Nation, Master of the World, Builder of Bridges, and Slasher of Taxes, do sentence you . . ." But he no longer wore his death sentence face. The exchange with Abu'l-Abbas had restored good humor to the mercurial ruler, and any sign of murderous intent was gone. "I sentence you," he repeated, "to look after the sultan's companion."

Across the table, Taj al-Mulk was waving his hands wildly, desperate to dissuade the sultan from this new course. It almost seemed like he would have preferred a death sentence.

"And exactly who is this nitwit, the sultan's companion?" Ghazali asked.

"Bring the sultan's companion," Malik-shah shouted.

Nush-tegin had already anticipated the Sahib al-Jalal's commands. He stood beside two page boys who between them carried a trunk, beautifully polished and held together with gold studs. "Open it," Malik-shah ordered.

They swung the lid open to reveal a doll, perhaps two cubits in height and dressed in a mustard-colored robe and white turban. The realism of its painted face was remarkable, with a jolly smile and a beard made of genuine hair. One of its hands was curled around the stem of a goblet, of the same design that everyone else at the table had, but smaller. "Professor Ghazali will be first," the sultan said.

It was such a curious item, Ghazali apparently forgot that in addition to alcohol, human images were also *haram*. When Nush-tegin held it out to him, Ghazali took it and cradled it in his lap.

"You have a new friend," Omar teased.

"All right," Ghazali said. "I'm looking after it. Now what?" His voice was brusque.

"The sultan's companion drinks with us, of course," Malik-shah said. Nush-tegin filled the sultan's goblet, tasted it, nodded, and handed it to the sultan, who, still standing, waited to drink until his cupbearer had taken care of the others around the table. Then he tilted his head back and nearly emptied his cup in a single gulp. The maroon liquid went over his tongue so fast, he barely tasted it. But the burn at the back of his throat and the warm place in his belly accelerated his slide down the path of good humor.

Around the table, the others sampled their own cups. "Those monks—they know a thing or two about fermentation," Omar said. "As for us, we might have had some animosity around this table tonight, but,

"The Grape that can with Logic absolute
The Two-and-seventy jarring Sects confute:
     The sovereign Alchemist that in a trice
Life's leaden metal into Gold transmute."[67]

As Omar recited the verse, the sultan fidgeted and squeaked like a child who had something really important to say but had already been warned twice not to interrupt the grown-ups. With the word "transmute" still hanging in the air, and before anyone else could start a verse of his own, Malik-shah burst out with, "Yes, yes, that's very good, Omar. But I want to show what the sultan's companion does."

He looked at each face around the table in turn, partly for dramatic pause and partly to make sure everyone was paying attention to the miraculous thing that was going to happen. "Now," he said, clapping his hands together for emphasis, "not counting our abstainer friends, we all tasted the wine, except for the sultan's companion. And like any good courtier, he soaks up his master's leftovers." Malik-shah handed his goblet to Ghazali with a flourish. "Let him satisfy his thirst with this."

Ghazali stared at the cup in his hand—there was still about a quarter of a serving left—and then at the doll sitting on his lap. Then he looked back at the cup, obviously puzzled. By way of explanation, the sultan pantomimed pouring from one imaginary goblet into another. Ghazali got the message: he poured the liquid at the bottom of the sultan's goblet into that of the mannequin. As the tiny cup filled, the sultan's companion lifted it to his mouth and tilted back his head. When he lowered his arm again, his cup was empty. He grinned his painted-on grin and nodded rapidly in approval of the delicious wine.

"That's an amazing feat of engineering," Omar exclaimed. "Let me try!"

He scrambled over to Ghazali, practically grabbed the mannequin out of his arms, and carried it back to his own place. Ghazali made a show of being happy to be rid of the thing.

"Second cup," the sultan cried. He drank and this time gave Omar the goblet. Once again the sultan's companion performed his drinking trick.

"The mouth is just red paint. Where does the wine go?" Omar muttered. Deep in thought, he added, "*Whither hurried hence?*"[68]

He insisted on another turn. This time he observed more closely. "Ah, I understand now," he said. "The wine flows out the *bottom* of the cup. The doll must have a tube inside his arm to conduct it away. Now, one more time."

But Malik-shah didn't want the Astronomer Royal to investigate the mechanism too closely. He commanded Omar to pass the sultan's companion to someone else. Old Tamimi got a turn, and then the poet Abu Ishaq Ghazi. Each time, the sultan announced how many cups he had drunk, swallowed another three-quarters of a goblet, and passed it on to whomever held the doll. Some of his guests matched the sultan drink for drink. Each time he raised his cup, they cheered boisterously.

On the sixth cup, Malik-shah pretended to look around the circle for a volunteer, but he already knew who the victim would be. "Humaydi," he said, quite serious all of a sudden. "You haven't had a turn." The others at the table noticed the change in his mood and simmered down.

"Toys are for children," Humaydi groused. "Pick someone else."

"No, I insist."

By now Taj al-Mulk had given up on hand gestures and spoke directly to his brother. "You're drinking too much."

"This is the last cup," the sultan promised.

"There's still time to stop this."

"Why would I stop it? Everybody's having such a good time."

"But that's about to change, isn't it?"

Humaydi held the automaton awkwardly, but with help from Nush-tegin he got it settled in his lap.

"Sixth cup," the sultan announced. He drank and handed the goblet to Ghazali, who passed it to Humaydi. Malik-shah watched intently as the grizzled scholar poured.

The sultan's companion drained his cup and bobbed his head one more time. "There," Humaydi said, "I did it. Someone take this *haram* thing away from me."

But the sultan didn't respond. He kept watching Humaydi.

Humaydi glared back. "Is there something else?" he asked.

Ten seconds passed.

Suddenly Humaydi cried out, "What *is* that?" He jumped to his feet, letting everyone see what had startled him: a wet, red stain that was spreading across his robe where the doll had been sitting.

The sultan pointed at Humaydi and laughed. "Ha! Ha! Ha! Ha!" He laughed so hard it sounded like coughing. "It *peed* on you! Ha! Ha! Ha! Ha!" Maybe it sounded like choking.

Ghazali stood indignantly. "Is this how a prominent scholar of the Hadith and deputy director of the Nizamiyya is treated in the sultan's pavilion?"

Omar, meanwhile, retrieved the sultan's companion, which had fallen to the carpet when Humaydi jumped up. The doll's legs flopped about as Omar removed its robe to reveal a panel on its back. He pried it open with his knife. "This is incredible," he said. "The person who built this was a genius. There's a reservoir for the wine, and when the wine fills it up, there's a siphon, which . . ."[69]

But no one else was interested in engineering. Not amid the chaos of Humaydi's outrage, and onlookers gathering to see what had happened, and slaves blotting spilled wine from the carpet, and Mu'ayyad al-Mulk's running commentary on the "failure of the Taj al-Mulk administration."

Through it all, the sultan kept laughing. "It looks like you're menstruating," he shouted. "You're a woman. And you're menstruating."

Ghazali flashed Malik-shah the glare that he reserved for misbehaving students, but it only encouraged the sultan. "He's on the rag!"

Turning to Humaydi, Ghazali said, "If we leave now, we can be back in Baghdad by morning."

The two scholars picked their way out of the pavilion, stopping frequently to acknowledge expressions of sympathy from members of the ulama who shared their outrage. Back at the sultan's table, Taj al-Mulk looked sadly at his brother and shook his head. He mouthed three words: "You blew it."

*   *   *

"Why? They *pissed* me off, that's why."

It was only Malik-shah and his inner circle—Taj al-Mulk, Terken Khatun, Yalbard, Amid ad-Dawla, Abu Nasir, and the new finance minister, Abu'l-Fadl Qummi.

The party guests had gone to bed and the slaves had finished cleaning up. They had cleared away the dishes and snuffed out most of the lights. The large circular trays that served as tabletops had been removed; only their stands remained. In the morning, the soldiers responsible for tearing down the pavilion would pack them up. Stretching into the darkness, the array of spindly brass frames seemed to go on forever. The council of war sat around one of them, isolated by the circle of light cast by the few lamps still burning.

Malik-shah had reached the stage of drinking where he wondered when the joy had faded and why it left an undigested lump of regret in its place. The hangover could go either way. "I couldn't listen to Ghazali lecture me anymore," he tried to explain. No one replied. Except for Terken Khatun, no one even made eye contact; the others all seemed to find something fascinating about their boots and slippers.

The gloom and silence made Malik-shah feel like he was supposed to keep talking. "I bring out the sultan's companion all the time," he said defensively. "The emirs love it."

"I tried to tell you before," Taj al-Mulk said sadly. "The ulama are not the emirs."

"There's no profit in reliving what happened tonight," Terken Khatun interjected. "We can't erase it now. We have some decisions we have to make." A modest silk veil covered her nose and mouth, a wall of separation from the men present. "Eid al-Fitr is a week away," she said. "Are we going to be ready or do we have to change our plans?"

"We can't move forward without the ulama," Taj al-Mulk replied. "And we lost them tonight."

"Don't exaggerate," Malik-shah said. "I spent the whole evening with Ghazali. He didn't impress me as a force to be reckoned with."

"Well, he is. A week from Friday, the Blind Imam will climb the steps under Mansur's dome and deliver his sermon. At the end he'll invoke the blessings of Allah on the rulers of the land. When he does that, if Mahmud's name isn't among them, then it's over for us. The people of Baghdad will think there's no legitimacy to what we did. There will be rioting in the streets."

"So the Blind Imam is the man we need. *Sik* Ghazali."

The sultan was a soldier and his inner circle was used to his profanity. But this was no way to talk about the head of the Nizamiyya. Someone needed to say something. They looked at one another, but it was Taj al-Mulk's bad luck to be the senior official present.

"There is a reason Chief Professor Ghazali is so widely respected," he said. "No one in all your kingdom knows Allah's law better than he does. And that's why, when this all happens, the Blind Imam will turn to him for advice—and do whatever he recommends. We can't pull this off without Abu Hamid Ghazali."

Malik-shah was on the verge of an angry outburst. But then he felt his wife gently take his hand in hers. He turned to her to see what advice she might offer.

"You know how much I want this for Mahmud," Terken Khatun said "But it's time to face some unpleasant facts." In the oval between her veil and her hijab, her frustration with the ulama was apparent in her eyes; it was a bond between her and her husband. "We lost this round," she continued. "We'll have to go through the motions in Baghdad. Pay your respects to al-Muqtadi, worship at a few shrines. But cut the visit short. Stay only as long as necessary to save face. Then journey back to Isfahan before the snows of winter block the mountain passes. We'll regroup and maybe next year we can try again."

"If only the Nizam were still alive," Taj al-Mulk said. "He would have known what to do."

That mournful thought seemed to be the final word. The meeting started to break up. The sultan's advisors stood, said their good-byes, and started various side conversations. But Taj al-Mulk had gotten the sultan thinking. *What* would *Nizam al-Mulk do?* Malik-shah didn't know. What he did know was *how* the Nizam would go about figuring it out. He had lectured the sultan a thousand times: "The Messenger—may the prayer and peace of Allah be upon him—was the greatest man in the history of the world. His knowledge came straight from Allah. And yet even he had advisors. If he needed them, then you and I, who have not been blessed with the gift of prophecy, need them that much more. Obtain wise ones and listen to them. Assemble them in the same room and force them to debate in your presence." Malik-shah had five advisors assembled around a tray stand, and so far he had heard from only two.

"Everyone return to your *sikking* cushions!" he commanded. "Now! This meeting isn't over until I say it is. And it's too dark in here. Abu Nasir, light some more lamps."

Everyone hastened to obey. While the others scrambled to their seats, the intelligence chief lit a wooden splint from one of the lamps and spread the flame to several others. By the time he returned to his cushion, the space around the sultan's circle was noticeably brighter.

Malik-shah scanned his advisors, their faces and robes so much more vibrant now. "Amid ad-Dawla," he said. "We haven't heard from you yet. You're the caliph's vizier. You know his mind. You know the minds of the people around him. How's the mood in the Dar Calipha?"

Something in the sultan's tone made Amid ad-Dawla feel he should stand to present his report. "There will be no trouble from the palace staff. Or the guards," he said.

"Why are you so certain?" the sultan asked.

"I fired everyone I could and replaced them with my own men."

"You see," the sultan said to Taj al-Mulk. "The situation isn't as bad as you make it sound."

Taj al-Mulk was more skeptical. "What about the caliph himself?" he asked. "We're counting on taking al-Muqtadi by surprise. Does he suspect anything?"

"Nothing," Amid ad-Dawla replied. "Since everyone around him works for me now, it's easy to control what he hears."

"As long as he trusts *you*."

261

"The caliph thinks I'm his faithful servant. It has never occurred to him that my real loyalty might be to the sultan."

"Thank you, Amid ad-Dawla," the sultan said. The caliph's vizier took that as his cue to sit again. "Let's hear from the finance minister next. Abu'l-Fadl, have you been in touch with the House of Samha? Ben Samha was essential to our plans. Is his son going to be able to step in and fill his shoes?"

Now that the precedent had been established to stand while reporting, Abu'l-Fadl Qummi rose in turn. "Saad intends to report to you as soon as his mourning week is complete. He assures me that he will be ready."

"Excellent. Intelligence Chief, you're next. Are the streets of Baghdad as tense as Taj al-Mulk would have us believe?"

"The situation is fluid," Abu Nasir said. "We saw that yesterday. One moment the mob was literally spitting its hatred at Yalbard. The next they were his enthusiastic supporters—and therefore yours. I expect the mood will change again when they hear how Professor Ghazali was treated here tonight."

"And which will be the mood on Eid al-Fitr?"

"There's time for them to change their minds three times between now and then."

"Can't you give me a more definite answer than that?"

"I apologize, O Sahib al-Jalal. It really is that fluid. I don't know what the mob will do in the end, but I promise you it will be heartfelt, spontaneous, and dumb."

"What can we do to sway them in our favor?"

"They respect Islam," Abu Nasir replied. "The more you show your piety, the better off you'll be."

"Sounds like it's not as cut and dry as my vizier would have me believe."

Abu Nasir tried to backpedal—he hadn't intended to contradict Taj al-Mulk—but the sultan cut him off. "Yalbard."

The emir snapped to his feet but not without cost; the wounds on his back were still fresh. He winced at the effort but managed to belt out, "Yes, O Sahib al-Jalal."

"You saw the crowd in Baghdad closer than any of us. If there was any trouble, could you handle it?"

"Yes, O Sahib al-Jalal." He considered it his job to spare the sultan the details, but Taj al-Mulk felt otherwise.

"With or without bloodshed?" the vizier asked.

"With," Yalbard replied. "A lot of it."

That was everybody. Malik-shah needed to say something now. He looked around the circle and, to his surprise, everyone was looking back expectantly. They were *waiting* for him to say something. A sense of responsibility to get it right weighed on him as if the whole success or failure of his sultanate depended on his next words. Outside, the camp was coming to life with the approaching dawn. He could hear voices that tried not to wake anybody—but sometimes forgot—the hollow thuds of wooden chests being stacked, and the noise of some sort of minor confrontation at the entrance to his pavilion; it sounded like the slaves had arrived to set up breakfast and the guards were making them wait. *Everyone* was waiting for the sultan this morning.

But he took his time. When he finally figured out what he wanted to say, he stood to address the group. Everyone snapped to their feet along with him.

"Thank you all for giving me your opinions," he said. "I understand what you're telling me. If we move against the caliph, we face considerable risk.

"No one is better than me at making decisions about risk on the battlefield. But political decisions are new to me. I always left such concerns to the Nizam. What I'm starting to figure out is that being the sultan means that no one can make these decisions for me. I can listen to what all of you say. But then it's up to me.

"So here's what we're going to do. We will go ahead, as planned, and move against the caliph. That gives us one week to undo the damage I did tonight and bring Ghazali over to our side. And I think I know someone who can help us.

"Taj al-Mulk, speak to Omar Khayyam. Cautiously at first. Just hint at what we plan to do and get a sense of whether he's sympathetic. If he is, tell him everything and get him to talk to Ghazali. They're friends; Ghazali might listen to him."

Abu Nasir looked around to see if it would be permitted to speak. As no one else seemed inclined to do so, he said, "Sahib al-Jalal, Omar Khayyam has left the camp. He—"

Taj al-Mulk cut him off. "I'm sure Omar has merely gone back to Baghdad," he said. "We'll catch up with him tomorrow."

"What happens if he can't convince Ghazali?" Terken Khatun asked.

"That's where it gets tricky," the sultan said with a smile, as if he actually looked forward to the challenge. "We go ahead with the plan anyway. We present it to Ghazali as a fait accompli and appeal for his help to prevent the spilling of Muslim blood."

Taj al-Mulk brightened for the first time in hours. "That could actually work," he said.

But Qummi shook his head. "I'm not so sure. He'll say, 'Do you seriously expect me to help you prevent bloodshed that you were so dimwitted as to be responsible for?'" He did a passable imitation of Ghazali.

"He'll say it," Terken Khatun replied. "But then he'll help us anyway. He doesn't want to see corpses in the courtyard of the Nizamiyya any more than we do."

The sultan was suddenly cheerful. He wasn't sure what it was he had done right, but for the first time since the Nizam had died, the people around him seemed to be functioning as a team. "That concludes our affairs for now," he said. "Anyone who wants to stay and eat the *suhur* with me is welcome."

*　　*　　*

Abu Nasir and Taj al-Mulk passed on *suhur*, pleading urgent business before departing for Baghdad. On leaving the sultan's pavilion, they strolled together a little way along the main road of the camp. Neither of them had slept, but they were energized by the job ahead and the promise of morning. The eastern sky was starting to brighten ever so faintly. Not enough to see by, but the half moon, high in the sky, took care of lighting up the world around them. The air had the heaviness that presaged a challenging and sticky day on the road, but for the time being, the temperature was comfortable and the birds sang cheerfully.

When they were out of earshot of the sultan's guards, Abu Nasir turned to the vizier and said, "I didn't want to contradict you a second time in front of the sultan, but Omar Khayyam didn't go back to Baghdad. He ordered a couple post horses and galloped off in the other direction with his assistant."

Taj al-Mulk sighed. "I expected that."

"Does the vizier want me to do anything about it?"

Taj al-Mulk waited to reply until a slave carrying a basket of flatbread on her head passed them. Then he asked, "Got a man in Qazvin?"

"Of course. He's keeping an eye on the Assassins."

"The Assassins can wait. Send a post rider up north. Give him a message for your man: take care of our friend."

CHAPTER 12

BISOTUN, KERMANSHAH PROVINCE
SATURDAY, 25 RAMADAN 485

14 Abán 471

30 October 1092

*O*mar wanted to put as much distance between himself and the sultan's camp as possible before his unauthorized mission was discovered. He and Baghdadi rode all night. The safe-conduct from Malik-shah was like a jinn in a fairy tale: its magic adjured fresh horses and refreshment to materialize at every post station. By midmorning the Iraqi plain ended abruptly and a mountain range sprang from the ground in front of them like the cover of a half-open book. It made the farming villages nestling in its shadow look small and helpless.

The mountains slowed the travelers' progress. The Khorasan Highway wound through the peaks in search of the gentlest terrain. Most of the day was spent plodding through rocky passes, hemmed in by cliffs that barely let the sun through. It was after dark when they arrived at Kermanshah City. Baghdadi wanted to stop for the night, but since the gates were already locked, Omar insisted on riding another few farasangs. It wasn't until they heard the gurgle of the Gamasiab River, just outside the village of Bisotun, that Omar finally agreed to pitch their tent and grab some sleep.

*   *   *

When he noticed the walls of the tent had turned from black to a pale gray, Omar was too excited to go back to sleep. Baghdadi, in contrast, slumbered on, curled under a blanket and no doubt dreaming of Khuld. *It's nice to be young*, Omar thought. He dressed as quietly as possible, so as not to wake his assistant, and emerged through the tent flap into the bright sunshine. The autumn morning was cold, the temperature a little above freezing. Omar closed the front of his fur-lined cloak, fastened the laces, and surveyed the scenery. They had pitched their little tent at the edge of the river. The water was low this time of year, exposing rock-pile islands and patches of reeds, their tips burned yellow by last summer's sun. From the riverbank, a meadow stretched to the Khorasan Highway. A single drop of dew sparkled on each blade of grass. Here and there, clusters of bare trees grew. The dry smell of fallen leaves filled the air. The meadow crossed the road before halting abruptly at the base of a cliff, whose jagged face, gold in the sun, soared into the sort of unpolluted azure sky that was a rare treat for a city dweller like Omar.

The night before, when Omar had insisted on pushing on past Kermanshah, it was not merely to make a little extra progress on the road to Qazvin. He had chosen this particular campsite for a reason. There was something nearby he wanted to see. He checked on the horses—they were grazing happily, their breath visible in the cold air—and then crossed the road to search for a famous set of stairs. His mother had told him the story of those stairs many times at bedtime, decades ago and half an empire away.

There once lived a sculptor named Farhad. This was during the reign of Khosrau the Second, the last great king of Persia before Arab invaders blessed the land with the Quran. The hardworking Farhad had the misfortune to fall in love above his station; the object of his affection was no less than the queen, Shirin. Eager to eliminate a rival, King Khosrau banished Farhad from his capital, commanding him not to return until he had carved a staircase into the cliff at Bisotun. It was an impossible task, but, eager to be united with his love, Farhad toted his hammer and chisel to the mountainside and was soon hard at work. Alas, Khosrau's plan backfired. As reports of Farhad's progress reached the palace, Queen Shirin began to have feelings for the humble man who sacrificed so much for her sake. Khosrau was not pleased and devised a new stratagem: he sent Farhad a letter, telling him that Shirin had died. Filled with grief, the love-stricken sculptor threw himself from the top of his staircase and plummeted to his death.

Farhad was dead, but as Omar soon discovered, his limestone staircase remained. Time had worn it down; Omar had to step carefully as he made his way up the cliff. About two hundred cubits above the road, Omar found what he had gotten up early to see: an ancient carving on the face of the cliff. The bas-relief depicted Khosrau, looking cocky with his long, rectangular beard and stylish robes, grinding his heel into the chest of a vanquished foe. Nearby, a string of captives were led before him in chains. The captives were, of course, much shorter than the king. Hovering above the scene, as if directing it, a guardian spirit rode a winged throne. He raised his hand as if to bless the triumphant monarch. Omar had seen the flying guardian motif before. It was called the *faravahar*, and fire worshippers had carved it into thousands of monuments all over Persia during the Time of Ignorance.

Around the scene, some sort of glyphs were etched into the stone. They were like little triangles with handles; Omar had seen these before too, on ancient clay tablets. Apparently they were gouged into the wet clay using a wedge-shaped tool. But gouging wet clay is easy. Carving a limestone cliff was far more difficult. Someone hundreds of years ago, possibly Farhad himself, had gone to a lot of trouble to transmit a message to future generations. There must have been a thousand lines of the neat writing. But the secret of the message had been lost during the long centuries: Omar was unable to read the ancient inscription. As far as he knew, there was no one alive who could. He opened his writing kit and began to copy a portion of the text; perhaps someday he would take a crack at deciphering it and learn who had carved the mysterious message and why.[70]

After he filled several pages with the symbols, Omar climbed down to the road and explored the rest of the site. Near his campsite he found the ruins of a palace. Some fifty rooms were arranged around a rectangular courtyard. Here and there pillars stretched skyward to support a roof that was no longer there. The walls, or what was left of them, were little more than knee-high. The stones were expertly fitted together. It was evident that the kings who built this place had hired only the most skilled craftsmen.

It was a peaceful spot. Grass sprouted from spaces that had once been floors. The scent of evergreen wafted from a nearby grove, where birds flitted from tree to tree. Omar thought of the ancient Arab poems, from the days before Muhammad. A common poetic device existed where a traveler, roaming the desert at night, stumbles on an abandoned campsite, which leads him to reflect on some long-ago romance—a lament on what was lost. Sitting on one of the walls, Omar indulged in some reflection on his own losses, albeit not of the romantic variety. It was quite moving to see the ruins in the wake of Nizam al-Mulk's death. *A poignant reminder of the transient nature of all we accomplish*, he mused. *Centuries ago, the world groveled in terror before the kings who ruled from this palace. And now broken walls are all that's left. Two weeks ago the world groveled in terror before Nizam al-Mulk. And now . . .*

A ringdove landed in the courtyard a few feet from Omar. Admiring her smooth, snowy feathers and the black ring that nearly circled her neck, Omar said, "You're a pretty little girl. And so brave. I'm not the first tourist you have associated with, am I? Let's see if I've got some bread for you." He fished in his pocket and found a crust he had been saving for later. He tore off a few crumbs and dropped them on the ground. The dove hopped from one to the next and pecked at them happily.

"You're not fasting for Ramadan, I see. I'm not either." Omar popped a morsel into his own mouth. "I don't have to, because I'm on an expedition. What's your excuse?" The dove looked around for more crumbs, and not finding any, jumped up onto the wall, perched next to Omar, and pecked at the bread in his hand.

"Do you ever reflect on the fate of kings?" Omar asked. The bird cocked its head and looked at him quizzically with reddish-brown eyes. "No, I suppose you don't."

Having satisfied its appetite, the ringdove settled into a crouch, puffed out its chest, and trilled pleasantly. Omar petted the bird gently on the head. Then he opened his pen case and began to write.

> The Palace that to Heav'n his pillars threw,
> And Kings the forehead on his threshold drew—
>   I saw the solitary Ringdove there,
> And "Coo, coo, coo," she cried; and "Coo, coo, coo."[71]

*　　*　　*

Omar was putting the finishing touches on his poem when a yawning Baghdadi stumbled out of the tent and found Omar among the ruins. Omar made a second trip up Farhad's staircase for Baghdadi's benefit. As he pointed out the various features of interest, his melancholy melted away and he became quite enthusiastic. "Observe the exquisiteness of the stonework," he said. "The expressiveness of the faces. The sadness in the prisoners. The nobility of the king. And look at these folds in the king's robes. Like real fabric draped over his thigh."

Back at the base of the cliff, they spread out a blanket in the ruins of the palace and enjoyed a picnic breakfast of flatbread and figs.

"I think, Khwaja, that you enjoyed being my tour guide," Baghdadi said.

"I did," Omar replied. "It's hard to explain to someone like yourself, someone who doesn't trace his nativity to Persia. But these ancient sites, they have great meaning for us. We're incredibly proud of them. Our forebearers built this amazing civilization centuries before the Arabs rode out of their peninsula to bless the world with Islam."

"Yes, I think I got some flavor of that from reading the *Shah-nama*. It actually seemed sad at the end when the Muslims came. All the Persian characters were in tears as they said their good-byes to one another."

"The *Shah-nama* changed the whole outlook for Persians. For four centuries we had been ruled by Arab caliphs, our history nearly forgotten. Then, as the caliphate was losing its grip, Ferdowsi wrote this wonderful epic poem that brought Rostam, and Bahram Gur, and all the other ancient heroes to life. And he wrote it in our own language."

Baghdadi looked around at the ruins. "The Persian kings must have been quite rich and powerful to build such remarkable monuments," he said. "It's truly a miracle of Allah that the early Muslims were able to defeat them."

It seemed to Omar that this was Baghdadi's way of asking to resume their lessons; they hadn't read a chapter of Aristotle together since before the fire at ben Samha's home. Omar couldn't think of anything Aristotle had to say that was relevant—the philosopher had little interest in history—but Omar did have a theory of his own. "The Muslims had something that the Persians didn't," he said. "They had an idea."

"What do you mean?" Baghdadi asked.

"Do you remember the episode in the *Shah-nama* about Qadisiyyah?"

"Of course. That was the battle that sealed the doom of the Persian kings."

"Right. So you remember that on the eve of the battle, the opposing generals went through the motions of trying to talk each other out of it and thereby avoid bloodshed. The Persian general wrote to his counterpart about the hopelessness of the Muslim cause. He boasted about the great wealth of the Persians and the nobility of lineage of their king, who commanded war elephants and hunting dogs and the moon. The Muslim general wrote back that jewels and elephants and hunting dogs were merely things of this world. He urged the Persians to embrace the vision of Muhammad and ensure a place for themselves in the Garden where rivers flow and houris serve wine and honey. The Muslims believed in something bigger, something more noble than jewels and hunting dogs.

"When a person takes a belief into his heart, it transforms him. He labors late into the night, depletes his wealth, pushes his body to its limits, and plunges into the midst of battle to achieve his vision, with his blood if necessary. This is how the Muslims differed from my Persian ancestors. They believed in something. They had a shining vision of heaven. The Persians, in contrast, had a proud history, but by then it was more of a burden than a source of strength. Perhaps their civilization had reached its natural limits. All they had to fight for was the status quo. And when the combat at Qadisiyyah went on longer than anyone expected, and became a battle of stamina, the Muslims had an edge that, in the end, let them smash the Persian forces and bring the word of Allah into Persia."

"But if the Muslims' idea was so much better," Baghdadi asked, "didn't Ferdowsi take a step backward by glorifying Persian history? Shouldn't we shun monuments like these, which date from the Time of Ignorance?"

"That's the genius of the Muslims," Omar replied. "Because—and now I speak as a Persian *and* a Muslim—we borrowed from our neighbors and the people that we conquered, and we made their ideas our ideas. Persia, India, and especially Greece are the foundation stones of our civilization— almost as much as the Quran. Did you know that when the caliph Harun ar-Rashid—three centuries ago—won battles against Rum, he demanded ancient Greek manuscripts as part of the tribute?

"We commenced with the faith of Muhammad and the Companions, and we fused it with the philosophy of Aristotle and the Greeks. We saw further than those who came before us, because we stood atop a tower of ideas that they constructed."

"Not everyone shares your view," Baghdadi pointed out. "Chief Professor Ghazali says that Greek ideas *polluted* Islam. He says we have to return to the 'pure' faith of the Messenger—may the prayer and peace of Allah be upon him."

"I know," Omar said. Suddenly he seemed tired, as if, like the Persian civilization, he too had run up against his natural limits. "A lot of people agree with him."

"Do you think they'll have an influence?"

"I'm sorry to say they already do. Sixty, eighty years ago Biruni was investigating whether the earth rotates. Ibn Haytham was figuring out how the eye works. Avicenna was making breakthroughs in . . . well, Avicenna made breakthroughs in everything. Now we still have scientists, but there's absolutely nobody of that caliber."

"There's you," Baghdadi said.

"See what I mean?" Omar replied. "Don't misunderstand me. Muslim science is still going strong, but it feels like it's past its peak. I loved Nizam al-Mulk as if he were my father, but there are times when I wish he had never built those damn Nizamiyyas. Now all the best minds go in for the study of shari'ah instead of science."

"Do you think Chief Professor Ghazali will have his way and Muslims will give up altogether on Greek science someday?"

"Allah have mercy on us if they do. Because . . ." Omar swept his arm in a semicircle in front of him, past broken pillars, collapsed walls, and moss-covered stones. "Well," he said, "you know what happens if you knock the foundation out from under a tower."

CHAPTER 13

BAGHDAD
SATURDAY, 25 RAMADAN 485
14 Abán 471
30 October 1092

*K*huld set down her pen and read through the letter. She shook her head with dissatisfaction. If only she had more to report. *In the Name of Allah, the Merciful and Compassionate*, it began.

Dear Father,

This is the first report of the mission you gave me, to spy on the women of the court and learn what I can about the murder of Nizam al-Mulk.

I'm sorry I didn't write yesterday. I had nothing to say. Terken Khatun and her entourage got to the palace late last night. It was chaos: a hundred ladies, with handmaids, eunuchs, and children in tow, all jockeying for the best rooms and trying to find their luggage. We had a token breaking of the fast, but Terken Khatun waited until tonight to hold the first "official" *iftar* of her stay in Baghdad.

It was a gala affair. You were right to make me get some new dresses—I really would have stood out otherwise. Once the guests were behind the walls of the harem, safe from prying eyes, they took off their chadors to reveal the stunning gowns underneath. The colors and fabrics were spectacular. All the leading ladies of the city and the court were here.

They're all idiots. Except Terken Khatun. I'm worried this mission is a waste of time; they don't know anything. I should have come to Qazvin with you. Khursheed—Professor Humaydi's third wife—could barely string a sentence together. She's about a hundred years old. She just sits there without saying anything. Which is a big improvement over Abu Shuja's wife, Kifah. She won't stop talking about how she's getting new carpets. Apparently her husband told her a few days ago and it was this big surprise. Until then he kept saying he couldn't afford it. Now colors and floral patterns are all she has on her mind. But the prize goes to Qurratulain, who is Mu'ayyad al-Mulk's principal wife. She spent the whole time bad-mouthing Taj al-Mulk. Clearly she wants Terken Khatun to use her influence with the sultan to get Taj al-Mulk fired and replaced with her husband. But she went about it so clumsily, it was obvious to everyone that's what she was doing. Stupidity and cunning don't mix. Qurratulain had a black eye, by the way—I'm not sure how she got it—but it was pretty clear that Terken Khatun wanted to give her another one to match.

I was going to write that I'm ashamed of my sex. But then I decided it's your sex that should be ashamed, because you made us that way. This is what you get when men don't give their daughters any education other than some basic reading of the Quran. Not you personally, of course, because you can't resist giving a lecture to anyone, but men in general.

Oh, Terken Khatun is trying to find out where you are. She's too clever to ask me directly. But she keeps starting conversations with "Your father was so much help when the sultan was angry with Taj al-Mulk. I hope I get a chance to thank him soon," or "Did your father ever visit Jerusalem? It's such a beautiful, historical city." She has also managed to slip Damascus, Hamadan, Isfahan, and, yes, Qazvin, into the conversation. I haven't told her anything.

I enclose a letter for Baghdadi. Don't read it! I expect you to take good care of him and not expose him to danger.

As she set the letter aside, the paper rustled gently and she realized something felt different about her surroundings. It took her a moment to figure out what: quiet. The jumble of female voices that had chattered continuously since early this morning was now hushed. Khuld rose from her cushion, tiptoed to the door of her room, and opened it noiselessly, just far enough to see what was going on in the hallway. It was a long arcade with candles at regular intervals flickering in brass sconces. Two black eunuchs stood sentry at the door to Terken Khatun's room, and two others patrolled the corridor, their slippers gliding noiselessly over the polished floor. Aside from these four men, the hallway was empty. The women of the harem had gone to bed. It was time for Khuld to begin her own patrol.

She didn't go out into the hallway, though. Not with the guards there. Instead, she closed her door and crossed the room to the far wall. Beneath the window, a wood panel adorned the wall, elaborately carved with interlinking hexagons. When she pressed one of the hexagons just so, the panel swung open to reveal the entrance to a secret passageway.

Khuld had known about this passage—and many others like it—for several days. After all, she had Terken Khatun's apartments practically to herself for almost a week. It had been the perfect opportunity to prepare for her mission. By the time the court arrived, Khuld had memorized every corridor, chamber, stick of furniture—and secret passageway. She discovered the latter because she had wondered why the outer walls of the palace were so thick—over two cubits in depth. A few minutes fiddling with the wood panel under her window had revealed the secret. These passages perforated walls throughout the palace like tunnels in an ant hill; this particular one stretched the entire length of the women's wing.

The floor of the passage was two or three cubits lower than the floor of Khuld's room. That had puzzled her for a while, until she realized it had been designed that way so that people traversing the tunnel could get past the windows—by walking under them.

The split-level arrangement did necessitate some minor gymnastics on Khuld's part, but she was well-practiced by now. She ducked into the opening, sat on the edge with her legs dangling, and let herself drop down. Then she closed the entrance panel behind her—it was now at eye level—and began her rounds.

The problem with secret passageways is that they're secret. The servants don't know about them—or at least they aren't supposed to—so no one cleans them and no one replaces the candles when they burn out. Those tales in *The Thousand and One Nights*, where the plucky hero discovers a hidden storeroom stuffed with gold and jewels, always seemed to leave out how dark and filthy such places were.

Khuld solved the darkness problem by bringing her table lamp. A special contraption she had bought on her last shopping trip with Baghdadi, it featured a set of louvers that she could adjust to control the brightness. When she showed it to her father, and he discovered that the flame kept burning even when the louvers were shut, it was all she could do to stop him from taking it apart. He kept saying, "I want to see how the air flow works."

As for the cleanliness problem, Khuld's solution was a strip of fabric over her nose and mouth to filter out dust and the odor of mildew. So her father had finally gotten her to wear a veil. On her feet she wore a sensible pair of shoes, an old pair, which she didn't mind getting dirty.

She walked to the end of the tunnel, her feet slipping now and then on the dusty floor. Although two cubits was wide for a wall, it was narrow for a passageway. Khuld practically held her breath to avoid brushing against the mixture of mortar dust and cobwebs that coated the bricks on either side of her. The lamplight skimmed dark panels set at regular intervals in the sand-colored brick—portals to the rooms of Terken Khatun and the other senior ladies. Khuld would explore them on the return trip.

She passed a dozen such apertures, and then the tunnel came to an abrupt end. Directly in front of her was one last panel. Khuld shut the louvers on her lamp so that the people on the other side wouldn't know she was there. Then she probed the panel with her fingertips until she felt what she was looking for: a tiny door, at eye level, about the size of a square on a chessboard. Opening it revealed a peephole into the room beyond. Khuld knew from her earlier reconnaissance that on the other side of the panel was a wooden carving, similar to the one in her own room. Hidden in the recesses of the carving, the peephole was invisible to all but those who looked for it.

Khuld peered through the opening into a large room where the most junior members of the harem—the slaves who did the serving and housekeeping—lived together. The viewing angle was odd; because of the geometry of the tunnel, Khuld had to look up into the room from a point knee-level above the floor. Still, she could clearly see piles of women's chemises, trousers, and robes. Apparently the slaves' duties kept them too busy to look after their own quarters. Most of them were sleeping, curled on blankets scattered among the stacks of clothing. A few snored; their rhythmic snuffles seemed loud in the otherwise silent room. Those who were still awake labored at various domestic tasks by lamplight—emergency sewing, mostly.

As nothing seemed to be happening, Khuld closed the peephole and started back in the direction she had come. As planned, she stopped at the first room she came to; it belonged to the sultan's concubines and was far more luxurious than the quarters of the domestic slaves. Khuld spied women drowsing on mattresses draped with beautiful quilted coverlets. No sewing, at least not in the parts of the room Khuld could see; other parts hid their secrets beyond the range of the peephole or behind silk curtains. No snoring either. This was not surprising, as the women had been screened not only for snoring but also for body odor, bad breath, and tummy gurgles. Indeed, Terken Khatun saw to the screening personally, bringing each prospective concubine into her own bed for a night before the candidate could be admitted to the harem.

Khuld was on her way to the next room, her lamp lighting the path ahead of her, when suddenly she heard the scrape of wood on wood. She felt a jolt of panic as the realization struck her that someone else was opening a panel and entering the passage. Khuld yanked the lever on her lamp to close the louvers again. Halfway down the hall, a trapezoid of light burst into view, and the shadow of another woman dropped into the passageway. She moved gracefully but without stealth; clearly she was not concerned about getting caught. The new arrival picked up a lamp that she had left in the entry, and Khuld recognized Terken Khatun, apparently on the same errand as Khuld. No wonder the sultan's wife knew everything that went on in the harem.

Khuld retreated to the shadows at the end of the hall, her sensible shoes gliding noiselessly over the stone floor. Terken Khatun, dressed in an open robe and silk chemise, held up her lamp and looked both ways. Pressed against the wall, Khuld prayed that the lamplight was too weak to give her away. She waited anxiously to see which way Terken Khatun would turn. If the sultan's wife went to the left, she would soon discover Khuld, trapped at the portal to the slaves' room.

Terken Khatun turned right. Away from Khuld. That gave Khuld more time, but she wasn't out of danger. Eventually, Terken Khatun would reach Khuld's room and discover through the peephole that it was empty.

Stupid! Khuld berated herself. *Why didn't I stuff some pillows under the coverlet?*

Stopping at the first panel beyond her own room, the sultan's wife viewed the scene on the other side of the peephole. Her lamp continued to burn as she did so. It didn't have louvers. Despite her predicament, Khuld couldn't help but congratulate herself for taking better precautions than a veteran sneak.

The room under surveillance belonged to the first lady-in-waiting, but apparently nothing was going on there, because Terken Khatun soon moved on to the next room, the one belonging to the second lady-in-waiting. Not a surprise—the first lady-in-waiting was seventy-five years old and had no doubt been asleep for hours. But it meant there was only one more room (the third lady-in-waiting's) before Terken Khatun got to Khuld's.

Khuld's mind raced. How to get out of this predicament? When Terken Khatun discovered Khuld's empty room, she would certainly go inside to investigate. That would give Khuld an opportunity to escape the secret passage through one of the other rooms. Then she could return to her own quarters through the front door; Terken Khatun would think she was coming from the water closet. She imagined how proud Baghdadi would be when she told him how brave and clever she had been. But which room could she use to make her getaway? Who would sleep through it or, failing that, who could she trust to keep her secret?

By now Terken Khatun was up to the third lady-in-waiting's room. Khuld's room was next. It occurred to her that Terken Khatun's own room was empty. Perhaps Khuld could escape through there.

Apparently there were some goings on in the third lady-in-waiting's room, because Terken Khatun lingered several long minutes at the peephole. Still huddled in the shadows at the far end of the corridor, Khuld desperately thought through all the things that could go wrong with her plan—and realized it couldn't possibly work. She had forgotten the two eunuchs standing guard outside Terken Khatun's door.

Terken Khatun was on the move again, her curiosity about the third lady-in-waiting satisfied. She approached Khuld's room and took hold of the tiny knob on the portal; the peephole cover swung open. The sultan's wife inclined her head closer to the aperture to get a better view.

The man in the passageway didn't have a lamp. That's how he got so close. Khuld wasn't even conscious of his presence in the tunnel until he was practically on top of Terken Khatun. He must have come from some other part of the palace through a connecting passageway. Apparently Terken Khatun didn't know he was there either, because when he materialized behind her and whispered something in her ear, she spun around, startled, and dropped her lamp. The flame sputtered out amid a musical crash of brass on stone; darkness spread and filled the passage.

Terken Khatun was in danger and Khuld didn't know what to do. Petrified, she felt like she was trapped in that cold-sweat moment between waking from a nightmare and figuring out it wasn't real. She heard whispered voices, wet sounds like slurping soup, and a series of brief female gasps. What was this strange man inflicting on the sultan's wife in a mildewed, claustrophobic secret passageway in the dark? Khuld's mind raced through a landscape of malignant possibilities.

When she finally hit on the answer, her mouth dropped open and she almost gave herself away with a gasp of her own. She felt warmth and the ability to move seep back into her body as she realized she had misread the situation. Those slurping noises were nothing more—and nothing less—than kisses. The only danger Terken Khatun faced was getting caught by her husband. Khuld had glimpsed the man in the corridor for only a moment before the light went out, not long enough to get a look at his face. But whoever he was, this lover of Terken Khatun, he definitely was *not* Malik-shah. For one thing, he was too tall. Besides, if the sultan wanted to kiss his wife, he didn't need to sneak around secret corridors.

Khuld heard footsteps and the swish of hands sliding along the wall as the two lovers felt their way down the corridor. They opened the panel to Terken Khatun's room and a dusty beam of light shot across the hallway. Lifting Terken Khatun by the waist, the man whirled her around and seated her on the ledge of the portal. Then he scrambled up after her and extended a hand to help her stand. The panel shut behind them and once again Khuld was in the dark.

Khuld scurried after them and squinted through the peephole into Terken Khatun's room. It occurred to her that the sultan's wife had been careless by not blocking it. Khuld smirked. For the second time tonight, she felt superior to her hostess.

As first wife, Terken Khatun merited the largest room, and it was huge. Five or six pointed arches took the measure of each wall. Scattered around the floor, forests of candles burned on iron stands and dozens of wooden chests spilled their cargos of silk-stuffs. But these luxuries were on the periphery of Khuld's field of view. The center was dominated by the bed, a carved wood monstrosity with an overstuffed mattress and heaps of pillows. Seen through the low peephole, it towered like some kind of siege engine.

Terken Khatun sat down on the edge of the bed and patted the mattress to invite the man to join her. But having come this far, crawling through hidden panels and navigating dusty passageways, he seemed unable to walk the last few feet. He stood at attention, his back to Khuld, unresponsive to Terken Khatun's come-hither glance.

"What's the matter?" the sultana asked.

"This is a mistake," he replied. "I shouldn't have come." The voice was familiar; Khuld was sure it was someone she had talked to in the past few days, but she couldn't place it.

"I'm glad you did," Terken Khatun replied in a sultry voice. "I missed you."

The man shook his head. "This thing," he said, "this thing between you and me. It's wrong. We both know it. For the love of Allah, you're my brother's wife."

Of course, Khuld thought. *Taj al-Mulk.*

"Perhaps I can change your mind," Terken Khatun said. She got up from the bed and walked around Taj al-Mulk so that she stood between him and the peephole. And then she started to peel off her clothes. From her vantage point, all Khuld could see of the sultana were the royal legs, wrapped in a silk robe. Then the robe slipped to the floor and crumpled in a heap by Terken Khatun's embroidered slippers. Next she pulled off her chemise. The garment jerked upward, out of sight, and then, like magic, rematerialized, sailing across the room. It landed on Taj al-Mulk's head; he pulled it off with one hand and gathered the fabric under his nose, the better to take in the scent of his lover. Earlier, in the passageway, Khuld had gotten a whiff of the sultana's perfume; she knew that Taj al-Mulk was inhaling a sticky brew of orange blossoms and musk, now infused with the acrid smoke of burning candles.

It was too much for him. He spun around and in an instant closed the distance between himself and Terken Khatun. Violently, he swept her up in his arms and carried her to the bed.

"Wait, my shoes," she squealed, squirming in his arms to kick the slippers off her feet. They landed on the floor just as he tossed her on to the mattress. Khuld thought it was the most romantic thing she had ever seen: the reluctant lover, overcome with passion, despite his better judgment.

But then he hopped up onto the bed himself, landing with a bounce, and for the first time since he had appeared in the secret passage, Khuld saw his face. He wore an expression of misery, the expression of a man who was too weak to resist temptation and too noble not to be ashamed of it. Not so romantic after all.

As for Terken Khatun, having conquered her lover, she was in no hurry to give him satisfaction. She sat back against the pillows, her naked breasts thrusting forward victoriously. Khuld had seen women's breasts at the baths many times, but this was the first time they appeared to her as something erotic. And Terken Khatun's were lovely. Not large, but firm and shapely, with dark nipples.

It was clear from the smile on her face that the sultana knew the effect she had on her brother in-law, but all she said was "Get your boots off the duvet."

"Fine," Taj al-Mulk replied, obedient and defiant at the same time. He shifted his position so that his feet hung over the edge of the mattress. "Is that any way to talk to the sultan's new vizier?" he asked with mock injury.

Terken Khatun ran one hand over the stubble of his shaved head and gently slapped each cheek to feel the week's worth of newly grown beard. "I don't like it," she said.

"I figured that if I were to be vizier, I should look the part."

"Where is it written that looking the part means looking like a Persian? The whole idea was supposed to be that you're the *Turkish* vizier."

"One step at a time. Let people get used to the idea—by giving in on the superficial things."

"You give in on too many things. And you worry too much about what people think. What about what *I* think? I miss your braids."

"Then I'll grow them back." He gave her another kiss. This one seemed to go on forever.

"I missed *you*," she added when she finally came up for air.

"We saw each other every day on the road."

"Not like this. Not alone. One beautiful night in my pavilion. That's all we had. The rest of the time I couldn't discuss things with you. I couldn't kiss you."

"Then we have missed kisses to make up for." But when he tried to kiss her again, she broke it off abruptly. "*Or* we could make up for missed discussions," he said, resigned. He rolled back against the pillows.

"I'm so frustrated," Terken Khatun said.

"Malik-shah?"

She nodded.

"Tell me about it," Taj al-Mulk said. "The meetings go on for hours. 'Taj al-Mulk do this. Taj al-Mulk do that.' His newfound passion for 'doing government' is fun." His sarcasm was evident.

But Terken Khatun wanted to talk about her own problems. "I can't get him to see my way about Mahmud."

"Does he still want to settle the succession on Berk-yaruq?"

"He won't budge."

"He'll budge," Taj al-Mulk said. "He always does eventually. Be patient."

The sultana jumped off the bed and spun around to confront her lover. "I can't afford to be patient," she said angrily. "If anything happens to Malik-shah, and Berk-yaruq becomes sultan, you know what will happen to me. Cast out of the palace and forced to live out my life on a pittance in some miserable house for dowagers. Unwanted. Powerless. And then, on those rare, 'special' occasions when I'm called upon to come to court, I'll be forced to watch that imbecile Zubayda flutter about as Queen Mother. How she will lord it over the rest of us." Terken Khatun wiped a tear from her cheek. "Is that the life you want for me?"

"Of course not." Taj al-Mulk took her arm and pulled her back onto the bed. "Do you want me to intervene with Malik-shah?"

"Good luck with that. He's been annoyingly independent lately. I think Omar Khayyam had something to do with it."

"I wouldn't worry about Omar Khayyam."

"He still thinks you're involved in the murder of Nizam al-Mulk."

"*Everyone* thinks I'm involved in the murder of Nizam al-Mulk," he said as he nuzzled the back of her neck. Then, in a whisper, he added, "*You* think I'm involved in the murder of Nizam al-Mulk."

She pulled away and jerked her head around to face him. "You need to take this seriously."

"You're so tense. Let me help." He kneeled on the bed behind her and massaged her shoulders. His fingers kneaded the sinews of her upper back, squeezing the tension away. "If it's any consolation, my brother is getting annoyed with Khwaja Omar," he said. "He's been asking for him all day—without a response. He's counting on Omar to intercede with Ghazali."

"Omar left the court at Nahrawan. Why hasn't anyone told my husband?"

"Why haven't you?"

"I want to find out where he is first."

"You don't know?" In his surprise, he stopped massaging her shoulders. "You're slipping."

"Did I give you permission to stop?" she replied. When he resumed the back rub, she added, "I tried to get information out of Khuld, but either she excels at keeping secrets or her father didn't tell her anything. Wherever Omar Khayyam has gone off to, no one seems to know."

"Almost no one," Taj al-Mulk said with a sly smile.

Terken Khatun spun around and slapped his chest backhanded. "Why didn't you tell me?"

"And miss out on getting slapped?"

She raised her hand to slap him again—on the face this time—but apparently he didn't like getting slapped *that* much. He grabbed her wrist and stopped her. Before she got a chance to try again with the other hand, he blurted, "Qazvin. Omar is on his way to Qazvin."

Terken Khatun wriggled free from her lover's grasp. "I thought I put a stop to this Qazvin business," she muttered. She poured herself a goblet of wine from the carafe on the nightstand. Then she got up and paced the room several times, sipping from the goblet and trying to think things through. "This isn't good," she said.

On her fourth lap past the bed, Taj al-Mulk grabbed her free hand. "If Omar thinks he can find the Nizam's killer by going to Qazvin, let him," he said. "What's that to you and me? *We* don't have anything to hide." Then he frowned, as if struck by a disconcerting idea. "Do we?" he asked.

"Don't we?" she replied with desperation.

Taj al-Mulk stood and looked at her reassuringly. Without breaking eye contact, he took the goblet from her, returned it to the nightstand, and, holding both her hands, said, "Don't worry. I have a man waiting for him in Qazvin. He'll keep an eye on things. Omar won't cause any trouble, I promise."

"That's not good enough! You have to stop him. Order your man to arrest him and turn him over to the governor."

"He can't do that. It'll blow his cover."

"The governor doesn't know who he is? Why not?"

"Because the governor is who he's there to spy on. Omar and the Assassins are just distractions."

"Fine. Tell the governor to arrest Omar."

"I can't do that. Omar hasn't done anything."

Terken Khatun's demeanor softened. She took one of Taj al-Mulk's hands and guided it over her breast. "Does there have to be a reason?" she asked. "Isn't it good enough that I asked for it?"

"It's just that—"

She didn't let him finish that thought. "I can make you do it," she said.

"And how will you do that?"

"Skills. I have skills."

"What skills?"

Instead of answering, she showed him. She wriggled out of her trousers, folded them, and placed then neatly on a nearby trunk. Then returning to the bed, she pushed him with splayed fingers against his chest, a chest made hard by decades with the bow. It was a gentle push, with a flourish at the end, but it was enough to send him sprawling backward on the bed. Then she stepped back to give him a better view of what was to come.

The only parts of Terken Khatun visible to Khuld now were her feet and calves, shimmering gold in the candlelight. But Khuld could see the rest of the sultana's nakedness reflected in Taj al-Mulk's expression. He tried to appear master of the situation, slowly taking off his clothes, pursing his lips as he assessed the sultana like a connoisseur appraising a fine piece of calligraphy. But his eyes betrayed him. They held no shame now, only passion. If Malik-shah were to burst in at that moment, Taj al-Mulk would have sprung from the bed, grabbed his sword, and cut his brother down with a stroke.

As Terken Khatun approached the bed, her firm bottom and well-defined back came into view. Khuld felt like she should look away and yet she couldn't. It wasn't the nudity that cast the spell on her; it was the way Terken Khatun carried herself—as if she controlled the situation and knew it. As part of her education, Khuld's father had taught her the biology of men and women, but it all seemed clinical, without much in it for the daughters of Eve. But he neglected to mention that for a woman who knew how to use it, sex was power. Physically, Taj al-Mulk was an epic hero, another Rostam. Yet for all his muscles he sat back helplessly on the mattress while Terken Khatun slinked toward him, her long, slender body dappled by candlelight. Khuld imagined that it was her bearing down on the bed, and Baghdadi lying there, skinnier than Taj al-Mulk for sure, but with the same mix of anxiety and desire on his face. She felt a warm glow deep inside.

Terken Khatun climbed onto the bed. Sitting astride Taj al-Mulk's midsection, she ordered him to remove her comb. Using both hands, Taj al-Mulk freed her hair from its ivory jailer. A spray of ebony tresses cascaded over her shoulders and down her back. The lovers' faces were close now, close enough to caress each other with their breath. Leaning in, she kissed him on the mouth; her hair fell forward and caught him in its net.

They kissed and nuzzled and stroked. Terken Khatun tugged playfully on the hairs under his arms and whispered into his ear. Khuld couldn't hear her words, but eventually the topic must have doubled back to the normally unsexy business of government, because Taj al-Mulk said, "I'm still going to need a reason."

"How's this for a reason?" Terken Khatun replied. She scooted lower on his body and rocked slowly, like riding a horse, but with greater deliberation. Her whole body moved as one, the muscles of her back and the cords of her biceps squeezing and releasing with the rhythm. Imperceptibly, she picked up the pace. Taj al-Mulk was breathing hard. Sweat glistened on his forehead.

Just as things seemed to be coming to a climax, she stopped.

The tension drained, the muscles smoothed. She dismounted her lover and retrieved her chemise from the floor. As she sat on the edge of the mattress, pulling the garment over her head, Taj al-Mulk asked angrily, "Why did you stop?" His voice caught as he struggled to hide that he was out of breath.

"You know why," she replied, popping her head through the chemise's neck hole and then guiding her hair through with her hands. It settled on her shoulders, sleek and black and perfectly arranged, as if her hairdresser had just finished with it.

"You *amm*!" he shouted. "Fine. Have it your way. You can have your damn arrest warrant. Now finish me."

Khuld knew that it was time to go back to her room. She had the dirt on Terken Khatun. Now there were several paragraphs she needed to add to the letter to her father. There was no time for delay; she had to encrypt it and send it off to Qazvin so that it arrived before the arrest warrant. But she couldn't tear herself away. She had to stay in the tunnel and watch Taj al-Mulk and Terken Khatun's illicit passion a little bit longer. At least—long enough to find out what "finish me" meant.

CHAPTER 14

QAZVIN
TUESDAY, 28 RAMADAN 485
17 Abán 471
2 November 1092

*T*he old woman took the stairs one at a time. She tested each step three times with the tip of her cane and then used it as a support while she slowly raised one foot to the new step, and then the other. All the while, she clutched the skirt of her long, black chador with her free hand to prevent herself from tripping over the hem. She was stooped, but an observer would be unable to tell whether that was because her spine was curved with age or because she was so focused on where she put her feet. She was right to be cautious. The outdoor staircase had no railing, and the sky was still dark. The sliver of moon was too feeble to light her way; she had to rely on whatever torchlight strayed from the enclosure below.

It was a large enclosure, walled in by four tall brick buildings and dotted with camels, donkeys, and mules, standing about patiently or jostling for position at the water troughs. Porters scurried among the animals, loading and unloading the wares of a dozen countries. And yet, for all the activity, there was room for more. Large patches of open ground were scattered around the courtyard. Clearly the khan had been built to handle far more business than it was getting. It was quieter than one would expect too. Sure, there was an occasional shout of "Mind your step" or "That's the wrong camel," and there was a buzz of haggling. But it was all conducted in subdued fashion, as if any unnecessary noise would cause delays. In a hurry to have their caravans out of town and on the road by dawn, the merchants of

Khan Ja'fari were far too busy to notice an old woman laboriously climbing the staircase.

At the third-floor landing, someone burst through the door and rushed past her down the stairs, nearly knocking her over. At least in *her* mind he nearly knocked her over. "Well, you go first, then," she yelled after him. She paused to recover from the near-death experience. It was a good excuse to catch her breath anyway. "Stupid mistress," she muttered. "Making me come all the way out here and climb all these stairs. And for what? She's not a child anymore; she's old enough to know better. It's not a good time to get involved."

She resumed her journey and reached the fourth floor at last. Passing through a rough wooden door, she entered a hallway lined with a dozen similar doors. Just her luck that the one she wanted was all the way down at the end. That's what the manager downstairs had told her. Omar Khayyam and his assistant were in the last room on the right. She shuffled to the end of the hallway and knocked on the door.

*   *   *

Omar and Baghdadi had arrived in Qazvin two days earlier. The eastern sky was orange and crimson with the approach of the sun as they galloped across the last farasang to the city walls. Just when they thought their long journey was nearly over, a traffic jam entering the city brought them to a standstill; the gates had just opened for the day and a crowd of farmers on their way to market, their donkeys laden with rice and vegetables, was trying to get through. Exhausted by their all-night ride and eager for sleep, Omar and Baghdadi were irritated by the delay. As they got closer, the reason for it became clear: the sentries were searching every sack and basket thoroughly.

Once inside the city, their search for lodgings didn't take long. A number of khans fronted a large plaza just beyond the gate. The Khan Ja'fari appeared to be the cleanest and best maintained. Omar and Baghdadi were ushered to a room and soon collapsed into states of blissful unconsciousness, free from the machinations of ministers, killers, and kings.

It was after noon when they awoke and headed to the city center to begin their inquiries. The brunt of the effort fell on Baghdadi, who surveilled the layout of the main bazaar and calculated a route to systematically hit every shop. But almost a third of them were closed, their roofs collapsing. Dried leaves, skitting at random over the pavement, blew into empty stalls and became trapped, piling up against the bases of the partitions. A new supply quickly took their places outside. Indeed there were far more leaves than people navigating the byways of the market, and what people there were tended to be soldiers on patrol instead of paying customers.

Baghdadi circulated the poster of Nizam al-Mulk's assassin around the stalls that were occupied. If the stall specialized in any sort of metalwork—armor, jewelry, cutlery—he showed the murder weapon as well. Most of the vendors insisted they were too busy to talk, despite the scarcity of customers. In one stall Baghdadi waited patiently for an armor dealer to finish a conversation with a Sufi. It seemed odd that a wandering mystic would have business with an armorer, but they spoke in whispers, so Baghdadi had no idea what that business might be. Whatever it was, the proprietor seemed agitated. The discussion ended abruptly when a soldier burst in and chased the Sufi away. In the next stall it was Baghdadi who was chased away—the proprietor came after him with a stick.

One of the few who were even willing to look at the poster was an old man who sat on the floor of a leather dealer's stall, carving a cowhide into strips for belts. When Baghdadi approached, he stopped working and listened attentively but held on to his knife, pointing the curved blade up in Baghdadi's direction, just in case. The old man studied the poster in silence for some time, which Baghdadi took to be a good sign. But when the old man finally handed it back, all he said was "'*Ask not about things which, if they be shown to you, will pain you.*'"[72]

For his part, Omar started out with the best of intentions to make his own inquiries at the Friday mosque. Like the market, the courtyard was nearly deserted, a bare, dusty, unpaved quadrangle under a featureless gray sky. Only a few leafless trees and a sad, undersize fountain broke up the expanse of dirt, and these were so isolated and desolate they made the vast courtyard seem vaster still. On the far side, a pointed arch, two stories high, marked the entrance to the building proper. Inside, Omar dredged up an imam and was going to show him the poster. But during the necessary exchange of pleasantries, the imam happened to mention that the building was almost three hundred years old, having been commissioned by none other than the great caliph Harun ar-Rashid. It was therefore of substantial historic interest. Omar insisted on a tour. That killed the afternoon.

Thus, Omar and Baghdadi both came up empty-handed. So that the day wouldn't be a total loss, they plastered some posters on pillars and walls. On the bottom of each sheet, they scribbled, *"Report any leads to the Khan Ja'fari."*

They had no better luck the next morning working the smaller markets near the city gates—even with Omar giving it his full attention. By midafternoon they were both frustrated with their lack of progress and cranky from fasting. It was then that Baghdadi asked, "Didn't you tell me that the murderer was obsessed with bankers?"

"That's right," Omar replied. "He spent a great deal of time loitering in the financial districts of Hamadan."

"Then maybe that's where we should focus our efforts here in Qazvin. The financial districts."

It was a good idea, despite the hike back to the city center. Omar wanted to visit the local branch of the House of Samha anyway to see if there was a letter from Khuld. They should have gone there first. Instead they stopped at several other banks on the way where they were greeted skeptically by snooty clerks with tightly wound turbans. *Too tightly*, Omar thought. *Their eyes bulge*. The clerks barely glanced at the posters, dismissing them with "No, I'm sure our institution does not serve such people."

But the welcome at the House of Samha was warm. The manager, a nearsighted Jew, perhaps thirty-five years old, with a tallith over his shoulders and ink stains on his cuffs, explained that ben Samha had written ahead, told him to expect them, and instructed him to render any and all et cetera, et cetera. Omar didn't understand how that was possible. Ben Samha would have had to send the instructions before Omar had even decided to go to Qazvin. Nevertheless, he was grateful for the cooperation.

It turned out there was no word from Khuld. The manager promised that if any message arrived he would send it over to the Khan Ja'fari right away. Then he took a good look at the poster and, not recognizing the killer, passed it around among his staff, giving his important visitors a tour of the facility in the process. The building was a smaller version of the flagship location in Baghdad—a front room for transacting business with the general public, a labyrinth of workshops and offices behind. The manager's office even sported the same style of wood cabinets, stuffed with ledger books and strongboxes, like those that had lined ben Samha's inner sanctum before the fire. The resemblance evoked a twinge of sadness in Omar. For a while he had to let Baghdadi do the talking.

With hindsight, they realized they should have questioned the porters first. The porters' station—at the main gate—gave them ample opportunity to watch the passersby. But the manager didn't bring Omar and Baghdadi back to the front until they had made the rounds of the rest of the establishment.

The older of the two porters—he was about seventy, with small, dark eyes set deep in a jovial, round face—was sure he recognized the man in the poster. "Oh, I see everyone who goes by," he said. "I have plenty of time to watch the traffic. Like that man over there. The one with the big nose." He pointed to an ugly man dressed as a workman. "He's walked by three times in the last hour."

"But what about the man in the poster?" Omar asked.

"Yeah, I used to see him go by," he said. "That was, oh, about a year ago maybe. Maybe less. Haven't seen him recently, though."

"Did you see where he came from?" Baghdadi asked.

"No, I never saw that."

"Where he went?"

"I only saw him walking past the gate here."

"Do you remember how he was dressed?"

"Now that you mention it, that was kind of a strange thing, his clothes. Because in your picture there he's dressed like a Sufi, but that's not how I saw him, at least not at first. No, when he first showed up he dressed pretty nice. His robe was made from good silk, well pressed, and he wore a yellow stole over his shoulders, like a student. I didn't see him in a Sufi robe until a couple of months later. And then it wasn't a blue robe, like in the picture. It was a black robe, like an initiate wears. I remember because I told Qalander here"—he pointed to his younger colleague—"I told Qalander, it looks like our boy found religion." The old man laughed raspily at his own joke.

"Yes, that's what you said," Qalander replied, joining the laughter. "'Looks like he found religion.'"

By now the sun was setting. As if choreographed, the gate swung open and the manager emerged at the exact moment the opening words of the *adhan* sounded from the minaret of the Harun ar-Rashid mosque. He carried the requisite bowl of dates for Omar and Baghdadi to break their fast. "I set aside a room where you can recite the evening prayer," he said. "You'll find a ewer and basin for washing, and a pair of prayer rugs. After you finish, please join me in my office for some refreshments."

"Some refreshments" turned out to be an understatement. When Omar and Baghdadi returned to the manager's office, *iftar* awaited them in the true spirit of Samha hospitality. By the time they reached the third course—a spicy stew of local game birds—Omar felt he had established enough of a rapport with the manager to ask some impertinent questions. "What happened here?"

The manager answered the question with a question. "What do you mean?"

"I mean here, in this city. Visitors searched. Markets and mosques practically deserted. People afraid to talk."

The manager looked away, suddenly preoccupied with getting the last bit of poultry off of a bone.

"I'm sure Saad wouldn't want you to withhold any pertinent information from us," Omar said.

"Very well," the manager replied. "You are looking at a city under siege. Not a literal siege, of course. There is no hostile army camped outside the city walls. The gates are open, part of the time at least, and people limp about their business as best they can. But a siege nevertheless."

"I don't understand," Omar said. "No one would dare aggress against a city under the protection of the Sahib al-Jalal."

But Baghdadi knew exactly who would dare. "The Assassins," he said.

The manager nodded. "We live in the shadow of Alamut," he said. He tossed the bone he had been picking onto a plate. "It's been this way for two years. Ever since the Sheikh of the Mountain took over the fortress. His people come into the city to recruit new members, shake down the merchants for supplies and 'taxes,' and kill anybody who speaks out against them. The governor wrote to Nizam al-Mulk to plead for help. The Nizam sent an army to besiege Alamut and for a while things got better. But when the army pulled back to the city to bivouac for the winter, it started all over again. They perform their acts of terror in secret now—they have to, with soldiers all over the street—but in a way that's worse. When something awful happens and you try to pin it on the Assassins, their supporters demand proof and ridicule you for 'conspiracy theories.' And now, with the Nizam gone..." The branch manager shrugged.

He shared many sad stories of families who had lost members to the Sheikh of the Mountain, either because they were killed or because they were recruited. "I don't understand the hold he has over them," he said. "I knew some of these kids. They were cheerful and respectful, and somehow he turned them into fanatics who stare at you with unblinking, angry eyes. There are more of them every day. It's as if he controls them with dark magic."

The tales put a damper on the rest of the meal. By the time dessert was eaten and the last good-byes exchanged, the other banks had closed and the already sparsely populated streets of the financial district were dark and deserted.

Their route back to the khan took them through a district of wine shops and restaurants. With the end of Ramadan in sight, the streets should have been crowded with raucous partygoers. Instead the shops were shuttered and there was barely a soul about. The gloom infected Baghdadi. "That was a complete waste of an evening," he complained.

"You wouldn't say that if you had sampled the wine," Omar replied. "Say what you will about the House of Samha, they know their vintages."

"Please be serious, Khwaja. We've been at this for two days—"

"A day and a half."

"Fine. A day and a half. We have only one lead and—" He stopped abruptly.

"What's the matter?" Omar asked.

"Didn't you hear that, Khwaja?"

"Hear what?"

"I think someone is following us."

Omar stopped to survey his surroundings; Baghdadi stopped at his side. They found they were in a little square lined with shops. Omar listened for footsteps, but all was silent and no one was in sight. Granted, there were plenty of places to hide. The recesses of darkened doorways around the square and the solitary ancient sycamore in the center cast plenty of convenient shadows for anyone who wished to disappear into the background. The tree had two main branches thrusting out from the trunk, giving it the appearance of a person reaching out to grab someone. Omar's gaze swept the square again, slowly this time, but as far as he could tell, the place was deserted.

He was turning to leave when suddenly he heard a noise. A paralyzing jolt shot through Omar and just as quickly released him. He let out a shout and spun to confront whatever was lurking in the night. And then he laughed to see a small shadow flit out of the sycamore and disappear beyond the rooftops. It was only a bird, the singer of the night, as startled by Omar as Omar was by the bird. "*The Nightingale that in the branches sang,*" he recited, "*Ah whence, and whither, flown again.*"[73]

They exited the square into a side street. "I tire of nightingales," Baghdadi grumbled. "All they do is keep people up at night. I don't know why the poets make such a fuss. They sound like any other bird to me."

"This city is getting to you," Omar replied. "Don't let it. We've done pretty well for a day and a half. Yes, we obtained only one lead, but it's an important one. It tells us we're looking in the right place. If Samha's porters saw the killer, so did other people in the district. Something will turn up tomorrow."

As if to prove his prophecy correct, the old woman knocked at their door the next morning.

*   *   *

She interrupted breakfast. Omar and Baghdadi sat on cushions on the floor, bareheaded, dressed in long-shirts and trousers, and savoring the pilaf; rice seemed to be the foundation of every meal in Qazvin. Omar had the *suhur* down to a science now. His body was used to getting up early, and he made sure to savor a hearty meal and drink plenty of water. He looked forward to an easy fast. With the approach of winter, the days were substantially shorter than they had been at the start of the month. And he enjoyed a psychological boost from that sliver of moon; through the little window of his room, he could spy it floating above the opposite wall of courtyard. It meant the end was in sight: tomorrow was the last day of Ramadan. Technically, Omar had some fasts to make up due to days missed for travel and smoke inhalation. But Khuld was 150 farasangs away, and it wasn't as if anyone else was going to check up on him.

Omar insisted on answering the knock himself, over Baghdadi's protests. "I'm done eating," Omar explained. "Finish your rice." When he opened the door and saw the old woman, he welcomed her, "*Ramadan Mubarak*," but she insisted on getting straight to business without returning his greeting.

"Are you the two who put up the posters?" she asked. In case there was any doubt which posters she meant, she took one from the pocket of her chador and held it out to Omar across the threshold with a hand gnarled by a lifetime of scrubbing floors and washing clothes.

"Yes, we are," Omar replied, taking the page from her. "Any information you have is most gladly received. Please come in."

But the old woman remained stubbornly in the doorway. "Come with me. My mistress wants to talk to you."

"Of course. Give me a moment to don my turban and robe and I'll be ready to depart."

Baghdadi was more suspicious. "Who is your mistress?" he demanded to know. "What does she want with us?"

"My mistress will explain everything," the old woman replied.

"Come, Baghdadi," Omar said. "Let's not keep a lady waiting."

Baghdadi jumped to his feet, but not to put on his robe. Instead, he joined Omar at the door. "Excuse us for a moment, please," he said to the woman, as politely as possible, given that the next thing he did was close the door in her face. He closed it gently, but that still left her standing alone in the hall, face-to-face with a closed door.

"How do you know this isn't a trap?" Baghdadi asked Omar.

"There's only one way to find out," Omar replied.

He reopened the door. The woman was still there, standing in the exact same position she was a moment ago. "Please accept my apologies," Omar said. "We'll be ready momentarily."

*   *   *

It took some effort to get the sack of rice up onto the camel's back. Hariri was too short to lift it gracefully. He was strong for a man pushing forty, especially in his legs, but he still had to give it a good heave. "I hate grainy days," he grumbled.

No one paid much attention as Hariri headed back to the storeroom for another load. Indeed there wasn't much anyone would want to pay attention to. It was difficult to pinpoint exactly what about his face made it so ugly—it might have been the nose that was a little too big, or the lips that were a little too thick, or the heavy-lidded eyes that made him look a little too sleepy. Most likely it was the combination. He was dressed for manual labor—ragged turban; shirt and trousers woven from rough, undyed wool; the skirts of his robe hiked up and tucked into his rope belt to leave his legs free. Indeed the only thing to distinguish him from the dozens of similarly dressed porters churning around the Khan Ja'fari was that he glanced a little too often at the fourth floor of the lodge.

In the storeroom he grabbed another sack and hoisted it onto his shoulder. As Hariri stepped through the door and back to the courtyard, the merchant's foreman made a tick mark on a slate. Hariri trudged over to the camels, sneaking another look at the lodge along the way. Through one window he noted the shadows skimming the walls.

There is definitely activity in Khayyam's room, he thought. *That has to be where the old woman went.*

A couple more trips back to the storeroom, but no change in the situation. The shadows kept moving, but that was it. Maybe Khayyam was still getting dressed. Since nothing seemed to be happening, Hariri gave himself permission to go over the poem one more time in his mind:

> How many were the gazelles at Hajir which fascinated with their eyes!
> How many the noble minds struck with amazement by fair maidens!
> How often did the graceful movements of a nymph, advancing with a stately gait, excite an ardent passion in my bosom!
> How many were the pretty cheeks whose aspect induced the censurer of foolish love to excuse me!
> How many pains combined to afflict my heart, when the ringlets of her I loved were unveiled and disclosed to sight![74]

Terrible, he thought, shaking his head. He heaved another sack of rice onto a camel. It landed with finality. *I have an ear for good poetry. And that poem I wrote, that is not good poetry. I would be better off if I had no ear at all. Then I wouldn't know better. I would think my poem was as good as anything out of the Golden Age. Hell, I probably would not even want to write poetry in the first place. Better to be a poetry dolt than to be cursed with mediocrity.*

"Hey, buddy," the foreman yelled. "I don't pay you to stand around."

Startled, Hariri looked around to see who the foreman was yelling at and realized it was him. And no wonder. He had become so absorbed in ridiculing his aspirations as a poet that he had come to a stop midway between the camels and the storeroom and was just standing there, plucking at his beard. *Careless*, he thought, *calling attention to yourself like that. You're not new at this. You stink as a poet. Don't stink at your other job too.* He broke into a jog to make up lost time.

Shortly after he resumed loading the camels, he saw the lamp go out in Khayyam's room. Something was happening. About a minute later, the door to the landing opened and three people emerged. They were too far away and it was too dark on the landing for Hariri to make out their faces, but obviously the stooped figure with the cane was the old woman. The other two had to be Khayyam and his assistant. The skinny one—the assistant—tried to help the woman with the stairs, but she kept stopping to argue with him; apparently she didn't want to be helped. It was clearly going to take awhile for them to reach the ground floor at this rate. Hariri easily had time to tote three more sacks and had just come out of the storeroom lugging a fourth when Khayyam and the others finally stepped off the bottom step into the courtyard. Hariri watched to see which way they went. North gate. Toward the city center.

"I warned you once," the foreman shouted. "Now you're out of here."

I already called attention to myself twice, Hariri thought. *Might as well go for broke.* "What are you trying to say?" he asked. "Are you giving me the sack?"

"You're damn right I am."

"Well, thank you. What should I do with the rice inside?"

"A joker, eh? You leave that sack here."

"Have it your way." Hariri dropped it at the foreman's feet. It kicked up a little cloud of rice dust as it hit the ground. "Thank you for a fun-filled morning."

The foreman erupted with something like "You pick that up," but with some choice Persian curses. Hariri wasn't really paying attention. He let a couple of moments go by to put some distance between himself and Omar's party. Then he slipped out the gate after them and shadowed them into the heart of Qazvin.

*　　　*　　　*

The crone escorted Omar and Baghdadi through the city streets to a large commercial structure in the financial district. The sign out front said *HOUSE OF JA'FAR*. When they entered the building, Omar couldn't help but notice the large number of guards. The old woman conducted her charges through a maze of offices, out to a courtyard, and up an outdoor staircase. They climbed several flights to a balcony that ran clear around the building. Built of wood, the covered walkway was painted green and carved in a way that reminded Omar of a Chinese painting. A pair of pine trees reached for the balcony from one corner of the courtyard; it was quite pleasant walking among the treetops in the cool morning air. As they passed open doors, they saw flashes of luxurious residential quarters, but the door to which their guide ushered them led to a room that was strictly functional. Bare white walls and practical, un-upholstered furniture. It was a place for work.

The old woman announced their arrival to her mistress rather ungraciously. As she shuffled off, she muttered something about half a morning's work piling up while she wasted time fetching people.

Speaking from behind a screen, the mistress of the house said, "Allow me to introduce myself. My name is Qutayya, daughter of Fakhr al-Ma'ali, and I am the last descendant of the House of Ja'far. My family has been the leading merchants of Qazvin for a hundred years. I own this commercial house, the khan where you're staying, a fleet of ships on the Khazar Sea, and a dozen other businesses in this town. I don't say this to brag, but I know there are not many women in this business. I want to prevent any misunderstandings about who I am. I learned from experience to make all of that clear at the beginning, before you say something to embarrass yourself because you thought I was merely the pampered wife of a wealthy man. But I know you didn't come here to learn who I am, Khwaja Omar. You want to know who the man in the poster is. Well, his name is Abu Tahir al-Arrani. But when we were growing up, everyone called him Wahid."

Omar caught glimpses of Qutayya through the lattice; he judged her to be quite young, probably in her late teens. In view of her age, he would have been surprised by the confidence with which she spoke if he didn't have a strong-willed daughter of his own. He wondered how long she had been so self-assured.

"You say you're the last of your line," he said. "How long has elapsed since your father passed through the Door of Darkness?"

"Not long," Qutayya replied. "Last year. But I'll get to that."

"Al-Arrani," Baghdadi said. "Arran is on the western shore of the Khazar Sea. Did this Wahid come from there?"

"Yes, in the Caucasus. He was born there. His father was a business associate of my father and wanted his son to get a better education than was possible in a place of wild mountain landscapes and wild mountain people. I think my father owed him a favor; I never knew what. All I know is that when I was five years old, my father returned from Arran with a caravan-load of Armenian carpets for the market and a new brother for me.

"We were the same age; maybe that's why we were inseparable as children. We used to run around the courtyard and play hide-and-seek in the storerooms. We learned to read together. Not long after that, Wahid was sent to the madrasa to learn the Quran, and later the Hadith. But after school, we still used to sit side by side at the dining room table, devouring the stories in the *Shah-nama*.

"Still, I don't think he was happy here. My father thought of him as a member of the family, but I don't think he ever thought of himself that way. He was always polite, a little too polite, like he was a guest in our house. And when he did get in trouble . . . I remember one time he and I were fighting with wooden swords. The battle started in the courtyard, but soon moved up the stairs and into an apartment where Wahid broke a vase. He received a beating for that, and afterward he told my father, through his little tears, 'Qutayya played in the house with a sword too, but you didn't beat her, because she's your *real* child.'

"Mostly Wahid was a good boy, though. He worked hard on his studies and soon became the star pupil at the madrasa. So it was only natural that eventually he would go off to the Nizamiyya."

"In Baghdad?" Omar asked.

"No, he didn't want to be that far from me," Qutayya replied. "He went to the one in Amol. We were thirteen when he left. There was some talk that when he returned, he and I would be married.

"In the meantime, since everyone expected Wahid to be a great scholar, my father had to look to someone else to learn the family business and be ready to take over after he died. And 'someone else,' it turned out, was me. He taught me accounting, and how to haggle, and judge the quality of a thousand different types of merchandise, and get the best terms for financing a caravan. Of course, I couldn't do everything from behind a screen. He hired an agent to be my eyes and ears. And that's how I met Mirza.

"Have you ever been in love, Khwaja Omar?"

"*I* have," Baghdadi piped up.

Omar laughed. "Stand down, Majnun," he said. "It was a rhetorical question."

"Majnun fell in love with Layla at first sight," Qutayya said. "People in poems *always* fall in love at first sight. Maybe in real life too; I wouldn't know. But what I do know is it wasn't like that for me and Mirza. My father impressed on me that I was taking on a lot of responsibility, especially for someone my age, and that I would have to work hard to learn everything I needed to know. So I was all business at first. Inventory lists and interest rates and the quality of wool and the price of a bolt of fabric. There were a great many documents that Mirza and I needed to go over together, and before long we decided it wasn't practical working through a screen. I let him come around to my side and we worked next to each other at the table, the way I used to sit with Wahid. It was all right; Mirza was close enough to the family, after all. And every once in a while, our arms would brush against each other as we both reached for the same page, and I would notice how handsome his face was. I didn't have these thoughts often, not at first, but they became more frequent as time went on. Later he told me that all the while he was wondering what my hair looked like under my hijab. We continued like this for four years.

"There was a caravan. Linen from Egypt, gold from the Sudan, brocade from Italy. The cost was astronomical. The merchandise came by mule, camel, and boat to Cairo, and from there it would come overland to Qazvin. My father organized a half dozen caravans a year like that, but this was the biggest one that Mirza and I had ever managed by ourselves. We had borrowed a considerable amount of money from the House of Samha to finance it—more than Mirza and I could pay back ourselves if the caravan didn't arrive. We didn't want to have to ask my father to bail us out in that case, but it was a real possibility. There were reports of bandits in the borderlands between the Fatimid and Seljuq territories raiding the caravans, plundering the merchandise, and killing the drivers. Day after day we anxiously checked the post for news.

"It was only a three-word letter. *Arrived in Baghdad.* Our worries were behind us. The roads between Baghdad and Qazvin are safe, so we had no concerns about that. Mirza came up with a carafe of wine, and we drank it and talked excitedly about how we would invest the profits. A caravan to India maybe. We even felt ambitious enough to talk about China. Mirza and I were both so happy that this was our life, working together at something we loved and were good at. We wanted nothing but for it to go on being our life.

"I don't remember the moment I decided to do it, or even if it was me that decided. But somehow Mirza and I were no longer talking; we were kissing.

"We approached my father about marriage. He had observed how Mirza and I behaved around each other for some time and was delighted.

"My father wrote to Wahid at the Nizamiyya and explained the situation. He assured him that he still looked upon him as a son and intended to see him well-situated. He suggested that if he had an opportunity to break away from his studies for a little while, he should come back to Qazvin. My father had several possible marriage prospects to discuss with him.

"Wahid left Amol right away, but not to discuss an engagement for himself. Rather, he intended to break up *my* engagement. But he arrived too late. Mirza and I were already married.

"It was a wonderful wedding. It went on for seven nights. So much food—pilafs, stews, roast meats, sherbets, and every kind of pastry. Mostly I celebrated here in the apartments with my women friends and relatives while the men had their party in the courtyard. But once each night, I was led out onto the balcony, and I made the circuit for the men to see. I had so much gold wire woven into my hair I could barely hold my head up. And of course I had a different gown each night—all made from the Italian and Egyptian fabrics from the caravan I told you about. It was like a symbol of our love, because, of course, that caravan was, in a sense, what brought us together."

Baghdadi and Omar glanced at each other. It was a remarkable transformation: the hardheaded businesswoman suddenly bubbling over about her big week, like any other teenage girl who had the rare luck to marry for love.

Observing her visitors through the lattice, Qutayya misinterpreted the look they exchanged. "Perhaps you think I digress," she said, serious once more. "But I want you to understand exactly what Wahid stole from me.

"By the time Wahid arrived, Mirza and I had been married for almost a week. Wahid spent some time talking to my father, but he wasn't interested in any of the marriage prospects that my father proposed. I expected him to go back to Amol at that point, but he didn't. I'm not really sure why not, but I was under the impression that he wasn't having much success at the Nizamiyya. He didn't fail, exactly, but he didn't stand out either."

As the resident expert on higher education, Baghdadi couldn't resist the opportunity to show off. "This is very common," he explained. "The Nizamiyyas attract the best students from all over the empire and they're fiercely competitive. So often students who were used to being at the top of their classes at their madrasas suddenly find out they're only average. And of course that limits their prospects. Instead of realizing their dreams of becoming brilliant scholars of the Shari'ah and joining the Nizamiyya faculties themselves someday, the best they can hope for is a position teaching the Quran to dimwitted boys at a provincial madrasa. Sometimes they have trouble coming to terms with that."

"That makes sense," Qutayya replied. "If Wahid was going through all that, on top of seeing his bride-to-be taken from him, it would explain why he didn't want to go back to Amol. For weeks he moped around. He didn't leave the house at all, except to go to mosque, which he started doing every day. He hardly ate anything, just picked at his food. At night I'd hear him knocking around the apartment, unable to sleep."

"Clearly a case of melancholia," Baghdadi said. "Too much black bile produced by excessive heat in the liver. You should have served him a steady diet of cooling foods, like celery."

Omar rolled his eyes. "After we get done with Aristotle," he said, "I'm going to start you on a steady diet of Avicenna. There are other ways to restore the humors than food. His psychological treatments were quite ingenious—especially where young men in love were concerned."

"I guess a psychological treatment is what my father had in mind," Qutayya continued. "He tried to cheer up Wahid by arranging for some of Wahid's old friends from the madrasa to visit. I think it made things worse, though. They had all graduated several years before and were making progress in their careers as shopkeepers or accountants or what have you, and I think that made Wahid feel like he hadn't accomplished anything. They had all expected that Wahid and I would get married one day, and I overheard one of them ask him why that didn't happen. Wahid replied, 'I decided Qutayya is too independent to make a good wife.'

"The one thing that interested him was calligraphy. He spent hours creating beautiful renderings of lines from the Quran. He was really quite good, but his choice of verses was . . . well, I'll show you."

Rising from her cushion, she retrieved three scrolls that waited on a nearby shelf. She opened a panel in the screen and passed them through to Omar, then shut the panel before the men could see anything of her other than a smooth-skinned hand emerging from a gold-trimmed sleeve.

Omar unfurled the scrolls on a nearby table, securing the corners with some books he found there. He stood and contemplated the artwork, stroking his long beard. Baghdadi got up, stood beside his *khwaja*, and studied the scrolls too, but he was unsure what he was supposed to look for.

They were things of beauty, as Qutayya said. There was a precision to them, the lines perfectly straight, each curly letter drawn exactly the same way every time it appeared, all the dots exactly the same size. Wahid must have obsessed over each scroll for days to get them perfect. Indeed, the only flaw was numerous rough spots on the surface of the parchment where Wahid had scraped away errors with a knife and tried again. The first scroll read, *The virtuous women, devoted, careful in their husbands' absence.*[75] The second, *If ye are patient and fear, their tricks shall not harm you.*[76] And finally, *Fight in Allah's way with those who fight with you, but transgress*

303

not; verily, Allah loves not those who do transgress. Kill them wherever ye find them, and drive them out from whence they drive you out.[77]

"*W'allah!*" Omar exclaimed.

"What is it, Khwaja?" Baghdadi asked.

"These three verses, taken from the Quran out of context and thrown together like this, create their own context, and it's disturbing: a young man who thinks that people, especially women, are out to destroy him. But if he's patient, Allah will make him powerful and he will exterminate his enemies. When Wahid was pacing this house at night, he was contemplating how everyone looks down on him and was dreaming about his revenge."

Qutayya sighed. "Sadly, that's exactly what he was thinking," she said. "As we found out.

"It was around that time that the Assassins came into the picture. For some time we had been seeing strange young men dressed as Sufis wandering around Qazvin. They were well-behaved and tended to keep to themselves. They did seem to be good Muslims. They lived simply, ate sparingly, didn't drink at all, gave generously to the poor, and never missed prayer. Those who talked to them found they were polite and well versed in the Quran and the Hadith.

"After the fortress at Alamut fell, the young men changed. Suddenly, the streets were filled with them. We soon found out that they had as much in common with Sufism as a dog has with a fruit basket. They came to the mosques and started arguments with the imams. They always traveled in groups of four or five and swarmed around their victims, so that when the imam tried to argue back, he would wear himself out trying to refute one false doctrine after another, after another. The arguments were never about anything important—minor points of the Shari'ah—but they made the imams look incompetent and impotent."

"'*Myself when young,*'" Omar recited,

"did eagerly frequent
Doctor and Saint, and heard great argument.
About it and about: but Evermore
Came in by the same door as I went."[78]

"If only the Assassins had your perspective, Khwaja Omar. Instead they declared that the doctors and saints were heretics, and they started setting up their own mosques. Nothing grand—little more than converted shops, but they were places where they could preach their own doctrine of hidden meanings in the Quran, known only to the Sheikh of the Mountain and the select few with whom he shared them. Some friends of Wahid took him to one of these mosques, and the prospect of being one of a select few had great appeal for him.

"That's when he started to change. He became more confident—but not in a good way. There was a smugness to him, as if he were more pious than the rest of us. He began to wear the Sufi robe, the black robe of an initiate, and he started calling himself Abu Tahir—the Father of Purity. And he was preachy about it. I should take care of my husband, he told me, not run a business. We shouldn't drink. We shouldn't be friends with Jews and Christians. It all had an apocalyptic ring to it. 'Cast away thy sins and prepare thy soul for the Day of Judgment, for no man knoweth the Hour that the Trumpet will sound, and when it is upon us, any would-be intercessor will be powerless to alter Allah's terrible decree.' That sort of thing.

"My father tried to reason with him. He showed the flaws in the Assassin doctrines point by point. He enumerated the misinterpretations of the Quran, the verses taken out of context, the concepts alien to Islam. But it was a frustrating exercise, because it seemed impossible to pin down what the Assassin doctrine *was*. It kept shifting. For example, Wahid seemed to think the Sheikh of the Mountain was *the* Imam, the true leader of the Muslims, if the Shiites are to be believed. So my father would cite various passages in the Quran and the Hadith and explain why they commanded loyalty to the caliph in Baghdad. But then Wahid would say, well, the Sheikh of the Mountain never claimed to be the Imam, he merely knew who the Imam was. Even when my father constructed a devastating argument, Wahid stubbornly clung to his ground. 'The Sheikh of the Mountain told me you would say that,' he insisted. It was as if the very fact that my father *refuted* the Assassins somehow *proved* they were right.

"I don't know if it's because they're confident in their beliefs or insecure. Probably a little of both. But whatever the reason, the Assassins don't tolerate contradiction. Anyone who opposes them must be swept from the field of battle. And my father had opposed them.

305

"It was about nine months ago. I was reviewing a contract here in my room one night when I thought I heard a noise outside. I went to the balcony to take a look. Snow was falling—it wasn't cold enough to stick to the paths, but there was a dusting on the ground and on the branches of the pine trees. No one was in sight. All was peaceful. I returned to my cushion and resumed my labors.

"I didn't hear him enter. All I knew was that one moment I was turning the page, and the next I felt a stinging sensation in my neck and the panic of gasping for air. Someone was standing behind me, pressing a knife against my throat. I grabbed for the arm that held the knife, but he batted my hands away with his free hand. 'Don't worry,' he said, and I recognized Wahid's voice. 'I'm not going to kill you. At least, not right away.'

"He ripped my cushion out from under me and I tumbled to the floor. Grinning an ugly grin, he pulled his robe over his head. It wasn't a novice's black robe anymore. It was blue—Wahid was a full-fledged Assassin now. He dropped the robe to the floor and stood over me, bare-chested. I tried to get up, but he kicked me in the side and began to lower his trousers. Then there was a crash and Wahid clutched at his head, and I realized Mirza was standing behind him, one half of a broken plate in his hand. The blow wasn't enough to render Wahid unconscious, though.

"He spun around and lunged at Mirza with his dagger. Mirza pivoted out of the way and the blade became tangled in his sleeve. While both men struggled to get control of the dagger—Wahid was at some disadvantage, because his trousers were around his ankles—I threw my inkwell in Wahid's face. He cried out and his hands went to his eyes, leaving Mirza with the weapon. He thrust the blade at Wahid's chest, but it didn't go in very far. It must have hit a rib, protecting Wahid from any real damage, but it left an ugly-looking wound.

"We ran. Mirza grabbed my hand and we charged out onto the balcony and toward the stairs. Wahid's wound stunned him briefly, but a moment later he was after us. We scurried down the slippery steps so fast it was more like falling than running. And then we saw two more Assassins running up the stairs toward us. We vaulted over the railing—we were only about one story above the ground at that point—and landed in the snow. But there was no time to lose.

"Across the courtyard, through the building, out into the street, we kept on running. We turned frequently in the twisted streets of the commercial quarter, hoping to lose anyone who might be following us. When it seemed that we had succeeded, I realized we were close to Abu Halwani's house—he's a sugar merchant—so we pounded on the door until someone answered. We rushed inside, the door closed behind us, and we were breathing hard but safe.

"'I have to go back,' Mirza said, turning to go out again.

"I grabbed his sleeve. 'No,' I shouted. 'They'll kill you.'

"'Your father is still there. I have to get him out.'

"'Don't go alone. Get the *shurat*.'

"'There isn't time.'

"'Then *I'll* get the *shurat*.'

"'They want you most of all. Stay here where you're safe.'

"In the end, Mirza agreed to take Abu Halwani, my merchant friend. But before they left, Abu Halwani quickly dispatched his servants on various errands: one brought me a blanket—I didn't realize how cold I was until it was snugly over my shoulders. Another fetched a doctor to look at the bruise where Wahid had kicked me. A third fetched the *shurat*. But they arrived too late.

"I won't burden you with the horrible details of what they found in the courtyard downstairs. There were dead bodies everywhere. My father. Mirza. Many of the servants. They smashed Abu Halwani's fingers with a hammer and only let him live so that he could tell us how brutal the Assassins were. Not that it was necessary—the state of the corpses told us everything. That and the instruments their torturers left behind. Razors, pliers, an iron poker. The poker was sitting next to a smoldering fire. You can imagine what they did with it."

Stunned, Omar and Baghdadi were at a loss for words. Qutayya opened the panel in the screen again, and for the first time they saw her face unobstructed. Her fine eyebrows, tilted up at the ends, gave her a look of great intelligence. But beneath them, her eyes were round and wide with bewilderment. It was as if she were reliving that terrible moment when they had come to her at Abu Halwani's house and given her the news that she would never plan a caravan with her beloved again or feel his lips against hers. Several seconds passed, and then a pair of sobs escaped her; they echoed in the silent room. A moment later she brushed her tears away and her expression hardened with fierce determination.

"I never used to give much thought to what the Quran said about hell," she said. "I was young and far too interested in living to worry about what happens after we die. But now I praise Allah every day for creating such a place. I'm sure that's where Wahid is now, and someday the Sheikh of the Mountain and the rest of the Assassins will join him there. I pray that with your help that day will be sooner rather than later. *'For them are cut out garments of fire, there shall be poured over their heads boiling water, wherewith what is in their bellies shall be dissolved and their skins too, and for them are maces of iron.'*[79]

"In the meantime, I am a widow at nineteen. I inherited my father's estates and run his businesses. It's something to keep me busy, to fill the years ahead. At my age I expect there will be a great many of them. I'm good at it; the business prospers, the dinars flow in. But the growing balances on the ledger sheets give me no pleasure. When Mirza died, I lost my world."

*   *   *

They argued as they passed between the massive double doors that guarded the House of Ja'far from the bustling traffic outside. Omar wanted to stay in the north and continue to investigate the Assassins. But Baghdadi insisted that short of an armed assault on Alamut, there was little they could do. Their best course was to ride back to Baghdad, report to the sultan, and let him worry about it. "This eagerness to return to Baghdad," Omar said. "It wouldn't have anything to do with a certain young lady who happens to be my daughter, would it?"

As it happened, someone decided for them. A palanquin waited by the entrance. It was a heavy vehicle, with wooden screens for sides instead of curtains. One was hinged and doubled as a door; it swung open, beckoning Omar and Baghdadi into the dark interior. Eight bearers stood by, ready to move out. The crowd gave them a wide berth, courtesy of the squad of soldiers that accompanied them. An officer approached the two scholars. The plume sprouting from the point of his Turkish helmet signified he was the commander. He was tall, with a long, thin face that was mostly nose, a low forehead, and a protruding brow that made Omar think of a bird of prey; his two braids hung from the back of helmet like a tail. "Omar Khayyam," he said, "you are required to come with us. You and your assistant."

He spoke softly and deliberately, yet his voice resonated in a menacing way. His tone didn't invite questions, but Omar asked one anyway. "What is this about?"

"My superiors will explain."

Omar fumbled in his pocket and drew out a scroll with the imperial seal on it. "I am embarked on a special mission at the command of the Sahib al-Jalal, Sultan Malik-shah. I insist that I be allowed go about my business."

The officer took the proffered document, read it, and smirked. "Forgers do such good work," he said. He rolled the paper up and slipped it into his cuirass. "It would be best if you got in the palanquin voluntarily," he added, "but one way or another, you're getting in." Lest there be any doubt what "one way or another" meant, he signaled to his men, who slid their swords out of their scabbards.

The inside of the vehicle was bare: no seats or cushions. Omar and Baghdadi took their places on the floor—Baghdadi sitting cross-legged, his posture rigid; Omar leaning casually against the wall with his knees propped up in front of him. "It looks like our unauthorized nighttime flight from the sultan's camp finally caught up with us," he said. For Baghdadi's sake, he did his best to sound unconcerned. But as if to contradict his reassurances, the door shut and they heard a wooden latch fall into place, locking them in the cabin from the outside.

The palanquin jerked as the bearers lifted it onto their shoulders and got under way. "Where do you think they're taking us?" Baghdadi asked.

"They'll probably take us to the governor. He'll question us and send us back to Baghdad. Which is where you want to be anyway."

That theory became untenable when the bearers trotted past the governor's palace and kept going. By the time they reached the north gate of the city, Omar realized something was very wrong. He shouted for help— Baghdadi joined him—but when five armed Turks are guarding prisoners inside a palanquin, the average citizen doesn't rush in to intervene. Omar and Baghdadi rocked inside the cabin and slammed their shoulders against the walls in the hope that it would cause the bearers to stumble. With luck they would drop the palanquin and the cabin would break open upon hitting the pavement. But the bearers were unfazed and all Omar and Baghdadi got for their trouble were painful jabs from a truncheon jammed through the lattice.

They cleared the city gates and sped through farm country. The harvest seemed to be winding down: only a handful of peasants were to be seen, gathering the last of the almond crop. Vines slithered over the trellises of grape arbors, bare of fruit, their leaves yellowing. Now and then a cluster of tents appeared—a military encampment—and Omar and Baghdadi held out hope that it was their destination. But each time, the bearers raced past it and the prisoners became ever more fearful about their predicament. In the distance, but getting closer with every step, a serpentine brown ridge stretched in front of them like a barrier to mark the end of the world.

It took about an hour, maybe a little more, to reach the chain of hills. The road pitched upward and the soldiers led the palanquin along switchbacks to the top of the ridge. From there Omar and Baghdadi glimpsed the country beyond through the lattice of their prison. It was a wild land, a land of deep ravines, snowy peaks, and inhospitable soil that produced little more than desert grasses.

As they crested the ridge and began their descent down the other side, Omar and Baghdadi realized they were crossing an invisible line, one that represented the limits of the sultan's protection. There would be no further outposts of the Seljuq state on the road ahead, no bastions of civilization where they could hope to be brought before a polite official who would treat an emissary of Malik-shah (even an emissary under a cloud) with respect. There was only one place they could be going now.

Alamut.

*   *   *

Once over the ridge, Omar and Baghdadi were released from their portable prison. A team of horses awaited them. They and the guards mounted up and headed off into the wilderness. They rode in close formation, with no opportunity for escape.

They traveled all day, tracing the curves of riverbeds and trotting along the rims of canyons. The gallop of the horses loosened small stones, which tumbled into the lightless abysses below. The party sped past meadows where sheep grazed and villages where flat-roofed houses huddled for protection in clefts at the bases of cliffs. There were few other travelers—mostly rice merchants whose mules were festooned with bells that announced their approach long before they plodded into view. Every couple of hours, they stopped and fresh horses suddenly appeared, seemingly out of nowhere; their hiding places behind rocks and inside caves were well chosen. Clearly the operation had been carefully planned.

By the time they reached Alamut, the sun had sunk behind the mountains, transforming them into jagged black outlines against a still pale sky. Omar needed only one glance at the geography to grasp why the siege earlier in the year had failed. Surprise was impossible: the only approach was through a narrow mountain pass. Any would-be enemy would suffer heavy casualties from a hail of rocks and arrows from the heights above. Once through the pass, the besiegers would find themselves hemmed inside a bowl-shaped valley. In the shadow of the northeast wall, a rocky crag, shaped like some beast of the sea, loomed four hundred cubits above the valley floor, with the castle itself perched on its head. The battlements on top of the ashen walls stabbed at the heavens as if they were spikes on an iron crown. There was no place to situate a ballista or other engine of siege, and anyone who tried would once again be subject to a barrage of deadly projectiles from above. The best an army could hope to do was pitch its tents a safe distance away, seal the pass to prevent supplies from reaching the castle, and wait, possibly for years, until starvation and thirst drove the fanatics from their stronghold.

At the base of the crag, a dusty stone staircase stretched upward into the twilight. It was too steep and narrow for the horses to pass; Omar and the others would have to hike the rest of the way.

After a day on horseback, Omar was grateful to stretch his legs. But his gratitude was short-lived. He soon learned that his nightly climb to the platform of his observatory was woefully insufficient training for a man of forty-four years to assault Alamut Rock. Before long his legs burned and he could feel his heart pounding in his chest. He reveled in any stretch of flat terrain—he practically ran down the path—only to be disappointed on rounding a curve and being confronted with yet another flight of stairs as vertical as Jacob's ladder.

It took an hour to reach the fortress. Passing through the main gate, Omar marked the intimidating doors—a pair of iron-studded behemoths that shut behind them with a decisive thud. Four guards manhandled the wooden crossbar into place and cut off Alamut from the outside world.

One of the soldiers conducted Omar and Baghdadi into a vast enclosure where dozens of men were hard at work. Their torches combined with cook fires and the inferno of a blacksmith's forge to light their efforts— a flickering, reddish, uncertain light, but bright enough to burn the stars out of the moonless sky and leave a smooth, charred expanse in their place. Numbed into compliance by years of mindless labor, a squadron of slaves, their bare chests shiny with sweat, mechanically heaped fuel onto the forge and worked the bellows to pump the flames higher. Nearby, skilled craftsmen played a concert of metallic rhythms as they beat their ploughshares into swords and their pruning hooks into spears.

Omar nudged Baghdadi and flicked his eyes in their direction. "That's why we came up empty-handed in the markets," he said. "The man who forged the murder weapon wasn't in Qazvin. He was here."

Their guide led them past training grounds where aspiring Assassins sparred with swords or crept up behind wooden mannequins to slit imaginary throats. Beyond that, a work crew hoisted buckets of earth out of the ground by means of a winch. Omar glanced into the hole but couldn't see the bottom—a cistern for the storage of water, no doubt. Clearly the Assassins were determined to be prepared for the return of the sultan's army and a new—and longer—siege, so determined that their preparations didn't sleep.

A modest, two-story residence squatted at the far end of the courtyard. Its façade boasted no tile or other ornament; the house was little more than a whitewashed box huddled under a flat, overhanging roof. Only a flicker of light escaped from the otherwise black rectangles of the windows. Whoever lived there cherished frugality when it came to lamp oil. Noticing Omar eyeing the structure, the guard explained, "The Sheikh of the Mountain's house." His charges could barely hear him, so hushed and awestruck were his tones.

In any case, they were not destined to meet the Lord of Alamut tonight. Instead, they veered off the path to his house and approached an opening in the ground. When they peered over the rim, they saw a limestone staircase forcing its way into the earth. The lower steps breathed orange light and fleeting shadow, the projection of whatever was down there.

It turned out to be a barracks, hewn out of the rock. Blue-robed Assassins slept on the floor or sat against the walls and ate by torchlight. Some kneeled on strips of carpet and chanted prayers. A few competed at flicking their daggers at a wooden target. The soldier led Omar and Baghdadi into an adjoining room—not much more than an alcove—and ordered them to sit. There were no cushions, only a few threadbare rugs, scattered around a low table. The soldier took his post at the entrance, in case Omar and Baghdadi had any ideas about wandering off.

The wait went on for some time. Omar had an empty feeling in his stomach—today's fast should have ended over an hour ago. When he remembered that this morning he thought it was going to go easy, he had to laugh. "'*The Worldly Hope men set their Hearts upon Turns Ashes*—'" he began.[80]

"Is this really the time for that?" Baghdadi demanded.

"What better time to light the lamp of wisdom than in our darkest hour?"

Still, Baghdadi worried him. The young man fidgeted on his rug—when he was seated, which wasn't often. He kept popping up to pace the room.

"When the time comes, I'll do the talking," Omar told his assistant, by way of reassurance.

But Baghdadi wasn't reassured. After half an hour of alternately sitting and pacing, he blurted out, "Why are they making us wait like this?"

"Is it making you nervous?" Omar asked.

"Yes!"

"That's why they're making us wait like this."

Eventually Officer Bird-of-Prey, the one who had led them from Qazvin, tramped into the room, stooping slightly on account of the low ceiling. Omar almost didn't recognize him. His cuirass and helmet were gone, replaced by a Sufi robe and turban. The two braids that had bobbed beneath his helmet during the day's journey had vanished—either they were wrapped under his turban or they had been a wig all along.

The soldier who had been guarding the door followed his commander into the room and stood behind Omar and Baghdadi. In one hand he carried a palm-branch switch.

The officer seated himself on a rug across the table from the prisoners. He didn't say anything at first. Instead he shuffled through a dozen or so documents that were waiting for him. He paused now and then to scrutinize one of them in more detail. When he finally did speak, it was without preamble, pleasantry, or looking up from his papers. "Why were you in Qazvin?" The word "why" echoed in the rocky chamber.

Omar saw no reason to lie. "The sultan commissioned me to inquire into the death of Nizam al-Mulk."

The officer turned over a page and skimmed the next one as he spoke. "You mean the *false* sultan commissioned you."

"Call him whatever you want," Omar replied. "That's the commission he imparted upon me. The trail led to Qazvin."

"And is that *all* you were doing there?"

"What else would I be doing?"

At last the officer looked up. He fixed his pale brown eyes on Omar and said, "You tell me."

Omar pressed his lips together in frustration. So this was their game. He was to be interrogated and not told about what. The way things were going, it was going to take some time too. Clearly the officer was in no hurry. He dragged out each syllable ominously as he spoke. But Omar had no intention of playing this game.

"The sun set hours ago," he said. "This would be much more pleasant on a full stomach."

"It's not supposed to be pleasant."

"Maybe some quail and a bit of pilaf."

The officer nodded to the soldier. The switch whistled and whacked Omar on the arm. It didn't hurt much. His sleeve protected him, and, in any case, the soldier had twisted his wrist at the last minute, so the switch landed on the flat side. Omar wondered about that. It was as if the order had come down not to harm the prisoners, and the lash was just for show. He decided to push a little more.

"I should introduce you to my old tutor," he told the soldier. "Now, *there* was a man who knew how to give a beating."

"We know all about your old tutor here," the officer said.

It was a peculiar thing to say, but Omar let it pass. Instead he asked Baghdadi, "Will you have anything to eat?"

The fear was obvious in Baghdadi's eyes. The young man was terrified at the possibility of provoking their interrogator. "What are you doing?" he asked with a mixture of apprehension and accusation.

"Ordering *iftar*."

"You apparently have mistaken me for a waiter," the officer interjected. "Let me set you straight. I am Abu Dhafir Misri, I am second only to the Sheikh of the Mountain here in Alamut, and I will have my answers. What was the real purpose of your visit to Qazvin?"

"I'll need something to wash it all down with, of course," Omar replied. "During our ramble through the countryside today, I noticed the grape arbors outside of Qazvin. There must be some stellar local vintages. Something on the lighter side, I should think, to complement the quail."

Now the officer actually did seem provoked. "The Sheikh of the Mountain is a holy man," he said indignantly. "There is no wine in his dominions."

"Really?" Omar surveyed his bleak surroundings—the low ceiling, the poor lighting, the walls that were part rock and part red dirt, and the bare furniture without style. "I would think there'd be a high demand here for the elixir of forgetfulness."

The soldier pulled back the switch to strike Omar again. Omar's arm shot up to fend off the blow, but what really averted it was quickly blurting out something relevant: "Finding the murderers of Nizam al-Mulk. That's my only mission." He was taking no chances that the second blow would fall as gently as the first.

Misri searched Omar's face for evidence of sincerity. When he broke off his scrutiny, he was still dissatisfied. "You're lying. You were in Qazvin to spy on us. The pretender al-Muqtadi and his lickspittle Malik-shah ordered you to learn about this castle and its defenses."

"Then it wasn't very bright of you to transport us here."

"You might as well tell me everything. The Sheikh of the Mountain knows all."

Omar rolled his eyes. "If he knows all, what difference does it make whether I tell you?"

"You doubt his power? Then how do account for the ease with which we found you?"

"I don't know," Omar replied. "Maybe the posters I plastered all over town with my address on it. Once you knew where I was staying, it would have been easy to follow me to the House of Ja'far."

Omar may have been skeptical, but Baghdadi was intrigued. "How *does* the Sheikh of the Mountain know so much?"

"Because he is humble," Misri replied. "I know your kind, Omar Khayyam. You spend your life trying to pile up knowledge by the labor of your own reason." Clearly Misri had researched Omar before he confronted him in Qazvin. "But how can knowledge come from ego? You glean what you can from the books of the Greeks, forgetting that Plato and Aristotle knew not the Messenger—may the prayer and peace of Allah be upon him— nor the Quran, nor the Shari'ah. How can knowledge come from ignorance? The Sheikh of the Mountain followed a different path. He submitted himself solely to the word of Allah and the discipline of a sheikh well versed in its hidden meanings. He escaped the twin traps of ego and ignorance by taking the words of the Quran into his heart: '*Verily, those who believe and do what is right,* and humble themselves to their Lord, *they are the fellows of Paradise; they shall dwell therein for aye.*'"[81]

For the first time since they had been brought in, the fear drained from Baghdadi's expression. He sat still on his rug, too absorbed in what Misri was saying to worry about himself. He had a thousand questions about the hidden meanings, but when he tried to ask them, Misri cut him off.

"I have other duties to attend to," Misri announced brusquely. "As for you, Omar Khayyam, I don't think you appreciate the gravity of your situation. Perhaps some time in a cell will give you both an opportunity to think it over."

He gestured to the guard with a flick of his thumb. "Take them away," he said.

The guard led Omar and Baghdadi to their new lodgings and locked them inside. Through the wooden bars of the gate, they watched him walk away, taking the only lamp with him. Omar had put on a brave front for Commander Misri. But now, as the light dimmed with each echoing footstep, Omar noticed his hands were trembling.

CHAPTER 15

BAGHDAD
THURSDAY, 1 SHAWWAL 485
19 Abán 471
4 November 1092

*T*he curtains were open. Tied back on either side of the dais with silk ribbons, they proclaimed to the world that the caliph Abu'l-Qasim al-Muqtadi B'illah, Commander of the Faithful and Scion of the House of Abbas, was holding court.

Only his son and his most senior officials were permitted to sit in his presence, of course. They occupied half a dozen chairs, arranged in order of precedence on either side of the brocade-covered throne. Protocol dictated that the other members of his "household" had to stand. More than a thousand of them packed the hall—relatives, bureaucrats, assorted hangers-on. Not that they were allowed to get too close. In front of the dais, and level with it, a rectangular golden pool separated the illustrious from the common. Flower petals floated on the surface of the water, suffusing their perfume into the room. On either side of the pool a set of five steps provided the chosen access to the dais.

For those condemned to remain in front of the pool, at least the floor was carpeted. The lush pile, woven with floral designs made from thread of real gold, was easy on the feet. Praise be to Allah for small comforts. The session was already long, and it was anyone's guess how much longer the courtiers would have to stand. They had already listened patiently to a long succession of petitioners. Now all eyes were trained on the Commander of the Faithful as he sat cross-legged on his high perch and chewed his breakfast.

"Much as I revere the month of Ramadan," he said, "it's a pleasure—now that it's over—to linger over a proper meal in the morning rather than having to wolf something down before the sun rises."

A slave girl kneeled in front of him and held out a serving dish. "So, my Daytime Sun," al-Muqtadi said, "what's the next course?" He leaned forward and lifted the cover; the escaping steam was tinged with aromas of lamb, onion, and baked fruit. Scooping out several morsels with a scrap of flatbread, he sampled the concoction. Four or five times. "This stew," he said at last. "This stew is a miracle. Truly excellent. Tell the cooks the spices are perfect. Just enough cinnamon to bring out the flavor of the apples, but not so much as to overpower it." Daytime Sun bowed her head and hurried off to deliver the caliph's message to the kitchen, leaving the lamb mixture on an end table beside the throne.

Al-Muqtadi took several more mouthfuls, with running commentary in between. "The apples aren't overcooked either. The perfect amount of resistance to the teeth . . . The meat is so tender . . . And what is that, saffron? . . . Excellent, excellent." All the while, the members of the court looked on, their gazes fixed on the caliph, afraid that if they made eye contact with their neighbors, they'd be unable to keep a straight face.

Indeed, it was hard not to smile at the sight of the caliph gobbling his stew. He just seemed to enjoy it so much. His courtiers wondered how he packed away such great quantities of food with such a small mouth. His upper lip was trimmed by a neat, brown mustache whose ends didn't quite reach his beard. It was a narrow semicircle of a beard, outlining a face that was well filled out with baby fat, making him look younger than his thirty-six years. As for his fair complexion and hazel eyes, they were inherited from the Armenian captive who had given birth to him.

The caliph didn't so much stop eating as slow down; eventually the pace was leisurely enough to permit some interaction with the people around him. He started with Abu'l-Abbas, who sat on his right, the epitome of good posture. "Remember, son," al-Muqtadi said. "The Quran teaches us that nothing happens except according to Allah's will. We have no ability to control the winds, the tides, or the vicissitudes of politics. So if Allah grants you some moment of peace to enjoy a little meal now and then, show your gratitude: see to it that the meal is a fine one."

"Yes, Father," Abu'l-Abbas replied.

His duty to impart wisdom to the young fulfilled, al-Muqtadi turned to business. "So," he said to Amid ad-Dawla, who was seated at his left. "Big day, big day."

"Indeed," his vizier replied.

"Let's review the plan."

"The first part of the day will be the same as in years past. There will be a procession to accompany you to the Mosque of Mansur. You will arrive in time for noon prayers. Then you return to the Dar Calipha by boat."

"And that's when I meet the sultan."

"Correct. He will time his arrival to coincide with your landing on the quay."

"Excellent. Do you have my sermon?"

Amid ad-Dawla held out a sheaf of papers to al-Muqtadi, who licked some sauce from his fingers before taking it. "What's the topic?" he asked, as he leafed through the pages.

"Chapter twelve, verse ninety-two of Allah's Holy Quran."

"Allah forgiving Joseph's brothers for selling him into slavery."

"Forgiveness is a suitable theme ahead of your meeting with the sultan."

"Very suitable. There is much that needs forgiveness—on both sides. Very well, then." He pushed his plate away and wiped his hands on a napkin. "I'd like to inspect the arrangements for this afternoon."

"At once, O Commander of the Faithful." The inspection would take the caliph clear across the Dar Calipha. Best that the out-of-shape al-Muqtadi save himself for this afternoon. Amid ad-Dawla beckoned to a quartet of bearers who approached the throne carrying a litter. The caliph had a little trouble hoisting himself into the brocade-covered seat; Amid ad-Dawla had to direct the bearers to hold it lower to the ground. But they were under way soon enough.

Amid ad-Dawla walked alongside the litter as they made their way along paths shaded by date palms. Al-Muqtadi was uncharacteristically quiet, as if turning over some doubts in his mind. When they were out of earshot of the bulk of the court, he asked Amid ad-Dawla, "Nizam al-Mulk was your father in-law, wasn't he?" Amid ad-Dawla nodded. "Did he ever take you into his confidence?"

"Sometimes," the vizier replied, sensibly cautious.

"Did he ever say anything to you about the sultan planning some conspiracy against me?"

"If the sultan were plotting against you, don't you think Nizam al-Mulk would have put a stop to it?"

"True, true," al-Muqtadi said thoughtfully. "But what about now? The Nizam is no longer there to interfere."

"The sultan treated Abu'l-Abbas and me with considerable warmth at Nahrawan," Amid ad-Dawla replied. "He even invited me to take part in the councils of his innermost circle. I have the utmost confidence in him."

"Abu Shuja didn't share your confidence. He warned me that Malik-shah was plotting against me."

"I cannot speak to my predecessor's opinions."

The brick expanse in front of them was the north wall of the palace. "You'll meet the sultan here at the Willow Tree Gate," Amid ad-Dawla explained.

The dark passage through the wall revealed only a patch of the sunlit plaza on the other side, but it was enough to see that a crowd had already gathered. A dozen caliphal mamelukes stood guard at the far end. Glimpsing the Commander of the Faithful through the gaps between the guards, one onlooker shouted, "It's him!" and the crowd broke into a cheer. The guards pulled into tighter formation and brandished their maces. The polished bronze heads of the weapons warned the public: no assassin would get close enough to the caliph to spoil Eid al-Fitr.

"Everything seems to be in order here," al-Muqtadi said. "Where will the sultan and I go from here?"

"The animal park is next on the schedule," Amid ad-Dawla replied.

They set off again. "What did they talk about?" al-Muqtadi asked.

Amid ad-Dawla gave the caliph a puzzled look. "I'm afraid the Commander of the Faithful has an advantage on me," he said.

"You said the sultan admitted you to his inner circle. What did they talk about?"

"People gave reports."

"Did my name come up at all?"

"Yes."

"And what did they say?"

Amid ad-Dawla looked around to make sure no one was in earshot. "They believe as long as Chief Professor Ghazali supports you, which he does, any move against you would be futile."

"Yes. Praise be to Allah for Chief Professor Ghazali. He has been a pillar of true Islam and his integrity is legendary. I rely on him greatly. And thank you for reassuring me. Because, of course, I don't want a war with the sultan. But there's something I don't understand. The sultan and his counselors. They talked about moving against me right in front of you?"

"Malik-shah thinks I'm Nizam al-Mulk's loyal son-in-law and therefore the sultan's loyal servant. It has never occurred to him that my real loyalty might be to you."

The animal park was a large, grassy enclosure surrounded by a high wall. Inside, four elephants covered in silk blankets crisscrossed the field like ships navigating a harbor. Their passage caused little concern to the giraffes, which were far too engrossed in munching leaves from the treetops to afford the elephants more than an occasional glance. Safely within the confines of a pen, a hundred lions lazed in the sun or gnawed at animal carcasses that had been lobbed over the fence for their breakfast.

Along the main path, evenly spaced on both sides, two dozen black-haired page boys stood at attention, each holding a leopard on a gold chain. The leopards were at attention too, sitting on their haunches, propped up on their front legs in a dignified fashion.

"I know how proud you are of those leopards," Amid ad-Dawla said. "I wanted to make sure we showed them off."

"Excellent," the caliph replied. He called over one of the keepers, who handed him a jeweled bowl filled with meat scraps. Then he ordered the bearers to carry him over to the closest leopard. He treated the big cat to a few scraps and ran his hand lovingly through her soft fur. The animal lay down and exposed her belly for the caliph to rub, but al-Muqtadi knew his pets far too well to fall for *that* trick. Instead, he scratched behind her ears. The leopard closed her eyes and purred. The sound was like the clack of wooden gears in a watermill during spring, when the current moves fast. The creature placed her paw lovingly over the caliph's hand and guided it to the itchy spots. "What a pretty girl you are," the caliph said. For Amid ad-Dawla's benefit, he offered a zoology lesson. "Did you know that in the wild, leopards carry their kill up into the trees?"

"I didn't know that."

"Oh, yes. They're incredibly strong and agile. I heard of one case, in Africa, where a leopard carried an entire giraffe—a little one—up a tree."

"Fascinating. You should be sure to tell the sultan about it."

The caliph gave the leopard's head one more caress and said, "What happens after we visit the animal park?"

"The formal audience."

"And where will that be?"

"In the Hall of Audience. In the Taj Palace."

The caliph gave that some thought. "Perhaps a less formal audience—in a less formal setting—would be more conducive to a renewal of friendship. Is the Palace of the Tree in any condition to receive visitors?"

"Let's see."

The reception room in the Palace of the Tree featured a circular pool lined with azure tiles. Growing from the depths of the water, an apple tree stretched to the high vaulted ceiling and endowed the building with its name. It was no common tree, however. The trunk, the branches, even the delicately veined leaves, were crafted entirely out of silver, enough of the precious metal to match the weight of twenty men. The fruit was pure gold, as were the dozens of birds that nestled among the branches and tended to their young.

"Everything seems to be in order," the caliph said. "Except the birds. They're not singing."

"They're water-powered," Amid ad-Dawla explained. "There's a tank at the top that needs to be filled. They'll sing this afternoon."

"And flap their wings?"

"Yes."

"Very good," the caliph said. "One thing more. I know you're confident that the sultan won't try to move against me. But let's take some precautions, just in case."

"What does the Commander of the Faithful have in mind?"

"While the sultan is here today, double the guards."

"Be assured, O Commander of the Faithful," Amid ad-Dawla replied. "I'll personally give the guards their orders."

THE THREAD OF REASON

*   *   *

The Willow Tree Gate took its name from a massive relic planted by al-Muqtadi's grandfather. Standing guard outside the walls of the Dar Calipha, it had witnessed the departure of dozens of holy day parades. Its tendrils drooped from its branches like strings of prayer beads.

By late morning the crowd had swelled into the thousands. Armies of mamelukes seemed to rival the number of the spectators. They held back the mob from the Willow Tree Gate and kept a path clear to the Later Bridge of Boats. A military band led the procession. Musicians on horseback cantered through the gate, blasting their long, straight horns and banging the kettle drums that were mounted on their saddles.

But it was the Commander of the Faithful that the crowd had come to see. Eager for a glimpse, onlookers craned their necks to see over the turbans of the people in front of them. At last al-Muqtadi appeared, riding atop a mule. As he emerged into the sun from the shadow of the passageway, a cheer raced across the plaza.

The caliph was wrapped in the Blessed Mantle, a simple, somewhat scratchy cream-colored robe of goat's hair that had belonged to the Messenger and been handed down through the centuries. Diamonds, rubies, and a few jumbo sapphires garnished his rings and studded his turban. Not that the crowd could see much of the latter: the caliph's headpiece was hidden under a shawl of black: the color of the Abbasid dynasty—and the color of death. A reminder, on this day of joy, that the Day of Judgment loomed in all our futures.

But despite the caliph's inky head cover, thoughts of death were far from the minds of the assembled masses. They were too wrapped up in identifying celebrities. At the caliph's side, his son, Abu'l-Abbas, marched on foot. Then came a slave carrying an inkwell on a velvet cushion, a squat cylinder made of silver, with gold inlay and a lid shaped like a crown. It was the symbol of office for the two men who marched in lockstep behind it, the viziers Amid ad-Dawla and Taj al-Mulk. Next in the procession were senior caliphal officials, followed by leading members of the ulama: Ghazali, Humaydi, Abu Ishaq . . . the presence of Qadi Shami and the Blind Imam, excited considerable comment. It was not lost on the crowd that these two men, who had not gone to greet the sultan at Nahrawan, were here to march

323

with the caliph. The spectators approved. Indeed, Shami earned back some of the respect he had lost over his tantrum in the Thirst Market. They were less approving of Abu Nasir ibn Ali. In their minds he was still *Abba* Nasir the Jew. Yes, al-Muqtadi had personally officiated at his conversion, but it had to be some Jewish trick.

The caliph led the procession across the Later Bridge and past the Castle Isa, one of the oldest structures in Baghdad. The road curved along the base of the castle walls, then opened up to a broad, straight avenue lined with towering palm trees and hordes of onlookers. Not content merely to look on, some of the crowd—banners in hand—jumped in at the end of the parade. The colorful fabric whipped above their heads as they marched. More banners fluttered on the sidelines or draped the façades of buildings. The cheers were impassioned. *"Allahu akbar! Allahu akbar!"* It was as if all of Islam spoke with one incredibly loud voice.

Al-Muqtadi soaked it up. Confined as he was to the Dar Calipha so much of the time, it warmed his heart to poke his head out one day a year and feel like part of a community—a loving community, drenched with charity, sanctity, and might. He waved his arms in encouragement and the noise surged to epic levels. *"Eid Mubarak! Eid Mubarak!"* Between his arm-waving and the jerky gait of the mule, the roly-poly Commander of the Faithful bounced comically in his saddle; Amid ad-Dawla was sure the caliph was going to fall off. But the worst that happened was that his turban kept slipping out from under the shawl and down over his eyes.

He pushed the headpiece back into place yet again, restoring his vision just in time to see a woman jump out into the road in front of him. Panic jolted the caliph, but the mule kept its presence of mind, stopping at the last possible moment. The procession came to a halt behind them, not without a few minor collisions. Among the casualties, Humaydi—knocked to the ground by a student of shari'ah who was engrossed in conversation about the law governing unjust trade practices and didn't stop quickly enough.

The cheering tapered off as all eyes turned toward the woman, who meanwhile had prostrated herself at the hooves of the caliph's mule and cried, "Help me! O Commander of the Faithful, help a poor old woman!" It was hard to gauge how old she actually was. Her clothes testified to a lifetime of poverty that would age anyone prematurely. A cheerful patch of some sort of tabby material was sewn onto her robe, but that only emphasized the drabness of the rest of the garment. Any other color the robe might have boasted at one time had faded amid hundreds of washings, leaving a uniform brownish gray. As for the color of her hair, it was concealed under a hijab, of course, and offered no clue as to how many years she had been toiling in this mortal world.

Two of the caliph's guards hastened to drag her out of the way, but al-Muqtadi commanded them to stop. So instead they helped her to her feet, surreptitiously frisking her for weapons as they did so.

The caliph looked down at the woman from his mount. "What is your suit, my child?" he asked, as gently as possible.

But the woman was tongue-tied. She blushed at what she had done. "It's . . . it's not important," she stammered.

"Then let me help you with something unimportant," the caliph replied kindly. A murmur of approval went through the spectators. But still the woman was afraid. "Tell me your name, child," the caliph said.

"My name is Izma. I am the wife of ibn Yasir the Rug Seller."

At the mention of ibn Yasir, Taj al-Mulk and Amid ad-Dawla exchanged glances. Him again.

"And this ibn Yasir," the caliph asked. "Is he here with you today?"

"No . . . no. That's the problem. My husband has disappeared. I haven't seen him in over a week."

It took some coaxing for the caliph to pry the story out of her. It was difficult to hear her over the buzz of the crowd, and what he could hear wasn't all that coherent. But eventually he pieced together that ibn Yasir had gone out to his carpet stall as usual the previous Wednesday morning. He had told Izma that he planned to work a few hours and then go over to the Thirst Market to watch the flogging. Izma insisted they couldn't afford for him to miss half a day's work. A squabble ensued. In the end, her husband stormed off and she hadn't seen him since.

"Why didn't you go to the *shurat*?" the caliph asked.

"I did!" Izma replied. "But they were of no help. They wouldn't listen to my story."

"Well, I'm listening, and I promise you, something will be done."

Taj al-Mulk offered his services. "This ibn Yasir is known to the government," he said. "We'll find him."

"As you wish," the caliph replied. "And where's my vizier?"

"I am here," Amid ad-Dawla replied.

"While Taj al-Mulk and his men look for ibn Yasir, I want you to talk to the Sahib ash-Shurat. It is unacceptable that a poor, unfortunate woman should be given the runaround like this. And see that she has money to meet her needs." He turned to Izma. "You see," he said. "We're already taking action. You were right to come to me."

"Thank you, O Commander of the Faithful!" Izma exulted, kissing one of his rings in gratitude. She looked happy and relieved that after so many days of worrying, she had finally shared the burden of an absent breadwinner. Suddenly her posture was straighter and she was more energetic. She disappeared into the crowd and the procession resumed.

Taj al-Mulk beckoned for Abu Nasir to join him. As they marched, he explained the situation and asked Abu Nasir to take charge of the search for ibn Yasir. "All this trouble over one missing carpet merchant?" Abu Nasir asked. "It hardly seems like a matter for the Intelligence Directorate."

"I have a hunch this has something to do with the murder of ben Samha," Taj al-Mulk replied.

"Perhaps. There was that altercation last year in the rug market."

"That's why I want you to look into it personally. Start right away."

"Very well," Abu Nasir replied. "And I'm pretty sure I know where to begin." He bade Taj al-Mulk farewell and headed upstream against the procession, back to the Later Bridge.

*   *   *

"As a matter of fact, he *did* come here," Hujayya said. "It surprised me after all the noise he made about flogging wine sellers."

The muezzin had not yet called noon prayers, but Hujayya's Tavern was already packed. It was as if everyone in Baghdad was determined to compensate for a month of daytime starvation in a single sitting. The tables filled up early, and latecomers had to squeeze in with strangers, but that only made it more of a party. Of course, the savory aroma of traditional roast goat filled the air, but Hujayya had plenty of other offerings as well. Hustling from the kitchen, loaded with skewers of charbroiled meats and platters of sticky pastries, Lina and the other serving girls were far too rushed to sing, flirt, or otherwise entertain. No one would hear them anyway above the raucous froth of holiday voices.

When Abu Nasir hopped off a water taxi and onto the quay next to the tavern, Hujayya had led him immediately to the best table, right at the edge of the patio, with an unobstructed view of the water. He had to break up a poetry contest and evict the competitors, but, then, it wasn't often that such a highly placed official graced his establishment. Besides, the wannabe versers had been there all morning and were still nursing their first goblets of wine. Hujayya invited Abu Nasir to partake in a drink—from a far better vintage than the poets were sipping—but the intelligence chief seemed insulted by the offer. *Converted Muslims are so much better Muslims than Muslims*, Hujayya thought. Still, he was able to entice Abu Nasir with some beef kabobs marinated in a cumin-ginger mixture and grilled with onions until they were nicely charred outside and perfectly pink and juicy in the middle. Once the intelligence chief was settled, Hujayya started to leave to tend to other customers, but Abu Nasir let him know his continued presence was required. And so Abu Nasir munched on kabobs and questioned Hujayya about the rug seller.

"It doesn't surprise me that he came back," Abu Nasir said. "Ibn Yasir no doubt wanted to finish what he started. When was this exactly?"

"That same day," Hujayya replied.

"The day we had the run-in with him in the square?"

"That's right, my friend."

"I am not your friend," Abu Nasir shouted, shaking Hujayya with his angry response. "I'm no friend to tavern keepers. This is an *official* inquiry. Perhaps your attitude would be more in keeping with that spirit if we conducted this interview in a jail cell."

Realizing that his overfamiliarity could destroy him, Hujayya did his best to capture the spirit Abu Nasir suggested by scrambling to his knees and knocking his forehead on the flagstones. It hurt. "I hear and obey, O Sahib al..." It took him a moment to remember the correct form of address. "O Sahib al-Ma'ali, sir," he said at last. He looked up to see if Abu Nasir was appeased.

Not yet. The intelligence chief sat stonily on his cushion. Abu Nasir pulled a writing kit out of his pocket, sharpened his pen, spread a piece of paper in front of him, and silently took a few notes. All of this was done slowly and deliberately, as if he thought Hujayya needed more time to reflect on the painful interrogation methods that the sultan's intelligence chief had the authority to inflict on a mere restaurateur if needed.

When he was satisfied that Hujayya had done enough reflecting, he resumed the questioning. "Now, then," he said, pen hovering over the page. "Our run-in with ibn Yasir happened on the day Yalbard was flogged. That would be Wednesday last. What time did he return?"

"About midnight, sir."

"*About* midnight? You cannot be more precise?"

Hujayya looked around the patio until he saw Lina, refilling a customer's goblet from a jug. "Lina!" he shouted. Lina approached, still carrying the jug. "What time did ibn Yasir come in last week?" Hujayya asked her. "It was midnight, wasn't it?"

"Just about," she told him. "I remember because I was wondering whether the muezzin had called midnight prayers yet." She turned to Abu Nasir to explain. "When it gets crowded in here, we can't hear the *adhan*."

"About midnight," Abu Nasir said. He wrote that down in his notes. "What happened when he arrived?"

"He was abusive," Hujayya said. "Almost swaggering. He demanded I show him to a table and bring a jug of my best wine."

"He asked for wine? After all the fuss he made earlier about drink being sinful?"

"That surprised me too. But what is *haram* in the morning is *halal* at night." Catching a whiff of disapproval from Abu Nasir, Hujayya added hastily, "At least in his mind."

"And what did you do?"

"I was going to throw him out, of course. He was already drunk. He must have visited several of my competitors before he came here. I run a high-class place. Someone like that is bad for business."

"You were *going* to throw him out. But you didn't?"

"He started yelling, 'What's the matter, Hujayya? Is my money not good enough for you?' Then he took a handful of coins out of his pocket and threw them in my face. There must have been fifteen dinars there."

"Fifteen dinars? Ibn Yasir never had fifteen dinars in his life."

"Well, he had fifteen dinars last Wednesday night. More. He was tossing dinars at the serving girls too."

"So you let him stay? Enough dinars makes a customer classy enough for Hujayya's?"

Hujayya smiled weakly. "I showed him to a table and sent Lina over with some wine and her guitar."

Abu Nasir turned to Lina. "Then what happened?" he asked.

"I poured a goblet for him," she replied. "He drained it immediately and demanded another. He went more slowly with the second one, so it was a good time for me to sing for him. I started with *Shirin's Lament for Farhad*."

"That's lovely," Hujayya interjected. "So sad and poignant."

"Ibn Yasir didn't like it," Lina continued. "He yelled at me, 'What do you think this is, Sweet Tits, a mosque? Give me something sexy.' So I tried a different, more upbeat song. It's called—"

But Abu Nasir was getting impatient. "I'm not interested in what songs you sang. Confine yourself to what the rug seller did."

"With each song I sang, the more riled he got," Lina said. "I know a thing or two about inspiring passion in men, and I've had more than my share of ogling, but this was different. It was resentment and malice, not passion, which I saw in his face. He said, 'Show me those tits, woman,' and made a grab for me. He ripped the bodice of my gown and . . . well, I don't wear a chemise underneath."

"Then what happened?"

"I smashed my guitar over his head."

Still kneeling on the pavement, Hujayya joined her in laughter. "It was quite a sight," he said. "His turban all tangled up in the strings."

"Boy, was he mad," Lina said. "And a crowd was starting to gather around us. Ibn Yasir pulled back his fist—like he was going to punch me—but a couple of the onlookers grabbed him by the arms. They dragged him to the door and threw him out into the square. We all followed, cheering them on. Ibn Yasir landed face-first, then stood up and turned around to us. 'I heard this was a classy place,' he said. 'Obviously I was misinformed. I'm off to find a really classy place. One where the staff doesn't break guitars on the customers' heads.' Then he walked away all dignified. Or it *would* have been dignified if he hadn't had a broken guitar stuck to his turban." She giggled.

"Quite a disturbance," Abu Nasir said. "Why didn't you call the *shurat*?"

"It all happened so quickly," Hujayya replied. "And after it was over, there didn't seem to be any point."

"You still should have reported it."

"Yes, O Sahib al-Ma'ali, sir." Hujayya knocked his head on the pavement again.

"Was that the last you saw of him?" Abu Nasir asked.

"He hasn't been back," Hujayya replied.

The intelligence chief looked over his notes. "I'd like to see the coins you received from ibn Yasir," he said.

Hujayya's mustache twitched. He knew these government officials and didn't like the direction this conversation was taking. "I no longer have them."

"Didn't you keep them?"

"Well, no. That was a week ago. They were mixed in with the rest of the receipts. Then I used them to pay the serving girls, the cooks, the wine merchants . . . a new guitar for Lina." Seeing Abu Nasir take another bite of kabob, he added, "And the butcher."

"But you must have kept some of them," Abu Nasir insisted. "You can't rule out that a few of ibn Yasir's dinars are still sloshing around the bottom of your cash box."

"It's not very likely."

"But not impossible. Whatever you received from him, I better have an expert look it over."

Hujayya was certain that Abu Nasir had no intention of turning the coins over to an expert—or anybody else. "And how am I to run a business without any cash?" he protested.

"I can't be responsible for every undercapitalized entrepreneur in Baghdad," Abu Shuja replied.

Hujayya wanted to argue further, but he was already on thin ice and it wouldn't do any good anyway. He pushed himself up off his knees with a middle-aged groan and headed inside for the cash box. Abu Nasir wiped his beard with a napkin and followed Hujayya. There would be no opportunity to squirrel away a few coins before Abu Nasir took possession of them. Along the way, Hujayya reassured impatient customers that someone would be right with them. Lina, scurrying in his wake with her jug of wine, did her best to keep that promise for him.

Inside the tavern, Hujayya pulled his clinking exchequer from its hiding place behind the counter and handed it over to Abu Nasir. "How long will you need to hold on to it?" he asked.

"Oh, not long," Abu Nasir replied. "In a day or two, go to the Dar Saltanah and inquire at the Registry of Outlays. They will make you whole, *inshallah*." If it be the will of Allah.

"I don't suppose there's any point in asking the Sahib al-Ma'ali for a receipt."

"You wouldn't want me to think you don't trust me, would you?" Abu Nasir replied. "Let me give you some friendly advice, Hujayya."

Hujayya resisted the temptation to say, "I thought you weren't my friend."

"Watch your step," Abu Nasir continued. "I take a most serious view of your failure to report the incident with ibn Yasir to the *shurat*. Especially now that ibn Yasir is missing. It seems you and your customers were the last people to see him."

*   *   *

Jamila was a very gentle camel. With her liquid brown eyes, she watched the faithful pour out of the Mosque of Mansur and gather in a circle around her. The expression on her face was almost human—as if she were bemused that so many people had come to see how pretty she was. Indeed she was extra pretty today, thanks to the string of red and blue beads that her keeper had placed around her elegant neck. The humans admired it and chattered the way humans do. Small boys wriggled to the front of the crowd for a better view of her, their shouts carrying above the conversation of the grown-ups. Jamila blinked coquettishly at her fans, her long eyelashes waggling.

Her keeper held her by a leash, but he didn't need to. Some men were hobbling her to prevent her from moving about. They didn't need to do that either. She stood perfectly still as they worked. They bent one of her front legs back and wound a rope around it, tying her hoof to her thigh. But she wasn't going anywhere anyway. Jamila was a good camel and she trusted her keeper. She would do whatever he wanted, even though what he now wanted was for her to stand on three legs.

One man in the group wasn't working, though. He merely wandered about. Despite being someone of obvious importance—he wore a jeweled turban with a black shawl over it—he behaved quite familiarly with the others, laughing with them and asking questions about their various tasks. Occasionally he ventured advice or clasped one of the men genially on the shoulder with one hand. The other he hid behind his back, holding something. The occasional glimpse of it kept drawing Jamila's gaze. Whatever it was, it glinted in the sun.

*   *   *

The sun sparkled on the cobalt-blue tiles of the mosque's façade as well. But under the arch of the entryway, all was darkness. Taj al-Mulk and Amid ad-Dawla lingered there, spying on the preparations from the shadows, patiently waiting out the last few stragglers as they filed out of the mosque and joined the crowd in the courtyard. It was only natural that the conversation would drift to the sermon. "The theme of Allah forgiving Joseph's brothers was appropriate," Taj al-Mulk said. "But what was he trying to say in the part about the leopards?"

"It wasn't in the prepared text," Amid ad-Dawla explained, a little embarrassed. "The caliph's own unfortunate improvisation."

"An improvisation should still have a point. Even an unfortunate one."

Amid ad-Dawla threw his hands up in frustration. "Not in this case. The Commander of the Faithful has leopards on the brain. He can't wait to show his pets to the sultan."

Taj al-Mulk peered into the interior of the mosque. It looked like everyone had gone. "Of course, I didn't stop you to talk about leopards," he said. "Where do things stand in the Dar Calipha? Does al-Muqtadi suspect anything?"

Amid ad-Dawla started to answer but abruptly reverted to his characteristic silence. Apparently someone had been out of the line of sight when Taj al-Mulk scanned the mosque. Because just then a short man with a too carefully trimmed beard approached on his way out. He looked vaguely familiar to Amid ad-Dawla, perhaps a minor functionary in the Registry of Correspondence. The man stopped to greet them. "*Eid Mubarak*, O Sahib al-

Ma'ali," he said, bowing low to Taj al-Mulk. He repeated the ritual with Amid ad-Dawla. "*Eid Mubarak*, O Sahib al-Ma'ali." Taj al-Mulk and Amid ad-Dawla returned the greeting, and the little man hurried on out to the courtyard, no doubt rehearsing the conversation in which he would impress his wife with the news that *both* viziers had wished him a blessed holiday.

"You were about to tell me about the caliph," Taj al-Mulk said when the man was gone.

"He's asking questions," Amid ad-Dawla replied, "which is unusual for him. I set his mind to rest, though."

"What did you tell him?"

"The truth. That Ghazali supports him and as long as that's the case, the sultan can't hurt him. That *is* still the case, isn't it?"

It was Taj al-Mulk's turn to throw his hands up. "I'm afraid so."

*　　　*　　　*

The man from the Registry of Correspondence joined the crowd in the courtyard and looked on as a fat-faced expert examined the patient camel. A butcher by trade, his clothes normally would have been stained with the bloody residue of his profession. But today was a special day; a clean robe of brilliant white covered his belly. His fingers were stubby but experienced; they probed Jamila's neck at the point where it joined her shoulder. The caliph, meanwhile, one hand still behind his back, stood next to the butcher and watched intently. The poking, tapping, and massaging went on for some time before the butcher found what he was looking for. Even then, he consulted with his assistant for a second opinion. It wouldn't do to get it wrong and embarrass the Commander of the Faithful. Finally, he pointed to a spot on the camel's neck and said, "There."

*　　　*　　　*

Under the archway of the mosque, Taj al-Mulk lamented his failure with Ghazali. "I sounded him out on our plan," he said. "In the most cautious and general terms, of course. And I don't see any way he's going to support the sultan against the caliph. Even if there hadn't been that unfortunate incident with the sultan's companion, Ghazali is too attached to the caliph

333

ideologically. He keeps repeating, 'Quran four fifty-nine,' over and over and over again. '*Obey Allah, and obey the Messenger and those in authority amongst you.*' To hear Ghazali tell it, when Allah said that, He was talking specifically about the caliph Abu'l-Qasim al-Muqtadi B'illah, Commander of the Faithful and Scion of the House of Abbas, in the year 485 of the Hijrah."

"Would it help if someone else talked to him?" Amid ad-Dawla asked. "Maybe if you got Omar Khayyam back?"

"At this point I don't think Ghazali will listen to *anyone* who represents the sultan."

The choice of words was accidental, but it seemed to Amid ad-Dawla there was something important in them. He became silent. The crowd noises from the courtyard floated into the archway and reverberated off the tiles. Finally, he said, "What if . . . ?" But the idea was still forming. Then he had it. *Of course*, he thought. *Why didn't we think of this before?* Out loud, he said, "What if Ghazali *thought* he was talking to someone who represented the caliph?"

Taj al-Mulk jerked his head in Amid ad-Dawla's direction. His reaction was plain on his face. *Brilliant*. But there was a flaw. "Ghazali is a smart man," he said. "If you lie to him, he'll see through it."

"I *never* lie," Amid ad-Dawla replied.

*   *   *

Al-Muqtadi hated this part. He delayed it for as long as he could. He caressed Jamila's neck with his free hand and spoke a few kind words to her. She really did have a very proud, human-like expression. Almost as if she were smiling. It was no way for her to die, to be robbed of her life for the glory of Allah. Maybe it wasn't even for the glory of Allah. Maybe it was merely for the ambition of men who claimed to speak for Allah. But al-Muqtadi was a good caliph, and twice a year he performed the sacred rite. It was expected of him. He pulled his other hand out from behind his back and revealed what he had been hiding: a short, flat sword with a jeweled handle, a legacy that, like his mantle, had come down to him through the centuries, in this case from one of his Abbasid ancestors. He pressed the point against the spot the butcher had shown him.

He was a very gentle caliph, but his secret was safe. He faced the camel; no one could see him close his eyes when he thrust the sword through the animal's jugular.

When he pulled the blade out, the blood came with it. It didn't ooze the way blood does when the barber nicks you. It poured. It poured like one of those churning mountain waterfalls that feed the Tigris. It splashed onto the pavement and spread in hot, frothy layers. The closest spectators dodged the growing crimson pool to keep their slippers from getting soaked.

At first Jamila did nothing. She just stood there, obedient as before. For a full six seconds, she stood there. Then she began to tremble. Her whole body shook, like a person about to cry. Her keeper had betrayed her. Angrily, she reared upward. The spectators scattered to avoid getting clobbered by her flailing front leg—the one that wasn't hobbled. But once they reached a safe distance, the circle re-formed and they went back to chatting pleasantly. Even the children. They looked on as if they were watching a boat tie up to the quay or a shopkeeper chase a beggar away. Something mildly interesting, a moment's distraction, but nothing out of the ordinary.

Jamila reared three more times. Then she gave up.

She lay down on her side. Or tried to. Her keeper wouldn't let her lie down completely. He pulled tightly on the lead to keep her head up. The blood wouldn't drain as fast if she didn't keep her head up.

It took her two minutes to die, suffering the whole time. At first she kicked, then she merely trembled. Then she stopped moving entirely and her keeper finally let her head sink to the pavement. The butcher took the sword from the caliph and wiped it on the camel's hairy side, now nothing more than a convenient towel.[82]

*   *   *

The quickest route from the Mosque of Mansur to the river was to double back to the Suq of the Booksellers and board a boat on the Sarat Canal. But al-Muqtadi's galley was far too large to squeeze into that cramped waterway: the span of the oars was wider than the channel. So after the sacrifice at the mosque, the caliphal procession resumed overland. This time it followed the Khorasan Highway northeast, through the Suq of the Hospital, then past the sprawling Adudi Hospital that gave the suq its name, until it intersected with the Tigris at the Main Bridge. There, tied up to the quay, the caliph's leviathan awaited its master.

No one would be accused of exaggeration if he called it a floating palace: it was certainly big enough and just as luxurious. The hull was painted a brilliant crimson and trimmed in gold. It was long and sleek and hugged the waterline along most of its length. But high up on the stern, on a raised platform, a charming pavilion looked out over the river, the city, and the rowers in the hull. The pavilion's outer walls and its barrel-shaped roof were inlaid with hexagonal designs rendered in mother-of-pearl; a team of craftsmen had taken five years to build it. On the inside, the walls were covered with richly embroidered satin curtains. Five half-moon balconies, two on each side and one in the back, curved out from the pavilion, offering secluded spots for lovers to coo, shy people to enjoy the view, and conspirators to conspire undisturbed.

Only the most senior officials and scholars were invited on board: Shami, Ghazali, the Blind Imam, and Amid ad-Dawla, of course, and a handful of others. They followed their host up the gangplank at a respectful distance, quite dignified in their somber-colored robes and turbans. Inside the pavilion the mood was less formal. The room bubbled with greetings and blessings, and there was a great deal of hugging. Daytime Sun and two other serving girls roamed among the guests with bowls overflowing with dates and gold cups cold with lemon sherbet.

Ghazali didn't know Amid ad-Dawla well—he was hard to get close to—but the chief professor had been impressed by him at Nahrawan. The caliph's vizier had managed to keep a refined demeanor during Malik-shah's boorish performance. Ghazali greeted him, "*Eid Mubarak*," but Amid ad-Dawla didn't seem to hear. Ghazali raised his voice. "*Eid Mubarak*, Sahib al-Ma'ali!"

It seemed to yank Amid ad-Dawla away from whatever it was he was thinking about. "*Eid Mubarak*," he mumbled perfunctorily. Then he wandered off. He didn't seem happy.

After the right amount of small talk, as dictated by protocol, the Commander of the Faithful made his way to the front of the pavilion, an open platform overlooking the rowers. Twenty-four benches stretched out beneath him; each bench accommodated six rowers. They sat patiently under the open sky, their backs straight, eyes forward, oars ready to be lowered into the water the moment the command was given.

A throne squatted stolidly near the edge of the platform. Al-Muqtadi took his place, standing in front of it, and signaled the pilot to cast off. Along the quay, a team of dockworkers pulled the gangplank free, untied the mooring lines, and pushed the ship out into the river with poles. When it had drifted clear, the pilot barked at the rowers. The galley unfurled its four dozen oars, twenty-four on a side, like some enormous, mythical bird from the *Shah-nama* spreading its majestic wings. On a second command, 144 rowers yanked their oars and the flame-red ship lurched forward, taking al-Muqtadi by surprise. He stumbled backward onto his throne, but the smiling good nature with which he accepted his mishap was infectious; everyone who saw it smiled with him. As the galley slowly picked up speed, the black banners of the Abbasids, mounted on poles at the corners of the roof, caught the breeze and fanned out proudly. The spectators erupted with shouts of "*Allahu akbar! Allahu akbar!* The peace of Allah upon the Commander of the Faithful!"

It was the biggest, loudest Eid al-Fitr crowd that al-Muqtadi could remember. Maybe it was the historic meeting about to take place that brought the people out, or maybe it was just the weather. It was certainly a beautiful day: bright sunshine, no haze. Spectators jammed the tiers of rooftops and balconies on both banks. The interior of Hujayya's was deserted as his customers moved out to the patio to watch the spectacle. On the top floor of the Dar Saltanah, Khuld, Terken Khatun, and other ladies of the court gathered on the catwalks and observed the pageantry from the privacy of latticed windows while slaves brought them wine in slender glasses. Other spectators lined up on the Bridge of Boats, connecting the two shores and converting that section of river into an enormous amphitheater, carved from the urban landscape, under a cloudless blue sky. The boldest children, frustrated with the lack of space at the bridge's railing, climbed down onto the pontoons and sat astride the bows; before long the less adventuresome ones followed in imitation. The crowd even spilled into the Tigris itself; hundreds of small craft escorted the caliphal ship, careful to give its formidable oars a wide berth. Only two areas were free of onlookers: the open waters ahead, beckoning the galley downstream, and the quays on either side—these had been cleared to make way for the sultan's troops.

An army marched along each shore, an honor guard to accompany the Commander of the Faithful. Boots tramped along the flagstones in time with the beating of drums, a bass line to the drone of the crowd. Unlike the Abbasids with their black flags, the Seljuqs had no official color. Black and yellow, red, green, and blue swirled together on banners that soared above soldiers' helmets. Taj al-Mulk, who had changed into his armor, led the troops on the west bank, happy to be away from his office and back on a horse. Malik-shah, on a more richly equipped horse, took the eastern shore, keeping pace with the river-borne al-Muqtadi as the two men approached their rendezvous.

Aboard the caliph's galley, Abu Hamid Ghazali watched the columns of soldiers from the windows of the pavilion. It was an impressive display of military might. And yet, despite the size of the sultan's forces, despite their impenetrable armor and their formidable discipline, Allah's will would prevail. And Ghazali had no doubt that it was Allah's will for the caliph to reign supreme. If it ever came to a conflict, the sultan's mamelukes would stand no chance against the Commander of the Faithful and his guards—backed by the common people of Baghdad. Even if the true Muslims were armed with nothing more than sticks, the outcome would be the same as it had been half a millennium ago, when the Messenger and his Companions—may the prayer and peace of Allah be upon them—crushed the Quraysh. The enemies of Islam had numbers and wealth on their side but not the power of Allah. Without that they were doomed, in their foolishness, to humiliating defeat.

Not everyone seemed to share Ghazali's faith in the ultimate victory of Allah. When he turned to rejoin the others, he noticed out of the corner of his eye Amid ad-Dawla, alone on the large balcony at the stern. The caliph's vizier stood staring down into the water and looking glum indeed. *What is the matter with him?* Ghazali wondered. First the barely mumbled greeting, now this. The rest of the caliph's guests were absorbed in conversation and honey-glazed pastries stuffed with raisins and chopped almonds. Ghazali was able to slip out the back door and join Amid ad-Dawla on the balcony unnoticed.

As it turned out, he was unnoticed even by Amid ad-Dawla. Ghazali waited patiently for the vizier to make the first conversational move. When

Amid ad-Dawla finally looked up from the water and saw Ghazali there, he said, "Oh, Professor. I didn't see you."

"I hope I didn't interrupt your meditations," Ghazali replied.

"It's just as well."

"What's the matter?"

"It's nothing. Really."

Now Ghazali *was* concerned. Amid ad-Dawla was even more reticent than usual. Ghazali tried to draw him out. "If there's anything I can help with . . ."

"As a matter of fact . . . No, I don't want to bother you."

"It's no bother."

"Well . . . how are staffing levels at the Nizamiyya?"

It seemed like a peculiar thing for the caliph's vizier to worry about. "Excellent," Ghazali replied. "We're fully staffed. Although if the sons of Nizam al-Mulk—your brothers-in-law—don't carry on their father's philanthropy, there may have to be some reductions."

"Then there's no chance of taking on someone new?"

"It's not promising. Although for the right someone . . . Who did you have in mind?"

"Me."

Ghazali was caught off guard. Was Amid ad-Dawla thinking of retiring to academia? He didn't really have any scholarly accomplishments. Sure, he had written a few poems, but everyone did that. Still, there was no one in Baghdad as well-connected.

"There's always a place for someone of your standing," Ghazali said. "Are you planning to leave the Dar Calipha?"

"Not by choice," Amid ad-Dawla said evenly.

When the shock wore off, Ghazali protested. "The Commander of the Faithful would never force you into retirement," he said. "He has nothing but praise for you."

"No, *al-Muqtadi* wouldn't push me out."

Ghazali's effort to figure it out was unmistakable. At first he stared over the stern, dumbfounded, his gaze drowning in the churn of the wake. Then he looked up and slowly scanned the west bank. Then the east. The hordes of Turks were still on the move, pounding their way to the Dar

Calipha. The realization filled him with sadness. "Those troops aren't merely for ceremony, are they?"

Amid ad-Dawla shook his head sorrowfully.

"Of course I knew something was in the works," Ghazali said. "Taj al-Mulk has been hinting at it all week, trying to get my support. But I never knew it was going to happen so soon."

Amid ad-Dawla stepped over to the door to the pavilion and peered inside. When he was sure no one was listening, he said, "We are witnesses to history, Professor. The last hour of the reign of the caliph al-Muqtadi. The books I read in school chronicled the ends of many kings. But they never captured the heartbreak."

Ghazali joined Amid ad-Dawla in the doorway and, standing at his side, followed his gaze. The man on the throne didn't seem heartbroken at all. Waving to the crowds, chatting with his friends, devouring the pastries—he was having the time of his life. "We have to warn him," Ghazali insisted.

Amid ad-Dawla grabbed Ghazali by the forearm to prevent him from bursting into the room. "Do you think that the Messenger's successor on earth doesn't already know everything?" he said.

"Look at him," Ghazali sputtered, waving one hand in the caliph's direction. "Does he act like he knows?"

"'Act' is a word with multiple meanings."

That grabbed Ghazali's attention. Snapping his head toward Amid ad-Dawla, he fixed his gaze on the vizier with the look of puzzled concentration that intelligent people reserve for the rare occasions when they are confronted by the unexpected.

"He doesn't want to cause a panic among the people," Amid ad-Dawla explained. "Their safety is far more dear to the Commander of the Faithful than his own."

The last time a major conflict had spilled blood within Abbasid territory, as opposed to on its borders, Abu Hamid Ghazali had been five years old. And that was a war among the Seljuqs; the Commander of the Faithful was never in danger. It was a lot to come to terms with.

Ghazali's gaze jerked from the caliph on his throne, to the crowds on the rooftops, to the soldiers marching down the quays, and back to caliph. *This is the fifth century. This can't be happening. It's been a hundred years since anyone fell so deeply into error that he overthrew the Messenger's successor on earth.*

At last he came to a resolution. Despite thirty years of peace—or perhaps because of them—he was certain the Quran commanded him to fight. He was ready to spring into action to enjoin good and forbid evil.

"We'll put a stop to it," he declared. "Bring the Blind Imam to me. He's over there, talking to the Shami. When we tell him what's happening, he'll denounce the sultan from the pulpit. It's Eid; there will be a big crowd at afternoon prayers. The people will listen to him. Then, as soon as we land, I'll go to the Nizamiyya and organize the students. They can arm themselves with—"

"Keep your voice down," Amid ad-Dawla cautioned in a firm whisper. "Before you panic everybody on board." Still holding Ghazali by the forearm, he pulled him from the doorway back onto the balcony. Then he closed the door, just to be on the safe side. He rested both hands on Ghazali's shoulders, looked him in the eye, and asked, "Do you think that's what the Commander of the Faithful wants?"

"He can fight this," Ghazali insisted. He swept his arm across the shore. "Look at those crowds. They adore him."

"He told me in no uncertain terms that he does not want a war with the sultan."

"Why not?"

"He doesn't want any Muslim blood spilled."

Ghazali was like a man who was all pumped up for a boxing match and suddenly learned that his opponent hadn't shown up. There was no one to hit. He took a couple of deep breaths and contemplated al-Muqtadi's hidden depths: the loving ruler, fully aware of how much danger he was in, yet not letting on for the safety of his subjects.

"He's right, of course," Ghazali said. "A truly great man. Naturally, I'll obey his wishes."

"He relies on you greatly," Amid ad-Dawla replied.

"That's kind of you to say."

"It's not me saying it. Those are the Commander of the Faithful's own words."

When you shoot to the top of your profession by age thirty-three, you get used to praise. Ghazali had had his share of it, from many highly placed officials, and even considered it his due. But he had never received it from anyone this high up. He was touched.

"I'm sure the Commander of the Faithful has more important things to worry about than me," he said with uncharacteristic modesty.

"Just this morning he told me, 'Praise be to Allah for Chief Professor Ghazali.'"

What a gracious man, Ghazali thought. *To think that with his world crumbling around him, he took the time to compliment a humble scholar. There must be something I can do for him.* He looked over to the west bank. It was the sight of Taj al-Mulk leading his troops along the quay that gave him the idea.

"Does the sultan's vizier know that the caliph doesn't intend to fight?" he asked. Without waiting for a reply, he answered his own question. "No, of course he doesn't. If he knew, he wouldn't be trying to strike a bargain with me."

Amid ad-Dawla started to say something, but Ghazali assured him, "Good news, Sahib al-Ma'ali. You can put off your retirement. I might not be able to save the caliph, but at least I can make sure that his sacrifice is not in vain. The sultan can have my cooperation. But he'll pay a price for it."

*   *   *

The two men rejoined the others inside the pavilion. Ghazali hoped that their talk had cheered Amid ad-Dawla some, but it was difficult to tell. The vizier stoically took his place behind the caliph's throne, his face a mask. In any case, Ghazali didn't have much time to think about it. At that moment, the passengers felt the deck shift abruptly under them; one or two of them had to grab a friend's shoulder or a piece of furniture to avoid stumbling forward. They moved up to the front of the platform to see what was going on and saw the palm trees and minarets of the Dar Calipha coming up on their left. The rowers had squared their blades in the water to slow the galley. On a command from the pilot, twenty-four port-side oars rose out of the river in unison; the starboard resumed rowing. With great dignity, the vessel curved toward the quay. Up ahead, Taj al-Mulk and his troops were already crossing the Later Bridge, breaking step to prevent the causeway from swaying out of control. The sultan, meanwhile, had fallen back to time his arrival to just after that of the caliph.

Protocol was executed with precision. After they descended the gangplank and stepped onto the quay, al-Muqtadi and his party had precisely enough time to form their ranks before Malik-shah cantered up at the head of his troops. He dismounted from his horse, handed the reins to a page boy, kneeled before the caliph, and kissed the paving stones. "In the name of Allah," the sultan said, "this most humble servant of the Commander of the Faithful begs to be admitted into his revered presence and permitted to kiss his blessed hand."

"The Commander of the Faithful welcomes his strong right arm into his presence," al-Muqtadi replied. "But permission to kiss his hand is denied."

Malik-shah, following the script, tried again. "In the name of Allah, may this most abject slave of the Commander of the Faithful be given the undeserved honor of kissing his sacred ring?"

Al-Muqtadi held out his hand to the sultan, who took it with his own and reverently touched his lips to the diamond that sparkled on the caliph's ring finger.

"Bloody hypocrite," Shami whispered to Ghazali.

But the caliph was the epitome of grace. "And in the name of Allah," he replied, "the Commander of the Faithful welcomes his loyal right arm and bids him rise."

Formalities dragged on for some time—protestations of not being worthy, wishes for a blessed Eid, prayers for each other's health, offers and acceptances of hospitality. Because of the limited space on the quay, most of the onlookers were soldiers, but a handful of courtiers was close enough to hear. They followed each line intently for any departure from the protocol, or even a slightly unusual intonation, ready to opine on what it meant. But they found none.

No one paid attention when Amid ad-Dawla slipped away for a side conversation with the captain of the caliph's guard. The two officials routinely had business to conduct, so a conference between them was not worthy of notice.

"You have done an excellent job today," Amid ad-Dawla said.

"I wish that were true, sir," the commander replied. "I take full responsibility for the altercation with the rug seller's wife."

"No harm has been done. You should be proud of your performance today, you and your men. I fully expected it. In fact, I arranged a treat for you. As soon as this welcoming ceremony is over, and the Commander of the Faithful is safely inside the Dar Calipha, you may all retire to your barracks and take the rest of the day off. And when you get there, you'll find a few jugs of something made from grapes." The commander started to protest. "I know," Amid ad-Dawla said, holding up one hand. "We're not supposed to. But your troops earned it."

"But who will guard the caliph? That's our sacred trust."

"That's part of the surprise. I arranged with Taj al-Mulk for the sultan's men to take over your posts for the remainder of the day."

"But that's not procedure, sir."

"I'm the vizier. I decide what the procedure is. It's a holiday. You and your men should enjoy it like the rest of us."

"Yes, O Sahib al-Ma'ali. And thank you."

By the time Amid ad-Dawla returned to the caliph's side, thirteen-year-old Abu'l-Abbas, gravely serious as always about his responsibilities, was wrapping up his own well-rehearsed litany. That concluded the ceremony. Crowds awaited sultan and caliph by the Willow Tree Gate and cheered to see the two men enter the Dar Calipha hand in hand. They were both short, but beyond that they were a study in contrasts: the swarthy, muscular Malik-shah in armor and pointed helmet, and the fair, pudgy al-Muqtadi in robes, turban, and shawl. Abu'l-Abbas entered behind them, followed by Taj al-Mulk and Amid ad-Dawla. The captain of the caliph's guard and his mamelukes followed on the way to their barracks. The Seljuq detachment tasked with taking their posts brought up the rear. After the last soldier disappeared into the dark passageway, the wooden gate shut behind him with a thud.

The Commander of the Faithful was cut off from the world.

CHAPTER 16

ALAMUT CASTLE
THURSDAY, 1 SHAWWAL 485
19 Abán 471
4 November 1092

*W*hen the predawn grayness woke them on the first morning of their captivity, Omar and Baghdadi finally got a good look at their new surroundings. It turned out to be more of a storeroom than a cell. Clean and dry, it even had a window. It was a decent-size room, and they had it to themselves, but three-quarters of the floor space was occupied by an army of waist-high clay urns. Like the office where they had been interrogated the previous night, the storeroom was an alcove carved into the mountain; three of the walls were rough-hewn rock. Unlike the office, the fourth wall was blocked by a row of wooden bars. No doubt built to prevent unauthorized personnel from getting in to pilfer supplies, they now kept the prisoners from getting out. The empty corridor on the other side was visible but out of reach; the gate was tightly secured to the door frame by a padlock and chain. Omar tried it anyway. There was no slack. As for the window, it was a bare, rectangular aperture in the rock, big enough for a man to squeeze through, with no shutters or bars to stop him. But any hope Omar had of escaping that way evaporated when he looked outside. They were high up on the cliff, a suicide drop hundreds of cubits to the valley floor. At least the window was good for a nice view of the jagged mountain landscape. In fact, the view was breathtaking.

In light of the bloodthirsty character of the Assassins, Omar was sure there were far more uncomfortable cells in Alamut. Just as with the palm-branch switch the night before, Omar sensed they were holding back, as if they wanted to impress Omar with his predicament but for some reason didn't want actual harm to come to him.

Omar and Baghdadi said their morning prayers and then made their *suhur* out of the leftovers from the meal the guards had brought them the previous night—some plain boiled rice and a few scraps of flavorless chicken. They finished well before sunrise. With nothing else to do, Omar started pulling the stoppers out of the urns to see what provisions shared their imprisonment.

"You won't find any," Baghdadi said.

"Any what?" Omar replied. "You don't even know what I'm looking for."

"Aren't you looking for wine?"

"Well, yes."

"You won't find any. You heard Commandant Misri last night. The Sheikh of the Mountain is a holy man and forbids wine in Alamut. As he should."

Omar shrugged. "No harm in looking," he said. "Besides, we don't know what else is in here that might be useful to us. Like food. Help me out—you search those urns over there."

It took half an hour to search them all. They found plenty of food but nothing they could eat: flour, olive oil, uncooked rice, dried peas. Some were filled with water; so *something* in the urns was useful. Their search complete, they sat down on the floor to wait for whatever was going to happen.

Omar thought a great deal and talked little; the day passed in relative quiet. Baghdadi was conscientious about observing the hours of prayer, and Omar joined in. Toward sunset, Omar went to the window to watch for the new moon. He didn't have long to wait—but, then, he knew approximately when to expect it. When the silver sliver finally flashed in the orange and purple sky, he had a verse ready:

> "As under cover of departing day
> Slunk hunger-stricken Ramadan away,
> > Once more within the Potter's house alone
> I stood, surrounded by the Shapes of Clay."[83]

"Is that what you've been thinking about all day?" Baghdadi asked. "I thought you were planning our escape. Now I find out you were composing poetry!"

"Do you like it?" Omar asked.

"No."

"Why not?"

"First of all, we're not in a potter's house, we're in a prison. Second, you're not alone. And third, we're *still* hunger-stricken!"

"But the *world* is a potter's house and we are, all of us, shapes of clay that the Celestial Potter molds, and uses, and returns to earth, to be made into a new pot, according to His will. So you see, I didn't forget you. You're a shape of clay."

"I'm flattered."

"As for still being hunger-stricken, yes, you got me there. But now that the sun has set, I'm sure the guard will visit us soon and bring some *iftar*."

Indeed it wasn't long. Rice with a bit of chicken again. As the guard slipped their meal through an opening in the bars, Baghdadi questioned him eagerly about whether he had any news about what the Sheikh of the Mountain had planned for them. But if the guard knew anything, he wasn't saying.

The skimpy meal did little to improve Baghdadi's mood. Omar tried to cheer him up, but Baghdadi was determined not to be cheered. He complained about their predicament; he complained about the rations; he complained about being separated from Khuld; he complained that the days of travel, investigation, and imprisonment interfered with his studies. "You promised to give me lessons," he griped. "You broke your promise."

Technically Omar had promised no such thing. All he ever said was "We ought to put the odd free moment to productive use." But he felt badly for Baghdadi, so rather than point that out, he said, "Let's do something about it."

Omar proposed a session on Aristotle, but Baghdadi's quest for knowledge no longer took him to foreign lands. "I've had enough of him," he said.

"How about the Shari'ah?" Omar asked.

"That would be all right."

Omar reckoned that the sections of the Hadith concerning Eid were suitable for today; working from memory, they debated the fine points in the dark until they were drowsy.

The second day promised to be much like the first, with the exception that now that hunger-stricken Ramadan had slunk away, there was a noontime meal. Then, as Omar and Baghdadi were chanting the final *raka'at* of their afternoon prayers, they unexpectedly heard the tramp of boots in the corridor. It was the guard again.

"Time for the midafternoon snack already?" Omar asked. Instead of replying, the guard turned his key in the padlock, swung the gate open, and gestured for the prisoners to follow him.

"Where are we going?" Omar asked, but again the guard was silent. "Fine," Omar said. "But if I'm dressed inappropriately for the occasion, don't blame me."

They climbed the steps into the open and breathed in the bright, cold fall afternoon. Omar was still wearing the fur-lined cloak he had worn in Bisotun. He took a moment to fasten the laces for added warmth, and they set off across the courtyard.

The castle appeared much different under the cloudless sky of day. Less hell-fiery, more dusty. All iron, brown Qazvin brick, and stone glowing gold in the sun. But day or night the labors of the Assassins didn't let up. Recruits hurriedly crisscrossed the courtyard on various errands, kicking up even more dust. Workmen spread plaster on the castle walls and fit lead sheets onto the ramparts to reinforce them. Others sparred, hammered weapons into shape, and otherwise shored up preparations for the inevitable day when the sultan's army returned.

One man, toting a stack of boards on his shoulder, bumped into Omar. "Watch where you're going, buddy," the man shouted. He was short and ugly, his nose too big, his lips too thick. Omar thought he had seen him before, hanging around the Khan Ja'fari, but that hardly seemed likely.

The answer to his question "Where are we going?" came soon enough as their guide hustled them past workshops, storage sheds, and even a humble mosque, until the only structure still ahead of them was the whitewashed house at the far end of the courtyard. The Sheikh of the Mountain's house.

They were obviously expected; the sentries waved them through the front door. They crossed a bare foyer and climbed a winding flight of stairs. On the second floor, they approached a room at the front of the house; the hallway split around it, allowing access from either side. The guard took the right fork and knocked on the door. "Come in," said a muffled voice.

It was the study of a scholar. Well, a poorly organized scholar. Papers and manuscripts were stacked haphazardly on chests and tables. The scent of fresh ink diffused from the inkwells that were strewn all over the room, chaperoned by pens and shakers of blotting dust. Books oriented every which way stuffed the shelves that hid nearly every square cubit of wall. The only areas free of reading matter were the two plank doors facing off on the side walls, and the large front window, handy for monitoring everything that went on in the castle.

Beneath the window, a lone man kneeled on the floor, praying. He was dressed as a Sufi master, in patched white robe and dingy white turban. His back was to his visitors, so they didn't see his face until he finished intoning the last syllables, rose, and turned to greet them. His beard was long but not full, as if too many years of fasting had left his body too enervated to produce much hair. The result was wispy and unkempt; it had clearly been a long time since he had bothered with anything as mundane as a visit to the barber. His eyes were large, brown, and sad, as if from a surfeit of meditation on his imprisonment in this sinful flesh. Indeed, everything about him screamed holy—a little too loudly—with two exceptions: The ring on his pale finger grasped a ruby far too large and expensive for any honest Sufi to afford. And the curl of his soft lips, with which he smirked at Omar, was the expression of a man who delighted in putting one over on someone more intelligent than he was.

Omar gaped at him in disbelief. This wasn't happening. "You?" he sputtered. "A Sufi?"

"Really, Omar Khayyam," the Sheikh of the Mountain replied in a high, gentle voice. "Is that any way to greet an old friend? Where are your manners?"

CHAPTER 17

BAGHDAD
THURSDAY, 1 SHAWWAL 485
19 Abán 471
4 November 1092

*O*nce through the Willow Tree Gate and out of the public eye, the sultan became a different person. The dutiful vassal transformed into the man of action in an instant. He let the caliph's hand drop from his and shot off toward the heart of the Dar Calipha. Pigeons and courtiers scattered at his approach.

"Our first stop will be the animal park," al-Muqtadi said, out of breath. The effort to keep up with Malik-shah was visible. "I'm sure . . . I'm sure my leopards will fascinate you."

Malik-shah stopped to consider. *A leopard hunt. That's worth a detour.* History could wait a couple hours. "What weapons do you use?" he asked.

"Weapons?" Al-Muqtadi was horrified. "My leopards are not for killing. They're for enjoyment. Pets."

Malik-shah snorted contemptuously and took off again.

"The turnoff is here," al-Muqtadi said. But the sultan kept on straight ahead. He traversed the length of the Dar Calipha. Chasing in the sultan's wake, al-Muqtadi kept protesting that they were going the wrong way and would miss the leopards. Malik-shah knew his destination, though: the Taj Palace. He had clearly been briefed on the layout; on entering he found the Hall of Audience without hesitation. Only al-Muqtadi, the two viziers, and a contingent of soldiers under Yalbard's command were permitted inside with him. Abu'l-Abbas and the coterie of officials that tried to follow found their way barred by more soldiers. Inside, a half dozen slaves on cleaning detail were gathering up the carpets to be taken outside and beaten. Yalbard ordered them to leave, and the great doors swung shut behind them.

Malik-shah stamped across the long hall, ascended the dais, and assumed the caliph's throne for himself. He didn't so much sit on it as lounge, reclining against one armrest with his boots dangling over the other. Marching behind their king, Taj al-Mulk and Emir Yalbard did an about-face and fell into position on either side of the brocade-covered chair. They stood at attention, awaiting orders. Al-Muqtadi objected to the sultan's lack of respect for the throne of the Abbasids. It was heretical, treasonous, and very impolite.

The Commander of the Faithful couldn't even get to the dais. Two of Yalbard's men were waiting at each set of steps; when al-Muqtadi approached, they crossed their spears smartly in front of him, blocking the way. He ordered them to stand down. In response, one of them gave him a shove that sent him sprawling on the bare floor and jarred the shawl and turban from his head. It was only then, lying there, that the caliph realized he did not recognize the faces or the armor of these soldiers. Somehow his loyal mamelukes had been replaced by imposters, as if by the magic of some evil jinn.

Barred from the dais, al-Muqtadi was stuck in front of the golden pool like a supplicant, with no one but Amid ad-Dawla to help him to his feet. That done, the vizier tried to help the little caliph with his turban as well, but it had become far too unwound to repair on the spot.

A yawning Malik-shah waited for the caliph to get settled and then waved casually for his brother to begin. Removing an official-looking scroll from his pocket, Taj al-Mulk held it up theatrically and declared, "Abu'l-Qasim al-Muqtadi, this is your Decree of Abdication." He paused to let the word "abdication" sink in. "There are a lot of *whereases* and *hereinafters*, and *in the Name of Allahs*. But the short version is this:

"Article the First: You confess that, through your officials, you repeatedly slandered the sultan's government and interfered with its legal and necessary operations. You further confess that you violated your contract of marriage with your wife Fulana bint Malik-shah by mistreating her and disinheriting the son she bore you, Mahmud.

"Article the Second: Having proved by your scandalous behavior that you are not a true Muslim, and therefore ineligible to lead the House of Islam, you resign from the caliphate immediately in favor of said Mahmud.

"Article the Third: The Dar Calipha, all properties therein, movable and immovable, the income of the date market and all other revenues pertaining to the caliphate, and any other caliphal assets will devolve upon said Mahmud.

"Article the Fourth: You renounce all future claim to the throne of the Abbasids.

"Article the Fifth: Your son, Abu'l-Abbas; his descendants; any issue you have in the future; and their descendants likewise renounce any such claims.

"The Sahib al-Jalal, Sultan Malik-shah, son of Alp Arslan the Seljuq, King of the East and the West, Glory of the Nation, Master of the World, Builder of Bridges, and Slasher of Taxes is peaceful and magnanimous. He recognizes that there flows in your veins the blood of Abbas, uncle to the Messenger. He has no desire to spill it, no matter how diluted. If you accept his terms, you will be permitted to travel to Basra this very night. You will be provided with an annual stipend sufficient to live out the rest of your life unmolested and in comfortable, albeit modest circumstances, subject to your good behavior.

"You may have thoughts of refusing this agreement. Be forewarned: the Master of the World is determined that the future of the Muslims be guided by a caliph who is worthy of the noble Abbasid bloodline, and combines it with that of the House of Seljuq. He will employ any means necessary to make it happen.

"Do you agree to these terms, Abu'l-Qasim al-Muqtadi?"

Al-Muqtadi was in denial. A sad figure, still girded by the Blessed Mantle, no turban, a receding hairline obvious in the stubble of his shaved head, he was reduced to staring at the floor and muttering. "No, no, no. That won't do. That won't do at all. I couldn't possibly go to Basra tonight."

"I need an answer."

"I mean, what's the weather like in Basra? I don't even know which robes to bring."

Malik-shah was fed up with this. He swiveled into a sitting position on the throne. With royal posture and his hands firmly clasping the armrests, he thundered, "Well, Muqtadi?"

"I need time to pack. And then there's my leopards. They would miss me. Who will look after my leopards when I'm in Basra?"

"Yes or no?"

"Commander of the Faithful," Amid ad-Dawla said. The gentle voice brought al-Muqtadi out of his trance. "The sultan is waiting for your answer."

Drawing himself up to his full height, such as it was, al-Muqtadi looked the sultan in the eye from across the golden pool and, in a voice of defiance, said, "I require more time."

"Absolutely not," the sultan insisted.

"Then my answer is—"

But Amid ad-Dawla interrupted. "O Sahib al-Jalal," he said, "may I approach the throne?" Malik-shah looked up at Taj al-Mulk with a puzzled expression. This wasn't in the script. Taj al-Mulk shrugged.

"Very well," the sultan replied. "Approach."

The soldiers let Amid ad-Dawla through and he climbed the five steps to the dais. Leaning over the throne to speak conspiratorially to Malik-shah, he beckoned Taj al-Mulk to do the same. "A delay could work to our advantage," Amid ad-Dawla said.

"Explain," Malik-shah demanded.

"Ghazali is ready to negotiate. With the delay, we could come to some understanding with him before the caliph's abdication is announced to the public."

"And why do you tell me this only now?"

"It only just happened."

Taj al-Mulk came to Amid ad-Dawla's rescue. "Amid ad-Dawla and I came up with a new tack a few hours ago. Apparently it was successful." He explained the plan that the two viziers had thought up at the mosque.

"*Sik* you!" the sultan shouted, jumping up from the throne. "*Sik* both of you! We had a plan that we all agreed to. We were going to force al-Muqtadi's abdication *today*. Now you're trying to get me to back down!"

"Keep your voice down," Taj al-Mulk said as forcefully as he could without raising his own. He glanced over toward the caliph, who still stood alone in his own Hall of Audience, able to hear every word of the sultan's outburst.

Malik-shah sat grudgingly. But there was still anger in his whisper. "Have you any idea how much risk I'm taking?" he said. "We can't afford to show weakness now."

"And we won't," Taj al-Mulk replied. "We'll be in a much stronger position if we do things this way."

"What of him?" Malik-shah asked, waving his hand contemptuously at al-Muqtadi. "And how will we keep this secret from a palace full of people?"

"The caliph is our prisoner. A prisoner in his own palace. I guarantee he won't cause any trouble. When his troops wake up tomorrow, hungover, they'll learn that they've been confined to their barracks by our men. But they won't know why. Only the people in this room know that."

"A delay can't possibly weaken our position if no one knows about it," Amid ad-Dawla added.

The sultan puffed out his cheeks in frustration. Nizam al-Mulk would have secured Ghazali's cooperation a week ago, and the sultan would not have been put in this impossible situation. But he *was* in this situation. "How long a delay are we talking about?" he asked.

"No more than two weeks," Amid ad-Dawla replied. The sultan looked at Taj al-Mulk, who nodded.

"That's a long time to keep secret what's going on here." Malik-shah looked over his shoulder at Yalbard and pointed to the soldiers. "Emir," he said, "can we rely on these men not to reveal what they've seen?"

"I guarantee it," Yalbard replied.

"Very well," the sultan said decisively. He glared at al-Muqtadi. "I am willing to entertain any concerns you have regarding the logistics of your departure. Taj al-Mulk will represent me in these discussions. Amid ad-Dawla will negotiate on your behalf. Chief Professor Ghazali will serve as mediator."

He paused and asked himself if there was anything else he needed to add. Of course—the deadline. Two weeks was too long. "He has ten days. That's what he gave ben Samha. Ten days."

CHAPTER 18

ALAMUT CASTLE
THURSDAY, 1 SHAWWAL 485
19 Abán 471
4 November 1092

R eally, Omar Khayyam," the Sheikh of the Mountain replied. "Is that any way to greet an old friend? Where are your manners?" He stood and spread his arms wide in welcome.

"Muhammad's tomb!" Omar exclaimed. In the past few weeks he had lost his mentor and patron, been ripped from the mathematical precision of his scientific instruments, and cast hundreds of farasangs away into the irrational chaos of court life. Then he was kidnapped; dragged to the bleakest, most remote spot on earth; interrogated; and imprisoned in a potter's house. All while fasting and on minimal sleep. And when the study door swung opened to reveal the instrument of the Nizam's annihilation, the villain turned out not to be Satan, or a jinn, or some other incarnation of evil, but someone he had known his whole life. In that surreal daze, Omar forgot that the apparition in front of him was the Sheikh of the Mountain; he was simply the companion of his childhood, and Omar was glad to see him. Stepping forward, Omar returned his friend's embrace, slapping his back and holding him tightly far longer than mere manners required.

Even when his friend released him, Omar didn't want to let him go. He held him at arm's length and looked him up and down. "I don't believe it," he said. "Hasan-i Sabbah. Fakhr al-Mulk told me you were lost at sea."

"And how is the third of the Three Professors?"

355

The question snapped Omar back across the decades, back into the present. "In mourning, thanks to you," he replied coldly.

"Oh, come now. Fakhr al-Mulk doesn't mourn. You mourn. You wallow in your wine and your poetry and your whores. But Fakhr al-Mulk doesn't mourn. Fakhr al-Mulk schemes. Fakhr al-Mulk hires accountants to tally up his father's estate to make sure none of his assets fall through cracks. Fakhr al-Mulk plots to discredit Taj al-Mulk and take the vizierate from him, which as far as Fakhr al-Mulk is concerned is merely one more asset in the estate of the Nizam, his by right of inheritance. But Fakhr al-Mulk doesn't mourn."

"Is that any way to speak of an old friend? Where are your manners?"

"Where are *yours*? I'm still waiting for you to introduce your young friend to me."

"I didn't think there was any necessity. Your trained bird of prey, Commander Misri, told me you know everything."

"But your young friend doesn't. So perhaps you'll introduce *me* to *him*."

Omar turned to his assistant. "Baghdadi, this is Hasan-i Sabbah," he said. "Fakhr al-Mulk, Hasan, and I were students together at the madrasa."

Baghdadi bowed his head in greeting to the Sheikh of the Mountain. "*Eid Mubarak*," he said.

"*Eid Mubarak*," Hasan replied. "You're a Nizamiyya student, I see. Is Abu Hamid Ghazali still chief professor?"

"Yes, sir."

"Then let me let you in on a secret. Old Abu Hamid is one of us."

"One of who? The Assassins?"

"Don't tell anyone."

"He keeps the secret well. He never gave any hint . . . I'm really surprised to hear it."

Omar piped up. "Professor Ghazali would be surprised to hear it too. That trick is beneath you, Hasan, saying such things when Ghazali isn't here to dispute it. I suppose when I'm not here, you tell people that Omar Khayyam is one of you."

Before Hasan could answer, the door swung open and Misri strode in, carrying a stack of papers. Omar couldn't help wonder whether Officer

Bird-of-Prey had been listening at the door and timed his entry to bail his sheikh out of an awkward conversation. "From Qazvin, my lord," Misri explained as he handed the papers to Hasan.

The Sheikh of the Mountain leafed through the documents. One in particular caught his attention. "Did you use the code I showed you?" he asked Misri.

"Yes, my lord."

The Sheikh of the Mountain turned to Omar. "My men collected your mail from the Khan Ja'fari," he said. "I took the liberty of having it decrypted. It was obliging of you to use the same code we used when we were children."

Omar looked a bit sheepish. "That was careless of me," he said. "When I taught it to Khuld, I never dreamed that her letters would be intercepted by one of the only two other people in the world who knew the damn thing."

"How is Khuld? She must be all grown up now."

"Willful as ever. What does she say?"

"All kinds of gossip from Baghdad. Apparently Mu'ayyad al-Mulk beats his wife. Abu Shuja is getting *his* wife new carpet. And it seems that Terken Khatun and Taj al-Mulk are steeped in sin. Your daughter is a most efficient spy. If she ever wants a position with the Assassins . . ."

"Did she mention me at all?" Baghdadi asked.

Hasan gave Baghdadi a questioning look, followed by a barely perceptible nod, as if he had just answered his own question. "No, no mention of you," he replied in a tone that seemed to share Baghdadi's pain. He read the page again with a slowness that made Baghdadi fidget with apprehension. "No mention at all," the Sheikh of the Mountain said at last.

But something in the letter had caught his eye. Pointing to a spot on the page, he turned to Misri and asked, "Is this true?"

Misri whispered something in his ear and handed him one last sheet of paper. Hasan laughed when he saw it. Addressing Omar, he said, "This is rich. I saved your hide by bringing you here, old friend."

"You astonish me," Omar replied.

"Don't take my word for it." Hasan held up the sheet of paper so that Omar could see it. It was a wanted poster, but not one of the ones that Omar had plastered all over Qazvin. This one featured a meticulous pen-and-ink drawing of Omar himself. "Apparently, there's a warrant out for your arrest," Hasan continued. "The sultan's men are looking for you all over Qazvin."

Omar took the poster and shrugged. "It isn't a very flattering likeness," he said. "Couldn't they have drawn me smiling? The man in this picture is positively grim."

Hasan tossed the rest of the documents onto an already cluttered table, all except Khuld's letter. That he crumpled and returned to Misri, whom he dismissed. When the door had closed behind his second in command, Hasan said, "In light of the danger you're in, Omar, you're welcome to stay here. In addition to your mail, my men retrieved your luggage from the Khan Ja'fari before the authorities arrived to confiscate it. You'll find it in your quarters."

"'Quarters' is a somewhat grandiloquent word for the storage room where you've locked us up for the last two nights."

"I must apologize for that," Hasan said. "I knew my men had brought a prisoner back from Qazvin, but I didn't find out until just now that it was you."

"And I thought you knew everything," Omar replied.

Hasan laughed, all good-natured now. "Of course I'll make it up to you," he said.

Omar didn't like the sound of that. It was as if the Sheikh of the Mountain were planning a long stay for him now that he knew all the secrets of Alamut. "Just so I can arrange my social calendar," he said, "How long a sojourn should I plan on?"

"Oh, we can talk about that later. For now, I ordered a room made up for you and Baghdadi here in the house, right next to mine. It's not luxurious, but you will no doubt find it an improvement over the storeroom. And I've arranged some refreshment for us," Hasan said, leading the way to a table that had already been set out.

"Your hospitality is overwhelming," Omar replied with abundant sarcasm. But inside, he cautioned himself to back off. *Careful, Khayyam*, he thought. *The Sheikh of the Mountain may resemble the Hasan you grew up with. But he's a different individual now. Someone very dangerous. Don't let his gentle manner fool you. You're his prisoner and his Assassins are fiercely loyal to him. One word from the Sheikh of the Mountain and it's the Door of Darkness for you and Baghdadi.*

It was a simple meal, a pilaf with dates. Once they had food in their bellies and cushions to relax on, Omar was surprised, despite his warning to himself, at how easily he and Hasan fell into their old patterns of friendship. They were two teenage boys again, talking late into the night about the things that seem important when you're young. They relived all the old arguments about Aristotle and Avicenna. The last mournful notes of evening prayers had long since faded before either of them asked the other what he had been doing the last fifteen years. Omar talked about the death of his wife, raising a daughter on his own, and building an observatory.

When it was Hasan's turn to tell of his adventures, he started by saying, "It's true, what Fakhr al-Mulk told you. I *was* lost at sea. I survived—obviously—but it was a turning point for me."

"But what happened before that?" Omar asked. "The last time I saw you, you had just resigned from the administration."

"Don't be so polite. You know perfectly well I didn't *resign*. I was fired. Do you remember why?"

"You wanted to demonstrate to the sultan that you could prepare a budget more swiftly than Nizam al-Mulk—and do a better job. But when you submitted it, the numbers didn't add up."

"They *did* add up. But just before I turned it in, that bastard Nizam al-Mulk stole several pages. I didn't notice until it was too late."

"So you needed a new professional situation."

"I went down to Egypt to serve the caliph—not al-Muqtadi, of course, but the *true* caliph—the Fatimid caliph. In Cairo I trained as a missionary. The plan was that when I finished, I would return to the east and proselytize for the Fatimid cause. And if, in the course of seeking recruits and showing them the light, any of my converts happened to give me information that was useful to the Fatimids, there were methods at my disposal to get it back to Cairo."

Omar turned to Baghdadi. "Let me translate that for you," he said. "My friend here planned to use religion as a mask so that he could become a spy for a foreign government."

Hasan objected. "When you gather and transmit information, old friend, you're a spy," he said. "When you recruit and train others to do it, you're a spy *master*. So that was my plan, but Allah, in His wisdom, placed a detour in my path."

"So I heard. You got in over your head in Egyptian politics and were arrested."

"They imprisoned me in Damietta, near the coast of the Sea of Rum. While I was there, one of the watchtowers in the prison collapsed. I was unharmed—actually I was nowhere near the tower at the time—but my friends exclaimed, 'It's a miracle!' Clearly, they said, Allah had great things planned for me. And so they arranged my escape.

"They put me on a ship to Morocco, but as you heard, it never got there. It was a small ship, no cabin. The crew, four passengers, and a cargo of glassware and linen, all out in an open boat. Two days out of port, a storm bore down on us from the west. As the wind picked up and the first drops of rain fell, we tied ourselves to the gunwales to prevent being swept overboard.

"Needless to say, we were soaked within minutes. Then the seasickness hit. We puked our guts into the ocean until we no longer had the strength to hang over the sides. Then we lay down and puked on the deck. Not that it mattered. Whatever we brought up was washed away moments later by the waves crashing down on us.

"For two days our little vessel was knocked around like a polo ball. With each new blow, the ship groaned and we were certain it was about to split in two. At one point there was a deafening crack and the mast broke in half. The falling timber narrowly missed killing the captain. The rest of us became tangled in rigging and sailcloth. Exhausted as we were, we had to clear it all away to avoid strangling in an errant rope.

"I don't know what came over me. I wasn't thinking straight anymore, although I had a vague idea that the others needed encouragement. So I said, 'Fear not.' Actually, I shouted it to be heard over the screeching wind and the driving rain. 'Fear not, for I am a holy man and Allah has a plan for me. He will not destroy His servant, so no harm can come to you as long as I am among you.' And I led the passengers and crew in prayer.

"Almost immediately the storm began to let up. Within an hour, the sun was poking through the clouds. Now I had two miracles to my name. And my first three disciples—my fellow passengers.

"With our sail gone, we were helpless in the water, but again Allah led me to my destiny. The currents drove us onto the Syrian shore. I was back in Seljuq lands. My friends in Egypt still needed intelligence. So I forgot about Morocco. Of course, the name 'Hasan-i Sabbah' was too well known, both to the Seljuqs and to my enemies in the Egyptian court. I needed a disguise, so I donned the Sufi robe, adopted the alias Deh-khoda, and began the mission I had trained for.

"I was rather good at recruiting. My reputation as a holy man, the air of mystery that surrounded me, and the esoteric doctrine I preached turned out to be valuable assets. My network of converts grew rapidly. Unfortunately, my success drew unwanted attention.

"I'm not sure what bothered Nizam al-Mulk more: our doctrine—he considered it heresy—or our espionage. Either way he was relentless. He put his intelligence chief, Abba Nasir, on my trail. That Jew must have practiced witchcraft. As soon as I could establish a new network, he would infiltrate it. Then a detachment of soldiers would show up to harass our converts, shut down our safe houses, and arrest our couriers. I realized I needed a secure base of operations, one the Nizam could never reach.

"For months I sent my men to infiltrate this castle. They snuck in, one or two at a time, filling positions as soldiers, bakers, carpenters—wherever there was an opening. When enough of them were in place, I appeared before the governor, revealed myself as the commander of the Assassins, and demanded that the castle be turned over to me. He had no choice; the castle was already mine. And thus Allah made me the lord of Alamut.

"With our new stronghold, we were secure enough to come out of the shadows. And that was when recruiting proceeded at a gallop. We sent missionaries into Qazvin and—"

But the call of the muezzin interrupted him. Hasan invited Omar and Baghdadi to join him in midnight prayers. Their worship went on for some time; Omar lost count of how many voluntary *raka'at* they chanted after the obligatory ones were completed.

When they finally rolled up their prayer rugs and returned to the table, Hasan said, "Omar, you and I have completely dominated the conversation. We've hardly heard a word from our young friend here."

"I was listening," Baghdadi said. "It was very interesting."

"What do you study at the Nizamiyya?" Hasan asked.

"Hadith and shari'ah."

"Not Quran?"

"I studied that before. In the madrasa."

"And what did you learn about it?"

"We had a comprehensive program. We started with—"

"For example, chapter twenty-four, verse thirty-five. Did you cover that?"

"'*Allah is the light of the heavens and the earth,*'" Baghdadi quoted. "'*His light is as a niche in which is a lamp, and the lamp is in a glass, the glass is as though it were a glittering star.*'"

"That's the one," Hasan-i Sabbah replied. "What does it mean?"

"Light is what makes the world visible to us. So the verse says that Allah is the source of knowledge."

"That's right, as far as it goes."

"What do you mean, 'as far as it goes'?"

"I mean why is the lamp inside a glass, and why is the whole apparatus tucked away in a niche—almost as if it were hidden?"

Baghdadi pouted, obviously disappointed with himself for not knowing the answer. He tried anyway. "I think it means—"

But the Sheikh of the Mountain didn't let him finish. "Or what about chapter seven, verse one forty-three?" he said. "Moses asked to look upon Allah and Allah told him, *'Thou canst not see Me; but look upon the mountain, and if it remain steady in its place, thou shalt see Me'; but when his Lord appeared unto the mountain He made it dust, and Moses fell down in a swoon! And when he came to himself, he said, 'Celebrated be Thy praise!'* What is the significance of this?"

"A few verses later,[84] the Quran speaks of an earthquake, so that's probably what caused the mountain to crumble."

"But why did Allah cause an earthquake? And without the earthquake, how might Moses have seen Allah simply by meditating upon a mountain?"

"I don't know. How?"

"Or what about chapter two, verse one eighty-five?"

"That's one of the verses that tell us to fast during Ramadan. It's straightforward enough. I doubt there are any hidden meanings there."

"There are hidden meanings in every verse, even the most seemingly innocuous ones. The Quran tells you to seek out a sheikh and he will guide you to them. '*None know the interpretation of it except Allah and those who are well-grounded in knowledge. They say, "We believe in it; it is all from our Lord.""*

Omar decided this had gone on long enough. "*Or* the Quran is telling you that there *isn't* any secret interpretation," he interjected. "None that a mortal can know, anyway. That power belongs to Allah alone, and Hasan here is reading the verse wrong. The correct reading is '*None know the interpretation of it except Allah. And those who are well-grounded in knowledge, they say, "We believe in it; it is all from our Lord.""*[85]

"I never understood how someone as painstaking as you in your study of the sciences nevertheless has no patience for delving into the mysteries of the Quran—its true mysteries," Hasan said.

Baghdadi tried to keep the peace. "May I ask a question?" he inquired of the Sheikh of the Mountain.

"Please do," Hasan replied. "I'm glad to see *someone* here wants to learn."

"There's something I don't understand. You said earlier that your success in recruiting was based solely on the strength of your message and your reputation as a pious man. Is that all?"

"I don't understand the question," Hasan replied. "What else would there be?"

Baghdadi hesitated to answer, so Omar did it for him. "That's his polite way of asking you about the Garden of the Assassins."

Baghdadi blushed, but Hasan laughed. "Oh, that," he said. "Since you're the student of my friend Omar, Baghdadi, I'll let you in on another of the secrets of Alamut. There is no Garden of the Assassins. Granted, if the public wants to believe that I have the magical power to send people to the Garden at will and bring them out again, far be it from me to rob them of that happy thought. But I really don't know how that story got started."

"I'll bet anything you made it up," Omar muttered.

"What was that?" Hasan demanded.

"I said I seem to have emptied my cup." He refilled it from the water pitcher.

Hasan, meanwhile, noted the look of disappointment on Baghdadi's face. "The Garden of the Assassins may be a lie," he said, "but the truth is even more wonderful."

"What is the truth?" Baghdadi asked.

"That the power of ideas—Allah's ideas—was all I ever needed." Baghdadi still looked skeptical. "You don't believe me?" Hasan asked. "Then let me prove how powerful an idea can be—when it comes from Allah."

He rose from his cushion and gestured for Baghdadi to follow him to the window. Putting one arm around Baghdadi's shoulders, he pointed out to the courtyard, where dozens of men were working by torchlight. "Every one of my Assassins is completely dedicated to our cause," Hasan said. "Pick one of them out—any one—and I'll show you how much."

Still at the table, Omar was absorbed in extracting the pit from a date when suddenly he jerked his head upward. He had just remembered something: a story from the history books. It gave him a bad feeling about where this was going. He scrambled to get to his feet and join the others at the window.

Baghdadi had made his selection. "That one," he said. He pointed to a young man stripped to the waist who was hustling across the courtyard at a good clip despite the two baskets of bricks hanging from a pole across his shoulders.

"You there," the Sheikh of the Mountain shouted. The porter dropped his burden and prostrated himself in the dust. "What is your bidding, O Sheikh of the Mountain?" he shouted back.

"I want you to climb the ramparts and—"

"Stop this right now," Omar said firmly.

Hasan looked in surprise at his old friend. "Why do you say stop? You don't even know what I'm going to tell him."

"You mean you're not planning to order him to jump off the castle wall?"

"Now you spoiled the surprise."

"What do you think? The Assassins is the first militant, esoteric movement in Islam? When Suleiman Janabi performed that demonstration—a century and a half ago—it was a surprise. Now it's just a cliché."

The porter, meanwhile, was on his feet, jogging to the nearest stairway to carry out his sheikh's orders.

"Your boy asked for a demonstration of the power of ideas," Hasan said. "I'm giving him one."

"We believe you," Omar replied. "Don't we, Baghdadi?"

But Baghdadi didn't seem to be listening. He was staring out the window, fascinated by the unfolding tragedy. The porter had reached the top of the stairs and waited on the platform for further instructions from the Sheikh of the Mountain.

"Climb the battlements," Hasan shouted.

The porter did as he was told. He pulled himself up into one of the square openings in the wall. But apparently he didn't think that was enough of a test of faith, because then he climbed even higher, onto the adjacent stone merlon. Once on top, he stood at attention, the torchlight creating the illusion that his pant legs were flapping in the breeze. Or was the wind really that gusty up there? He stared out straight across the valley at the blue-white stars hanging over the black silhouettes of mountains. He didn't even bother to look down at the jagged rocks below, not that he could see them on the moonless night, reaching up like teeth about to grind their dinner to a bloody stain.

Omar said very evenly, "Baghdadi . . ."

Startled, Baghdadi practically jumped. "Yes, Khwaja," he said.

"Tell the Sheikh of the Mountain that you are convinced by his demonstration."

"Oh, yes. Of course. It was an effective show of power."

Hasan ordered the porter to return to the courtyard and resume hauling bricks. Indifferent, the youth climbed down from the wall. "I suppose it's just as well," Hasan said. "Bricks do need to be hauled."

Hasan closed the shutters and he and his prisoners returned to the table, Baghdadi deep in thought, Omar downright mad. "You have no right to wear that robe, Hasan," he said. "A Sufi is a spiritual being. You're no Sufi."

"You don't know what you're talking about, Omar. You can see I live abstemiously. I follow the Quran and the Hadith and learn their hidden meanings. What part of what we do here isn't Sufi?"

"How about the part where you exterminate your fellow Muslims? Or did your pursuit of hidden meanings in the Quran cause you to overlook its *overt* meanings. '*And whoso kills a believer purposely, his reward is hell, to dwell therein for aye; and Allah will be wrath with him, and curse him, and prepare for him a mighty woe.*'"[86]

Hasan pointed to the window. "That fellow?" he asked. "I didn't kill him."

"You were going to."

"No, I wasn't. And if he killed himself, how is that *my* sin?"

"And what about murder for hire? Is that a sin? Who paid for the assassination of Nizam al-Mulk?"

Hasan gave Omar his most intimidating glare. But when Omar held his gaze and didn't back down, Hasan said, "Nizam al-Mulk sent an army into my lands, besieged my castle, and killed my people. So I had plenty of motive to retaliate, all on my own, without anyone else paying me for the job. Besides, it was an act of love."

"Love?" Omar said skeptically. "You felt love for the Nizam?"

"Of course I loved him," Hasan replied. "He was my mentor. But he sinned. By cutting his life short, I cut short his sinning. He's in a slightly cooler region of hell now because of me. It was an act of compassion."

What was so nauseating was that Hasan's soft voice contained no trace of irony. Omar could imagine Fakhr al-Mulk speaking of killing his enemies out of love. It would have been a joke, though, twisted pride in his own villainy. But Hasan meant it. He truly believed he had acted in the Nizam's best interest.

Omar was determined to set him straight. "It was you who sinned," he said. "You killed a believer."

"Never believe the propaganda," Hasan replied. "Nizam al-Mulk went to great lengths to convince the world that he was the guardian of orthodoxy. But he didn't live up to his own propaganda. In fact, he wasn't even an unbeliever; he was something worse. He was one who disbelieved after believing. An apostate. If he's no longer Muslim, that verse you quoted no longer applies. You know perfectly well that the penalty for apostasy is death."[87]

"Nizam al-Mulk, apostate? That's absurd."

"Why absurd? It's the same argument he used against me: 'Shiism isn't Islam.'"

"He guided two generations of sultans to revere and protect the caliph."

"A false caliph—who he kept under his thumb."

"He spent a fortune endowing universities to teach shari'ah."

"To teach heresy, you mean."

"And what about his decades waging jihad against unbelievers?"

"I'm surprised he found the time, what with the drinking parties and the wars against our brother Muslims: The Qarakhanids. The Fatimids. Me."

"And that's what this is really about, isn't it? Nizam al-Mulk was an obstacle to your ambitions. So you became an agent of the Egyptian government—a foreign power—and returned to Persia to sow chaos under the guise of religion."

"I did no such thing. The Assassins were a denomination of peace until Nizam al-Mulk persecuted us. We have a right to defend ourselves, old friend."

"*W'allah!* I'd offer my sympathy, except for one difficulty."

"What's that?"

"It's completely and utterly ludicrous. Your grievances exist only in your own mind. Nizam al-Mulk did you nothing but good. He gave you a seat at his dinner table, he gave you a position in his administration, he gave you the benefit of his advice. So stop pretending to be the victim. Sending an assassin—a cowardly sneak, hiding in a crowd with a dagger—was very, very wrong."

"Nizam al-Mulk had the whole Seljuq Empire at his disposal. All I had was this castle and the surrounding countryside. I couldn't possibly defeat him on the field of battle. So I had to employ . . . unorthodox means."

"And who made you Nizam al-Mulk's judge?"

"The Quran. Chapter three, verse one ten: '*Enjoin good and forbid evil.*'"

"I hardly think that means stabbing the sultan's vizier on the highway."

"'*Kill them wherever ye find them, and drive them out from whence they drive you out.*'"

"And how are we to have any peace or order if every man is free to decide who's a believer, and who's not a believer, and murder the ones they decide against? There would be chaos."

"I profit from chaos."

"That's the most truthful thing you said since I got here. But you didn't answer my argument."

"I don't have to. That argument isn't in the Quran. It's your own reasoning."

"Reason is the sure road to truth."

"Then why do so many sects divide the House of Islam? If reason is such a sure road, every man who travels it should arrive at the same place."

"Sometimes the traveler takes a wrong turn, even on the best marked roads. But even so, he's better off sticking to the roads than charging off across uncharted countryside. Reason is one of the faculties that Allah gave us. He wants us to use it."

"If Allah wanted us to use reason, He would have said so."

"He did. Chapter ten, verse one hundred of the Holy Quran: '*Allah puts horrors on those who do not reason.*'"

"But you left out the first half of the verse: '*It is not for any person to believe save by the permission of Allah.*' Allah will make you believe, or not, according to His will. Your reason is your attempt to obtain knowledge without Allah's permission and ultimately can have no effect. Clearly, when you see the verse in context, '*those who do not reason*' should be understood as '*those who have no sense*' or '*those who do not understand.*' The Quran is not talking about Aristotelian deduction here. You're just trying to impose reason on the text where it doesn't exist."

Omar started to protest, but the Sheikh of the Mountain had hit his stride and kept going. "I've known you my whole life, Omar, but I don't understand you. I know you believe—quite rightly—that the Quran is the word of Allah. And yet you think you need something more, reason, to understand the world. I suspect sometimes you would ignore the word of Allah entirely if your 'reason' told you different."

That hit the target. *Is he right?* Omar wondered. *Do I really hold reason in higher esteem than the Quran? And is that why I work so hard to hide from myself that they're in conflict?* His very being rebelled against the idea and pushed it out of his head. He could wink at drinking wine. And he could squirrel away bread in his pockets during Ramadan. But the line had to be drawn somewhere, and the idea that the Quran was anything less than the complete, final, and perfect testament of Allah was too blasphemous to contemplate.

Hasan, meanwhile, continued in more subdued tones. "You disappoint me, Omar," he said. "I thought you would be capable of appreciating what I have built here in Alamut. I've done no less than recreate the first generation of Islam, the Islam of the Messenger and his Companions—may the prayer and peace of Allah be upon them. A true

Muslim community, the fulfillment of the Quran. I even had hopes that you would choose to join us. Well, no matter. You will still serve my purpose."

"I'd love to serve your purpose," Omar replied. "But I really have to get back to Baghdad."

"I'm afraid that will be quite impossible," Hasan replied.

This is it, Omar thought. *The part where the Sheikh of the Mountain tells me I will never leave Alamut*. "Why is it impossible?" he asked out loud. "I'd think you'd want me to return to Baghdad so that I could tell the world how mighty you have become. So much so that it was you who struck down the great Nizam al-Mulk."

"Oh, I have propagandists for that. They'll reveal the truth to the public when the time is right. In any case, you're the wrong messenger. I doubt your account would be very flattering."

"You're not wrong."

"But the real problem is that you're one of the few people who know my true identity. Mystery is the secret of my power. I really can't have it getting out that the mighty Sheikh of the Mountain is just little Hasan from the city of Ray."

"So, then, I'm a prisoner here."

"You'll be treated well. As I said, I have provided quarters for you here in the house. And I do need an astronomer. There will be plenty for you to do—chart the course of the moon to fix the dates of the new months and the holidays, for starters. And then there's the mosque—I assume you saw it." Omar recalled the modest structure he had seen when the guard led him through the courtyard. "I was never satisfied that we put the mihrab in the right place," Hasan continued. "We took bearings for the direction of Mecca as best we could, but if you could check the calculations. And naturally there will be more mosques as the Assassin state expands, and they'll all need mihrabs. But you will never leave Assassin lands."

"And my research?"

"You mean your inquiries into the so-called *Greek* sciences? There is no place in the Assassin state for the science of the unbelievers. I'm sure you understand." He rose from his cushion. "Welcome to your new home," he said. "Let me show you to your quarters. I think you'll agree they're the best Alamut has to offer."

*　　　*　　　*

"The best Alamut has to offer" turned out to be a gloomy cube. Not much bigger than a closet, its cracked and whitewashed walls were bereft of decoration. The musty odor of mildew choked the claustrophobic space. A beat-up old chest, a couple of threadbare cushions, a bedroll for Baghdadi, and a saggy mattress for Omar grudgingly ceded a few hand widths of scuffed bare floor to the purposes of navigation.

Omar stood at the window, an unscreened rectangle that showed him just enough of the outside world to tease him. The torchlight that flooded the courtyard washed away most of heaven's dome. As long as the Assassins labored through the night, Alamut would prove a poor home for an astronomer. Only the brightest objects shined through the yellow haze: Some of the more luminous stars. The planets, of course. Saturn floated high in the western sky. *It mocks me with its freedom*, Omar thought. *Well, its metaphorical freedom, anyway*; despite the poet in him, he knew perfectly well that all the planets were slaves to laws of motion. Those laws dictated that tomorrow Saturn would go into retrograde. He had trained his staff well; the team in Isfahan would chart the planet reversing course with an accuracy unprecedented in human history, with or without Omar there to supervise. But he had hoped it would be with.

Unfortunately, staring at Saturn wasn't going to bring him any closer to home. He turned away from the window to see what Baghdadi was up to. The young man lay on his bedroll, his arms flopped at his sides, his eyes open, staring at nothing in particular. It was as if all the spirit had been drained out of him. He wore only his long-shirt; his student robe had been cast aside and lay in a heap on the floor.

"I told you to watch the door," Omar said.

"What difference does it make?" Baghdadi replied glumly.

"We need to learn the guards' routine if we're ever going to get out of here."

"We know their routine. They patrol the hallways. Not that it matters. We're never getting out of here."

"You mustn't think like that."

"You heard the Sheikh of the Mountain. 'Welcome to your new home.'"

There had to be something that would cheer Baghdadi up. Maybe something in the saddlebags that the Assassins had retrieved from Qazvin. Omar rummaged through long-shirts and *miswak* twig toothbrushes. He was angry, but not surprised, to discover that the blade that killed Nizam al-Mulk had been confiscated. But on the plus side, Baghdadi's copy of the *Prior Analytics* was still there. "Look," Omar said, waving the leather-bound prize. "We can do some studying."

"No, thank you."

"It's Aristotle."

"With all due respect, Khwaja, you are one of the foremost scholars of Aristotle in the world, and it didn't do you any good. You're a prisoner here, just as I am."

"We'll find a way out."

"And how are we going to do that? Even if we snuck past the guards and escaped from the house, how would we escape from the castle? And I don't suppose you're hiding a couple of horses in those saddlebags. Or did you plan to walk to Qazvin? Try it. *They* have horses. They would catch up to us in no time and drag us back here."

Inwardly, Omar was forced to admit that the boy had a point. Imprisoned in the fortress, surrounded by Hasan's fanatics, a day's journey to the nearest outpost of law and civilization: their predicament was grim. But Omar was the adult in the room. He had a responsibility to keep up Baghdadi's spirits. "We'll come up with a plan," he said. "We'll get back to Baghdad."

"And what if we do? There's nothing for me there anymore."

"Muhammad's tomb! What are you talking about? You have your studies in the Nizamiyya. You have a career as a scholar after that. And you have Khuld."

"Don't you understand?" Baghdadi yelled, choking back tears. "Miss Khuld has forgotten me!"

Young love, Omar thought. Out loud he said, "Is that what this is about? We left Baghdad exactly a week ago. I assure you, Khuld hasn't forgotten you."

"How can you be so sure?"

"Because Khuld never forgets anything."

"Then why hasn't she written to me? Why didn't she even mention me when she wrote to you?"

"Why do you assume Hasan told us the truth?"

"The Sheikh of the Mountain is a holy man. He would never lie."

"Oh, wouldn't he?"

"We'll never get to go back to Baghdad and find out, thanks to you."

"This isn't my fault."

Baghdadi sat up on his bedroll. "Whose fault do you think it is?" he shouted. "You're the one who dragged us to Qazvin. I told you it was too dangerous, but you insisted on coming. All that mattered to you was the mystery. It was this big intellectual puzzle and you wanted to solve it. You didn't give a damn whether anybody else got hurt! That's why you drink so much. So that you don't have to face what you do to people!"

The arrow hit the target. Omar sat down on the edge of his mattress. *Is the boy right?* he wondered. *Am I pure intellect with no regard for anyone else?*

Without warning, the door popped open. A guard in a leather helmet poked his head in. "Is there a problem here?" he asked. "I heard shouting."

"Everything is splendid," Omar replied. "Thank you."

The guard left, closing the door behind him.

But Omar was not feeling splendid. All the fatigue of the past three weeks suddenly caught up with him. Desperate to catch a murderer before any other loved ones were killed, he had galloped hundreds of farasangs on horseback to beat his head against mystifying political barriers, tenuous as smoke, yet somehow able to stand in his way. He had made friends and lost friends. Now all he wanted was to sleep. He curled up on the mattress and tried to nod off, but sleep cannot be caught by chasing it. Doubts chattered in his mind, and there was no wine in Alamut to silence them. Baghdadi was right about that much. To Omar, a goblet of ruby liquid really was *"the Cup that clears TO-DAY of past Regrets and future Fears."*

The maddening part was that he had succeeded. He had solved the mystery. But it made no difference. He knew who had wielded the dagger that murdered Nizam al-Mulk: the petulant loser Abu Tahir Arrani. Pulling his strings was the Sheikh of the Mountain, Hasan-i Sabbah. Abu Tahir was drowning amid feelings of inferiority and rejection. Hasan had twisted that young man's insecurities to his own ends by holding out a branch of community and purpose, which Abu Tahir had eagerly grasped. Now Hasan planned to brag to the world about his crimes, and would have done so even if Omar had stayed home and measured planetary coordinates instead of wearing himself out following the trail to Alamut. No doubt the only reason Hasan had not already trumpeted his role in it to the world was that he intended to make good on his threat against the sultan first. For despite Omar's efforts, Malik-shah was still in danger, and Omar had no way to warn him about where the threat originated. Nor would there be a Day of Justice for Hasan. He was ensconced on his mountain, free from fear of reciprocation, at least for this lifetime. Possibly the next.

It wouldn't be so bad if it were merely Omar who was destined to live out his life as a prisoner. He had had decades of practice resigning himself to fate. *"The first Morning of Creation wrote What the Last Dawn of Beckoning shall read."*[88] But apparently it was also written on the first Morning of Creation that he would drag Baghdadi into prison with him, thwart the young man's ambitions, and separate him from Khuld when he still burned with the thrill of new love.

And speaking of Khuld, what kind of life had he given her? She had looked after him since she was eleven years old. She had cooked his meals and washed his clothes and combed Isfahan's whorehouses for him when he didn't come home. She had given up starting a family of her own for his sake. Yes, it was her choice. But he was her father, he could have put his foot down, he could have refused to allow it. Instead he had scarcely paid attention to her. He was too absorbed in arc minutes, and rhyming quatrains, and tavern wenches. *If she ever does get married*, he thought, *I won't even know about it*. A tear slid off his cheek and was absorbed by the pillow as he thought of the grandchildren he would never see. He would have liked to have grandchildren, to play little games with them and teach them arithmetic. Hell, he would have liked to have Khuld nag him, just one more time.

Maybe someday he would escape from Alamut, see his daughter again, and tell her how proud he was of her. But there were others whom he'd never see: Nizam al-Mulk, the patriarch of so many family dinners, holidays, and outings when Omar and Fakhr al-Mulk were growing up together. And ben Samha, who barely knew Omar, but who always had a smile for him. Omar had arrived in Baghdad clueless about the dangerous political currents and the hidden reefs that could spell disaster for the unwary; ben Samha had taken it upon himself to pilot Omar safely through them.

Why had ben Samha been killed? Was that Omar's fault too? If Omar hadn't poked his beard into things, would ben Samha still be alive?

Wait a minute, Omar thought. He sat up on the mattress. *Why* had *ben Samha been killed?*

"Why was ben Samha killed?" he asked out loud.

Still sulking on his bedroll, a startled Baghdadi jerked his head up and looked at Omar. "Huh?" he asked.

"Why was ben Samha killed?" Omar repeated, more excited this time.

"Who cares? The case is over. Anyway, it's not like we can bring him back."

"No, we can't bring him back. But we can still bring his killer to justice." Omar jumped to his feet and clasped Baghdadi on the shoulder. "What are you sitting around for? We came up north to find evidence. Let's go find it."

"What difference does it make?"

"All the difference in the world, perhaps. Come on! Get up! Put your robe on!" Omar glided between the bedroll and the mattress and opened the door a crack to check for guards. The hallway was empty.

"Even if we find anything," Baghdadi said. "What would we do with it? We're still prisoners here."

"Let's take one problem at a time."

Baghdadi shook his head. "You just can't help yourself, can you? After all the tragedy, after everything I said to you, you still have to investigate things. And I think you enjoy it."

Baghdadi's words were obviously intended to hurt Omar. But Omar didn't feel hurt. In fact, he felt happy. "That's who I am," he said as he yanked the door handle. Framed in the open doorway, the entrance to Hasan's study awaited them across the hall. "As for who you are," Omar said, "you are my capable assistant whose help I require. So let's go."

*   *   *

"What are we looking for?" Baghdadi asked.

374

"I'm not sure," Omar replied. "Anything that might tie the Assassins to someone on our suspect list. Letters, bank receipts, schematics for mannequins that drink wine and urinate."

They were alone in Hasan's study. The room was dark now, with only their lanterns for illumination. The sputtering oil flames cast a brownish tint on any chests or tables that fell within the circles of their light. It was quieter now as well. Everyone else in the house—everyone except the guards, that is—had gone to bed. The daytime racket of household staff carrying out their chores and messengers rushing through the halls was silent now. But from out in the courtyard, the metallic ring of blacksmiths' hammers and the rhythmic scrape of construction saws washed relentlessly against the shutters, which muffled the sounds but could not keep them out.

Baghdadi raised his lamp to reveal how much clutter of paper and books littered the room. "This will take forever," he complained.

"Then we better get started. You search that table. I'll take these shelves over here."

"What if the guards find us?"

Omar was growing impatient. "You watched them yourself," he said. "They just patrol the corridors. As long as there's no disturbance, they don't intrude into the rooms."

"But what if they do?"

"There are two doors. If they come in one, we abscond through the other."

Baghdadi seated himself on a cushion at one of the tables and started looking through a stack of papers. But he got no further than the second sheet when he had another question. "What makes you think there's a connection to any of our suspects? The Sheikh of the Mountain said he acted alone. He certainly had a motive. Why do you think he isn't telling the truth?"

"Because even though he had a motive to exterminate Nizam al-Mulk, there was a second murder, and I'm convinced that's the key to the mystery."

"Ben Samha."

"Right."

"Maybe the Sheikh of the Mountain killed him too."

"No. I'm sure he didn't."

"Why not?"

"Because for *that* murder, he had no motive." Baghdadi looked puzzled, so Omar explained. "It wasn't ben Samha who cheated Hasan out of his position in the administration. And it wasn't ben Samha who sent an army against Alamut. There was no connection between Hasan and ben Samha."

"Maybe the two murders aren't related."

"They have to be. Ben Samha told me the sultan has a master plan. He never revealed what it was, but he was definitely in the middle of it. Now go back to work."

Baghdadi looked through a few more pages. One of them caught his attention. "I suppose this is yours," he said. "Not that it matters anymore."

"What's that?" Omar asked.

"Your safe-conduct. The one from the sultan that Misri confiscated from you."

"Give it to me."

Baghdadi did as he was told. "We'll need this if we ever get out of here," Omar said.

"What's the use?" Baghdadi replied sullenly. He gestured at the stacks of documents. "What's the use of any of this? You heard the Sheikh of the Mountain. We'll be here the rest of our lives. He knows the hidden meanings in the Quran. That makes him powerful. We can't fight him."

Omar approached Baghdadi and grabbed him roughly by the shoulders, squashing the safe-conduct as he did so. "Listen to me," he said firmly. "We *will* get out of this. I've known Hasan my whole life. I've seen him make a fool of himself in front of a classroom. I've seen him shoplift in the bazaar. I've even seen him naked in the bath. He's just a man, like us. He doesn't have any mystical powers derived from hidden meanings in the Quran. Allah endowed us with reason because that's the tool He wants us to use to understand the universe. Not hidden meanings. There are no hidden meanings."

Baghdadi looked disappointed, but whether it was with Hasan or Omar, Omar couldn't tell. In any case, he went back to sifting through papers.

Omar rolled up the safe-conduct and tried to slide it into his pocket, but it jammed. Something was in the way. That surprised him; the Assassins had searched him and confiscated everything he was carrying the night he

376

and Baghdadi were brought in. He fished into the pocket and discovered that the obstruction was nothing more than a bit of scrap paper. Puzzled, he held it under the lamp and laughed. All that was written on it was two numbers: 46. 31.

"Muhammad's tomb!" he exclaimed. "Make a liar out of me. There are hidden meanings in the Quran, after all."

"It's not nice to make fun of me," Baghdadi replied.

"I'm not." Omar handed him the note. Baghdadi read it and shrugged.

"Don't you get it?" Omar asked. "Chapter forty-six, verse thirty-one of Allah's Holy Quran. "*Believe in Him and He will deliver you.*' Help is on the way."

"What kind of help? Who wrote it? How did it end up in your pocket?"

"I have no idea."

"If someone wanted to tell you that help is on the way, why wouldn't he give you a note that said, 'Help is on the way,' instead of a secret code?"

"I don't know. Maybe he likes secret codes. Maybe he was worried it would be intercepted. Maybe he didn't have time. Look at the handwriting— it looks like he scratched it out in a hurry."

"I suppose so. So now what do we do?"

"We keep searching Hasan's study. I don't know what form help will take or the hour it will arrive, but when it does, we may have to leave in a hurry. I want our business here to be complete."

Suddenly, Baghdadi froze.

"What's the matter?" Omar asked.

"Keep your voice down, Khwaja," Baghdadi whispered. "I thought I heard someone coming."

They listened in silence. There were definitely footsteps in the main hall. But whoever it was passed the turnoff to the study and kept on going. Just another of the regular patrols.

"Khwaja?" Baghdadi said sheepishly.

"Yes, what is it?"

"I'm sorry about before, in our room. It was not my place to criticize you."

Omar laughed. "I *hired* you to criticize me," he replied.

"You're making fun of me again."

"No, really. Don't you remember the night we met?"

"We went to Hujayya's. You drank wine."

"And you tried to talk me out of it. That's why I took you on. Because you argued with me. You weren't intimidated by the august personage of the Astronomer Royal."

"I didn't know you felt that way. I promise in the future I'll argue with you whenever possible."

"Thank you. I think."

For several minutes, they didn't speak; the only sound was the rustle of paper. But then something else bothered Baghdadi. "Do you think the Sheikh of the Mountain really didn't know that you were the prisoner his men brought back from Qazvin?"

"Of course he knew," Omar replied. "That's why he locked us up in that storeroom instead of some damp, rat-infested cell."

"But why lock up his old friend at all?"

"He wanted to mess with our heads. He wanted us to know that he had us in his power. And he wanted us to have gratitude when later he 'rescued' us."

"I guess that makes sense."

Omar continued rifling through the documents on the bookshelves. There was no order to them. Sketches of planned buildings stacked with reports from Assassin agents, with draft essays about hadith in between. It could take days to find what they were looking for. But at most they had three hours until the sun rose and the house came to life.

After a while, Omar noticed that Baghdadi hadn't asked any questions recently. The drumbeat of shuffling paper gave way to the occasional turn of a page. Omar looked over to the table and saw Baghdadi absorbed in reading a manuscript.

"What's that?" Omar asked.

"An autobiography," Baghdadi replied.

"Of who?"

"The Sheikh of the Mountain, of course."

"After all that fuss he made about keeping his identity a secret?"

"It surprised me too."

"Ego, I suppose. If he can't let the world know who he is while he's alive, he can at least make sure there's a record of it after he passes through the Door of Darkness. What does he write?"

"This chapter is about you."

"He must have been hard up for something to say. Anything interesting?"

"He talks about how you went to school together . . . I didn't know you were at school with Nizam al-Mulk too."

"Nizam al-Mulk?" Omar scoffed. "*W'allah!* Who does he think he's kidding?"

"Khwaja, please, your voice."

"I attended school with *Fakhr* al-Mulk," Omar said, speaking more softly now. "The *son* of Nizam al-Mulk. Nizam al-Mulk! How old do you think I am?"

"That's what it says here."

"Let me see that." He took the manuscript from Baghdadi and began to read out loud:

> "Omar Khayyam, Nizam al-Mulk, and I studied together in a school in Nishapur. And we agreed in principle, according to the strictest rules of honesty and right conduct, to make a pact— sealed by drinking each other's blood—"

"Eww," said Baghdadi.

> "—that whichever of us became the greatest would strengthen and reinforce the other two."

As Omar read, he absentmindedly parked himself on a cushion at the table. Baghdadi, looking over his shoulder, followed along with him.

> "And so it happened, as told in the annals of the Seljuqs, that Nizam al-Mulk came into the vizierate. Omar Khayyam came to pay court to him and reminisce about their childhood together. Remembering the old pact, Nizam al-Mulk said, 'I will make you the governor of Nishapur and the surrounding territories.'

"But Omar replied that the life of a great man is one of wisdom, virtue, and learning. 'You have aspirations to rule an empire,' he said. 'But to hand down prohibitions to the common people? I have no such ambitions. Set me on the road to fame and give me an annual stipend.'"

"That doesn't sound like you at all," Baghdadi observed. "There isn't a 'Muhammad's tomb!' or a '*W'allah!*' in the entire speech."

"Does anyone sound like himself in the history books?" Omar asked in reply. "They weren't my exact words. But he got the gist of it." He continued reading:

"And Nizam al-Mulk bestowed upon him ten thousand dinars from the tax revenue of Nishapur, and this stream has flowed every year since then without decrease or obligation.

"And I also came, from the city of Ray, to pay court to the Nizam.

"I reminded him, 'Your eminence made me a promise.'

"Nizam al-Mulk replied, 'You shall have authority from Ray to Isfahan.' I was an excellent choice for the job, but I wasn't satisfied with the offer and I turned it down. What I was expecting was a high-ranking position in the ministry. Nizam al-Mulk (who was backed into a corner) said, 'Then you shall attend the Sahib al-Jalal, the Sultan.'

"But because he knew that I aspired to the same dignity and level in the ministry that he held himself, he kept a close eye on me."[89]

"Hasan didn't hold back," Omar said when he finished reading. "See how he insinuates his own greatness by associating himself with the pious and powerful. But the notion that Nizam al-Mulk went to the madrasa with us is ludicrous—he was thirty years older than we were."

"So there never was a pact?"

Omar chuckled. "I haven't thought about that in years. Yes, there was a pact. But it was Hasan and Fakhr al-Mulk who made the pact with me, not Nizam al-Mulk. He wasn't a party to it. Although in the end he was the one who assisted all three of us; it wasn't one of us assisting the other two.

So in truth the pact was moot." His head jerked rapidly as he searched the table.

"What are you looking for?" Baghdadi asked.

"A pen. I'm going to correct the manuscript."

"You can't do that."

He found a pen wedged inside a volume of poetry; apparently Hasan had been using it as a bookmark. Omar dipped it into an inkwell, shook off the excess ink, and held it poised over the page as he pondered where to start. "This won't take long," he explained. "The story is basically true. It's only the details that need some adjustments."

"If you mark up the manuscript, the Sheikh of the Mountain will know we were here."

Omar hesitated for a moment, then set the pen down. "You're right, of course," he said. He looked over the manuscript one more time, disappointed. "It'll just have to be something for future historians to puzzle over."

"What else does it say?" Baghdadi asked.

Omar waved his hand over the manuscript dismissively. "Only the story he already told us. How he tried to make Nizam al-Mulk look bad, but the Nizam got the better of him: '*After several years with no problems, the sultan came to Nizam al-Mulk. He wanted to set a budget. Nizam al-Mulk asked for some time, but I said—*'"

This time the footstep in the corridor was just outside one of the doors.

"Khwaja—" Baghdadi started, in a panic.

"I heard it," Omar replied, dropping the manuscript on the table. "Let's get out of here."

The door creaked as it opened. But by then Omar had shoved Baghdadi out through the other door and leaped out after him. They dived across the hall to their own room. Omar yanked the door closed behind them as quickly as he could, careful to pull back at the last moment so that it met the door frame noiselessly. They snuffed out the flames in their lamps, jumped onto their respective mattresses and bedrolls, and pulled the covers over themselves.

A moment later the bedroom door opened and a ray of lamplight pierced the dark. Omar and Baghdadi snapped their eyes shut and pretended to sleep. They were out of breath, but they regulated their breathing as best they could. Whoever the intruder was—presumably one of the guards—he hovered in the doorway for a while. A minute went by, then another. Then they heard the guard's footsteps, and Omar felt him brush past as he followed the narrow path to the chest where they had left their lamps. *Muhammad's tomb!* Omar thought. *They're still hot. If he touches them* . . . But apparently the guard didn't, because he turned around and left. For whatever reason, he had satisfied himself that nothing was amiss. He closed the door behind him.

The creak of boots in the corridor faded away.

*   *   *

There was an intruder in the room.

At first Omar was fuzzy about where he was. But then he saw Baghdadi curled up on his bedroll, noiselessly slumbering, the way young people do. And there was the window, still yellow with torchlight. Not the gray light of dawn. If Omar had slept, it hadn't been for very long. Had someone entered the room? The guard maybe? Or had Omar dreamed that? He didn't remember dreaming, but—

Suddenly an arm was flung across his chest and a hand was cupped over his mouth. An ugly, round face, half cloaked in shadow, peered down on him from a few inches away. Terrified, Omar thrashed about, desperate to twist free. "None of that," his assailant said, quietly but firmly. He leaned his weight into his arm, pinning Omar to the mattress. Omar struggled to breathe against the crushing pressure. "Don't cry out," the intruder whispered. "I'm a friend. Taj al-Mulk sent me. Nod if you understand."

Omar nodded with exaggerated vigor.

The intruder released the hold he had on Omar. As Omar's panic subsided, he sat up on the bed and took a good look at his guest. The man was short but powerfully built. He dressed like any of the Assassins: white turban, blue robe, patches. As for his face, the initial impression of ugliness wasn't wrong, but it also held a great deal of intelligence, especially around the eyes; they warned Omar not to raise any disturbance. Omar was certain he had seen this face before—more than once—but he couldn't remember where.

The visitor waved one hand vaguely in Baghdadi's direction. "Wake him," he ordered. Omar shook his assistant gently by the shoulder. Rolling over on his back, Baghdadi smiled and muttered, "What, again, Khuld? How many times a night can you—?" But then dreams retreated in the face of reality and Baghdadi's eyes widened as he realized it was Omar looking down at him. "I'm so sorry, Khwaja," he said, mortified. "I—"

But Omar cut him off with a finger placed over Baghdadi's lips. He neither needed nor wanted an explanation. "We have company," he whispered.

As a puzzled Baghdadi eyed the visitor suspiciously, Omar said, "All right, he's up. Now, who are you?"

"My name is Hariri," the visitor replied. "Abu Muhammad Qasim al-Hariri al-Basri. I came to assist your escape."

"Are you the man who introduced the note into my pocket?" he asked. "Forty-six, thirty-one?"

"Yes."

"So what's the plan?"

"We must leave. Now. I have three horses hidden down in the valley."

Omar's gaze settled on the saddlebags. "Leave them," Hariri said. "Take only what you can't replace—provided it fits in your pockets."

Omar thought for a moment. He couldn't replace the sultan's safe-conduct, obviously. He patted his robe to make sure it was still in the pocket. *Is there anything else?* he wondered.

Baghdadi read his thoughts. "What about the murder weapon?" he asked.

"Our Assassin friends took it," Omar said. "They're determined to keep us away from sharp objects. No matter. We still have its twin in Baghdad. All right, then, we're ready to—" Then he remembered. "Wait. We can't go yet."

"We have to," Hariri replied.

"No, I have to return to Hasan's study. There's evidence there, I know it."

"Do you really think the guard that was here didn't notice your lamps were still hot?" Hariri asked, patiently. "He reported it to his superior, and the information is working its way up through the ranks as we speak. In one hour, with the approach of dawn, the muezzin is going to chant the call to prayer, and this house is going to come to life. What do you think is going to happen when the Sheikh of the Mountain receives his morning briefing and finds out you were in his study?

"There are going to be guards in the hallway, guards in the study, and guards on you. You have one chance to get out of here, and that's now. Unless you want to spend the rest of your life calculating the start of holidays and the positions of mihrabs."

"You're right, of course," Omar said. "Baghdadi, let's go."

But Baghdadi didn't move. He sat on his bedroll, deep in thought, his head held between his palms.

"Come on, son," Omar said as he followed Hariri to the door. "We're leaving."

"I'm not going," Baghdadi replied.

Omar stopped in his tracks. "Of course you're going," he said. "Why aren't you going?"

"I think I can learn more if I stay here. Please don't misunderstand me, Khwaja, I'm very grateful for all you taught me about Aristotle and logic, but the Sheikh of the Mountain, he *knows*. Everything that happens, the hidden meanings."

"Muhammad's tomb! There aren't any hidden meanings! I already explained that. If you interpret the verse correctly, it says—"

But Hariri didn't let Omar finish. He pushed past him, back into the room, and approached Baghdadi. Without warning, his leg shot out and his boot made contact with Baghdadi's jaw—hard. The force of the kick knocked Baghdadi over backward, onto the bedroll. He was out cold. "Let's go," Hariri said.

A stunned Omar looked down at Baghdadi's unconscious body. "*W'allah!* Why did you do that?" he demanded.

"He is no longer your assistant. He's one of them."

"But you didn't have to render him unconscious."

"Yes, I did. Otherwise, he would sound the alarm. Now we have to get out of here. I want to be three farasangs away when he wakes up."

The young man lay helplessly on the bedroll, his legs still crossed. Omar couldn't help thinking how uncomfortable that would be—if Baghdadi were conscious. His sleeves had ridden up, revealing his scrawny forearms.

Omar had hoped the young man would someday be his son-in-law. Apparently that was not to be. Khuld would be heartbroken, but Omar had to concede the inevitable. Baghdadi couldn't possibly come with them now even if he wanted to—which he didn't.

"How do we sneak out of the house?" he asked. "There are guards at the front door."

"That will not be a problem," Hariri replied. "We are not going through the front door."

*   *   *

Instead they went up. An outdoor staircase, accessible from a side door, took them directly from the second floor to the top of the building. They bolted across the roof to the back of the house and came face-to-face with the castle wall. A ladder waited for them, to take them even higher. Omar didn't know what Hariri intended to do once they got up to the battlements, but whatever he had in mind, it had been meticulously planned.

They climbed the ladder. "Stay in the shadows," Hariri said when they reached the top. He didn't want anyone down below in the courtyard to spot them.

"Where do we go now?" Omar asked.

Hariri gestured toward the wall with one hand. Up and over.

"And how do we do that without plummeting to our deaths?" Omar demanded.

Hariri approached a niche in the wall and drew out the end of a rope that had been coiled neatly out of sight.

"You've got to be kidding me," Omar said.

"Getting down is easy," Hariri replied. "You should have seen what I went through to get *up* the wall. Face me," he ordered. He wrapped the rope around one of the stone merlons and then threaded it around Omar—over his shoulder, around his waist, between his legs. "Now up you go," he said. "Into the embrasure."

Omar climbed into the gap between two merlons and glanced over his shoulder down into the valley. It was too dark to see the bottom. Maybe it was better that way. "*W'allah!*" he exclaimed. "Are you sure this is safe?"

"You'll be surprised," Hariri replied. "Step backward."

Cautiously, Omar took a couple steps back until he reached the edge of the precipice and his heels hung over empty space. Only his toes still gripped the stonework.

"Lean back," Hariri said.

"I'll break my neck," Omar replied.

"Trust me."

Nervously, Omar put his weight into the rope. To his astonishment, it held. "It works!" he exulted.

"Feed a little of it through your hands," Hariri said.

Omar gave it a try and now had some slack to take a couple of steps downward, bracing his feet on the vertical wall face. He tried it again and took a couple more steps. "This is amazing. It's just like walking," he said, delighted.

"I told you you'd be surprised," Hariri replied. "Now keep going. I'll be right beside you." He secured a second rope around the next merlon over.

It didn't take him long to catch up with Omar. Together, they made their way downward. Omar was slow at first, but with practice he picked up speed. It wasn't *just* like walking, though. Far more tiring. Soon his arms ached with the effort.

They had been descending for what seemed like an eternity when Hariri abruptly froze and whispered, "Wait."

"What is it?" Omar asked.

"Shhh."

Looking up, Omar spied something moving above them on the ramparts and realized why Hariri was on sudden alert. A guard was passing on patrol. He stopped at each embrasure, looked out across the valley, and then leaned over to check for anyone scaling the walls. Then he disappeared behind the adjacent merlon before reemerging at the next embrasure to repeat the procedure. Omar held his breath. Any movement by him or Hariri risked attracting the guard's attention. If they were spotted, two slashes of the guard's knife would be all it would take to sever the ropes and send Omar and Hariri plummeting in terror. Would he actually feel his skull shatter against the rocks, Omar wondered, or would instant death spare him that agony? *"We know not if we shall breathe out the very Breath we now breathe in."*[90]

386

A second patrol appeared, this one from the opposite direction. The two guards met right above the climbers and stopped to converse. The discussion went on for several minutes. Obviously Omar couldn't keep holding his breath. The pressure of air in his lungs was too intense. He tried to let it out as quietly as possible, but it sounded to him like wind howling through a canyon. That must have been his imagination, though, because up on the battlements, the guards kept talking as if nothing were amiss. The ropes strained against Omar's back and dug into his palms. He worried how long he could hold on. His arms convulsed with the struggle.

Then he slipped.

He plunged toward the rocks. Air rushed at him. His stomach flew upward. Terror welled inside him like an icy liquid. Desperately, he fought to clamp down on his scratchy lifeline. As it skidded through his palms, the rope seared his flesh like a red-hot razor.

After several failed attempts, Omar got a grip on the rope. The slack tensed and yanked him to a bone-rattling stop.

At first he was too panicked to think. His heart pounded and he gasped for air. But as the surge of adrenalin subsided and his breathing and heart rate steadied, he could begin to assess his situation. He was dangling from the rope, swinging gently in the night. Before he fell, Hariri had been beside him. Now Hariri was fifteen cubits above. Which meant that was how far Omar had dropped. He could see the ground now. He only had about a third of the way to go. Not that far, really. Those rope burns were going to smart like a son of a bitch the rest of the way, though. And his whole side ached—he vaguely remembered slamming into the wall at some point. He was pretty sure he had cried out when that happened.

The guards—had they heard it? Apparently so. They peered over the wall, trying to locate the source of the noise. They waved their torches below them to light up any intruder. Omar realized that their light was the reason he could now see the ground. He kept very still, but there wasn't much he could do about the swinging of the rope. Seconds passed.

Suddenly a screech rang out, like the cry of an eagle, and a black shape shot away from the castle wall and glided into the night. "Just a bird," one of the guards said, shrugging. The screech repeated four or five times, fainter each time. The guards resumed their patrols.

With the guards out of sight, Hariri called down to Omar. "Are you all right?" he asked, barely audible.

"Yes, I'm fine," Omar replied. "What's taking you so long? I'm all the way down here." He rocked back and forth a few times until he had enough momentum to maneuver his feet back onto the wall.

The escapees resumed their descent. Soon Hariri was level with Omar again. "Lucky for me that bird decided to go for a flight when she did," Omar said. Hariri laughed. Omar wasn't sure why.

At last they touched down at the base of the castle wall. "The most difficult part is behind you now," Hariri said. He helped Omar untangle himself from his rope. Then he pulled both ropes down from the wall, carefully coiled them, and hid them under some brush.

Compared to the rappel down the wall, scrambling down the crag was easy. Along the way, Hariri snagged a leather pouch that was wedged between two rocks. "Here's your 'bird,'" he said. "Nothing lucky about it."

"Huh?" Omar replied.

Hariri let out a screech. His eagle call was spot on.

The trip down the crag was a lot faster than the trip up. It took only twenty minutes to reach the valley floor. "Our transport is over there," Hariri said, pointing to a copse of willow trees; their drooping branches hid three horses from the lookouts on the castle wall. They were already saddled and ready to go. Hariri tethered the spare one to his own, and he and Omar mounted up. A flick of the reins and a gentle pressure of their heels, and they were galloping toward the narrow pass and out of the Valley of the Assassins.

CHAPTER 19

A gray light was spreading from the east when Lina stepped out through the door of her client's house. *What a pervert*, she thought. *That's the last time I take a job from an egg merchant.*

The house had been stuffy, and rich with the odor of frying eggs. Grateful to be out of there and into the fresh, predawn air, she bounced along the street, her new guitar strapped across her back, her colorful silks fluttering in the breeze.

She decided on the river route. The quay had a forlorn, morning-after look. Ramadan was over. Yesterday's celebration had drawn huge, raucous crowds that stayed out for hours after midnight. But now the streets were hushed as the city slept off its collective hangover—a metaphorical hangover for the majority of Baghdadis, but, in the opinion of Shami and Ghazali, a literal hangover for far too many. In any case, there were only a few other people in sight. Lina passed a street sweeper who was cleaning up food wrappers, pistachio shells, and the odd little mound of broken pottery that until the previous night's revelry had been a wine jug. Up ahead, a solitary figure drove a mule across the Main Bridge. The riverfront was silent, except for the swish of Lina's slippers on the paving stones and the wash of the waves against the quay.

But as she approached the Gate of the Arch, a new sound intruded. Something in the water was bumping against the quay.

Bump.

Bump.

Bump.

When she looked over the edge, it appeared to be a sack filled with—well, she couldn't tell. It kept trying to float out into the river, but the waves kept pushing it back against the quay.

Bump.

Bump.

Bump.

Then she realized it had a head.

The head was submerged face down in the Tigris, flopping from the neck like a broken branch. What Lina had mistaken for a sack was actually a man's robe, the seams stressed by the bloated carcass inside. The fabric was mottled with patches of mud and inflated like an overfilled, person-sized wineskin. The corpse's arms and legs were tangled in various aquatic weeds. Where the skin was exposed—mainly around the hands and feet—it had taken on a grayish tinge.

The stink invaded Lina's nostrils suddenly, catching her off guard. It was a cross between rotting meat and low tide. Before she knew what was happening, the contents of her stomach rebelled. She barely had time to kneel at the edge of the quay.

CHAPTER 20

ALAMUT CASTLE
FRIDAY, 2 SHAWWAL 485
20 Abán 471
5 November 1092

C ommander Misri reported to the Sheikh of the Mountain's study as soon as he was certain. "Omar Khayyam has escaped."

The Sheikh of the Mountain took the news calmly. He was seated on a cushion, making notations in an account book. "That is not possible," he replied without looking up. "I gave orders that Omar was not to leave the house." He completed an entry in the ledger, generously inking a tail on the last letter with a swoop of his reed pen. "Surely my orders were not disobeyed."

Misri stood stiffly at attention. "He is nowhere to be found, my lord."

"This is most unwelcome news." He sprinkled some dust on the page to blot the wet ink. Only then did he set the book aside and give his full attention to his second in command. "You'd better start at the beginning," he sighed.

"It was right after sunrise. A servant went to Khayyam's room with his breakfast. Khayyam was gone and his assistant had been knocked unconscious. The servant notified one of the guards and we immediately began a search of the castle—"

"Which would explain the activity outside my window."

"We looked inside and out."

"And . . . ?"

"No sign of Khayyam. But we did find this." He beckoned to one of his men who was waiting out in the hallway. The Assassin lugged a long coil

391

of rope into the study. He dropped it on the floor next to the Sheikh of the Mountain. "Hidden under some brush," Misri explained. "At the base of the east wall."

Hasan looked skeptical. "Omar is hardly the athletic type," he said. "What makes you think this is his?"

Misri gestured into the hallway again. A second Assassin entered with another coil. He dropped it on top of the first one. "He had help," Misri replied.

Puzzled, the Sheikh of the Mountain contemplated the rope. "Omar is fiercely loyal," he said. "It's not like him to leave his assistant behind. Have you been able to get anything out of the boy?"

"Not yet. He's come to, but he's still groggy. So he hasn't told us anything useful. He will, though."

"I understand," Hasan said. "Very well." He stood and brushed some blotting dust off his robe. "Get your fastest riders together and have them on the road in five minutes. Don't take any chances. I want Khayyam apprehended before he can reveal our secrets. As for anyone he's been in contact with . . ."

"At once, my lord." Misri pivoted smartly on his heels and double-timed it to the exit. His two men hoisted the coils of rope over their shoulders and fell in behind him.

They were almost out of the study when the Sheikh of the Mountain added, "Oh, and Commander . . ."

Misri halted in the doorway and looked back questioningly at his chief. "Yes, my lord?" he asked.

"When they bring Omar back . . . he doesn't *have* to be alive."

CHAPTER 21

BAGHDAD
FRIDAY, 2 SHAWWAL 485
20 Abán 471
5 November 1092

It was only a half session today. Shami was going to have to wrap things up before noon—with enough time to spare for the porters to drag the judges' thrones off to the side before midday prayers began.

The Commission of Inquiry and Justice in the Murder of Nizam al-Mulk was still limping along. But after Yalbard had been flogged so viciously, witnesses had grown understandably scarce. Whenever the bailiffs tried to serve a summons, the summonee had conveniently left town on urgent business for the sultan and no one knew when he'd be back. Commission sessions were still convened, but they were intermittent, desultory, and brief. The crowds in Shami's court thinned out as the public sought entertainment venues that promised more action.

But clearly something was up today. Not only had Shami resorted to the unusual expedient of calling a Friday session, but word on the street—industriously orchestrated by Mu'ayyad al-Mulk—was that there was going to be a break in the case. The exact nature of the break was a little vague; lack of information made the members of the public all the more insistent that their pet theories were correct. Among Nizamiyya students the leading theory was that Omar Khayyam had returned from a covert operation with shocking new evidence. Nearby, in the date market, merchants told their customers that the sultan's second wife, Zubayda, had been smuggled out of Isfahan in a sealed palanquin carrying secrets that until now had been shrouded by the walls of the harem. But across the river, in the Street of the

Pitch Workers, they knew better. It wasn't Zubayda, the second wife, but rather Safariyya, the third wife, who was going to testify. The only thing everyone agreed on was that a surprise witness was involved and it was someone who had just arrived in Baghdad.

Eager for a show, the spectators returned to the Mosque of Mansur. Anyone entering the main hall, confronted with the solid mass of robes and turbans in front of him, would have been certain there was no place for him. Yet, pushed on by the crush of people behind him, he would find one anyway. The tide of humanity washed up against the stone pillars and the three judges' thrones like foam on the surface of a turbulent ocean.

The din of theorizing stopped instantly when Shami and Ghazali entered the hall. Silence reigned as they proceeded down the aisle and took their places on their thrones. It wasn't really necessary for Shami to bang his staff on the platform to call the session to order—he already had the audience's complete attention—but he followed the form.

"Bring in the witness," he ordered the bailiffs.

The rear door opened to reveal a middle-age man, elegant and austere like a younger version of his father, but with a smirk on his face as if he had put something over on someone. Fakhr al-Mulk.

The murmurs that rippled through the crowd were half gloating ("See I told you") and half self-deprecation ("Fakhr al-Mulk. Of course. *I* should have thought of that"). Fully aware of the sensation he was causing, Fakhr al-Mulk took his time making his way up the aisle. He wore a plain linen robe, solid beige, with no pattern or embroidery; he was far too smart to provoke Shami's prejudice against silk and other forms of ostentation. Under his arm he carried a sheaf of papers; it bounced jauntily in his ringless fingers. He reached the front of the mosque and bowed low to the qadis.

"Rise," Shami said. "And allow me to commend you for the example you set in carrying out your civic responsibilities by coming here—without having to be summoned—so soon after the death of your father. I know you've had a long trip from Isfahan—we will try to make this as quick and painless as possible. You sent me word that you had important evidence bearing on his murder. What have you brought us?"

With both hands, Fakhr al-Mulk held up the sheaf of papers over his head. "This," he said. "*The Book of Politics*—"

"I can get that in any bookseller's stall."

"Not volume two."

It took a moment for that to sink in, but then court erupted in a chorus of eager voices. In a city with as many bookstores, libraries, and universities as Baghdad, the announcement of a sequel to *The Book of Politics* would have been an event under any circumstances. When the circumstances were a crowded and high-stakes court hearing, excitement bubbled over. "I had no idea!" "When does it go on sale?" "I already knew. My cousin in the government told me in confidence. He says it's even more insightful than the first volume."

Raqim, who had been dispatched by Taj al-Mulk to keep an eye on the proceedings and report back, was sitting next to a former classmate who happened to be in the book business. "I thought you were my friend," his classmate reproached him. "How can you do this to me?"

"What are you talking about?" Raqim asked in reply.

"The thing's going to be the biggest best seller since the *Shah-nama*, and you didn't get me an advance copy."

Raqim was spared the need to reply by Shami pounding his staff on the platform and thundering, "Silence!" It took several minutes, but finally the room settled down, and the qadi instructed Fakhr al-Mulk, "Start at the beginning."

Fakhr al-Mulk rehashed what he had told Omar in the sultan's camp: that he had found the eleven new chapters among his father's papers and that it warned that enemies of Islam had infiltrated the government and were conspiring to overthrow the Commander of the Faithful. He smiled as he spoke, like a chess player sitting on a game-ending move just to see how long he could string along his opponent.

"And what do you conclude from all of this?" Shami asked.

"Clearly my father found out about this conspiracy and tried to put a stop to it, but he was killed to prevent him from interfering."

"Let me see that." Shami gestured impatiently for the clerk to pass the manuscript to him. "I take a most serious view of this accusation," he said.

"I marked the page in question," Fakhr al-Mulk offered helpfully.

Shami read the section indicated. His scowl became more pronounced as he grumbled over each damning phrase. "'*Odious enemies to the religion of Muhammad . . . propaganda for the Shiite creed . . . spirit of evil intentions . . . intrigues . . . ruses . . .*'" When he completed the passage, he savagely ransacked the rest of the document but couldn't find what he was looking for. "What are the names of these malefactors?" he demanded.

"My father doesn't say, Qadi," Fakhr al-Mulk replied, not the least bit perturbed by the judge's ill humor. "But the way I see it, there is only one person it *could* be. The man who now has my father's job: Taj al-Mulk."

CHAPTER 22

ALBORZ MOUNTAINS
FRIDAY, 2 SHAWWAL 485
20 Abán 471
5 November 1092

*E*very bump in the saddle was torture. Omar's ribs ached where he had slammed into the castle wall, and his palms smarted so severely from rope burn that he could barely hold the reins. But Hariri refused to slow down. Not until he and Omar had put a good hour of riding between themselves and Alamut. Only then did he finally pull back on the reins and say, "Rest the horses."

They dismounted at the top of a rise. It was a desolate spot but tactically sound: no one could approach from either direction unobserved. The sky was overcast and an icy wind kissed the lichen-covered rocks as it sped over the landscape. On either side of the road, patches of larkspur pierced the terrain, the blooms long since withered, leaving only dead stalks to remember them. "*The Flower that once is blown forever dies,*"[91] Omar observed.

"Never mind that," Hariri replied, his breath visible in the cold morning air. "Show me your hands."

Omar extended his arms and let Hariri examine his palms. "Those burns look pretty bad," Hariri said, plucking at his beard in thought. "Are they causing you much pain?"

"I don't suppose you've got any ointment in your saddlebags," Omar said.

"No," Hariri replied. "But there is *something* we can do." He slid his knife out from the sheath on his belt.

"Whoa," Omar said, backing away from the steel blade. "There's no need to do anything drastic. They feel much better now."

Hariri drew the knife back, behind his head, and sawed the ends off his turban. As he held up the two strips of fabric in front of him, his well-worn face broke into a smile. "Bandages," he said.

He took one of Omar's hands and set to work wrapping it. "I had planned to take you back to Qazvin," he said, "but there's a complication."

"The warrant for my arrest," Omar replied.

"You know about that."

"Hasan showed me the wanted poster."

"Hasan?"

"The Sheikh of the Mountain."

Hariri frowned. Three days in Alamut and Omar had learned things that Hariri had failed to find out in a year. "When we get back on the road," he said, "you're going to have to tell me what else you know." He finished wrapping one of Omar's hands. "How is that?"

Omar flexed his hand. "Perfect," he said. "You're a bandaging professional." The padding was thick enough to give him some protection against the reins but not so thick as to impede his range of motion. "So Qazvin is out," he said. "Where do we flee instead?"

Hariri started on the other hand. "We'll have to take the long way. We'll bypass Qazvin and circle around until we rejoin the Hamadan Road south of the city. There's a post station there. They won't be looking for you, and you'll be able to get a fresh horse to go wherever you want."

"That'll work," Omar replied. "But if you don't mind a stupid question—and don't think I don't have any gratitude for all you've done—but why don't you arrest me yourself? You're an agent of the sultan. You would be well rewarded by your superiors if you brought in the fugitive astronomer."

"My superiors ordered me to protect you. Until they tell me otherwise, that's what I'm going to do." He looked around to take his bearings. "All the villages around here are under the control of Alamut," he said. "So a change of horses anytime soon is out of the question. We have a spare. That will help. The animals can take turns carrying the load. But we're going to have to pace ourselves and hope that we have enough of a head start to get back to Seljuq-controlled territory before the Assassins catch up to us. So don't dawdle."

Omar looked down the road, back in the direction of Alamut. Hariri was right, of course. As soon as Hasan realized Omar was gone, he would send his armed thugs to bring Omar back.

Hariri knotted the second bandage. "I'm finished dressing your wounds," he said. "Let's saddle up."

As planned, Hariri debriefed Omar about Alamut while they rode. He asked about everything, and in painstaking detail: the meeting with the Sheikh of the Mountain, what Omar and Baghdadi found when they searched his study, even the contents of the storeroom where they had spent their first two nights.

It took almost two hours, but once that formality was out of the way, Hariri loosened up and, in fact, turned out to be quite an agreeable traveling companion. "You mentioned flowers before," he said. "The Flower dies forever or something like that."

"'*The Flower that once is blown forever dies.*'"

"That was it. Is it from one of your poems?"

"'*Man was created weak*,'"[92] Omar replied. "As fragile as a flower. And like a flower, he only lives once."

"I'd be honored if you recited it for me."

Omar obliged:

"Oh threats of Hell and Hopes of Paradise!
One thing at least is certain—*This* Life flies:
　　　One thing is certain and the rest is Lies;
The Flower that once is blown forever dies."

A friendly theological debate followed. Hariri argued that "threats of Hell and Hopes of Paradise" *are* certain. "They are in the Quran hundreds of times," he said. "They are the essence of our religion."

When that subject was exhausted, Omar asked Hariri to return the favor and recite a verse of his own. Hariri was reluctant. "I have one on which I have been working," he said. "But it is not very good."

"Recite it anyway," Omar replied. "Maybe it will appeal to me." Hariri recited the poem about the gazelles at Hajir. When it was finished, Omar said, "You're right—that isn't very good."

Hariri laughed. "I tried to warn you," he replied, and then added, "I know some stories."

It turned out "know some stories" was an understatement. Hariri was a treasure trove of stories—most of them merely scandalous, a few utterly filthy, all delivered in complete sentences of perfectly grammatical Arabic. One of them concerned an old man who dragged his young wife in front of the qadi to petition for a divorce on the grounds of lack of intimacy. When the qadi asked the wife why she refused to have sex with her husband, she said, "Because he insists on prowling around the back door of the house."

"It is necessary," the old man replied in his defense. "The front door is wider than the Tigris and more filthy than a menstrual rag."

But the old geezer and his wife were merely getting warmed up. With the whole court looking on, obscene puns and metaphors shot back and forth like bombardments of Greek fire. "I would not ride you if you were a saddle," he hollered. "I would not let you in my prayer niche if you were an imam," she retorted. Finally the qadi got fed up with both of them and gave them each a dinar just to go away. "But, then, that was what they wanted in the first place," Hariri explained.

"A scam!" Omar exclaimed.

Hariri nodded, impishly grinning. "As for the qadi," he said, "he was such a miser, and it pained him so much to be separated from his cash, that he had to adjourn court so he could go home and mourn. For two days he stayed inside, unable to eat. You might say he missed his two dinners."[93]

"Great story. Dreadful pun," Omar said. "Seriously, though, *this* is the kind of writing you should do. Clever con men. Miserly qadis. You have a natural feel for Arabic, Hariri, but you're wasting it on the gazelles of Hajir."

That gave Hariri something to think about and they rode through the mountains in silence for a while, the only sound the clop of the horses and the screech of an occasional eagle.

But Omar was thinking about something too and finally had to ask. "Tell me, Hariri," he began. "You said that the reason you didn't incarcerate me is that you are following orders. Is that all there is to it?"

"As a matter of fact, there is more to it," Hariri replied. "There has been talk about the way you have conducted your investigation. It even reached us in Qazvin. You are the one person looking into the death of the Nizam who is trying to find out the truth with no political axe to grind."

"Were you fond of him?" Omar asked. "The Nizam, I mean."

"A lot of us in the government were fond of him. Because he actually cared about the people who worked for him. You know I am from Basra, and there was an incident there—it must have been about twelve or thirteen years ago. Have you ever heard of ben El the Tax Collector?"

"No. Who's that?"

"A man who excelled at his vocation. He brought in about four hundred thousand dinars a year. But despite his unfortunate choice of profession, and despite being Jewish, he was well-loved in Basra, he and his wife both. As a matter of fact, when she died, the whole city came out for her funeral procession. Well, almost the whole city. The qadi stayed home. But everyone else came out.

"Tragically for ben El, the emir Gohara'in wanted to undermine the Nizam. And since ben El was Nizam al-Mulk's man, Gohara'in plotted against him. He went hunting with Malik-shah and convinced the sultan to order ben El drowned, and the sentence was carried out."

"It is sad," Omar said, "that an innocent person should be consumed in the crossfire."

"It was," Hariri replied. "But here is my point about the Nizam: When ben El was killed, Nizam al-Mulk went into mourning for the Jew. I don't mean he put on a show for public consumption. I mean he seriously grieved. He locked himself in his house and refused to conduct any business. That went on for three days until the sultan ordered him to go back to work. And even then Nizam al-Mulk had to ease himself into it. At first he confined himself to ceremonial duties like parades. But when he was fully recovered, he took Malik-shah to task for the terrible thing he had done, and he didn't mince words."

Memories of the Nizam weighed heavily on Omar and Hariri. Once again they plodded in silence for a spell. But then the clouds melted away, and just over a rise a colorful panorama greeted the travelers. Beneath them a valley sprawled, a gentle fertile plain that contrasted with the stark mountain ranges on either side of it. A river lazed through a band of fields bordered by poplar trees whose leaves were as yellow as lemons. Whatever they grew there had already been harvested, exposing a rich patchwork of burnt-orange soil to the bright autumn sun.

Hariri stopped to point out the crystal-sharp boundary between the brown mountains on the other side of the valley and the blue sky above them. "That is it," he said. "Qazvin is over that ridge. We will ford the river and then follow the chain of mountains. But we will stay on this side of them to be out of sight of the sentries around the city. About three farasangs down, there's a place where we can cross over and bypass Qazvin unobserved." They tugged the reins and began to make their way down into the valley.

They were about halfway down the hill when an arrow whistled just overhead and planted itself in the dirt a few cubits in front of them. The riders' heads spun backward. Over their shoulders they spied a dozen or so Assassins charging down the hill after them. Several had bows drawn and arrows nocked, ready to let fly.

"We have to move!" Hariri shouted as he prodded his horse to a gallop. Omar scrambled to keep up.

It seemed like a matter of seconds for them to careen down the slope. The racket of hoofbeats was like an army of kettledrums hammering out an advance. Arrows streaked past them, their iron points perforating the ground. Mostly. One embedded itself in Omar's saddle, a finger's breadth from his thigh. Another struck Hariri in the shoulder but fortunately it only grazed him.

Hariri yanked his knife out of its sheath and cut the spare horse loose. The panicked mare spun around and bolted at the Assassins, who took her down with a barrage of arrows. Bucking in pain, she collapsed on the road. Her killers scattered chaotically to avoid stumbling over the corpse, only to close ranks again once they sped past.

The river was only a hand's breath deep this time of year. Omar and Hariri dashed across in an instant, the horses' hooves kicking up a spray of muddy water.

Once Omar and Hariri were across, the mountains came up on them fast. Hariri slowed just enough to let Omar pass and start up the cliff first. The climb curbed their pace markedly while the Assassins, still speeding across the flats, closed the gap between them.

402

And it kept closing, even after the Assassins reached the base of the mountains and began their ascent. No doubt they rode fresh horses, courtesy of some friendly (or, more likely, terrorized) village along the way, while Omar and Hariri's horses had been on the trail since before dawn. Hariri kept looking nervously over his shoulder as the Assassins closed in. The moment he realized that there was no hope of escape was plainly visible on his face: his expression hardened with resolution. He stopped looking behind him and started looking ahead—for defensible terrain.

He picked his spot, tugged the reins, and was off his horse before it had come to a complete stop. The lay of the land was ideal. One side of the road was hemmed in by a wall of limestone forty cubits high. On the other side, a cliff dropped off treacherously. The approach was narrow and steep. The Assassins would have to slow and come at him single file. Hariri would have the high ground and the luxury of taking them on one at a time. He caught up to where his horse was waiting for him. Two swords hung from its saddle, one on each side. Hariri slid one from its scabbard and, with deadly speed, wrote his name in the air as a warm-up. Abu Muhammad Qasim ibn Ali al-Hariri al-Basri.

Omar, meanwhile, noticed that the hoofbeats on his tail had faded away. He glanced over his shoulder and saw the riderless horse and, beyond that, Hariri dotting his *ya*'s with a stab from his sword. Grasping the situation, Omar looked for a place to turn around, but the road was too narrow. Instead he stopped.

"Keep going!" Hariri yelled.

But Omar paid no mind. He dismounted and ran back along the mountain road, toward Hariri.

"I said, keep going!" Hariri shouted.

"You need assistance," Omar replied as he squeezed past Hariri's horse. He held out his hand and said, "Give me a sword and I'll fight."

Hariri slapped Omar's bandaged hand with the flat of his own sword. Omar's arm jerked backward in pain. "You can't even hold a sword," Hariri said, "much less fight with one. So stop talking nonsense and get back on your horse."

"But—"

"Go!"

Omar still hesitated. Hariri put his free hand on Omar's shoulder and looked him in the eye. "My mission is to protect you," he said. "Let me do it."

Omar felt the tears well. "Look," he said. "If I don't encounter you again, I want you to know—"

Hariri cut him off. "None of that," he said. "I'm not so easy to get rid of. Now, go!"

Reluctantly, Omar returned to his horse. "Remember," Hariri shouted after him. "Don't go to Qazvin. Stay on this side of the ridge. Ride three farasangs and then cross over."

Omar mounted up and galloped away. The road climbed for a bit and then switched back. He quickly reached an overhang with a view of the battle. Pulling up to the edge of the cliff, he saw that one of the Assassins already lay motionless on the road, a dark bloodstain spreading over his blue robe. Hariri was exchanging sword thrusts with a second man. He lunged forward, but the enemy saw the move coming and blocked Hariri's sword with a downward thrust of his own. Then he swung at Hariri's midsection. Hariri quickly sucked in his stomach and the blade sliced air. As the two men alternated jabs and parries, their cries of *"Allahu akbar!"* and the ring of blade on blade carried up to Omar.

There was one thing Omar could do to help. Just beyond the fighting, the rest of the Assassins were bunched up in a confusion of men and horses. Some nocked arrows in their bows, but an officer ordered them to stand down. "You'll hit our own man," he shouted. Omar jumped off his horse and hurled rocks down at them as fast as he could pick them up. The Assassins instantly organized and constructed an ad hoc shelter by interlocking their shields above their heads. The rocks bounced harmlessly into the ravine.

Hariri's opponent, meanwhile, drew back his sword and charged. Hariri gracefully sidestepped his foe, grabbed his arm, and swung him over the edge of the cliff. The Assassin's screams were sickening.

Hariri took a step back to catch his breath and assess his situation before his next assailant attacked. One of the Assassins had stepped out from under the shelter formation and was aiming a loaded bow at something above him. Hariri followed the man's line of sight and spied Omar on top of the cliff. He hurled his sword at the archer like a javelin and ran him through the chest. "Get *out* of here!" he shouted at Omar.

Omar realized he was distracting Hariri. He jumped back onto his horse and tugged the reins to steer the animal away from the cliff edge. The last thing he saw before the battle vanished from sight was an Assassin with a dagger charging a swordless Hariri.

Omar galloped off again. Beyond the next switchback, he reached a fork in the road. The path to the right led up and over the ridge to Qazvin, where there were thousands of Seljuq soldiers and certain arrest. The path to the left continued along the ridge to freedom. Omar knew what he had to do. He veered to the right. To Qazvin.

Cresting the ridge, Omar saw the brown brick buildings of the city clustered in the distance. The parti-colored tents of half a dozen military encampments dotted the fields between it and the mountains. Omar steered his horse toward the closest one.

His descent took far longer than he would have liked. The cliff face was steep, and the winding road dragged out the distance immeasurably. Wherever the terrain allowed, he cut off the switchbacks and hurtled straight down the rocky mountainside. His horse skidded more than it galloped, its hooves setting loose cascades of dirt and pebbles until it regained the path below.

Omar didn't stop until he reached the gate of the camp. Yanking the safe-conduct out of his pocket, he waved it at the sentry on duty. "Escort me to your commander at once," he ordered. One glance at the imperial seal and the guard hastened to obey. Out of breath, Omar ran into the commander's tent. He thrust the safe-conduct into the commander's hand and, between panting, said, "There are a dozen Assassins trying to kill a man, just over the ridge."

The camp had been a little sleepy when Omar rode in, but with the chance to see some action, it woke fast. Men scurried around, barking orders, saddling horses, strapping on armor, grabbing weapons. When the soldiers chosen for the rescue team were mounted on their horses and assembled for their briefing, Omar warned them that Hariri was dressed the same as the Assassins. He carefully described Hariri's build and appearance so that they wouldn't kill the wrong man. *Praise be to Allah that Hariri's face is so ugly*, Omar thought. After what seemed like endless questions about the geography of the battlefield and the strength of the enemy forces, the detachment finally moved out. Two dozen men on horseback galloped through the main gate, their banners streaming in the wind.

Standing in the tent flap, Omar and the commander watched the rescue party until it disappeared over the ridge. "We can wait inside," the commander said. They sat down on cushions next to a tray stand and he dispatched an orderly for refreshments. "We know the spot you described," he assured Omar. "It isn't far. They'll get there soon."

"I hope it's soon enough," Omar replied.

The orderly hurried back carrying a tray loaded with pilaf, wine, and paperwork and set it in the stand. The commander pushed the dishes over to Omar and kept the paperwork for himself. "Go ahead and chow down," he said, apologizing for his rudeness in not joining in the repast. By way of explanation, he added, "Those *amm*-grabbers at headquarters never let up."

While Omar dug into the rice, the commander dug into the stack of documents. One of them got his attention. He glanced back and forth between it and Omar several times, as if trying to verify something. Omar wondered what it was that the commander found so interesting—although he had a bad feeling he already knew. He looked over and, sure enough, it was as he suspected.

"I still say they should have drawn me smiling," he said.

CHAPTER 23

BAGHDAD
FRIDAY, 2 SHAWWAL 485
20 Abán 471
5 November 1092

*T*he face was badly bloated from being in the river so long," Taj al-Mulk explained. "But his wife identified his clothes, along with a birthmark on his thigh. No doubt about it, it was definitely the corpse of the rug seller, ibn Yasir."

The sultan ducked under the hot water, cutting himself off from his vizier. He wished Taj al-Mulk wouldn't bother him while he was bathing.

The Nizam had always complained about the "burden" of government (usually in the context of "If the Master of the World is dissatisfied with my services, I'll be more than content to lay down my burden and live out my life sweeping the Kaaba"). Malik-shah used to shrug off Nizam al-Mulk's bellyaching. But now that some of that burden had been thrust on his own shoulders, he wondered how the Nizam had done it all. Meetings pursued ceremonies, which pursued audiences, which pursued more meetings, one after the other, late into the night, at a pace as frenzied as a horse zigzagging across a polo field. Which was why Malik-shah hadn't been to any actual polo fields since he had arrived in Baghdad. Or hunting expeditions. Or drinking parties. His only refuge was his daily bath.

Granted, if one needed a refuge, the sultan's bath chamber was an excellent place for it. In a city of architectural wonders, it was a jewel. Corinthian columns and potted palms outlined a pool twenty cubits long. The walls were coated with humidity-proof pitch that, when hardened, gave the appearance of black marble. There were no windows per se, but high overhead an array of eight-pointed stars had been cut through the walls. They let in just enough of the late afternoon sun to create the illusion that the stars were shining.

Lined up at one end of the pool, a half dozen concubines in low-cut chemises and silk trousers stood in attendance, ready to provide soap, towels, music, refreshments, scrub brushes, or anything else the sultan might demand.

A starlit night, a haven from the afternoon glare, time for repose from the day's labors: it was Malik-shah's sanctuary, a place where he could take a few minutes' break from the constant demands of courtiers and petitioners and loll in hot water with beautiful women. And yet here was Taj al-Mulk, grimly standing fully dressed at the edge of the pool; the surface of the water made him look all wavy. *Does he really* sikking *expect me to do government twenty-four hours a day?* the sultan wondered.

Malik-shah stayed underwater as long as he could. But inevitably the pressure in his lungs grew unbearable. He shot through the surface and gulped at the air. The steam felt suffocating.

Taj al-Mulk had apparently kept right on talking while Malik-shah was submerged. "The *shurat* reported bruising around the neck and shoulder," he was saying. "Six stab wounds in his belly." As the vizier continued with the details of the postmortem examination, Malik-shah paddled over to the shallow end and reclined against the wall of the pool. Puffing his bare chest at the ersatz night sky, he silently dared the stars to challenge him.

He beckoned to the concubine who was holding the tray of refreshments. A sweet lass, barely in her teens, she sashayed over to serve the sultan. Her long, raven hair, gathered and tossed over one shoulder, bounced over the curves of her neck and bosom as she walked. The other women followed her movements with malice in their eyes. She had some nerve, to be yummier to the sultan than they were. Kneeling at the edge of the pool, she leaned over to feed dates to Malik-shah, her soft breast brushing his cheek, her musky perfume pungent in the steamy room. One at a time, she slid the fruits between his lips. But when she reached into the bowl for another, he said, "Not so fast." He took her by the forearm and guided her hand back toward him so that he could suck the date stickiness from her fingers. Then he yanked her arm and pulled her into the pool with him. Hot water splashed onto the tile floor. Without missing a beat in his corpse report, Taj al-Mulk took a step backward to keep his slippers dry.

The woman laughed, a sexy laugh, from deep in her throat. *Most girls her age would have giggled*, Malik-shah thought. *Or screamed.* She clasped one arm over the sultan's shoulder to steady herself while she jumped onto his lap and straddled him with her wet thighs. She was about to feed him another date, but at the last moment she snatched it away and popped it into her own mouth instead. "Now I don't have one," Malik-shah said. She remedied that: she pressed her mouth against his and gave it to him. Her lips were full and soft. "You're not shy," he observed through a mouthful of sugary date flesh. A seductive alabaster smile was her answer.

The sultan felt her heft on his groin and her breasts pushing up against the muscles of his chest. His *huyar* stirred; it lengthened, sliding along the taut, wet silk of her chemise. The sensation was devastating. *This one is an enchantress*, he thought. *Terken Khatun outdid herself when she found her*. He looked up at Taj al-Mulk. His brother was being so businesslike; he had no idea what was going on under the surface of the water. The sultan had to laugh at that.

"Get a present for my wife," he ordered. "Something with emeralds. And see to it that—" He turned back to the concubine. "What's your name?" he asked.

"Sanjeeda," she replied.

"See to it that Sanjeeda finds her way to my bed tonight."

"As you wish, O Sahib al-Jalal," Taj al-Mulk replied. "Now, about the money."

"What money? Isn't Sanjeeda paid for?"

"The rug seller's money."

"Oh, him."

"You will no doubt recall the reports that ibn Yasir was in possession of a large sum of money before he disappeared. In fact, we suspected him in the murder of ben Samha because of that. But when they fished his body out of the river, the money was gone. So we think he was killed in a robbery. No surprise there. With him tossing dinars all over town like a *huyar*, it was only natural that he would attract the attention of thieves. But there was one thing in his pocket: ben Samha's key ring. Saad identified it. So I can say with confidence that the murder of ben Samha is solved."

"So justice was done," Malik-shah replied. He spat out a date pit, over Sanjeeda's shoulder and into the pool. "Good."

"Next order of business," Taj al-Mulk said. He consulted a sheet of paper with the list of topics he wanted to cover. "I'm sure you're eager to hear about my negotiations with Ghazali."

"Only if there's progress," Malik-shah replied in a tone of voice that insinuated there had better be.

He turned to Sanjeeda. "Wine," he demanded. She held a golden goblet to his lips and he drank. The wine tasted sour after the sweet dates. He took the goblet from Sanjeeda, tipped out the remaining liquid, and refilled it from the pool. Then he rinsed his mouth from the goblet and spit the water out in a long arc.

"I spent yesterday evening with the chief professor," Taj al-Mulk said. "He gave me his initial list of demands."

"That's as far as you got? What have you been doing all day?"

"Professor Ghazali has been tied up in court. The Commission of Inquiry and Justice in the Murder of Nizam al-Mulk."

"What a waste of time that turned out to be. All right, what are his demands?"

"Number one, retain Amid ad-Dawla as vizier to the new caliph."

Malik-shah laughed. "We were going to do that anyway."

"Second, release Abu Shuja Rudhrawari from house arrest."

"What do you think?"

"As long as he stays out of trouble . . ."

"Fine."

"Third, address the lax enforcement of shari'ah in Baghdad."

"I agree. Shari'ah *should* be enforced."

"There are some specifics . . ."

"Am I going to like them?"

"The closure of all wine shops and the banishment of singing girls from Baghdad."

"Is he *sikking* joking?" the sultan asked. "Do you have any idea how many people are employed in wine shops?"

"No, Sahib al-Jalal, how many?"

"Well, I don't know. But I am certain it's a lot. What will become of them? Are they going to beg in the streets? Or does Ghazali expect *me* to feed them? And by the way, Nizam al-Mulk would have known how many there are. You need to be on top of these things."

"I apologize, O Sahib al-Jalal."

Sanjeeda refilled the goblet and offered it to the sultan, but he was no longer thirsty for wine and he waved it away. He noticed with disappointment that he was no longer thirsty for Sanjeeda either. "What else does Ghazali want?" he demanded. Taj al-Mulk hesitated.

"I'm waiting," the sultan said.

"Enforcement of the Ordinance of Omar," Taj al-Mulk replied. "And the dismissal of all Jews and Christians from government service."

A moment of calm on the sultan's part only served to underscore the tirade that followed. "No!" he shouted. "The director of the Nizamiyya does *not* get to *sikking* dictate who *I* can have in my *sikking* administration. Who does that *amm* think he is?"

Now he was too aggravated to relax; he clambered out of the pool, nearly tipping Sanjeeda into the water. A slave rushed up with a towel; Malik-shah wrapped it around himself without interrupting his tirade.

"Nizam al-Mulk said hire the best people, and that's what I intend to do." He strode out of the room. Taj al-Mulk hurried to keep up. Emerging from the comforting steam of the bath chamber into the chill of the cooling room was a shock. "Is this your idea of negotiating?" the sultan yelled. "You told me Ghazali was ready to deal."

"And he is. This is his initial offer. We'll make a counteroffer and—"

"It better be a counteroffer with no restrictions on who I hire. As for wine shops—"

But Yalbard's arrival interrupted the rant. The emir was in a state. His face was flushed, his helmet dented, and there was some sort of food stain on his armor.

"Is this how you present yourself to your sultan?" Malik-shah shouted.

"It couldn't wait, O Sahib al-Jalal," Yalbard replied, with no hint of apology.

"What couldn't wait? Don't talk in *sikking* riddles."

"The city. It has erupted in rioting. It started at the Mosque of Mansur and has spread all over West Baghdad."

411

The sultan turned to his brother. "You assured me that if we negotiated with Ghazali, you could keep the city under control."

"Let's figure out what's going on before we start assigning blame," Taj al-Mulk replied. "I'll take a detachment out and reconnoiter."

"Don't reconnoiter! Stop the damn violence. With violence if you have to. And secure the bridges. Don't let it spread to this side of the river."

"Sahib al-Jalal," Yalbard interjected. "It would be better if someone else led the troops."

"Why someone else? Taj al-Mulk is the damn vizier. It's his job to deal with this mob."

"Well, the thing is, Sahib al-Jalal . . ."

"What?"

"He's the one the mob is after."

*   *   *

By the time the troops got organized, the sun had set. Malik-shah took charge of the sortie in person. Armed and mounted on his white Arabian stallion, he rode out from the palace, Yalbard at his side, an army of Turkish cavalry behind them. The Square of the Arch was deserted; an eerie hush had settled over the darkened shops and restaurants. The army proceeded cautiously through the Gate of the Arch and across the Bridge of Boats. They moved so quietly that they could hear the creak of the chains as the pontoons rocked with the current. Yalbard ordered a detachment to remain at the bridge and control access across the Tigris while the main force continued along the Khorasan Highway, into the neighborhoods of West Baghdad.

The area around the Adudi Hospital was deserted as well. Or so it seemed. A loud splat startled everyone as a rotten orange found its mark on the sultan's cuirass. He jerked his head to see where it had come from and spotted a man running away. Two soldiers were ordered in pursuit. Malik-shah watched them chase the culprit around the corner of the building and out of sight.

"What do you want to do with him when we catch him?" Yalbard asked. "Flog him or execute him?"

"Enlist him," Malik-shah replied. "There's no point in wasting someone whose aim is that good."

But the point was moot: the two soldiers returned empty-handed. A page boy wiped the orange pulp from the sultan's armor and buffed the steel plates until they gleamed in the torchlight, despite the sultan's fidgeting.

"I think I hear something up ahead," the sultan said. "Forward!"

The something started as a low drone but soon swelled to a noisy mash-up of shouts, chants, and official voices issuing threats. Around a bend in the road, a scene of chaos confronted the army.

A line of two dozen city *shurat* was pitted against a mob in a moving face-off, the *shurat* retreating slowly in lockstep, the rioters instantly pouring into the gap. Truncheons and shields lay abandoned on the road; clearly the *shurat* had started out with more men, but their numbers had dwindled as deserters fled—in far too much of a hurry to be bogged down with equipment.

The officer in charge demanded that the mob break up. "You are ordered to disperse immediately," he bellowed. "Those who do not obey will be subject to arrest." But only those closest to him could make out his words over the chanting of the crowd.

"The Muslims—united—will never be divided!"

"The Muslims—united—will never be divided!"

"The Muslims—united—will never be divided!"

The officer was visibly relieved when his deputy tapped him on the shoulder and nodded in the direction of the imperial troops riding to the rescue. He ordered his men to withdraw, glad to turn their places over to the military. An imposing figure in the saddle, the sultan by his mere presence commanded silence in the rioters. But they were silent for only a moment. Then a new chant started.

"Death to Taj al-Mulk."

"Death to Taj al-Mulk."

"Death to Taj al-Mulk."

From atop his horse, Malik-shah surveyed the tactical situation. The organized marchers were only a fraction of the assembled mob, far outnumbered by onlookers who merely milled about. Many were children, eager to gawk at the non-routine. At the back of the mob, a mother dragged her little boy away from the scene of danger.

As in any crowd, there were troublemakers who mistook anonymity for license. Some of them climbed onto barrels, high ground for chucking rocks and vegetables at any target within range, with no distinction between friend and foe. Others set mounds of trash ablaze. Malik-shah could see eight or nine such fires. Rioters danced helter-skelter around them like demons. Their fiendish antics mocked the banners, still draped over the buildings from the day before, whose festive calligraphy earnestly wished a blessed Eid upon the City of Peace.

On one side of the road, in the Suq of the Hospital, looting was in full swing. Men dashed in and out of stalls, their arms loaded with crutches, bandages, jars of ointments, sacks of medicinal herbs, and anything else they could carry. Not to mention a few things they couldn't. Two men lugged a wooden cabinet but, finding it too heavy, abandoned it in an aisle, allowing its load of glass vials to cascade noisily and shatter on the pavement. Another looter was positively giddy to have plundered a balance scale, but he didn't take the counterweights, so it was unclear how he intended to weigh anything with it. Nearby, an overweight proprietor tried to defend his meager inventory of therapeutic moss by jabbing at the looters with a paring knife. They were far too spun up to let a little thing like that stop them, though. They swarmed the merchant, wrestled him to the ground, and kicked his prone body, over and over again. Others smashed the bamboo partitions that marked the boundaries of his stall. Oblivious to the pandemonium around him, one old codger with a cane slowly hobbled his way through the market, intent on some errand, ignored by merchants and looters alike.

Malik-shah ordered a detachment to take control of the market and secure his flank. They rescued the merchant with the paring knife and began the work of chasing looters away. But it seemed like whenever one was scared off, scattering purloined medical supplies in his wake, two more popped out of a stall with a new collection of loot. The shifting currents of the rioters, as they sought to flee the soldiers, caused them to collide with each other, adding to the confusion.

Meanwhile the sultan swiveled his attention to the main mass of demonstrators. He picked up where the *shurat* had left off. "You are ordered to disperse," he roared. "Those who disregard this order will be dispersed by overwhelming force."

But the crowd kept on chanting.

"I repeat," the sultan boomed. "You are ordered to disperse!"

"Death to Taj al-Mulk!"

"You have until a count of ten."

"The Muslims—united—will never be divided!"

Malik-shah signaled to Yalbard. "One!" the emir bellowed.

The mob paid no heed. Malik-shah scanned the faces in front of him. Most were contorted with rage. But one man actually seemed to enjoy his newfound freedom from the constraints of civilization. He jumped up and down on top of a barrel and pumped his fists in the air, more in celebration than in anger. As the crowd chanted, he joined in with a bit more gusto than everyone else, especially on the word "Death!"

Fury grew inside Malik-shah; there is no more potent fuel for anger than watching someone you hate celebrate.

"Two!" Yalbard continued.

The rioter on the barrel caught the sultan glaring at him. Pleased with the attention, he hopped down onto the pavement and tried to charge the imperial troops. But there were too many people in the way; he was soon stopped by the crush of other rioters. Undeterred, he clawed at the paving stones, trying to pry one loose.

"Three!"

Finally the hooligan succeeded in dislodging one of the flat stones. He hurled it over the heads of the other rioters, targeting Malik-shah's face. But it fell short and landed at the feet of the sultan's horse. The well-disciplined animal didn't condescend to flinch.

"Four!"

I'm going to cut that one down myself, Malik-shah thought, grinning maliciously. *I'll slice off his head and use it as a polo ball.* He drew his sword in anticipation.

"Five! . . . Six!"

The sultan took a good look at the face of his prospective victim. He fantasized how it would look when he whacked it with a mallet and watched it bounce down the field and through the goalposts.

And that's when Malik-shah had a realization: this human being he was about to kill was just a kid whose beard hadn't even begun to fill in. He couldn't have been more than fourteen years old. An obvious product of poverty, he wore a ragged turban and his robe had been patched many times.

"Seven! . . . Eight!"

Memories of Nizam al-Mulk echoed in the sultan's head. The Nizam had impressed upon him a thousand times "The sultan is the father of his people. It is for them that this government exists." If that were true, then to raise his sword against this child would be to murder one of his own sons. He wondered how Berk-yaruq or Sanjar would have turned out if they had been born in a hovel instead of a palace. Would they be here today, chucking the paving stones?

"Nine—"

"Stand down," Malik-shah ordered Yalbard.

The emir stopped counting and gave the sultan a questioning look. "If we don't end this riot," he said, "it will consume all of West Baghdad."

"We'll find another way."

"There's only *one* other way. You know what you're going to have to do."

"Yes."

"He's your brother."

"I know."

CHAPTER 24

QAZVIN
SATURDAY, 3 SHAWWAL 485
21 Abán 471
6 November 1092

O mar was treated with the utmost respect. He was transferred from the military camp to the City of Qazvin, where he was confined to a pleasant room in the governor's mansion, with a view of the Harun ar-Rashid Mosque. There was a comfortable mattress, a low table for eating, and even a small collection of books. Dinner consisted of an excellent pilaf with grilled lamb chops, washed down with a fine local vintage. "Compliments of the House of Ja'far," the guard explained when he brought it. "When news reached Mistress Qutayya that you were a prisoner here, she sent it over immediately."

Omar asked whether there was any news about the battle on the ridge. Had the detachment reached Hariri in time to rescue him from the Assassins? But either the guard was not important enough to keep informed or he had orders not to tell, because all he said was "Sorry. First I heard of it." Omar even tried a bribe—a cup of wine. The guard enjoyed it immensely, but it failed to loosen his tongue.

The escape from Alamut, the chase through the mountains, making a new friend only to lose him again—Omar was exhausted. He went to bed right after dinner and slept until morning.

He spent most of the next day working out his next step. While his situation wasn't as dire as it had been in Alamut, and his present accommodations were far better, he was still a prisoner. Somehow he needed to smooth things over with the sultan. It occurred to him that Taj al-Mulk owed him a favor. Omar had, after all, helped soothe the sultan's anger over Yalbard's flogging. Clearly the best approach to Malik-shah was through his vizier. Omar found pen, paper, and ink in a cabinet and began to compose a letter to Baghdad. The bandages on his hands made it difficult to write, but with practice he could produce something sufficiently legible that someone would be able to copy it over before it was sent.

By midafternoon he had torn up several drafts and was about to start another when he was summoned into the presence of the governor. A fiftyish man with military bearing, the governor sat on his throne, much like a qadi, but holding a spear rather than a staff. He inquired whether all of Omar's needs had been met and then said, "I've received a carrier pigeon with new orders. You are to be escorted back to Baghdad. You leave immediately." Before Omar could ask any questions, there was a knock at the door. "That will be your escort now," the governor said.

A guard opened the door to the Hall of Audience, revealing a short, powerfully built man, dressed for travel. The new arrival didn't seem to be bothered by the cuts and bruises that covered his face and hands; his thick lips grinned and his heavily lidded eyes were merry.

"Hariri!" Omar exclaimed.

"I told you I'm not that easy to get rid of," Hariri replied.

Omar rushed over to the door and embraced Hariri warmly. "*As-salamu alaykum*," he said, meaning it. Peace upon you, friend. "Are you my escort?"

"I've been ordered back to Baghdad for reassignment," Hariri replied. "Apparently someone blew my cover."

CHAPTER 25

ALAMUT
SATURDAY, 3 SHAWWAL 485
21 Abán 471
6 November 1092

*A*nd when you arrived at the spot, the bodies were just lying there, exposed on the mountainside?" the Sheikh of the Mountain asked.

"Yes, my lord," Commander Misri replied indignantly. "Unburied. No doubt it was intended as a message for us. The unbelieving dogs."

"Do not be angry with the unbelievers," the sheikh replied in his soft voice. "'*Dost thou reckon that most of them will hear or understand? They are only like the cattle, nay, they err more from the way.*'[94] But how is this possible? You told me that someone helped Omar escape. How do two men kill twelve of my warriors? Especially when one of them is an astronomer."

"They appear to have had help, my lord. A wealth of hoofprints scarred the road from Qazvin."

"Malik-shah's men?"

"Probably."

The sheikh folded his arms thoughtfully and leaned back slightly on his cushion. "Where is Omar now?" he asked.

"He was taken under guard to the governor's mansion. I sent a man to watch the house. He just reported back. Omar was released this afternoon. He left Qazvin, headed south."

"Back to Baghdad, no doubt." The Sheikh of the Mountain absentmindedly flipped through a few pages of a book that was on the table in front of him. "We can't let him report to Malik-shah," he said. "He knows the defenses of this castle. He knows my true identity."

419

"To prevent it, we'd have to—"

"Can it be done?"

"We can try to overtake him on the road. But by now he must have a forty-farasang head start. And once he gets back to Baghdad, well, we might have a little time before he receives an audience with anyone who matters. A few hours, maybe. Days if we're lucky. Then he'll spill everything he knows. And all the while he'll be safely ensconced behind the walls of the Dar Saltanah."

"Don't we have anyone on the inside?"

"Our client was getting information from someone. But we don't know who."

The Sheikh of the Mountain stood and paced his study. After several laps, he stopped at the window and stared thoughtfully at the battlements. That was a neat trick he had played the other day—demonstrating his power to Baghdadi by nearly getting one of his men to jump off. And speaking of Baghdadi . . .

"How's Omar's ex-assistant doing?" he asked.

"He is completely recovered from his injury," Misri replied. "He's responding well to our indoctrination."

"I told you he would. He's the type. You spout some nonsense about the seven planets being the seven prophets, and they think they've been let in on the esoteric secrets of the universe. I was right to recruit him."

"You did it right under Khayyam's nose too."

"And at the madrasa they said *I* was the slow one."

"Khayyam never had a clue what you were up to. But why do you bring up Baghdadi?"

The Sheikh of the Mountain gave Misri a look like Misri was the slow one. "Oh," Misri said. "I don't recommend it."

"Why not?"

"He's only been here a few days. We don't know if he's loyal."

"I can think of no better way to test him."

"He's untrained."

"Do you have anyone else who can get inside the Dar Saltanah and close to Omar?"

"Not in time."

"Then that settles it."

"Even with Baghdadi, it's a long shot," Misri said.

"We don't have a choice," the Sheikh of the Mountain replied. "If there's even the slightest chance of killing Omar before he reports back, we have to take it. Send for the boy."

CHAPTER 26

BAGHDAD
TUESDAY, 6 SHAWWAL 485
24 Abán 471
9 November 1092

*O*n their journey back to Baghdad, Hariri entertained Omar with more of his bawdy stories. When they tired of that, he and Omar held contests to improvise various forms of trick poetry. Omar matched Hariri verse for verse in alternating dotted and undotted letters, but Hariri was the undisputed master of the pun. Still, it was a long trip, and inevitably there were lulls in the conversation. Omar used these times to admire the scenery and ponder the identity of his benefactor. Who had ordered his release from incarceration in Qazvin? It had to be someone senior. Taj al-Mulk? Malik-shah perhaps?

He received his answer almost immediately upon arriving at the Dar Saltanah. Hariri turned him over to a guard, who escorted him through corridors and across courtyards. Omar was struck by how busy the place was—guards everywhere, page boys and officials running about on one errand or another. A marked change since his previous sojourn. It didn't take long to realize where the guard was taking him: the harem.

Terken Khatun didn't talk like a benefactor. "I stood in your way from the beginning," she said through a curtain. "I wanted you to fail in your investigation. I did everything I could to place obstacles in your path and send you on wild goose chases. I burned your wanted posters. I even tried to use your own daughter as a spy against you. You should be proud of her; she told me nothing. I pointed you to ben Samha in order to steer you in the wrong direction. And when it turned out to be the *right* direction, the direction of Qazvin, it was I who persuaded Taj al-Mulk to issue a warrant for your arrest."

She had abandoned her cloistered mother act: no handwringing over the well-being of the sultan's children, no carefully timed interruptions from grandchildren, no wine or pastry. Today she was all business and confidence.

And yet something was hiding in her tone of voice, like a catfish skulking among the reeds at the bottom of a muddy pond. Barely visible, but if you look for it, you'll see it move about. Omar attempted to identify what he was hearing. *It isn't toughness*, he thought. *Or deception. It's a kind of tension of the voice mixed with . . . fear? No, it isn't fear either. Something stronger.*

Panic.

"I opposed you because I thought Taj al-Mulk was guilty of murdering the Nizam," she continued. "I wanted to protect him. And now I have brought you back because he needs your help."

So that was it. No apologies. She spoke as if she had a right to lead Omar astray and then, having changed her mind, had an equal right to his assistance. She didn't even feel the need to justify her extraordinary protectiveness of her brother-in-law, but, then, Omar already knew the reason for that, thanks to Khuld's extraordinary spycraft. And yet there was something touching about it. Because Omar now realized that Taj al-Mulk was not merely a sexual plaything for her. Nor was he merely a cat's paw in her game of imperial politics. She really cared about him. She loved him.

"Why doesn't Taj al-Mulk ask me for help himself?" Omar asked.

"You haven't heard?" Terken Khatun replied. "Taj al-Mulk has been arrested. He's been charged with the murder of the Nizam. There's to be a trial in front of the qadi and the Commission of Inquiry and Justice."

It made sense now: Terken Khatun's change of heart, the summons from Qazvin, her not-quite-convincing iciness. Still, Omar was stunned. From the beginning, Taj al-Mulk was on everyone's suspect list, including Omar's. Omar never really believed it, though. The sultan's brother always tried to do the right thing, even when he was in over his head. That wasn't an attribute of a murderer. Taj al-Mulk wouldn't misappropriate a dirham, much less murder the great Nizam. Still, there was something that puzzled Omar. "Everyone suspected Taj al-Mulk," he said. "But there was never any proof. What changed?"

"There is new evidence. Fakhr al-Mulk arrived in Baghdad with a book he found in his father's papers."

"*The Book of Politics*. Volume two."

"How did you know?"

"He showed it to me when we were in Sahneh."

"And you kept quiet about it. I appreciate your discretion. What did you think of it?"

"It was inconclusive. The Nizam definitely believed someone in the sultan's court was out to get him. But he named no names. It was everybody and nobody."

"So the book doesn't actually prove anything?"

"No."

"Can you convince the other commissioners of that?"

"Shami has it in for the sultan. He's going to jump at the chance to get at him through his brother. But Ghazali, he's a scholar. He'll be open to arguments. They just better be damn good ones."

"Then think of some quickly. The trial starts tomorrow morning."

* * *

Omar had hoped for an opportunity to report what he found at Alamut to the sultan as soon as he returned. But his interview with Terken Khatun changed his priorities. He had eighteen hours until the commission reconvened for the trial of Taj al-Mulk, and he needed to make the most of them. Unfortunately, he wasted the first four trying to get his hands on the manuscript. Shami had custody of it and was reluctant to let it go. It was only after Ghazali interceded with a hastily scribbled fatwa that the qadi was forced to concede that, as a commissioner, Omar had a right to examine it. All of this involved a great deal of riding in litters, waiting for messengers, and quoting from the Quran.

In the course of rushing around Baghdad, Omar ran into Yalbard, who filled him in on what he had missed during his travels—the Eid al-Fitr parade, the showdown between the sultan and the caliph, and the riot the following day.

"You should have seen Malik-shah," Yalbard said. "He faced down the mob and declared in a booming voice, 'People of Baghdad, I have heard your petition. Let it be known that I take a most serious view of the allegations against my brother. No one is above the Shari'ah. Not me. Not him. I will therefore bind him over to the qadi to be tried for the crime of which he is accused. May justice be done!' Mounted atop his horse, his armor gleaming, he was so regal and so commanding, it seemed like he was clothed in victory. It didn't occur to anyone in the crowd that he had surrendered completely. They marched at his sides all the way back to the palace, heaping praises on his name with every step. Then they dispersed peacefully and returned to their homes."

Yalbard drew himself up to his full, considerable height as he spoke. Clearly he was proud to be an emir in the service of Malik-shah.

Of course Omar had left a message for Khuld as soon as he finished his interview with Terken Khatun, but with all the running around, they kept missing each other. So he didn't see her until she arrived in his room with dinner. He firmly intended to keep the resolution he had made in Alamut to tell her how proud he was of her, but she didn't give him a chance.

"I brought enough for you and Baghdadi both," she said cheerfully. She actually seemed to be singing to herself as she bustled about, laying out the dishes. Suddenly she stopped, looked up, and glanced around the room. "Where *is* Baghdadi?" she asked.

It was a conversation Omar had been dreading. "Baghdadi," he said. "Well, he's not here."

"I don't know why you have to send him out on errands right before dinner. When will he be back?"

"Um, the thing is," Omar replied, "the time came to leave Alamut, and Baghdadi made a decision."

"What sort of decision? He's all right, isn't he?"

"Oh, yes, he's fine. Actually he was out cold when I last saw him, but I'm sure he's fine now."

"Out cold?"

"—but that isn't the point. It's just that, well, you know how learning is so important to him."

"Yes, that's why he'll be a great scholar someday."

"Right. A *great* scholar."

"But you still haven't told me why he isn't here."

"When it was time to leave, he thought through his options—"

"Options? What options?"

"I'm getting to that. He thought through his options, and he decided the best way to continue his education—"

"Yes?"

"—was to remain in Alamut and become an Assassin."

Khuld froze. She was silent for a long, uncomfortable moment. Then she said, very evenly, "Father, it's not nice to tease me like that."

Still seated, Omar took her hand and held it to his cheek. Her skin was rough from the years of domestic labor she had devoted to him. He looked up into the face of his child and, matching her even tone, said, "I'm afraid this time I'm not teasing."

It was heartbreaking to see the switch in Khuld. One moment she had been eagerly anticipating her reunion with her love; the next her dreams of the future had been cruelly ripped away. Tears brimmed in her eyes; her shoulders slumped.

But Omar saw the misery on her face for only a moment. Because then she turned away. She rearranged a lock of curly, black hair that had come loose from her hijab. "You should have told me earlier," she said brusquely. "Now his food will go to waste."

She went back to laying out the meal. No singing now, just the clatter of dishes being slammed onto the table.

As it turned out, Baghdadi's dinner did get eaten. Hariri showed up. He sensed he had come at a bad time and tried to cut his visit short. But Omar thought a distraction would be good for Khuld—or maybe for himself. He insisted that Hariri stay for the meal.

Hariri tried to cheer Khuld up with tales of Omar's heroism during the battle on the ridge, which couldn't be done without bragging a little about his own. "The Assassins were fanatically eager to die in the name of the Sheikh of the Mountain," he said, "but their officer had his mission to think about. By the time I had slain six of his men, he ordered the rest to break off the attack. The delay gave me a chance to regain my strength.

"My enemies were right below me. I was so close I could smell the sweat of their bodies and the manure from their horses. I could hear every word of their deliberations. They intended to wait me out. They knew I was trapped there. If I returned the way I had come, I would walk right into their swords. But if I went the other way, up the ridge, I would soon find myself on less favorable ground, unable to defend myself from a renewed attack. So we waited.

"As the sun dropped low in the sky, the Assassins realized the flaw in their strategy: once protected by the cover of night, I could easily make my escape. They had to make their move now. Three of them broke away from the others and attempted to scale the cliff face with the intent of reaching the road above me. One of them slipped and fell to his death; the other two achieved their objective. Now the Assassins attacked from both sides. Their swords jabbed at me. I parried as best I could, but still they got their cuts in, slicing my arms, slashing my cheeks. I managed to dispatch one more to hell, but the remaining four were closing in. They formed a semicircle around me, with my back up against the rock. By this point I was exhausted and barely able to lift a sword. I didn't know how much longer I could hold out.

"And then suddenly one of the Assassins gave out a cry and staggered backward into the ravine. I later found out that I owed a debt of gratitude to an archer on the cliff above me whose shaft had flown so true. A moment later, twenty or so Turks came galloping around the bend to my rescue. If your father hadn't sent them—sacrificing his own freedom—I would certainly have died, friendless and alone at the hands of the enemies of right religion."

"What happened to the last three Assassins?" Khuld asked.

"Two of them tried to flee. But a dozen horses—their own horses—blocked the narrow road and trapped them there. The Turks cut the fugitives down in an instant. As for the third, he was so surprised to see the rescue party that he let his guard down. I put the last of my energy into one terrific thrust and plunged my sword into his heart—just before I collapsed."

*   *   *

Shami had no legal grounds to withhold the manuscript from Omar, but he could make obtaining it as painful as possible. After dinner the clerk of the court showed up in Omar's room with a whole battery of paperwork that had to be reviewed and signed: receipts, pledges of secrecy, acknowledgments of instructions for proper handling. When Omar's signet was finally affixed to the last document, he was permitted to take possession of the book, and the clerk went on his way. Khuld left shortly after—Hariri escorted her back to the harem—leaving Omar alone with *The Book of Politics*, volume two.

He started by scrutinizing the manuscript itself. The pages were uniform in size and made of the same high-quality paper that Nizam al-Mulk had always used, which Omar recognized from the numerous official communications he had received from the Nizam over the years. The ink was a rich sepia and consistent in color throughout. As for the handwriting, it was definitely the Nizam's. In a world where the ability to write was a foot in the door, a beautiful hand catapulted many ambitious young men to brilliant careers. Nizam al-Mulk's distinctive calligraphy flowed like a thousand rivulets that etched the desert sands and planted life after a rainfall.

On to the reading. Omar figured he might as well get comfortable. He removed his robe and turban, poured himself a goblet of wine, stretched out on the bed in his long-shirt, and started on the first page. Eleven chapters and four goblets later, he felt that he had accomplished nothing. The text was much as he remembered it from the quick read-through he had done in Sahneh.

He could feel the alcohol now. It was not the feeling he so coveted, the wave of happiness washing over him. Instead it was that other drunk feeling, the feeling that he was wooly-headed and clueless as to what he was supposed to do next.

Scraps of paper, covered in his notes, were scattered all over the bed. At least he could arrange them into some semblance of order. One by one, he picked them up from the coverlet, read them, and sorted them into six neat stacks. Most of them were excerpts from the text and questions for himself; they had all seemed terribly important when he had written them down, but now, as he reread them, he felt like he was grasping at straws.

As he turned over yet another note to add it to the appropriate stack, he noticed writing on the back. This wasn't surprising, as he often reused paper. Still, he read it to see what it was.

> Khayyam, who stitched the tents of science,
> Has fallen in grief's furnace and been suddenly burned.

The poem he had written at Hujayya's. He remembered that night fondly; it was the first night he had spent with Lina. Reading the poem again, he had to laugh at himself. Even in the depths of "grief's furnace," he couldn't resist his little joke: referring to himself in the third person. It reminded him of one of the passages in *The Book of Politics*:

> Sultan Toghril had Abu Nasir Kundari; Alp Arslan and Malik-shah had Nizam al-Mulk, and there were a great many others.

Like Omar, Nizam al-Mulk also referred to himself in the third person. That was an odd thing for anyone who didn't share Omar's sense of humor to do; Omar had certainly never known the Nizam to indulge in it. Perhaps the book contained other odd passages, ones that Omar had overlooked.

The poet in him was distracted by the moonlight streaming in at the window. He got out of bed for a better view. The moon was nearly half full, hovering above the city. He recited a verse:

> "But see! The rising Moon of Heav'n again
> Looks for us, Sweet-heart, through the quivering Plane:
>   How oft hereafter rising will she look
> Among those leaves—for one of us in vain!"[95]

It was actually a setting moon—the room had a southwestern exposure—but such details shouldn't get in the way of a good poem. Whoever she was trying to find, she didn't look among the leaves but rather in the construction site spread out below. Her light transformed brick foundations into a magical silvery white. If she were looking for the carpenters and masons, they had long since left for the day, but the abundance of ladders, tools, and building materials they left behind reminded Omar of what a bustling place it was during working hours.

Perhaps the moon was searching for ben Samha. It was a tragedy that after he had planned the buildings, procured the financing, and supervised the construction, he hadn't lived to see the finished product. Omar tried to imagine it: a dozen palatial homes, complete with gardens, the Mosque of the Sultan as the focal point, a Seljuq encroachment in the heart of the Abbasid city. Which was what made him think of another passage in *The Book of Politics* that didn't make sense:

They talk the Master of the World into the idea of annihilating the Abbasid dynasty.

Now that the dam had broken, Omar realized there were a lot of passages that bothered him. They rushed at him like a flood:

> One will not know the extent of their intrigues and their ruses until I am gone, and one will know only then the extent of my loyalty to this victorious government, and the worry which the existence and the projects of this sect have given me.

> Every time royal women offer their counsel, it was suggested to them by people with bad intentions.

> No Jew, Christian, or heretic would have the audacity even to enter a Turkish camp, much less serve a great lord.

> The Jew is dead.

Suddenly Omar's alcoholic haze cleared. It was obvious now.

Omar dashed to the door, bumping into the bed and upsetting several of his stacks of notes in the process. He ran out into the corridor, oblivious to the fact that his head was bare and he was dressed only in his long-shirt. He dodged from one dimly lit, deserted hallway to the next, turning corners at random, until he finally found a page boy.

"Son," he said, grabbing the boy by the shoulders. "I have necessity of your assistance. I want you to raid the supply chests and procure for me bottles of ink."

"Ink?" the boy replied. "What kind of ink?"

"Why, *every* kind of ink."

CHAPTER 27

BAGHDAD
WEDNESDAY, 7 SHAWWAL 485
25 Abán 471
10 November 1092

*E*verything had been in perfect order when Abu Ismail Toghrai closed up last night. All the glassware had been washed and put away, the tools stowed in their compartments in the tool chests, the fire extinguished, and the ashes swept clean. But when he had returned to the Nizamiyya this morning and opened the door to his laboratory, a vista of chaos assaulted him. The workbenches were littered with mortars, pestles, scissors, funnels, books, open bottles of chemicals, pots without lids, crucibles filled with some sort of pulpy mash, bubbling cauldrons, and twisted bits of tubing. The acrid odor of vinegar hung in the air. Standing over a smoking hearth, a middle-age man held a flask over the fire with a pair of tongs and watched intently to see what the liquid inside would do when he heated it. It didn't do anything.

The intruder was known to Toghrai, who should have guessed. Who else would do something like this? And although his "guest" was widely respected for significant contributions to many fields of science, chemistry wasn't one of them.

"You," Toghrai greeted him. "Get out."

"Ah, Abu Ismail," Omar Khayyam replied. "You're just in time. How do you get alkaloids to precipitate out of a solution?"

"What are you doing here?"

"I borrowed some of your chemicals. I knew you wouldn't mind. Old friends and all."

431

"I do mind. Look at this mess. And by the way, we're not friends. My life has been serene and orderly since we stopped being friends. I intend to keep it that way. Not to mention that I'm free of hangovers now."

"I'm hurt. But I assure you, you'll find this of interest. And it's for a good cause. I'm trying to contrive tests to identify different kinds of ink."

"And your plan was to randomly mix chemicals until you figured it out? Have you been at it all night?"

Omar looked around at the open bottles that covered the workbenches. He was forced to admit that he had helped himself to a plethora of powders and liquids.

"Well, you know," he said. "Chemistry. One must experiment."

"Leave," Toghrai replied.

"This is important."

"I said leave!"

Omar sat down on a box. All flippancy gone, he said, "I could really use your help. A man's life is at stake. Literally. *'Whoso saves one life, it is as though he saved all men together.'*"[96]

Omar's abrupt mood swing caught Toghrai off guard. He knew Omar was capable of being serious, even pious. It was always inside him. *If only it came to the surface more often*, Toghrai fretted. Out loud he said, "Very well. Tell me what you're trying to do and I'll help you. But you have to promise me something in exchange."

"Name it. Whatever you want."

"You will never enter my lab again as long as you live for any reason whatsoever."

"Obviously I won't come for a return engagement if you're not here, but if you were here . . ."

"Regardless of whether I'm here or not. You're banned."

"Fine. I agree," Omar said. "I'll never, ever come back. Just help me." There was pleading in the last sentence.

Toghrai was satisfied. "What are you trying to do?" he asked.

Omar explained his problem.

"That's tough," Toghrai replied. "There are lots of tests to identify inks, but you have to know what you're looking for. There are hundreds of ink recipes. It can be made from soot, pomegranate, indigo, wine dregs, peach pits, nutshells, chalcanthite, oak gall—the government uses oak gall."

"Then let's commence with that," Omar replied. "What reacts with oak gall?"

Toghrai walked over to a bookcase and scanned the titles. "What did you do with Pliny?" he asked, irritated. "*Naturalis Historia*."

"Which volume?" Omar replied.

"Thirty-four."

"It's over there, on the bench."

Toghrai thumbed through the book, stopping now and then at a section that seemed relevant. One passage in particular captured his attention. Absentmindedly, he sat down on a stool and started to read.

"Well?" Omar asked impatiently. "Is there a test for oak gall?"

"Uh-huh," Toghrai replied, still reading.

"What is it?"

"Verdigris."

Unfortunately, Toghrai was fresh out of verdigris. "Go to a pharmacist," he said. "They use it in some medicines."

"I know," Omar replied. "Avicenna was a fan. It's one of the ingredients in his Ointment of the Apostles."

Toghrai scribbled a name on a scrap of paper. "Here's the man I use," he said, handing the note to Omar. "Abu Ali Bashir. He has a stall in the Suq of the Hospital. You can rely on him. He'll never sell you a tainted product."

Omar was already running late and he had to stop at the Dar Saltanah to change his clothes on the way. He started to put on the scratchy, black, woolen caftan he had worn during his previous court appearance, but then changed his mind and wrapped himself in his silk robe of honor instead. The garment was quite colorful, sporting bands of crimson, blue, and gold. It had been bestowed on him by Malik-shah thirteen years ago, upon completion of the Jalali calendar. *To hell with Shami*, he thought.

When he finally got to the Suq of the Hospital, he found to his dismay that Abu Ali's stall was closed.

Omar inquired at a neighboring vendor and was told, "Yes, he usually makes the rounds of his suppliers this time of day."

"When do you expect him to return?" Omar asked.

"Could be any minute now—"

"I'll wait, then."

"Or could be in an hour. Hard to say. Perhaps I have what you're looking for."

The stakes were too high to gamble on anything other than pure verdigris. Omar mumbled something about how his business was with Abu Ali personally. "I'll wait," he repeated.

"I'll be here if you change your mind." The words were friendly but the vendor sounded put out.

Omar paced in front of Abu Ali's stall, scrutinizing each person who approached to determine whether he might be a conscientious pharmacist. Alas, Omar was disappointed as one candidate after another hurried past on some errand that led elsewhere. He couldn't help but notice that some of them gave him sidewise glances, and it was no wonder. With his parti-colored robe of honor, he was conspicuously out of place among the working-class women desperately buying medicines for their sick children and the burly carpenters repairing the damage from last week's riot. "I look like a parrot," he grumbled to himself. "The country parrot who visited the city and now has to loiter in the marketplace while he waits for the city parrot to return with supplies. And also he has bandages on his claws."

Actually, the wait wasn't that long—not more than a quarter of an hour. It only seemed longer. Abu Ali turned out to be a slender septuagenarian with an immaculate robe and a fastidiously trimmed white beard. His stock of verdigris had survived the looting, and he jumped at the opportunity to help a friend of Abu Ismail Toghrai. (Granted, "friend" wasn't the word Toghrai would have used, but the pharmacist didn't need to know that.) As far as Omar was concerned, Abu Ali was *too* helpful: the pharmacist insisted on briefing Omar about safe handling of the material and then walked him through its use. Omar was irritated by all of this—he hadn't slept, he was in a hurry, and it wasn't that complicated anyway—but he had to admit afterward that the practice session paid off.

With *The Book of Politics* under his arm and a bottle of verdigris and a brush in his pocket, Omar ran down the Khorasan Highway to the Mosque of Mansur, dodging pedestrians and pack animals all the way. The cape on his robe flapped in the breeze behind him, eliciting more than one giggle from the people he passed. Arriving at the mosque, he sprinted across the courtyard and through the door at the last moment possible.

Shami and Ghazali were already in place at the entrance, about to proceed into the hall. Instead of a greeting, Shami merely pointed to the manuscript and said, "I'll take that."

Bracing himself on his knees as he tried to catch his breath, Omar was in no condition to reply; he held out the book to the qadi without saying a word.

"I trust it's in pristine condition," Shami said. The plus side of Omar's last-minute arrival was that the qadi was in too much of a hurry to check the pages. He didn't even have time for criticism of Omar's silk attire beyond a sidewise glance and a cluck of his tongue.

The three judges passed through the colossal double doors and made their way down the center aisle. Once again the mosque was packed. And the crowd wasn't friendly to Taj al-Mulk.

Representing the caliph's faction, Humaydi, Tamimi, the Blind Imam, and a host of other clerics and academics had come to witness the downfall of a member of the sultan's inner circle—his own brother, no less. Abu Shuja was unable to attend, of course—he was still under house arrest—but Omar noticed he had sent his servant, the one who had been "fired" during Omar's visit to the house near the Gate of Degrees. He hung back, near the doors, so that when the time came, he could make a hasty exit and his sahib would be among the first to learn the verdict.

The contingent from the sultan's faction was smaller but no friendlier to the defendant. In the front row, Fakhr al-Mulk stood ready to grab at the second chance to succeed to his father's old job, as soon as a guilty verdict rendered the post vacant. He was flanked by his brother, Mu'ayyad al-Mulk, and the new finance minister, Abu'l-Fadl Qummi, who no doubt harbored fantasies about stepping up to the post themselves, in the event that things fell through for the front-runner.

As for Taj al-Mulk, he stood at the foot of the qadis' thrones, dressed in civilian clothes, calmly awaiting judgment, to all appearances unaware that he was hemmed in by his enemies.

As executor of his father's estate, and therefore the representative of the aggrieved party, it fell to Fakhr al-Mulk to present the evidence for the prosecution, which he did at great length. Omar nodded off twice—he had been up all night, after all. Each time, the qadi jolted Omar back into the swing of things by leaning over and poking him with his staff. The court recessed for noon prayers, followed by lunch (a welcome change, now that Ramadan had given way to Shawwal), and then the prosecution case concluded.

By the time Shami opened up the floor to his fellow commissioners for questions, it was late afternoon. Sunbeams streamed through the windows of the mosque, as if Allah Himself had taken an interest in the proceedings and chosen to grace them with His Holy Light. There were a few argumentative questions from Ghazali, and then the qadi recognized Omar, who began, "My good friend Fakhr al-Mulk has put together a compelling case that the sultan's vizier, Taj al-Mulk, is responsible for the murder of his father. As we heard, the case relies heavily on a manuscript, a written document that purports to be a previously unknown second volume of *The Book of Politics*."

"Purports?" Shami grumbled. "What do you mean, 'purports'? Are you trying to suggest the manuscript isn't genuine? Because we had testimony from Fakhr al-Mulk as to its impeccable provenance. You would have heard it, Khwaja Omar, had you been awake."

"I have no doubt that Fakhr al-Mulk discovered the manuscript among his father's papers as he testified," Omar replied. "But did Nizam al-Mulk write it? And if not, how did it get there? As Taj al-Mulk's judges we have an obligation to question the witnesses against him."

"The 'witness,' as you call it, is a sheaf of paper. Just how do you propose to question it?"

"With science," Omar replied.

"Science!" Shami scoffed. "I assume you mean *Greek* science."

"If you please."

"No, I don't please. This is a court of shari'ah. There is no place for foreign theories here."

Grumbles surged through the crowd as hundreds of spectators suddenly became experts on science. The names of Plato and Aristotle, al-Farabi and Avicenna, echoed in the mosque.

"Allah is not bound by causation," one man insisted.

"But the Mu'tazilites—" another began.

"It's all the same thing. Allah is Supreme Intellect."

Shami leaned over toward Ghazali. "Back me up on this," he said in a low voice.

"It has been my experience," Ghazali replied, "that Greek science is limited in its application. It is often incoherent and it certainly can't tell us the great truths of Islam."

The caliph's party purred with approval.

"You see," Shami said. "Limited in its application."

"But that doesn't mean it's not useful," Ghazali continued. "As long as science stays within its limitations and doesn't contradict the Quran, it can sometimes demonstrate minor truths. The cause of eclipses is a good example. There are good geometric arguments for that. Now, there are certain foolish people who believe they advance the cause of religion by attempting to undermine those arguments. But the scientific proofs in these cases are quite robust, so these supposed friends of Islam foolishly expose themselves for the bigots that they are. In doing so, they harm the very cause they had hoped to advance."

As Omar listened, his hopes rose. Ghazali seemed to be leaning in favor of allowing the demonstration to proceed. But then Ghazali's argument abruptly changed direction.

"As I said," he continued, "science does have limited applications. But I sincerely doubt that they have anything to do with our business here. Unless Omar is going to tell us that the guilt or innocence of Taj al-Mulk has something to do with eclipses."

A laugh passed through the mosque and Omar remembered why Ghazali was such a dangerous opponent. Shami had antagonized the crowd with his intransigence. But by conceding that science had some valid applications, however limited, Ghazali came off as reasonable and won the spectators to his side.

Fortunately, Omar still had one arrow in his quiver. "I thank the chief professor for that thoughtful summary of the role of science in legal testimony," he said. "But it is nevertheless testimony. And as the chief professor well knows, Allah's Holy Quran commands us, '*Conceal not testimony. For he who conceals it, verily, sinful is his heart.*'"

Annoyed by the suggestion that there were any sinful hearts in his courtroom, Shami gestured for Ghazali to approach him. The chief qadi and the chief professor consulted for some time. There was a great deal of whispering, gesturing, head shaking, and shrugs. Gradually it dawned on

Omar what was taking so long. Shami and Ghazali had no arguments. They were going to have to allow the demonstration!

At last the discussion tapered off, Ghazali returned to his throne, and Shami announced his decision. "Now that Khwaja Omar has advanced a *legal* argument," he grumbled, "the matter appears in a different light. This court is always willing to bow to the Shari'ah. Proceed with your scientific...thing. Just stay within your limitations."

"Thank you, Chief Qadi," Omar replied. "If the clerk of the court would be so kind as to hand me the manuscript . . ."

The clerk retrieved the sheaf of papers from the qadi and passed it to Omar, who leafed through it until he found the page he was looking for. Holding the sheet of paper up for all to see, Omar explained, "This is from the fifth chapter, toward the middle of the manuscript. It's the passage where Nizam al-Mulk warns darkly of *'damaging and odious enemies to the religion of Muhammad.'* The heart of the prosecution case is that these enemies are none other than then finance minister, now vizier, Taj al-Mulk and his followers."

With his free hand, Omar reached into his pocket and pulled out the bottle he had brought from the pharmacy. The spectators looked curiously at the blue-green liquid that sloshed around inside.

"What is that?" Ghazali asked.

"Verdigris," Omar replied. "Copper filings dissolved in vinegar. Watch what happens when I treat the text with it." He dabbed some of the reagent onto the paper with a brush. The ink ran a bit, but aside from that, nothing happened. Omar signaled the clerk, who took the page and brought it to Professor Ghazali and Qadi Shami in turn.

"It didn't do anything but make a green stain on the page," Shami scoffed. "So much for science." He smirked and rolled his eyes. Scornful laughter erupted from the crowd and echoed from the dome.

"Indeed, Chief Qadi," Omar replied. "But now let me demonstrate what happens when I perform the same test on a page from the first chapter."

"You've already damaged one page in the manuscript, without any benefit. I really can't countenance damaging another."

"It's a small area, Chief Qadi. No bigger than a fingernail. And it will reveal the truth." He selected a sheet of paper from the manuscript and gave it to the clerk to pass around.

The qadi scanned the page. "This is about the caliph Harun ar-Rashid and his wife," he said. "May Allah have mercy upon them. He sought out her advice . . . she gave millions to charity . . . No, there's nothing here that has anything to do with this case. Unless you're going to claim that Harun ar-Rashid murdered the Nizam." The audience tittered weakly.

"Praise be to Allah," Omar replied. "He was truly looking out for the interests of justice when He appointed you the leader of this commission. Your fairness in sniffing out points in favor of the defendant is extraordinary." Omar hoped that would put Shami sufficiently off balance to shut him up for a while. "What I want you to observe, however, is not the *content* of the page, but rather the *page* itself. Same paper as the first page I gave you. Same handwriting, same sepia-colored ink. The text, of course, is different, but aside from that, as far as the eye can see, the two pages are identical."

Holding both sheets directly in front of his eyes, Shami peered at them carefully to make sure it wasn't a trick. "That's right," he said at last. "The two sheets of paper are identical. Except one has a green stain on it."

So much for shutting him up. "Oh, why don't you just shove it up your rear?" Omar muttered.

"What was that?" the qadi demanded.

"I said, give me a minute and all will be clear. Now, if I could get that second page back." The clerk of the court shuttled the sheet of paper back to Omar, who painted a small area with the verdigris. He stood on the platform, turned to Shami and Ghazali, and held the page so they could see it.

"That's remarkable," Ghazali said.

The green liquid had mingled with the sepia ink and turned black.

Shami had been certain the experiment was a waste of time. When something actually happened, he was stunned. Speechless seconds dragged on as the spectators, who couldn't see the page, grew restless. Their whispers reminded the qadi that he had a court to preside over. He made an anemic attempt to take back control of the proceedings. "Yes. Well," he said. "The stain changed color. I suppose that proves something and wasn't intended merely to show off your knowledge of chemistry."

"Indeed it does, Chief Qadi," Omar replied. "It proves that this second page was written in oak gall ink. Verdigris turns black in the presence of this kind of ink. I still have some testing to do, but I have reason to believe that Nizam al-Mulk always employed oak gall ink."

"And what about the first page you showed me?"

"It *wasn't* written in oak gall ink. That undeniably has some bearing on the issue."

"What issue?"

"The issue of the authenticity of the manuscript. I think we can now say, with some confidence, that volume two of *The Book of Politics*—or to be precise, *a portion* of volume two—is a forgery."

A moment of silence hovered over the mosque as the significance of that sunk in. Then Fakhr al-Mulk cried out, "I'm the victim of a fraud!" The rest of what he said was drowned out in the general ruckus. There was indignation, and catcalls, and accusations of shenanigans. Others merely shook their heads.

"Shami is too softhearted," Humaydi said. "He never should have acquiesced to such an un-Islamic travesty of a demonstration."

"Silence!" Shami bellowed with enough fury and authority to shut the crowd down. "Khwaja Omar has the floor."

"Thank you, Chief Qadi," Omar said as he resumed. "It's clear what transpired. The first few chapters—and by the way, the last few as well—were written by the Nizam. But someone forged the chapters in the middle—the ones that implicate Taj al-Mulk. Then someone snuck into Nizam al-Mulk's pavilion and slipped them into the manuscript. I believe it was Abu Tahir, the assassin himself. He must have done it just before the murder, while everyone was at *iftar*. As for the forger, I don't know his identity and probably never will. Whoever he was, he was a genius. He duplicated Nizam al-Mulk's handwriting, paper, even the color of the ink he used. But not its chemical composition. That was his mistake. He used the wrong ink.

"Therefore, *The Book of Politics* is completely worthless as evidence. But without it there is no case against Taj al-Mulk. Qadi Shami, Chief Professor Ghazali, we have no choice. We have to acquit him."

CHAPTER 28

BAGHDAD
THURSDAY, 8 SHAWWAL 485
26 Abán 471
11 November 1092

*T*he people of Baghdad wanted answers.

The last week had been chaos incarnate—the riots, the trial of Taj al-Mulk, his dramatic vindication. And then, when the smoke cleared, they noticed something else: no one had seen the Commander of the Faithful since Eid al-Fitr. By itself that wasn't unusual; the caliph rarely made public appearances. But Seljuq troops continued to occupy the Dar Calipha. No one knew whether they were there to protect the caliph or to keep him prisoner, or even if he were still alive. So when it was announced that Malik-shah intended to hold court, rich and poor alike flocked to the Dar Saltanah and jammed the Hall of Audience in the hope that he would shed some light on al-Muqtadi's whereabouts.

They milled about, eager for the massive curtain that stretched across the front of the hall to rise and reveal the dais, the signal that the sultan's court was open for business. A hunting scene from the *Shah-nama* was woven into the curtain's fabric. Mounted on a camel, Prince Bahram Gur galloped across the drapery as he brought an ostrich to bay, his bow drawn, taut for the kill. All around the prince, other ostriches fled while lesser humans marveled at his prowess. Today was the first royal audience since ben Samha had renovated the palace, and most of the visitors hadn't seen the new curtain. It excited considerable criticism from the more religious element. Professor Ghazali quoted the Hadith: "'*The people who will receive the severest punishment on the Day of Resurrection will be those who try to*

441

make the like of Allah's creations.'"[97] But the threat of hellfire didn't deter the curtain. The brocade obstacle, forbidden image and all, was stubbornly unmoved by the disapproval of the ulama.

Standing nearby, dressed in his parti-colored robe of honor, Omar only half listened to the lecture on the law concerning representational art. In his pocket was a royal command to be in attendance; it had been delivered to his room by a page boy that morning. Scanning the crowd, Omar wondered who else had been summoned and who was merely curious. If Omar had received a summons, Ghazali probably had too. Humaydi was no doubt merely tagging along with Ghazali. Taj al-Mulk didn't need to be sent for; attending the sultan was his job. Shami—definitely summoned; in view of his well-known antipathy for the sultan, there was no other reason he would be here. As for Abu Shuja Rudhrawari, Omar didn't know what to make of his presence. There he was, leaning on his ivory-handled walking stick and wearing one of his trademark tailored caftans. Had he been pardoned and freed from house arrest? Or was he merely on furlough for the day? All around Omar, the chatter of anticipation told him that others had the same questions he did.

At last the curtain began to rise, its motion slow and dignified. A hush fell over the court. At the center of the dais, Malik-shah appeared; he sat on his throne with impressive posture. Two empty chairs, one on each side of the throne, awaited whomever he intended to honor with the privilege of sitting in his presence. His robe, tailored from dark blue silk, was far less ornate than was his custom, ornamented with only some restrained gold trim around the sleeves and down the front. His headdress, a sort of four-pointed crown, was fashioned from the same blue fabric and trimmed with gold as well. The simplicity of his garb clad him in a gravitas that astonished those who knew him.

"All kneel before the Sahib al-Jalal, Sultan Malik-shah," an usher announced in a powerful voice. "Son of Alp Arslan the Seljuq, King of the East and the West, Glory of the Nation, Master of the World, Builder of Bridges, and Slasher of Taxes." But the announcement was scarcely necessary. The spectators had already fallen to their knees and prostrated themselves before the Master of the World.

"You may rise," the sultan said. His words had the form of permission, but his tone left no doubt that they were a command. When all the audience was on its feet, he said, "Taj al-Mulk may approach the throne."

"The honored vizier Abu'l-Ghana'im Tutush ibn Alp Arslan," the usher called out.

There were subdued cheers—mostly from his own retainers—as Taj al-Mulk climbed the dais. They had been scarce at court during his imprisonment and trial, but now that he was back in favor, they came crawling from their hiding places to squeal their approval. Needless to say, Fakhr al-Mulk didn't join in. He stood silently at the front of the crowd with his arms folded; his followers took their cue from him. At least he was silent until he found himself on the receiving end of a sharp glance from the sultan. Then he shrugged and, with an innocent smile, added his voice to the chorus. The gesture of reconciliation between the rivals won such admiration from the crowd that everyone joined in, cheering for Taj al-Mulk and Fakhr al-Mulk alike.

Taj al-Mulk, meanwhile, had reached the top of the stairs and was kneeling before his brother. His beard was coming in nicely—not bad for less than a month of growth. Malik-shah stood and extended his hand to help his brother rise. Then they embraced. It wasn't the embrace of two brothers. Rather, it was the embrace of a king and a subject. The sultan initiated it and the sultan decided when to break it off. "You are welcome back in our presence," he said. "Now you may sit."

Taj al-Mulk took the chair on the sultan's left while Malik-shah turned to the audience and said, "Let it be known that throughout the lands of the Seljuqs no one is above the law. Those of my subjects, no matter how noble, who are accused of a crime will be tried accordingly. If they are found guilty, they will be punished as spelled out in the Shari'ah. If innocent, it will give me great joy to see them freed—as my brother has been freed. For that I owe a debt of gratitude to the members of the Commission of Inquiry and Justice in the Murder of Nizam al-Mulk. Khwaja Omar, Chief Professor Ghazali, and Chief Qadi Shami may approach the throne."

"Khwaja Abu'l-Fath Omar ibn Ibrahim Khayyam," the usher commanded. "Chief Professor Abu Hamid Muhammad ibn Muhammad al-Ghazali. His Honor the Chief Qadi Abu Bakr Muhammad ibn Muzaffar ash-Shami."

The crowd didn't need any sharp glances from Malik-shah to shout their praise for the commissioners. Ever since the day before, in the palaces and in the streets, all anyone in Baghdad had talked about was how the three men had carried out their assignment with diligence and integrity. "The blessings of Allah upon them!" rang out through the hall. "Allah bless Shami! Allah bless Ghazali! Allah bless Khayyam!"

When the last echo of the spectators' accolades finally faded away, it was the sultan's turn. "Gentlemen," he said, "I will be forever indebted to you for the fair and impartial way you conducted the trial of my brother. And in recognition of your single-minded pursuit of the truth, I award each of you a robe of honor."

Omar and Ghazali were already wearing robes of honor. Two page boys approached and helped to remove them.

"I suppose I could use a new one," Omar said, smiling at Malik-shah. "It's been thirteen years."

The sultan smiled back, but only superficially. The joke wasn't that great, and he was all business today anyway. Three other page boys carried in the new robes, which the sultan draped over the commissioners' shoulders himself.

Omar couldn't help noticing that they were made of silk. *I guess the qadi won't be getting much utility out of his*, he thought. They each had cream-colored *tiraz* armbands around the sleeves with inscriptions in old-style Kufic script embroidered in gold thread: "*In the name of Allah. May He shower His blessings upon the Commander of the Faithful, Uniter of the Houses of Abbas and Seljuq, the Caliph Mahmud ibn Abu'l-Qasim al-Muslih B'illah, and his honored vizier, Amid ad-Dawla Jahir. Given at Baghdad in the year 485 of the Hijrah.*"

Omar and Ghazali exchanged glances when they read it. The caliph al-Muslih. It seemed like the sultan was being premature in assigning a regnal name to Mahmud and memorializing his accession to the caliphate in *tiraz* bands. Omar wondered what he had up his sleeve that filled him with such confidence.

The sultan asked the three commissioners to remain while he summoned Abu Shuja to the throne. "Abu Shuja Muhammad ibn al-Husain Zahir ad-Din ar-Rudhrawari."

Abu Shuja climbed the dais and kneeled before the sultan, a bit stiff in his tight-fitting clothes.

"You may rise," Malik-shah told him. "Chief Professor Ghazali has pleaded your cause to me. He has told me of your piety and your scholarship. You are hereby paroled from your house arrest, contingent upon your good behavior."

"Thank you, O Sahib al-Jalal," Abu Shuja replied, bowing his head. "And be assured that my behavior toward you will always be as your great position merits."

"I have no doubt about it. I'm planning a little hunting party tomorrow. I hope you'll join me."

"I would not miss it."

Turning to the three commissioners, Malik-shah added, "The invitation is for all of you as well, of course."

"We'll be there," Ghazali replied on behalf of the group.

The sultan dismissed Omar, Shami, and Abu Shuja. Ghazali he invited to remain. As he watched Abu Shuja and the others descend the stairs, Ghazali commented, "O Sahib al-Jalal, your mercy is praiseworthy. And you did me honor by taking my poor advice."

Malik-shah offered him the vacant chair, the one on his right. The place of honor. The two men took their seats and chatted for a while. Ghazali reeled off several hadith about the early caliphs and how they took advice from their wise men. He spoke enthusiastically, leaning forward and gesticulating excitedly as he talked. To the surprise of everyone who had witnessed the fiasco at Nahrawan, the sultan not only listened solemnly but actually kept up his end of the conversation. He waited patiently for Ghazali to taper off before bringing up the real reason for their meeting.

"It has been brought to my attention," he said, "that the death of Nizam al-Mulk has created some embarrassment for you."

This wasn't in the script. It threw Ghazali off his game. "Embarrassment?" he asked, puzzled. "For me?"

"For the Nizamiyya, I mean," the sultan replied. "Financial embarrassment. As I understand it, the Nizam was your primary benefactor."

"He was most generous."

"I'm sure his absence is keenly felt. I have, therefore, decided to do something about it. I have instructed my finance minister, Abu'l-Fadl

Qummi, to provide you with whatever funds you need to ensure that the Nizamiyya remains the Seljuq Empire's premier institution of higher learning."

Ghazali looked like a man who had just been told by his doctor that he didn't have terminal cancer after all. He broke into a grin, his shoulders relaxed, and no one would have been surprised if he had gotten up and started to dance. It was only with effort that he resumed a courtly demeanor. "Thank you, O Sahib al-Jalal," he said, sincere in his gratitude.

"It is only as you deserve, in light of your tireless custodianship of the Nizamiyya during the last year—and your lifetime of brilliant scholarship in the service of Islam."

"You honor me."

"Perhaps the greatest honor I can give you is not to detain you any longer. I'm sure you have many things to do."

"That's true," Ghazali replied. "As a matter of fact, I was just going to speak to the Blind Imam. I thought I'd have a few words with him about his sermon next week. I think some changes are needed near the end—the part where he beseeches Allah to bestow health and victory upon the caliph."

Waves of murmuring rippled through the audience as the insiders explained to their friends what that meant: Mahmud would be named as caliph in the sermon. It was all over for al-Muqtadi.

"Then don't let me detain you, Chief Professor," Malik-shah said. "You're dismissed."

As Professor Ghazali descended the stairs from the dais, Malik-shah leaned over to Taj al-Mulk and whispered, "And that, my brother, is how you get the support of the intellectuals."

*   *   *

It was nearly dinnertime when Khuld showed up in her father's room. Omar was seated on a cushion, scratching some notes on a piece of paper on his lap. All the evidence in the murders of Nizam al-Mulk and Abba Saad ben Samha was scattered on the table in front of him: the Sufi robe and the eighty-five gold dinars found sewn in its hem; ben Samha's keys; the charred ledger book with the pages torn out; *The Book of Politics*, volume two; stacks of miscellaneous documents; and the dagger that had been found in Malik-shah's tent. The only thing missing was the other dagger, the actual murder weapon, the one that the Assassins had confiscated.

"You were out late last night," Khuld said as she came through the door. "I stopped by and you weren't here. Guzzling Hujayya's best lamp oil I suppose?"

Omar grunted a yes without looking up from his notes.

"And after that?" Khuld went on. "I suppose little Lina took you home."

Another grunt from Omar.

"That's nice," Khuld said.

Khuld had never before passed up an opportunity to call Lina's profession "disgusting." Omar looked up from his work to find out who this imposter was. It *looked* like Khuld. But she was *smiling*. She was dressed up too. Instead of her usual cotton house dress and apron, she wore a new silk robe, one of those he had made her buy when she embarked on her mission to spy on Terken Khatun.

She set about straightening the room. Omar's two robes of honor, the old one and the new one, lay discarded on the bed. She folded each one carefully and packed them in a chest. As she worked, she sang softly to herself—some love song that was popular in the taverns this week.

"And where have *you* been gallivanting about?" Omar asked.

"Visiting shrines," Khuld said. "You should see the tomb of Maruf Karkhi. He was a Sufi in the second century. Over the casket there's a beautifully carved—"

"Did you get someone to escort you? Someone to at least *pretend* to be your brother?"

"Oh, Hariri took me," she replied, a little too casually.

Ah, that explains it, Omar thought. Khuld and Hariri had been spending a lot of time together since Omar's return to Baghdad.

"And how is my friend Hariri?" he asked.

"He's wonderful," Khuld said happily. "Sightseeing with him is like sightseeing with you. He knows everything too. He told me all about the architecture of the tomb and the life of Maruf Karkhi . . ." She launched into a story about the *maruf's* conversion from Christianity to Islam.

"And what else did you converse about?" Omar asked when she finished.

"Your verdigris experiment. Actually, everyone in town is talking about that. They say it was brilliant."

"It had a certain amount of dramatic flair."

"What I wonder is how you knew that the ink wouldn't match."

"I cheated," Omar replied with a guilty smile. "Abu Ali the Pharmacist and I performed a trial run in his shop before I went to court."

"That's not what I meant. How did you get the idea to test the ink in the first place? What made you suspect that the manuscript had been tampered with?"

Omar grabbed *The Book of Politics* and flipped through the pages until he found what he was looking for.

"This is what first got my attention," he said, showing Khuld the suspicious passage. "'*Sultan Toghril had Abu Nasir Kundari; Alp Arslan and Malik-shah had Nizam al-Mulk, and there were a great many others.*' Nizam al-Mulk referred to himself in the third person."

"So what?" Khuld asked. "You do that all the time."

"Yes, but I do it as a joke," Omar replied. "For most other people it's a strange thing to do. Once that occurred to me, I realized how many other passages in the manuscript didn't ring true."

"Like what?"

"The tone, for one thing. It wasn't like Nizam al-Mulk to complain. Then there was the warning against taking advice from a woman, coming three chapters after praising Harun ar-Rashid for taking advice from a woman. Another problem was Nizam al-Mulk's attitude toward the Jews."

"What's wrong with the Jews?"

"According to the manuscript, they don't know their place. It said that the Nizam longed for the good old days, when no Jew would dare enter a Turkish camp, much less be appointed to a high office. But we know of at least two instances when Nizam al-Mulk had not only appointed Jews to high office, but taken their side when they came into conflict with Muslims. Hariri told me about the first one: years ago in Basra, when Gohara'in convinced the sultan to have ben El the Tax Collector drowned. The second, of course, was last year here in Baghdad: Abu Shuja's clash with ben Samha."

Khuld continued to putter around the room as she took in her father's deductive brilliance—putting stray books away, straightening the bedclothes, fluffing the pillows with her usual violence.

"You said that the person who forged the manuscript was a genius," she said. "But it sounds like he made a lot of mistakes."

"He was a genius at paper, handwriting, and the color of the ink. But someone else probably instructed him what to write. And, yes, whoever that was got careless about this third-person business; there's no doubt about that. Perhaps he was in a hurry. But the rest was done intentionally."

"Why?"

"To mislead us."

"Mislead us? About what? Who the murderer was?"

"Oh, something much more important than the murder of one man. The murder of an institution. Something that would alter the whole future of Islam."

Khuld stopped her straightening. "The future of Islam?" she asked.

"That's what this is all about," Omar replied. "The successor to the Messenger. His representative on earth."

"The caliph?" she asked.

"The Commander of the Faithful himself. It's all in the manuscript. *'Damaging and odious enemies to the religion of Muhammad'* who *'talk the Master of the World into the idea of annihilating the Abbasid dynasty.'* It implied that Taj al-Mulk was trying to convince the sultan to remove al-Muqtadi from office and replace him with the sultan's own grandson, over Nizam al-Mulk's objections."

"How do you know that's not how it happened?"

"Have you any idea how much planning a coup like that entailed? The tactical problem alone was considerable. The sultan needed to get physical control of the Dar Caliph and al-Muqtadi's person. But that was only the initial step. Do you see all the construction going on outside that window? What do you think it's for? Once he had the caliphate under his control, Malik-shah intended to make himself the master of Baghdad. His new capital. Maybe just his winter capital; I don't know. But some kind of capital. Either way it was a huge undertaking. Construction started a year ago, so the plot was under way for at least that long. I have suspicions it was longer. All the way back to when the marriage of the sultan's daughter to al-Muqtadi disintegrated—three years ago. Nizam al-Mulk controlled the levers of government. No undertaking of that magnitude could have possibly taken place in Seljuq lands if he opposed it. Besides, one of those houses being built was for him.”

“Good point.”

“Anyway, he practically admitted his complicity in the conspiracy.”

“When did he do that?” Khuld asked.

“When he fired Abu Shuja,” Omar replied. “Do you remember what he told the caliph? Abu Shuja was ‘interfering with the plans of the regime.’ I asked ben Samha what plans he was talking about, but he died before he could tell me. Now we know. Ben Samha was in charge of the building program—constructing houses for Seljuq officials, renovating the palace, raising the Mosque of the Sultan. Nizam al-Mulk knew history; he knew that in the days of the Arab conquest, a mosque was a symbol that the Muslims controlled a city. The Mosque of the Sultan was going to be the symbol that Malik-shah controlled Baghdad. Ben Samha was the central figure in all of these building projects. He was integral to the plan to overthrow the Abbasids. That’s the plan that Abu Shuja interfered with when he tried to humble ben Samha.”

“But Malik-shah must have known the truth,” Khuld said.

“Of course he knew,” Omar replied. “That’s why he laughed when Fakhr al-Mulk revealed the manuscript to him.”

“Why didn’t he say something when the manuscript was revealed to the public?”

“How could he? He still didn’t have a deal with Ghazali. Riots were breaking out in Baghdad. Looters overran the markets. The whole conspiracy was coming apart at the seams. If he admitted the extent of his involvement at that point, the mob, the ulama, they all would have been united in going after his head. And on top of that, I think that despite what he knew, there was some little part of his mind that nagged at him and crippled him with doubt. Could the manuscript be telling the truth? Did Nizam al-Mulk support the plan, or was it all Taj al-Mulk’s doing? I can just picture Malik-shah trying to remember who said what at all those meetings when he wasn’t paying attention.”

“But he did the right thing in the end.”

“He was brilliant. He surprised everyone. Now al-Muqtadi is packing his baggage, and Malik-shah towers over the political landscape like the Colossus of Rhodes.”

Khuld resumed her war on clutter. She advanced across the room to lay siege to her father's papers.

"Don't touch those," Omar said.

"It's almost dinnertime," she replied without stopping. "I need to clear the table."

"I'm in the middle of something."

"What could you possibly be in the middle of? The case is over. Taj al-Mulk is innocent."

"We know that Taj al-Mulk didn't do it. But we still don't know who did."

"Oh, of course," Khuld said. She put a sheet of paper back down onto the table and stared dumbfounded at it. "I should have thought of that. I don't know what's wrong with me today."

"You have other concerns on your mind," Omar replied.

"What's that supposed to mean?"

"You're spellbound by love."

Khuld turned away. But before she did, Omar could swear he saw her blush. He never thought he'd see *that*.

"Yes, well, we should concentrate on the case," Khuld said.

"What's this 'we'? Are you my assistant now?"

"It's obvious you need one. Look at this mess. What are you doing with all of these papers?"

"I'm trying to compose a new list of suspects. I thought if I laid out everything in front of me—"

"What was wrong with your old suspect list?"

"It's completely worthless."

"Why do you say that?"

"Do you remember who was on it?"

"Malik-shah. Terken Khatun. Taj al-Mulk. Nizam al-Mulk's sons. Abba Saad ben Samha. Abu Nasir. Maybe Amid ad-Dawla. All people who had power in the government, because that's what Nizam al-Mulk wrote in his . . . oh."

"Yes, you figured it out. When I compiled that list, I still believed that the manuscript was genuine. What a stroke of luck! Nizam al-Mulk reached out to me from beyond the grave and told me who to suspect. With lots of cryptic warnings about Shiite conspiracies, so that after the fact,

451

Hasan-i Sabbah could boast that the great Nizam al-Mulk was afraid of him. But let me ask you this: if Nizam al-Mulk didn't write it, who did? Who wanted to create chaos by putting Taj al-Mulk, Terken Khatun, Abba Saad ben Samha, and the other Seljuq insiders under suspicion? Who would want to mislead us into thinking that the Nizam opposed the plan to overthrow the Commander of the Faithful?"

Khuld wasn't so spellbound by love that she couldn't put it all together. "Someone who wanted to protect the caliph."

"Bull's-eye! Whoever was behind it hoped that without Nizam al-Mulk at his side, Malik-shah wouldn't have the skill, or the courage, or the brains to go ahead with the plan. But in case the murderer was wrong about that, the manuscript was his insurance. If the public believed that their beloved, pious, recently martyred Nizam al-Mulk opposed the plan, they would start a revolution rather than let the sultan get away with it."

"And they nearly did," Khuld observed. "It might have worked if you hadn't found out the truth. Who is on the new suspect list?"

Omar shuffled through the papers until he found the one he was looking for. He handed it to Khuld, who read aloud: "'One. Abu Abdullah Humaydi.'"

"He's fiercely partisan on the side of the caliph," Omar explained. "And as deputy director of the Nizamiyya, he has the school's budget at his disposal. So he had the means to employ the Assassins."

Khuld continued reading: "'Two. Qadi Abu Bakr Shami.' He certainly was hostile to Nizam al-Mulk. What does this say, next to his name?"

Omar leaned over to decipher his nearly illegible scrawl. "Oh, I made a note to investigate his finances and see if he could afford the services of Alamut. A qadi can become quite rich if he's corrupt. I think Shami is honest, but I don't know him that well."

Khuld looked back at the paper, but there were only the two names. She turned it over. Blank. "That's it?" she asked. "Humaydi and Shami?"

"That's all I could think of," Omar replied.

"There are plenty of other people in Baghdad who support the caliph. What about Abu Shuja Rudhrawari?"

"I considered him, but the sultan took almost everything he had when he fell from power. He doesn't have the means."

"How do you know that?"

Omar felt like an idiot. "He told me so," he replied sheepishly. "And I forgot to judge harshly everything I hear. Okay, you can be my assistant. Write him down."

Khuld took a seat on a cushion and, holding the page on a piece of pasteboard across her lap, added Abu Shuja to the list along with a note to look further into his finances.

"Why does it have to be a partisan of the caliph?" she asked. "Why not the caliph himself? He obviously has a motive to save his own skin. And he has towers filled with gold."

"The accumulated treasure of a dozen generations of Abbasids. Makes the Nizamiyya budget look like the revenue of a fruit stand," Omar replied. "But from everything I hear, al-Muqtadi isn't very good at doing things. He's bright enough, but no one ever lets him try. The real power in the Dar Calipha is Amid ad-Dawla."

"Should I write him down?"

"Might as well."

They mulled over several other possible suspects, but none of them seemed likely. Ghazi, Tamimi, and some of the other professors at the Nizamiyya were outspoken in their opposition to the sultan, but they didn't have the purse to pull off a world-altering assassination.

"What about Ghazali?" Khuld asked. "He had access to the Nizamiyya funds, just like Humaydi. And look at the way he took over your investigation. It's almost as if he wanted to lead you down the wrong path. What better way to cover his own crime?" Observing the sad expression on her father's face, she added, "Yes, I know, he's your friend. It pains you to even consider him. But as you would say, the truth is a friend, and Abu Hamid Ghazali is a friend."

"But the truth is a truer friend?" Omar asked. "No, it's not simply friendship. I just don't believe it, that's all. Until a year ago, Ghazali was definitely the sultan's loyal servant. Granted, since he came to Baghdad, he's been more sympathetic to the caliph. But I don't think he's become so blinded by al-Muqtadi's cause that he would commit murder. On top of that, the death of the Nizam has left Ghazali scrambling for funding for the Nizamiyya. So he would seem to have an interest in the Nizam being alive."

After a moment of hesitation, he added, "I suppose I should be thorough, though. Write him down."

That gave them five names: Professor Humaydi, Qadi Shami, Abu Shuja, Amid ad-Dawla, and Professor Ghazali.

"Humaydi stands out," Khuld observed. "He's the only one that we know for sure had both motive and means."

"He only appears to stand out because we have so many questions about the others," Omar replied.

"What about Amid ad-Dawla? He's the only name on both of your lists."

"I wish I knew who he's really loyal to."

At an impasse, Khuld declared it was time for her to fetch dinner. She made her father promise to clear the table by the time she got back. As she tied on her hijab and headed to the door, Omar pondered the list of suspects one more time and realized there *was* one name that stood out. A name that he would have missed if it hadn't been for Khuld. The name of the man who had lied to him.

He called to Khuld.

She turned in the doorway to see what he wanted. "Yes?" she asked.

"I'm proud of you."

She didn't answer right away. And when she did answer, there was a catch in her voice.

"Never mind that," she said. "Get the table cleaned up."

*   *   *

Baghdadi had no trouble getting past the palace guards. One of them even greeted him by name. "Hey, Muhammad, where've you been?" Apparently, the word hadn't gone out that he had defected. But, then, why would it? No one expected him to return to Baghdad.

The jagged peaks of the Alborz and the Zagros, the walled cities of Qazvin, Hamadan, and Kermanshah—they had all blurred together on the return trip. The Sheikh of the Mountain's network of safe houses dispensed sustenance and fresh horses almost as efficiently as the sultan's post stations. Despite Khwaja Omar's head start, Baghdadi calculated that he had galloped into Baghdad no more than two days behind the Astronomer Royal.

He stabled his horse at a safe house in Karkh. The hideout was run by an angry-looking florist who was expecting him. Baghdadi was certain that the same carrier pigeon who had tipped off the florist to Baghdadi's imminent arrival had also brought orders to keep an eye on him.

Baghdadi crossed the Main Bridge back to the east bank and the Dar Saltanah. He cut through the courtyard to the wing where Omar's room was located and bounded up the stairs. As he hurried along the corridor, it occurred to him that his days on the road had rendered him disheveled. He paused for a moment outside Omar's door to catch his breath and adjust his robe, stole, and turban. *Khwaja Omar is going to be shocked enough to see me*, he thought. *It won't do to enter his room looking like I escaped from the lunatic ward at Adudi.* He checked that the dagger was still in his sleeve and that the document he had brought from Alamut was still in his pocket. That was the most important thing. With everything in order, he reached out and pushed the door open.

*   *   *

With Ramadan over, the royal kitchens didn't serve quite as sumptuous feasts every night. Still, the chefs had concocted a delicious-smelling roast chicken stuffed with an apricot-date mixture; a vinegar-lime sauce offset the sweet stuffing. Khuld was sure her father would like it. She carried it up to his room on a tray along with a plummy red wine from the coast of the Sea of Rum.

Her hands full, she eased open the door with her foot and was furious at what she saw. She had asked her father to do one simple thing—clear the table—and he hadn't done it. His books and papers were still scattered all over the tabletop, and he just sat there, poring over some document. Typical. He was so wrapped up in what he was reading that he didn't even notice that Baghdadi was standing over him with a bloodstained dagger.

Baghdadi was standing over him with a bloodstained dagger.

When it finally registered, Khuld didn't so much drop the tray as hurl it at the floor. It clattered on the polished stone, spraying wine, sauce, and chicken parts in all directions. She charged Baghdadi, shoved him across the room, and pinned him against the wall with her forearm. With her free hand, she twisted his wrist until he cried out in pain and dropped the dagger.

"Assassin!" she shouted. "I'll kill you!"

"I'm not an Assassin," Baghdadi gasped hoarsely, forcing the words out against the pressure of Khuld's arm across his throat.

"You lie!" she yelled, pushing down even harder.

Behind her, someone said, "Khuld," in a patient voice, but she had other things on her mind. "All you ever do is lie!" she went on.

Again, "Khuld."

"I can't believe I loved you."

She felt a gentle hand on her shoulder and jerked her head to see who was there. It was her father, and he was trying to tell her something.

"You're . . . you're all right," she stammered.

"Khuld, listen to him," he said firmly.

She let up the pressure on Baghdadi's larynx just enough for him to whisper, "I'm not an Assassin."

Through her tears, Khuld looked to her father for guidance. Omar nodded.

"He didn't betray you?" Khuld asked.

"It's the truth," Omar replied. "Our friend Baghdadi fooled everybody."

Confused, Khuld turned back to Baghdadi. She made eye contact with him, and he held her glance with such a look of sincerity that it erased all of her doubts.

"That's wonderful!" she exclaimed. She had her Baghdadi back. She threw her arms around him in a warm embrace and squeezed him so hard that once again he struggled for air.

"*W'allah!*" Omar exclaimed, "Let the poor fellow breathe."

"Oh," Khuld replied, laughing. "I'm sorry." She let up on him—but only slightly.

Suddenly a threatening voice demanded, "Get away from her!"

Still in a happy dream, Khuld turned her head—resting it on Baghdadi's shoulder—and there was Hariri standing in the doorway.

"Qasim!" she said cheerfully. Whether the smile on her lips was for Hariri or Baghdadi, she couldn't have said.

The scowl on Hariri's face was entirely for Baghdadi. "I said, get away from her!" he ordered, brandishing a dagger; its steel blade flashed angrily in the lamplight. "I took you down once. I can do it again."

"You certainly did," Baghdadi replied. "And for that I am eternally grateful."

*   *   *

"I wasn't grateful at the time, of course," Baghdadi explained. "But you did me an enormous favor, Hariri. After the kick in the face you gave me, no one could doubt that I was loyal to the Assassins. I was unconscious for an hour and groggy for several hours after that. When I said I was serious about defecting, the Sheikh of the Mountain had to believe me."

The reasonably civil conversation was courtesy of Omar, who had stepped in to prevent Hariri from thrashing Baghdadi a second time. "Trust me," Omar assured his new friend. "The young man isn't a threat."

Then Khuld had taken charge and ordered Baghdadi to clean up the sticky mess of chicken parts, broken crockery, wine, and vinegar-lime sauce. "It was your fault, after all," she said. "What were you thinking, surprising me like that?" He did the best he could, but someone was going to have to go over the stonework again with a scrub brush in the morning. Meanwhile Khuld had marched back down to the kitchen and returned with enough victuals for four. Planted at the table between her two suitors, she relished her dinner as she interrogated Baghdadi about his adventures among the Assassins.

"But why did you do it?" she asked. "You could have escaped with my father and Hariri. Why remain in Alamut?"

"So I could finish searching the Sheikh of the Mountain's study."

Omar had already told Khuld about the attempt to search through Hasan's papers and how it had been cut short by one of the guards. "Wasn't it dangerous to go back there?" she asked. Her words expressed concern for Baghdadi's safety, but her tone betrayed her admiration for his bravery.

"Khwaja Omar had told me how certain he was that there was important evidence there," Baghdadi replied. "So when Hariri showed up to rescue us, I knew that I had to stay behind until I had another opportunity to search the study."

"But why did you tell my father you wanted to join the Assassins?"

"Because I knew that if I told him the real reason I wanted to stay behind, he wouldn't let me. I had to convince him that he and I were through as *khwaja* and pupil. As it was, your father tried to talk me out of it, but then Hariri ended the discussion with that brutal kick of his."

"And did you find anything?"

Omar answered for him. "Just this." He handed a sheet of paper to Hariri. "Pass that to Khuld," he said. It was the document he had been studying so intently when Khuld had burst into the room and launched her assault on Baghdadi.

"Be careful, Khwaja," Baghdadi said. "You're getting sauce on it."

Hariri glanced at the text as he passed it on. "Hebrew," he said knowingly.

"Aramaic," Baghdadi replied. He noticed Hariri giving him a dirty look from across the table. *I guess some people don't like being corrected*, he thought. He tried to make Hariri feel better by adding, "It's an easy mistake to make. The alphabet is the same."

But that only made Hariri angrier. "Don't patronize me, boy," he growled.

Khuld, meanwhile, held the document out in front of her as if she had forgotten it. Omar reminded her. "That piece of paper you have in your hand," he said, "is a letter of credit. For fifty thousand dinars." He paused to let that sink in. None of them had ever seen fifty thousand dinars in one place. Not even Omar, who had managed the budget to build the royal observatory. "To be precise," he went on, "it's a *receipt* for a letter of credit. The letter itself has already been cashed and returned to the bank. And look whose seal is at the bottom."

Hariri knew without looking. "The House of Samha," he said.

Khuld studied the wax impression under the lamp. "You're right," she exclaimed. "How did you know?"

"It's the only bank in Qazvin big enough to handle a transaction of that magnitude."

Khuld beamed at him. Her eyes sparkled with pride. Baghdadi saw her expression reflected in Hariri's face. *What's with these two?* he wondered.

"This is how the Assassins got paid for the murder of Nizam al-Mulk," Omar continued. "Someone deposited the funds with ben Samha here in Baghdad, and the Assassins were able to withdraw them from his Qazvin branch."

"But there's still something I don't understand," Khuld said. She turned to Baghdadi. "If you weren't really an Assassin, why were you standing over my father with a dagger?"

Baghdadi got up, retrieved the dagger from on top of a chest, and handed it hilt-first to Khuld for a closer look. "It's the murder weapon," he said. "The one that killed Nizam al-Mulk. The Assassins confiscated it from us, but I stole it from Commander Misri's office. I was just bringing it back."

Khuld examined the dagger for a moment and then laid it down on the table in order to take up the letter of credit again. She had to ask Baghdadi the meaning of a couple of words, but overall she did pretty well with the Aramaic.

At last she burst out, "You did it. You solved the case!"

Much as he enjoyed the praise, Baghdadi couldn't help but notice that Hariri was glaring at him again. Khuld must have picked up on that too, because she said, "Aw! Someone's feeling left out. My father and Baghdadi would both still be prisoners in Alamut if it weren't for you," she said. "Thank you."

Omar smiled indulgently; it wasn't often that he got to see his daughter so happy. But there was still business to attend to. "I hate to be the rain that washes out the celebration," he said, "but let's not get ahead of ourselves. The case isn't solved. Not yet, anyway. This document is a huge step forward. It's our first proof of something we suspected for a week: that the Assassins didn't act alone in the murder of Nizam al-Mulk. Someone paid them. But we still don't know who. All we know is that it was someone in Baghdad who had funds on deposit with the House of Samha."

"That could be almost anyone," Khuld said. "So how do we settle it?"

"I'll pay Saad a visit tomorrow morning," Omar replied. "It's time he and I had a talk."

CHAPTER 29

BAGHDAD
FRIDAY, 9 SHAWWAL 485
27 Abán 471
12 November 1092

K hwaja Omar," said Saad, "You know perfectly well that I won't tell you anything. I'm sure my father explained to you that the House of Samha must respect the confidentiality of its clients."

They sat under the shade of an awning that had been set up in front of the Samha residence. It was one of the many makeshift shelters jammed into the courtyard. The entire staff was now working in the open air. Their furniture was an incongruous mix of ad hoc contrivances—here some planks were propped up on wooden blocks to use as a worktable, there a costly antique chair that had somehow survived the fire. Spread out in front of them, a team of workmen removed the rubble from what once had been the bank. Bricks and other reusable building materials were brushed, rinsed, sorted, and piled at the edges of the lot. Everything else was shoveled into baskets. A steady stream of mules hauled full baskets away and returned with empty ones. It was dusty work; a hazy cloud hovered over the site. Saad and most of his staff wore the ends of their turbans over their noses and mouths. Despite the hardships in rebuilding Abba Saad's empire, his spirit continued to guide it. Hanging from the awning, in a spot where Saad could see it from his chair, was the Tree of Life tapestry that Omar had remarked on during his first visit. The fabric was blackened by smoke damage, and yet the flames had failed to destroy it.

"Even if I wanted to tell you," Saad continued, "I couldn't. I don't know who the client was. My father handled this transaction. I knew nothing about it. And any record we had burned in the fire."

Omar sighed. He and Saad had been going in circles for three-quarters of an hour. At least he didn't have to argue on an empty stomach. His host had been kind enough to provide him with some wine and a few lamb-filled pastries. "I know how much you liked those when you were here before," Saad had explained when the old servant Daniel brought them out. Omar was delighted that the Samha hospitality had been passed on to the next generation. Alas, the Samha stubbornness had gone with it.

Omar wondered whether Saad was telling him the truth or covering for his client. He sipped from his goblet and considered his next move. He had one last gambit to play. It was time to play it.

Reaching into his pocket, Omar produced the murder weapon, unwrapped the protective cloth, and showed it to Saad. "Do you remember this?" he asked.

"Of course," Saad replied. "It's the dagger that killed Nizam al-Mulk. That was the reason you came here the first time. You wanted to see if my father could determine its origin."

"And do you remember what happened?"

"He looked at the sapphire under his magnifying glass and said that it came from Qazvin."

"What did you think of that?"

"Actually it surprised me. Most sapphires come from India. I wanted to get a look at it myself, but before I got a chance, my father gave you the magnifying glass as a gift."

"You were right to be surprised," Omar said, rising from his chair. "There was a reason your father didn't let you look. Let me demonstrate."

He led his host to the smoking jeweler's forge at the edge of the courtyard. There he placed the dagger on the stone rim and asked Saad to hold it steady. He picked up a hammer and chisel that someone had left behind. The bandages were finally off his hands; it was easy for him to knock the sapphire out of its setting with a single blow. He dropped it in a ceramic crucible and, with a long pair of iron tongs, put the crucible to bed at the center of the glowing coals.

461

About a minute passed, but nothing happened. The blue jewel just sat there. "I think it has necessity for more heat," Omar said. He pumped the bellows, breathing tenuous life into the embers; they exhaled wispy orange flames.

"Can I help with something?" Saad asked.

"Keep watching the gemstone," Omar replied as he continued to work the bellows.

Another minute passed. Suddenly Saad gasped in surprise. A pool of liquid had formed at the base of the stone. It was melting. "That's no sapphire," he said.

"Do you remember when your father told me about the impurities in the stone," Omar replied. "I said they looked like bubbles in a piece of glass. Well, that's exactly what they were." He dropped the handles of the bellows. By now the stone was a glowing orange puddle at the bottom of the crucible.

Saad prodded it with an awl; the molten glass was thick like pine sap. "So not only was it not an elusive Qazvin sapphire," he said. "It wasn't a sapphire at all. Why would my father lie like that?"

"Guilt. He knew that the House of Samha was the instrument that financed the murder of Nizam al-Mulk." Saad started to protest, but Omar reassured him. "Of course, he didn't do it intentionally. It was just one of the numerous financial transactions he handled every week. He had no way of knowing what the funds were going to be used for. When he realized what he had done, he must have been horrified. But he was in a bind. The reputation of the House of Samha was built on protecting its clients' secrets. He couldn't tell me who the client was. But he managed to convince himself that if he pointed me in the right direction—the direction of Qazvin—and I figured it out on my own, then he could make things right without violating his professional creed. Maybe that was a valid loophole, or maybe he just rationalized it. I'm hardly one to condemn anyone for rationalization. In any case, he was killed because he knew the identity of the murderer—an identity he would never reveal explicitly. But I believe his last wish was that I would reveal it for him."

Omar had given it his best shot. But had it found its mark? Clearly his words had an effect on Saad, who stared into the crucible, stirring the molten glass. Of course he had to be thinking about his father. Missing him terribly. Wondering what advice he would impart. His face glowed orange in the light of the fire. Grief's furnace. Omar saw his own heartache reflected in Saad's expression. Heartache for Abba Saad ben Samha. Heartache for Nizam al-Mulk.

When Saad finally spoke, he said, "I believe you, Khwaja Omar. I think you're right, that my father's dying wish was to see the murderer brought to justice. I want to help you. I really do. But I can't tell you what I don't know."

Omar felt a surge of frustration. He had been so excited when Baghdadi showed up with the letter of credit. Now it looked like another dead end. Perhaps Saad was lying; perhaps he really didn't know. Either way, they were at an impasse. But Omar wasn't ready to give up. He had a job to do. "I still need to know who the client was," he said.

Saad looked up from the glowing coals, obviously surprised that Omar wouldn't let it go, visibly annoyed that Omar wouldn't leave him to mourn in peace.

"So," Omar continued. "What are we going to do about it?"

*   *   *

"Whatever possessed you to have him arrested?" Abu Shuja exclaimed in disbelief.

"I didn't see any other way," Omar replied. "I'm sure that once Saad has sat in the sultan's dungeon for a few days, he'll reconsider his position."

They mingled with the other guests in the sultan's pavilion. It was a small group; only a select few among the members of the hunting party had been honored with an invitation to join the sultan afterward.

The hunt itself had been thrilling—while it lasted. At first light Malik-shah and his entourage had galloped out of Baghdad along the Damascus Highway toward the open country northwest of the city. The cloudy skies portended perfect hunting weather: no solar glare, not too hot. For hours the horses disconcerted farmers' oxen and trampled newly planted fields as they chased down their quarry. Over six dozen antelope fell prey to the rapid-fire onslaught of arrows. The sultan slew sixty-three of the graceful creatures himself, a few shy of his personal best, but not bad. Alas, a late afternoon cloudburst soaked the hunting party, the dogs lost the scent of the herd, and a somewhat soggy Malik-shah called it a day.

In a clearing near the center of camp, an army of butchers carved up the carcasses; the meat was to be distributed among Baghdad's poor. The choicest animals, of course, were set aside for tonight's feast. They turned on spits over open flames, protected from lingering showers by an awning. The mingled aromas of wood smoke, roasting meat, and damp earth filled the air.

While they waited for their dinner to reach a nice, juicy pink in the middle, the guests in the sultan's pavilion milled about, talking of recent events. A section of the tent had been partitioned off for their use by hanging carpets woven with appropriate hunting motifs. It was a small area compared to the tent as a whole—large enough so that the assembled company didn't feel crowded but close enough to maintain a sense of intimacy. For those who drank wine, Nush-tegin kept the goblets full. A trio of serving girls poured iced fruit drinks for the others.

The guests were scrubbed and perfumed. Baths had been provided to cleanse them of the dirt and sweat of a day in the saddle. The sultan had proclaimed tonight's event to be "informal." While a novice courtier might interpret that as "come as you are," those of wisdom and experience understood it to mean "wear your *second*-best getup." So although there were no actual robes of honor in evidence, the guests wrapped themselves in a colorful panorama of linens and silks. Omar wore gold brocade with a pattern of stylized ringdoves. Malik-shah, in keeping with his newfound gravitas, opted for a solid—a subdued maroon silk. But as always, the fabric was of the finest quality. The dignified trim—made from thread of real gold—sparkled under the plethora of lamps. Abu Shuja's tailored caftan sported a floral pattern; the brocade roses perfectly matched the color of the massive ruby on his finger. Only the austere Qadi Shami and the Blind Imam shunned color altogether; they stuck to their usual black wool.

The group around Omar was skeptical that he had arrested a citizen as prominent—and as essential to the regime—as the head of the House of Samha. "Don't take my word for it," Omar said. "Taj al-Mulk, you tell them."

"It's true," the vizier replied. "Khwaja Omar came to me this morning and requested an arrest warrant. Fortunately I hadn't left for the hunt yet. I arranged for the document to be prepared and sent a squadron of mamelukes to the Suq of the Goldsmiths. They brought the banker in. It was all finalized before the muezzin called noon prayers."

"Since you signed in my name," Malik-shah said as he pushed into the group, "I should know what the charges were."

"Conspiracy to commit murder," Taj al-Mulk replied.

"And there's evidence of this?"

"The letter of credit that Khwaja Omar showed me is evidence enough."

Abu Shuja still had his doubts. "Do you really think time in jail will loosen the Jew's tongue?" he asked.

"If it doesn't," Yalbard interjected, "say the word, and I'll spend a few minutes with him. He'll talk."

The conversation lagged as the group pondered the implications of this latest twist in the case of Nizam al-Mulk. Humaydi, who never could get a word in when more celebrated individuals were talking, took advantage of the opportunity. "I don't care what the evidence is," he burst out. "Or whether the Jew talks or not. The fact that he's a banker is reason enough to lock him up."

A lively debate ensued. Ghazali held forth on whether the Quran's prohibition on charging interest applied to Jews. Taj al-Mulk conceded that he wasn't a scholar of shari'ah, but as the former finance minister, he knew government funding inside and out. The regime couldn't possibly function without credit.

As the others argued back and forth, Fakhr al-Mulk drew Omar aside and said, "I must tell you, old friend, I'm impressed that you arrested the banker. I didn't think you had it in you to play rough."

"It's been a rough month," Omar replied. "And you didn't help any."

"I suppose you're referring to the little episode of the manuscript."

"That damn manuscript cost me weeks of wasted effort. It led me down a completely wrong path."

"I don't see how you can blame me," Fakhr al-Mulk said innocently. "I was the victim. The victim of a fraud."

"You must have suspected something. After all, you knew your father spearheaded the conspiracy against al-Muqtadi. Didn't it strike you as peculiar that he condemned it in his manuscript?"

"Now that you mention it, it was a little odd."

"And yet you didn't say a thing about it."

"How could I? It was a state secret."

"And that was the only reason?"

"I have no idea what you're trying to imply, Omar Khayyam. I've been nothing but a good citizen."

"Good citizen," Omar repeated skeptically.

"Absolutely," Fakhr al-Mulk replied. "I found a piece of evidence and I turned it over to the proper authorities. It would have been presumptuous of me to judge it myself."

"You promised to consult with me before you went public with it."

"How could I consult? You ran off to Qazvin. No one knew where you were. Ghazali and Shami were your partners in the investigation. I reasoned that consulting them was the next best thing."

"And if it happened to benefit you personally by removing a rival from your path . . ."

"That was just a lucky coincidence."

It was plain from the expression on Omar's face that he was in no mood for Fakhr al-Mulk's facetious villain act tonight.

Fakhr al-Mulk tried a more serious tack. "So, you and me," he said. "Are things all right between us?"

"The Two Professors?"

"There used to be three."

Omar sighed wearily. "Hasan-i Sabbah has transformed himself into something deplorable," he said. "A terrorist. He presides safely on his mountaintop and sends impressionable losers out to commit suicide killings in his name. He's a first-class shit cowering behind a Quran. As for Nizam al-Mulk and Abba Saad ben Samha, they're dead. Passed beyond the Door of Darkness. That's three friends I have lost this month. I couldn't bear to lose another. '*Behold the Heav'n's iniquitous Play; Behold the World—empty: Friends pass away . . .*'"

Fakhr al-Mulk finished the verse for him: "'*Canst thou live for thyself for a moment? Seek not for TO-MORROW; behold TO-DAY!*'"[98]

"Good plan, friend," Omar replied.

Fakhr al-Mulk opened his arms and embraced the companion of his youth. Omar hugged him back. They held fast to each other until unborn Tomorrow and dead Yesterday were as if they never existed. Struck from the calendar.[99]

By then they had attracted the attention of their host. "If you two lovebirds aren't too busy," Malik-shah called to them, "get your asses over here. I have a few announcements to make."

The other guests had gathered in a circle. Omar and Fakhr al-Mulk found an open space between Mu'ayyad al-Mulk and Professor Ghazali and stepped in to close the gap. Taj al-Mulk, meanwhile, who had been consulting with Nush-tegin on some logistical matter, found that the ring had closed on him. He squeezed in between Ghazali and Humaydi, jostling them and forcing everybody else to adjust their positions.

When at last the circle stabilized, Malik-shah said, "Now that I finally have everyone's attention, first things first. I understand that I killed sixty-two antelope today."

"Sixty-three, Sahib al-Jalal," Yalbard corrected him.

"Sixty-three it is. Now, some of you might not be aware of this, but Nizam al-Mulk used to lecture me about certain topics—"

"Just a little," Yalbard called out.

"—and one of those topics was hunting. He said that while a certain amount of hunting was desirable for the recreation and training of the Master of the World, and it showed humility for the Master of the World to provide for his own table, I was taking it to excess—I think the word he used was 'obsession.' I needed to cut back, he said. As with many things, I didn't listen to him."

The guests were sympathetic. Every one of them had, at one time or another, fantasized about not listening to Nizam al-Mulk.

"Nevertheless," Malik-shah continued, "he did convince me of one thing: that to kill an animal for my own pleasure, rather than from the necessity of feeding myself, was wrong. To atone for that sin, I resolved that for every animal I killed, I would donate one dinar to the poor." Nush-tegin handed a purse to the sultan, who pressed it into the hand of the Blind Imam. "Please see that this make its way to the poor box."

"May Allah bless you, O Sahib al-Jalal," the imam replied.

"Yalbard," the sultan said as he returned to his place in the circle. "How many dinars does that make it since I first made this resolution?"

"Including the sixty-three for today," Yalbard replied, "it comes to ten thousand, one hundred, sixty-two."

Some of the guests agreed with the Nizam that the sultan needed to devote more time to governing and less time to hunting. But even they couldn't help but be impressed. A murmur of admiration went around the circle.

But Malik-shah wasn't finished with inciting admiration. "Now that business is out of the way," he said, "let me welcome all of you to my home. For my tent is my true home, far more so than any structure of brick and mortar.

"As you know, the genius of Nizam al-Mulk was that he was able to unite the diverse and sometimes conflicting factions that make up the Great Seljuq Empire. I have to confess that during the past month there were times when it seemed that his accomplishment was unraveling. So it does my heart good to see you all here tonight—you who represent the pillars of our community: the mosque, the university, the bench, the military, and the vizierate. I am proud to look on you as my friends."

"The new Malik-shah," Ghazali whispered to Omar. "Grace befitting a king. He's full of pleasant surprises tonight."

"To put it in Aristotelian terms," Omar whispered back, "the potentiality was always there. He merely had necessity of kinesis to transform it to actuality."

"Bah! You and your Greek science."

The next surprise wasn't as pleasant for the chief professor. Malik-shah called to Nush-tegin, who brought the sultan an extra-large jeweled goblet, which he filled from a ewer. Malik-shah held the goblet high and said, "My friends, I invite you to share a cup with me, to honor the memory of the Nizam." A rumble of disapproval welled up from the general direction of Humaydi, Shami, and Abu Shuja, but the sultan paid it no mind. He handed the goblet to Yalbard, who took a gulp and passed it on.

Abu'l-Fadl Qummi was next, followed by Mu'ayyad al-Mulk and Fakhr al-Mulk. The latter raised the cup, turned toward Taj al-Mulk, and said, "In the spirit of unity, which was so important to my father, I'm honored to share this token of goodwill with his successor."

A hush fell over the company, silent respect for a heartfelt gesture of reconciliation from a defeated rival.

When the moment had passed, Fakhr al-Mulk held out the cup to Omar. But just as Omar started to reach for it, Fakhr al-Mulk pulled it back and said, "Not so fast, my friend. There's a price."

"Are you short of cash already?" Omar asked sarcastically. "Your inheritance didn't endure very long, did it?"

"Nothing so crass as dinars. The price I seek is of a different nature. If you want a drink, you must buy it with a poem." The demand brought the other guests back to life. With one voice, they chanted, "Poem! Poem! Poem!"

Omar obliged:

"Were it not Folly, Spider-like to spin
The Thread of present Life away to win—
    What? for ourselves, who know not if we shall
Breathe out the very Breath we now breathe in!"[100]

Fakhr al-Mulk looked around the circle to gauge the reaction. "It appears the assembled company is unsatisfied, old friend," he said, continuing to hold on to the goblet. "Too gloomy. You can do better, Omar. This is a drinking party, after all. I know you've written a poem or two about drinking."

"Oh, all right," Omar replied with mock annoyance. He smiled impishly and recited:

"I drink Wine; my Enemies, high and low,
Say—'Do not drink it; 'tis Religion's Foe.'
    When I learned wine was a Foe, I answered—
''Tis permitted to drink the Foe's Blood, though.'"[101]

Guffaws burst out and filled the small compartment with joy. Malik-shah in particular relished the joke. Satisfied with the response, Fakhr al-Mulk finally relinquished the goblet. Omar took a swig and passed the cup to the next guest.

The laughter stopped abruptly. Because the next guest was Chief Professor Ghazali.

Ghazali stood stone-faced, holding the goblet at arm's length, as if it were bubbling over with some noxious brew of chemicals. All eyes turned to him to see what he would do. If he drank, he was the foe of religion. If he didn't, he was the foe of Malik-shah. It would be like throwing the new spirit of unity back in the sultan's face. Not to mention insulting the memory of Nizam al-Mulk. Aware that many looked to him for leadership, he froze with uncertainty.

Then Taj al-Mulk whispered in his ear, "Think about the Nizamiyya," and Ghazali knew what he had to do. He raised the goblet to his lips and tipped it slightly. Everyone could tell that he didn't really drink. But that didn't matter. It was sufficient that he had gone through the motions.

After Taj al-Mulk took his turn, which featured a gracious response to Fakhr al-Mulk's olive branch, the goblet moved on to the remaining members of the ulama. Humaydi and Shami were both disappointed in Ghazali, but they followed his example anyway: they pretended to drink. Only the Blind Imam, who couldn't see what Ghazali had done, passed the goblet on untouched. The sultan made allowances for the old man's infirmity and chose not to take offense.

Abu Shuja was last. Holding up the cup, he said, "The real proof of the new spirit of unity is that I am here at all, released from house arrest. Again I offer my gratitude to the Sahib al-Jalal for that." He waved the goblet in the direction of Malik-shah, who nodded. "But there is someone else I should thank as well," Abu Shuja continued. "Chief Professor, I owe you a debt. As do we all. You not only obtained *my* freedom, but you also, more than anyone else, worked tirelessly to negotiate a settlement between the sultan and the caliph and thereby free this city from the tyranny of civil unrest. It was you who made this historic occasion possible."

"That's nice," Omar muttered to no one in particular. "Wasn't that nice?" Ghazali had been put through hell tonight, and Omar was pretty sure there would be more to come, some of it at Abu Shuja's hands. Maybe it had to be, but Omar was still glad to see his friend get some respect.

All eyes turned to Ghazali, eager for his response. He was clearly moved. Tears glistened in his eyes as he said, "I merely do what Allah commands me. *'If the two parties of the believers quarrel, then make peace between them.'*"[102]

"To Abu Hamid Ghazali," everyone replied in unison.

"To Abu Hamid Ghazali," Abu Shuja echoed. He pretended to drink and passed the goblet to the sultan.

"And to unity," Malik-shah added with a sweeping gesture that took in everyone in the compartment. Glancing into the bowl of the goblet, he smiled slyly to see that it was half full. He had forced the ulama to submit and still got to keep their wine. He raised the goblet to his thick lips and drained the contents dry.

*   *   *

Amid ad-Dawla had to skip the sultan's celebration. He was tied up making sure that it wasn't premature. Since Eid al-Fitr, he had latched himself on to al-Muqtadi, alert for the smallest signs that the caliph had suddenly discovered independence and intended to renege on his abdication. But there weren't any.

After Malik-shah left the Dar Calipha, al-Muqtadi had remained standing in the Hall of Audience for almost an hour, too stunned to move. Then, abruptly, he ran off to his chambers and shed his holiday robes in favor of a garment of sackcloth. He shut himself up in the Mosque of the Caliph and spent the next nine days in nearly continuous prayer and fasting. He saw no one other than Amid ad-Dawla and Professor Ghazali; the latter stopped by once a day to update the Commander of the Faithful on the status of negotiations.

As for what the caliph hoped to gain from his sudden turn to Allah, the worldly Amid ad-Dawla was stumped. Guidance? Forgiveness? Deliverance? Immersed in the repetitive chant of his prayers, the caliph kept his own counsel.

Then that night, while the vizier was at supper, al-Muqtadi left the mosque and gave his guards the slip. Amid ad-Dawla hastily called out a half dozen squadrons of the sultan's mamelukes to scour the grounds for the caliph. When they finally found the fugitive, Amid ad-Dawla would have laughed had he been prone to such displays. It should have been the first place they looked: the animal park.

Al-Muqtadi was sitting peacefully on a bench, nuzzling the head of one of his prize leopards. "Oh," he said, surprised to discover that he wasn't alone. "Amid ad-Dawla. Sit." He gestured to the empty space next to him on the bench.

Amid ad-Dawla dismissed the mamelukes and joined the caliph.

"Ghazali didn't come today," al-Muqtadi said. "It's over, isn't it?"

Amid ad-Dawla nodded.

"That's it, then," al-Muqtadi said. "Tomorrow is day ten. I'll have to leave for Basra." He stroked the fur on the leopard's neck. "I wanted to say good-bye to the cats. Somebody told me that my retirement estate isn't big enough for an animal park."

"Yes, I know," the vizier replied sadly. He was the somebody who had told the caliph that. The caliph must have forgotten. "They'll be well cared for." He observed that al-Muqtadi had lost a little weight, thanks to his days of fasting. He looked good, actually.

"I put in a word for you with Chief Professor Ghazali," al-Muqtadi continued. "He convinced the sultan to keep you on as vizier to Mahmud."

"I'm grateful to the Commander of the Faithful."

"It's nothing less than you deserve. You have been so loyal to me." Suddenly his voice failed him. He buried his face in his hands. Sobs convulsed his body. Amid ad-Dawla wanted to comfort him with a reassuring hand on his shoulder. But to touch the Commander of the Faithful uninvited was forbidden. It took a minute or so, but eventually al-Muqtadi recovered enough to talk. "You and Ghazali," he said, his cheeks streaked with the trails of tears. "You both stuck by my side long after everyone else abandoned me. I couldn't ask for two finer men to look after my interests."

Amid ad-Dawla wasn't prone to guilt, but al-Muqtadi made him feel like a first-rate heel. All he could say was, "Thank you, O Commander of the Faithful." His voice was choked with sadness.

In a friendly gesture, al-Muqtadi placed a hand on his vizier's knee. "There's no need for formality," he said. "Not anymore."

"You're still the Commander of the Faithful. For one more day, anyway."

"You know I wasn't always the Commander of the Faithful. There was a time when I was just Abdullah. I suppose I will be again now. That's what my mother called me."

Amid ad-Dawla placed his hand over the caliph's and gave it a squeeze. "Thank you, Abdullah," he said.

"My father died before I was born," Abdullah continued. "As for my grandfather, he was busy being the Commander of the Faithful, Scion of the House of Abbas, the caliph al-Qaim B'illah. So my mother was really all I had growing up. Her name was Urjuman. She was from humble origins. A slave. Captured as a girl in Armenia on some raid or other."

"You were young when she died. Do you remember her?"

"Not well. I remember she was pretty. I suppose you have to be pretty to be sold into the harem of a caliph's son. And she tried to pass her humility on to me. When I was six or so, people would play a game. They would challenge me by asking, 'Who are you?' just to hear me answer back in my most imperious little voice, 'I'm the next caliph!' My mother wasn't amused. 'Be humble, Abdullah,' she said. 'You may be the next caliph, but you're still the son of a slave. Never forget that.' I was too young. I didn't really know what 'humble' meant. I guess I'll learn now."

Amid ad-Dawla had only a weak smile to offer by way of consolation.

The two men sat side by side on the bench and looked out at the animal park. They didn't talk. The sky had cleared partially. The stars were visible in some spots; in others they were hidden by clouds. The moon was out, two-thirds full. The trees and grass were damp from the earlier showers; droplets of water glistened in the moonlight like spent tears. The rich smell of damp earth mixed with a whiff of animal droppings. Somewhere in his pen a lion roared. The caliph's other pets stirred for a moment and then went back to sleep, the elephants huddled close to each other, the giraffes with their necks curled up against their bodies. Abdullah's leopard lay her head down in his lap. She purred as he scratched behind her ears.

Maybe there's something to prayer after all, Amid ad-Dawla thought. Whatever the reason, Abdullah had made peace with his future.

CHAPTER 30

BAGHDAD
SATURDAY, 10 SHAWWAL 485
28 Abán 471
13 November 1092

*H*e bribed one of the page boys to tell him where Saad was being held. But the labyrinth of torch-lit corridors and urine-soaked stairways would have confounded Theseus. A series of wrong turns had him retracing his steps several times through the bowels of the Dar Saltanah. Every moment he wasted could be the moment that Saad betrayed his identity. He wanted to curse in frustration, but cursing was blasphemous.

When he finally found the doorway he was looking for, there were no guards. That was a problem. He had counted on there being guards he could bribe to unlock the door. But then he raised his lantern to examine the door more closely and discovered there wasn't a lock. What kind of prison was the sultan running?

He pushed the door open. The sudden onslaught of bright light forced him to shut his eyes in a hurry. He had expected to find a dark cell. What was going on? He blinked several times until his eyes adjusted and it was no longer painful to view the surprising scene.

It was a pleasant, sunlit room at ground level. Clearly his confusion in getting here, combined with how the palace was situated (it cascaded down a hill), had disoriented him. He hadn't descended nearly as far as he thought. The wall opposite him sported a row of open doors that looked out on a charming courtyard, lushly planted with orange and yellow chrysanthemums; he caught the scent of their perfume. At the center, a fountain tinkled soothingly. The room itself was furnished with a low table that held a chess set, a pair of pitchers—one filled with wine, one with water—and four goblets. Seated cross-legged on cushions, Saad and Omar Khayyam faced off across the chessboard. Between them, Professor Ghazali kibitzed. Opposite Ghazali, an empty cushion awaited the newcomer.

A guard stood watch in one corner. Without looking up from the game, Omar pointed to the visitor in the doorway and said to the guard, "Search him."

*   *   *

After a few moments, the guard said, "He just had this," holding up a dagger.

"Thank you," Omar replied. "Wait outside, please."

Hastening to obey, the guard pivoted on his heels and tramped out to the corridor, taking the dagger and lantern with him.

Omar closed the door and then looked his guest up and down. The newcomer wore a tailored, solid black caftan; his garb was considerably more subdued than was his custom. No shimmering silk or elaborate patterns with roses. But that made sense; he wouldn't want to be conspicuous in the dungeon corridors. The only remnant of what he had been wearing the night before was the massive ruby on his finger.

"Abu Shuja Rudhrawari," Omar said. "I was expecting you."

"I can see that," Abu Shuja replied, nodding toward the empty cushion.

"You should exercise caution with knives. You could hurt someone. But, then, you already hurt so many people."

Abu Shuja was so eager to show off how quickly he had grasped his predicament that he didn't bother to deny the accusation. Instead, he said, "I congratulate you, Omar Khayyam. It was an ingenious trap."

Omar was sure that with a little flattery Abu Shuja would confess everything, purely out of vanity. "We may be here awhile," Omar replied. "Please, have a seat."

"You can take over my position," Saad offered.

"I would not want to disrupt the game," Abu Shuja replied.

"I wish you would. Khwaja Omar is positively humiliating me." He scooted down to the place opposite Ghazali, taking his goblet of wine with him.

"Very well," Abu Shuja said. He settled on Saad's cushion and surveyed the board while Omar filled a goblet with water for him.

Abu Shuja's position in the game was every bit as bad as Saad claimed. He was down an elephant and two pawns compared to Omar, whose chariots and vizier had Abu Shuja's shah in a three-way check. "I take it it's my move," Abu Shuja said.

Omar nodded. Abu Shuja slid his shah diagonally one square, taking Omar's vizier. That got him out of immediate danger, but his position was still precarious.[103] "So what betrayed me?" he asked as he puzzled over how to get out of the jam he was in. "How did you know it was me?"

"At first I didn't. I assumed the murderer had to be someone in the sultan's party. Like everyone, I was completely fooled by that manuscript of yours."

"Writing a few new chapters for *The Book of Politics* was definitely one of my cleverer ideas."

"Until I figured it out."

"Yes, your verdigris demonstration was devastating."

"It changed everything," Omar replied. "That was when I realized that Nizam al-Mulk was murdered to protect the caliph. From there it wasn't hard to figure out that you were the man behind the assassination." He moved a horse. Abu Shuja was in real trouble now. Checkmate was a move away. "The thing I still haven't figured out," Omar went on, "was how you knew Nizam al-Mulk planned to depose the caliph. The plot against al-Muqtadi was secret, known only to the sultan's inner circle."

"For a smart man, you can be rather dense, Omar Khayyam. If it was known only to the sultan's inner circle, then obviously someone in the sultan's inner circle told me."

Abu Shuja had a point. Omar ran through the sultan's intimates. *Nizam al-Mulk, Terken Khatun, Taj al-Mulk, ben Samha, Yalbard . . .* "Of course," he said. "Abu Nasir. The intelligence chief. You put a price on his conversion to Islam, didn't you?"

"Last year, when I reintroduced the Ordinance of Omar, Abu Nasir—he was Abba Nasir then—became rather gloomy about his future as a

Jew amid the revival of true Islam. So I dangled the possibility of conversion in front of him. I offered to have al-Muqtadi preside at the ceremony personally. But there was nothing so commercial as a 'price' on his conversion. Granted, I may have mentioned to him that to be Muslim was to be completely loyal to the Commander of the Faithful. Abu Nasir jumped at the opportunity and has been feeding state secrets to me ever since." Abu Shuja was on the offensive now. He moved one of his chariots halfway across the board to the square next to Omar's shah. "Check," he said.

Omar was disappointed. He had expected to make the winning move on this turn, but now he had to deal with Abu Shuja's chariot instead. Still, it was more an annoyance than a threat. "You're just prolonging the inevitable," he said, as he easily captured it with his shah. "I suppose it was also Abu Nasir who told you when Malik-shah and Nizam al-Mulk would travel to Baghdad."

"Abu Nasir was a fountainhead of useful information. I duly passed it on to the Assassins. But you still haven't told me why you suspected me. There were others in Baghdad who wanted to protect the caliph. Qadi Shami, Professor Humaydi. Even Chief Professor Ghazali."

Ghazali gave Abu Shuja *the look*—the one he usually reserved for disruptive students.

"Oh, I suspected them too," Omar said. He turned to Ghazali and put a reassuring hand on his forearm. "Although in your case, my friend, I never seriously believed it." Looking back at Abu Shuja, he continued. "But of all the suspects, you stood out. There were a lot of circumstantial things. Like the murder occurring exactly one year to the day after you were placed under house arrest. But what really got my attention was the lie you told me."

"I must be slipping. When did I do that?"

"At our first meeting. You told me you were broke and needed to borrow money because of the bad harvest in Rudhrawar."

"And how did you know that was a lie?"

"Because I had *been* to Rudhrawar. I rode through on the way to Baghdad and watched congregations of happy peasants harvest a bumper crop of saffron."

"How careless of me."

"So if you were expecting a financial windfall from Rudhrawar, I wondered why you were in such dire straits. Then I realized it was because you had already consumed the money. Fifty thousand dinars to the Assassins for the murder of Nizam al-Mulk."

Abu Shuja smiled. "Is that all? Were there no other errors on my part?"

"It was a brilliant murder."

"You are too kind."

"It's the truth. So many intermediaries stood between you and Nizam al-Mulk that it took me a month—and considerable personal danger—to peel back all the layers. Ben Samha, Hasan-i Sabbah, Abu Tahir Arrani—we didn't even know his name at first. Brilliant. Of course you had a year to plan it and the twisted mind of Hasan-i Sabbah to help you.

"But the second murder—ben Samha—that was sloppy. There were clues everywhere. Whoever was behind it had to be someone who knew the operations of the bank. A client, most likely. Which you were. And since ibn Yasir the Rug Seller actually ignited the fire, it had to be someone connected to him. Which you were. It was all very ad hoc. You must have planned it in great haste."

"And yet for all my 'sloppiness,' you still could not prove anything. You had to set a trap for me."

"The House of Samha was always your Achilles' heel. I was sure that if I announced Saad was going to rat you out, you would have come here to add him to your compendium of victims. It's still your move, by the way."

"Oh," said Abu Shuja. He quickly moved his elephant, leapfrogging over his horse. "Check," he said.

At first, Omar couldn't see where the threat came from. Then he realized that with the elephant out of the way, Abu Shuja's remaining chariot had a clear path to Omar's shah. *Another delaying tactic*, Omar thought as he moved his shah a square, out of danger.

"The way I figure it," Omar said, "you presumed you were being quite clever by going to the House of Samha. You blamed Abba Saad for your fall from the vizierate and your subsequent arrest. But now you would get your vengeance. You would make him your unwitting instrument to finance the Nizam's assassination.

"But it all came unraveled when you found out that the Commission of Inquiry and Justice planned to call ben Samha as a witness. You couldn't take a chance on letting him testify. So you were forced into another murder.

"At that point you must have been in a panic. You couldn't kill ben Samha yourself, as you were confined to your house. And you couldn't bring in the Assassins again. You were out of time and out of money. But then you remembered there was someone in Baghdad who hated ben Samha as much as you did. And he was just stupid enough for you to talk him into doing your dirty work. So you told your wife a fairy tale about buying new carpets, which gave you the excuse to invite ibn Yasir to your home.

"You briefed him on everything he needed to know: where to hide, how to get out, where ben Samha kept his keys, and, most important, which records to burn. The tragic thing was that it was so unnecessary. Ben Samha had no intention of appearing before the commission. He was preparing to flee at the very moment he was killed.

"So you were rid of ben Samha, who knew too much. But now you had to contend with ibn Yasir, who knew too much. And he was far less discreet than ben Samha. I haven't figured out how you killed him. My theory is that you lured him back to your house by promising to pay him after the murder, but when he came to collect, you stabbed him and shoved his corpse out a window into the Tigris. But that seemed far-fetched. Too many people would know that he came to your house and never left. Besides, he was found upstream from your home."

"That *was* my plan," Abu Shuja replied, "and you are right, it was not a very good plan. But then I got lucky. Instead of coming back, the idiot rug seller helped himself to ben Samha's cash box and started throwing dinars all over town like a Jew. It was only a matter of time before someone robbed the robber and sank his body in the river."

Two murders. A third one planned. Arson. The sacred ceremony of conversion subverted. As Abu Shuja's catalog of crimes grew thicker, Professor Ghazali looked increasingly disgusted. At last he couldn't keep his silence. "And to think I thought of you as my friend," he said.

Ghazali's outburst wasn't surprising. But Omar knew where this path led and longed to spare Ghazali the heartbreak. Desperate to create a distraction, he reminded Abu Shuja that it was his move.

"Chariot to shah's chariot eight," Abu Shuja said. "Check."

Undeterred, Ghazali plowed on. "You murdered a brother Muslim in cold blood. '*Whoso kills a believer purposely, his reward is hell, to dwell therein for aye; and Allah will be wrath with him, and curse him, and prepare for him a mighty woe.'"*

"My cup is empty," Omar said. "Who needs a refill?" He rose from his cushion and made the rounds of the table, topping off everyone's goblets from the two pitchers. Water for Ghazali and Abu Shuja. Wine for Saad and himself.

"How could you be so foolish as to fall this deeply into error?" Ghazali continued. "Where did you possibly get the idea that Allah would countenance it?"

"Do you not know?" Abu Shuja asked, smiling.

Ghazali shook his head.

"I got the idea from you," Abu Shuja said.

There was no turning back now. Omar set the pitchers on the table and sat down in defeat.

"What?" Ghazali spat out. He was finished with Abu Shuja. He got up and started to walk away. But he had to have the last word; his combativeness was his undoing. He stopped, turned around, and said, "I never told you any such thing."

Abu Shuja smiled. "Did you not?" he said. "You came to my house, you delivered your lectures, and I listened. You said, *'Obey Allah, and obey the Messenger and those in authority amongst you.'* Well, al-Muqtadi is in authority amongst us, and Nizam al-Mulk rebelled against him time and again—until *I* put a stop to it. You said, *'Enjoin good and forbid evil.'* Nizam al-Mulk was on the verge of committing an unforgivable evil. I forbade it. You said it was permitted to kill a ruler who was an unbeliever. Nizam al-Mulk's unbelief will weaken the community no longer. You said, *'Fight those who believe not in Allah.'*[104] I fought the unbeliever ben Samha and I defeated him. You said to emulate the Messenger and his Companions—may the prayer and peace of Allah be upon them. Well, the Messenger and his Companions slaughtered their enemies to advance the cause of Islam, and so did I. I did everything you taught me to, so don't stand there looking shocked and threatening me with hellfire and the wrath of Allah. You have no right to judge me. You are nothing but talk. While you gave lectures, I lived the life of the Messenger."

Ghazali stood for a long, uncomfortable moment, too stunned to talk, an expression of misery on his guileless, round face. When he finally spoke, it was to mutter, "No. No. It wasn't my fault." He shuffled out of the room, a pathetic figure.

Omar wanted to go after him and comfort his wounded friend. But he couldn't. The game with Abu Shuja had to play out to the end. "Whose move is it?" he asked.

"Yours," Abu Shuja replied. "You're still in check."

It was another easily escapable predicament. "Shah takes chariot," Omar said.

The others were relieved to have their attention returned to chess. The scene they had just witnessed was too uncomfortable to dwell on. But inwardly, Omar was puzzled. Abu Shuja was bleeding men. *Why does he keep smiling?*

Calm as a pond at sunrise, Abu Shuja said "Pawn to shah's horse seven. Check."

It was a move of only one square. But it put Omar's shah in danger that he hadn't foreseen. Perplexed, he studied the configuration of the chessmen.

As he considered his options, he was distracted by movement out of the corner of his eye. Abu Shuja was helping himself to the pitcher. Something was wrong about that. It took Omar a moment to realize what: it was the wrong pitcher—the one filled with wine, not water.

Thinking fast, Omar latched onto Abu Shuja's wrist and wrenched it away from the wine. A shower of white powder fell from Abu Shuja's ring and landed on the table. It came from a secret compartment, behind the ruby, which Abu Shuja had popped open while Omar and Saad were focused on the game.

Omar twisted the ring off Abu Shuja's finger. "I'll keep that," he said.

No doubt the poison was deadly; Omar didn't take any chances. He set the pitcher and ring aside on a nearby chest for evidence—and to prevent him and Saad from touching them absentmindedly. Using the edge of a piece of paper as a scraper, he collected the spilled powder into a bowl. That went onto the chest as well. He washed away any residue from the table with water from the other pitcher and dried it with his handkerchief, which then joined the other tainted objects. Finally, he went out to the courtyard and scrubbed his hands in the fountain.

"Shah to shah's horse eight," he said as he rejoined the others at the table and moved his shah out of harm's way. "You failed, Abu Shuja Rudhrawari. You won't poison any witnesses today. In fact, you failed at everything. You counted on Malik-shah to be weak. You were sure that he wouldn't go through with the plan to depose the caliph without the Nizam at his side. Especially after you threatened his life with the second dagger and tried to sway public opinion with the fake manuscript. But the sultan showed more strength of will than any of us expected. Before today is over, al-Muqtadi will be exiled to Basra, and a new caliph will reign in Baghdad."

"Oh," Abu Shuja said with a smile. "I wouldn't be so sure of that. Horse to shah's chariot six. Checkmate."

A dumbfounded Omar stared at the board. Abu Shuja was right. Omar's shah was pinned. The game was over.

He looked over at Abu Shuja's ring, the pitcher of wine, and the bowl of toxic powder. Then back at the board. When he raised his head, Abu Shuja was grinning at him maliciously. "So," Abu Shuja said, "the brilliant Omar Khayyam figured it out at last."

Omar kept his head long enough to send Saad home and issue orders to the guard in the hallway. "Abu Shuja Rudhrawari is under arrest. Don't let him leave under any circumstances."

"By whose authority?" the guard asked.

"The sultan's," Omar replied. He shoved his safe-conduct into the guard's hand by way of authorization. "And don't touch the items on the chest," he added.

Then he ran.

*   *   *

The beat of his horse's hooves rumbled like an entire regiment on the march. Omar galloped down the Damascus Highway, grateful to be in open country. The ride across the city had seemed interminable. One delay after another: slow-moving mules, oblivious pedestrians, bottleneck intersections. Now, as he raced past farms and jumped irrigation ditches, he dug his heels into his horse's sides to prod the animal to go just a little bit faster and make up for lost time. He had told the stable boys repeatedly that he had to have a horse with speed and stamina; the horse didn't disappoint. The chestnut steed pushed itself to its limits, despite the steam of sweat rising off its body and the ring of foam gathering around its mouth.

When the cluster of tents finally came into view, Omar steered off the road and cut across the adjacent farms. He flew through the camp at full speed; he didn't slow until he had reached the sultan's pavilion. Before the horse had even come to a complete stop, Omar had dismounted and was running into the tent. The abandoned steed trotted a little farther and then wandered aimlessly until a soldier took him by the reins and led him to a nearby pasture.

Gloom pervaded the cavernous main hall, the only light a grayish haze that filtered through the fabric of the roof. It was empty of humans, except for Yalbard and a pair of soldiers, who guarded the entrance to the inner compartment. The emir nodded Omar through.

In the sultan's bedchamber, the atmosphere was solemn. About a dozen men milled about, speaking in hushed tones. Most of them were doctors, but Taj al-Mulk and a few other senior officials were in attendance as well. An unpleasant odor, a mixture of vomit and diarrhea, lingered in the air.

Malik-shah lay limply in his bed, his head bare, his eyes closed, his body piled with blankets to sweat the fever out of him. Omar gently placed a hand on the patient's forehead. It felt hot and clammy. When he drew back one of Malik-shah's eyelids, the pupil was dilated excessively. Reaching under the blankets, he found the sultan's wrist and placed two fingers on the pulse point. Fast and erratic. Omar looked questioningly at the head physician. The despondent doctor returned Omar's gaze and shook his head sadly.

The prodding caused Malik-shah to stir. He opened his eyes, but it took him awhile to focus and recognize his visitor. "Omar," he said at last. He seemed happy to see him.

"I heard you were sick," Omar replied. "But this, this is nothing. I should have stayed in Baghdad."

"Scientists make the worst liars," said Malik-shah, then broke into a fit of coughing. He extracted his arm from under the covers and waved desperately at something on the cluttered nightstand with a shaking hand.

Omar realized the sultan was pointing to a pitcher. He splashed some water into a goblet and held it to the mouth of his friend. Grabbing the bowl of the cup with both hands, Malik-shah managed a few sips. Then he pushed it away. Omar noticed that the sultan's bare forearms were splotched with some kind of rash.

When he could speak again, Malik-shah asked, "Did you get him?"

"Yes," Omar replied. "It was Abu Shuja."

"And he did this to me?"

"Last night. The poison was in his ring."

"Good. He and I can go to hell together."

"You aren't going anywhere, Sahib al-Jalal. You're far too tough to die from a minor illness like this. And when it *is* your turn, many years from now, you'll enter the Garden, '*beneath which rivers flow; where they are provided with fruit . . . and there are pure wives for them therein, and they shall dwell therein for aye.*'"[105]

"You can't fool me. You don't believe in the Garden."

"Today I want to." Omar fished in his pocket for his handkerchief to dry the tears that flowed freely down his cheeks. But then he remembered. He had left it in Baghdad, soaked with the same toxins that had poisoned Malik-shah.

The sultan grasped Omar's hand and used it to pull himself up into a sitting position. "Listen," he said, a bit stronger now. "I summoned the emirs. I still have to settle the matter of my successor." Omar tried to protest but the sultan was firm. "This is important. I'm going to name Berk-yaruq. He's young. He's going to need wise counselors."

"He'll have them. He'll have dozens of them from all over the empire."

"I want you to be one of them. I know he respects you. Advise him. The way you always advised me."

He sank back on the pillow and closed his eyes. His breathing was shallow but steady. He tightened his grip on Omar's hand. Omar kneeled beside the bed and the two men stayed like that, not speaking, for several minutes. Then Malik-shah opened his eyes again and looked at Omar. "Do you really think I'll enter the Garden?" he asked.

"Of course you will," Omar replied, holding his friend's gaze. "You were a good man."

"But was I a king? I mean, in the end."

"In the end, you were a king."

EPILOGUE

BAGHDAD
FRIDAY, 16 SHAWWAL 485
4 Azar 471
19 November 1092

*O*mar never saw Malik-shah again.

Terken Khatun had the sultan carried back to Baghdad in a palanquin and installed him in her quarters. There were no announcements on the status of his health, and no one was permitted to see him. But Omar still had his spy in the harem; Khuld brought regular reports to his room. The sultan was slipping away.

Terken Khatun, meanwhile, held a steady stream of secret meetings with emirs and senior officials. It was obvious what she was trying to do: beg, badger, and bribe them into throwing their support behind Mahmud and elevate him to the throne of Seljuq in Berk-yaruq's place.

It must have been more difficult than she expected, because when the sultan died, almost a week later, Terken Khatun kept it a secret, evidently in a bid to buy herself more time. Omar found out right away, of course, thanks to Khuld. She felt her father's grief keenly and asked him whether he needed anything. No, Omar replied. He wanted to be left alone.

She came back a couple of hours later to check on him and found he had gone out. On the table, he had left behind a single sheet of paper with a poem on it:

> But that is but a Tent wherein may rest
> A Sultan to the realm of Death addrest;
>   The Sultan rises, and the dark Servant
> Strikes, and prepares it for another guest. [106]

THE THREAD OF REASON WILL CONTINUE.

Glossary of Foreign Expressions

ADHAN (Arabic)—the call to prayer. Familiar to anyone who has ever watched a movie or TV show that takes place in the Muslim world: there's always an establishing shot of a panoramic view of the city with the voice of the muezzin carrying over the housetops as he chants the *adhan*.

ALLAHU AKBAR (Arabic)—the watchword of the Muslim faith. Literally "Allah is the greatest," though often translated, "Allah is great," it is a versatile phrase which may be heard in numerous contexts, including at the opening of the call to prayer, in times of stress, upon completion of a public flogging, when a missile strikes its target, and as an expression of determination.

AMM (Turkish)—vagina

AS-SALAMU ALAYKUM (Arabic)—"Welcome, friend." A common greeting

BARAKA (Arabic)—literally a blessing, in Sufism it refers to the flow of divine gifts that results from mystic practice.

BURQA (Arabic)—a women's outergarment. From the word, *barqa'a*, meaning to veil or drape, a burqa typically covers the entire head, face, and body, leaving only the eyes visible.

CHADOR (Persian)—an outer garment worn by women, especially in Persia, to preserve their modesty. Typically it consists of a large piece of fabric which is draped over the head and reaches to the feet.

DHIMMI (Arabic)—literally a "protected person." A non-Muslim living under Muslim rule. According to the Shari'ah, in exchange for the protection of his Muslim rulers, a *dhimmi* must pay a special tax, the *jizyah*, and be subject to restrictions such as wearing distinctive clothing as a badge of his inferior status.

EID (Arabic)—festival

FATWA (Arabic)—a legal opinion. A fatwa is more than a brief but less than a court ruling. Any qualified scholar of shari'ah may issue a fatwa, but it is typically binding only on that scholar's own followers.

HAJJ (Arabic)—the pilgrimage to Mecca, which observant Muslims make at least once during their lifetimes

HADITH (Arabic)—literally a narrative or a telling—in other words, a story. Typically it's a story about something Muhammad did or said, but sometimes it's about one of his companions. I've never seen an estimate of how many hadith exist, but it must be in the hundreds of thousands. In the early years of Islam, scholars compiled what they considered the most reliable hadith into six collections that were canonized (or seven, depending on the school of thought). In Sunni Islam these collections, together with the Quran, form the basis of the Shari'ah or law.

HALAL (Arabic)—permitted, especially with regard to what foods and beverages are permitted by the Shari'ah.

HARAM (Arabic)—forbidden, especially with regard to those things forbidden by the Shari'ah. When uttered as an interjection, it means "Shame!" and is often used to express sympathy. It can also mean something sacred and inviolable, and thus is related to *harem*, the quarters for the female members of a household.

HAVDALAH (Hebrew)—literally a "separation," the Jewish ceremony held on Saturday evening to mark the end of the Sabbath and the beginning of the work week

HIJAB (Arabic)—a veil or covering, especially a head covering used by women to preserve their modesty

HIJRAH (Arabic)—a departure or emigration, in particular the flight of Muhammad from Mecca to Medina in 622 AD. The Muslim calendar is dated from this event.

HOURI (Arabic)—a virgin who dwells in the Garden of Paradise, as a reward for the faithful, as promised in the Quran

HUYAR (Turkish)—penis (literally, cucumber)

IFTAR (Arabic)—During Ramadan, observant Muslims fast from sunup to sundown. *Iftar* is a feast that marks the end of each day's fast. As with the English word *breakfast*, it is derived from the word *break*.

IMAM (Arabic)—derived from the word *to lead,* the use of *imam* varies somewhat within the Muslim world. Among Sunnis, it generally refers to any person who is qualified to lead the five-daily prayers. But to Shiites it means *the* Imam, the leader of all Muslims, similar to the caliph. The word is generally capitalized when used in the Shiite sense.

INSHALLAH (Arabic)—If it be the will of Allah.

JIHAD (Arabic)—literally a struggle, jihad is commanded by the Quran. A great deal of ink has been expended as to whether it means an armed conflict against the unbeliever, or a personal, spiritual struggle for self-improvement. I cover the topic in my blog at http://michael-isenberg.blogspot.com/2017/07/so-what-does-jihad-mean.html.

JIZYAH (Arabic)—a tax on non-Muslims living under Muslim rule

KHAN (Persian)—also called a caravanserai, a khan was a place where a caravan could stop, rest for the night, and obtain supplies.

KHWAJA (Persian)—master

LA ILAHA ILLA-LLAH (Arabic)—"There is no god but Allah." In testifying to Allah's oneness, this expression is the cornerstone of Islam, and comprises the first part of the *shahada* or profession of faith.

MADRASA (Arabic)—school

MAMELUKE (Arabic)—literally an "owned person," a Mameluke was a soldier in one of the slave armies that were common in the Muslim world during the Middle Ages.

MARUF (Arabic)—literally a person who knows, the term is used as an honorific for Sufi masters.

MIHRAB (Arabic)—the niche in a mosque, often beautifully decorated, which indicates the *qibla*, or direction of Mecca. Muslims face this direction to pray.

MUBARAK (Arabic)—blessed

MUEZZIN (Arabic)—the person who chants the *adhan* or call to prayer

MUHTASIB (Arabic)—an official responsible for overseeing a market. He ensures that order is maintained, weights and measures are honest, and the Shari'ah is enforced

PEECH (Turkish)—bastard

QADI (Arabic)—a judge

RAK'A (pl. *RAKA'AT*) (Arabic)—literally a bowing or kneeling, the *rak'a* is the basic building block of Muslim prayer

SACHMALIK (Turkish)—nonsense, bullshit

SAHIB (Arabic)—master, owner. Often used as part of an honorific such as Sahib al-Jalal (His Majesty) for a sultan, Sahib as-Sumu al-Malaki (His Royal Highness) for a prince, and Sahib al-Ma'ali (His Excellency) for a senior minister

SHARI'AH (Arabic)—Muslim law

SHURTA (pl. *SHURAT*) (Arabic)—policeman

SIK (Turkish)—the sex act. *SIKKER* and *SIKKING* are not, of course, actual Turkish words, but rather adaptations I made for the benefit of English-speaking readers.

SUFI (Arabic)—a mystic. The origin of the term is controversial. The leading theories are that it comes from *suf*, meaning wool, after their garments, or *safa'*, meaning purity. For background about the history and practice of Sufism, I recommend *Early Islamic Mysticism* by Michael Sells and *The Shambhala Guide to Sufism* by Carl Ernst.

SUHUR (Arabic)—the pre-dawn meal eaten during Ramadan before the beginning of the day's fast

SUQ (Arabic)—market, bazaar

TALLITH (pl. TALLITHIM) (Hebrew)—a fringed shawl, worn by observant Jews, as commanded by the Torah

TIRAZ (Arabic)—literally meaning embroidery, to receive a *tiraz*, an armband with an embroidered inscription, was a great honor.

ULAMA (Arabic)—the Muslim intellectual class

W'ALLAH (Arabic)—By God!

YA (Arabic)—the last letter of the Arabic alphabet. It represents a sound similar to the English *Y*.

Units of Measure

1 FARASANG = the distance a caravan can travel in an hour; around 3.5 miles or 5.6 kilometers

1 CUBIT = the distance from the elbow to the tips of the fingers; around 1.5 feet or 0.5 meter

1 MAUND = between 3.5 and 6.0 pounds (1.6 to 2.7 kilograms); sources vary on the exact amount

1 DIRHAM = around 0.1 ounces or 3 grams; also a silver coin of that weight

1 DINAR = a gold coin of around 0.15 ounces or 4.25 grams. The exchange rate between gold and silver coins varied with market conditions and purity but was typically between 10 and 15 dirhams per dinar.

Notes

¹ Winston S. Churchill, *A History of the English-Speaking Peoples*, vol. 1, *The Birth of Britain* (New York: Dodd, Mead & Company, 1956), 202.

² The *Shah-nama*, or *Book of Kings*, is the national epic of Persia. Written by Abu'l-Qasim Ferdowsi (ca. 940–1020), this monumental work—it's the longest poem ever written by a single person—covers the history and heroes of Persia from their origins, shrouded in myth, through the real-life Sasanian kings who were ultimately swept away by the Muslim conquest in 651. Like other national epics, the *Shah-nama* was instrumental in forging both a vernacular literature and a sense of national identity. To get some sense of its significance for Persians, see the conversation between Omar and Baghdadi in chapter 12.

³ *Sahih al-Bukhari*, trans. M. Mushin Khan (2009), vol. 7, book 72, no. 838. Other versions of the story occur in vol. 1, book 8, no. 371; vol. 3, book 43, no. 659; vol. 7, book 72, no. 842; and vol. 8, book 73, no. 130.

⁴ A roughly cubical structure (hence the name: Kaaba/cube), some forty-three feet high, the Kaaba in Mecca is the holiest site in Islam. Muslims all over the world face the direction of the Kaaba during their five daily prayers and seek to visit it at least once in their lifetimes as the centerpiece of the pilgrimage, or hajj.

⁵ Quran, trans. Edward Henry Palmer (1880), http://www.sacred-texts.com/isl/htq, 2:275. I'm partial to the Palmer version of the Quran, because, unlike many more recent translations, it doesn't whitewash the violent and intolerant passages. Many twenty-first-century Muslim scholars seek to interpret the Quran in a gentler way—and that's healthy—but it was not how most Muslims of the eleventh century viewed things. For consistency with the rest of the text, and also the original Arabic, I changed "God" to "Allah" and "Apostle" to "Messenger" wherever they appeared.

⁶ Quran, 47:4–6; 78:32–34. The translation of the phrase that I give here as "young girls with swelling breasts" is a matter of some controversy. The Arabic is *kawa'ib aturaban*. The first word is often translated "young girls" or "youthful companions" but in fact means, as Palmer rendered it, "girls with swelling breasts." It comes from the word *ka'aba*, meaning "to swell or be round." The second word, *aturaban*, means "of the same age as themselves," and that's how Palmer translated

it. But it seemed to me that "youthful" better captured the spirit of what the Quran was trying to say, so I took one of my rare departures from Palmer.

[7] Ibid., 5:90.

[8] *The Rubaiyat of Omar Khayyam*, trans. E. Fitzgerald (London: Bernard Quaritch), ii. A *ruba'i* is a quatrain, a poem of four lines. The term comes from the Semitic word *arba*, meaning four. *Rubaiyat* is the plural. It is, therefore, a collection of poems rather than a single long poem. Fitzgerald's translations of Omar Khayyam's *Rubaiyat* may generously be described as loose. Many quatrains are composites of multiple verses in the original manuscripts, and a handful don't seem to map to anything Khayyam wrote at all. However, some scholars of Persian insist that Fitzgerald captured the *spirit* of Khayyam far better than more scholarly translators who accurately rendered Khayyam's meaning word for word and produced lifeless verse that falls on the ear with a wooden thud. The translations and numbering are from Fitzgerald's second edition (1868), except where otherwise indicated.

[9] Ibid., lxxviii.

[10] Ibid., xxxiv.

[11] *Rubaiyat*, Ousley manuscript #140, 108. The translation here is a composite of Fitzgerald, lxxiii, and the one in *The Rubaiyat of Omar Khayyam*, ed. and trans. E. Heron-Allen (Boston: L. C. Page & Co., 1898). As I noted above, Fitzgerald's translations aren't particularly accurate. For verses where I thought that Fitzgerald didn't capture the right shade of meaning, I used Heron-Allen's translations instead. I also used them for verses that Fitzgerald didn't include in his collection at all. However, since Heron-Allen's translations are in a very different style from Fitzgerald's—they don't even rhyme!—it was necessary for me to adapt them for consistency with the rest of the text.

[12] *Rubaiyat*, trans. Fitzgerald, xxi.

[13] Ibid., lxvii.

[14] Abu Ali ibn Sina (980–1037), or Avicenna as he's known in the West, was the epitome of a Renaissance man, centuries before the Renaissance. Arguably the most prominent philosopher in Islam, he was also a physician, poet, naturalist, vizier to the Emir of Hamadan, and occasional fugitive. His *Canon of Medicine* was *the* handbook for doctors for centuries, both in the Muslim world and in Europe. Omar Khayyam, in his treatise *On Being and Obligation*, referred to Avicenna as his mentor. Although he evidently meant that figuratively (as best we can tell, their lifetimes did not overlap), it is clear that Avicenna heavily influenced Omar's philosophical writings.

[15] *Rubaiyat*, trans. Fitzgerald, xxix.

[16] Nizam al-Mulk, *Siasset Namèh ou Traité de Gouvernement (The Book of Politics or Treatise on Government)*, Angers: Imprimerie Orientale de A. Burdin et Cie, (1893), trans. Charles Schefer, 243–44. The translation from the French is mine. *Siasset Namèh* is Persian; the book is also known by its Arabic name, *Siyar al-Muluk*, or *The Conduct of Kings*.

[17] *Rubaiyat*, trans. Fitzgerald, l, li.

[18] Considered by many Muslims to be the pinnacle of the Abbasid dynasty, Harun ar-Rashid is known to Westerners as the caliph whose incognito travels among his people led to many humorous situations in *The Thousand and One Nights*.

[19] Nizam al-Mulk, *Siasset Namèh*, 213.

[20] Ibid., 223.

[21] Ibid., 206.

[22] Ibid., 220.

[23] Ibid., 220–22.

[24] Ibid., 231–32.

[25] Ibid., 231.

[26] Ibid., 291.

[27] Ibid., 307.

[28] *Sahih al-Bukhari*, vol. 8, book 76, no. 470.

[29] *Rubaiyat*, trans. Fitzgerald, xxii.

[30] Ghazali's views regarding legitimacy and authority in Islam may be found in his treatises *Exposing the Batiniyyah* and *The Book of Counsel for Kings* and continue to be influential to this day. In fact, in a 2014 propaganda pamphlet called "Extend your Hands and Pledge Loyalty to Baghdadi" (https://archive.org/details/baghdadi-001), ISIS quoted *Exposing the Batiniyyah* in support of its claim to have established a legitimate caliphate.

[31] In Islam one may recite additional prayers beyond the number prescribed for the five daily sessions. These "extra" prayers are called *nafl*, which literally means something that goes beyond the requirements; it is commonly translated as "optional," "voluntary," or the absolutely awful word, "supererogatory." Such prayers are believed to strengthen the relationship between Allah and the worshipper.

[32] *Rubaiyat*, trans. Fitzgerald, 3rd ed., xii.

[33] Quran, 3:118.

[34] Proverbs 3:18. King James Version.

[35] There is some debate among modern scholars whether the so-called Ordinance of Omar really originated with the caliph of that name. But there is no doubt that scholars of Omar Khayyam's time believed it did and considered it legally binding. The particular provisions may be found in Ghazali's *Kitab al Wagiz fi Fiqh*

Madhab al-Imam al-Shaf'i (A Compendium of the Jurisprudence of the Imam Shaf'i).

[36] *Rubaiyat*, trans. Fitzgerald, introduction. The suggestion that Omar wrote this verse while grieving for Nizam al-Mulk came from T. H. Weir's 1926 monograph, *Omar Khayyam the Poet*.

[37] *Rubaiyat*, Ousley manuscript #140, 137, trans. adapted from Heron-Allen (see note 11).

[38] Ibid., 93.

[39] Ibid., 87.

[40] Ibid., 81.

[41] "Chapters on Manners," Sunnah.com, http://sunnah.com/tirmidhi/43.

[42] Quran, 3:110.

[43] In Omar's time these love stories were well-known folk tales that had been kicking around for hundreds of years. It would be another century, however, before they got their definitive forms, in the poems *Khosrau and Shirin* and *Layla and Majnun* by Nizami Ganjavi (ca. 1141–1209).

[44] Abu Shuja Rudhrawari, *The Experiences of the Nations*, in *The Eclipse of the 'Abbasid Caliphate; Original Chronicles of the Fourth Islamic Century*, trans. H. F. Amedroz and D. S. Margoliouth, vol. 6 (Oxford: Basil Blackwell, 1921), 210. Minor edits made for consistency with the present work.

[45] "Chapters on Knowledge," Sunnah.com, http://sunnah.com/tirmidhi/41, book 41, no. 2.

[46] Ghazali's repulsive views about women, including the comment about the advantages of a short wife, may be found in his writings, specifically *The Book of Counsel for Kings, Marriage and Sexuality in Islam*, and *The Alchemy of Happiness*.

[47] Abu Shuja Rudhrawari, *The Experiences of the Nations*, 268.

[48] Ibid., 90.

[49] Ibid., 253.

[50] Ibid., 107.

[51] The tales of Kalila and Dimna were hugely popular in the medieval Islamic world—and the modern one—as well known as, say, "Cinderella" or "Little Red Riding Hood" in the West. Like its Western counterparts, the tales of Kalila and Dimna have spawned a whole industry of picture books and children's cartoons.

[52] Abu Shuja, *Experiences of the Nations*, 142–43. Minor edits made for consistency with the present work.

[53] Ibid. Minor edits made for consistency with the present work.

[54] Quran, 24:31.

[55] Ibid., 2:283.

[56] Ibid., 2:184–85.

[57] *Sahih Muslim*, trans. Abd al-Hamid Siddiqui (2009), book 17, Hadith numbers 4226–31.

[58] From Abu Ali ibn Haytham, *Doubts Concerning Ptolemy*, quoted in "Ibn al-Haytham wa Ishamatih fi al-Ulum al-Haditha (Ibn al-Haytham and his Contributions to Modern Science)", *Mudawanat as-Sirdab (Underground Blog)*, April 2012, http://asirdabe.blogspot.com/2012/04/blog-post_20.html; translated by me.

[59] *Rubaiyat*, trans. Fitzgerald, xxvi.

[60] Ibid., lxxvii.

[61] Quran, 75:14.

[62] *Rubaiyat*, trans. Heron-Allen, 44.

[63] Quran, 47:15.

[64] Ibid., 78:31–34.

[65] *Rubaiyat*, trans. Fitzgerald, lxvii.

[66] This story is very famous and has been recounted by many authors, both medieval and modern. However, the oldest version of it that I've been able to find is the one in Ghazali's *Nasihat al-Muluk* (Book of Counsel for Kings).

[67] *Rubaiyat*, trans. Fitzgerald, lxi.

[68] Ibid., xxxiii.

[69] Drawings of the sultan's companion, and a description of the mechanism, may be found in *The Book of Knowledge of Ingenious Mechanical Devices* by Badi'al-Zaman al-Jazari, who lived from 1136 to 1206.

[70] Had Omar been able to decrypt the writing, which modern readers will recognize as cuneiform, he would have learned that the monument was more than a thousand years older than he thought. The king depicted was not, in fact, the Sasanian Khosrau II, who reigned from AD 590 to 628. Rather, the monument was built to commemorate the defeat of the pretender Gaumata by Darius the Great in 521 BC. Unfortunately for Omar, the Bisotun inscription would not be deciphered until the nineteenth century. In contrast to the famous bas-relief and inscription, the nearby palace does date from the time of the Sasanians.

[71] *Rubaiyat*, trans. Fitzgerald, xx.

[72] Quran, 5:101.

[73] *Rubaiyat*, trans. Fitzgerald, civ.

[74] Abu'l-Qasim al-Hariri, "How Many Were the Gazelles at Hajir," in Shams al-Din Abu Al-'Abbas ibn Khallikan, *Ibn Khallikan's Biographical Dictionary*, trans. B. MacGuckin de Slane, vol. 2 (Paris: Oriental Translation Fund of Great Britain and Ireland, 1843), 492.

[75] Quran, 4:34.

[76] Ibid., 3:120.

[77] Ibid., 2:190–91.

[78] *Rubaiyat*, trans. Fitzgerald, xxx.

[79] Quran, 22:19–21.

[80] *Rubaiyat*, trans. Fitzgerald, xvii.

[81] Quran, 11:23.

[82] Animal sacrifice remains a part of Islam to this day; one can see videos of it on YouTube. I do not recommend them for the squeamish. Readers familiar with modern practices will object that the sacrifice of an animal is not the ritual for Eid al-Fitr, but rather Eid al-Adha, some two months later. However, the Eid al-Fitr practice seems to have differed in the Abbasid era. In his account of his travels in Iraq in the 1160s, the Spanish Jew Benjamin of Tudela writes of al-Muqtadi's great-great-grandson al-Mustanjid sacrificing a camel at the Mosque of Mansur during the "Festival after Ramadan"—clearly Eid al-Fitr. Incidentally, Benjamin's *Itinerary* is also notable for being the first book in Europe to mention China.

[83] *Rubaiyat*, trans. Fitzgerald, lxxxix.

[84] Verse 155.

[85] Quran, 3:7. At the time the Quran was first set to paper, and even in Omar's day, written Arabic did not use punctuation. Hence the ambiguity.

[86] Ibid., 4:93.

[87] *Sahih al-Bukhari*, vol. 4, book 52, no. 260. *The Prophet said, "If somebody—a Muslim—discards his religion, kill him."*

[88] *Rubaiyat*, trans. Fitzgerald, lxxix.

[89] *Sarguzasht-e Sayyidna (Story of our Lord)*, in Rashid ad-Din Tabib, *Jami al-tavarikh: qismat-i Isma'iliyyan, va Fatimiyyan, va Nazariyyan, va Da'iyyan, va Rafiqan (Compendium of History: Sections on the Ismailis, Fatimids, Christians, Daiyyan, and Rafiqan)*, ed. Muhammad Mudarrisi and Muhammad Danish'pazhuh (Teheran: Nashr-i Kitab, 1959), 110–11; translated (loosely) by me.

[90] *Rubaiyat*, trans. Fitzgerald, xiv.

[91] Ibid., lxvi.

[92] Quran, 4:28.

[93] Abu Muhammad al-Qasim al-Hariri, *The Assemblies of Al Hariri*, trans. F. Steingass, vol. 2, Fortieth Assembly (London: Royal Asiatic Society, 1898), 101–108.

[94] Quran, 25:44.

[95] *Rubaiyat*, trans. Fitzgerald, cix.

[96] Quran, 5:32. Palmer renders the passage as *"Whoso saves one, it is as though he saved men altogether."* I modified it slightly for clarity.

[97] *Sahih al-Bukhari*, vol. 7, book 72, no. 838.

[98] *Rubaiyat*, Ousley manuscript #140, 126, trans. adapted from Heron-Allen.

[99] *Rubaiyat*, trans. Fitzgerald, lix.

[100] Ibid., xiv.

[101] *Rubaiyat*, Ousley manuscript #140, 38, trans. adapted from Heron-Allen.

[102] Quran, 49:9.

[103] As the reader will observe, in the world of medieval Islam, the game of chess was similar but not identical to our modern game. Obviously, there was no piece called a bishop in that non-Christian society; it was called an elephant instead. The other inhabitants of the board were the shah (king), vizier (queen), horse (knight), chariot (rook), and pawn. The chessmen moved according to the same rules as in the modern game, with a few exceptions. Among these were that the vizier moved only one square at a time, and only diagonally, and the elephants moved two squares at a time, also diagonally, and could jump over other pieces. For a complete account, see David Parlett, *The Oxford History of Board Games* (Oxford: Oxford University Press, 1999), 296 99.

[104] Quran, 9:29.

[105] Ibid., 2:25.

[106] *Rubaiyat*, trans. Fitzgerald, lxx. Fitzgerald's version used the Arabic/Persian word *Ferrásh*, but since it is unknown to most Western readers, I substituted the English translation, "Servant."

www.ingramcontent.com/pod-product-compliance
Lightning Source LLC
Chambersburg PA
CBHW030541020726
47494CB00005B/1448